Praise for #1 *New York T...*
bestselling author Linda Lael Miller

"Miller tugs at the heartstrings as few authors can."
—*Publishers Weekly*

"Miller's name is synonymous with the finest in Western romance."

DISCARD —*RT Book Reviews*

"Linda Lael Miller creates vibrant characters and stories I defy you to forget."
—#1 *New York Times* bestselling author Debbie Macomber

"Miller is one of the finest American writers in the genre."

—*RT Book Reviews*

Praise for *New York Times* bestselling author
Maisey Yates

"Fans of Robyn Carr and RaeAnne Thayne will enjoy [Yates's] small-town romance."
—*Booklist* on *Part Time Cowboy*

"Passio...
person...
...owboy

"Wraps... to
read m...

—*Publishers Weekly* on *Bad News Cowboy*

LINDA LAEL MILLER

MAISEY YATES

Cowboy
Ever After

HQN™

ISBN-13: 978-1-335-52382-2

Recycling programs for this product may not exist in your area.

Cowboy Ever After

Copyright © 2018 by Harlequin Books S.A.

The publisher acknowledges the copyright holders of the individual works as follows:

Big Sky Mountain
Copyright © 2012 by Linda Lael Miller

Bad News Cowboy
Copyright © 2015 by Maisey Yates

CONTENTS

BIG SKY MOUNTAIN

Linda Lael Miller

In loving memory of my cherished beagle-dog, Sadie.

I'm grateful for every second
of our eleven years together.

CHAPTER ONE

A FINE SWEAT broke out between Hutch Carmody's shoulders and his gut warned that he was fixing to stumble straight into the teeth of a screeching buzz saw. The rented tux itched against his hide and his collar seemed to be getting tighter with every flower-scented breath he drew.

The air was dense, weighted, cloying. The small church was overheated, especially for a sunny day in mid-June, and the pews were crammed with eager guests, a few weeping women and a fair number of skeptics.

Hutch's best man, Boone Taylor, fidgeted beside him.

The organist sounded a jarring chord and then launched into a perky tune Hutch didn't recognize. The first of three bridesmaids, all clad in silly-looking pink dresses more suited to little girls than grown women—in his opinion anyhow—drag-stepped her way up the aisle to stand beside the altar, across from him and Boone.

Hutch's head reeled, but he quickly reminded himself, silently of course, that he had to live in this town—his ranch was just a few miles outside of it. If he passed out cold at his own wedding, he'd still be getting ribbed about it when he was ninety.

While the next bridesmaid started forward, he did

his distracted best to avoid so much as glancing toward Brylee Parrish, his wife to be, who was standing at the back of the church beside her brother, Walker. He knew all too well how good she looked in that heirloom wedding gown of hers, with its billowing veil and dazzling sprinkle of rhinestones.

Brylee was beautiful, with cascades of red-brown hair that tumbled to her waist when she let it down. Her wide-set hazel eyes revealed passion, as well as formidable intelligence, humor and a country girl's inborn practicality.

He was a lucky man.

Brylee, on the other hand, was not so fortunate, having hooked up with the likes of him. She deserved a husband who loved her.

Suddenly, Hutch's gaze connected with that of his half brother, Slade Barlow. Seated near the front, next to his very pregnant wife, Joslyn, Slade slowly shook his head from side to side, his expression so solemn that a person would have thought somebody was about to be buried instead of hitched to one of the choicest women Parable County had ever produced.

Hutch's insides churned, then coalesced into a quivering gob and did a slow, backward roll.

The last bridesmaid had arrived.

The minister was in place.

The smell of the flowers intensified, nearly overwhelming Hutch.

And then the first notes of "Here Comes the Bride" rang out.

Hutch felt the room—hell, the whole planet—sway again.

Brylee, beaming behind the thin fabric of her veil,

nodded in response to something her brother whispered to her and they stepped forward.

"Hold it," Hutch heard himself say loudly enough to be heard over the thundering joy of the organ. He held up both hands, like a referee about to call a foul in some fast-paced game. "Stop."

Everything halted—with a sickening lurch.

The music died.

The bride and her brother seemed frozen in mid-stride.

Hutch would have sworn the universe itself had stopped expanding.

"This is all wrong," he went on miserably, but with his back straight and his head up. It wasn't as if he hadn't broached the subject with Brylee before—he'd been trying to get out of this fix for weeks. Just the night before, in fact, he'd sat Brylee down in a vinyl upholstered booth at the Silver Lanes snack bar and told her straight out that he had serious misgivings about getting married and needed some breathing space.

Brylee had cried, her mascara smudging, her nose reddening at the tip.

"You don't mean it," she'd said, which was her standard response to any attempt he made to put on the brakes before they both plummeted over a matrimonial cliff. "You're just nervous, that's all. It's entirely normal. But once the wedding is over and we're on our honeymoon—"

Hutch couldn't stand it when a woman cried, especially when he was the cause of her tears. Like every other time, he'd backed down, tried to convince himself that Brylee was right—he just had cold feet, that was all.

Now, though, "push" had run smack up against "shove."

It was now or never.

He faced Brylee squarely.

The universe unfroze itself, like some big machine with rusted gears, and all hell broke loose.

Brylee threw down her bouquet, stomped on it once, whirled on one heel and rushed out of the church. Walker flung a beleaguered and not entirely friendly look in Hutch's direction, then turned to go after his sister.

The guests, already on their feet in honor of the bride, all started talking at once, abuzz with shock and speculation.

Things like this might happen in books or movies, but they *didn't* happen in Parable, Montana.

Until now, Hutch reflected dismally.

He started to follow Brylee out of the church, not an easy proposition with folks crowding the aisle. He didn't have the first clue what he could say to her, but he figured he had to say *something*.

Before he'd taken two strides, though, Slade and Boone closed in on him from either side, each taking a firm grip on one of his arms.

"Let her go," Boone said quietly.

"There's nothing you can do," Slade confirmed.

With that, they hustled him quickly out of the main chapel and into the small side room where the choir robes, hymnals and Communion gear were stored.

Hutch wondered if a lynch mob was forming back there in the sanctuary.

"You picked a fine time to change your mind about getting married," Boone remarked, but his tone was light and his eyes twinkled with something that looked a lot like relief.

Hutch unfastened his fancy tie and shoved it into one coat pocket. Then he opened his collar halfway to his breastbone and sucked in a breath. "I tried to tell her," he muttered. He knew it sounded lame, but the truth was the truth.

Although he and Slade shared a father, they had been at bloody-knuckled odds most of their lives. They'd made some progress toward getting along since the old man's death and the upheaval that followed, but neither of them related to the other as a buddy, let alone a brother.

"Come on out to our place," Slade said, surprising him. "You'd best lay low for a few hours. Give Brylee—and Walker—a little time to cool off."

Hutch stiffened slightly, though he found the invitation oddly welcome. Home, being Whisper Creek Ranch, was a lonely outpost these days—which was probably why he'd talked himself into proposing to Brylee in the first place.

"I have to talk to Brylee," he repeated.

"There'll be time for that later on," Slade reasoned.

"Slade's right," Boone agreed. Boone, being violently allergic to marriage himself, probably thought Hutch had just dodged a figurative bullet.

Or maybe he was remembering that Brylee was a crack shot with a pistol, a rifle, or a Civil War cannon.

Given what had just happened, she was probably leaning toward the cannon right about now.

Hutch sighed. "All right," he said to Slade. "I'll kick back at your place for a while—but I've got to stop off at home first, so I can change out of this monkey suit."

"Fine," Slade agreed. "I'll round up the women and meet you at the Windfall in an hour or two."

By "the women," Slade meant his lovely wife, Joslyn, his teenage stepdaughter, Shea, and Opal Dennison, the force-of-nature who kept house for the Barlow outfit. Slade's mother, Callie, had had the good grace to skip the ceremony—old scandals die hard in a town the size of Parable and recollections of her long-ago affair with Carmody Senior, from which Slade had famously resulted, were as sharp as ever.

Today's escapade would put all that in the shade, of course. Tongues were wagging and jaws were flapping for sure—by now, various up-to-the-minute accounts were probably popping up on all the major social media sites. Before Slade and Boone had dragged Hutch out of the sanctuary, he'd seen several people whip out their cell phones and start texting. A few pictures had been taken, too, with those same ubiquitous devices.

The thought of all that amateur reporting made Hutch close his eyes for a moment. "Shit," he murmured.

"Knee-deep and rising," Slade confirmed, sounding resigned.

KENDRA SAT AT the antique table in her best friend Joslyn's kitchen, with Callie Barlow in the chair directly across from hers. The ranch house was unusually quiet, with its usual occupants gone to town.

A glance over one shoulder assured Kendra that her recently adopted four-year-old daughter, Madison, was still napping on a padded window seat, her stuffed purple kangaroo, Rupert, clenched in her arms. The little girl's gleaming hair, the color of a newly minted penny, lay in tousled curls around her cherubic face and Kendra felt the usual pang of hopeless devotion just looking at her.

This long-sought, hard-won, much-wanted child.

This miracle.

Not that every woman would have seen the situation from the same perspective as Kendra did—Madison was, after all, living proof that Jeffrey had been unfaithful, a constant reminder that it was dangerous to love, treacherous to trust, foolish to believe in another person too much. But none of that had mattered to Kendra in the end—she'd essentially been abandoned herself as a small child, left to grow up with a disinterested grandmother, and that gave her a special affinity for Madison. Besides, Jeffrey, having returned to his native England after summarily ending their marriage, had been dying.

Some men might have turned to family for help in such a situation—Jeffrey Chamberlain came from a very wealthy and influential one—but in this case, that wasn't possible. Jeffrey's aging parents were landed gentry with a string of titles, several sprawling estates and a fortune that dated back to the heyday of the East India Company, and were no more inclined toward child-rearing than they had been when their own two sons were small. They'd left Jeffrey and his brother in the care of nannies and housekeepers from infancy, and shipped them off to boarding school as soon as they turned six.

Understandably, Jeffrey hadn't wanted that kind of cold and isolated childhood for his daughter.

So he'd sent word to Kendra that he had to see her, in person. He had something important to tell her.

She'd made that first of several trips to the U.K.,

keeping protracted vigils at her ex-husband's hospital bedside while he drifted in and out of consciousness.

Eventually, he'd managed to get his message across: he told her about Madison, living somewhere in the U.S., and begged Kendra to find his daughter, adopt her and bring her up in love and safety. She was, he told her, the only person on earth he could or would trust with the child.

Kendra wanted nothing so much as a child and, during their brief marriage, Jeffrey had denied her repeated requests to start a family. It was a bitter pill to swallow, learning that he'd refused her a baby and then fathered one with someone else, someone he'd met on a business trip.

She'd done what Jeffrey asked, not so much for his sake—though she'd loved him once, or believed she did—as for Madison's. And her own.

The search hadn't been an easy one, even with the funds Jeffrey had set aside for the purpose, involving a great deal of web-surfing, phone calls and emails, travel and so many highs and lows that she nearly gave up several times.

Then it happened. She found Madison.

Kendra hadn't known what she'd feel upon actually meeting her former husband's child, but any doubts she might have had had been dispelled the moment—the *moment*—she'd met this cautious, winsome little girl.

The first encounter had taken place in a social worker's dingy office, in a dusty desert town in California, and for Kendra, it was love at first sight.

The forever kind of love.

Months of legal hassles had followed, but now, at long last, Kendra and Madison were officially mother and daughter, in the eyes of God and government, and Kendra knew she couldn't have loved her baby girl any more if she'd carried her in her own body for nine months.

Callie brought Kendra back to the present moment by reaching for the teapot in the center of the table and refilling Kendra's cup, then her own.

"Do you think it's over yet?" Kendra asked, instantly regretting the question but unable to hold back still another. "The wedding, I mean?"

Callie's smile was gentle as she glanced at the clock on the stove top and met Kendra's gaze again. "Probably," she said quietly. Then, without another word, she reached out to give Kendra's hand a light squeeze.

Madison, meanwhile, stirred on the window seat. "Mommy?"

Kendra turned again. "I'm here, honey," she said.

Although Madison was adjusting rapidly, in the resilient way of young children, she still had bad dreams sometimes and she tended to panic if she lost sight of Kendra for more than a moment.

"Are you hungry, sweetie?" Callie asked the little girl. Slade's mom would make a wonderful grandmother; she had a way with children, easy and forthright.

Madison shook her head as she moved toward Kendra and then scrambled up onto her lap.

"It's been a while since lunch," Kendra suggested, kissing the top of Madison's head and holding her close. "Maybe you'd like a glass of milk and one of Opal's oatmeal raisin cookies?"

Again, Madison shook her head, snuggling closer

still. "No, thank you," she said clearly, sounding, as she often did, more like a small adult than a four-year-old.

They'd arrived by car the night before and spent the night in the Barlows' guest room, at Joslyn's insistence.

The old house, the very heart of Windfall Ranch, was undergoing considerable renovation, which only added to the exuberant chaos of the place—and Madison was wary of everyone but Opal, the family housekeeper.

Just then, Slade and Joslyn's dog, Jasper, heretofore snoozing on his bed in front of the newly installed kitchen fireplace, sat bolt upright and gave a questioning little whine. His floppy ears were pitched slightly forward, though he seemed to be listening with his entire body. Joslyn's cat, Lucy-Maude, remained singularly unconcerned.

Madison looked at the animal with shy interest, still unsure whether to make friends with him or keep her distance.

"Well," Callie remarked, getting to her feet and heading for the nearest window, the one over the steel sink, and peering out as the sound of a car's engine reached them, "*they're* back early. They must have decided to skip the reception."

Jasper barked happily and hurried to the door. Joslyn had long since dubbed him the one-dog welcoming committee and at the moment he was spilling over with a wild desire to greet whoever happened to show up.

With a little chuckle, Callie opened the back door so Jasper could shoot through it like a fur-covered bullet, positively beside himself with joy. There was a little frown nestled between the older woman's eyebrows, though, as she looked toward Kendra again. "This is odd," she reiterated. "I hope Joslyn is feeling all right."

Shea, Slade's lovely dark-haired stepdaughter, just turned seventeen, burst into the house first, her violet eyes huge with excitement. "You're not going to *believe* this, Grands," she told Callie breathlessly. "The music was playing. The bridesmaids were all lined up and the preacher had his book open, ready to start. And what do you suppose happened?"

Kendra's heart fluttered in her chest, but she didn't speak.

A number of drastic scenarios flashed through her mind—a wedding guest toppling over from a heart attack, then a cattle truck crashing through a wall, followed by lightning boring its way right through the roof of the church and striking the bridegroom dead where he stood.

She shook the images off. Waited with her breath snagged painfully in the back of her throat.

"What?" Callie prodded good-naturedly, studying her step-granddaughter. She and Shea were close— the girl worked part-time at Callie's Curly Burly Hair Salon in town, and during the school year, Shea went to Callie's place after the last bell rang, spending hours tweaking the website she'd built for the shop.

"Hutch called the whole thing off," Shea blurted. "He stopped the wedding!"

"Oh, my," Callie said. The door was still open, and Kendra heard Joslyn's voice, then Opal's, as they came toward the house. Slade must have been with them, but he was keeping quiet, as usual.

Kendra realized she was squeezing Madison too tightly and relaxed her arms a little. Her mouth had dropped open at some point and she closed it, hoping no one had noticed. Just then, she couldn't have uttered a word if the place caught fire.

Opal, tall and dressed to the nines in one of her home-sewn and brightly patterned jersey dresses, crossed the threshold next, shaking her head as she unpinned her old-fashioned hat, with its tiny stuffed bird and inch-wide veiling.

Slade and Joslyn came in behind her, Joslyn's huge belly preceding her "by half an hour," as her adoring husband liked to say.

By then, the bomb dropped, Shea had shifted her focus to Madison. She'd been trying to win the little girl over from the beginning, and her smile dazzled, like sunlight on still waters. "Hey, kiddo," she said. "Since we missed out on the wedding cake, I'm up for a major cookie binge. Want to join me?"

Somewhat to Kendra's surprise, Madison slid down off her lap, Rupert the kangaroo dangling from one small hand, and approached the older girl, albeit slowly. "Okay," she said, her voice tentative.

Joslyn, meanwhile, lumbered over to the table, pulled back a chair and sank into it. She looked incandescent in her summery maternity dress, a blue confection with white polka dots, and she fanned her flushed face with her thin white clutch for a few moments before plunking it down on the tabletop.

"Do you need to lie down?" Callie asked her daughter-in-law worriedly, one hand resting on Joslyn's shoulder.

Madison and Shea, meanwhile, were plundering the cookie jar.

"No," Joslyn told her. "I'm fine. Really."

Opal tied on an apron and instructed firmly, "Now

don't you girls stuff yourselves on those cookies with me fixing to put a meal on the table in a little while."

A swift tenderness came over Kendra as she took it all in—including Opal's bluster. As Kendra was growing up, the woman had been like a mother to her, if not a patron saint.

Slade, his blue gaze resting softly on Joslyn, hung up his hat and bent to ruffle the dog's ears.

"Poor Brylee," Opal said as she opened the refrigerator door and began rummaging about inside it for the makings of one of her legendary meals.

"Sounded to me like it was her own fault," Slade observed, leaving the dog in order to wash his hands at the sink. He was clad in a suit, but Kendra knew he'd be back in his customary jeans, beat-up boots and lightweight shirt at the first opportunity. "Hutch said he told Brylee he didn't want to get married, more than once, and she wouldn't listen."

For Slade, this was a virtual torrent of words. He was a quiet, deliberate man, and he normally liked to mull things over before he offered an opinion—in contrast to his half brother, Hutch, who tended to go barreling in where angels feared to tread and consider the wisdom of his words and actions later. Or not at all.

Joslyn, meanwhile, tuned in on Kendra's face and read her expression, however guarded it was, with perfect accuracy. They'd been friends since they were barely older than Madison was now, and for the past year, they'd been business partners, too—Joslyn taking over the reins at Shepherd Real Estate, in nearby Parable, while Kendra scoured the countryside for Jeffrey's daughter.

"Thank heaven he came to his senses," Joslyn said,

with her usual certainty. "Brylee is a wonderful person, but she's all wrong for Hutch and he's all wrong for her. They wouldn't have lasted a year."

The crowd in the kitchen began to thin out a little then—Shea, the dog and Madison headed into the family room with their cookies, and Callie followed, Shea regaling her "Grands" with an account of who did what and who wore what and who said what.

Slade ascended the back stairway, chuckling, no doubt on his way to the master bedroom to change clothes. Except for bankers and lawyers, few men in rural Montana wore suits on a regular basis—such get-ups were reserved for Sunday services, funerals and... weddings, ill-fated or otherwise.

Opal, for her part, kept murmuring to herself and shaking her head as she began measuring out flour and lard for a batch of her world-class biscuits. "Land sakes," she muttered repeatedly, along with, "Well, I never, in all my live-long days—"

Joslyn laid her hands on her bulging stomach and sighed. "I swear this baby is practicing to be a rodeo star. It feels as though he's riding a bull in there."

Kendra laughed softly, partly at the image her friend had painted and partly as a way to relieve the dizzying tension brought on by Shea's breathless announcement. *Hutch called the whole thing off. He stopped the wedding.*

"The least you could do," she teased Joslyn, trying to get a grip on her crazy emotions, "is go into labor already and let the little guy get a start on his cowboy career."

As serene as a Botticelli Madonna, Joslyn grinned. "He's taking his time, all right," she agreed. The briefest frown flickered in her shining eyes as she regarded Kendra more closely than before. "It's only fair to warn you," she went on, quietly resolute, "that Slade invited Hutch to come to supper with us tonight—"

Joslyn continued to talk, saying she expected both Slade and Hutch would saddle up and ride the range for a while, but Kendra barely heard her. She flat-out wasn't ready to encounter Hutch Carmody, even at her closest friend's table. Why, the last time she'd seen him, after that stupid, macho horse race of his and Slade's, she'd kicked him, hard, in the shins.

Because he'd just kissed her.

Because he'd risked his life for no good reason.

Because hers was just one of the many hearts he'd broken along his merry way.

Plus she was a mess. She'd been on the road for three days, and even after a good night's sleep in Joslyn's guest room and two showers, she felt rumpled and grungy.

She stood up. She'd get Madison and head for town, she decided, hurry to her own place, where she should have gone in the beginning.

Not that she planned to live there very long.

The mega-mansion was too big for her and Madison, too full of memories.

"Kendra," Joslyn ordered kindly, "sit down."

Opal could be heard poking around in the pantry, still talking to herself.

Slade came down the back stairway, looking like himself in worn jeans, a faded flannel shirt and boots.

Passing Joslyn, he paused and leaned down to plant a kiss on top of her head. Kendra sank slowly back into her own chair.

"Don't start without me," Slade said, spreading one big hand on Joslyn's baby-bulge and grinning down into her upturned face.

It was almost enough to make a person believe in love again, Kendra thought glumly, watching these two.

"Not a chance, cowboy," Joslyn replied, almost purring the words. "We made this baby together and we're having it together."

Kendra was really starting to feel like some kind of voyeuristic intruder when Opal came out of the pantry, looked Slade over from behind the thick lenses of her glasses, and demanded, "Just where do you think you're going, Slade Barlow? Didn't I just say I'm starting supper?"

Slade straightened, smiled at Opal. "Now don't get all riled up," he cajoled. "I'm just going out to check on the horses, not driving a herd to Texas."

"Do I look like I was born yesterday?" Opal challenged, with gruff good humor. "You mean to saddle up and ride. I can tell by looking at you."

Slade laughed, shook his head, shoved a hand through his dark hair before crossing the room to take his everyday hat from a peg beside the back door and plop it on his head. "I promise you," he told Opal, "that the minute that dinner bell rings, I'll be here."

Opal huffed, cheerfully unappeased, then waved Slade off with one hand and went back to making supper.

"You might as well stay here and face Hutch," Joslyn told Kendra, as though there had been no interruption in their conversation. "After all, Parable is a small town, and you're bound to run into him sooner rather than later. Why not get it over with?"

The twinkle in Joslyn's eyes might have annoyed Kendra if she hadn't been so fond of her. Like many happily married people, Joslyn wanted all her friends to see the light and get hitched, pronto.

An image of Brylee Parrish bloomed in Kendra's mind and she felt a stab of sorrow for the woman. Loving Hutch Carmody was asking for trouble—she could have told Brylee that.

Not that Brylee would have listened, any more than *she* had long ago, when various friends had warned her that she was marrying Jeffrey on the rebound, had urged her to take time to think before leaping feetfirst into a whole different world.

"I need to get Madison settled," Kendra fretted. "There are groceries to buy and I've been away from the business way too long as it is—"

"The business is just fine," Joslyn said reasonably. "And so is Madison."

As if on cue, the little girl gave a delighted laugh in the next room.

It was a sweet sound, all too rare, and it made the backs of Kendra's eyes scald. "I don't know if I can handle it," she confessed, very softly. "Seeing Hutch again right away, I mean. I was counting on having some time to adjust to being back—"

Joslyn reached out, took her hand. Squeezed. "You can handle it," she said with quiet certainty. "Trust yourself, Kendra. Nothing is going to happen between you and Hutch unless you want it to."

"That's just the trouble," Kendra reflected miserably, careful to keep her voice down so Madison wouldn't overhear. "Wanting a man—wanting *Hutch*—and knowing better the whole time—well, you know—"

"I do know," Joslyn said, smiling.

"I have a daughter now," Kendra reminded her friend. "I want Madison to grow up in Parable, go to the same schools from kindergarten through high school. I want to give her security, a real sense of community, the whole works. And getting sucked into Hutch's orbit would be the stupidest thing I could possibly do."

"Would it?" Joslyn asked, raising one delicate eyebrow as she waited for a reply.

"Of course it would," Kendra whispered fiercely. "The man broke my heart into a gazillion pieces, remember? And now he's dumped some poor woman virtually at the altar, which only goes to prove he hasn't changed!"

"Did it ever occur to you," Joslyn inquired, unruffled, "that Hutch might have 'dumped' Brylee for the simple reason that she's not you?"

"No," Kendra said firmly, shaken by the mere possibility, "that did *not* occur to me. He did it because he can't commit to anything or anyone long-term, because Whisper Creek Ranch is all he really cares about in this world—*because* he's a heartless, womanizing *bastard*."

Before Joslyn could offer a response to that, Madison, Shea, Callie and the dog trailed back in the kitchen, making further discussion of Hutch Carmody impossible.

Kendra was still flustered, though. Her heart pounded and her throat and sinuses felt strangely thick—was she coming down with something? Every instinct urged her to get the heck out of there, *now,* but the idea seemed cowardly and, besides, Madison was just starting to let herself be part of the group.

If they rushed off to town, the little girl would be understandably confused.

So Kendra decided to stay, at least until after supper.

She was a grown woman, a mother. Joslyn had been right—it was time she started trusting herself. Hutch had always held an infuriating attraction for her, but she was older now, and wiser, and she had more self-control.

The next hour was taken up with getting ready, coming and going, table-setting and a lot of companionable, lighthearted chatter. Slade returned from the barn as he'd promised and, after washing up in a downstairs bathroom, made the whole crew promise not to pester Hutch with questions about the interrupted wedding.

As if, Kendra thought. She probably wouldn't say more than a few polite words to the man. If she spoke to him at all.

She felt strong, confident, ready for anything.

Until he actually walked into the ranch house kitchen, that is.

Seeing her, he tightened his jaw and shot an accusatory glance in his half brother's direction.

"Didn't I mention that Kendra's here?" Slade asked, breaking the brief, pulsing silence. There was a smile in his voice, though his blue eyes conveyed nothing but innocent concern.

Hutch, his dark blond hair sun-kissed with gold, recovered his normal affable manner within the space of a heartbeat.

He even smiled, flashing those perfect white teeth and setting Kendra back on her figurative heels.

"Hello, Kendra," he said with a nod, after taking off

his hat. Like Slade, he was dressed "cowboy" and the look suited him.

Kendra replied with a nod of her own. "Hutch," she said, turning from the chopping board, where she'd been preparing a salad, and wished she'd cleared her throat first, because the name came out like a croak.

His gaze moved straight to Madison, and Kendra read the questions in his eyes even before he hid them behind a smile. Madison, meanwhile, raised Rupert, as if presenting him to this stranger for inspection.

"Howdy, there," he said, all charm. "Do my eyes deceive me or is that critter a kangaroo?"

CHAPTER TWO

THE WAY HUTCH figured it, a solid week should have been plenty long enough for the fuss over the wedding-that-never-was to die down, but when Saturday afternoon rolled around again and he sat down at his computer to get a quick read on the gossip situation, tired from rounding up strays with the ranch hands since just after dawn, he was promptly disabused of the notion.

This jabber-fest was getting worse by the moment.

Apparently he'd made every "jerk" list in cyberspace, not just locally, but worldwide. Indignant females from as far away as the Philippines thought he ought to be tarred and feathered, and a couple of Brylee's girlfriends, bless their vengeful little hearts, had set up a page on one of the major networking sites solely for the purpose of warning every woman with a pulse to steer clear of Hutch Carmody.

The reverse version, he supposed, grimly amused, of an old West "Wanted" poster.

Of course, this being the digital age, there were pictures up the wazoo—Bride-Doll Brylee, flushed and furious in her over-the-top dress, stomping on her bouquet in the church aisle. Brylee, outside in the bright June sunshine, probably only moments after the first shot was taken, wrenching the taped-on "Just Married" sign from the back of the limo that would have carried the two of them over to the Community Center for the reception, ripping the cardboard in two and flinging the pieces into the gutter. Brylee, later still, hair pulled back and caught up in a long, messy ponytail, face puffy and scrubbed clean of makeup, her gown swapped out for jeans and a T-shirt bearing the motto Men Suck. She was surrounded by a dozen or so of her friends, at a table in the center of the Boot Scoot Tavern, the jukebox lit up behind her. No doubt, it was playing a somebody-done-me-wrong song.

Hutch sighed. He hadn't escaped the amateur paparazzi himself—these days, every yahoo and his Aunt Bessie had a smart phone, and they were mighty quick on the draw with them.

One memorable image showed him standing in the center of the sanctuary, clearly uncomfortable in the penguin get-up he'd rented from Wally's Wedding World, over in Three Trees, the neighboring town, looking pale and bleakly determined not to get married no matter what he had to do to avoid it. And those were just the stills—there were videos, too. In one thirty-second wonder, he could be seen climbing into his rusted-out pickup truck, right there in the Presbyterians' gravel parking lot, and in the next, he was heading for the horizon, a dust plume spiraling behind his rig.

Yep, that was him all right, beating a hasty retreat, like a yellow-bellied coward on the run.

That impression rested sour on the back of his tongue.

Someday, he suspected, when Brylee met up with her own personal Mr. Right, got hitched for real, and had herself a houseful of kids, she'd thank him for stopping the wedding and thereby preventing certain catastrophe.

At present, though, that particular "someday" seemed a long way off.

Weary to the aching marrow of his bones, Hutch logged off the internet, pushed back from the rolltop desk that had been in his family since the Lincoln administration, and stood up, stretching luxuriously before retrieving his coffee mug and ambling out of the little office behind the ranch house kitchen.

Taking Slade's advice, he'd kept a low profile since the day that, like the bombing of Pearl Harbor and the 9/11 attacks, would forever live in infamy. Against his own better judgment, he hadn't gone to see Brylee in person, called her on the phone, or even sent her an email.

He hadn't done much guilt-wallowing, either, which might be proof that he really *was* a "selfish, heartless, narcissistic bastard," as members of Team Brylee universally agreed, at least online. By now, the group probably had its own secret handshake.

Hutch regretted hurting Brylee, of course, and he certainly wished he could have spared her the humiliation of that very public breakup, but his overriding emotion was a sense of relief so profound that it still made his head reel even after a week.

Train wreck, averted.

Apocalypse, canceled.

Check and check.

Running into Kendra Shepherd at Slade and Joslyn's place after the debacle had *definitely* thrown him, however—slammed the wind out of him as surely as if he'd been hurled off the back of a bad bull or a sun-fishing bronco and landed on hard ground.

He'd loved Kendra once and he'd believed she loved him.

He'd expected to spend the rest of his life with the woman, happy to make babies, run Whisper Creek Ranch with Kendra at his side, a full partner in every way.

Instead, enter Jeffrey Chamberlain, he of the nominal titles and English estates, practically a prince to a woman like Kendra, brought up in a small Montana town by a grandmother who resented the responsibility of raising her errant daughter's child. Chamberlain had been visiting friends at the time—Hollywood types with delusions of living the ranching life in grand style—and damned if Sir Jeffrey hadn't struck up a conversation with Kendra at the post office one fine day and parlayed that, over the coming weeks, into a romance so epic that it could only have ended badly.

Not that Kendra had fallen for Chamberlain right away—at the get-go, she'd insisted he was just a friend, interesting and funny. Hutch, though nettled, had reluctantly—okay, *grudgingly*—accepted the explanation.

Down deep, he'd been out-of-his-gourd jealous, though, and soon enough the bickering commenced.

Chamberlain, knowing full well what he'd set in motion, had found excuses to stay on in Parable and he just bided his time while things got worse and worse between Hutch and Kendra.

Inevitably, the bickering escalated to fiery yelling matches and, worse, single words, terse and biting, punctuated by long, achy silences.

Eventually, Kendra had given Hutch an ultimatum—trust her or leave her.

He'd chosen the latter option, being a stubborn, hard-headed cowboy from a long line of stubborn, hard-headed cowboys, never really thinking she'd go at all, let alone stay gone; everybody knew they belonged together, he and Kendra. After a semidecent interval, though, she'd hauled off and eloped with Jeffrey.

There were still days—moments, really—when Hutch couldn't believe it had come to that, and this was one of them.

Now, standing in his kitchen, he closed his eyes, remembering.

Kendra had called him three days after tying the knot down in Vegas.

Even then he'd wanted to say, "This isn't right. Come home."

But he'd been too cussed proud to take the high road.

He'd wished "Lady Chamberlain" well and hung up in her ear. Hard. They'd seen each other numerous times afterward, the way things shook out, especially after Chamberlain bought his way out of the marriage and crossed the pond to resume his Lord-of-the-manor lifestyle while Kendra remained in Parable, rattling around in that hotel-sized mansion on Rodeo Road.

Small as Parable was, he and Kendra had come close to patching things up a few times, making another start, but something always went wrong, probably because neither one of them trusted the other any further than they could have thrown them.

They'd been civil last Saturday night at Slade and Joslyn's noisy supper table, but Kendra had looked ready to jump out of her skin at any moment, and as soon as the meal was over and the dishes were in the machine, she'd grabbed up her little girl and boogied for town in her boxy mom-car.

What had happened to that little BMW convertible she used to drive?

"She wasn't expecting to see you tonight," Joslyn had explained, touching his hand once Kendra and the child were out of the house.

Hutch had slanted an evil look at his half brother. "I know the feeling," he'd said.

Slade had merely looked smug.

Now with another long, dirty workday behind him and lunch a distant memory, Hutch stood there in his stupidly big kitchen and tried to shift his focus to rustling up some kind of a supper, but the few budding science experiments hunkered down in the fridge held no appeal. Neither did the resoundingly empty house—by rights, the place should have been bursting with noisy ranch kids and rescued dogs by now. Instead it was neat, cold and stone silent.

Hutch sighed, shoved a hand through his hair. Stepped back from the refrigerator and shut the door.

Upstairs he took a quick shower and donned fresh jeans, a white shirt and go-to-town boots.

He'd hidden out long enough, damn it.

By God, he was through keeping a low profile—he meant to fire up one of the ranch trucks, drive into Parable to the Butter Biscuit Café, claim one of the stools at the counter and order up his usual cheeseburger, shake and fries. As for the joshing and the questions and the speculative glances he was bound to run into?

Bring it, he thought.

KENDRA HAD HAD a week to put that off-the-wall encounter with Hutch the previous Saturday night behind her and she was mostly over it.

Mostly.

She'd been busy, after all, overseeing the move of her real estate company from the mansion on Rodeo Road to the little storefront, catty-corner from the Butter Biscuit Café, enrolling Madison at the year-round preschool/day-care center and scanning the multiple-listings for cozy two-bedroom houses within a reasonable radius of Parable.

In a town like that one, smaller properties were always hard to find—people didn't necessarily sell their houses when they retired to Florida or Arizona or entered a nursing home. They often passed them down to the next generation.

At present, Kendra's choices were a double-wide trailer in the very court where she'd grown up so unhappily with her grandmother—no possible way—what resembled a converted chicken coop on the far side of Three Trees, which was thirty miles away, or the cramped apartment over old Mrs. Lund's garage on Cinch Buckle Street, which rented for a tidy sum and didn't even have its own entrance.

With her fifteen-thousand-square-foot mega-mansion on the market, already swarming with cleaning people and painters these days in preparation for showing—she and Madison had taken up temporary residence in the estate's small guesthouse.

Given that two different potential buyers, both highly qualified, had already expressed interest in the main residence, Kendra had no intention of getting too settled in the cottage, cheery and convenient though the place was. Upscale homes were much easier to sell than regular houses, at least in that part of Montana, because so many jet-setters liked to buy them up and visit them once in a blue moon.

For now, though, the guesthouse was sufficient for their needs. Madison loved the big yard, the thriving flower gardens and the swing on the mansion's screened-in sun porch. The four-year-old was content to share the cottage's one bedroom with Kendra, take meals in the tiny, sun-splashed kitchen, and ease, an hour or two at a time, into the preschool program, where there were plenty of playmates around her own age.

Already Madison's fair skin was golden, having absorbed so much country sunshine, and she didn't cry at the prospect of even the shortest separation from Kendra.

Tara Kendall stopped by the real estate office just as Kendra was about to close up for the day. She and Madison planned on picking up a takeout meal over at the Butter Biscuit, then eating at the small white wrought-iron table at the edge of the rose garden on Rodeo Road.

"Can we get a dog now?" Madison was asking for the umpteenth time, when Tara breezed in, pretty with her shoulder-length brown hair expertly layered and her perfect makeup that looked like no makeup at all.

"Do I have an offer for you," Tara said, with a broad grin. She wore a sleek yellow sundress that flattered her slight but womanly figure, and her legs were so tanned she didn't need panty hose. "My golden retriever, Lucy, just happens to have a sister who still needs a home."

"Gee," Kendra drawled, feeling self-conscious in

her jeans and T-shirt. "Thanks so much for that suggestion, Tara."

Madison was already jumping up and down in anticipation. "My very own dog!" she crowed.

Tara chuckled and reached out a manicured hand to ruffle Madison's bright copper curls. "Oops," she said, addressing Kendra in a singsong voice that sounded warmly insincere. "Did I just put my foot in my mouth?"

"More like your entire leg," Kendra replied sweetly. Tara, a relative newcomer to Parable, had fit right in with her and Joslyn, turning a duet into a trio—the three of them had been fast friends from the beginning. "We're not ready for a dog yet, since we don't really have a place to—" She paused, looked down at Madison, who was glowing like a firefly on a moonless night, and reconsidered the word she'd intended to use, which was "live," diverting to "permanently reside."

"We have the cottage," Madison pointed out. "There's a yard and Lucy's sister could sleep with us."

"Says you," Kendra said, but with affection. She remembered how badly she'd wanted a pet as a little girl, but her grandmother had always refused, saying she had enough on her hands looking after a kid. She wasn't about to clean up after a dog or a cat, too.

"You promised," Madison reminded her sagely. She was so like Jeffrey—she had his eyes, his red hair, his insouciant certainty that everything good would come to him as a matter of course—including golden retriever puppies with sisters named Lucy.

"I said we could get a pet when we were settled," Kendra clarified patiently after shooting a see-what-

you've-done glance at a singularly unrepentant Tara.
"We'll be moving soon."

"So will the dog," Tara put in lightly. "Martie Wren
can only keep her at the shelter for so long, then it's off
to—well—wherever."

"Thanks *again,* Tara," Kendra said. She knew her
friend meant well, but the woman wasn't known for
her good judgment. Hadn't she given up a great job in
New York, heading up a world-class cosmetics company, to buy, of all things, a dilapidated chicken ranch
on the outskirts of Parable, Montana?

Huge tears welled in Madison's eyes. "Nobody *wants*
Lucy's sister?"

At last, Tara looked shamefaced. "She's a beautiful
dog," she told the little girl gently. "Somebody will
adopt her for sure."

"You, for instance?" Kendra said.

"I guess she could live with Lucy and me for a
while," Tara decided, shifting her expensive hobo bag
from her right shoulder to her left.

Madison grabbed Kendra's hand, squeezed. "We
could just *look* at Emma, couldn't we?"

"Emma?" Kendra echoed, dancing on ice now,
Bambi with all four limbs scrabbling for traction.

"That's what we'd call Lucy's sister," Madison said
matter-of-factly, her little face shining more brightly
than the sunset gathering in shades of pink and orange
at the rims of the mountains to the east. "Emma."

Emma. It was Madison's birth mother's name. Did
she know that?

How could she? She'd been only a year old when
Emma gave her up.

"Why 'Emma'?" Kendra asked carefully, hoping to hide her dismayed surprise from the child.

Tara, she instantly noted, had already read her face, though she couldn't have known the significance of the name, and she looked way beyond apologetic.

"It's a pretty name," Madison said. "Don't you think so, Mommy?"

"It's lovely," Kendra conceded. "Now, shouldn't we pick up our supper and head for home?" She glanced at Tara. "Join us? Nothing fancy—we're getting takeout—but we'd love to share."

Tara blinked, clearly uncertain what response she ought to give. "Well—"

"And it would be fun to meet Lucy," Madison went on. "Is she with you?"

"As a matter of fact," Tara said, "yes. She's in the car. We just came from the vet's office and—"

"You're both welcome," Kendra insisted. Firstly because Tara *was* a dear friend and secondly, because she was enjoying the other woman's obvious discomfort. "You *and* Lucy."

"Well," Tara murmured, with a weak little smile, "okay."

Kendra smiled. "Let's go, then," she said, jingling the ring of keys she'd just plucked from her purse.

She shut off the inside lights, stepped out onto the sidewalk and locked up behind them. Leaving Kendra's Volvo in the parking lot out back, they crossed the street to the Butter Biscuit Café. Tara's flashy red sports car was parked on the street in front of the restaurant, the yellow dandelion-fluff dog, Lucy, pressing her muzzle against the driver's-side window, steaming up the glass.

Kendra's heart softened at the very sight of that dog,

while Madison rushed over to stand on tiptoe and press the palms of both hands against the window.

"Hello, Lucy!" Madison cried gleefully.

Lucy barked joyously, her brown eyes luminous with impromptu adoration. She tongued the window where Madison's right palm rested.

Tara laughed. "See?" she said, giving Kendra a light elbow to the ribs. "It's fate."

"I'll get you for this," Kendra told her friend with an undertone.

"No, you'll thank me." Tara beamed, all confidence again. "I'm counting on Emma to win you over." She whispered that last part.

They practically had to drag Madison away from the car, and the dog, each adult gripping one of her small hands as they approached the entrance to the Butter Biscuit Café.

The place was rocking, as always, with dishes clinking and waitresses rushing back and forth and the juke-box blaring an old Randy Travis song.

All the noise and busyness subsided though, at least for Kendra, when her gaze found and landed unerringly on Hutch Carmody.

He sat alone at the counter, ridiculously handsome in ordinary jeans, a white shirt and black boots. A plate sat in front of him, containing half a cheeseburger, a few French fries and some pickles.

It wouldn't have been so awkward if he hadn't noticed Kendra—or at least, if he'd *pretended* not to notice her—but he turned toward her immediately, as though equipped with Kendra-detecting radar.

A slow smile lifted his mouth at one corner and his greenish-blue eyes sparked with amused interest.

Madison rushed straight toward him, as if they were old friends. "We're getting a dog!" she piped. "Well, *maybe*."

Hutch grinned down at the child, his expression softening a little, full of a kindness Kendra had never seen in him before, not even in their most private and tender moments. The man definitely had a way with kids.

"Is that so?" he asked companionably. "Is this dog purple, like your kangaroo?"

Madison giggled at this question. "No, silly," she said. "Dogs are *never* purple!"

Hutch chuckled. "Neither are kangaroos, in my experience. Not that we have a whole lot of them hopping around the great state of Montana."

"They mostly live in Australia," Madison told him solemnly. "Rupert is only purple because he's a *toy*."

"I guess that explains it," Hutch replied, his gaze rising slowly to reconnect with Kendra's. Electricity arced, potent, between them. "I'm glad to have the purple kangaroo question settled. It's been troubling me a lot."

And that wasn't the only thing he'd been wondering about, Kendra suddenly realized. He wanted to know how she'd managed to produce a child without ever being pregnant.

As if that were any of his business.

"Hello, Hutch," Kendra said, her voice strangely wooden.

He merely nodded.

Tara spoke up. "How have you been?" she asked him nervously.

Something flickered in Hutch's eyes; it was obvious that he'd figured out what Tara really wanted to know. "I've been just fine, Tara," he replied evenly and without rancor. "Except, of course, for that whole non-wedding thing."

Tara blushed.

So did Kendra.

"G-good," Tara said.

"We'd better place our order," Kendra added, and immediately felt like a complete fool. A well-spoken person otherwise, she never seemed to know what to say around Hutch. "B-before the café gets any busier, I mean—"

"Plus Lucy's locked up in the red car outside," Madison put in.

"Plus that," Kendra said lamely.

"Lucy?" Hutch asked, raising one eyebrow.

"My dog," Tara explained.

"Right," Hutch answered. His gaze remained on Kendra, stirring up all sorts of totally unwanted memories, like the way his hands felt on her bare thighs or the touch of his lips gliding softly over the tops of her breasts. "Nice to see you again," he added casually.

When he looked at her that way, Kendra always felt as though her clothes were made of cellophane, and that got her hackles up. Not to mention her nipples, which, thankfully, were well hidden under the loose fabric of her T-shirt.

Even though she turned away quickly and began studying the big menu board on the wall behind the cash register, Kendra was still acutely aware of Hutch, of little Madison, who so clearly adored him, and of Tara, who was trying to pick up the dangling conversational thread.

"Rodeo Days are almost upon us," Tara said brightly.

Every Independence Day weekend since the beginning of time, Parable had hosted the county rodeo, fireworks and carnival. People came from miles around to eat barbecued pork and beef in the park, root for their favorite cowboys and barrel-racing cowgirls, and ride the Ferris wheel and the Whirly-Gig. "The cleanup committee is looking for volunteers. Shall I put your name down to help out, Hutch?"

The woman was wasted as a chicken rancher, Kendra thought, pretending to puzzle between the café's famous corn-bread casserole and deep-fried catfish. Tara should have been selling ice to penguins.

"Sure," she heard Hutch say.

Kendra settled on the corn-bread casserole, preferring to avoid deep-fried *anything,* slanted a glance at Tara and raised her voice a little to place the order with a waitress. "To go, please," she added, perhaps a touch pointedly.

She heard Hutch chuckle, low and gruff.

What was funny?

Tara edged over to Kendra's side, digging in her purse for money.

"My treat," Kendra said, watching out of the corner of her eye as Madison tore herself out of Hutch's orbit and joined the women in front of the cash register.

The food was packed for transport, handed over and paid for, all in due course. As they were leaving, Madison turned back to wave at Hutch.

"I like that cowboy man," she announced, to all and sundry, her little voice ringing like a silver bell at Christmas.

An affectionate group chuckle rippled through the café and Kendra hid a sigh behind the smile she turned on her daughter. "Let's go," she said, taking Madison's small and somewhat grubby hand in hers before they crossed the street to get to Kendra's Volvo.

"Meet you at your place," Tara called, unlocking her car door and then laughing as she wrestled the eager puppy back so she could slide into the driver's seat and take the wheel.

Kendra nodded and, when the Walk sign flashed, she and Madison started across the street.

"Don't you like the cowboy man, Mommy?" Madison asked, wrinkling her face against the bright dazzle of afternoon sunshine.

The question surprised Kendra so much that she nearly stopped right there in the middle of the road. "Now why on earth would you ask such a thing, Madison Rose Shepherd?" she asked, keeping her tone light, almost teasing.

"If he looks at you," Madison observed, as they stepped up onto the sidewalk and started toward the Volvo, "you look away."

Thinking it was uncanny, the things children not only noticed but could verbalize, Kendra turned up her inner-smile dial a notch and squeezed Madison's hand gently. "Do I?" she countered, knowing full well that she did.

Madison nodded. "He looks at you a lot, too," she added.

Mercifully they'd reached the car, and the next few minutes were taken up with settling Madison in her booster seat and placing the take-out bag carefully on the floor, so the food inside wouldn't spill.

A four-year-old's attention span being what it was, Kendra had reason to hope the subject would have

changed by the time she'd buckled herself in behind
the wheel and started the car with an unintended roar
of the motor.

"Do you know if the cowboy man likes dogs?" Madison ventured, from her perch in the backseat.

Kendra calmly took her foot off the gas pedal, shifted
into Drive and steered carefully into the nonexistent
traffic. "Yes, I think so," she replied, as matter-of-factly
as she could.

"That's good," Madison said happily.

Kendra wasn't about to pursue that observation.
"Have you ever been to a rodeo?" she asked, a way of
deflecting the topic away from dogs and Hutch Carmody.

"What's a rodeo?" Madison asked.

Kendra took the short drive home to describe the
phenomenon in words her small daughter might be expected to understand.

"Oh," Madison said when Kendra was finished.
"Will the cowboy man be there?"

LUCY THE GOLDEN RETRIEVER turned out to be a real
charmer, with her butter-colored fur and those saintly
brown eyes dancing with intermittent mischief.

After supper, served as planned at the metal table
beside the rose garden, Madison and the pup ran madly
around the yard, celebrating green grass and vivid colors and the cool breeze of a summer evening.

Watching them, Tara smiled. "I'm sorry if I put you
on the spot before," she said to Kendra, after taking a
sip from her glass of iced tea. "About Lucy's sister, I
mean."

"That was her birth mother's name," Kendra reflected, watching the child and the dog as they played in the gathering twilight.

Tara set the glass down. "What? Lucy?"

Kendra shook her head. "No," she said, very softly. "Emma. Do you suppose Madison remembers her mother?"

"*You* are Madison's mother," Tara replied.

"Tara," Kendra said wearily.

"From what you've told Joslyn and me, Madison's been in foster care since she was a year old. How could she remember?"

Kendra lifted one shoulder slightly, then let it fall. "It seems like a pretty big coincidence that Madison would choose that particular name. She must have overheard it somewhere."

"Probably," Tara allowed. Then she added, "Kendra, look at me."

Kendra shifted her gaze from drinking in the sight of Madison and Lucy, frolicking against a backdrop of blooming flowers of every hue, to Tara's concerned face.

"You're not afraid she'll come back, are you?" Tara prompted, almost in a whisper. "This Emma person, I mean, and try to take Madison away?"

Kendra shook her head. She was at once comforted and saddened by the knowledge that Madison's biological mother hadn't wanted her baby enough to fight for her.

The woman had demanded money, naturally, but she'd signed off readily enough once Jeffrey's American lawyers got the point across that the buying and selling of babies was illegal.

"She's relinquished all rights to Madison," she finally answered.

Tara sighed. "It's hard to understand some people," she said.

"Impossible," Kendra agreed. Oddly, though, she wasn't thinking of Madison's birth mom anymore, but of Hutch.

The man was a mystery, an enigma.

He fractured women's hearts with apparent impunity—there always seemed to be another hopeful waiting in the wings, certain she'd be the exception to the rule—and yet kids, dogs and horses saw nothing in him to fear and everything to love.

Was he actually a good man, underneath all that bad-boy mojo and easy charm?

"Still planning to sell this place, then?" Tara asked with a gesture of one hand that took in the mansion as well as the grounds.

Kendra nodded. "I'll be putting the proceeds in trust for Madison," she said. She hadn't told Joslyn and Tara everything, but they both knew Jeffrey had fathered the little girl. "It's rightfully hers."

Tara absorbed that quietly and took another sip from her iced tea. "You won't miss it? The money, I mean? Living in the biggest and fanciest house in town?"

Kendra's smile was rueful. "I'm not broke, Tara," she said. "I've racked up a lot of commissions since I started Shepherd Real Estate." She looked back over one shoulder at the looming structure behind them. "As for missing this house, no, I won't, not for a moment. It's a showplace, not a home."

Tara didn't answer. She seemed to be musing, mulling something over.

"So," Kendra said, "how's the chicken ranch coming along?"

At that, Tara rolled her beautiful eyes. "It's a disaster," she answered with honest good humor. "The nesting-house roof is sagging, the hens aren't laying—I suspect that's because the roosters are secretly gay—and Boone Taylor still refuses to plant shrubbery to hide that eyesore of a trailer he lives in so it won't be the first thing I see when I look out my kitchen window every morning."

"Regrets?" Kendra asked gently. Madison and Lucy seemed to be winding down; moving in slow motion as the shadows thickened. After a bath and a story, Madison would sleep soundly.

Tara immediately shook her head. "No," she said. "It's hard, but I'm a long way from giving up."

"Good," Kendra said with a smile. "Because I'd feel guilty if you were having second thoughts, considering I was the one who sold you the place."

"You might have warned me about the neighbors," Tara joked.

"Boone isn't so bad," Kendra felt honor-bound to say. She'd known him since childhood, known his late wife, Corrie, too. He'd lost interest in life for a long time after Corrie's death from breast cancer a few years back, but last November he'd up and run for sheriff and gotten himself elected by a country mile. "He's just stubborn, like most of the men around here. That's what gets them through the hard times."

Tara's eyes widened a little. "Does that apply to Hutch, too?"

Kendra stood up, beckoned to her tired daughter. "Time to get ready for bed," she called to Madison, who meandered slowly toward her—proof in itself that she was exhausted. Like most small children, she normally resisted sleep with all her might, lest she miss something.

The puppy trotted over to Tara, nuzzling her knee, and she laughed as she bent to ruffle her ears.

"If you think Lucy's perfect," she said, instead of goodbye, "just wait till you meet her sister."

CHAPTER THREE

THE NEXT MORNING after church, Kendra gave in to the pressures of fate—and her very persistent daughter—and drove across town to Paws for Reflection, the private animal shelter run by a woman named Martie Wren.

Martie, an institution in Parable, oversaw the operation out of an office in her small living room, surviving entirely on donations and the help of numerous volunteers. She'd converted the two large greenhouses in back to dog-and-cat housing, though she also took in birds and rabbits and even the occasional pygmy goat. The place was never officially closed, even on Sundays and holidays.

A sturdy woman with kindly eyes and a shock of unruly gray hair, Martie was watering the flower beds in her front yard when Kendra and Madison arrived, parking on the street.

"Tara said you might be stopping by," Martie sang out happily, waving and then hurrying over to shut off the faucet and wind the garden hose around its plastic spool.

Kendra, busy helping Madison out of her safety rigging in the backseat, smiled wryly back at the other woman. "Of course she did," she replied cheerfully.

"We're here to see Lucy's sister," Madison remarked.

Martie, at the front gate by then, pushing it wide open in welcome, chuckled. "Well, come on inside then, and have a look at her. She's been waiting for you. Got her all dolled up just in case the two of you happened to take a shine to each other."

Kendra stifled a sigh. She wanted a dog as much as Madison did—there had been a canine-shaped hole in her heart for as long as she could remember—but she'd hoped to find a permanent place to live before acquiring a pet. Get settled in.

Alas, the universe did not seem concerned with her personal plans.

She and Madison passed through the gate, closing it behind them, and Martie led the way onto the neatly painted front porch and up to the door.

The retriever puppy did indeed seem to be waiting—she was sitting primly on the hooked rug in the tiny entryway, with a bright red ribbon tied to her collar and her chocolate-brown eyes practically liquid with hope.

Kendra immediately melted.

Madison, meanwhile, placed her hands on her hips and tilted her head to one side, studying the yellow fluff-ball intently.

The puppy rose from its haunches and approached the little girl, looking for all the world as though it were smiling at her. *Where have you been?* the animal's expression seemed to say. *We're supposed to be having fun together.*

Madison turned her eyes to Kendra. "She's so pretty," she said, sounding awed, as though there had never been and never would be another dog like this one.

"Very pretty," Kendra agreed, choking up a little.

She saw so much of her childhood self in Madison and that realization made her cautious. Madison was Madison, and trying to soothe her own childhood hurts through her daughter would be wrong on so many levels.

Martie, an old hand at finding good homes for otherwise unwanted critters, simply waited, benignly silent. She believed in letting things unfold at their own pace—not a bad philosophy in Kendra's opinion, though she'd yet to master it herself.

As a little girl she'd had to fight for every scrap of her grandmother's attention. In her career she'd been virtually *driven* to succeed, believing with all her heart that nothing good would happen unless she *made* it happen.

Now that Madison had entered her life, though, it was time to make some changes. Shifting her type-A personality down a few gears, so she could appreciate what she had, rather than always striving for something more, was at the top of the list.

Madison was still gazing at Kendra's face. "Can we take her home with us, Mommy?" she asked, clearly living for a "yes." "Please? Can we name her Daisy?"

Kendra's eyes burned as she crouched beside her daughter, putting herself at eye level with the child. "I thought you wanted to call her Emma," she said.

Madison shook her head. "Daisy's not an Emma. She's a Daisy."

Kendra put an arm around Madison, but loosely. "Okay," she said, very gently. "Daisy it is."

"She can come home with us, then?" Madison asked, wide-eyed, a small, pulsing bundle of barely contained energy.

"Well, there's a procedure that has to be followed," Kendra replied, looking over at Martie as she stood up straight again, leaving one hand resting on the top of Madison's head.

"Daisy's had her shots," Martie said, "and I've known you since you were the size of a bean sprout, Kendra Shepherd. You'll give this dog a good home and lots of love, and that's all that matters."

Something unspoken passed between the two women. Martie was probably remembering other visits to the shelter, when Kendra was small. She'd been the youngest volunteer at the shelter, cleaning kennels, filling water bowls and making sure every critter in the place got a gentle pat and a few kind words.

"You get a free vet visit, too," Martie said, as though further persuasion might be required.

Madison's face shone with delight. "Let's take Daisy home right now," she said.

Kendra and Martie both laughed.

"There are a few papers to be signed," Martie said to the child. "Why don't you and Daisy come on into the office with your mom and me, and keep each other company while we grown-ups take care of a few things?"

Madison, though obviously eager to take Daisy and run before one of the adults changed their mind, nodded dutifully. "All right," she said, her hand nestled into the golden fur at Daisy's nape. "But we're in a hurry."

Martie chuckled again.

Kendra hid a smile and said, *"Madison Rose."*

"We'll be very quick," Martie promised over one shoulder.

They all trailed into Martie's office, Daisy sticking close to Madison's side.

"It isn't polite to rush people, Madison," Kendra told her daughter.

"You *said,*" Madison reminded her, "that the church man took too long to stop talking, and everybody wanted to get out of there and have lunch. You wanted him to hurry up and finish."

Kendra blushed slightly. She *had* said something along those lines as they were driving away from the church, but that was different from standing up when the sermon seemed never-ending and saying something like, "Wrap it up, will you? We're in a hurry."

Explaining that to a four-year-old, obviously, would take some doing.

Martie chuckled again. "Lloyd's a dear, but he does tend to run on when he's got a captive audience on a Sunday morning," she remarked with kindly tolerance. "Bless his heart."

The Reverend Lloyd Atherton, like Martie, was a fixture in Parable. Long-winded though he was, everybody loved him.

Kendra made a donation, in lieu of a fee, listened to a brief and heartrending explanation of Daisy's background—she'd literally been left on Martie's doorstep in a cardboard box along with six of her brothers and sisters—and signed a simple document promising to return Daisy to Paws for Reflection if things didn't work out.

"Is Daisy hungry?" Madison wanted to know. It was a subtle nudge. *We're in a hurry.*

Martie smiled. "Puppies always seem to *think* they

are, but Daisy had a bowl of kibble less than half an hour ago. She'll be just fine until supper time."

Madison nodded, apparently satisfied. She was staring raptly at the little dog, stroking its soft coat as she waited for the adoption to be finalized.

Soon enough, the details had been handled and Madison was in the back of the Volvo again, buckled into her booster seat, with Daisy sitting alertly beside her, panting in happy anticipation of whatever.

They made a quick stop at the big discount store out on the highway, leaving Daisy waiting patiently in the car with a window partly rolled down for air while they rushed inside to buy assorted gear—a collar and leash, a package of poop bags, a fleecy bed large enough for a golden retriever puppy to grow into, grooming supplies, a few toys and the brand of kibble Martie had recommended.

Daisy was thrilled at their return and when Kendra tossed the bed into the backseat, the animal frolicked back and forth across the expanse of it, unable to contain her delight, causing Madison to laugh in a way Kendra had never heard her laugh before—rambunctiously and without self-consciousness or restraint.

It was a beautiful thing to hear and Kendra was glad there were so many small tasks to be performed before she could put the car in motion, because her vision was a little blurred.

Back at the guesthouse, Kendra put away the dog's belongings while Madison and Daisy ran frenetically around the backyard, both of them bursting with pent-up energy and pure celebration of each other.

"We need a poop bag, please," Madison announced

presently, appearing in the cottage doorway, a vision in her little blue Sunday-school dress.

Smiling, Kendra opened the pertinent package, followed Madison outside to the evidence and proceeded to demonstrate the proper collection and disposal of dog doo-doo.

Afterward, she insisted they both wash their hands at the bathroom sink.

Daisy looked on from the doorway, wagging her tail and looking pleased to be in the midst of so much interesting activity.

Lunch, long overdue by then, was next on the agenda. Madison and Kendra made peanut butter and jelly sandwiches in the impossibly small kitchen, and Kendra poured a glass of milk for both of them.

Daisy settled herself near Madison's chair, ears perked forward, nose raised to sniff the air, probably hoping that manna, in the form of scraps of a PB and J, might fall from heaven.

Martie had been adamant on that point, though. No people food and very few treats. The treat a dog needed most, she'd said, was plenty of love and affection.

When the meal was over and the table had been cleared, Madison announced, yawning, that Daisy had had a big morning and therefore needed a nap.

Amused—Madison normally napped only under protest—Kendra suggested that they ought to change out of their church clothes first.

Madison put on pink cotton shorts and a blue short-sleeved shirt, and Kendra opted for jeans and a light-weight green pullover. When she came out of the bedroom, Madison and Daisy were already curled up together on the new fleece dog bed, and Kendra didn't have the heart to raise an objection.

Lie down with dogs, get up with fleas, she heard her grandmother say.

Shut up, Gramma, was her silent response.

"Sleep tight," she said aloud, taking a book from the shelf and stepping outside, planning to sit in the shade of the maple trees and read for a while.

The scene was idyllic—bees buzzing, flowers nodding their many-colored heads in the light breeze, the big Montana sky sweeping blue and cloudless and eternal overhead.

Kendra relaxed as she read, and at some point, she must have dozed off, because she opened her eyes suddenly and found Hutch Carmody standing a few feet away, big as life.

She blinked a couple of times, but he didn't disappear.

Not a dream, then. Crap.

"Sorry," he said without a smidgeon of regret. "Didn't mean to wake you."

Kendra straightened and glanced toward the open doorway of the cottage, looking for Madison. There was no sign of either the child or the dog, but Kendra went inside to check on them anyway. They were both sleeping, curled up together on Daisy's cloud-soft bed.

Quietly, Kendra went back outside to face Hutch.

How could she not have heard him arrive? His truck was parked right there in the driveway, a stone's throw from where she'd been sitting. At the very least, she should have heard the tires in the gravel or the closing of the driver's door.

"What are you doing here?" she whispered, too rattled to be polite.

Hutch spread his hands wide, grinning. "I'm unarmed," he said, sidestepping the question. He was, she recalled, a master at sidestepping any topic he didn't want to discuss. "Don't shoot."

Kendra huffed out a sigh, picked up her book, which she'd dropped in the grass when she'd woken up to an eyeful of Hutch, and held it tightly against her side. "What. Are. You. Doing. Here?" she repeated.

He gestured for her to sit down, and since her knees were weak, she dropped back into her lawn chair. He drew another one up alongside hers and sat. They were both gazing straight ahead, like two strangers in the same row on an airplane, intent on the seat belt/oxygen mask lecture from an invisible flight attendant.

"Tell me about your little girl," Hutch finally said.

"Why should I?" Kendra asked reasonably, proud of her calm tone.

"I guess because she could have been ours," he replied.

For a moment, Kendra felt as if he'd elbowed her, hard, or even punched her in the stomach. Once the adrenaline rush subsided, though, she knew there was no point in withholding the information.

A person could practically throw a rock from one end of Parable to the other and juicy stories got around fast.

"You'll hear about it soon enough," she conceded, though ungraciously, keeping her voice down in case Madison woke up and somehow homed in on the conversation, "so I might as well tell you."

Hutch gave a long-suffering sigh and she felt him

looking in her direction now, though she was careful not to meet his gaze. "Might as well," he agreed quietly.

"Not that it's any of your business," Kendra pointed out.

He simply waited.

Distractedly, Kendra wondered if the man thought she'd given birth to Madison herself and kept her existence hidden from everyone in Parable all this time.

"Madison is adopted," she said. It was a simple statement, but it left her feeling as though she'd spilled her guts on some ludicrous tell-all TV show.

"Why do I think there's more to the story?" Hutch asked after a pause. His very patience galled Kendra— what right did he have to be *patient?* This was a courtesy explanation—she didn't owe it to him. She didn't owe him *anything* except maybe a broken heart.

"Madison's father was my ex-husband," Kendra said. Suddenly, she wanted to cry and it had nothing to do with her previous hesitation to talk about something so bruising and private. Why couldn't Madison have been born to *her,* as she should have been?

"And her mother?"

Once again, Kendra looked to make sure Madison hadn't turned up in the cottage doorway, all ears. "She was one of Jeffrey's girlfriends."

Hutch swore under his breath. "That rat bastard," he added a moment later.

Kendra stiffened her spine, squared her shoulders, jutted out her chin a little way. "I beg your pardon?" she said in a tone meant to point out the sheer irony, not to mention the audacity, of the pot calling the kettle black.

"Could we not argue, just this once?" Hutch asked hoarsely.

"Just this once," Kendra said, and one corner of her mouth twitched with a strange urge to smile. Probably some form of hysteria, she decided.

"I'm sorry I called your ex-husband a rat bastard," Hutch offered.

"You are not," Kendra challenged, still without looking at him. Except out of the corner of one eye, that is.

"All right," Hutch ground out, *"fine."* He sighed and shoved a hand through his hair. "Let me rephrase that. I'm sorry I didn't keep my opinion to myself."

A brief, sputtering laugh escaped Kendra then. "Since when have you ever been known to keep your opinion to yourself?"

"You're determined to turn this into a shouting match, aren't you?"

"No," Kendra said pointedly, bristling. "I am *not* planning on arguing with you, Hutch Carmody. *Not ever again.*"

"Kendra," Hutch said, "you can hedge and stall all you want, but eventually we're going to have this conversation, so we might as well just go ahead and get it done."

She made a swatting motion in his general direction, as though trying to chase away a fly. Now she was digging in her heels again and she couldn't seem to help it. "Madison is *my* daughter now, and that's all that matters."

"You're an amazing woman, Kendra," Hutch told her, and he sounded so serious that she swiveled on the seat of her lawn chair to look at him with narrowed, suspicious eyes.

"I mean it," he said with a gruff chuckle, the sound gentle and yet innately masculine. "Some people couldn't handle raising another woman's child—under those circumstances, anyhow."

"It isn't Madison's fault that Jeffrey Chamberlain was a—"

Hutch's mouth crooked up at one corner and sad mischief danced in his eyes. "Rat bastard?" he finished for her.

"Yes," she said. "That's about the size of it."

He grinned full-out, which put him at an unfair advantage because when he did that, her bones turned to jelly and her IQ plummeted at least twenty points. "Well now," he said. "We finally agree on something."

"Go figure," Kendra remarked, going for a snippy tone but not quite getting there.

"We're on a roll."

"Or not."

He laughed, shook his head. "I'm about to say something you'll have to agree with, whether you want to or not," he warned.

She felt a weird little thrill and could have shaken herself for it. "Is that so?"

Hutch nodded toward the cottage doorway, where Madison finally stood, rubbing her eyes and yawning, Daisy at her side. "You're lucky to have that little girl in your life, however it came about, and the reverse is true, too. You were born to be a mother, Kendra—and a good one."

"Damn it," Kendra muttered, at a loss for a comeback.

Hutch grinned as Madison's eyes widened—she was slowly waking up—and a glorious smile lit her face. She scrambled toward them.

"Hello, cowboy man!" she whooped, feet still bare, curls rumpled, cheeks flushed.

Hutch laughed again. "I guess you might as well call me that as anything else," he said. He exuded the kind of quiet, wholesome approval little girls crave from daddy-types.

Not that Hutch was any such thing.

"Do you like dogs?" Madison asked earnestly.

As if she'd already made her own decision on that score, Daisy suddenly leaped into Hutch's lap in a single bound, bracing her forepaws on his shoulders and licking his face.

"Yep," he said from behind all that squirming dog. "And, as you can see, they're inclined to like me, too."

"Good," Madison said.

Kendra felt unaccountably nervous, though she couldn't have said why. "Madison—" she began, but her voice fell away.

"Do you like kids, too?" Madison pressed.

Kendra groaned inwardly.

Hutch set Daisy carefully on the ground, patting her still-bouncing head. "I like kids just fine," he said.

"Do you have any?"

Hutch shook his head. "Nope."

"Madison," Kendra repeated, with no more effect than before.

"Do you like my mommy, too?"

Kendra squeezed her eyes shut.

"As a matter of fact," Hutch replied easily, "I do. Your mother and I are old friends."

Kendra squirmed again and forced herself to open her eyes.

Even rummaged up a smile that wouldn't quite stick.

Before she could think of anything to say, however, Hutch unfolded himself from his lawn chair with Madison standing nearby, still basking in his presence. "I guess I'd better head on home before I wear out my welcome," he drawled, and there was a twinkle in his eyes when he snagged Kendra's gaze. "See you around," he added.

Madison caught hold of his hand. "Wait," she said, in a near whisper.

He leaned down, resting his hands on his knees. "What?" he asked, with a smile in his voice.

"Will you be at the rodeo thing?" Madison continued.

"Sure enough," Hutch said, his tone and manner so void of condescension that he might have been addressing another adult. Maybe that was his gift, that he treated children like people, not some lesser species. "Never miss it. After all, I'm a cowboy man."

Madison beamed, evidently satisfied, and when Daisy bounded off in pursuit of a passing butterfly, her small mistress gamboled after her, arms wheeling as if she might take flight.

"Cowboy man," Kendra reflected thoughtfully.

"I've been called worse," Hutch joked.

"That's a fact," Kendra said brightly. She could have listed half a dozen names she'd called him over the years, to his face and in the privacy of her own head.

Whistling some ditty under his breath, and still grinning, Hutch turned and headed for his truck, lifting a hand in farewell as he went.

He got behind the wheel and drove away, and Kendra didn't watch him go.

"YOU'RE WAY TOO pregnant to be at work," Kendra told Joslyn the next day, stepping into the storefront office after dropping Madison off for the morning preschool session and leaving Daisy at Tara's for a doggy playdate with Lucy, only to find her business partner already there, tapping away at the keyboard of her computer.

Joslyn flashed her a smile as she looked up from the monitor. "So I hear," she said. She sighed good-naturedly. "From Slade. From Opal. From Callie."

"And now, from me," Kendra replied, setting her handbag on the edge of the desk since she'd be going out again as soon as she'd checked her messages. She was due at her lawyer's office at ten-thirty, which was why she hadn't brought Daisy to work with her.

Madison had been beside herself at the thought of Daisy being left at home alone because, as she'd explained it, "Daisy is a puppy and a puppy is the same as a baby and a baby needs somebody with it at all times."

Kendra had given in, at least temporarily.

"You're supposed to be on maternity leave, remember?" she prompted, happy to see her friend for whatever reason, all protests aside.

"Ouch," Joslyn said out of nowhere, spreading a hand over her zeppelin of a belly and making a wincey face.

"Is the little guy practicing his rodeo moves again?" Kendra asked, smiling. If only every baby could be born into a union as loving and warm as Joslyn and Slade's—it would be a different world.

"It would seem he's switched to pole vaulting," Joslyn said in a tone of cheerful acceptance. After a few slow, deep breaths, she focused on the computer monitor again. "Come over here and check out this listing, Kendra. It's a rental, but I think it might be exactly what you've been looking for."

Immediately interested, Kendra rounded her friend's desk to stand behind her and peer at the small white house on the screen. She recognized it, of course; she had at least a passing knowledge of every piece of property in Parable County, be it residential or commercial.

This charming little one-story colonial, with its white clapboard walls and green shutters and wrap-around porch, was situated across the street from the town park, just two blocks from the public library. Both Madison's preschool and the new real estate office were within easy walking distance.

"Why didn't I know about this?" Kendra mused, studying the enticing image on the monitor.

Joslyn raised and lowered one shoulder, very slightly. "You've been out of town," she replied. "Plus we only *sell* real estate, we don't manage rentals."

Kendra's brain sifted through the facts she already knew: the colonial had belonged to attorney Maggie Landers's late aunt, Billie. Upon Billie's death, at least a decade before, Maggie had inherited the property. She'd had some much-needed renovations done, Kendra recalled, but never actually lived in the house herself. She'd rented it out to a schoolteacher, long-term. Now, apparently, it was empty—or about to be.

She practically dived for the telephone. Sure she already had an appointment with Maggie about Madison's trust fund, but she didn't want someone else snapping up the house.

Maggie's front office assistant put Kendra through to the boss right away.

"Tell me you're not canceling our appointment,"

Maggie said without preamble. "If you do, you'll be the third one today."

Kendra's heart had begun to pound. "No," she said quickly, smiling. Hoping. "No, it isn't that—I'll be there at ten-thirty, like we agreed—"

"Kendra," Maggie broke in, sounding concerned now. "What on earth is the matter? You sound as though you've just completed a triathlon."

"Your house—the rental—Joslyn just showed me the listing on the internet—"

Maggie gave a nervous little laugh and Kendra could see her in her mind's eye, fiddling with that strand of priceless pearls she always wore. "Yes? What about it?"

"Is it still available?"

Maggie sounded relieved when she answered, "Of course. The ad just went up today."

"I'll take it," Kendra burst out. Her own recklessness left her gasping for breath—she never did reckless things. Well, not reckless things that didn't involve Hutch Carmody, anyway.

"Sight unseen?" Maggie echoed.

"It's perfect for Madison and me," Kendra said, relaxing a little.

"Don't you even want to know how much the rent will be?"

Kendra strained to see Joslyn's monitor again and scanned quickly for the price. "That won't be a problem," she nearly chimed.

Maggie was quiet for a few moments, taking it all in. "All right," she said finally. "Come early and we'll go over the details of the trust fund, then run over to the house so you can have a look inside before you commit yourself to a year's lease—"

Kendra bit back a very un-Kendra-like response, which would have gone something like this: *I'm committing right now. Do you hear me? Right now!*

"Fine," she said moderately. "But please don't show it to anyone else in the meantime."

"In the meantime?" Maggie echoed, with a friendly little laugh. "As in, say, the next half hour? Relax, Kendra—if you want the house, it's yours."

Joslyn was grinning throughout the whole conversation.

"Thank you," Kendra said, near tears, she was so excited. She said goodbye, hung up and grabbed her purse from the corner of her desk.

"Kendra," Joslyn said, "take a breath. It's meant to be."

"That," Kendra retorted lightly, already on her way to the door, car keys in hand, "is what you said about Hutch and me. Remember?"

"Oh," Joslyn answered breezily, "I haven't changed my mind on that score. Sooner or later, I'm sure you'll both come around."

Kendra shook her head, gave a rueful chuckle. "Don't work too hard," she said, opening the office door. "If you're still here when I get back, I'll buy you lunch at the Butter Biscuit."

"One more lunch at the Butter Biscuit," Joslyn said, "and I'll be a butter*ball*. Anyway, I promised to meet Shea at the Curly Burly at one—we're going shopping."

Kendra nodded and rushed out.

Five minutes later, she was seated in Maggie's office, on the very edge of her chair.

Maggie had already warned her that building a legal structure that would protect Madison's considerable financial interests would require a series of meetings, if only because of the complexity of the task.

Kendra listened to Maggie's explanations and suggestions as patiently as she could, but her mind was on the one-story colonial with the fenced backyard. This, too, was unlike her—she usually focused keenly on whatever she was doing at the time, but today, it was impossible.

Maggie, a pretty woman with short hair, gamine eyes and very nice clothes, finally chuckled and laid down her expensive fountain pen.

"You're not getting a word of this, are you, Kendra?" she asked.

Kendra smiled and shook her head. "I'm sorry. From the moment I realized the house might be available, I've been fidgety."

Maggie collected her handbag from a drawer of her desk. "Then let's go and do the walk-through," she said. "Then we'll come back here and take another shot at running the numbers for Madison's fund."

"I'd like that," Kendra said, feeling almost giddy.

"Follow me, then," Maggie said, jangling her car keys.

The cottage had been freshly painted, Kendra noticed with a pang of sweet avarice, and so had the picket fence out front. The flower beds were in full bloom and the lawn, newly mown, smelled sweetly of cut grass.

It was so easy to imagine herself and Madison living here.

"I knew you were selling the mansion, of course," Maggie said when they got out of their cars and met on the sidewalk in front of the colonial. "But I guess

I thought you'd be in the market to buy a place, rather than rent."

"I did plan on buying," Kendra answered, letting her gaze wander over the sleeping-in-the-sunshine face of that perfect little house, "but I'm learning that it's wise to be open to surprises."

Maggie smiled and opened the creaky gate. "Isn't that the truth?" she responded.

CHAPTER FOUR

WHEN HUTCH FINALLY caught up with Brylee, she was in her small but well-organized warehouse on the outskirts of Three Trees, helping to stack boxes as they were unloaded from the back of a delivery truck.

Clad in jeans, sneakers and a blue U of M pullover, she looked more like a teenager than a thirty-year-old woman with a successful business and a bad-luck wedding day to her credit. Her russet-brown hair hung down her back in a long, fairly tidy braid, and she hadn't bothered with makeup.

She didn't notice Hutch right away and he used those moments to gather his resolve, all the while wishing he *felt* something for Brylee—God knew, she was beautiful and she was sweet and she was smart. She was definitely wife and mother material—but she didn't stir him down deep where it counted and that was a deal-breaker.

At last Brylee stilled, like a doe catching the scent of some threat on the wind, she turned her head his way and saw him standing just a few feet inside the roll-up doorway of the warehouse,

Her large eyes, bluish today because of the color of the shirt she was wearing, looked hollow as she took him in and he knew she was weighing her options—seriously considering walking away without deigning to speak, if not shooting him down where he stood or running him over with the first handy forklift.

Brylee had a temper and she could be as hardheaded as any statue, but she was no coward. She spoke sotto voce to the other workers, all female, all of whom were staring now, as though Hannibal Lector had just appeared in their midst, wearing the leather mask and holding a plate of fava beans, and then came slowly toward him.

Brylee ran a small but thriving party-planning company that sold home decor items and various gifts. She had a network of sales people that covered a five-state area, holding lucrative little gatherings in people's homes, and operated a thriving online store, as well.

"Hello, Hutch," she said, indicating her nearby office with a nod and leading the way.

He fell into step with her after muttering a gruff "hello" of his own.

The office was small and furnished in early army surplus. Brylee evidently reserved her creative capacities for choosing and photographing products, training her "independent home decor consultants" and coming up with innovative marketing strategies. Here, in this little room off the warehouse, she handled the practical end of things.

"I wondered when you'd show up," she said once they were inside her enclave with the door closed against listening ears.

"I wanted to come and see you right after the—well, after—but I was persuaded that it wouldn't be a good idea," Hutch replied. He stood with his back to the door, while Brylee perched on the edge of her beat-up steel desk, with her arms folded and her head tipped to one side in skeptical anticipation.

"I could have spared you the trouble of paying a visit," Brylee replied quietly. She looked strained, exhausted, a little pale, but pride flashed in her changeable hazel eyes and stiffened her generous mouth. "I don't have anything to say to you, Hutch. Nothing I'd want written in the Book of Life, anyway."

"Well," he drawled, after stifling a wry chuckle, "it just so happens that I have something to say to you."

Brylee arched one eyebrow and waited. She looked bored now, but wary, too. What, she might have been wondering, was this yahoo going to spring on her now?

Hutch shoved a hand through his hair. He'd left his hat in the truck, but otherwise he was dressed as usual in work clothes and boots. Whisper Creek Ranch practically ran itself these days, well-staffed and well-organized as it was, but he still felt the need to get up every morning before the sun rose and tend to the business of herding cattle, mending fences and all the rest.

Today he hadn't been able to keep his mind on the routine, though, and it was a damn confusing situation, too. He thought about Kendra 24/7, but he'd been drawn to Brylee ever since that broken-road wedding that didn't quite come off.

"I can't say I'm sorry for what I did," he said straightforwardly. "Going through with that ceremony would have been the mistake of a lifetime—for both of us."

"Yes, you made that pretty clear," Brylee answered, her tone terse. "Is that what you drove all the way from Whisper Creek to tell me?"

"No," Hutch said, standing his ground. "I came to say that you'll find the right man, no matter what you think now, and when you do, you'll be damn glad you didn't marry me and wreck your chances to be happy."

"Maybe I'm *already* 'damn glad I didn't marry you,'" Brylee reasoned tartly. "Did you ever consider *that* possibility?"

He grinned. "That one did occur to me, believe it or not," he said. "I should have made you listen to me, Brylee, before things went as far as they did."

"That was my grandmother's dress I was wearing," she said, after a short pause. "It had to be restored and altered and specially cleaned. I spent a fortune on the cake and the invitations and the flowers and all the rest. It's going to take *weeks,* even with help from my friends, to send back all those wedding gifts." Her shoulders moved in the ghost of a shrug. "But, hey, what the heck? You win some, you lose some. And besides, who needs six toaster ovens anyhow?"

Tears brimmed in her eyes and she looked away, fiercely dignified.

"Brylee," Hutch said, not daring to touch her or even take a step in her direction. "I know you're hurt. I'm sorry about that—sorrier than I've ever been about anything in my life. And I'm more than ready to reimburse you for any of the costs—"

"I don't want your *money!*" she flared suddenly, looking straight at him now, with fire flashing behind the pride and sorrow in her eyes. "This was never about money—I have plenty of my own, in case you haven't noticed."

"I know that, Brylee," he said gently.

"Then what did you expect to accomplish by coming here?" She held up an index finger. "Wait, let me answer for you," she added. "Your conscience is both-

ering you—what *passes* for a conscience with you—
and you want me to say all is forgiven and we can be
friends and go on as if nothing happened." With that,
Brylee slipped past him and jerked the office door open
wide. "Well, you can just go to hell, Hutch Carmody,
and take your lame apologies with you." A sharp, indrawn breath. *"Get out."*

"You might want to try *listening* to what's really
being said to you, Brylee, instead of just the parts you
want to hear," he told her calmly, not moving. "It would
save a lot of wear and tear on you and everybody else."

"Get. Out." Brylee parsed the words out. *"Now."*

He spread his hands in an "I give up" gesture and
ambled past her, across the warehouse, which was as
still as a mausoleum, and out through the doorway into
the sunshine.

Walker Parrish, Brylee's brother, had just driven up
in a big, extended-cab pickup with his stock company
logo painted on the doors. He raised rodeo stock on
his ranch outside of Three Trees, where he and Brylee
had grown up.

Hutch stopped. He frankly wasn't in the mood for
any more yammer and recrimination, but he wouldn't
have it said that he'd tucked his tail and run from
Walker or anybody else.

"We-e-e-l-ll," Walker said, dragging out the word.
"If it isn't the runaway bridegroom."

Hutch wasn't about to give an inch. "No autographs,
please," he retorted dryly. He wasn't looking for a fight,
but if Walker wanted one, he'd come to the right man.

Walker chuckled and shook his head. Hutch knew
women found Brylee's big brother attractive, with his
lean but wide-shouldered build and his rugged fea-

tures, but so far he'd managed to steer clear of marriage, which should have made him at least a little sympathetic to Hutch's side of the story, and clearly hadn't.

"I can't imagine what you're doing on my sister's property right now," Walker observed, his water-gray eyes narrowed as he studied Hutch.

Hutch took his time shaping a reply. "I felt a need to offer an apology," he finally said, his tone level, even affable. "She wasn't in the frame of mind to accept it."

"I don't reckon she would be," Walker said. "Far as I'm concerned, Brylee always was half again too good for you, and in the long run you probably did her a favor by calling off the wedding. None of which means I wouldn't like to smash your face in for putting her through all that."

While Hutch privately agreed with much of what Walker had just said, he wasn't inclined to explain his repeated attempts to put the brakes on before he and Brylee and half the town ended up in the church on that fateful Saturday afternoon. And he'd come to Three Trees to apologize to Brylee, not her brother.

"If you want a fight, Walker," he said, "I'll give you one."

Walker appeared to consider the pros and cons of getting it on right there in the warehouse parking lot. In the end, though, he shook his head. "What goes around, comes around," he finally said. "You'll get what's coming to you." Then, as an apparent afterthought, he added, "You planning on entering the rodeo this year?"

"Don't I always?" Hutch answered, mindful that Walker provided the bulls and broncos for such events all over the West, including the one in Parable. He was well-known for breeding almost unrideable critters.

Walker grinned. "Here's hoping you draw the bull I have in mind for you," he said. "He's a real rib-stomper."

"Bring him on," Hutch replied, grinning back.

With that, the two men, having said their pieces, went their separate ways—Hutch heading for his truck, Walker going on into the warehouse.

Behind the wheel of his pickup, Hutch ground the key into the ignition.

He didn't know what he'd expected of this first post-disaster encounter with Brylee, but he'd *hoped* they could at least begin the process of burying the hatchet.

After all, neither of them were going anywhere.

Parable and Three Trees were only thirty miles apart, and the two communities were closely linked. In other words, they'd see each other all the time.

He sighed and drove away. Maybe there was something to Brylee's accusation that, in coming on this fool's errand, he'd been more interested in soothing his own conscience than making any kind of amends, but at least he'd tried—again—to set things right, so they could at least be civil to each other.

He figured it was probably too soon and wondered if the anti-Hutch internet campaign would ramp up a notch or two, since several of the key players—Brylee's friends and employees—had basically witnessed the confrontation.

These days everybody was an ace reporter.

"Well, cowboy man," he muttered to himself, "you're batting a thousand. Might as well go for broke."

Reaching the highway, he rolled on toward Parable. And Kendra.

MADISON WAS THRILLED with the new house when Kendra sprang the surprise on the little girl after picking her up at preschool that afternoon, and Daisy was thrilled with the spacious backyard.

The small colonial boasted two quite spacious bedrooms, plus a little cubicle Kendra planned to use as a home office, and two full baths. The kitchen was sunny, with plenty of cupboard space and a small pantry, and there was a large, old-fashioned brick fireplace in the living room. Closer inspection revealed small hooks in the wooden mantel for hanging Christmas stockings.

All in all, the place was perfect—except, of course, for being a rental and therefore impermanent. Kendra had asked Maggie about buying the house, but Maggie was understandably reluctant to sell. She said it would be like putting a price on her childhood, and she couldn't do that.

"This is my room!" Madison exulted now, standing in the center of the space with window seats and built-in bookshelves and shiny plank floors worn to a warmly aged patina. The folding closet doors were louvered, and the overhead light fixture was small but ornate.

Daisy gave a single joyous bark, as though seconding Madison's motion and making a claim of her own.

Kendra laughed. "Yes," she said to both of them. "This is your room."

"Am I going to have a bed?" Madison inquired matter-of-factly.

"Of course," Kendra replied. "We'll visit the furniture store over in Three Trees and you can pick it out yourself."

The town of Three Trees was actually smaller than Parable by a couple of thousand people, but it boasted a large outlet mall that drew customers from all over that part of the state, along with a movie house, a large bookstore and a Main Street lined with shops.

"Can we go *now?*" Madison asked.

"I don't see why not," Kendra replied. Her gaze fell on Daisy. Shopping for furniture with a puppy in tow didn't mesh.

The next question was inevitable, not to be forestalled. "Can Daisy come with us?" Madison wanted to know.

Sadly, Kendra shook her head. "That won't work, sweetie. But she'll be fine at the guesthouse, I promise."

Madison mulled that over, then her face brightened again. "All right," she said. "Daisy must be tired from playing with Lucy all day. She can take a nap while we're gone."

"Good thinking," Kendra said, holding out a hand to her daughter. "Let's get going."

Daisy was remarkably cooperative when they got back to the guest cottage. She lapped up half the water in her bowl, munched on some kibble, went outside with Madison to take care of dog business and returned to settle on her soft bed in the kitchen, yawning big.

Kendra's heart swelled into her throat as Madison crouched next to the puppy, patting its head gently and whispering, "Don't be scared, okay? Because Mommy and I will be back before it gets dark."

For the thousandth—if not millionth—time, Kendra wondered what life in that series of foster homes had been like for Madison. Had she felt safe, secure, loved?

According to the social workers, Madison's care had been exceptional—most foster parents were decent, dedicated people, generous enough to make room in their homes and their hearts for children in crisis.

Still, Madison had been passed around a lot, shuffled from one stand-in family to another. How could she *not* have been affected by so many changes in her short life?

Kendra was pondering all these things as she fastened the child into her booster seat in the backseat of the Volvo, and then as she slipped behind the wheel and started the engine. "I'm not going anywhere, you know," she felt compelled to say, making an effort to keep her voice light as they pulled out onto Rodeo Road.

She didn't so much as glance at the mansion either as they passed it or in the rearview mirror; it might have been rendered invisible.

Maybe, as some scientists claimed, things didn't actually exist until someone looked at them.

"Yes, you are *too* going somewhere," Madison responded, after a few moments of thought. "You're going to Three Trees so we can buy a bed!"

Kendra laughed, blinked a couple of times and focused her attention on the road, where it belonged. "That isn't what I meant, silly."

"My first mommy left," Madison said, perhaps sensing that Kendra's conversation was leading somewhere.

"Yes," Kendra said gently. "I know."

"But you won't leave," Madison said with reassuring conviction. "Because you *like* being a mommy."

Kendra sniffled. Blinked again, hard. "I love being *your* mommy," she replied. "You're the best thing that's ever happened to me, kiddo. Remember that, okay?"

"Okay," Madison said, her tone almost breezy.

"Some of the kids at preschool have daddies, not just mommies."

The ache of emotion slipped from Kendra's throat to settle into her heart. Part of the child's remark echoed to the very center of her soul. *Not* just *mommies.*

"My daddy died," Madison went on. It was an exchange they'd had before, but repeating the facts seemed to comfort the little girl somehow, to anchor her in a new and better present. "He's in heaven."

"Yes," Kendra said, thick-voiced. She considered pulling over for a few moments, in order to pull herself together. "But he loved you very much. That's why he sent me to find you."

Thank you for that, Jeffrey. In spite of everything else, thank you for bringing Madison into my life.

The topic ricocheted with the speed of a bullet. "Is the cowboy man somebody's daddy?"

The question pierced Kendra's heart like an arrow. They were near the park, and she pulled over in the shade of a row of hundred-year-old maples, all dressed up in leafy green for summer, to regain her composure.

"I don't think so," she managed, after swallowing hard.

"I like the cowboy man," Madison said. A short pause followed and when she spoke again she sounded puzzled. "Why are we stopping, Mommy?"

Kendra touched the back of her right hand to one cheek, then the other. "I just needed a moment," she said.

"Are you crying?" Madison sounded worried now.

"Yes," Kendra answered, because it was her policy never to lie to the child, if it could be avoided.

"Why?"

"Because I'm happy," Kendra said. And that was the truth. She *was* happy and she was grateful. She had a great life.

Still, there was the daddy thing.

As a little girl, lonely and adrift, tolerated by her grandmother rather than loved, Kendra had longed for a father even more than she had for a dog or a kitten. She could still feel the ache of that singular yearning to be carried, laughing, on strong shoulders, to feel protected and cherished and totally safe.

She was all grown up now, perfectly capable of protecting and cherishing her daughter as well as looking after herself and a certain golden retriever puppy in the bargain. But could she be both mother and father to her little girl?

Was she, and the love she offered, enough?

"I don't cry when I'm happy," Madison said as Kendra pulled the car back out onto the road. "I *laugh* when I'm happy."

"Makes sense," Kendra conceded, laughing herself.

They drove on to Three Trees, parked in front of the furniture store and hastened inside, hand in hand.

And they found the perfect bed almost immediately— it was twin-size, made of gleaming brass, with four high posts and a canopy frame on top. A dresser, a bureau and two night tables, all French provincial in style, completed the ensemble.

Kendra paid for their purchases—the pieces were to be delivered the next day, bright and early—and before they knew it, they were almost home again.

Madison, seemingly deep in thought for most of the drive, piped up as they pulled into the driveway. "Mommy, we forgot to buy a bed for *you*."

"I already have one, honey," Kendra responded, stopping the car alongside the guesthouse. She'd selected a few modest pieces from the mansion to take along to the new place. Most of the furniture in the main house was too big and too fancy for the simple colonial. There was a queen-size bed in one of the guest rooms that would work, a floral couch in the study, and they could use the table and chairs from Opal's old apartment.

Kendra wanted to leave room for some new things, too.

She parked the car and turned Madison loose, and they raced each other to the guest cottage, where Daisy met them at the door, barking a happy greeting.

Kendra set aside her purse, washed her hands, and searched the cottage fridge for the makings of an evening meal. She was chopping the vegetables for a salad, to which she would add leftover chicken breasts, also chopped, when she heard a vehicle coming up the driveway.

Peering out the kitchen window, she saw Hutch Carmody getting out of his truck.

Her stomach lurched and her heartbeat quickened as she hurriedly wiped her hands on a dish towel and went outside. Daisy and Madison, who had been playing in the kitchen moments before, rushed out to greet him.

Soon they were all over him.

He laughed at their antics and swung Madison off the ground and up onto his shoulders, where she clung, laughing, too.

The last of the afternoon sunlight caught in their hair—Hutch's a butternut color, Madison's like copper flames—and the dog circled them, barking her excitement.

Kendra couldn't help being struck by the sight of the man and the little girl and the dog, looking so happy, so *right*.

She went outside.

"I was here earlier," Hutch told her, easing Madison off his back and setting her on her feet, where she jumped, reaching up, wanting to be lifted up again. "You weren't home."

Kendra couldn't speak for a moment, knowing, as she somehow did, that she might never get the image of the three of them together out of her head. It had been unspeakably beautiful, like some otherworldly vision of what family life *could* be.

"Hello?" Hutch teased, when she didn't say anything, standing close to her now, his head tipped a little to one side, like his grin. All the while, Madison was trying to climb him like a bean pole and he finally swung her back onto his shoulders.

"Come in," Kendra heard herself say, her voice all croaky and strange.

He nodded and followed her into the guest cottage, ducking so Madison wouldn't bump her head on the door frame. This time when he put the child down, she seemed content just to hover nearby.

He accepted the chair Kendra offered him at the small dining table and the coffee she brought him— black, the way he liked it.

Funny, the things you didn't forget about a person— mostly small and ordinary stuff, like coffee preferences and the way they always smelled of sun-dried cloth, even after a day spent hauling cattle out of mud holes or digging postholes.

Kendra gave herself a mental shake, sent a protesting Madison off to wash her hands and face before supper. Daisy, of course, tagged along with her small mistress, though she cast a few glances back at Hutch as she went.

"Join us for supper?" Kendra asked, hoping she sounded—well—neighborly.

Hutch shook his head. "No, thanks," he said, offering no further explanation, which was like him.

Kendra could hear Madison in the bathroom, running water in the sink, splashing around, talking non-stop to Daisy about the new house and the new bed and whether or not they'd be allowed to watch a DVD that night before they had to go to bed.

"Why are you here?" she finally asked very quietly. And this time, it wasn't a challenge. She was too tired for challenges, too wrung-out emotionally from the things Madison had said in the car.

Hutch sighed.

The distant splashing continued, as did the child-to-dog chatter.

"I'm not entirely sure," he said at some length, taking Kendra aback a little.

She couldn't remember one single instance in all the time she'd known Hutch Carmody when he hadn't been completely sure of everything and everybody, especially himself.

"That's helpful," she said mildly.

Any moment now Madison would be back in the room, thereby curtailing anything but the most mundane conversation.

"Joslyn tells me there's a cleanup day over at Pioneer Cemetery on Saturday," he finally said, after casting about visibly for something to say. "There'll be a town picnic afterward, like always, and, well, I was just wondering if you and Madison and Daisy might be interested in going along." He paused, cleared his throat. "With me."

Kendra was astounded, not so much by the invitation as by Hutch's apparent nervousness. Was he afraid she'd say no?

Or was he afraid she'd say yes?

"Okay," she agreed, as a compromise between the two extremes. She wanted, she realized, to see how he'd react.

Would he backpedal?

Instead he favored her with a dazzling grin, rose from his chair and passed her to set his coffee cup, still mostly full, in the sink. Their arms brushed and his nearness, the hard heat of his very masculine body, sent a jolt of sweet fire through her.

"Okay," he said with affable finality.

Madison was back by then, holding up her clean hands for Kendra to see but obviously more interested in Hutch than in her mother.

"Very good," Kendra said approvingly, and began moving briskly around the infinitesimal kitchen, setting out plates and silverware and glasses—which Madison promptly counted.

"Aren't you hungry, cowboy man?" she asked Hutch when the tally was two places at the table, rather than three.

He looked down at Madison with such fondness that Kendra felt another pang of—*something*. "Can't stay," he said. "I have horses to look after and they like their supper served on time, just like people do."

Madison's eyes widened. "You have *horses?*" From her tone she might have asked, "You can walk on water?"

"Couldn't very well call myself a cowboy if I didn't have horses," Hutch said reasonably.

Madison pondered that, then nodded in agreement. Her eyes widened. "Can I ride one of your horses sometime? Please?"

"That would definitely be your mother's call," Hutch told her. It was grown-up vernacular, but Madison understood and immediately turned an imploring face to Kendra.

"Maybe sometime," Kendra said, because she couldn't quite get to a flat-out no. Not with all that ingenuous hope beaming up at her.

Remarkably, that noncommittal answer seemed to satisfy Madison. She scrambled into her chair at the table and waited for supper to start.

"See you on Saturday," Hutch said lightly.

And then he tousled Madison's hair, nodded to Kendra and the dog, and left the house.

"*Are* we going to see the cowboy man on Saturday?" Madison asked eagerly. Once again, it struck Kendra that, for a four-year-old, the child didn't miss much.

"Yes," Kendra said, setting the salad bowl in the center of the table and then pouring milk for herself and Madison. Daisy curled up on her dog bed in the corner, rested her muzzle on her forepaws, and rolled her lively brown eyes from Madison to Kendra and back again. "The whole town gets together every year to spruce the place up for the rodeo and the carnival.

Lots of people like to visit the Pioneer Cemetery while they're here, and we like it to look presentable, so you and I and Hutch will be helping out there. After the work is done, there's always a picnic, and games for the kids to play."

"Games?" Madison was intrigued. "What kind of games?"

"Sack races." Kendra smiled, remembering happy times. "Things like that. There are even prizes."

"What's a sack race?" Madison pursued, a little frown creasing the alabaster skin between her eyebrows.

Kendra explained about stepping into a feed sack, holding it at waist level and hopping toward the finish line. She didn't mention the three-legged race, not wanting to describe that, too, but she smiled at the memory of herself and Joslyn tied together at the ankles and laughing hysterically when they lost their balance and tumbled into the venerable cemetery grass.

"And there are prizes?" Madison prompted.

Kendra nodded. "I won a doll once. She had a real camera hanging around her neck by a plastic strap. I still have her, somewhere."

Madison's eyes were huge. "Wow," she said. "There were cameras when you were a little girl?"

Kendra laughed. "Yes," she replied, "there were cameras. There were cars, too, and airplanes and even TVs."

Madison pondered all this, the turning gears in her little brain practically visible behind her forehead. "Wow," she repeated in awe.

After supper, Madison had her bath and put on her pajamas, and Kendra popped a favorite DVD of an animated movie into the player attached to the living room TV.

Madison snuggled on the floor with Daisy, one arm flung companionably across the small dog's gleaming back, and the two of them were quickly absorbed in the on-screen story.

Kendra, relieved that she wouldn't have to sit through the movie for what must have been the seventy-second time, set up her laptop on the freshly cleared kitchen table and booted it up.

She'd surf the web for a while, she decided, and see if there were any for-sale-by-owner listings posted for the Parable/Three Trees area. She was, after all, a working real estate broker, and sometimes a well-placed phone call to said owners would produce a new client. Most folks didn't realize all that was entailed in selling a property themselves—title searches and tax liens were only *some* of the snags they might run into.

Alas, despite her good intentions, Kendra ended up running a search on Hutch Carmody instead, using the key word *wedding*.

The page that came up might as well have been called "We Hate Hutch."

Kendra found herself in the odd position of wanting to defend him—and furiously—as she looked at the pictures.

Brylee, the discarded bride, heartbroken and furious in her grandmother's wedding gown.

Hutch, standing straight and tall and obviously miserable midway down the aisle, guests gawking on either side as he held up both hands in a gesture that plainly said, "Hold everything."

The condolence party over at the Boot Scoot Tavern, Brylee wearing a sad expression and a T-shirt that said Men Suck.

Beware, murmured a voice in the back of Kendra's mind.

But even then she knew she wouldn't heed her own warning.

After all, what could happen in broad daylight, in a cemetery, with Madison and half the county right there?

CHAPTER FIVE

"DOES THIS SEEM a little weird to you?" Kendra asked Joslyn on Saturday morning as they helped Opal and a dozen other women set out tons of home-prepared food on the picnic tables at Pioneer Cemetery. "Holding what amounts to a party in a graveyard, I mean?"

Joslyn, who looked as though she might be having trouble keeping her center of gravity balanced, smiled and plunked herself down on one of the benches while the cheerful work went on around her. "I think it's one of the best things about small towns," she replied. "The way life and death are integrated—after all, they're part of the same cycle, aren't they? You can't have one without the other."

Thoughtful, Kendra scanned the surrounding area for Madison, something that came automatically to her now, and found her and Daisy industriously "helping" Hutch, Shea and several of the older girl's friends from school pull weeds around a nearby scattering of very old graves. The water tower loomed in the distance, with its six-foot stenciled letters reading "Parable," its rickety ladders and its silent challenge to every new generation of teenagers: *Climb me.*

"I guess you're right," Kendra said very quietly, though by then the actual substance of her friend's remark had essentially slipped her mind. An instant later, though, at some small sound—a gasp, maybe—she turned to look straight at Joslyn.

Joslyn sat with one hand splayed against either side of her copiously distended stomach, her eyes huge with delighted alarm. "I think it's time," she said in a joyous whisper.

"Oh, my God," Kendra replied, instantly panicked, stopping herself just short of putting a hand to her mouth.

Opal stepped up, exuding a take-charge attitude. "Now everybody, just stay calm," she commanded. "Babies are born every second of every day in every part of the world, and this is going to turn out just fine."

"G-get Slade," Joslyn managed, smiling and wincing at the same time. "Please."

No one had to go in search of Joslyn's husband; he seemed to have sonar where his wife was concerned.

Kendra watched with relief as he came toward them, his strides long and purposeful, but calm and measured, too. He was grinning from ear to ear when he reached Joslyn and crouched in front of her, taking both her hands in his.

"Breathe," he told her.

Joslyn laughed, nodded and breathed.

"It's time, then?" he asked her, gruffly gentle. His strength was quiet and unshakable.

"Definitely," Joslyn replied.

"Then let's get this thing done," Slade replied, straightening to his full height and easing Joslyn to her feet, supporting her in the curve of one steel-strong arm as they headed for the parking lot.

Opal took off her apron, thrust it into the hands of

a woman standing nearby and hurried after them, taking her big patent leather purse with her.

Shea materialized at Kendra's side with Madison and Daisy and leaned into her a little, her expression worried and faintly lost.

Kendra wrapped an arm around the teenage girl's slender shoulders and squeezed. "Everything's going to be all right," she said softly. "Just like Opal said."

"They forgot all about me," Shea murmured, staring after her stepparents and Opal as they retreated.

"No, sweetheart," Kendra said quickly. "They're just excited because the baby's coming and maybe a little scared, that's all."

Shea bit her lower lip, swallowed visibly, and rummaged up a small, tremulous smile. "A baby brother will be hard to compete with," she reflected. "Especially since he really belongs to them and I don't."

Kendra knew Shea adored Slade—her mother, his ex-wife, was remarried and living in L.A.—and she also knew that Slade loved this girl as much as if he'd fathered her himself. And Joslyn loved her, too.

"You belong to them, too, Shea," Kendra assured the girl. "Don't forget that."

Madison, perhaps sobered by Shea's mood—the two had been hanging out together since Madison and Kendra had arrived with Hutch—slipped her hand into Kendra's and looked up at her with wide, solemn eyes.

"Are babies better than big kids?" she asked very seriously.

Kendra's heart turned over. "Babies are very special," she answered carefully, "and so are the big kids they turn into."

As she spoke, Hutch stepped into her line of sight,

and something happened inside Kendra as she watched him watching Slade and Joslyn's departing vehicle. Opal sat tall and stalwart in the backseat.

What *was* that look in his eyes? Worry, perhaps? Envy?

Back in high school, Kendra recalled, Joslyn had been Hutch's first love and he hers. Most people had expected them to marry at some point, perhaps after college, but they'd grown apart instead, from a romantic standpoint at least. They had remained close friends.

She, Kendra, had been his *second* love.

Maybe that was why he hadn't stepped in when she threw herself into an ill-fated relationship with Jeffrey Chamberlain, way back when. Possibly, letting her go had been easy because he hadn't really been over Joslyn at that point.

In fact it could well be that he *still* wasn't over her, even though she was happily married to his half brother and about to give birth to their first child.

Now you're just being silly, Kendra scolded herself silently, straightening her spine and raising her chin. Besides, what did it matter who Hutch Carmody did or did not love? He'd hurt every woman he'd ever cared about—except Joslyn.

"Do you want me to drive you to the hospital?"

The question had come from Hutch and he was looking at Shea as he spoke. Although he and Slade were still working on being brothers, he was already an uncle to Shea and she was a niece to him.

Shea shook her head, slipped away from Kendra's side and held out a hand to Madison. "The three-legged race is starting soon," she said to the little girl. "Want to be my partner?"

Madison nodded eagerly and crowed, "Yes!" for good measure, in case there might be any ambiguity in the matter.

"Let's go check out the prize table then," Shea said. And just like that, they were off, racing through the grass, Daisy and Jasper, the Barlows' dog, bounding after them.

"Slade and Joslyn do realize," Kendra began, without really meaning to say anything at all, "that Shea is worried that they won't love her as much once the baby is here?"

Hutch, standing nearer than she'd thought, replied quietly, "Slade and I may have our differences," he said, "but the man is rock-solid when it comes to loving his family." A pause followed, then a wistful, "Not a trait he learned from our dad."

Picking up on the pain in his words, she looked at him directly.

They were essentially alone together, under those leafy, breeze-rustled trees, because everyone else had gone back to what they were doing before Joslyn had gone into labor—setting out food, pulling weeds, mowing grass, generally getting ready for the festivities that would follow on the heels of the cleanup effort.

Hutch, meanwhile, looked as though he regretted the remark about John Carmody, not because he hadn't meant it, but because it revealed more than he wanted her or anyone else to know.

"Tell me about your dad," Kendra said, pushing the envelope a little. She remembered the elder Carmody clearly, of course, but she hadn't really known him. He'd been a grown-up, after all, and a reserved one at that, handsome like Slade and almost religious about minding his own business.

Hutch took her hand, and she let him, and they drifted away from the others to sit on rocks overlooking the town of Parable, nestled into the shallow valley below. "Not much to tell," he said in belated reply to her earlier request. "The old man and I didn't see eye to eye on most things, and he made it pretty plain that I didn't measure up to his expectations."

"But you loved him?"

"I loved him," Hutch confirmed, staring out over the town, past the church steeples and the courthouse roof. "And I guess, in his own way, he probably loved me. Do you remember your dad, Kendra?"

She shook her head. "He was long gone by the time I was born," she said.

Remarkably, as close as they'd been, she and Hutch hadn't talked much about their childhoods. They'd been totally, passionately engrossed in the present.

Now Kendra thought about her mother, Sherry, beautiful and flaky and too footloose to raise a little girl on her own. In a moment, Kendra was right back there, like a time traveler, standing in the overgrown yard in front of her grandmother's trailer, clutching Sherry's fingers with one hand and gripping the handle of a toy suitcase in the other.

She'd been five years old at the time, only a few months older than Madison was now.

"I'll be back soon, I promise," she heard Sherry say as clearly as if a quarter of a century hadn't passed since that summer day. "You just sit there on the porch like a good girl and wait for your grandma to get home from work. She'll take care of you until I can come and get you."

Maybe the suitcase, hastily purchased in a thrift store, should have been a clue about what was to come, but Kendra was, after all, a child and a trusting one at that. She hadn't known she was being lied to, not consciously at least.

Most likely Sherry hadn't known she was lying, either. Never mean, Sherry had always meant well. She just had trouble following through on her better intentions.

In the end, she'd leaned down, kissed Kendra on the top of her head, promised they'd be together again soon, this time for good. They'd get a house of their own and a dog and a nice car.

With that, Sherry waggled her fingers in farewell, climbed into her ancient, smoke-belching station wagon and drove away.

Kendra simply sat and waited—it wouldn't have occurred to her to wander off or run after Sherry's car.

When her grandmother arrived home a couple hours later, she got out of her car, lit up a cigarette and drew deeply on the smoke. Then she crossed the overgrown yard to stand there frowning down at Kendra.

With her bent and buckled plastic suitcase beside her, Kendra looked up into her grandmother's lined and sorrow-hardened face, and saw no welcome there.

"Just what I need," the old woman had said bitterly. "A kid to take care of."

But Alva Shepherd *had* given Kendra a home, however reluctantly.

She'd put food on the table and kept a roof over their heads and if love and laughter had been lacking from the relationship, well, nobody had everything. If Sherry hadn't dropped her off that day, she probably would have been killed in the car accident that took her mom's life six months later.

After that, her grandma had been a little nicer to her, not out of compassion—she didn't seem to grieve over losing a daughter or Kendra's loss of her mother, apparently regarding it as a fitting end to a misspent life—but because Kendra became eligible for a small monthly check from the government. That made things easier all around.

"Kendra?" Hutch tugged her back into the here and now, still holding her hand.

"There are too many broken people in this world," she said, thinking aloud.

Hutch simply gazed at her for a long, unreadable moment. "True enough," he agreed finally, almost hoarsely. "But there are plenty of good ones, too, built to stay the course."

Happy noises in the distance indicated that the games were about to start and picnic food was being served. Hutch was right, of course—these sturdy people all around them were the proof, teaming up to tend the grounds of a decrepit old cemetery, to serve potato salad and hot dogs and the like to old friends and new, to hold races for children who would remember sunny, communal days like this one well into their own old age.

In that moment, Kendra felt a wistful sort of hope that places like Parable would always exist, so babies could be born and grow up and get married and live on into their golden years, always in touch with their own

histories and those of the people around them, always a
part of something, always belonging somewhere.

It was what Kendra had wanted for Madison, that
kind of stability, and what she wanted for herself, too—
because her story hadn't ended with her overwhelmed
grandmother on the rickety porch of a double-wide that
had, even then, seen better days. Because Opal had
taken her into her heart and Joslyn had been the sister she'd never had, and the generous souls who called
Parable home had taken her into their midst without
hesitation, made her one of them.

Tears brimmed in her eyes.

Hutch, seeing them, stopped and cupped a hand
under her chin. "What?" he asked with a tenderness
that made Kendra's breath catch.

"I was just thinking how perfect life is," Kendra admitted, "even when it's *im*perfect."

He grinned. "It's worth the trouble, all right," he
agreed. "Want to enter the three-legged race? I can't
think of anybody I'd rather be tied to at the ankle."

She laughed and said yes, and threw herself headfirst into the celebration.

PARABLE COUNTY HOSPITAL was small, with brightly
painted white walls, and most of the staff had been
born and raised within fifty miles of the place, so folks
felt safe when they were sick or hurt, knowing they'd
be cared for by friends, or friends of friends, or even
kinfolk.

Hutch hadn't been there since his dad died, but now
there was the baby boy, born a few hours before, ratch-
eting up the population by one. The numbers on the sign
at the edge of town were magnetic, so they could be

altered when somebody drew their first breath, sighed out their last one or simply moved to or from the community.

Slade, standing beside him, rested a hand briefly on his shoulder. After the races and the picnic and the prizes, he'd dropped Kendra and Madison and that goofy dog of theirs off at their new digs before heading home to shower, shave, put on clean clothes and make the drive back to town.

"You done good, brother," Hutch said without looking at Slade.

Slade chuckled. He hadn't taken his eyes off that little blue-bundled yahoo in the plastic baby bed since they'd stepped up to the window. "Thanks," he replied, "but Joslyn deserves at least some of the credit. She handled the tough part."

Hutch smiled, nodded. The kid hadn't even been in the world for a full day and he was already looking more like John Carmody, as did Slade, by the second. He guessed it was the old man's way of keeping one foot in the world, even though he was six feet under. "What are you going to call him?" he asked.

"Trace," Slade answered, with a touch of quiet awe in his voice, as though he didn't quite believe his own good fortune. "Trace Carmody Barlow."

Hutch wasn't prepared for the "Carmody" part. While Slade was technically as much a Carmody as Hutch himself was, their dad hadn't raised him, hadn't even claimed him until his will was read.

Slade interpreted his half brother's silence accurately. "It's a way of telling the truth," he said. "About who Trace is and who I am."

Hutch swallowed. Nodded. "How's Joslyn?" he managed to ask.

"She's ready to take the boy and head home to Windfall," Slade said with another chuckle. "Opal and I overruled her, insisting that she spend the night here in the hospital, just to make sure she and the baby don't run into any hitches."

Windfall was the aptly chosen name of Slade and Joslyn's ranch, which bordered Hutch's land on one side. Slade had bought the spread with the proceeds from selling his share of Whisper Creek to Hutch and, as convoluted as the situation had been, Hutch would always be grateful. He was a part of that ranch and it was a part of him, and losing half of it would have been like being chopped into two pieces himself.

"I see you brought Kendra and her little girl to the cleanup today," Slade remarked lightly.

Hutch looked straight at him. "Some first date, huh?" he joked, not that it actually *was* a first date, considering that he and Kendra had once been a couple. "A picnic at a cemetery."

Slade grinned. "I took Joslyn to a horse auction the first time we went out," he reminded Hutch. "Maybe chivalry runs in the family."

"Or maybe not," Hutch said, and they both laughed. Shook hands.

"Thanks for showing up to have a look at the boy," Slade said.

Hutch nodded, said a quiet goodbye and turned to go while Slade stayed behind to admire his son for a little while longer.

Shea and Opal were standing in the corridor when

Hutch got there, talking quietly with a beaming Callie Barlow.

"That's one fine little brother you've got there," he told Shea.

Apparently over her earlier angst at no longer being the only bird in the nest, Shea smiled brightly and nodded in happy agreement. Callie hugged her step-granddaughter, her own eyes full of tears.

"He's the best," Shea murmured.

"Congratulations," Hutch said to Callie. It was, if he recalled correctly, the first word he'd ever said to the woman, even though he'd always known her. It wasn't that he'd judged her—he supposed she'd loved the old man once upon a time, since she'd had a child with him—but Hutch's mother's heartache and rage over the affair was still fresh in his mind. Until Trace, acknowledging Callie would have seemed like an act of disloyalty to his mom, as crazy as that sounded. After all, she'd died when he was twelve.

"Thank you, Hutch," Callie said, dashing at her wet eyes with the back of one hand.

"You look skinnier every time I see you," Opal put in, giving Hutch the once-over and frowning with devoted disapproval. To Opal, everybody in Parable was her concern, one way or the other. "You need me to come out to Whisper Creek and cook for you for a couple of weeks. Put some meat on those bones. And who ironed that shirt—a chimpanzee?"

Hutch grinned, though he felt a thousand years old all of a sudden and bone-weary in the bargain. "Nobody ironed it," he said, even as he wondered why he'd risen to the bait. "It's permanent press." He'd taken the garment out of the dryer and pulled it on just before leaving the house to drive back to town.

"There's no such thing as 'permanent press.'" Opal sniffed. "A shirt ought to be *ironed*."

That seemed like a good time to steer the conversation in another direction. "I appreciate your offer, Opal," he said honestly, "but Joslyn's going to need you to help take care of Trace."

"Joslyn's mama is on her way to Parable as we speak," Opal replied succinctly. "She'll provide all the lookin' after that family needs, at least for a week or two. I'll be at your place first thing tomorrow morning with my suitcase, so be ready for me."

Hutch opened his mouth, closed it again.

There was no point in arguing with Opal Dennison once she'd made up her mind, which she obviously had. If she meant to take over his house—or his whole life, for that matter—she'd do it. She was about as stoppable as a tornado gobbling up flat ground.

Best to just get out of the way and wait for the dust to settle.

"See you tomorrow," he finally said.

"Pick up some spray starch on your way home," Opal ordered. "And a decent iron, too, if you don't have one."

He pretended not to hear and walked off toward the elevator.

THE ELEVATOR DOORS opened, and Kendra came face-to-face with Hutch when she stepped out.

Even after spending much of the day in his company over at the Pioneer Cemetery, she felt startled by the encounter. Unprepared and very nervous.

"Where's Madison?" he asked, his gaze drifting

lightly over Kendra's cotton print sundress, which she changed into after the picnic, and then back to her face.

Kendra found her voice. Stepping past him, she remembered that she'd come to the hospital on a mission—to see her best friend's brand-new baby for the first time. "Downstairs," she answered automatically. "The receptionist is looking after her."

"I'll say howdy to her on my way out," Hutch replied.

He entered the elevator. The doors whispered shut between them and Kendra was left with the odd sensation that she'd imagined the whole exchange, if not the whole crazy *day*.

Had she really entered—and lost—a three-legged race at a cemetery picnic?

Seeing Callie and Shea and Opal in a happy huddle, she joined them.

"How's the new mama?" she asked.

Shea rolled her eyes. She was flushed and twinkly with excitement, like a girl-shaped topiary draped in fairy lights. "Would you believe Joss wants to go home—*right now?* Dad and Opal are making her stay the night, though—just to be on the safe side."

"So I guess that means Joslyn's doing just fine," Kendra said, smiling.

"She's amazing," Callie put in. "And so is little Trace. Lordy, he looks just like his daddy. Slade Barlow in miniature, that's him."

"Dad's walking about a foot off the ground," Shea said, pleased.

"Hutch's mama would roll over in her grave if she saw him wearing that wrinkled shirt out in public," Opal fretted, her gaze focused on the closed elevator doors. "She took pride in things like that."

Kendra blinked, confused.

"Don't mind Opal," Shea said in a conspiratorial whisper, slipping an arm through Kendra's. "She's suffering from a laundry fixation at the moment—it'll pass."

"Oh," Kendra said, no less confused than before but allowing herself to be swept into Joslyn's room.

Her friend was sitting up in bed, hair brushed, face scrubbed and glowing, eyes lively with joy. "Did you see him yet?" she asked, her tone happy and urgent.

Kendra laughed. "Not yet," she admitted. "I just got here a minute ago."

That dazed feeling, as if she couldn't quite catch up with herself, was still with her.

There were flowers everywhere, making the small quarters look and feel more like a garden than a hospital room.

Joslyn beamed. "I can't wait to have another one," she said.

"Whoa," protested Slade, from the doorway, grinning. "We just got out of the delivery room a couple of hours ago, woman."

"Come here and kiss me," Joslyn told him.

Shea laughed and made a face. "Gross," she said fondly.

By that time, Slade had crossed the room, bent over Joslyn, and touched his mouth to hers. The air crackled with electricity.

Kendra, still befuddled, remembered the bouquet of yellow carnations she was carrying and found a place for it among the tangle of color filling the room nearly to overflowing.

A nurse brought little Trace in then and placed him

gently in Joslyn's waiting arms. The sight of the three of them—father, mother and child—was a poignant one to Kendra and she felt a warm twinge of affection—along with a touch of envy. The latter was followed by a swift plunge into guilt, because she loved Madison so fiercely, and wanting to bear a child of her own seemed almost greedy.

Joslyn's gaze over the baby's downy head rested warmly on Kendra for a moment and the kind of understanding only close friends can share passed between them.

Shea took a cautious step forward. "Could—could I hold him?" she asked.

Joslyn smiled at the girl. "Of course," she replied easily. "Here—let me show you how to support his head…."

As simply, as beautifully, as that, Shea took her place in this newly expanded family—and then there were four.

Kendra was so choked up she nearly fled the room, fearing she'd cry and Joslyn would misunderstand.

"I'll pay you a visit when you get home," she told her friend, aware of Callie and Opal entering the room behind her. The walls were starting to close in; she needed fresh air and space to recover her equilibrium.

What was wrong with her, anyway?

"Wait," Joslyn said when Kendra would have made her exit. "There's something I want to ask you before you go and it's important."

Kendra, mystified and strangely hopeful, approached the bedside. Shea, holding the baby expertly, made room for her in the small, cozy circle, and Slade looked at her with a smile in his eyes.

Up close, Trace was so beautiful that he claimed a piece of Kendra's heart, right then and there, and she knew she'd never get it back, never even *want* to get it back.

"Will you be Trace's godmother?" Joslyn asked softly, reaching out to cover Kendra's cool and somewhat unsteady hand with her own warm one. Her grasp was firm.

The request was a simple one and yet it touched Kendra to the center of her soul, an unexpected grace. "I'd be proud," she managed in a ragged voice.

Joslyn squeezed her hand. "Good," she said, tearing up herself. "That's good."

Overcome, Kendra touched Trace's tiny head, turned and hurried out of Joslyn's hospital room. The instant she crossed the threshold, the tears came in rivers and she ducked into the women's restroom to pull herself together.

At one of the sinks, she splashed cold water on her face, not caring that she'd ruined her mascara. She used a moist paper towel to wipe away the dark trails on her cheeks, drew a deep breath and squared her shoulders, ready to face the world.

For the most part, anyway.

Downstairs Madison was ensconced at the main desk, coloring importantly and enjoying being the center of attention.

It threw Kendra a little when she realized that Hutch was there, too, chatting amicably with the receptionist. Barely out of her teens, the young woman, whose name tag read Darcy, looked up at him with an expression that resembled wonder, hanging on his every word.

Kendra found herself withdrawing slightly—she

might have been able to hide her puffy eyes from Madison, but Hutch was another matter. He noticed right away and she knew he probably wouldn't ignore the only-too-obvious fact that she'd been crying, very recently and a lot.

He might even deduce that, while she was very happy for Slade and Joslyn, she was feeling oddly hopeless at the moment, and that would make her too vulnerable to all that cowboy charm.

"Maybe I ought to drive you and Madison home in my truck," he said, straightening and stepping back from the tall reception counter. "I can call one of the ranch hands to bring your car back over to your place."

Hutch's attention had fully shifted by then, entirely focused on Kendra, and the receptionist seemed not just miffed but crestfallen, as though the sun had suddenly stopped shining for good.

"Mommy cries when she's happy," Madison announced. "She told me so, when we went to buy my bed at the store in Three Trees."

Hutch's mouth quirked upward at one side. "Crying and driving don't mix very well," he said easily, huskily. "Especially when there's precious cargo aboard."

"What's precipitous car-blow?" Madison asked.

"It's what you are," Hutch told the child, though his eyes hadn't left Kendra's face.

There was no question of refusing to accept his offer of a ride home; that would make her look like a careless mother, willing to risk her daughter's safety in order to protect her pride, which, of course, she wasn't. And never mind that she was perfectly capable of operating a motor vehicle; it wasn't as if she'd been drinking, for Pete's sake.

For these reasons, and others not so easy to recognize, she gave in.

She even said, "Thank you."

Outside Hutch sprinted over to the Volvo to fetch Madison's car seat from the back, and within a few moments he was installing the gear inside his extended cab truck. His hands moved with a deftness Kendra well remembered as he hoisted Madison into the seat—he, the bachelor rancher and local heartthrob, might have performed the task a million times before.

Madison loved being fussed over by a daddy type—what little girl didn't?—and if she'd been wearing a dress instead of those little jeans and a T-shirt, she probably would have stood right there in the hospital parking lot and twirled her skirt.

A softness settled over Kendra's heart as she looked on, but it was soon replaced by a flicker of dread. She could certainly prevent herself from falling in love with Hutch Carmody, but could she prevent *Madison* from buying into the illusion?

Hutch, despite his wild ways, was decent through and through. He genuinely liked people, particularly children, and he talked to them with a rare, enfolding ease that naturally made them feel special, even entirely unique.

It wasn't a deception, Kendra concluded sadly, not really. The problem was that, to Hutch, *every* child was special and every woman. Every dog and horse, too.

She tried to shake off these thoughts as she climbed into the front passenger seat, once Madison was settled, and buckled herself in for the short ride home.

If she didn't allow herself to care too much for this

man, she reasoned fitfully, as Hutch took the wheel and started the truck's engine, maybe Madison wouldn't care too much for him, either.

CHAPTER SIX

MADISON, AFTER GREETING a wildly joyful Daisy the moment they entered the new house, where there were still boxes all around, accumulated over several days of moving, took Hutch by one hand and practically dragged him from one room to another, showing the place off. Of course the dog followed them, occasionally putting in her two-bits with a happy little bark.

Kendra, emotionally winded from a long and eventful day, remained in the kitchen doing busywork, washing her hands at the sink, debating whether or not she ought to brew some coffee. The stuff could keep her up half the night, but as she remembered only too well, Hutch could drink the strongest java at midnight and still enjoy the sleep of the innocent and the just.

Talk about ironic.

Still Hutch had brought her and Madison safely home from the hospital visit to see the newest member of the Barlow clan—she was going to be Trace's godmother and the honor humbled her—and she owed the man the courtesy of a cup of coffee if he wanted one.

He'd pretty well gone to the wall that day, Hutch had, and he'd been a big part of some very memorable experiences for both her and Madison. At his suggestion, she'd left the keys to her Volvo at the hospital reception desk, and a couple of his ranch hands were already en route from Whisper Creek to pick up the vehicle and bring it to her.

Yes, the least she could do was offer the man coffee.

She didn't dare think about the *most* she could have done.

In the distance she heard Madison's ringing laugh, the dog's excitement at having the family intact and a visitor thrown in as a bonus, and Hutch's now-and-again comment, all along the lines of, "Well, isn't *that* something."

By the time the three wayfarers got back to the kitchen, Kendra had brewed a coffee for Hutch and an herbal tea for herself, using the one-cup wonder machine brought over from the big house. The device looked massive in this much smaller room, and way too fancy, but it served its purpose and for now that was enough.

"This is quite a change from the mansion," Hutch observed quietly as Madison hurried for the back door, calling over one shoulder that Daisy needed to go outside, and quick!

Kendra merely smiled and held out the cup of black coffee.

"Don't mind if I do," Hutch said, taking the mug. It looked fragile as a china teacup in his strong rancher's hands. "Thanks."

She inclined her head toward the table and he drew back a chair, but waited until she sat down with her tea before he took a seat himself.

His manners were yet another of Hutch's contradictions: he would leave a woman practically at the altar, wearing her heirloom wedding dress, break her heart right there in the presence of all her friends and family, but he opened doors for anyone of the female persuasion, whatever her age, and his male elders, too.

Through the open screen door, with its creaky hinges, Madison could be heard encouraging Daisy to hurry up and be a good girl so they could go back inside and be with the cowboy man.

Hutch grinned across the expanse of the tabletop and Kendra grinned back.

"This has been quite a day," she said, wondering if Hutch had the same odd mixture of feelings as she had where Slade and Joslyn's new baby was concerned. He was clearly happy for the Barlows, but she knew he wanted kids, too—it had been a favorite topic between them, back in the day, how many children they'd have, the ideal ratio of boys to girls, and even what their names would be.

A weary sort of sorrow overtook Kendra, just for that moment, and nearly brought tears to her eyes.

She shook it off. No sense getting all moody and nostalgic.

"That it has," Hutch agreed in his own good time, which was the way he did everything. The habit could be exasperating, Kendra reflected, except in bed.

Whoa, she thought. *Don't go down that road.*

A warm flush pulsed in her cheeks, though, and he noticed, of course. He always noticed what she'd rather have hidden, and overlooked things that should have caught his attention.

She looked away for a moment, recovering from the sexual flashback.

Madison and the dog came back inside, which helped Kendra calm down, and Madison sort of hovered around Hutch like a moth around a lightbulb.

Kendra finally sent Madison into the living room to watch the cartoon channel for the allowed half-hour before bath and bed, not because she wanted to get rid of her, but because the child's obvious adoration for Hutch was so unnerving.

Only cartoons could have distracted Madison from this admittedly fascinating man and even then she was reluctant to leave the room.

As soon as they were alone, Kendra opened her mouth and stuck her foot in it. "Don't let her get too attached to you, Hutch," she heard herself almost plead, in a sort of fractured whisper. "Madison's already lost so much."

Hutch looked stunned; he even paled a little, under his year-round tan, but in a nanosecond, he'd gone from stunned to quietly furious.

"What the hell is *that* supposed to mean?" he demanded, and though he kept his voice low, it rumbled like thunder gathering beyond the nearby hills.

Kendra let out a long breath, closed her eyes briefly, and rubbed her temples with the fingertips of both hands. "I wasn't saying—"

He leaned slightly forward in his chair, his bluish-green eyes fierce on her face. "What *were* you saying, then?" he pressed. She knew that look—he wasn't going to let this one go, would sit there all night if he had to, until he got an answer he could accept as the unvarnished truth.

"Madison is only four years old," she said weakly. Carefully. "She doesn't understand that your charm, like sunshine and rain, pretty much falls on everybody." She tried for more clarity and spoke with more strength now. "I don't want her getting too fond of you, Hutch.

You're so nice to her and she might read things into that that aren't there."

Hutch shoved a hand through his hair in a gesture of pure annoyance. His jawline went a bloodless white, he was clenching his back molars together so tightly. "You think I play *games* with people—with kids?" he finally asked, as though the concept had come out of left field and mowed him down. "You think I get some kind of kick out of making them believe I care so I can kick their feelings around later, just for the fun of it?"

Kendra hiked up her chin and met his gaze straight on. "Maybe not with children," she allowed evenly, "but do you 'play games' with women? That's a definite yes, Hutch. And I'm sure Brylee Parrish isn't the only person who'd be willing to back me up on the theory."

"You believe all that—" he paused, looked back over one shoulder, probably to make sure Madison hadn't wandered back into earshot and, seeing that she hadn't, finished with "—*crap* on the internet?"

Kendra's chuckle was light, but edged with a degree of bitterness that surprised even her. "Pictures don't lie," she said. "Besides, this goes back a lot further than your infamy on the web. Maybe you've forgotten that one of those broken hearts was mine?"

He looked as though he couldn't believe what he was hearing. "And maybe *you've* forgotten that we had something good going for us before you decided to kick off the traces and become Lady Chamberlain."

"It wasn't like that at all!" Kendra whispered.

"Go ahead and rewrite history to suit yourself," Hutch rasped, pushing back his chair and standing up, his half-finished coffee forgotten. He made the move so quietly that his chair didn't so much as scrape the floor, but rage was hardwired into every lean, powerful line of him. He set his hands on his hips and looked down at her for a long moment, then added, "The fact is, sweetheart, *you* walked out on *me*."

A knock sounded at the screen door just then, and a man's face appeared on the other side of the mesh. "Brought the car," he said, jangling the keys.

Hutch crossed the room, yanked the screen door open, and stormed right past the guy without even glancing at him.

The ranch hand looked at him curiously and extended the Volvo keys to Kendra, who had followed Hutch as far as the threshold, even though she had no intention of pursuing him. All the things she wanted to say to Hutch—okay, *scream* at him—were lodged painfully in the back of her throat, where she'd barely managed to stop them.

"Thank you," Kendra said mildly, taking the keys from the visitor's hand.

"You're mighty welcome," the weathered cowboy replied with a practiced tug at his hat brim. A mischievous twinkle lit his eyes. "Seems like this wouldn't be a good time to hit the boss up for a raise."

Kendra smiled at the joke. "You're probably right," she replied.

Hutch's truck started up with a roar, and both Kendra and the ranch hand winced a little when the tires screeched as he pulled away from the curb.

The cowboy shook his head, smiled ruefully and turned toward the other Whisper Creek truck waiting in the short driveway alongside the house, a second man at the wheel.

Kendra waved, closed the screen door, then its inside counterpart, hung the keys on a nearby hook and turned to find herself facing her daughter.

Madison and Daisy stood side by side, in the middle of the kitchen, their heads tilted at exactly the same angle, their gazes questioning and worried.

Kendra had to smile at the picture they made, even though she was still so irritated with Hutch that she felt like tearing out hanks of her own hair.

"The cowboy man didn't say goodbye," Madison said, and her lower lip wobbled slightly.

It was one of those rare times when only a lie would do, Kendra decided ruefully. "Actually, Mr. Carmody was in a big hurry, and he asked me to tell you goodbye and say he was sorry he had to rush off."

Madison, being an intelligent child, looked skeptical and unappeased, but she accepted the fib—to a degree. "I heard mad voices," she challenged Kendra after a few beats.

They'd been so careful not to yell, she and Hutch, though she'd *wanted* to and it was probably safe to assume Hutch had, as well. Madison had picked up on the energy of the exchange, rather than the actual words.

"It's time for your bath and a story," Kendra said moderately, striving for normalcy. How could Hutch claim, for one *moment,* that she'd been the one to break them up? He'd virtually *handed her over* to Jeffrey and walked away whistling.

"You should be nice to people," Madison lectured. "That's what you always tell me."

Kendra placed splayed fingers gently between her

daughter's shoulders and started her in the direction of the main bathroom. "Let's have this discussion another time, please," she said.

Daisy's toenails clicked on the hardwood floor behind them as she and Madison headed down the hall, Madison resisting ever so slightly as they went.

"But you forgot *supper*," the child reasoned.

Sure enough, Kendra realized, the evening meal had completely slipped her mind. "You're right," she replied, at once chagrined and glad to find common ground, even if it was a little shaky. "Tell you what— we'll feed Daisy and then, after you've had your bath, I'll whip up a couple of grilled cheese sandwiches for us. How would that be?"

Madison looked up at her and something in her small, obstinate face relented. "I like grilled cheese sandwiches," she admitted.

Kendra smiled. "Me, too," she said.

With Madison stripping and Daisy supervising the whole enterprise, Kendra managed to prepare the little girl's bath—a few inches of warm water with bubbles.

Madison climbed in and Daisy rested her muzzle on the edge of the bathtub, watching her small mistress, brown eyes shining with love.

"Can Daisy get into the tub, too?" Madison asked, reaching for her pink sponge and the duck-shaped bar of soap she favored.

"Not this time, sweetie," Kendra said, since that seemed better than a flat no.

Madison huffed out a sigh and began her ablutions, perfectly capable of bathing herself.

A few minutes later, she announced, "I'm clean now, Mommy!"

Smiling, despite the quiet but persistent ache in the region of her heart Hutch still claimed, Kendra gave her a kiss and reached for a towel.

HUTCH HAD ALWAYS been good at letting stuff roll off his back—he'd had to be—but that tangle with Kendra back at her place made him want to fight.

With anybody, about anything.

When the lights of Boone's cop car flashed behind him, just before the turn-in at Whisper Creek, it almost pleased him to pull over.

"What?" he snapped, rolling down the window on the passenger side of the truck so Boone could peer in at him.

"You headed for a fire?" Boone countered. "I clocked you at fifty in a thirty-five back there."

Hutch swore under his breath, tightened his grip on the steering wheel. "Sorry," he lied, glaring through the windshield at the dirt road ahead. It did some twisting and turning, that old road, before it joined the highway and rolled right on into Idaho and Washington.

At the moment, he sure felt like following it till it ended at the Pacific Ocean.

"Look at me, Hutch," the sheriff said, and he sounded dead serious.

Hutch turned his head, met Boone's gaze. "Write the ticket and be done with it," he growled.

"Well, who spit in *your* oatmeal this morning?" Boone asked, folding his arms against the base of the window and studying Hutch intently.

"I've got a lot on my mind right now," Hutch snapped. "All right?"

Boone sighed, shoved a hand through his dark hair.

"I know that," he said, "but I can't let you go speeding around my county, now can I? Pretty soon, folks will be saying I turn a blind eye when my friends break the law and I can't have that, Hutch. You know I can't."

"So *write the ticket*," Hutch reiterated. He just wanted to be gone, to be moving, to be riding hard across darkening ground on a horse or climbing Big Sky Mountain on foot—*anything* but sitting still.

"Have it your way," Boone said. He took his ticket book from his belt, scrawled on a piece of paper, ripped it free, and held it out to Hutch, who snatched it from his hand and barely managed to keep from chucking it out his own window out of sheer cussedness.

"Thanks," Hutch told him, glaring.

Boone laughed. "I'd say 'you're welcome,' but that would add up to one too many smart-asses per square yard." He wouldn't unpin Hutch from that penetrating gaze of his. "I'm off duty and I was headed for home until you went shooting by me like a bat out of hell," he said companionably. "Why don't you follow me back over to my place? We'll have a couple of beers and feel sorry for ourselves for a while."

Hutch had to chuckle at that, though it was against his will and he resented it. "All right," he agreed at last, and grudgingly. "Long as you promise not to run me in for drunk driving after plying me with liquor."

"You have my word," Boone said with a grin. "See you over there."

With that, he backed away from the window and strolled back to his cruiser where the lights were still swirling, blue and white, causing the few passersby to slow down to gawk.

Boone's land, situated on the far side of Parable

from where they started, was prime, fronting the river and sloping gently up toward the foothills, but it had the look of a place bogged down in hard times. The double-wide trailer was ugly as sin, and there were a couple of junked-out cars parked in the tall grass that surrounded it.

The double-wide had rust around its skirting, the makeshift porch dipped in the middle, and there was an honest-to-God toilet out front, with a bunch of dead flowers poking out of the bowl. Boone and his wife, Corrie—she'd never have stood for a john in the yard— had planned to live in the trailer only until they'd built their modest dream house, but when Corrie died of breast cancer a few years back, everything else in Boone's life seemed to stall.

If he'd had a dog, folks said, he'd have given it away. He *had* sent his two young sons, Griffin and Fletcher, off to live with his sister and her family in Missoula, where he probably figured they were better off.

Running for sheriff, after Slade announced that he wouldn't be seeking reelection, had been the first real sign of life in Boone since Corrie was laid to rest and for a while optimistic locals had hoped he'd get his act together, bring his kids home to Parable where they belonged, and just generally get on with things.

Parking behind the cruiser, Hutch felt an ache of sorrow on his friend's behalf—Boone had loved Corrie with all he had, from first grade on through college and in some ways, it was as if he'd just given up and crawled right into that grave with her.

"I swear this place looks worse every time I see it," Hutch remarked after getting out of the truck. There should have been two little boys running to greet their dad after a day at work, he thought, and a dog barking in celebration of his return, if not a woman smiling on the porch of the new house.

Instead it was dead quiet, like a graveyard with rusted headstones.

"You sound like the chicken rancher," Boone responded dryly, cocking a thumb in the direction of the neighboring place where Tara Kendall had set up housekeeping the year before. "She says this place is an eyesore."

Hutch had to grin. "She has a point," he said. Then, aware that he was pushing it, he added, "How are the boys?"

Boone, starting toward the sagging porch, tossed him a look. "They're just fine with their aunt and uncle and their brood," he said. "So don't start in on me, Hutch."

Hutch pretended to brace himself for a blow from his oldest and best friend. "You won't hear any relationship advice from me, old buddy," he said. "These days, I'm on America's Ten Most Unwanted list, which hardly makes me an authority."

"Damn straight," Boone grumbled. "And that's where you belong, too. On a master shit-list, I mean. I knew all that womanizing was bound to catch up with you someday."

Hutch laughed and followed his friend into the trailer. Boone always said what he thought; nobody was required to like it.

The inside of the double-wide was clean enough, but it was dismal, too. Full of shadows and smelling of the bachelor life—musty clothes left in the washing machine too long, garbage in need of taking out, the remains of last night's lonely pizza.

Boone opened the refrigerator and took out two cans of beer, handing one to Hutch and popping the top on another, taking a long drink before starting back outside again to sit in one of the rickety lawn chairs on that sorry excuse for a porch.

Hutch joined him.

"Old friend," Hutch ventured, looking out over what passed for a yard, "you need a woman. And that's just the start."

Boone grinned ruefully. "So do you," he said. "But you keep running them off."

Hutch sipped his beer. It was icy cold and it hit a dry spot, way down deep, unknotting him a little. "Slade's a dad now," he remarked, letting the gibe pass. "Can you believe it?"

"Hell, yes, I can believe it," Boone responded. They had a three-cornered alliance, Slade and Hutch and Boone. Slade and Hutch, being half brothers, hadn't gotten along until after the old man died, but Boone was close friends with both of them and always had been. "One look at Joslyn and Slade was a goner. Mark my words, they'll have a houseful of little Barlows before too long."

Hutch chuckled, but his thoughts had taken a somber turn just the same. "I reckon they enjoy the process of making them, all right," he said. A pause followed and another slow sip of cold beer. "What do you suppose it is about Slade, that's missing in you and me?" he asked.

Boone didn't pretend not to understand the question, but he took his time answering. "I hate to admit it," he finally replied, "but I think it's just plain-old backbone. Slade's not afraid to throw his heart in the ring and risk getting it stomped on. You and me, now, we're a couple of cowards."

Hutch absorbed that for a while. It was a tough truth to acknowledge—he wasn't afraid of anything besides climbing the water tower in town and giving up a chunk of his ranch to some vindictive ex-wife—but he couldn't deny that Boone had a point. Therefore, he didn't take offense. "What scares you the most, Boone?" he asked quietly.

Boone studied the horizon for a few moments, weighing his reply. "Loving a woman the way I loved Corrie," he said at long last. "And then losing her in the same way I lost Corrie. I don't honestly think I could take that, Hutch."

They were quiet for a long time, beers in hand, gazes fixed on things that were long ago and faraway.

"Your boys are growing up, Boone," Hutch ventured, after a decent interval. "They need you."

"They *need* what they have," Boone said, his voice taut now, his grip on his beer threatening to crush the can between his fingers, "which is a normal life with a normal family." He paused, swore, shook his head. "Hell, Hutch, you know I can't take care of them the way Molly does."

Hutch bit back the obvious response—that if Boone would just get his act together, he could make a home for himself and his boys, like millions of other single parents did. But who was he to talk about having it together, after all?

He didn't have kids and a wife waiting at home, either.

Didn't even have a dog, for God's sake, since Jasper had moved in with Slade.

For whatever reason, Boone didn't point out the holes in Hutch's own story, but that didn't mean he'd let him off the conversational hook, either.

Fair was fair and Hutch had been the one to set this particular ball rolling.

"That's quite a hubbub Brylee's friends are stirring up on the web," Boone said.

Hutch swallowed a sigh—and a couple more gulps of beer. "I am," he replied gravely, "a casualty of the digital age."

Boone laughed outright at that. "And innocent as the driven snow on top of it all," he added, before swilling more beer. As Slade had done when he held the office, Boone rarely wore a uniform—he dressed like any other Montana rancher, in jeans, boots and shirts cut Western-style. Now he unfastened the top two buttons of his shirt and breathed in as if he'd been smothering until then. "You and me," he said, "we're destined to be crusty old bachelors, it seems."

Kendra filled Hutch's mind just then. He saw her in the kitchen at his place, starting supper. He saw Madison, too, and even the dog, Daisy, hurrying out of the house to greet him when he got out of his truck or climbed down off his horse.

"I guess there are worse fates," Hutch allowed, but his throat felt tight all of a sudden and a little on the raw side.

"Like what?" Boone asked, gruffly companionable, still reflective. He was probably remembering happier days and hurting over the contrast between then and now.

"Being married to the wrong woman," Hutch said with grim certainty.

Boone sighed, finished his beer and stared solemnly at the can. "I wouldn't know about that," he answered, and though his voice didn't actually break, there was a crack in it. He'd been hitched to the *right* woman, was what he meant.

Finished with his own beer, Hutch stood up. He had work to do at home and besides, the emptiness would be there waiting, no matter how long he delayed his return, so he might as well get it over with. "We're a pair to draw to," he said, tossing the can into a wheelbarrow overflowing with them in roughly the place where Corrie used to set flowers in big pots.

Boone stood, too. Tried for a grin and fell short.

"You signed up for the bull-riding again this year?" he asked, referring to the upcoming rodeo. The Fourth fell on a Saturday this year, a convenient thing for most folks if not for Boone, who would surely have to bring a few former deputies out of retirement to make sure Parable County remained peaceable.

"Course I am," Hutch retorted, feeling a mite touchy again. "Walker Parrish promised me the worst bull that ever drew breath."

"I'll just bet he did," Boone said with another chuckle, throwing his own beer can in the general direction of the wheelbarrow and missing by a couple of feet. "When it's your turn to ride, I reckon a few of the spectators will be rooting for the bull."

Hutch started toward his truck. Twilight was gathering at the edges of the land, pulling inward like the top of a drawstring bag, and his horses would be wondering when he planned on showing up with their hay and grain rations. "No different than any other year," he said. "Somebody's *always* on the bull's side."

"You might want to think about that," Boone answered, and damn if he didn't sound serious as a heart attack. *Him,* with his sons farmed out to kinfolk, however loving, and the weeds taking over, threatening to swallow up the trailer itself.

Hutch stopped in his tracks. "Think about *what?*" he demanded.

"Life. People. How time gets away from a man and, before he knows it, he's sitting in some nursing home without a tooth in his head or a hope in his heart that anybody's going to trouble themselves to visit."

"Damned if you aren't dumber than the average post," Hutch said, moving again, jerking open the door of his truck and climbing inside.

"At least I know my limitations," Boone said affably.

"Thanks for the beer," Hutch replied ungraciously, and slammed the truck's door.

He drove away at a slower pace than he would have liked, though. Boone had already written him up for speeding once and he wasn't above doing it again.

By the time he got back to Whisper Creek, he'd simmered down quite a bit, though what Boone had said about the pair of them being cowards still stuck in him like barbed wire.

A familiar station wagon, three years older than dirt, was parked next to the house when he pulled in.

Opal, he realized, had arrived early.

He muttered something under his breath, got out of the pickup and went directly into the barn, where he spent the better part of an hour attending to horses.

It was almost dark by the time he'd finished, and the

lights were on in the kitchen, spilling a golden glow of welcome into the yard.

Stepping inside, he nodded a howdy to Opal, refusing to give her the satisfaction of demanding to know what the hell she was doing in his house. For one thing, he already knew—she was frying up chicken, country-style, and it smelled like three levels of heaven.

"Wash up before you eat," Opal ordered, tightening her apron strings and eyeing him through the big lenses of her glasses.

"I generally do," Hutch said mildly, running water at the sink and picking up the bar of harsh orange soap he kept handy.

"Look at those boots," Opal scolded with that strange, gruff tenderness she reserved for people in need of her guidance and correction. "Bet the soles are caked with manure."

Hutch sighed. He'd scraped them clean outside, on the porch, as he'd been taught to do around the time he started *wearing* boots.

"With you over here," he quipped, "who's going to nag Slade Barlow?"

"Shea's mama got in early," Opal replied, spearing pieces of chicken onto a platter with a meat fork. "So I figured I might as well get started setting things to rights around here."

Hutch dried his hands on a towel and grinned at her. "You're off to a good start with supper," he conceded.

She chuckled. "I made mashed potatoes and gravy, too, and boiled up some green beans with bacon and onion to boot. Sit yourself down, Hutch Carmody, and eat the first balanced meal you've probably had in a month of Sundays."

He waited until all the food was on the table and Opal was seated before taking a chair, wryly amused to recall that this was just the scenario he'd imagined for himself earlier.

Only the woman was different.

CHAPTER SEVEN

THE MANSION ON Rodeo Road seemed strangely hollow the next morning when Kendra stepped through the front door, even though most of the original furniture remained and there were painters and other workers in various rooms throughout.

Standing in the enormous entryway, she tipped her head back and looked up at the exquisite ceiling, waited for a pang of regret—some kind of sadness was to be expected, she supposed, given that she'd spent part of her life here. She'd wanted so much to live in this house, long before she'd met and married Jeffrey Chamberlain, and after her marriage a number of dreams had lived—and died—right here in these rooms.

Somewhat surprisingly, what Kendra actually felt was a swell of relief, a healthy sense of letting go, of moving on, even of becoming some more complete and authentic version of herself.

There was comfort in that, even exhilaration.

When she'd first set foot in the place, as an awe-struck little girl recently dumped on the porch of a rundown double-wide on the wrong side of the railroad tracks, Joslyn had been the one who lived here, along with her mom, Dana, and stepfather, Elliott, and, of course, Opal.

To Kendra the place had seemed like a castle, especially at Christmas, with Joslyn as resident princess.

During her childhood and her teens, the mere scope of that house had amazed Kendra—there were rooms not just for sleeping or eating or bathing, like in most homes, but ones set aside just for plants to grow in, or for playing cards and watching TV, or for reading books and doing homework or simply for *sitting*. Her grandmother's trailer had closets, of course, but here there were *dressing* rooms, too, with glass cubicles for shoes and handbags, and what seemed like a million bathrooms. There had even been a nook—several times larger than the living room in the double-wide—set aside for wrapping gifts, tying them up with elaborate bows, decorating them with small ornaments or glittery artificial flowers.

To a child who was handed money and told to buy her own birthday and Christmas presents, the mere concept of such finery had been magical.

Alas Kendra had been quick enough to realize, once she became the mistress of this monstrosity of a place, that it was never the structure itself, or any of its fancy trappings, that she'd wanted.

Instead it was the family, the sense of fitting in and belonging somewhere, of being a valued part of something larger.

Seen from the outside, Joslyn's life had certainly *seemed* happy in those early days, even enchanted, although a shattering scandal would eventually erupt, leaving everything in ruins.

Before her stepfather's financial fall from grace, when he'd ripped off friends and strangers alike, Joslyn had had it all—and while some people had been jealous of her and thought of her as spoiled and self-centered, Kendra had seen a different side of Joslyn. She'd shown empathy for Kendra's very different situation, but never pity, and she'd been willing to share her toys and her skates and, later on, her beautiful clothes.

More importantly, Joslyn had shared her mom and Opal and the little cocker spaniel, Spunky. Elliott Rossiter, the stepfather, had come and gone, funny and affable and generous, but always busy doing something important.

Stealing, as it turned out.

As an adult, Kendra had hoped to fulfill at least a part of her own dream with Jeffrey—the formation of a family—and in a roundabout way, she'd succeeded, because she had Madison now.

"Hello?" The voice startled Kendra out of her musings, even though she'd known she wasn't alone, having seen the painters' and cleaning service's vans in the driveway.

Charlie Duke, who ran Duke's Painting and Construction, stepped into view, clad in splotched overalls and wiping his hands on a shop rag. He grinned, showing the wide gap between his front teeth.

"Mornin', Ms. Shepherd," he said. "Here to see how the place is comin' along, are you?"

Kendra smiled. "Something like that," she replied. She'd known Charlie and his wife, Tina, for years and in the post office or the grocery store or over at the Butter Biscuit Café, either one of them would have addressed her simply as "Kendra," but the Dukes were old-fashioned people. When Charlie was on the job, all exchanges were formal, and Kendra was "Ms. Shepherd."

"We've about finished up in the main parlor," Charlie told her, with quiet pride, leading the way along the corridor. He wore paper booties over his work boots, and his T-shirt had a hole in the right shoulder, only partially covered by one of his overall straps.

Kendra followed, like someone taking a tour of some grand residence in an unfamiliar country.

It was almost as though she'd never been inside the place before, which was crazy of course, but such was her mood—reflective, calmly detached.

The parlor had been her office, as well as the main reception area for Shepherd Real Estate, and what furniture she hadn't moved over to the storefront was still in place, though covered by huge canvas tarps. The walls, formerly a soft shade of dusty rose, were now eggshell, neutral colors allegedly being the way to go when a house was on the market, in the hope of appealing to a broader spectrum of potential buyers.

Kendra did a quick walk-through—no small undertaking in a house the size of the average high school gymnasium—greeted Charlie's two sons, who were busy painting the kitchen a very pale yellow, and various members of the cleaning team, perched stoutly on high ladders, polishing window glass, and then went back to her car, where Daisy waited patiently in the passenger seat. They'd dropped Madison off at preschool first thing, the two of them, and the next stop was Kendra's office.

Upon arriving there, she took Daisy for a quick turn around the parking lot and then they both entered through the back way.

While Daisy explored the space—she'd been there before but, in her canine brain, there was always the exciting possibility that something had changed since the last visit—sniffing at silk plants and file cabinets and windowsills, Kendra booted up her computer, unlocked the front door and turned the Closed sign around to read Open.

She was in the tiny, closed-off kitchenette/storage room, starting a pot of coffee brewing, when she heard someone come in from the street. Daisy's low, almost inquisitive growl made her hurry back to the main part of the office.

The man standing just inside the door was strikingly handsome, wearing the regulation jeans, boots, Western-cut shirt and hat, as most men in Parable did.

He removed the hat, acknowledging Kendra with a cordial nod, and grinned down at Daisy, who by then must have decided he didn't represent a threat after all. Far from growling at him, she was nuzzling the hand he lowered for her to inspect.

It was a moment or two before Kendra placed the man—not a stranger, but not a resident of Parable proper, either. Of course, some new people could have moved into town while she was traveling, somehow managing to escape her notice, but that didn't seem very likely. After all, it was her business to know what was going on in the community, who was moving in and who was moving out, and she'd kept pretty close tabs on such local doings, through Joslyn, even while she was away.

The visitor smiled and recognition finally clicked. His name was Walker Parrish, and he was a wealthy rancher with a place over near Three Trees. Besides raising prize beef, he bred bulls and broncos for rodeos, as well.

And he was brother of the almost-bride, Brylee Parrish, Hutch's latest casualty-of-the-heart.

Surely, Kendra thought, a little desperately, he didn't think *she'd* been a factor in the wedding-day breakup? Everyone knew she'd been involved with Hutch at one time, but that had been over for years.

Still, what other business could Parrish have with her? He already owned a major chunk of the county, so he probably wasn't looking to acquire property, and since his place had been in his family for several generations, she couldn't imagine him selling out, either.

She finally gathered enough presence of mind to smile back at him and ask, "What can I help you with today, Mr. Parrish?"

"Well," he said with a grin that cocked up at one side, "you could start by calling me by my given name, Walker."

Daisy, by that time, had dropped to her belly in what looked like a dog-swoon, her long nose resting atop Walker's right boot, as though to pin him in place so she could stare up at him forever in uninterrupted adoration.

"All right," Kendra said. "Walker it is, then." As a somewhat flustered afterthought, she added, "I'm Kendra."

Again, the grin flashed. "Yes," he said. "I know who you are." He cleared his throat. "I came by to ask you about the house on Rodeo Road. I understand you're getting ready to sell it."

Kendra nodded, surprised and hoping it didn't show. Maybe she'd been wrong earlier, deciding that Walker hadn't come to buy or sell real estate. "Yes," she said, at last summoning up her manners and offering him one of the chairs reserved for customers while she moved behind her desk and sat down. "What would you like to know?"

Daisy sighed and lifted her head when Walker moved away, then wandered off to curl up in a corner of the office for a snooze.

Once Kendra was seated, Walker took a seat, too, letting his hat rest, crown to the cushion, on the chair nearest his. There was an attractive crease in his brown hair where the hatband had been, and it struck her, once again, how handsome he was—and how, oddly, his good looks didn't move her at all.

She reviewed what she knew about him—which was almost nothing. She didn't think he had a wife or even a girlfriend, but since the impression was mainly intuitive, she couldn't be sure.

Wishful thinking? Perhaps. If he *was* single, the question was, why? Why was a man like Walker Parrish still running around loose? Evidently the good ones *weren't* already taken.

"I guess I'd be interested in the price, to start," Walker replied with a slight twinkle in his eyes. Had he guessed what she was thinking in regard to his marital status? The idea mortified her instantly.

Her tone was normal when she recited the astronomical numbers.

Walker didn't flinch. "Reasonable," he said.

The curiosity was just too much for Kendra. "You're thinking of moving to Parable?" she asked.

He chuckled at that, shook his head. "No," he said. "I'm here on behalf of a friend of mine. She's—in show business, divorced, and she has a couple of kids she'd like to raise in a small town. Wants a big place because she plans to set up her own recording studio, and between the band and the road crew and her household and office staff, she needs a lot of elbow room."

Kendra couldn't help being intrigued—and a little wary. It wasn't uncommon for famous people to buy land around Parable, build houses even bigger than her own and landing strips for their private jets, and proceed to set up "sanctuaries" for exotic animals that didn't mix all that well with the cattle, horses, sheep and chickens ordinary mortals tended to raise, among other visibly noble and charitable efforts. Generally these out-of-towners were friendly enough, and the locals were willing to give them the benefit of the doubt, but in time the newcomers always seemed to stir up trouble over water rights or bounties on wolves and coyotes or some such, alienate all their neighbors, and then simply move on to the next place, the next adventure.

It was as though their lives were movies and Parable was just another set, instead of a real place populated by real people.

"Anybody I might have heard of?" Kendra asked carefully.

Something in Walker's heretofore open face closed up just slightly. "You'd know her name," he replied. "She's asked me not to mention it right away, that's all. In case the whole thing comes to nothing."

Kendra nodded; she'd had plenty of practice with this sort of thing. Most celebrities were private nearly to the point of paranoia, and not without reason. Besides the paparazzi, they had to worry about stalkers and kidnappers and worse. Safety—or the illusion of it—lay in secrecy, and safety was usually what made places like Parable and Three Trees attractive to them.

"Fair enough," she said easily. "There are always a few upscale properties available in the county…." She could think of two that had been standing empty for a while; one had an Olympic-size indoor pool, and the other boasted a home theater with a rotating screen and plush seats for almost a hundred. The asking prices were in the mid-to-high seven-figure range, not surprisingly, but it didn't sound as though that would strain Walker's mysterious friend's budget.

But Walker was already shaking his head. Being a local, he knew as well as anybody which properties were for sale, what kind of shape they were in, and approximately what they'd cost to buy, restore and maintain—and he'd asked specifically about the house on Rodeo Road. "She wants to be in town," he said. Then a frown creased his tanned forehead. "Is there some reason why you don't want to show your house just yet?"

"No, no," Kendra said, "it's nothing like that. We can head over there right now if you want. It's just that—" She stopped in the middle of the sentence because she couldn't think of a diplomatic way to go on.

"Show business people are sometimes unreliable," Walker finished for her. The frown had smoothed away and he was grinning again. "I remember that rock band a few years back—the ones who built a pseudo haunted house, trashed the Grange Hall in Three Trees one night when they were partying and then nearly burned down a state forest, conducting some kind of crazy ritual. But it wouldn't be fair to hold that against everybody who sings and plays a guitar to earn a paycheck, would it?"

Kendra let out a long breath, shook her head no. Walker was right—that *wouldn't* be fair—and besides, hadn't he *said* this woman wanted to raise her children in a small town? That gave her at least one thing in common with Kendra herself, and with most of her friends, too.

Parable had its problems, like any community, but the crime rate was low, people knew each other and down-to-earth values were still important there. In a very real sense, Parable was a *family*. And it was cousin to Three Trees.

The two towns were rivals in many ways, but when trouble came to one or the other, they stood up to it shoulder to shoulder.

"If you have time," she reiterated, "I can show you through the house right now."

"That would be great," Walker said, rising from his chair. "I was there a few times when I was a kid, for parties and the like, but I don't remember too many of the details."

Kendra stood, too, simultaneously reaching for her purse and Daisy's leash. She blushed a little, imagining the state of the Volvo's interior. Pre-Madison and pre-dog, she'd kept her vehicles immaculate, as a courtesy to her clients, but now...

"I'm afraid my car needs vacuuming. The dog..."

Walker laughed. "Given my line of work," he said, "I'm not squeamish about a little dog hair. Matter of fact, I have three of the motley critters myself. But I'll take my own rig because I've got some other places to go to this morning, after we're through at your place."

Kendra nodded, clipped on Daisy's leash and indicated that she'd be leaving by the back way, so she'd need to lock up behind Walker after he stepped outside.

"Meet you over there," he said, and went out.

She nodded and locked the door between them.

Daisy paused for a pee break in the parking lot, and then Kendra and the retriever climbed into the Volvo and headed for Rodeo Road for the second time that morning.

"AT THIS RATE," Hutch grumbled good-naturedly, surveying the meal Opal had just set before him—a late lunch or an early supper, depending on your perspective, "I'll be too fat to ride in the rodeo, even though it's only a few days away."

Opal laughed. "Oh, stop your fussing and sit down and eat," she ordered.

She'd been busy—had the ironing board set up in the middle of the kitchen, and she must have washed and pressed every shirt he owned because she'd evidently been hard at it all day. Except, of course, for when she took time out to build the meat loaf she'd just set down in front of him. The main dish was accompanied by creamed peas and mashed potatoes drowning in gravy; and just looking at all that food, woman-cooked and from scratch, too, made his mouth water and his stomach growl.

But he didn't sit, because Opal was still standing.

With a little sigh and a sparkle of flattered comprehension in her eyes, she took the chair indicated and nodded for him to follow suit.

He did, but he was still uncomfortable. "Aren't you going to join me?" he asked, troubled to notice that she hadn't set a place for herself.

Opal's chuckle was warm and vibrant, vaguely reminiscent of the gospel music she loved to belt out when she thought she was alone. "I can't eat like a cowboy," she answered. "Be the size of a house in no time if I do."

Hutch was fresh out of self-restraint. He was simply too hungry, and the food looked and smelled too good. He took up his knife and fork and dug in. After complimenting Opal on her cooking—by comparison to years of eating his own burnt sacrifices or his dad's similar efforts, it seemed miraculous they survived—he asked about Joslyn and the baby.

"They're doing just fine," Opal said with satisfaction. Her gaze followed his fork from his plate to his mouth and she smiled like she might be enjoying the meal vicariously. "Dana—that's Joslyn's mother, you remember—is a born grandma, and so is Callie Barlow. Between the two of them, Slade, Shea and of course the little mama herself, I was purely in the way."

"I doubt that," Hutch observed. Opal, it seemed to him, was more than an ordinary human being, she was a living archetype, a wise woman, an earth mother.

And damned if he wasn't going all greeting-card philosophical in his old age.

"I like to go where I'm needed," she said lightly.

Hutch chuckled. "So now I'm some kind of—case?" he asked, figuring he was probably that and a lot more.

Opal's gaze softened. "Your mama was a good friend to me when I first came to Parable to work for old Mrs. Rossiter," she said, very quietly. "Least I can do to return the favor is make sure her only boy doesn't go around half-starved and looking like a homeless person."

That time, he laughed. "I look like a homeless person?" he countered, at once amused and mildly indignant. Living on this same land all his life, like several generations of Carmodys before him, letting the dirt soak up his blood and sweat and tears, he figured he was about as *un*homeless as it was possible to be.

"Not exactly," Opal said thoughtfully, and in all seriousness, going by her expression and her tone. "A *wifeless* person would be a better way of putting it."

Hutch sobered. Opal hadn't said much about the near-miss wedding, but he knew it was on her mind. Hell, it was on *everybody's* mind, and he wished something big would happen so people would have something else to obsess about.

An earthquake, maybe.

Possibly the Second Coming.

Or at least a local lottery winner.

"You figure a wife is the answer to all my problems?" he asked moderately, setting down his fork.

"Just most of them," Opal clarified with a mischievous grin. "But here's what I'm *not* saying, Hutch— I'm not saying that you should have gone ahead and married Brylee Parrish. Marriage is hard enough when both partners want it with all their hearts. When one doesn't, there's no making it work. So by my reckoning, you definitely did the right thing by putting a stop to things, although your timing could have been better."

Hutch relaxed, picked up his fork again. "I tried to tell Brylee beforehand," he said. He'd long since stopped explaining this to most people, but Opal wasn't "most people." "She wouldn't listen."

Opal sighed. "She's headstrong, that girl," she reflected. "Her and Walker's mama was like that, you know. Folks used to say you could tell a Parrish, but you couldn't tell them much."

Hutch went right on eating. "Is there anybody within fifty miles of here whose mama you *didn't* know?" he teased between bites. He was ravenous, he realized, and slowing down was an effort. *Keep one foot on the floor, son,* he remembered his dad saying, whenever he'd shown a little too much eagerness at the table.

"I don't know a lot of the new people," she said, "nor their kinfolks, neither. But I knew *your* mother, sure enough, and she certainly did love her boy. It broke her heart when she got sick, knowing she'd have to leave you to grow up with just your daddy."

Hutch's throat tightened slightly, making the next swallow an effort. He'd been just twelve years old when his mother died of cancer, and although he'd definitely grieved her loss, he'd also learned fairly quickly that the old man believed in letting the dead bury the dead. John Carmody had rarely spoken of his late wife after the funeral, and he hadn't encouraged Hutch to talk about her, either. In fact, he'd put away all the pictures of her and given away her personal possessions almost before she was cold in the grave.

So Hutch had set her on a shelf in a dusty corner of his mind and tried not to think about the hole she'd left in his life when she was torn away.

"Dad wasn't the best when it came to parenting," Hutch commented belatedly, thinking back. "But he wasn't the worst, either."

Opal's usually gentle face seemed to tighten a little, around her mouth especially. "John Carmody was just plain selfish," she decreed with absolute conviction but no particular rancor. To her, the remark amounted to an observation, not a judgment. "Long as he got what he wanted, he didn't reckon anything else mattered."

Hutch was a little surprised by the bluntness of Opal's statement, though he couldn't think why he should have been. She was one of the most direct people he'd ever known—and he considered the trait a positive one, at least in her. There were those, of course, who used what they liked to call "honesty" as an excuse to be mean, but Opal wasn't like that.

He opened his mouth to reply, couldn't think what to say, and closed it again.

Opal smiled and reached across the table to lay a hand briefly on his right forearm. "I had no business saying that, Hutch," she told him, "and I'm sorry."

Hutch found his voice, but it came out gruff. "Don't be," he said. "I like a reminder every once in a while that I'm not the only one who thought my father was an asshole."

This time it was Opal who was taken aback. "Hutch Carmody," she finally managed to sputter, "I'll thank you not to use that kind of language in my presence again, particularly in reference to the departed."

"Sorry," he said, and the word was still a little rough around the edges.

"We can either talk about your daddy and your mama," Opal said presently, "or we can drop the whole subject. It's up to you."

His hunger—for food, at least—assuaged, Hutch pushed his mostly empty plate away and met Opal's gaze. "Obviously," he said mildly, "you've got something to say. So go ahead and say it."

"I'm not sure what kind of father Mr. Carmody was," she began, "but I know he wasn't up for any awards as a husband."

Offering no response, Hutch rested his forearms on the tabletop and settled in for some serious listening.

When she went on, Opal seemed to be picking up in

the middle of some rambling thought. "Oh, I know he wasn't actually married to your mother when he got involved with Callie Barlow, but she had his engagement ring on her finger, all right, and the date had been set."

Hutch guessed the apple didn't fall far from the tree, as the old saying went. He hadn't cheated on Brylee, but he'd done the next worst thing by breaking up with her at their wedding with half the county looking on.

"That was hard for Mom," he said. "She never really got over it, as far as I could tell."

Opal nodded. "She was fragile in some ways," she replied.

Hutch felt the sting of chagrin. He'd loved his mother, but he'd always thought of her as weak, too, and maybe even a mite on the foolish side. She'd gone right ahead and married the old man, after all, knowing that he'd not only betrayed her trust, but fathered a child by another woman.

A child—Slade Barlow—who would grow up practically under her nose and bear such a resemblance to John Carmody that there could be no doubt of his paternity.

"I guess she liked to think the whole thing was Callie's fault," Hutch reasoned, "and Dad was just an innocent victim."

"Some victim," Opal scoffed, but sadly. "He wanted Callie and he went after her. She was young and naive, and he was good-looking and a real smooth talker when he wanted to be. I think Callie really believed he loved her—and it was a brave thing she did, barely grown herself and raising Slade all by herself in a place the size of Parable."

Hutch recalled his encounter with Callie at the hospital, how happy she was about the new baby, her grandson. And his heart, long-since hardened against the woman, softened a little more. "I reckon most people are doing the best they can with whatever cards they were dealt," he said. "Callie included."

"It's a shame," Opal said after a long and thoughtful pause, "that you and Slade grew up at odds. Why your daddy never acknowledged him as his son is more than I can fathom. It just doesn't make any sense, the two of them looking so much alike and all."

Hutch considered what he was about to say for a long moment before he actually came out with it. Opal knew everybody's business, but she didn't carry tales, so he could trust her. And he didn't want to sound as if he felt sorry for himself, because he knew that, for all of it, he was one of the lucky ones. "When it was just Dad and me," he finally replied, "nobody else around, he used to tell me he wished I'd been the one born on the wrong side of the blanket instead of Slade. I guess by Dad's reckoning, Callie got the better end of the deal."

Opal didn't respond immediately, not verbally anyway, but her eyes flashed with temper and then narrowed. "Slade is a fine man—Callie did a good job bringing him up and no sensible person would claim otherwise—but he's no better and no worse than you are, Hutch."

Hutch just smiled at that, albeit a bit sadly. Sure, he wished his dad had shown some pride in him, just once, but there was no point in dwelling on things that couldn't be changed. To his mind, the only way to set the matter right was to be a different kind of father himself, when the time came.

He pushed back his chair, stood up and slowly carried his plate and silverware to the sink.

Opal was right there beside him, in a heartbeat, elbowing him aside even as she took the utensils out of his hand. "I'll do that," she said. "You go on and do whatever it is you do in the evenings."

Hutch smiled. "I was thinking I might head into town," he said. "See what's happening at the Boot Scoot."

"I'll *tell* you what's happening at that run-down old bar," Opal said, with mock disapproval. "Folks are wasting good time and good money, swilling liquor and listening to songs about being in prison and their mama's bad luck and how their old dog got run over when their wife left them in a hurry."

"Why, Opal," Hutch teased cheerfully, "does that mean you don't want to go along as my date?"

"You just hush," Opal scolded, snapping at him with a dish towel and then giving a laugh. "And mind you don't drink too much beer."

CHAPTER EIGHT

AFTER TAKING A quick shower and putting on clean clothes, Hutch traveled a round-about road to get to the Boot Scoot Tavern that night—a place he had no real interest in going to—and the meandering trail led him right past Kendra Shepherd's brightly lit rental house.

In simpler times, he wouldn't have needed a reason to knock on Kendra's door at pretty much any hour of the day or night, but things had certainly changed between them, and not just because she had a daughter now. Not even because he'd almost married Brylee Parrish and Kendra *had* married Sir Jeffrey, as Hutch privately thought of the man—when he was in a charitable frame of mind, that is.

No, there was more to it.

The whole time he'd known Kendra, she'd coveted that monster of a house over on Rodeo Road. As a kid, she'd haunted it like a small and wistful ghost, Joslyn's pale shadow. As a grown-up, she'd found herself a prince with the means to buy the place for her and after the divorce she'd held on to it, rattling around in it all alone for several years, like a lone plug of buckshot in the bottom of a fifty-gallon drum.

Now all of a sudden, she'd moved into modest digs, rented from Maggie Landers, opened a storefront office to sell real estate out of and switched rides from a swanky sports car to a *Volvo,* for God's sake.

What did all of that mean—beyond, of course, the fact that she was now a mother? Did it, in fact, mean *anything?* Women were strange and magnificent creatures, in Hutch's opinion, their workings mysterious, often even to themselves, never mind some hapless man like him.

Kendra had, except for staying put in Parable, turned her entire life upside down, changed practically everything.

Was that a good omen—or a bad one?

Hutch wanted an answer to that question far more than he wanted a draft beer, but since he could get the latter for a couple of bucks and the former might just cost him a chunk of his pride, he kept going until he pulled into the gravel-and-dirt parking lot next to the Boot Scoot.

The front doors of that never-painted Quonset hut, a relic of World War II, stood open to the evening breeze, and light and sound spilled and tumbled out into the thickening twilight—he heard laughter, twangy music rocking from the jukebox, the distinctive click of pool balls at the break.

With a smile and a shake of his head, Hutch shut off the headlights, cranked off the truck's trusty engine, pushed open the door and got out. The soles of his boots crunched in the gravel when he landed, and he shut the truck door behind him, then headed for the entrance.

Once the place would have been blue with shifting billows of cigarette smoke, hazy and acrid, but now it was illegal to light up in a public building, though the smell of burning tobacco—and occasionally something else—was still noticeable even out in the open air. He caught the down-at-the-heels Montana-tavern scent of the sawdust covering the floor as he entered, stale sweat overridden by colognes of both the male and female persuasions, and he felt that peculiar brand of personal loneliness that drove folks to the Boot Scoot when they had better things to be doing elsewhere.

Hutch nodded to a few friends as he approached the bar and then ordered a beer.

Two or three couples were dancing to the wails of the jukebox—he thought of Opal's description of the tavern and smiled at its accuracy—but most of the action seemed to center around the two pool tables at the far end of the long room.

Hutch's beer was drawn from a spigot and brought to him; he paid for it, picked up the mug in one hand and made his way toward the pool tables. By the weekend, when the rodeo and other Independence Day celebrations would be in full swing, the crowds would be so thick in here, at least at night, that just getting from one side of the tavern to the other would be like swimming through chest-deep mud of the variety Montanans call "gumbo."

Finding a place to stand without bumping elbows with anybody, Hutch watched the proceedings. Deputy Treat McQuillan, off duty and out of uniform but still clearly marked as a cop by his old-fashioned buzz haircut, watched sourly, pool cue in hand, while another player basically ran the table, plunking ball after ball into the appropriate pocket.

Never a gracious loser, McQuillan reddened steadily throughout, and when the bloodbath was over, he turned on one heel, rammed his cue stick back into the wall-rack with a sharp motion of one scrawny arm and stormed off.

A few of the good old boys, mostly farmers and ranchers Hutch had known since the last Ice Age, shook their heads in tolerant disgust and then ignored McQuillan, as most people tended to do. Getting along with him was just too damn much work and consequently the number of friends he could claim usually hovered somewhere around zero.

For some reason Hutch couldn't put his finger on—beyond a prickle at the nape of his neck—he was strangely uneasy and getting more so by the moment. He watched the deputy shoulder his way toward the bar, evidently impervious to the good-natured joshing of the people he passed.

Hutch had never liked McQuillan, and he certainly wasn't in the minority on that score, but in that moment he found himself feeling a little sorry for the man, if no less watchful. The very air had a zip in it, a sure sign that something was about to go down, and it probably wasn't good.

Halfway across the sawdust-covered floor, McQuillan stopped at a table encircled by women, put out his hand and jerked one of them to her feet, hard against his torso and into a slow dance. At first, Hutch couldn't make out who she was, with folks milling in between.

A scuffle ensued—the lady evidently preferred not to participate, at least not with Treat McQuillan for a dancing partner—and the other females at the table rose as one, so fast that a few of their chairs tipped over backward.

"Stop it, Treat," one of them said.

And then, as people shifted and pressed in on the

scene, Hutch recognized the woman who didn't want to dance. It was Brylee.

He plunked down his mug on another table and instinctively headed in that direction, ready to take McQuillan apart at the joints like a Sunday-supper chicken just out of the stewpot. But right when he would have reached the couple, an arm shot out in front of his chest and stopped him as surely as if a steel barricade had slammed down from the ceiling.

"My sister," Walker Parrish said evenly, "my fight."

Hutch hadn't spotted either Walker *or* Brylee when he came in, so he hadn't had a chance to square away their presence in his mind. He felt a little off-balance.

In the next instant, Parrish shoved McQuillan away from Brylee, hard, hauled back one fist and clocked the deputy square in the beak.

That was it. The whole fight. Though in the days to come it would grow with every retelling, eventually becoming almost unrecognizable.

McQuillan's eyes rolled back, his knees buckled and he went down.

Walker, meanwhile, gripped Brylee firmly by one arm, barely giving her a chance to retrieve her purse from the floor next to her chair, and propelled her toward the exit.

"We're going home now," he was heard to say in a tone that left no room for negotiation.

"Damn it, Walker," Brylee yelled in response, struggling in vain to yank free from her brother's grasp. "Let me go! I can take care of *myself!*"

In spite of everything, Hutch had to smile a little, because what Brylee said was true—she *could* take care of herself and in the long run she'd be just fine.

Oh, the woman had spirit, all right. Life would have been so much simpler all around, Hutch thought, if only he could have loved her.

Moments later, the Parrishes were gone and somebody was helping McQuillan back to his feet. He was rubbing his jaw and had one hell of a nosebleed going, but he looked all right, otherwise—no obvious need for any wires, stitches or casts, anyhow.

"I'm pressing charges!" McQuillan raged. "You're all witnesses! You all saw what Walker Parrish did to me!"

"Ah, Treat," one man drawled, "let it go. You put your hands on the man's *sister,* and after she told you straight out she didn't care to dance—"

McQuillan's small, beady eyes flashed fire. He was trying to staunch the nosebleed with the sleeve of his shirt, but not having much luck. Some of the sawdust on the floor would definitely have to be shoveled out and replaced.

"I mean it," he insisted furiously. "Parrish assaulted an officer of the law and he's going to face the consequences!"

Hutch, standing nearby, flexed his fist slowly and waited for the urge to drop McQuillan right back to the floor again to pass.

Presently, it did.

The show was over and Hutch turned, meaning to go back for the beer he'd set aside minutes earlier. He nearly collided with Brylee's best friend, Amy Jo Du-Pree in the process.

"You have your nerve coming in here, Hutch Carmody!" Amy Jo seethed, standing practically toe-to-toe with him and craning her neck back so she could look up at him. Five-foot-nothing and weighing a hundred pounds soaking wet, Frank and Marge DuPree's baby girl was a pretty thing, but feisty, afraid of nothing and no one.

Montana seemed to breed women like that.

Hutch arched an eyebrow. "Excuse me?" he countered, raising his voice a little as the jukebox cranked up and Carrie Underwood took to extolling the virtues of baseball bats and kerosene-fueled revenge.

Maybe that was what was making the whole female sex seem more impossible to deal with by the day, Hutch speculated fleetingly. Maybe it was the inflammatory nature of the music they listened to on their iPods and other such devices.

"You heard me," Amy Jo all but snarled through her little white teeth, and gave him a light but solid punch to the solar plexus.

Intrigued and, okay, a little pissed off at the injustice of it all, Hutch took Amy Jo by the arm and squired her outside.

The parking lot was hardly quieter than the interior of the bar, what with Walker and Brylee yelling at each other and then peeling away in Walker's truck, and then Boone arriving with his lights flashing and his siren giving a single mournful whoop in case the blinding strobe left any doubt he was there.

"Hell," Hutch breathed, watching as the sheriff climbed, somewhat wearily, out of his cruiser and came toward the doors of the Boot Scoot. "McQuillan's really going to do it—he's going to press charges against Walker."

"Somebody ought to press charges against *you*," Amy Jo huffed out, but she wasn't quite as steam-powered as before. "How could you, Hutch? How could you let things go so far and then humiliate Brylee in public the way you did? Do you even know how much a wedding *means* to a woman? She looks forward to it her whole life, from the time she's a little bit of a thing, and then——"

Boone passed them, nodded in grim acknowledgment as he went inside the tavern to investigate the scene of the crime, as McQuillan, who must have gotten right on his cell phone to report the event, would no doubt term it.

By now the damn idiot had probably taped off a body-shape in the sawdust, to mark the place where he'd fallen.

Hutch turned his attention back to Amy Jo. "Just exactly what is it," he asked, exasperated, "that you people want me to do, here?"

Amy Jo jutted out her spunky little chin. "'You people'? You mean Brylee's friends?"

"I *mean*," Hutch bit out tersely, "that all this Team Brylee crap is getting old. I've always lived here and I always will, and I will be *damned* if I'll stay away from the Boot Scoot or anyplace else I want to go, just because you and the rest of Brylee's bunch think I ought to be ashamed of what I did." He leaned in, and Amy Jo's eyes widened. "Here's a flash for you—pass it on. Post it on that stupid website. Print up T-shirts, put fliers on windshields, whatever. *I'm not going anywhere. Deal with it.*"

Amy Jo blinked. She wasn't a bad sort, really. It was just that she and Brylee had grown up as close friends, the way Kendra and Joslyn had. The way he and Slade might have, if it hadn't been for the old man's cussed determination to ignore one of them and browbeat the other.

Loyalty was an important quality in a friend, even when it was the bullheaded kind like Amy Jo's.

"Nobody expects you to move away or anything," Amy Jo said belatedly and in a lame tone.

"Good," Hutch sputtered, as another ruckus of some kind erupted inside the Boot Scoot. "Because when hell freezes over, I'll still be right here in Parable."

Amy Jo swallowed, nodded and went back into the tavern to find her friends.

Although Hutch's better angels urged him to get in his truck and go home, where he should have stayed in the first place, he figured Boone might need some help settling things down, so he followed Amy Jo inside.

McQuillan was out of control, waving his free arm and guarding his gushing nose with the other, yelling in Boone's face.

Boone, for his part, calmly stood his ground. "Now, Treat," he reasoned, amiable but serious, "I would hate to have to run one of my own deputies in for drunk-and-disorderly and creating a public nuisance, but I'll do it, by God, I'll throw you straight into the hoosegow if you keep this up."

At the periphery of his vision, Hutch saw Amy Jo and the rest of the Brylee contingent quietly gather their purses and other assorted gear and trail out of the tavern. Probably a wise decision, given the incendiary mood McQuillan was creating.

"Arrest *me?*" the deputy bellowed. Treat never had known when to keep his mouth shut, which was part of his problem. "I'm the *victim* here! I was *assaulted!*"

"We'll discuss that," Boone assured him, "but not until you calm down."

"I'd have knocked you on your ass, too, McQuillan," a male voice contributed from somewhere in the dwindling crowd. "You can't expect any different when you grab on to a woman in a goddamn cowboy bar!"

"Harley," Boone said, recognizing the speaker immediately, and without looking away from McQuillan's bloody, temper-twisted face, "shut up."

Hutch, looking on, privately agreed with Harley. Manhandling a lady was asking for trouble pretty much anywhere, but square in the middle of cowboy-central, it was close to suicidal.

Just the same, he positioned himself at Boone's left side, not quite in his space but close enough to jump in if the shit hit the fan.

Boone slanted a brief glance in his direction. "You involved in this?" he asked.

Hutch folded his arms, rocked back slightly on his heels. "Now Boone, I am downright *insulted* by that question. I just happened to be here, that's all."

Boone's expression remained skeptical, but only mildly so. He sighed heavily. "Come on, Treat," he said to his disgruntled deputy. "I'll give you a lift over to the hospital, get them to check you out, and take you home. No way you're in any condition to drive."

Treat was all bristled up, like a little rooster with his feathers brushed in the wrong direction. "I'd rather walk," he replied coldly. Boone might have been McQuillan's boss, but he was also the man who'd trounced him at the polls last Election Day and he clearly wasn't over the disappointment. McQuillan had wanted to be sheriff from the time he was little, never mind that he was constitutionally unsuited for the job.

"Whatever you say, Treat," Boone responded. "But leave your rig right where it's parked until morning."

"I'll be filing charges against Walker Parrish as soon as the courthouse opens," McQuillan maintained, but he was on the move as he spoke, headed for the doors.

The onlookers finally lost all interest and dispersed, going back to their pool playing and their beer drinking and their armchair quarterbacking.

Boone turned to Hutch. "What happened here?" he asked.

The incident, though it had already drifted into the annals of history, still chapped Hutch's hide a little. He wasn't in love with Brylee Parrish, but standing around watching while some drunken bastard strong-armed her into something she didn't want to do went against his grain in about a million ways.

Hutch told Boone the story, leaving out the part about how he'd meant to go after McQuillan himself but Walker had stepped in and thrown a punch of his own.

"Well," Boone said on a long breath, "that's fine. That's just *fine*. Because if McQuillan doesn't cool off overnight—and experience tells me that won't happen— I'll probably have to charge Walker with assault."

"Come on," Hutch protested. "I told you what happened—McQuillan brought that haymaker on himself."

Boone was on his way toward the exit and Hutch, tired of the bar, tired of just about everything, followed. "Walker had the right to defend his sister," the sheriff allowed quietly, over one shoulder, "but he took it too far. He's half again McQuillan's size and whatever my personal opinion of old Treat might be, he *is* a sworn

officer of the court. Landing a punch in the middle of
his face, though a sore temptation at times, I admit, is
a little worse in the eyes of the law than if Walker had
decked, say, for instance—*you*."

They were in the parking lot by then. The lights on
top of Boone's squad car still splashed blue and white
over everything around them in dizzying swirls.

"He's welcome to try," Hutch said, hackles rising
again. Did *everybody,* even his best friend, think he
had a fat lip and a shiner coming to him just because
he hadn't gone through with the wedding?

Boone opened his cruiser door, leaned in and shut
off the lights, which was a relief to Hutch, who was
starting to get a headache. "Go home, Hutch," Boone
said. "I've got one loose cannon on my hands in Treat
McQuillan and I don't need another one."

"I'm not breaking any laws," Hutch pointed out, putting an edge to the words. There it was again, somebody telling him where to go, what to do. Damn it, the
last time he looked, he'd still lived in a free country.

"True," Boone agreed. "But if Walker hadn't gotten
to McQuillan first, you'd have clocked him yourself,
and don't try to claim otherwise, because I *know* you,
Hutch. You've got *pissed-off* written all over you, and if
you hang around town on the lookout for trouble, you're
bound to find some." The sheriff sighed again. "It's my
job to keep the peace and I mean to do it."

Hutch's strongest instinct was to dig in his heels
and stand up for his rights, even if Boone *was* making
a convoluted kind of sense. And it still stung a little,
remembering how Walker had gotten in his way back
there when McQuillan crossed the line with Brylee. He

felt thwarted and primed for action at the same time—not a promising combination.

Before he could say anything more, though, Boone changed the subject in midstream by announcing, "My boys are coming for a visit. Spending the Fourth of July weekend with me."

Hutch went still. Grinned. "That's good," he said, pleased. Then, after a pause, "Isn't it?"

"Hell, no, it isn't good," Boone answered, looking distracted and miserable. "That trailer of mine isn't fit for human habitation. I wouldn't know what to feed them, or what time they ought to go to bed, or how much television they should be allowed to watch—"

Hutch laughed, and it was a welcome tension-breaker. The muscles in his neck and shoulders relaxed with a swiftness that almost made him feel as though he'd just downed a double-shot of straight whiskey.

"Then maybe you ought to clean the place up a little," he suggested. "As for bedtime and TV, well, it shouldn't take a rocket scientist to figure those things out. These are kids we're talking about here, Boone, not some alien species nobody knows anything about."

Boone ground some gravel under the toe of his right boot. "That's easy enough for you to say, old buddy, since you don't have to do a damn thing except share your infinite wisdom with regard to parenting."

Hutch slapped Boone's shoulder. "What if I told you, *old buddy,* that if you can take a day or two off from sheriffing, I'll come over and help you dig out?"

Boone narrowed his eyes. "You'd do that?"

Hutch pretended injury. "You doubt me? You, who was almost the best man at my almost wedding?"

Boone eased up a little himself, even chuckled, albeit hoarsely. "I'll have to deal with McQuillan, one way or the other, but I can take tomorrow off and part of the next day, too."

"Fine," Hutch said. "Give me a call when you're ready to start and I'll be at your place with a couple of machetes and some dynamite."

Boone laughed, this time for real. "Machetes and dynamite?" he echoed, taking mock offense. "No flame gun?"

"Fresh out of flame guns," Hutch answered, walking away, getting into his truck and starting up the engine.

He honked the horn once and headed for home.

KENDRA, HAVING JUST dropped Madison off at preschool and Daisy at Tara's for a doggy playdate with Lucy, stopped by the Butter Biscuit Café to buy a chocolate croissant and a double-tall nonfat latte before heading to the office the next morning. She was in a buoyant mood, since Walker Parrish had shown definite interest in the mansion the day before when she'd taken him through it. He hadn't come right out and said the place was exactly what his mystery friend was looking for, but Kendra's well-honed sales instincts had struck up an immediate *ka-ching* chorus.

No offer had been made, she reminded herself dutifully, as she waited at the counter to place her take-out order. And a deal was only a deal, at least in the real estate business, when the escrow check cleared the bank.

Thus focused on her internal dialogue, Kendra didn't notice Deputy McQuillan right away. When she did, she saw that he sat nearby at the long counter with open spaces on both sides of him, crowded as the Butter Biscuit always was during the breakfast rush, his nose not only bandaged, but splinted and both his eyes blackened.

"I'm pressing charges," he said to everyone in general, his tone as stiff as a wire brush. He had the air of a man just winding up a long and volatile oration.

The café patrons politely ignored him.

"Don't mind Treat," the aging waitress whispered to Kendra when she reached the counter, order pad in hand. "He's just running off at the mouth because he made a move on Brylee Parrish last night, over at the Boot Scoot Tavern, and Walker let him have it, right in the teeth."

Kendra winced at the violent image. "Ouch," she said, keeping her voice down.

"Broke his nose for him," the waitress added unnecessarily and with a note of satisfaction.

McQuillan must have overheard because his gaze swung in their direction, and Kendra felt scalded by it, as though he'd splashed her with acid.

"Go ahead, Millie," he growled at the still recalcitrant waitress. "Tell the whole world *Walker's* side of the story."

"It's everybody's side of the story," Millie said, undaunted. "You made a damn fool of yourself at the Boot Scoot and that's a fact. Ask me, you're just lucky Walker got to you before Hutch Carmody did."

Hutch's name, at least in connection with an apparent bar brawl over one Brylee Parrish, caught in Kendra's throat like rusty barbed wire snagging in flesh.

McQuillan's face flamed, and his full attention shifted, for whatever reason, to Kendra. "You'd do well to think twice before you take up with Carmody again," he informed her. "He's no good."

Kendra couldn't speak, she was so galled by McQuillan's presumption. Who the *hell* did the man think he was, talking to her like that?

"Shut up, Treat," Millie said dismissively. "All these good people are trying to enjoy their morning coffee or catch a quick breakfast. Why don't you let them?"

A terrible tension stretched taut across the whole café, like massive rubber bands. The snap-back, if it happened, would be terrible.

Chair legs scraped against the floor as men in various parts of the room pushed back from tables, ready to intercede if the situation went any further south.

"All I wanted to do," McQuillan went on, as an ominous, anticipatory silence settled over the place, "was help Brylee forget about her broken heart. Dance with her a little, maybe buy her a drink." He pointed to his battered face with one index finger. "And *this* is what I got for my trouble."

Just then, Essie, the long-time owner of the Butter Biscuit and a no-nonsense type to the crepe soles of her sensible shoes, trundled out of the kitchen, wiping her hands on her apron and advancing until she stood opposite Treat McQuillan with only the counter between them. Her eyes, with their Cleopatra-style liner and shadow, were hot with temper.

"I've had just about enough out of you, Treat," she said, her voice ringing off every window and wall. "You behave yourself, or I'll call Boone and have you hauled out of here!"

McQuillan flushed a dangerous crimson. "You'll have to call Slade instead," he retorted bitterly, apropos of who-knew-what, "because he's filling in for Boone.

Guess he didn't quite get being sheriff out of his system, old Slade."

"I'll call the damn *President,* if I have to," Essie answered back, "and don't you sass me again, Treat McQuillan. I knew your mama."

I knew your mama.

Kendra almost smiled at the familiar phrase, in spite of the tinderbox climate in the Butter Biscuit Café that sunny and otherwise beautiful late June morning. In Parable, the bonds of friendship and enmity both ran deep, intertwining like tree roots under an old-growth forest until they were hopelessly tangled.

"I knew your mama" was enough to shut most anybody up.

Sure enough, McQuillan subsided, spun around on his stool, stepped down and strode out of the cafe, looking neither to the right nor the left.

The chuckles and comments commenced as soon as the door closed behind him.

"I'm not sure that man is entirely sane," Essie observed, watching him go.

Nobody disagreed.

Kendra ordered her latte and croissant, waited, paid for her purchase and left the restaurant, still feeling strangely shaken by the episode.

Walking back to the office, she got out her cell phone and speed-dialed Joslyn's number, hoping she wouldn't wake her friend up from a post-partum nap or something equally vital.

Joslyn answered on the first ring, though, sounding too chipper to have delivered a baby so recently or to be contemplating a nap. "Hi, Kendra," she said. "What's up?"

"I'm not sure," Kendra answered honestly. Why *was* she calling Joslyn?

Joslyn simply waited.

"I hear Slade is standing in for Boone," Kendra finally said, reaching her storefront and fumbling with her keys. "As sheriff, I mean." She was used to juggling purses and briefcases, cell phones and coffee, but her fingers seemed slippery this morning.

Joslyn replied cheerfully. "Boone's sons are coming for a visit, so he needed some time off to get his place ready. Slade offered to take over the job for a few days."

"Oh," Kendra said, opening the office door and practically fleeing inside. What was she going to say if Joslyn wanted to know why she'd bother to ask about something so clearly not her concern in the first place?

"Why do you ask?" Joslyn said, right on cue.

Kendra sighed, dropping her purse onto her desk, then setting down the coffee and the bag with the croissant inside, too. Even with those few extra seconds to think, she didn't come up with a plausible excuse for the inquiry.

The truth was going to have to do. "Deputy McQuillan was making a big fuss when I stopped in at the Butter Biscuit a little while ago. Going on about how Walker Parrish assaulted him last night and he's going to see that he's charged."

Joslyn sighed. "There was a little scuffle at the Boot Scoot last night, as I understand it," she said with just a touch of hesitation.

"And Hutch was involved," Kendra said.

"Indirectly," Joslyn confirmed.

"Not that it's any business of mine, what Hutch Carmody does." Kendra was speaking to herself then, more than Joslyn.

Joslyn gave a delighted little chuckle. "Except that you do seem a little worried," she observed. "Why don't you just admit, if only to me, your main BFF, that you still have a thing for the guy?"

"Because I *don't* 'have a thing for the guy.'"

"Right," Joslyn replied.

"I'm a mother now," Kendra prattled on, unable, for some weird reason, to stop herself. "I have a dog and a Volvo, and I need to make a life."

This time, Joslyn actually laughed. "All of which means—*what,* exactly? That you don't need a little romance in this life you're making? A little sex, maybe?"

"Sex?" The word came out high-pitched, like a squeak. "Who said anything about sex?"

"You did," Joslyn replied with good-humored certainty. "Oh, not in so many words. But you're feeling a little jealous, aren't you? Because you have some scenario in your head of Hutch defending Brylee's honor at the Boot Scoot Tavern?"

"I wouldn't call it…jealousy," Kendra finally replied, her tone tentative.

"Okay," Joslyn agreed sunnily. "What *would* you call it?"

"You're no help at all," Kendra accused, further deflated, but smiling now. Talking to Joslyn always made her feel better, even when nothing was really resolved.

"Let's do lunch in a couple of days," Joslyn said, "after Mom goes back to Santa Fe and things return to normal around here. Maybe Tara can join us."

Still feeling like an idiot, Kendra replied that she'd enjoy a girlfriend lunch, said goodbye and hung up.

She spent the morning noodling around on her computer, carefully avoiding the "Down With Hutch Carmody" webpage, along with the temptation to add a thing or two, and answered a grand total of two inquiries by phone.

By ten forty-five, she felt so restless that she set the business phone to forward any calls to her cell, locked up the office and drove out to Tara's chicken ranch, intending to pick up Daisy and go home. Madison still had a couple of hours to go at preschool, which she was starting to enjoy, and Kendra didn't want to disrupt the flow by taking her out early.

Tara was outside when Kendra pulled into her rutted dirt driveway, wearing red coveralls and wielding a shovel. Daisy and Lucy frolicked happily nearby, playing catch-tumble-roll with each other.

"Don't tell me," Tara chimed mischievously, approaching Kendra's car on the driver's side. "You're here to help me clean out the chicken coop! What a true friend you are, Kendra Shepherd."

Kendra laughed. "You wish," she said. It was a relief to stop thinking about Hutch Carmody and sex for a while. They were two separate subjects, of course, but she hadn't been able to untangle one from the other since her phone conversation with Joslyn.

"Then what *are* you doing here?" Tara asked, looking like half of "American Gothic," except young and pretty instead of severe.

"Can't I visit a friend?" Kendra bantered back, pushing open the door and stepping somewhat gingerly into the muck of the barnyard. She wished she'd swapped out her Manolos for a pair of gum boots before leaving town.

Not that she actually *owned* gum boots.

Tara laughed at Kendra's mincing steps, pointed out a relatively clean pathway nearby and paused to lean her shovel against the wall of the chicken coop before following Kendra toward the old farmhouse she'd been refurbishing over the past year.

The woman was the very personification of incongruity, to Kendra's mind, with her model's face and figure and those ridiculous coveralls.

They settled in chairs on Tara's porch, since the weather was so nice and the dogs seemed to be having such a fine time dashing around in the grass, two flashes of happy gold, busy being puppies.

Once seated, Tara nodded in the direction of Boone Taylor's place, which neighbored hers. "He's finally cleaning up over there," she said in a tone that struck Kendra as oddly pensive. "I wonder why."

CHAPTER NINE

WHEN HUTCH ARRIVED at Boone's place that morning, he brought along plenty of tools, a truck with a hydraulic winch for heavy lifting and half a dozen ranch hands to help with the work. Opal followed in her tank of a station wagon, bucket-loads of potato salad and fried chicken and homemade biscuits stashed in the backseat.

Boone, standing bare-chested in his overgrown yard, plucked his T-shirt from the handle of a wheelbarrow where he'd left it earlier, now that he was in the presence of a lady.

Hutch grinned at the sight, and backed the truck up to a pile of old tires and got out.

Boone walked over to greet him, taking in the other trucks, the ranch hands and Opal's behemoth vehicle with a nod of his head. "You always were something of a show off, Carmody," he said.

"Go big or go home," Hutch answered lightly. "That's my motto."

"Along with 'make trouble wherever possible' and 'ride bulls at rodeos till you get your teeth knocked out'?" Boone gibed.

"Is there a law, Sheriff Andy Taylor, that says I can only have one motto?" Hutch retorted. The Maybury reference had been a running joke between them since the election results came in last November.

"Reckon not," Boone conceded, looking around at the unholy mess that was his property and turning serious. "I appreciate your help, old buddy," he said.

"Don't mention it," Hutch replied easily. "It's what friends do, that's all."

Boone nodded, looked away for a moment, cleared his throat. "What if Griff and Fletch get here and want to turn right around and head back to Missoula?" he asked, keeping his voice down so the ranch hands and Opal wouldn't overhear.

"One step at a time, Boone," Hutch reminded him. "Seems like the first thing on our agenda ought to be making sure the little guys don't get lost in all this tall grass."

Boone's chuckle was gruff. "I laid in plenty of beer," he said.

"Well," Hutch replied, heading around to the back of his pickup to haul out shovels and electric Weedwackers, "don't bring it out while Opal's around or we'll get a rousing sermon on the evils of alcohol, instead of all that good grub she was up half the night making."

Boone's chuckle was replaced by a gruff burst of laughter. "If she's brought any of her famous potato salad, she can preach all the sermons she wants," he answered, and went to greet the woman as she climbed out of her car and stood with her feet planted like she was putting down roots right there on the spot.

Out of the corner of his eye, Hutch watched as Boone leaned down to place a smacking kiss on Opal's forehead.

Pleased, she flushed a color she would have described as "plum" and pretended to look stern. "It's about time you got your act together, Boone Taylor," she scolded. Right away, her gaze found the toilet with the flowers growing out of the bowl and her eyes widened in horrified disapproval. "That commode," she announced, "has *got* to go."

She summoned two of the ranch hands and ordered them to remove the offending lawn ornament immediately. Two others were dispatched to carry the food and cleaning supplies she'd brought into Boone's disreputable trailer.

"If it isn't just like a man to put a *toilet* in his front yard," she muttered, shaking her head as she followed her willing lackeys toward the sagging front porch. "What's wrong with one of those cute little gnomes, for pity's sake, or a big flower that turns when the wind blows?"

"Does she always talk to herself like that?" Boone asked, helping himself to a Weedwacker from the back of Hutch's pickup.

"In my limited experience," Hutch responded, reaching for a plastic gas can to fill the tank on the lawnmower, "yes."

The next few hours were spent whacking weeds, and the result was to reveal a lot more rusty junk, numerous broken bottles and the carcass of a gopher that must have died of old age around the time Montana achieved statehood.

Opal occasionally appeared on the stooped porch, shaking out her apron, resting her hands on her hips and demanding to know how any reasonable person could live in a place like that.

"She thinks you're reasonable," Hutch commented to Boone, who was working beside him, hefting debris into the backs of the several trucks to be hauled away.

"Imagine that." Boone frowned, shaking his head in puzzlement. He'd worked up a sweat, like the rest of them, and his T-shirt stuck to his chest and back in big wet splotches.

"And don't think I didn't notice all that beer in the fridge!" Opal called out, to all and sundry, before turning and grumbling her way back inside that sorry old trailer to fight on in her private war against dust, dirt and disarray of all kinds.

"Beer," one of the ranch hands groaned, his voice full of comical longing. "I could sure use one—or ten— right about now."

Later on, when the sun was high and all their bellies were rumbling, Opal appeared on the porch again and announced that the kitchen was finally fit to serve food in, and the thought of her cooking rallied the troops to trail inside, take turns washing up at the sink and fill plates, buffet style, at the table.

The ranch hands each sneaked a can of beer from the fridge—Opal turned a blind eye to those particular proceedings—and wandered outside to eat in the shade of the trees.

Opal sat at the table in the middle of Boone's freshly scrubbed kitchen, and Boone and Hutch joined her.

"You're a miracle worker," Boone told her, looking around. The place was still scuffed and worn, just this side of being condemned by some government agency, but all the surfaces appeared to be clean.

"And you've been without a woman for way too long," Opal retorted, with her trademark combination of gruffness and relentless affection.

Boone loaded up on potato salad—he probably hadn't had the homemade version since before Corrie got sick—and helped himself to a couple of crunchy-coated chicken breasts. "I'm surprised at you, Opal," he teased. "To hear you tell it, women are made to clean up after men. If *that* gets out, militant females will burn you in effigy."

She expelled a huffy breath and waved off the remark for the foolishness it was. After a moment or two, her expression turned solemn and she studied Boone as though she'd never seen him before, peering at him through the lenses of her out-of-style eyeglasses.

"This isn't what Corrie would want, Boone," she said quietly. "Not for you and certainly not for those two little boys of yours."

Boone put down his fork, still heaping with potato salad, and stared down into his plate in silence. He looked so stricken that Hutch felt a crazy need to come to his friend's rescue somehow, but he quelled it. Intellectually, he knew Opal was right; maybe she could get through to Boone where he and Slade and a lot of other people had failed.

"We weren't planning to live in this trailer for more than a year," Boone said without looking up. "It was just a place to hang our hats while we built the new house."

"I know," Opal said gently. "But don't you think it's time you moved on—built that house, brought your boys home where they belong and maybe even found yourself a wife?"

At last, Boone looked up. The misery in his eyes made the backs of Hutch's sting a little.

"I can't marry a woman I don't love," he said hoarsely, "and I'm never going to love anybody but Corrie."

A silence fell.

Boone took up his fork again, making a resolute effort to go on eating, but his appetite was clearly on the wane.

"It was a hard thing, what happened to you," Opal allowed after some moments, her voice quiet and gentle to the point of tenderness, "but Corrie's gone for good, Boone, and you're still alive, and so are your sons. They need their daddy."

"My sister—"

"I know Molly loves them," Opal said, when Boone fell silent after just those two words. "But they're *yours,* those precious boys, flesh of your flesh, bone of your bone, blood of your blood. *They belong with you.*"

Boone pushed his chair back, looking as though he might bolt to his feet, but in the end stayed put. "I truly appreciate your hard work, Opal," he said, without looking at her *or* at Hutch, "and I mean no disrespect, but you don't know what you're talking about. You don't know how good Griff and Fletch have it with their aunt and uncle and all those cousins."

"I'm sorry, Boone," Opal said. "You didn't ask for my opinion and I should have kept it to myself."

Boone left the table then, left the kitchen, without a backward glance or a word of parting. The screen door, half off its hinges, crashed shut behind him.

"It's progress, Opal," Hutch told the woman quietly, painfully aware of the tears gathering in her wise old eyes. "That Boone will let the boys come back to Parable even for a holiday weekend—it's a big thing. Last Christmas, he went to Missoula, rather than bring them here. Now he's cleaning up the place and he's letting us help, and that's something he's resisted for a long, long time, believe me."

Opal sniffled, swatted at Hutch, and stood up to clear away her plate and Boone's. "When did you get so smart?" she countered. "I'd have sworn you didn't have a lick of sense yourself, entering rodeos, stopping weddings, living all by yourself like some fusty old codger twice your age."

"Why sugarcoat anything, Opal?" Hutch joked, and commenced eating again. "Tell me how you really feel."

The food was good, after all, and there wasn't a damn thing wrong with *his* appetite, whatever might be going on with Boone's.

"The man's depressed," Opal fretted, scraping the plates clean and setting them in the newly unearthed sink. "He puts on a fine show, as far as being sheriff, but he's got to be feeling pretty darn low to let things come to this."

"Try not to worry," Hutch said. "Corrie's death threw Boone for a loop and that's for sure, but he's coming around, Opal. He's finally coming around."

"I hope you're right," Opal fussed, sounding unconvinced.

"You'll see," Hutch answered, wondering where he was getting all this confidence in his best friend's future all of a sudden. He and Slade and plenty of other people had been worried about Boone for years.

Running for sheriff was the first sign of life he'd shown since losing Corrie, and there had been precious little reason to be encouraged since then.

Boone knew his job—even as Slade's deputy, he'd been a standout, steady, dependable, honest to the bone. His clothes were pressed, his boots polished and he got his hair trimmed over at the Curly Burly salon once a month like clockwork.

But then he came home to a hellhole of a trailer and did God knows what with his free time.

"He'd be a good match for Tara Kendall, you know," Opal speculated aloud, her tone wistful. "Both of them lonely, with their places bordering each other the way they do—"

"They hate each other," Hutch said.

"Same way you and Kendra do, I reckon," Opal shot back, smiling.

Hutch felt a slow flush climb his neck to pulse hard under his ears, which were probably red by then. "I don't hate Kendra," he informed his friend gravely. He couldn't say whether or not Kendra hated *him,* but he sure hoped not, because that was just too desolate a thing to consider.

"And Boone doesn't hate Tara, either," Opal went on, self-assured to the max. "She makes him feel some things he'd rather not feel, and that scares the heck out of him, and the reverse is true, too. Tara's as scared of Boone Taylor as he is of her." She paused, probably for dramatic effect, then delivered the final salvo. "Just like you and Kendra."

Hutch was suddenly too exasperated to eat, even though he was still a little hungry after working like a field hand all morning. Ranching involved some effort, but these days he spent more and more of his time supervising the men who worked for him, driving around in his pickup, riding horseback for the fun of it instead of rounding up strays or driving cattle from one feeding ground to another, or checking fence lines.

If he didn't watch out, his own prediction would prove true and he'd be too fat to compete in the rodeo by the end of the week.

He excused himself, rose stiffly from the table and carried his dishes and silverware toward the sink. He scraped his plate into the trash, set it in the hot, soapy water Opal had ready, and left the kitchen.

"GO OVER THERE?" Kendra repeated, peering through the pair of binoculars Tara had brought out onto the porch so they could spy on the doings over at Boone's place. Heat surged through her as she watched Hutch haul his shirt off over his head, revealing that lean, rock-hard chest—the one she'd loved to nestle against once upon a time. "Are you crazy?"

"It would be the neighborly thing to do," Tara replied, appropriating the binoculars and raising them to her face. Lucy and Daisy, having run off all that energy chasing each other around Tara's yard and trying to catch grasshoppers, were asleep in the shade of a gnarl-trunked old apple tree nearby.

"Since when are you and Boone on 'neighborly' terms?" Kendra countered. Damned if she didn't want to get a look at Hutch Carmody, up close and shirtless, but damned if she'd indulge the whim, either.

"We're not," Tara admitted. "But after all the verbal potshots I've taken at the man for maintaining an eyesore, the least I can do is encourage him to stick with the cleanup campaign." She handed the binoculars back to Kendra, who immediately used them. "Besides, Opal is over there, working her fingers to nubs. Maybe she could use some help from us."

"Right," Kendra said, thinking of her business suit and high-heeled shoes. "I'm certainly dressed for it." She watched, heartbeat quickening, as Hutch used the T-shirt to wipe his forehead and the back of his neck.

Muscles flexed in his arms and shoulders, making her mouth water. "You, on the other hand, look like a fugitive from a rerun of *Green Acres,* so you might as well go right on over there with your bad self."

"Not without backup," Tara said.

"Opal is backup enough for anybody," Kendra replied. It was almost as though Hutch knew she was watching him from afar; he seemed to be overdoing the whole manly thing on purpose just to rile her up.

Take the way he walked, for instance, with the slow, rolling gait of an old-time gunslinger, like his hips were greased, like he owned whatever ground he set his foot down on. And the way he threw back his head and laughed at something Opal called to him from the porch of Boone's trailer.

"Scared?" Tara challenged.

"No," Kendra lied, lowering the binoculars with some reluctance. She needed a few moments to process the sight of Hutch Carmody walking around half-naked. "I'm supposed to pick Madison up at preschool. And there's supper to think about, and—"

"You're supposed to pick Madison up in *two hours,*" Tara pointed out.

"Why do you want to do this?" Kendra asked, almost pitifully. She felt cornered by Tara's calm logic. "You can't *stand* Boone Taylor."

"Like I said," Tara replied with a self-righteous air, "good behavior should be encouraged. Besides, I'm dying to know why he's suddenly so interested in all this DIY stuff."

Kendra sighed, recalling her phone conversation with Joslyn earlier that day. "Well, *I* can tell you that," she said importantly. "Boone's boys are coming to stay

with him for the weekend. He's getting the place ready
for them."

"Boone has *children?*" Tara looked honestly surprised.

"Two," Kendra replied, wondering how Tara could
have lived around Parable for so long without knowing
a detail like that. "They've been living with his sister
and her family in Missoula since his wife died."

"I knew he was a widower," Tara mused sadly. "But
kids? The man just packed his own children off to his
sister's place after they lost their mother?"

"Well, I don't think it was as cut and dried as
that...." Kendra began, but her voice fell away. She
liked Boone, and felt a need to take his side, if sides
were being taken, though like just about everyone else
he knew, she could have shaken him for turning his
back on a pair of small, motherless boys the way he had.

"He's even more selfish than I thought," Tara said
decisively. She got out of her chair, still holding the
binoculars, and went into the house, returning without
them a few moments later. Evidently their spy careers
were over. "Who *does* a thing like that?" she ranted
on under her breath as she plunked back into her chair.

Compassion for Boone welled up in Kendra's chest.
"You weren't here when his wife died," she said quietly. "It was *terrible,* Tara. Corrie was in so much pain
toward the end and Boone couldn't do a thing to help
her. That would be hard for anybody, but especially for
a man who's been strong all his life."

"You can bet it was hard for those little boys, too,"
Tara pointed out, but her tone had softened somewhat
by then. "How old are they?"

Kendra made some calculations, "Probably five and

six," she said. "Something like that. Cute as can be—both of them look just like their dad."

A deep sadness moved in Tara's lovely eyes.

Kendra considered the possibility that her own mother might have abandoned her not because she didn't love her, but because she was overwhelmed by life in general. Maybe she'd suffered from depression, like Boone, and become trapped in it.

Maybe, maybe, maybe.

"Don't be too hard on Boone," she said, deciding it was time she and Daisy headed back to town. "He and Corrie married young, and they loved each other so desperately."

Tara nodded slowly. She was looking in the direction of Boone's trailer, although at that distance, with no binoculars to bring them closer, the people appeared tiny and it was hard to tell one from the other.

"Hey," Kendra said to her distracted friend, preparing to descend the porch steps, call for Daisy and head for her car. "Why don't you and Lucy come into town later and have supper with us?"

Tara smiled, rose from her chair, came to stand at the porch railing, resting her hands on top of it. "Thanks," she said, with a little shake of her head. "Maybe some other time."

Kendra nodded, and moments later she and Daisy were in the Volvo, heading down the driveway toward the main road.

Her thoughts and emotions were jumbled—visions of Hutch, bare-chested in the afternoon sunlight, predominated, but there were images of Boone at Corrie's funeral, too. It had rained that gloomy late-winter day, and a bitterly cold wind had driven all the mourners from the graveside the moment the last "Amen" had been said—except for Boone. He'd simply stood there, all alone, with his head down, his hands folded and his suit drenched, gazing downward at his wife's coffin.

Finally Hutch and Slade and a few others had gone out there to collect him, and he'd swung at them, shouting that he wasn't going to leave Corrie alone in the rain. They'd finally prevailed, but it was a struggle, Boone saw to that.

Since then, he'd never been the same.

He worked hard—it was common knowledge that he sent a lot of his paycheck to his sister for the boys' support—and then he went back to that sad piece of land he'd once had such great plans for, and that was all.

It grieved the whole town, because Parable was, after all, a family, and Boone, like Hutch and Slade, was a favorite son.

When Boone ran for sheriff, everyone's hopes rose—maybe things were finally turning around for him—but until today, when the cleanup effort had apparently begun, there had been no further indication that anything much had changed.

At home, Kendra changed into khaki walking shorts, a green tank top and sandals. Then she brushed her shoulder-length hair, caught it up in a ponytail and checked the contents of her refrigerator, considering various supper possibilities.

She'd stopped thinking about Boone's situation, which was a relief, but Hutch refused to budge from her mind no matter how she tried to distract herself.

And she definitely tried.

She tossed an old tennis ball for Daisy in the back-yard for at least fifteen minutes, then collected the day's mail from the box attached to her front gate. Nothing but sales fliers and missives addressed to "occupant"— everything had to be forwarded from her old address on Rodeo Road.

Not that she received a lot of mail in this day of instant electronic communication.

She chucked everything into the recycle bin and booted up her computer, a streamlined desktop set up in her home office. Nothing there, either.

Finally it was time—or close enough to it—to drive over to the preschool and collect Madison. Daisy rode shotgun in the Volvo's front seat, panting and taking in everything they passed with those gentle brown eyes, as if there might be a quiz later on what she'd seen and she wanted to be ready for any question.

The preschool occupied a corner of the community center, a long, rambling building that also housed the Chamber of Commerce, along with several conference rooms and a performance area with a stage. The local amateur theater group used the latter, as did the art and garden clubs, and dances, wedding receptions and other events were held there, too. Outside, there was a pool, a tennis court and a baseball field.

The town was justifiably proud of the whole setup, and maintaining the place was a labor of love, done mostly by volunteers.

Kendra parked near the baseball field, her usual place, and walked Daisy around on a leash, poop bag at the ready, while they waited for Madison's "class" to be dismissed for the day.

The bell rang and children catapulted through the open doors of the preschool, releasing pent-up energy as they laughed and jostled each other, celebrating their freedom.

Kendra, standing beside the car with Daisy, smiled as she watched Madison's head turn in her direction, watched her smile broaden as she raced over, waving a paper over her head.

"Look what I drew!" she crowed, shoving the sheet of paper at Kendra and then dropping to her knees in the grass to cover Daisy's muzzle with kisses and ruffle her silken ears.

Kendra looked down at her daughter's artwork and felt a wrench in the center of her heart. Madison had drawn a house with green crayon, recognizable as the one they lived in, with four distinct figures standing in the front yard—a little girl with bright red hair, a yellow dog, a stick-figure rendition of Kendra herself, notable for an enormous necklace of what seemed to be blue beads, and a tall man wearing jeans, a purple shirt, brown boots and an outsize cowboy hat.

Hutch.

"It's a *family!*" Madison said excitedly. "One with a cowboy daddy in it."

Kendra swallowed. "I can see that," she said quietly, before handing the paper back to Madison. "That's a very nice picture," she added, afraid to say more, lest the sudden tears pressing behind her eyes break free.

"Can we tape it to the 'frigerator?" Madison asked, her huge gray eyes solemn now, as though she expected a refusal and was already bracing to argue the point.

"Sure," Kendra said with a smile after clearing her throat.

She spent the next five minutes getting Madison, the dog and herself squared away in the Volvo.

"My friend Brooke has a daddy," Madison announced, once they were in motion. "So do lots of the other kids."

Give me strength, Kendra thought prayerfully. "Yes," she said.

"They put daddies in their pictures, so I did, too," Madison explained. "I made mine a cowboy."

"Does this cowboy have a name?" Kendra ventured. She couldn't just shut the child down, after all, and there was no use trying to change the subject before Madison was ready because she'd pursue it.

"Cowboy man," Madison said in a cheery, who-else tone of voice. "He has lots of horses, and I get to ride one of them sometime."

"That will be exciting," Kendra agreed, smiling.

"He said that," Madison chimed from her place in the backseat, Daisy beside her. "You heard him say that, didn't you, Mommy? That I could ride one of his horses if you said it was okay?"

"I heard," Kendra said. Did Hutch even remember making the offer? Or had he simply been making conversation, telling the child what he thought she wanted to hear at that particular moment?

To him, it was probably just small talk.

To Madison it was a promise, sacred and precious.

Kendra bit her lower lip, thinking. She could play the heavy, of course, say she'd rather Madison didn't get on a horse until she was a little older—conveniently, that was the truth—but one, she didn't want to raise a fearful child and, two, why should *she* be the one to disappoint Madison, while Hutch came off as the good guy, the one who'd tried to make the dream happen and would have succeeded, if not for her?

No.

This time, for once in his life, he was going to follow through.

Madison would have her horseback ride; Kendra would make sure of that, for her little girl's sake.

As soon as they got home, Madison fetched a roll of cellophane tape from Kendra's office, climbed onto a chair and proudly affixed her "family" drawing to the refrigerator door.

"There," she said, getting down and standing back to admire the installation.

Kendra admired it, too. "You'd better make some more pictures," she said thoughtfully. "That one looks a little lonely all by itself."

Madison readily agreed and ran off, Daisy on her heels, to find her crayons.

Kendra returned the chair to its place at the table, got out her cell phone and bravely keyed through stored numbers until she found Hutch's. When was the last time she'd dialed *that* one?

"Hello?" he said after the second ring.

"We need to talk," Kendra answered, employing a clandestine whisper. "When can we get together?"

CHAPTER TEN

WE NEED TO TALK. When can we get together?

To say Kendra's words had caught Hutch off guard would be the understatement of the century, but he hoped his tone sounded casual when he replied, "Okay, sure. I'm just leaving Boone's place—I've got some chores to do at home, and I could really use a shower."

TMI, he thought ruefully. *Too much information.* The woman hadn't asked for a personal hygiene report, after all.

Because he disapproved of other people talking on their cell phones while they drove, Hutch pulled over to one side of Boone's weed-shorn yard and let the men he'd brought over from Whisper Creek pass on by him in their trucks, and Opal, too.

Probably thinking there might be trouble, Opal stopped her big station wagon and started to roll down her window to ask if everything was all right, but Hutch grinned and waved her on.

Kendra sounded a little flustered when she answered, as though she might be wishing not only that she hadn't phrased the invite the way she had, but that she'd never called him at all. "Tonight, tomorrow—whenever," she stumbled.

Hutch felt better, aching muscles and ravenous hunger notwithstanding. Obviously, he wasn't the only one feeling a little out of their depth at the moment and he had to admit, the "we need to talk" part intrigued him in a big way.

"So this is nothing urgent," he concluded with a smile in his voice. He didn't need to see Kendra to know she was blushing to the roots of her pale gold hair; practically every emotion showed plainly on the landscape of her face and usually her inner climate did, too.

Kendra Shepherd might look like a Nordic ice queen, but Hutch knew she was capable of tropical heat.

Meanwhile, Kendra struggled bravely on, determined to make her point, whatever the heck *that* was. "No—I mean—well, I suppose we could discuss it now—"

"That's fine, too," Hutch said amiably, relishing the exchange.

"Yes, Madison," she said to her daughter, who could be heard asking questions in the background, "you *do* have to wash your hands before supper. You've been petting the dog, for Pete's sake."

Hutch chuckled at that. "I'll stop by later tonight," he offered. "What time does Madison go to bed?"

"Eight," Kendra said weakly.

"Then I'll be there around eight-thirty."

There was a pause, during which Hutch half expected Kendra to change her mind, tell him there was no need to come over in person because she could just say what she had to say right there on the phone.

Except that, for whatever reason, Kendra didn't seem to want Madison to be privy to what was said.

"Eight-thirty," Kendra confirmed, sighing the words.

Hutch agreed on the time, set his phone aside and

hurried home, where he fed the horses, took a shower, wolfed down cold chicken and potato salad, leftovers from the meal Opal had served over at Boone's earlier in the day, and checked the clock about every five minutes.

It wasn't even six yet.

He'd done everything that needed doing at warp-speed, it seemed. What the hell was he supposed to do with the two and a half hours still to go before he could show up on Kendra's doorstep?

"You've sure got a burr under your hide about something," Opal commented, putting away the remains of the feast. She'd left some of the overflow with Boone and given shares to the ranch hands who'd helped out with the work, too. Nobody turned down Opal's potato salad, ever. "Jumpy as a cat on a griddle, that's what you are."

Good-naturedly, Hutch elbowed her aside and took over the job she'd been doing, shoving chicken and potato salad every which way into the fridge. "Why don't you take the night off?" he asked companionably, when he thought enough time had elapsed so the question wouldn't sound contrived.

"Given that I don't work for you in the first place," Opal informed him, "that's an interesting suggestion. What are you up to, Hutch Carmody? You planning on heading back to the Boot Scoot Tavern again tonight, looking to drum up some more trouble?"

He laughed. "No," he said. "I'm *not* going to the Boot Scoot, and never mind that, it's none of your business if I do."

Opal's eyes were sly, even suspicious. "There's Bingo tonight," she said. "I never miss a game, especially when I'm on a lucky streak. Since I'm headed into town anyway, I could drop you someplace, pick you up later on."

"I do my own driving these days," he reminded her dryly. "Have been since the day I got my license."

"Fine," Opal said with a sniff, untying her apron and heading for her part of the house, presumably to get dolled up for a big night wielding Bingo daubers in the basement of the Elks' Club. "*Don't* tell me what's going on. It isn't as if I won't find out sooner or later. All I've got to do is keep my ear to the ground and sure enough, somebody will mention seeing you tonight, and they'll have the details, too."

Hutch laughed again, shook his head. He'd have sworn he'd never miss being nagged by a woman, but he surely had. Having Opal around was like having a mom again—a good feeling, even if it was a bit on the constricting side. "I'm going to see Kendra," he admitted. "And don't ask me why, because the whole thing was her idea and I don't have the first clue what she wants."

Opal's eyes were suddenly alight with mischievous supposition. "Well, now," she said. "Kendra wants to see you. As for what she wants, anybody but a big dumb cowboy like you would know that from the get-go." She paused to reflect for a few moments, and at the tail end of the thought process, she was looking a little less delighted than before. "You get on the wrong side of her again? Is that it?"

"I'm always on the wrong side of Kendra," Hutch said lightly. *But the view is good from any direction.*

Opal shuffled past him, yanked open the refrigerator, and neatly rearranged everything he'd just shoved

LINDA LAEL MILLER 189

in there. "Make sure you pick up some flowers on your way over," she instructed, dusting her hands together as she turned to face him again. "That way if you *are* in the doghouse, which wouldn't surprise me, Kendra might forgive you quicker."

"Forgive me?" Hutch echoed, pretending to be offended. "I haven't done anything she needs to forgive me *for.*"

"Maybe not recently," Opal conceded, with another sniff and a glance that begrudged him all grace. "But you did enough damage to last a lifetime back in the day. Get the flowers. There were some nice Gerbera daisies at the supermarket when I was there yesterday."

Hutch executed a deep bow of acquiescence.

Opal gave a scoffing laugh, waved a hand at him and went off to get ready for a wild night of Bingo.

KENDRA PEERED INTO the yellow glow of the porch light and caught her breath.

She'd been expecting Hutch, of course, but for some reason, every encounter with the man, planned as well as unplanned, made her feel as though she'd just taken hold of the wrong end of a cattle prod.

He wore newish jeans, a crisply pressed and possibly even starched cotton shirt in a pale shade of yellow, polished boots and a good hat instead of the usual one that looked as though it had just been trampled in a stampede or retrieved from the bed of a pickup truck.

And he was holding a colorful bouquet of flowers in his left hand.

He must have misunderstood her phone call, she thought, with a sort of delicious desperation. Her heart hammered against her breastbone, and her breathing was so shallow that she was afraid she might hyper-ventilate if she didn't get a grip.

After drawing a very deep breath, Kendra opened the front door; he'd seen her through the frosted oval window, so it was too late to pretend she wasn't home.

He took off the hat with a deftness that reminded her instantly of other subtle moves he'd made, under much more intimate circumstances, way back in those thrilling days—and nights—of yesteryear.

"The flowers were Opal's idea," he said first thing.

Kendra's mouth twitched with amusement. Hutch was doing a good job of hiding the fact, but he was as nervous as she was, maybe even more so.

"No wine?" she quipped. "You're slipping, cowboy."

He let his gaze range over her, just briefly, as she stepped back so he could come inside. "I figured that would be pushing my luck," he said, and she couldn't tell if he was kidding or serious.

Kendra led the way through the house to the kitchen and offered him a seat at the table. She'd long since cleared away all evidence of supper, supervised Madison's bath, read her a story and heard her prayers, and she'd checked on the child a couple of times over the past half hour, as well.

Both Madison and Daisy had been sound asleep each time she looked in.

Kendra accepted the flowers, found a vase and arranged them quickly. The colors, reds and maroons, oranges and deep pinks and purples, thrilled her senses, a riot of beauty.

When she turned around with the bouquet in hand, she nearly collided with Hutch.

Color climbed her cheeks and she stepped around him to set the flowers in the middle of the kitchen table.

"There's coffee, if you'd like some," she told him, feeling as shy as if he were a stranger and not a man who'd made love to her in all sorts of scandalous places and positions.

Stop it, she scolded herself.

Hutch's eyes twinkled as he watched her—he was seeing too much. Although he could be infuriatingly obtuse, he had a perceptive side, too. One that generally worked to his advantage. "Thanks," he said, "but I've had plenty of java already. One more cup and I'll be up all night putting a new roof on the barn or something."

Kendra smiled at the image, calming down a little on the inside. "I'll just look in on Madison once more," she said, and beat a hasty retreat for the hallway. What *was* it about Hutch that made all her nerves rise to the surface of her skin and sizzle there, like some kind of invisible fire?

He said nothing as she hurried away, but she would have sworn she felt the heat of his gaze wherever her shorts and tank top left her skin bare—on the backs of her arms and calves, on her nape.

Madison, she soon discovered, was still asleep in her "princess bed," or doing a darned good job of playing possum. Daisy, curled up by Madison's feet, raised her downy golden head, yawned and descended back into the realm of doggy dreams.

Since there was no excuse for lingering—and she'd been the one to suggest this rendezvous in the first place—Kendra forced herself to go back to the kitchen and face Hutch.

He was still standing in the center of the room, hat

in hand, and he pulled back a chair at the table for her as adeptly as if they'd been in some fancy restaurant instead of her own modest kitchen.

She sat, interlaced her fingers on the table top and silently wondered why she'd gotten herself into a situation like this—it wasn't like her. The pop-psychology types would probably say she had an unconscious agenda—sex, for instance.

Definitely not true.

Sex was out of the question with Madison in the house.

Thanks to this particular cowboy, though, the small kitchen seemed charged with the stuff, even electrified.

While Kendra's brain was trying to make sense of her own actions, Hutch hung his hat from a peg beside the back door and came to sit down across from her. He watched her in silence for a few moments, his expression solemn, and finally uttered a mildly plaintive, *"What?"*

Kendra, all fired up over his promise to take Madison for a horseback ride earlier, felt silly now. Why hadn't she simply said what she wanted to say while they were on the phone before?

Because she'd wanted to *see* Hutch, that was why. Ever since she'd watched him on Tara's porch, through those binoculars, he'd been on her mind. She *was* trying to prevent Madison from being disappointed over a much wanted horseback ride that didn't ever quite happen—any mother would feel the same—but in retrospect, the requested meeting looked...well... transparent.

God, this was embarrassing.

"This is really no big deal," she began awkwardly. "It's just—"

And then she couldn't force out another word. Her face burned and she wanted to look away from Hutch's face, but pride wouldn't let her take the easy way out.

"I'm listening," he reminded her quietly.

"Madison is really counting on a horseback ride," Kendra blurted, still awkward.

He raised one eyebrow in silent question. *"And?"* his expression prompted.

"I'm getting this all wrong," Kendra fretted. "It seemed like such a good idea before, to get everything out in the open and all that, but now—"

Hutch looked genuinely puzzled, maybe even flummoxed. If Kendra hadn't felt like such an idiot the look on his face would have made her laugh.

"But now?" he urged, his voice low and baffled. "You've decided against letting Madison go for a horseback ride?"

Suddenly, she giggled. It was some kind of nervous reaction, of course, but the release of tension was welcome, even though it did feel a lot like the spring of an old-fashioned watch breaking and spinning itself unwound. "No, that isn't it," she managed, after a moment of recovery. "I just got to thinking that you might forget what you told Madison, about going riding, I mean, and she's—"

"She's counting on it," Hutch confirmed, looking only slightly less confused than before. "Kendra, what the hell are you talking about?"

This time the giggle came out as a half-hysterical little laugh. She put a hand over her mouth and rocked, hoping the mysteries of incontinence would not be revealed to her. *Especially* in front of Hutch Carmody.

Before she could frame an answer, though, Hutch's eyes darkened with realization, reminding her of a sky working up a booming spate of thunder that might last for a while instead of blowing over quickly.

"You just automatically assumed I'd let her down, is that it?" he demanded, leaning in a little. His eyes flashed with indignation.

Kendra straightened her spine. Lifted her chin a notch or two. "Not exactly," she hedged. *"Not exactly?"* mocked a voice in the back of her mind. Come on. He'd just verbalized her precise thoughts on the matter. She'd been afraid he'd hurt and disappoint her little girl, and decided not to let it happen—that was the size of it.

"If you'll remember," Hutch went on, filling her in in case she hadn't noticed the figurative skywriting arching across the firmament overhead, "I told Madison she could ride one of my horses if it was all right with you. *You're* the one who didn't want to commit to a straight-out 'yes' and just barely settled for 'maybe.' And now it's *my* fault for letting her down?"

Kendra swallowed miserably. Looked away.

"Kendra," Hutch insisted. Just that one word, just her name, was all he said, but it carried weight.

"All right," she whispered, meeting his gaze again. "I'm sorry. I was wrong. Can we just get past that, please?"

His mouth smiled, but his eyes were solemn, even sad. "I meant what I said before," he finally replied. "If you're agreeable, we'll put Madison on the gentlest horse I own and she'll have her ride. Or she can ride with me, whatever you think best."

Kendra's throat tightened and she had to look away once more before reconnecting. Those eyes of his seemed to see into the deepest part of her, seeking and finding every secret she'd hidden away over the years, even from herself.

"When?" she asked, still mortified by her own behavior but trying to put a good face on things. "Madison will expect specifics."

He smiled again, this time with his whole face. "Whenever you say," he answered.

Kendra sighed. The ball was in her court and he wasn't going to let her forget that. "Tomorrow?" she threw out tentatively. "After she gets out of preschool?"

"That'll work," Hutch said, watching her. "About what time should I expect you and the munchkin to show up on Whisper Creek?"

"Three-thirty? Is that too early? I know you probably have a lot of work to do and I wouldn't want to impose or anything."

Lame. Of *course* she was imposing—but she was in too deep and there was no other way out.

"Three-thirty," Hutch agreed. Then, unexpectedly, he reached across the table and closed his fingers gently around her hand. "One question, Kendra. Why was it so hard for you to get all this said? We have a history, you and I, and not all of it was bad—not by a long shot."

"I'm—not sure," Kendra admitted softly.

"That's an honest if inadequate answer," he said, but his grin, if slight, was genuine. He got up, walked over to retrieve his hat, held it in one hand as he looked back at Kendra. "Tomorrow, three-thirty, Whisper Creek Ranch?"

"If it's inconvenient for you, another time would be fine, honestly—"

Hutch narrowed his eyes, not in anger, but bewilderment, as though by squinting he might make out some aspect of her nature he hadn't spotted before. "Women," he said with a note of consternation in his voice.

Kendra got to her feet, led the way back through the house toward the front door. *"Men,"* she retorted with a roll of her eyes.

She'd never planned for it to happen, and maybe Hutch hadn't either, but once they'd stepped beyond the cone of light thrown by the porch fixture, into the soft, summery shadows, they found themselves standing close to each other—too close.

Hutch curved a hand under Kendra's chin, lifted her face and kissed her, as naturally as they would have done in the old days.

And Kendra kissed him back, her body coming awake as both new and very familiar sensations took hold, expanding and contracting, soaring and then plummeting.

Kendra gave a silent gasp. It was still there, then, all of it, the passion, the need, the wildness, the things she'd tried so hard to forget over the years since their breakup.

She knew she ought to change directions, put on the brakes before they collided in the train wreck of the century—but she just couldn't.

She was lost in that kiss, lost in the way it felt to have Hutch's arms around her again, strong and sure, holding her close.

Her knees went weak, and she knotted her fists in the fabric of his shirt and held on, and still the kiss continued, seemingly taking on a life of its own, now playful, now deep and commanding.

"Mommy?"

The word, coming from just beyond the screened door, sliced down between them like a knife.

Both of them stepped back.

"You didn't tell me the cowboy man was here," Madison said innocently, rubbing away sleep with one hand even as she pressed her little nose against the worn screen, looking curious but nothing more. Her sidekick, Daisy, did the same.

"I didn't want to wake you up," Hutch said chivalrously. "Your mom and I were deciding on when you ought to take that horseback ride we talked about."

Madison's eyes instantly widened, and she stepped back far enough to open the screen door so she and Daisy could bolt through the gap.

"Really?" the child cried. *"When? Where?"*

Hutch lifted her easily, naturally into his arms, grinned. "Really," he said. "Tomorrow afternoon, at my ranch."

"I told you she'd ask for specifics," Kendra managed to say. Her face was still flaming, her heart was pounding, and she was frantic to know how much Madison had seen, and understood, before interrupting that foolish, *wonderful* kiss.

Madison literally squealed with delight. "Yes!" she cried, punching the air with one small, triumphant fist.

Hutch chuckled and set her back on her bare feet, tousled her tumbling copper curls lightly, though by then his gaze was fixed on Kendra again. She couldn't read his expression very well, since he was standing on the fringes of the glow from the porch light, but she saw the white flash of his teeth as he smiled.

"I guess that's settled, then," he said. He set his hat on his head, tugged at the brim in farewell and added, "Good night, ladies. I'll see you tomorrow."

And he turned to go.

"Wait!" Madison blurted, and Kendra was relieved to realize she hadn't been the one to speak, because that exact same word had swelled in the back of her throat and very nearly tumbled out over her tongue.

Wait.

Wait for what? A second chance? A miracle? Some passage opening between now and the time when everything had been good and right between them?

You're losing it, Kendra thought to herself.

Hutch paused at the top of the steps, turned to look back over one shoulder and waited quietly for the little girl to go on.

Kendra had forgotten that quietness in him. Hutch was still a rowdy cowboy inclined toward the rough-and-tumble and that probably hadn't changed, but he carried a vast silence inside him, too, as though he were somehow anchored to the core of the universe and drew confidence from that.

"Can Daisy come, too?" Madison asked earnestly.

"It's all right with me if it's all right with your mother," Hutch replied almost gruffly.

Kendra didn't dare say anything, so she nodded. She wanted Hutch to stay, though. She wanted more of his kisses, and still more, and she ached to return to the sweet, secret places where she knew they would take her.

But it wasn't going to happen, she told herself. Not tonight, anyway.

Hutch went his way—down the walk, through the gate, around to the driver's door of his truck; and she went to hers—back into the house, with Madison and Daisy.

HEADED HOME TO the ranch through a pale purple summer night, Hutch felt exuberant and scared shitless, both at the same time. The aftereffects of the kiss he and Kendra had shared on her porch still reverberated through his system like bullets ricocheting around inside a cement mixer and every instinct urged him to get far away from the woman, fast.

Except that there was nowhere to go.

He rolled down the window, switched on the radio and sang along with a country-western drinking song at the top of his lungs for the first mile or so, and by the time he was about to round the last bend, some of the adrenaline had ebbed and there was at least a remote possibility that he could think straight.

He wasn't speeding—the ticket Boone had given him was still fresh in his mind—but he nearly hit the critter sitting in the middle of the road anyhow.

He swerved, screeched to a stop, shut off the engine but not the headlights, and shoved open the door. Sprinting around the back of the truck, he was surprised—and relieved—to see that the animal, either a black dog or a very skinny bear, was still in one piece. The creature hadn't moved from the middle of the road, and as he approached, it whimpered low in its throat and cowered a little.

"You hurt?" Hutch asked, mindful that another rig

could come around the bend at any moment and send both him and what turned out to be a dog headlong into the Promised Land. Swiftly, he crouched, ran experienced rancher's hands over the creature's matted back and all four legs. He stood up again. "Come on, then," he said, satisfied that nothing was broken. "Let's see if you can walk."

Hutch started slowly back toward the truck.

The dog got up and limped after him.

Carefully, he hoisted the stray into the passenger's seat of his truck.

"You oughtn't to sit in the road like that," he said, once he was behind the wheel again and turning the key in the ignition. "It's a good way to get killed."

Here he was, talking to a dog.

A strange thing to do, maybe, but it felt good.

The dog turned to look at him with weary, limpid eyes and shivered a little.

Hutch debated turning around, taking the stray back to town, to the veterinary clinic, or at least to Martie Wren's place, so she could take a look at it, maybe check for one of those microchips that served as canine GPS. He'd been around horses and dogs and cattle all his life, though, and he knew instinctively that this one was sound, underneath all that dirt and deprivation.

Pulling in at the top of his driveway, Hutch was relieved to see Opal's station wagon parked up ahead. Evidently Bingo was over for the night, because she probably wouldn't have left the Elks' basement before the last number was called.

He parked, lifted the dog out of the truck and set him on his four thin, shaky legs. "You're going to be all right, fella," he told the animal gruffly. "You've got my word on that."

They went inside.

Opal was at the table, drinking tea and reading from her Bible.

"Land sakes," she said, at the sight of the dog, "what *is* that?"

Hutch gave her a wry look. "Just a wayfarer fallen on hard times," he said.

Opal closed her Bible, stood up, removing her glasses, polishing them with the hem of her apron, and putting them back on again, so she could examine the dog more closely. "Poor critter," she said. "Let's have us a good look at you."

Next she moved her teacup and Bible and draped a large plastic bag over the table.

"Heft him on up here," she said.

Hutch complied.

The dog stood uncertainly in the middle of the table, convinced, no doubt, that he was breaking some obscure human law and would be punished for it. He took to shivering again.

"Nobody's going to hurt you now," Opal told him, with gentle good humor, as she began to examine and prod. "Just look at that rib cage," she remarked, finally stepping back. "When's the last time you had anything to eat, dog?"

Hutch put the critter back on the floor, went to the cupboard for a bowl, filled it with water at the sink, and set it down in front of the newcomer.

The animal drank every drop and looked up at Hutch, asking for more as surely as if he'd spoken aloud.

Hutch refilled the bowl.

Opal, meanwhile, washed her hands and proceeded to ferret around in the fridge, finally emerging with two pieces of chicken and a carton of cottage cheese.

Deftly, like she cared for starving strays every day of her life, she peeled the meat off the bones and broke the chicken into smaller chunks. She mixed in some of the cottage cheese and set the works down on the floor on a plate.

The dog, lapping up water until then, fell on that food like he was afraid it would vanish before his eyes. He made short work of the meal, and Hutch would have given him another helping, but Opal nixed the idea.

"His poor stomach has all it can do to deal with what's already in there," she said.

After that, Hutch bathed the dog in the laundry room sink, helped himself to a couple of towels fresh from the dryer and rubbed that bony mutt down until his hide gleamed and his fur stuck out in every direction.

When he and the dog got back to the kitchen, Opal had cleared the table and resumed her Bible reading and her tea drinking. She tapped at the Good Book with one index finger and said, "Leviticus. That's the perfect name for our friend here."

"How so?" Hutch asked, washing up at the kitchen sink. The whole front of his good shirt was muddy and wet from giving the dog a bath, but he didn't care.

"Because that's what I was reading when you brought him in."

Hutch smiled to himself. He remembered when he was a kid and his mom would read through the whole Bible every year, a day at a time. She always said if a person could get through the book of Leviticus, they could get through anything.

"I take it Bingo was a bust?" he ventured, watching as Leviticus ambled over to the pile of old blankets Opal must have put out for him, settled himself, gave a sigh and closed his eyes.

"I won the blackout," Opal informed Hutch proudly with a smile and a shake of her head. "Five hundred dollars. So I'm pretty flush."

Hutch looked at the now sleeping dog and felt a space open wide in his heart to accommodate him. "Speaking of money," he said, "I owe you some for all you've done around here, and over at Boone's place today, too."

Opal executed another dismissive wave of one hand. "I don't want your money, Hutch," she said. "And didn't I just now tell you I've got five hundred beautiful dollars in my wallet at this very moment?"

He chuckled, shook his head. "You," he said, "are one hardheaded woman."

"All the more reason not to argue with me," Opal replied. She arched both eyebrows and Hutch saw the question coming before the words left her mouth. "How did things go over at Kendra's?"

Hutch folded his arms, leaned back against the counter alongside the sink. "Well enough that she and Madison will be coming out here tomorrow afternoon for a horseback ride," he said. It was more than he would have told most people, but he owed Opal, and besides, talking to her was easy.

Opal beamed. "They'll stay for supper," she announced. "I'll make my famous tamale pie. Kendra always loved it and so will that sweet little girl of hers."

Hutch spread his hands. "You'd better be the one to offer the invitation," he said, remembering the kiss. By now the regret would be setting in, Kendra would be wishing she'd slapped him instead of kissing him right back. "If it comes from me, she's more likely to say no than yes."

"Now why do you suppose that is?" Opal pretended to ponder, but her gaze found the dog again and she smiled. "You mean to keep Leviticus, don't you?" she asked.

"Unless somebody's looking for him," Hutch replied. "I'll check with Martie tomorrow."

"Nobody's looking for Leviticus," Opal said with sad certainty. "He'd have a collar and tags if he belonged to someone."

Hutch felt a peculiar mixture of sympathy and possessiveness where Leviticus was concerned. The dog was bound to be nothing but trouble—he'd chew things up and he probably wasn't housebroken—but Hutch wanted to keep him, wanted that more than anything except to find some common ground with Kendra, so they wouldn't be so jumpy around each other.

Tomorrow couldn't come soon enough to suit him.

CHAPTER ELEVEN

"I'LL NEED BOOTS," Madison announced the next morning at breakfast. "Can we buy some, please? Today?"

Practically from the moment she'd opened her eyes, Madison had been fixating on the upcoming horseback ride out at Whisper Creek Ranch. Even as she spooned her way diligently through a bowlful of her favorite cereal, her feet were swinging back and forth under the table as though already carrying her toward the magic hour of three-thirty in the afternoon.

"Let's wait and see," Kendra said, sipping coffee. She didn't normally skip breakfast, but that day she couldn't face even a bite of toast. She had orchestrated this whole horseback riding thing, set herself up for yet another skirmish with Hutch and now the reality was almost upon her—and Madison.

What had she done?

More importantly, why *had she put herself and her daughter in this position?*

"Everybody at preschool has boots," Madison persisted. Daisy, having finished her kibble, crossed the room to lay her muzzle on the child's lap and gaze up at her with the pure, selfless love of a saint at worship.

"Most of those children have been riding since they were babies," Kendra reasoned, making a face as she set her coffee cup down. Usually a mainstay, the stuff tasted like acid this morning. "Suppose you get on that horse today and find out you hate riding and you never want to do it again?"

"That won't happen," Madison said with absolute conviction. Where did all that certainty come from? Was it genetic—some vestige of all those English ancestors riding to the hunt, soaring over hedges and streams?

Kendra shook off the thought. She hadn't slept all that well the night before, imagining all the things that might go wrong today, and now she was paying the price. Her thoughts were as muddled as her emotions.

"What makes you so sure of yourself, young lady?" she challenged with a small smile.

Madison grinned back at her. "You're always saying it's good to try new things," she said with a note of triumph that underscored Kendra's impression that the child was only *posing* as a four-year-old—she was really an old soul.

Busted, Kendra thought. She *was* always telling Madison that she shouldn't be afraid—of preschool, for instance, or speaking up in class, or making friends on the playground—and now here she was, projecting her own misgivings onto her daughter. Speaking to the frightened little girl she herself had once been, instead of the bold one sitting across from her on a sunny, blue-skied morning full of promise.

"I'll make a deal with you," Kendra said, brightening. "If you still want boots after this first ride, we'll get you a pair." She wondered if the child had visions of racing across the open countryside on the back of some gigantic steed, when she'd most likely wind up on a pony or an arthritic mare.

"Okay," Madison capitulated, not particularly pleased but willing to negotiate. "But I'm still going to want those boots."

Kendra laughed. "Hurry up and finish your breakfast," she said. "Then go and brush your teeth while I let Daisy out for a quick run in the backyard. You need to be on time for preschool and I have to get to the office."

The spiffing-up process over at the mansion was winding down, according to reports from the painting and cleaning crews, and she already had two appointments to show the place, one at noon and one the following morning.

Things were moving along.

Why did it suddenly seem so difficult to keep up?

Madison set her spoon down, wriggled off her chair, and carried her mostly empty cereal bowl over to the sink. She stood on tiptoe to set it on the drainboard, humming under her breath as she headed back toward the bathroom.

Daisy started to follow her small mistress, but when Kendra opened the back door, the dog rushed through it, wagging her tail. Kendra followed.

The morning was glorious—the grass green, with that fresh-cut smell, and lawn sprinklers sang their rhythmic songs in the surrounding yards. Birds whistled in the branches of trees and a few perched on Kendra's clothesline, regarding Daisy's progress with placid nonchalance.

Madison returned to the kitchen just as Daisy and Kendra were coming in from outside. She opened her lips wide to show Kendra her clean teeth.

Kendra pretended to be dazzled, going so far as to

raise both hands against the sudden glare, as if blinded by it.

Madison giggled, this being one of their many small games. "You're silly, Mommy," she said.

Kendra tugged lightly at one of Madison's coppery curls and bent to kiss the top of her head. "Have I mentioned that I love you to the moon and back?" she countered, taking Daisy's leash from its hook and snapping it to the dog's collar.

"I love you *ten* times that much," Madison responded on cue.

"I love you a hundred times that much," Kendra pronounced, juggling her purse, car keys and a leash with an excited puppy at the other end.

"I love you *the last number in the world* times that much," Madison said.

"I love you ten thousand times that much," Kendra told her as they trooped outside and headed for the driveway, where the trusty Mom-mobile was parked.

"That isn't fair," Madison argued. "I said the last number in the world."

"Okay," Kendra answered, smiling. "You win."

HUTCH MOVED FROM one stall to the next, assessing every horse he owned.

They were ordinary beasts, most of them, but they all looked too big and too powerful for a four-year-old to ride.

Was it too late to buy a pony?

He chuckled at the idea and shook his head. Whisper Creek was a working ranch and the horses pulled their weight, just as the men did. He'd be laughed right out of the Cattleman's Association if he ran a Shetland on the same range as all these brush cutters and ropers. The sweet old mare he'd reserved for greenhorns had passed away peacefully one night last winter and much as he'd loved the animal, it hadn't occurred to him to replace her. It was a matter of attrition.

Opal stepped into the barn just as he turned from the last stall, dressed for going to town. She wore a jersey dress, as usual, but a hat, too, and shiny shoes, and she carried a huge purse with a jeweled catch.

"I've got a meeting at the church," she informed him. "After that, I thought I'd look in on Joslyn's bunch, see how they're doing."

Hutch smiled, walked slowly in her direction. He'd already sent the ranch hands out onto the range for the day, assigning them to the usual tasks, which left him with nothing much to do other than look himself up on the internet and see how he was faring in the court of public opinion.

Not that he couldn't have guessed. Team Brylee was probably still on the warpath, and so far a Team Hutch hadn't come together.

"You don't work for me," he reminded Opal affably, as she had recently reminded him. "No need to explain your comings and goings."

Opal stood stalwartly in his path, clutching her purse to her chest with both hands as though she expected some stranger to swoop in and grab it if she relaxed her vigilance for a fraction of a second. "I'm living under your roof," she said matter-of-factly, "so it's just common courtesy to tell you my plans."

Hutch stopped, cleared his throat, smiled again. "All right," he agreed. "You've told me. It was unnecessary, but I appreciate it just the same."

Opal didn't move, though she might have loosened her grip on her handbag just a little; he couldn't be sure. "You and Boone," she mused, sounding almost weary, even though it hadn't been an hour since breakfast. "I declare, the two of you will worry me right into an early grave."

Hutch's chuckle sounded hoarse. He shoved a hand through his hair. "That would be a shame, Opal," he said. "Boone will be fine and so will I."

"Just the same," Opal replied, "I sometimes wonder if I'm *ever* going to be able to cross you off my active prayer list."

Hutch felt his mouth quirk at one corner. "We're on your prayer list?" he responded. "Why, Opal, I'm both touched and flattered."

"Don't be," she told him gruffly. "It means you're a hard case, and so is Boone."

"I see," Hutch said, though he didn't really. He wanted to laugh, but some instinct warned him that Opal was dead serious about this prayer list business. "Well, then, maybe I'm not flattered after all," he went on presently. "But I'm still touched."

She smiled that slow, warm smile of hers, the one that seemed to take in everybody and everything for miles around, like a sunrise. "There may be hope for you yet," she said, her tone mischievously cryptic. "I'll be back in plenty of time to make supper for you and Kendra and that sweet little child of hers. Try not to say the wrong thing and drive them off before I get back."

Hutch merely nodded and Opal turned, her purse still pressed to her bosom, to leave the barn.

He'd fed the horses earlier; now he began the process of turning them out of their stalls and into the pasture—

all except Remington, that is. He heard Opal's station wagon start up with a gas-guzzling roar, listened as she drove away, tires spitting gravel.

Opal did everything with verve.

He smiled as he fetched his gear from the tack room, carried it back to where the gelding waited, patiently chewing on the last of his grain ration.

Hutch opened the stall gate, and Remington stepped out into the breezeway—he knew the drill, and suddenly he was eager to be saddled, to leave the confines of that barn for the wide-open spaces.

Five minutes later, Hutch was mounted up, and the two of them were moving over the range at a graceful lope, headed for Big Sky Mountain.

Reaching the base of the trail Hutch favored, the horse slowed for the climb, rocks scrabbling under his hooves as he started up the incline.

Hutch bent low over the animal's neck as they passed through a stand of oak and maple trees, the branches grabbing at both man and horse as they went.

The mountain was many things to Hutch Carmody— for as long as he could remember, he'd gone there when he had something to mourn or something to celebrate, or when he simply wanted to think.

From a certain vantage point, he could see the world that mattered most to him—the sprawling ranch lands, the cattle and horses, the streams and the river and, in the distance, the town of Parable.

After about fifteen minutes of fairly hard travel, he and Remington reached the small clearing that was, for him, the heart of Whisper Creek Ranch.

It was here that, as a boy of twelve, he'd cried for his lost mother.

It was here that he'd raged against his father, those times when he was too pissed off or too hurt or both to stay put in school or in his room or out in the hay-scented sanctuary of the barn.

And it was here that he and Kendra had made love for the first time—and the last.

He sighed, swinging down from the saddle and leaving Remington to graze on the tender grass.

The pile of rocks was still there, of course—waist-high and around six feet long, resembling a tomb, he thought wryly, or maybe an altar for Old Testament–style offerings to a God he didn't begin to understand and, frankly, didn't much like.

Opal definitely would not approve of such an attitude, he thought with a smile. She'd keep him on her hard-case prayer list for the duration.

No doubt, he belonged there.

After taking a moment to center himself, he walked over to the improvised monument, laid his hands on the cool, dusty stones on top and remembered. Every one of those rocks represented something he'd needed to say to John Carmody and never could, or something he *had* said and wished he hadn't.

High over his head, a breeze whispered through the needles of the Ponderosa pines and the leaves of those stray maples and oaks that had taken root in this place long before he was born. Remington nickered contentedly, his bridle fittings jingling softly.

A kind of peace settled over Hutch.

"You were hard to love, old man," he said very quietly.

John Carmody wasn't actually buried under those rocks—he'd been laid to rest in the Pioneer Cemetery—

but this was where Hutch came when he felt the need to make some connection with his father, whether in anger or in sorrow.

The anger had mostly passed, worn away by intermittent rock-stacking sessions following the old man's death, but the sorrow remained, more manageable now, but still as much a part of Hutch as the land and the fabled big sky.

And that, he decided, was all right, because life was all of a piece, when you got right down to it, a jumbled mixture of good and bad and everything in between.

He turned his back to the rock pile then, folded his arms and drew the vast view into himself like a breath to the soul.

In the distance he could see the spires of Parable's several small churches, the modest dome of the courthouse, with the flag rippling proudly at its peak. There was the river, and the streams breaking off from it, the spreading fingers of a great, shimmering hand.

His gaze wandered, finally snagged on the water tower.

Like the high meadow where he stood, that rickety old structure had meaning to him. He'd ridden bulls and broncos, ranging from mediocre to devil-mean, over the years, breaking a bone or two in the process. He'd floated some of the wildest rivers in the West, raced cars and skydived and bungee jumped, you name it, all without a flicker of fear.

And then there was the water tower.

Like most kids growing up in or around Parable, he'd climbed it once, made his way up the ancient ladder, rung by weathered rung, with his heart pounding in his ears and his throat so thick with terror that he could hardly breathe.

Reaching the flimsy walkway, some fifty feet above the ground, he'd suddenly frozen, gripping the rail while the whole structure seemed to sway like some carnival ride gone crazy. A cold sweat broke out all over him, clammy despite the heat of a summer afternoon and, just to complete his humiliation, Slade Barlow had been there.

Slade, his half brother, and at the time, sworn enemy, had dared him to make the climb in the first place. Ironically, Slade had been the one to come up that ladder and talk him down, too, since there was nobody else around just then.

Thank God.

Even now, after all his time, the memory settled into the pit of Hutch's stomach and soured there, like something he shouldn't have eaten.

He forced his attention away from the tower—most folks agreed that, being obsolete anyhow, the thing ought to be torn down before some darn-fool kid was seriously hurt or even killed, but nobody ever actually *did* anything about the idea. Maybe it was nostalgia for lost youth, maybe it was plain old inertia, but talking seemed to be as good as doing where that particular demolition project was concerned.

Hutch sighed, a little deflated, wondering what he'd expected to achieve by coming up here, approached Remington and gathered his reins before climbing back into the saddle.

He stood in the stirrups for a moment or two, stretching his legs, and then he headed for home, where no one was waiting for him.

AT NOON, KENDRA showed the mansion to the first potential client, a busy executive from San Francisco who was looking, he said, for investment opportunities. His wife, he told Kendra, had always wanted to start and run a bed-and-breakfast in a quaint little town exactly like Parable.

She'd smiled throughout, listening attentively, asking and answering questions, and finally telling the man straight out that there were already three bed-and-breakfasts in town, and they were barely staying afloat financially.

The man had nodded ruefully, thanked Kendra for her time and driven away in his rented SUV. Most likely he'd promised his wife he'd take a look, and now he'd done that and could dismiss the plan in good conscience. Instinctively she knew no offer would be forthcoming, but she wasn't discouraged.

Kendra had returned to the office afterward, where she'd left Daisy snoozing contentedly in a corner, and eaten lunch—a carton of yogurt and an apple—at her desk.

Taking a client through the mansion, although almost certainly a fruitless enterprise, had served as a welcome distraction from her mixed-up thoughts about Hutch and that afternoon's horseback ride, but now she was alone in her quiet office, except for Daisy, and her imagination threatened to run wild.

The phones were silent.

The computer monitor yawned before her like the maw of a dragon, ready to suck her in and devour her whole.

She was ridiculously grateful when the mailman

dropped in with a handful of fliers and bills, thrilled when the meter reader put in a brief appearance.

"I'm losing my mind," she confided to Daisy, when the two of them were alone in the silent office again. "You've been adopted by a crazy woman."

Daisy yawned broadly, closed her lovely brown eyes, and went back to sleep.

"Sorry if I'm boring you," she told the dog.

Daisy gave a soft snore.

By the time three o'clock rolled around, Kendra was practically climbing the walls. She attached Daisy's leash to her collar, shut off the lights, locked the front door and all but raced out the back way to her car.

When she arrived at the community center, Madison was waiting for her, along with her teacher, Miss Abbington.

Miss Abbington did not look like a happy camper.

"What's wrong?" Kendra asked as soon as she'd parked the car and gotten out.

"I think Madison should answer that," Miss Abbington said. She was a small, earnest woman with pointy features that made her look hypervigilant—a quality Kendra appreciated, especially in a person who spent hours with her daughter every day.

Madison flushed, but her chin was set at an obstinate angle. "I was incordiable," she told Kendra.

"Incorrigible," Miss Abbington corrected stiffly.

"What happened?" Kendra asked the little girl, at once alarmed and defensive. How could a four-year-old child be described as "incorrigible?" Wasn't that word usually reserved for hard-core criminals?

"I misrupted the whole class," Madison said, warming to the subject.

"*Dis*rupted," Miss Abbington said.

Kendra gave the woman a look, then refocused her attention on her daughter. "That isn't good, Madison," she said. "What, specifically, did you do?"

Madison squared her small shoulders and tugged her hand free from Miss Abbington's. "I borrowed Becky Marston's cowgirl boots," she admitted without a hint of shame. "When she took them off to put on her sneakers for gym class."

"Without permission," Miss Abbington embellished, looking down her long nose at Madison. "And then, when Becky asked for her boots back, you told her you weren't through wearing them yet."

"Madison." Kendra sighed. "We talked about the boot thing, remember? This morning at breakfast?"

"I just wanted to see what they felt like," Madison said, but her lower lip was starting to wobble and she didn't look quite as sure of her position as before. "I would have given them back tomorrow."

Kendra looked at Miss Abbington again. Miss Abbington's gaze connected with hers, then skittered away.

"I'll take it from here," Kendra told the other woman.

"Fine," Miss Abbington said crisply.

"It's wrong to take someone else's things, Madison," Kendra told her daughter. "You know that."

From the car, Daisy poked her muzzle through a partly open window and whimpered.

Madison's eyes filled with tears, real ones. She was a precocious child, but she didn't cry to get her way. "Are you mad at me, Mommy?"

"No," Kendra said quickly, trying not to smile at the image of her little girl clomping around the schoolroom in a pair of purloined boots. *This isn't funny,* she scolded herself silently, but it didn't help much.

"Do I still get to go to the cowboy man's house and ride a horse?"

Canceling the outing would have made sense, giving Madison reason to think about her behavior at preschool, but Kendra privately nixed the idea on two counts. One, she knew Madison's disappointment would be out of all proportion to the misdemeanor she'd committed and, two, she'd have to reschedule the ride and she didn't think her nerves could take the strain.

She was a wreck as it was.

"Yes," she said, leading Madison to the car and helping her into the safety seat in back. Daisy was on hand to lick the little girl's face in welcome. "You can still ride Mr. Carmody's horse. But tomorrow, as soon as you get to school, you will apologize to Miss Abbington *and* to Becky for acting the way you did." A pause. "Fair enough?"

Madison considered the proposition as though it *were* a proposition and not an order. "Okay," she agreed. "But I still think Becky is a big crybaby."

"Don't push your luck, kiddo," Kendra warned.

She got behind the wheel, fastened her seat belt, started the engine.

"None of this would have happened," Madison offered reasonably, "if I had my own cowgirl boots."

Kendra closed her eyes for a moment, swallowed a laugh. She wanted Madison to be spirited and proactive, yes. But a demanding brat? No way.

"One more word about those boots," she said, glancing at the rearview mirror to read her daughter's face, "and there will be no visit to Mr. Carmody's ranch, no horseback ride and definitely no day at the rodeo."

Madison's jaw clamped down tight. She obviously had plenty more to say, but she was too smart to say it.

She wanted that ride.

Half an hour later, after a quick stop at home, where Kendra and Madison both changed into jeans and T-shirts and gave Daisy a chance to lap up some water and squat in the backyard, the three of them set out for Whisper Creek Ranch.

On the way, Kendra told herself silently that she was making too big a deal out of this. Nothing earthshaking was going to happen; Hutch would lead a horse out of the barn, Madison would sit in the saddle for a few minutes and that would be it.

She and Madison could turn right around and come home, none the worse for the experience.

Big Sky Mountain loomed in the near distance as they drove on toward the ranch, towering and ancient. If there was one thing in or around Parable that made Kendra think of Hutch Carmody, it was that mountain.

How many times had they gone there, on horseback and sometimes on foot, to be alone in that hidden meadow he loved so much, to talk and laugh and, often, to make love in the warmth of the sun or the silvery glow of starlight?

A blush climbed her neck and pulsed in her cheeks.

Too many times, she thought glumly.

It had been wonderful.

Her grandmother had found out about the trysts eventually—probably by reading Kendra's diary—and said, "You're just like your mother. I can't trust you out of my sight any more than I could trust her. You turn up pregnant, girl, and I'll wash my hands of you."

Kendra had taken great care *not* to get pregnant, but not because of her grandmother's threat—the old woman had long since washed her hands of her daughter's child. No, it was because she hadn't wanted to trap Hutch, force him into marriage because she was having his baby. A few of the other girls in school had gone that route with their boyfriends, and the consequences were sobering, to say the least.

Though she'd loved Hutch, and sometimes feared that she still did, Kendra had wanted to go to college. Yes, she'd wanted children, but at the right time and in the right way. Knowing what it felt like to be a living, breathing burden, she'd been determined to wait, to start her family when she and Hutch were both ready.

Instead she'd gotten involved with Jeffrey Chamberlain. It had been an innocent friendship at first—she'd been fascinated by Jeffrey's accent, his dry British sense of humor, his style and manners.

Still, she hadn't married him out of love, not really. She'd *wanted* to love him, wanted the fairy-tale life he offered, wanted things to be *settled,* once and for all, so she could get on with her life.

But right up until the moment she'd said, "I do," she'd expected Hutch to step in, to reclaim her, to be willing to slay dragons to keep her.

He'd done none of those things, of course. And she'd been a dreamy-eyed fool to expect him to.

Now nearing the gate at the base of Hutch's long driveway, Kendra put the past firmly out of her mind.

That was then. This is now.

Hutch was in front of the barn, and he'd saddled

three horses—two regular-size ones and a little gray pony with black-and-white spots.

Daisy began to bark, noticing the shy black dog lurking nearby, and Madison, spotting the pony, gave a delighted squeal.

But Kendra was still counting the horses.

By her calculations, there was one too many.

She barely got the car stopped before Madison was freeing herself from the restraint of her safety seat, pushing open the rear door, scrambling out.

Daisy leaped out after her, and Hutch laughed as both the dog and the little girl bounded toward him and the horses. He introduced his own dog, Leviticus, who stayed a little apart, looking on cautiously.

"That's the *littlest* horse in the whole world!" Madison raved, having barely noticed the dog, stopping finally to stare at the pony in wonder.

"Maybe," Hutch agreed, grinning. His gaze rose slowly to Kendra's face and locked on with an impact she actually felt.

"I'm little, too," Madison chattered on eagerly.

Hutch looked serious, thoughtful. "Now, isn't that a coincidence?" he asked. "You and the pony being so suited to each other, I mean?"

Kendra tightened her fists at her sides, forcibly relaxed them. She knew next to nothing about the day-to-day operation of Whisper Creek Ranch, but she was ninety-nine percent sure there was no job here for such a tiny horse.

Everything about the animal was miniature, even by pony standards, including the Lilliputian saddle and bridle.

"Simmer down," Hutch said to Kendra in a near

whisper, though he was still grinning. "I borrowed the horse from a neighbor. She's as gentle as they come."

Kendra swallowed. "Oh," she said.

Hutch's attention shifted back to Madison. The little girl basked in the glow of his quiet approval. "Want to give this thing a try?" he asked her.

Madison nodded wildly. Daisy had lost interest by then, and gone off to sniff the surrounding area for heaven only knew what. Leviticus followed her, as if to make sure she behaved throughout the visit.

Once again, Hutch's eyes rested on Kendra's face. He was waiting for her permission.

"You're sure this animal is tame?" she asked him.

"Sure as can be," Hutch assured her.

"Well—" She stopped, bit her lower lip. "All right, then."

Hutch chuckled, put his hands to Madison's waist and swung her easily into the saddle. He put the reins in her small hands, told her how to hold them, explaining quietly that she shouldn't pull on them too hard, because that was hard on the pony's mouth.

Madison, for her part, looked not just overjoyed, but transported.

"Look, Mommy!" she cried. "I'm on a horse! I'm on a *real* horse!"

Kendra had to smile. "Yes," she agreed. "You certainly are."

Hutch led the pony around in slow but ever widening circles, there in the barnyard, letting Madison get the feel of riding. The child seemed spangled in light, she was so happy.

I'm on a horse! I'm on a real horse!

Inwardly, Kendra sighed.
Madison was hooked.
And that meant she was, too.

CHAPTER TWELVE

HUTCH WATCHED KENDRA watching her daughter ride, on her own now, and he was glad he'd "borrowed" Ruffles from a family up the road, even though he was sure to get a joshing from the ranch hands, among others. The plain truth of the matter was that he'd bought the pony outright—the Hendrix kids were grown and gone and the little mare had been "mighty lonely these last few years," according to Paula Hendrix.

He moved to stand alongside Kendra, close enough but not too close.

Her eyes brimmed with happy tears, and she fairly glowed with motherly pride. "She's loving this," she murmured so softly that Hutch wasn't sure if she was talking to him at all.

"Madison's a natural, all right," he agreed quietly. "A born rider."

"You went to a lot of trouble," Kendra went on, still not looking his way. "Borrowing a pony and everything, I mean." She was pleased, he knew, but there was a tension in her, too—she was ready to spring into action if anything went wrong, rush in to save her baby. And there was something else, too—a kind of wariness that probably didn't have much to do with either Madison or the horse.

Just then, Hutch felt a strange ache in a far corner

of his heart. In a perfect world, Madison would have been their child, his and Kendra's. Her last name would be Carmody, not Shepherd or Chamberlain or whatever it was, and riding a horse wouldn't be a rare adventure, it would be part of her daily life, like it was of any ranch kid's.

But then, this *wasn't* a perfect world, now was it? It was the real deal, and that meant things would go wrong, and people could get sidetracked, screw up their whole lives because of things they should or shouldn't have said or done.

"Ready to ride?" he asked, to get the conversation rolling again.

"I haven't been on horseback in years," Kendra confessed. "Not since—"

Her words fell away into an awkward silence, and she blushed.

She was obviously remembering what *he* was remembering—all those wild rides they'd taken, back in the day, in and out of the saddle.

"It's like riding a bike," he said mildly, throwing her a lifeline. "Once you learn how to sit on a horse, you never forget."

She turned her gaze back to Madison, who was riding in their direction now, beaming. The pup had fallen into step with Ruffles—Leviticus watched from the shade of the barn—and they sure made a picture, all of them, an image straight off the front of a Western greeting card.

When Kendra spoke, she jarred him a little. "How do we get past this, Hutch?" she asked very softly.

"This what?" Hutch asked just as quietly.

Her shoulders moved in a semblance of a shrug.

"The awkwardness, I guess," she said, and there was the smallest quaver in her voice. She paused, shook her head slightly, as if to clear her brain. "I can't pretend that nothing happened between us," she went on as Madison and Ruffles and the dogs drew nearer. "But I keep trying to do just that and it makes me crazy."

Hutch chuckled. "Well, then," he reasoned, "why don't you stop trying and just let things be what they are? It's not as if any of us have much of a choice in the matter, anyhow."

She sighed and kept her eyes on Madison, but she seemed a little less edgy than before. "You're right," she said. "Much as we might want to change the past, we can't."

He wanted to ask what she would change, if she could, but Opal's station wagon pulled through the gate just then and came barreling up the driveway.

"Look!" Madison called, as Opal got out of her car. "I'm riding a horse!"

"You sure enough are," Opal agreed, her smile wide. Her gaze swept over Hutch and Kendra, and the two other horses waiting to be ridden. "You about done with riding now?" she asked the child. "Because I've got supper to start and I could sure use a hand with the job."

Madison, Hutch suspected, could have stayed right there on Ruffles's back for days on end, given the opportunity, but she turned out to be the helpful sort.

"I guess I'm done," she said. "For right now, anyway."

Hutch approached and lifted her down off Ruffles's back. "You go on ahead with Opal," he told the little girl when she looked up at him in concern. He could guess what she was thinking. "I'll tend to Ruffles, and show you how to do that another time."

Madison nodded solemnly and patted the pony's nose. "I wish you were my very own," she told Ruffles. Then she smiled up at Kendra, waiting for a nod.

Kendra did nod, a little reluctantly, Hutch thought.

Opal put out a hand to Madison, Madison took it without hesitation, and they headed toward the house, chatting amicably, the dogs ambling along behind them.

"That was slick," Kendra observed with wry amusement, watching as the four disappeared through the kitchen doorway.

Hutch took Ruffles's reins and led the pony toward the barn door. "I didn't put Opal up to anything, if that's what you mean," he said, grinning back at her. "Make sure those horses don't take off. I'll be right back."

I'll be right back.

Kendra sighed. Now she'd have to go riding—alone with Hutch Carmody, no less—and she had nobody to blame but herself. She'd put herself in this position, sealed her own fate.

She *was* crazy.

Gingerly, she gathered the reins of the two horses and waited for Hutch to unsaddle Ruffles and tuck her away in a stall. And she waited.

She recognized the big gelding as Remington, Hutch's favorite mount, but the long-legged mare was a stranger.

"I have a child to raise and a business to run," she told the mare in a hurried undertone. "I cannot afford to break any bones, so don't try anything fancy."

The mare nickered companionably, as if promising to behave herself.

Hutch came back before Kendra was ready for him to, taking Remington's reins from her hands. "That's Coco," he said, nodding at the mare. "She's a roper, so she's lively and fast, but she's fairly kindhearted, too."

"Fairly?" Kendra echoed, waiting for muscle memory to kick in so she could mount up without making an even bigger fool of herself than she already had.

Hutch laughed, steadied the mare for her by taking a light hold on the bridle strap. "This isn't a dude ranch," he pointed out, clearly enjoying her trepidation. "Except for Ruffles, all these horses earn their keep, one way or another."

Having nothing to say to that—nothing civil, that is—Kendra reached up, gripped the saddle horn with damp palms, shoved her left foot in the stirrup and hoisted.

Hutch gave her a startling boost by splaying one hand across her backside and pushing.

She gasped, surged skyward and landed in the saddle with a thump.

He laughed again, mounted Remington and reined in alongside Kendra. "Ready?" he asked.

Her face was on fire, and she refused to look at him on the ridiculous premise that if she couldn't see him, he couldn't see her, either. "Ready," she confirmed, stubborn to the end.

"Good," he said, and he and Remington were off, leading the way, heading for the open range at a slow trot.

Kendra's horse followed immediately, her rider bouncing hard in the saddle with every step. Kendra concentrated on syncing herself with Coco and, when they'd traveled a hundred yards or so, she found her stride.

Hutch's gelding clearly wanted to run—*please, God, no*—but he held the horse in check with an ease that was both admirable and galling. Everything seemed to come easily to this man, and it wasn't fair.

"Where to?" he asked, grinning over at her as Coco matched her pace to Remington's.

"Anywhere but the high meadow," Kendra answered and was immediately embarrassed all over again. Talk about your Freudian slip—Hutch hadn't suggested riding to their secret, special place, now had he? *She'd* been the one to bring it up.

He chuckled at her miserable expression. "Tell me, Kendra," he began easily, "who are you more afraid of—me or yourself?"

"Don't be ridiculous," she sputtered. "It's just that I haven't ridden in a long time and the meadow is halfway up the mountain and—"

"Easy," Hutch admonished good-naturedly. Was he addressing her or his horse?

It had damned well *better* be the horse.

Alas it turned out to be her, instead. "Kendra," he went on, "I'm not fixing to jump your bones the second we're alone. We're two old friends out for a horseback ride, and that's all there is to it."

Maybe for you, Kendra thought peevishly. The answer to his earlier question was thrumming in her head by now, all too obvious. She was afraid of herself, not him. Afraid of her own desires and the way her intelligence seemed to take a dive whenever he turned on the charm.

Not that he'd been obvious about it.

Still the damage was done.

Whether he knew it or not—and it would be naive to think he didn't—Hutch had been in the process of seducing her almost from the moment she and Madison had arrived at the ranch. All he'd had to do to melt her resolve was to act like what Madison wanted most right now—a daddy.

They rode in silence for a while, the horses choosing their direction, or so it seemed to Kendra, the animals pausing alongside a stream to lower their huge heads and drink.

Hutch's expression had turned solemn; he seemed far away, somehow, even though he was right beside her. Sunlight danced on the surface of the creek as the water whispered by.

"Why did you come here, Kendra?" he finally asked, narrowing his eyes against the brightness of the late-afternoon sun as he studied her face.

"To the ranch?"

"To Parable," Hutch said.

She bristled. "Because it's home," she said tightly. "Because I want to raise Madison in a place where people know and care about each other."

Hutch dismounted, stood beside Remington, looking up at her. "And you were so happy here as a child that you figured Madison would be, too?" he asked. It wasn't a gibe, exactly, but he knew all about Kendra's life with her grandmother, so the remark hadn't been entirely innocent, either.

"Not always," she admitted, her tone a little distant. She was tempted to get down off the horse and stand facing him, but that would mean getting back *on* again and her legs felt too unsteady to manage it. "Nobody's happy all the time, are they?"

He gave a raspy chuckle, gazing out over the rippling water that gave his ranch its name—Whisper Creek. "That's for sure," he said.

She shifted uncomfortably in the saddle. No way around it, she was going to be sore after this ride, unaccustomed as she was.

Oh, well. Better achy body parts she could soak in a hot bathtub with Epsom salts, she figured, than an achy heart.

"I lied about the pony," Hutch said out of the blue. He bent as he spoke, picked up a pebble and skipped it across the busy water with an expert motion of one hand.

Kendra frowned, confused. Everything about this man confused her, in fact. "What?" she asked.

"I didn't borrow Ruffles," he replied, meeting her gaze again. "I bought her. The kids she used to belong to grew up and went away, and she's been lonely."

Something softened inside Kendra. Finally she began to relax a little. "Well, then," she said. "Why didn't you just say so in the first place?"

He cleared his throat. "Because I figured you'd think I was trying to get to you through Madison," he told her.

Some reckless Kendra took over, pushed the day-to-day Kendra aside. "Were you?" she asked. "Trying to get to me through my daughter, that is?"

She saw his jaw tighten, release again.

"That would be wrong on so many levels," he said. He was clearly angry, which was rich, considering he'd been the one to raise the topic in the first place. "Madison's not a pawn. She's a person in her own right."

"I quite agree," Kendra said, sounding prim even in her own ears.

That was when Hutch reached up, looped an arm around Kendra's waist and lifted her down off Coco's back. She came up against him, hard.

"If I want to 'get to' you, Kendra," he informed her, "I *can*—and without using an innocent little kid or anybody else."

She stared up at him, startled, breathless and without a thought in her head.

And that was when he kissed her, not gently, not tentatively, but with all the hunger a man can feel for a woman, all the need and the strength and the hardness and the heat.

Instantly she turned to a pillar of fire. Her arms slipped around Hutch's neck and tightened there, and she stood on tiptoe, pouring herself into that kiss without reservation.

This was what she had feared, some vague part of her knew that.

This was what she had *longed for.*

It was Hutch who broke away first. His breath was ragged, and he thrust the fingers of his right hand through his hair in a gesture that might have been frustration. "*Damn* it," he cursed.

Kendra, all molten passion just moments before, went ice-cold. "Don't you *dare* blame me for that, Hutch," she warned, in a furious whisper. "*You* started it."

He didn't answer, didn't even look at her.

No, he turned away, gave her his back.

"I'm sorry," he said, after a long time, his voice rough as dry gravel.

He was *sorry?* He'd rocked her to the core, thrown the planet off its axis, changed the direction of the tides with that kiss. And he was *sorry?*

"So much for two old friends just out for a simple horseback ride," she heard herself say. Humiliation and anger combined gave her the impetus to get back on Coco with no help from Hutch Carmody, thank you very much.

Hutch turned then, glowering up at her. "Don't," he warned. "Don't be flippant about this, Kendra. Something just happened here, something important."

"Yes," Kendra said lightly. He was standing and she was mounted and that gave her a completely false sense of power, which she permitted herself to enjoy for the briefest of moments. "You *kissed* me, remember?"

"I'm not talking about that," Hutch told her.

"Then what *are* you talking about?"

"We're not finished, you and I," Hutch said. "*That's* what I'm talking about."

"That's where you're wrong," Kendra retorted, coming to a slow simmer. "We are *so* finished. So over. So done. So through. We have been for years, in case you haven't noticed."

"The way you just kissed me says different," he replied, mounting up at last, reining the gelding around so that he and Kendra were facing each other.

"You kissed *me,"* she reiterated, almost frantic.

"You're damn right, I did," Hutch answered. "And you kissed me right back. If we'd been up at the meadow where it's private, instead of down here on the open range, we'd be making love right now, hot and heavy. Just like in the old days."

"Your ego," she snapped, "is exceeded only by your

ego. I'm not one of—one of *those* women, the kind you can have whenever you want!"

He laughed, but it was a tight sound, a challenge, a promise. "Prove it," he said.

Kendra was practically beside herself by then. She wanted to get back to the barn, get off this damnable horse, collect her daughter and her dog, and race for home, where she could reasonably pretend none of this had ever happened. "What do you mean, 'prove it'?" she practically spat.

"Opal is looking after Madison," he said. "Let's ride up the mountain, Kendra—just you and me. Right now."

"Absolutely *not*," Kendra shot back loftily, amazed at how badly she wanted to take him up on what would surely be, for her, a losing bet.

"Scared?" he asked, leaning in, almost breathing the word. His mouth rested lightly, briefly, against hers, setting her ablaze all over again.

"Yes," she said in a burst of honesty.

"Of me?"

Kendra swallowed hard, shook her head from side to side. He'd been right before—she was afraid of herself, not him—but she wasn't going to admit that out loud.

"It's probably inevitable," Hutch said, sounding gleefully resigned. "Our making love, I mean."

"Think what you like," Kendra bluffed, her tone deliberately tart. "But I've been down that road before, Hutch, and I'm not going back. I'm not a gullible young girl anymore. I'm a responsible woman with a daughter."

"And that means you can't have a sex life?"

"I will *not* discuss this with you," she bit out, turning Coco around and heading back toward the house and the barn and Madison. Back toward sanity and good sense.

Of course Hutch had no difficulty catching up. He looked cocky, riding beside her, all cowboy, all *man*.

She was in big trouble here.

Big, *big* trouble.

SHE AND MADISON had to stay for supper—Opal wouldn't hear of anything else, and besides, Kendra knew that leaving in a huff would reveal too much.

So she stayed.

She left Hutch to put the horses away by himself, except for his devoted shadow, Leviticus, then went into the house and washed her hands at the kitchen sink while Madison, swaddled in an oversize apron and elbow-deep in floury dough, regaled her with her new knowledge of cooking.

"She's ready for her own show on the Food Channel," Opal put in proudly, standing next to Madison at the center island and supervising every move.

"I don't doubt that for a moment," Kendra agreed, hoping her coloring had returned to normal by now.

"I'm making *biscuits,*" Madison said.

"Impressive," Kendra replied. "Will you teach me how to make them, too?"

Madison giggled at that. "Silly Mommy," she said. "You just need to look in a cookbook and you'll *know* how."

Kendra kissed her daughter's flour-smudged cheek. "You've got me there," she said, with a little sigh.

"Coffee's fresh," Opal said with a nod in the direction of the machine. "Mugs are in the cupboard above it."

"Thanks." Kendra needed something to do with her

hands, so she got out a cup, poured herself some coffee and took a slow sip, hoping it wouldn't keep her awake half the night, thinking about the most recent go-round with Hutch. She was jangly enough as it was.

"How was the ride?" Opal asked, and her attempt to put the question casually was a total flop.

"Fine," Kendra replied noncommittally.

"Where's Mr. Hutch?" Madison wanted to know.

So, Kendra thought. He'd graduated from cowboy man to Mr. Hutch. What was next—Daddy?

"He's looking after the horses," Kendra answered, leaning against the counter and taking another sip of coffee. Oddly the caffeine seemed to be settling her down rather than riling her already frayed nerves, and she was grateful for this small, counterintuitive blessing.

"When can we get my boots?" Madison chimed in.

Kendra laughed. "Does that mean you want to go riding again?" she hedged.

Madison nodded eagerly, still working away at the dough she'd been kneading in the big crockery bowl in front of her. "I want to ride *far*," she said. "Not just around and around in the yard, like a little kid."

"You *are* a little kid," Kendra teased.

"I reckon that biscuit dough is about ready to be rolled out and cut," Opal put in. Without missing a beat, she gently removed Madison's hands from the bowl, wiped them clean with a damp dish towel and lifted the child down off the chair she'd been standing on.

"I can help," Madison offered.

"Sure you can," Opal agreed.

The woman was the soul of patience. Kendra smiled at her, mouthing the words "Thank you."

"But first I need to say good-night to Ruffles," Madison said.

"After supper," Kendra answered.

Hutch came in then, rolling up the sleeves of his shirt as he stepped over the threshold in stocking feet, having left his dirty boots outside on the step. His hair was rumpled, and there were bits of hay on his clothes. Kendra was struck by how impossibly good he looked, even coming straight from the barn.

He nodded a greeting to Opal and Kendra in turn, then spared a wink for Madison as he used an elbow to turn on the hot water in the sink. He lathered his hands and forearms with a bar of pungently scented orange soap, rinsed and lathered up again.

To look at him, nobody would have guessed that less than an hour before he'd kissed Kendra as she'd never been kissed before—even by him—and thrown her entire being into sweet turmoil in the space of a few heartbeats. He'd plundered her mouth with his tongue and she'd not only allowed it, she'd *responded,* no question about it.

He'd said it was inevitable that they'd make love. Dared her to ride up the mountain with him, to that cursed, enchanted meadow where heaven and earth seemed to converge as their bodies converged.

Stop it, she told herself sternly.

"I made the biscuits," Madison was saying to Hutch as he turned away from the sink, drying his hands on a towel. "Well, I *helped,* anyway."

Opal chuckled. She'd gotten out a rolling pin and a biscuit cutter. "Get back up on this chair, young lady, and I'll show you what to do next."

Madison scrambled to obey.

Opal gave the child's hands another going over with a damp cloth.

Together they rolled the dough out flat, used the cutter to make circles, placed these on a baking sheet lined with parchment paper.

Hutch crossed to the oven and reached for the handle on the door.

"Don't you open that oven," Opal immediately commanded. "You'll let out all that good steam."

For a moment Hutch looked more like a curious little boy than a man. "Whatever it is, it sure smells good," he said.

"It's my special tamale pie, like I said I'd make," Opal replied briskly, "and I'll thank you not to go messing with it before we've even sat down to say grace."

Hutch grinned, spread his hands in a conciliatory gesture. "Yes, ma'am," he said. "Far be it from me to mess with supper."

"And don't you forget it," Opal said, evidently determined to have the last word.

It was a mundane exchange, but Kendra enjoyed the hominess of good-natured banter between people who cared for each other as if they were family. When she was growing up, meals had been catch-as-catch-can affairs, and if her grandmother did bother to cook, she slammed the pots and pans around in the process, letting Kendra know it was an imposition. That *she* was an imposition.

Those days were long gone, she reminded herself. She'd come through okay, hadn't she? And she was a good mother to Madison, at least partly because she wanted things to be different for her.

"I'd sure like to know what's going on in that head

of yours right about now," Hutch said, surprising her. When had he crossed the room, come to stand next to her, close enough to touch? And why did he have to be so darned observant?

"I was just thinking how lucky I am," she said.

He grinned, watching as Madison "helped" slide the biscuits into the extra oven built into the wall beside the stove. "You definitely are," he said, and there was something in his voice that took a lot of the sting out of things he'd said earlier.

That was the thing she had to watch when it came to Hutch.

He could be kind one moment and issuing a challenge the next.

Most of the time, he was impossible to read.

Soon enough, they all sat down to supper, Opal and Madison, Kendra and Hutch, and it felt a little too *right* for comfort. After struggling so hard to regain her emotional equilibrium, Kendra was back on shaky ground.

She was hungry, though, despite her jumpy nerves, and she put away two biscuits as well as an ample portion of Opal's delectable tamale pie.

Madison had had a big day, and by the time supper was over, she was fighting to stay awake. "Mommy said I could say good-night to Ruffles," she insisted, yawning, when the table had been cleared and the plates and silverware loaded into the dishwasher.

Hutch lifted the child into his arms, though he was looking at Kendra when he spoke. "And your mommy," he said, "is a woman of her word. Let's go."

What was *that* supposed to mean? Was there a barb hidden somewhere in that statement?

Kendra decided not to invest any more of her rapidly waning energy wondering. She thanked Opal for supper and for letting Madison help with the preparations, and followed Hutch, Madison and the ever-alert Daisy out the back door. They crossed the yard, headed for the barn, and Madison, half-asleep by then, rested her head on Hutch's shoulder.

Hutch flipped on the light as they entered, and carried Madison to Ruffles's stall.

Kendra watched, stricken with a tangle of bittersweet emotions, as Madison leaned over the stall door to pat the pony's head.

"Good night, Ruffles," she said, keeping her other arm firmly around Hutch's neck. Solemnly, she instructed the little horse to sleep well and have sweet dreams.

Kendra's heart turned over in her chest and her throat tightened.

Too late, she realized that Hutch was watching her and, as usual, seeing more than she wanted him to see.

"We'd better go now," she said, forcing the words out.

Hutch nodded. Still carrying Madison, he led the way back outside, setting the child in her car seat as deftly as if he'd done it a thousand times before, chuckling when the dog joined them in a single bound.

Kendra resisted the urge to double-check the fastenings on the car seat, just to make sure he'd gotten it right.

Of *course* he'd gotten it right. He was Hutch Carmody, and he got just about everything right—when he chose to, that is.

"Thanks," Kendra said, standing beside the car, hugging herself even though the night was warm. Since she didn't want him jumping to the conclusion that her thank-you included that soul-sundering kiss beside Whisper Creek, she added, too quickly, "For letting Madison ride Ruffles, I mean."

A slow grin spread across Hutch's face as he watched her. Overhead, a million gazillion silvery stars splashed across the black velvet sky and the moon glowed translucent, nearly full.

"Anytime," he said easily, Leviticus waiting quietly at his side.

"Right," Kendra said, at a loss.

Hutch opened the driver's door for her, waited politely for her to slip behind the wheel, fumble in her bag for the keys, fasten her seat belt and start the engine.

Madison was already asleep—if she hadn't been, Kendra knew, she would have been asking when she could come back and ride Ruffles again.

When Hutch remained where he was, Kendra rolled down her window. She had her issues with the man, but she didn't want to run over his feet backing out. "Was there something else?" she asked, hoping she sounded casual.

He leaned over to look in at her. "Yeah," he said. "You planning on coming to the rodeo? You and Madison?"

She nodded, smiled. "There's no way I could get out of it even if I wanted to," she said. "Madison's never been and she's looking forward to the whole weekend, rodeo, fireworks and all."

Speaking of fireworks, she thought, as the memory of that kiss coursed through her, hot and fierce, causing her heart to kick into overdrive.

"I'm entered in the bull-riding on Saturday afternoon," Hutch said, "but I'd sure like to buy the two of you supper and maybe take Madison on a few of the carnival rides before taking in the fireworks."

All she had to do was say no, take time to step back and regain her perspective.

Instead she said, "Okay." Immediately.

Hutch grinned. "Great," he said. "I'll be in touch, and we'll work out the details."

She nodded, as though nothing out of the ordinary had happened that day.

Maybe for *him* nothing had.

Dismal thought.

Kendra murmured good-night, Hutch stepped away from the car and she put the Volvo in motion.

At home, she unbuckled Madison, awake but sleepy, and carried her into the house. She helped the child into her pajamas, oversaw the brushing of teeth and the saying of prayers, tucked her daughter in and kissed her forehead.

"Good night, Annie Oakley," she said.

Daisy, probably needing to go outside, fidgeted in the doorway.

"Who's that?" Madison asked, yawning big again, but she was asleep before Kendra had a chance to answer.

Leaving Madison's bedroom, she followed Daisy back to the kitchen and stood on the porch while the dog did what had to be done.

As soon as she was back inside the house, Daisy headed straight for Madison's room.

Kendra, a little too wired to sleep, tidied up the already tidy house, watered a few plants and finally retreated to her home office and logged on to the computer. She'd check her email, both business and personal, she decided, and then soak in a nice hot bath, a sort of preemptive strike against the saddle soreness she was bound to be feeling by morning.

She weeded out the junk mail—somehow some of it always got past the filter—and that left her with two messages, one from Tara and one from Joslyn. Both had attachments—forwards, no doubt.

She clicked on Joslyn's, expecting a cute picture of the new baby.

Instead she was confronted with a page from a major social-media site, a photo someone had snapped of her and Hutch running the three-legged race at the cemetery picnic the previous weekend. Both of them were laughing, pitching forward into the fall that sent them tumbling into the grass.

The caption was short and to the point. "Up to his old tricks," it read. "Already."

CHAPTER THIRTEEN

KENDRA STIFFENED IN her chair, staring at the computer monitor and the picture of her and Hutch, feeling as though she'd been slapped across the face. She clicked back to the main body of Joslyn's email and read, "Now they've gone too far. This means war."

The second message, from Tara, was similar.

The anti-Hutch campaign was one thing, as far as Kendra's two closest friends were concerned, but dragging her into it was one step over the line. Clearly they were prepared to do battle.

She sat back, drew a few long, deep breaths, releasing them slowly, and reminded herself that this wasn't such a big deal—the page was a petty outlet for people who apparently had too much free time on their hands, not a cross blazing on her front lawn or a brick hurled through her living room window.

She answered both Tara's and Joslyn's emails with a single response. "I'll handle it." Then, calmer but no less indignant at some stranger's invasion of her privacy, she printed out a copy of the webpage, folded it carefully into quarters and took it back to the kitchen, where she'd left her purse. She tucked the sheet of paper away in the very bottom, under her wallet and cosmetic case, looked in on her daughter once more and retreated to the bathroom for that long soak she'd promised herself.

The warm water soothed her, as did the two over-the-counter pain relievers she took before crawling into bed. She hadn't expected to sleep, but she did, deeply and dreamlessly, and the next thing she knew, sunlight was seeping, pink-orange, through her eyelids.

Her thighs and backside were sore from the horse-back ride, but not sore enough to matter.

She threw herself into the morning routine—getting Madison up and dressed and fed, making sure Daisy went outside and then had fresh water and kibble. She skipped her usual coffee, though, and sipped herbal tea instead.

"You look pretty, Mommy," Madison said, taking in Kendra's crisp linen pantsuit. Lately, she'd been wearing jeans.

"Thank you," Kendra replied lightly, pausing to bend over Madison's chair at the breakfast table and kiss the top of her head. "I have an appointment this morning—a client is coming to see the other house—so hurry it up a little, will you?"

"About my boots," Madison began.

So, Kendra thought wryly, she'd been right to suspect that, while genuine, the compliment on her outfit had its purposes.

"There will be all sorts of vendors—people who sell things—at the rodeo this weekend. We'll check out the boots then."

Madison beamed, but then her face clouded over. "But I still have to say sorry to Miss Abbington and Becky," she recalled.

"Absolutely," Kendra said firmly. "Suppose Becky

had taken *your* boots, without permission, and then re-fused to give them back. How would you feel?"

"Bad," Madison admitted.

"And so?" Kendra prompted.

"Becky felt bad," Madison said. Then something flashed in her eyes. "But I didn't wear Miss *Abbington's* shoes. Why do I have to say sorry to her?"

"Enough," Kendra said, softening the word with a smile. "You know darn well why you need to apologize to Miss Abbington."

"I do?" Madison echoed innocently.

Kendra simply waited.

"Because I was misruptive in class," Madison fi-nally conceded.

"Bingo," Kendra said.

An hour later, with Madison at preschool and Daisy minding the office, Kendra showed the mansion to the second client, a representative of a large investment group with an eye to turning the place into an apart-ment complex.

Kendra knew right away that there would be no ac-tual sale, but that didn't matter. The real estate business was all about showing places again and again, until the right buyer came along. Generally, she had to bait a lot of hooks before she caught a fish.

Work was the furthest thing from her mind anyway, with that printout of the webpage burning a hole in the bottom of her purse.

At lunchtime, she locked up the office, loaded the always adventuresome Daisy into the Volvo and headed for the neighboring town, Three Trees.

She didn't know Brylee Parrish well—the two of

them were barely acquainted, with a five-year gap in age, and they'd grown up in separate if closely linked communities—but she knew exactly where to find her. Brylee, with her flourishing party-planning business, was the original Local Girl Makes Good—she had a large warehouse and offices just outside Three Trees.

During the drive, Kendra didn't rehearse what she was going to say, because she didn't know, exactly. She doubted that Brylee personally was behind the webpage photo and the remark about Hutch being up to his old tricks, but she'd know who was.

Arriving at Brylee's company, Décor Galore, Kendra rolled down one of the car windows a little way, so Daisy would have air, and promised the dog she'd be back soon.

A receptionist greeted her with a stiff smile and several furtive glances stolen while she was buzzing the boss to let her know that Kendra Shepherd wanted to see her.

"She'll be here in a couple of minutes," the receptionist said, hanging up. Now, for all those sneak peeks, the young woman wouldn't look directly at Kendra. She nodded toward a small and tastefully decorated waiting area. "Have a seat."

"I'll stand, thank you," Kendra said politely.

When Brylee appeared, opening a side door and poking out her head, Kendra was immediately and oddly struck by how beautiful she was, with those huge hazel eyes and that glorious mane of chestnut-brown hair worn in a ponytail today.

"Come in," Brylee said, and her cheeks flared with color, then immediately went pale.

Kendra followed Brylee through a long corridor,

through the busy, noisy warehouse and into a surprisingly plain office. The furniture—a desk, two chairs, some mismatched file cabinets and a single bookcase—looked as though it had come from an army surplus store. There were no pictures or other decorations on the walls, no knickknacks to be seen.

"Sit down—please," Brylee said, taking the chair behind her desk.

Kendra sat, opened her purse, dug out the folded sheet of paper and slid it across to Brylee.

Brylee swallowed visibly, and her unmanicured hands trembled ever so slightly as she unfolded the paper and smoothed it flat.

Kendra felt a brief stab of sympathy for her. After all, losing Hutch Carmody was a trauma she well understood, and it had probably been worse for Brylee, all dressed up in the wedding gown of her dreams, with all her friends and family there to witness the event.

Brylee, meanwhile, gave a deep sigh, closed her eyes and squeezed the bridge of her nose between one thumb and forefinger. Then, rallying, she squared her slender shoulders and looked directly at Kendra.

"I don't expect you to believe me," she said with dignity, "but I didn't know about this."

"I have no reason not to believe you," Kendra replied moderately. She drew in another deep breath, let it out and went on, feeling her way through her sentence word by word. "Some people—maybe a lot of them—would say it's just a harmless photograph and I ought to let it go at that. If this is as far as it goes—fine. I can deal with it. But I have a four-year-old daughter to think about, Ms. Parrish, and—"

Brylee put up a hand. She still looked wan, but a

friendly sparkle flickered in her eyes. "Please," she interrupted. "Call me Brylee. We're not enemies, you and I—or, at least, I hope we're not—and I totally get why this bothers you." She paused, bit her lip, studying Kendra's face with a kind of broken curiosity. "Really, I do."

"Then we don't have a problem," Kendra said, wanting to be kind and at the same time picking up on just how much Brylee wanted to ask if she and Hutch had some kind of "thing" going. "Just ask whoever put this up on the web to take it down, please, and leave me alone."

Brylee arched one perfect eyebrow. "What about Hutch?"

"What about him?" Kendra countered mildly.

"Never mind," Brylee said miserably, looking away for a long moment.

Kendra was relieved when Brylee didn't press the point. *What about Hutch?* Indeed. She had no idea what, if anything, was happening between her and Hutch Carmody. Sure, he'd kissed her, and made her want him in the process, but he was on the rebound, after all. He must have cared for Brylee at some point or he'd never have asked her to marry him.

The realization struck her like a face full of cold water; she grew a little flustered and fumbled with her purse as she rose from her chair. "I'd better go—my dog is in the car and—"

Brylee stood, too, her smile sad but real. "I'm sorry, Kendra. About the webpage, I mean. It seemed pretty innocent at first—all my friends were mad at Hutch and so was I—but enough is enough. I'll see that they take the page down."

To Kendra's mind, Hutch was a big boy and he could fight his own battles; her only concern was that she'd been featured. "Thank you," she said.

Brylee walked her back along the corridor, through the reception area and out into the parking lot. She smiled when she saw Daisy poking her snout through the crack in the window, eager to join in any game that might be played, but Kendra felt edgy. She knew there was something else Brylee wanted to say to her.

Sure enough, there was.

"I don't think Hutch ever really got over you," Brylee said quietly, and without malice. "I should have paid more attention to the signs—he called me by your name once or twice, for instance—but I guess I was just too crazy about him to see what was happening."

Kendra felt another tug of sympathy, even as all the old defenses rose up inside her. "Thanks again," she said, and climbed into her car.

Daisy whimpered in the backseat, either because she needed to squat in the grass or because she'd taken a liking to Brylee, or both, but the dog was going to have to wait. No way was Kendra going to let Daisy christen Brylee's parking lot right in front of the woman—it might seem, well, like a symbolic gesture.

Brylee waved, watching as Kendra drove away and Kendra waved back.

Thoughts assailed her as she pulled onto the highway leading home to Parable; she heard Brylee's words, over and over again. *I don't think Hutch ever really got over you—he called me by your name once or twice—*

"Stop it," Kendra told herself, right out loud.

Daisy whimpered again, more urgently this time.

Kendra pulled over when she came to a wide spot in

the road, got out of the car, leaned into the backseat to hook Daisy's leash to her collar and took the dog for a short walk in the grass.

By the time they were on their way again, she was starting to feel foolish for confronting Brylee with that printout at all. She'd probably overreacted.

Before pulling back onto the highway, Kendra got out her cell phone and called Joslyn.

"Were you asleep?" she asked, first thing.

Joslyn laughed. "I'm a new mother," she said. "We don't sleep."

Kendra laughed, too. "Is your mom still visiting?"

"She left this morning," Joslyn answered. "Mom was a lot of help—Callie has been, too—but it's time things got back to normal around here. Besides, Slade and Shea are great with the baby."

"Good," Kendra said.

"You called to find out if I was sleeping?" Joslyn teased. "Is this about that stupid webpage? Five minutes after I hit Send, I wished I hadn't just sprung the thing on you like that. Tara feels the same way."

"It's all right," Kendra said, watching as cars and trucks zipped by on the highway. "But, yeah, that's the reason I called. I've just been to see Brylee."

"Come right over," Joslyn commanded cheerfully. "Immediately, if not sooner. I want to hear all about it."

"Nothing happened," Kendra put in lamely. It wasn't as if she and Brylee had gotten into a hair-pulling match or anything; they weren't a pair of junior high schoolers fighting over a boy.

"Be that as it may," Joslyn replied, "you obviously need some BFF time or you wouldn't have called. *Come over.*"

"I'll be there in twenty minutes," Kendra capitulated, grateful.

"Good," Joslyn answered.

When Kendra and Daisy arrived at Windfall Ranch, Tara's sports car was parked alongside the main house, next to Joslyn's nondescript compact. Slade's truck was nowhere in sight—maybe he'd driven his mother-in-law to the airport.

Joslyn and Tara both appeared on the back porch as Kendra got out of the car and freed Daisy from the confines of the backseat. Lucy, Tara's dog, was on hand to greet her and the pair frolicked, overjoyed at their reunion.

Joslyn smiled and waved, but Tara looked worried.

"Have I just made a world-class fool of myself or what?" Kendra fretted as she approached the porch. By now, of course, Joslyn would have told Tara about the visit to Brylee's office.

Tara finally smiled. "I'm not sure," she joked. "Come inside, and we'll figure it out over coffee and pastry."

They all trooped into Joslyn's recently remodeled kitchen, including Lucy and Daisy, who greeted Jasper, Slade's dog, and were roundly snubbed by Joslyn's cat.

Baby Trace lay in his bassinet, gurgling, his feet and hands busy as he tried to grab hold of a beam of sunlight coming in through a nearby window.

Joslyn smiled, tucked his blanket in around him, and bent to plant a smacking kiss on his downy head. "I love you, little cowboy," she said softly.

The backs of Kendra's eyes scalded a little, in the wake of a rush of happiness for her friend. Joslyn had built a successful software company on her own, sold it for a fortune and righted an old wrong that wasn't even hers in the first place. But *this*—Slade, his step-daughter, Shea, the baby, the ranch, all of it—was her dream come true.

And it had been by no means a sure thing.

Now, though, she absolutely shone with fulfillment.

Tara, following Kendra's gaze, smiled and said quietly, "There she is, the world's happiest woman."

Kendra nodded and blinked a couple of times, and they all sat down to enjoy the tea Joslyn must have brewed in advance. There were doughnuts with sprinkles waiting, too.

"Do you miss your mom, now that's she's gone home to Santa Fe?" Kendra asked Joslyn, deciding to skip the doughnuts because her stomach was still a little touchy.

"Of course I do," Joslyn said. "It was lovely, having her here, but she has a life to get back to and, besides, we're sure to see her again soon."

"We shouldn't have forwarded that webpage to you," Tara interjected, looking fretful again. "I don't know what we were thinking."

"It's all right," Kendra said truthfully. "I would have seen it sooner or later anyway, and it was better that it came from the two of you."

"You really went to see Brylee Parrish?" Joslyn asked, wide-eyed.

"No," Kendra joked. "I just said that to get a rise out of you. *Yes,* I went to see Brylee, and I feel like an idiot. One of those people who are always on the look-out for something to raise a fuss about."

"I'd say you had reason to raise a fuss," Tara said, loyal to the end. "Sometimes things like that picture of you and Hutch being posted with a snarky comment start out small and then mushroom into a major hassle."

"Well, anyway, it's done," Kendra went on with a little shrug. "Brylee is actually a very nice person, you know. She's going to make sure the page gets taken down—so no harm done."

"Did she ask if you and Hutch are involved?" Joslyn asked. No sense in pulling any punches; cut right to the chase—that was Joslyn's way.

"She wanted to," Kendra said, "but she didn't."

"Are you?" Tara prodded.

"Am I what?" Kendra stalled.

"Involved. With. Hutch. Carmody," Tara said with exaggerated patience.

"No," Kendra said, thinking, *not if you don't count that hot kiss by Whisper Creek yesterday afternoon.*

"I heard he bought a pony for Madison," Tara persisted.

"Who told you that?" Kendra wanted to know.

"Word gets around," Tara said.

"Opal," Kendra guessed, and knew she was right by the looks of fond chagrin on her friends' faces.

"Don't be mad at Opal," Joslyn was quick to say. "We were talking on the phone and it just slipped out that Hutch bought a pony for Madison to ride and, well, it's only natural to draw some conclusions."

"Which, of course, you did," Kendra pointed out sweetly. "It just so happens that you're wrong, though. Hutch bought the pony because the people who owned it before said it was lonely, with their kids grown up and gone from home."

Tara and Joslyn exchanged knowing looks.

"Every hardworking cattle rancher needs a pony named Ruffles," Joslyn observed dryly and with a twinkle.

"It means nothing," Kendra insisted.

"Whatever you say," Tara agreed, grinning.

"You two are impossible."

"At least we're objective," Joslyn said. "Unlike some people I could mention."

Kendra picked up her teacup and took a measured sip. "You are *so* not objective," she said at some length.

"We want you to be happy," Tara said.

"Well, I want you to be happy, too," Kendra immediately replied. "So why aren't we trying to throw *you* together with somebody—like Boone Taylor, for instance?"

Tara turned a fetching shade of apricot-pink. "Oh, *please,*" she said.

Joslyn, comfortably ensconced in her own marriage and family life, grinned at both of them. Happy people could be downright insufferable, Kendra reflected, especially when they were trying to make a point. "There was a time," she reminded them, "when I couldn't *stand* Slade Barlow. And look how that turned out."

"Oh, right," Tara said grumpily. Her teacup made a clinking sound as she set it back in her saucer. "We'll just go out and find men we absolutely cannot abide, won't we, Kendra, and live happily ever after. Why didn't *we* think of that?"

Joslyn's eyes shimmered with mischievous amusement. "You might be surprised if you gave Boone even the slightest encouragement," she said before turning her gaze on Kendra. "And as for *you,* Ms. Shepherd, we all know that Hutch Carmody makes your little heart go pitty-pat, so why try to pretend otherwise?"

Kendra sighed a long, sad sigh. "Maybe he does," she confessed, almost in a whisper. "But that doesn't mean things will work out between us. They didn't before, remember."

"You do feel something for him, then," Joslyn pointed out kindly, patting Kendra's hand.

"I don't know *what* I feel," Kendra said. "Except that he scares me half to death."

"Why?" Tara asked. Her tone was gentle.

"Once burned, twice shy, I guess," Kendra answered. She glanced down at her watch, partly as a signal that she didn't want to talk about Hutch anymore. "I'd better get back to the office," she added, "before people decide I've gone out of business because I'm never there."

Nobody argued. Both Tara and Joslyn rose to hug their friend goodbye.

Kendra called to Daisy and within minutes the two of them were on the road again.

When she reached the office and checked her voice mail, Kendra learned that three prospective new listings were in the works. She called back each of the people who'd decided to sell their property, arranging meetings for the afternoon, glad to be busy.

The first of the three was a modest ranch-style house with a big yard, a detached garage and plenty of space for flower beds and gardens. The owner, an aging widower named John Gerard, had decided to share a condo in Great Falls with his brother. The place had been impeccably maintained, but it needed some upgrading, too—it would make a good starter home for a young couple, with or without a family.

Kendra and Mr. Gerard agreed on an asking price and other details, and papers were signed.

The second property was commercial—a spooky

old motel that would be difficult to sell, given the dilapidated state it was in, but Kendra liked challenges, so she took that listing on, too, mainly because it was in a good location, almost in the middle of town.

By the time she visited the third offering, a double-wide trailer in her grandmother's old neighborhood, she was getting anxious. She had to be at the preschool by three o'clock to pick up Madison, that being the present arrangement, and she couldn't be late.

The owner—in her distracted state Kendra hadn't connected the dots—was Deputy Treat McQuillan. His face was still colorfully bruised from the set-to with Walker Parrish the other night at the Boot Scoot Tavern. By now the incident had assumed almost legendary proportions in and around Parable and she wondered, a little nervously, if Deputy McQuillan had followed through on his threat to press charges against Walker for assault.

In uniform, McQuillan was waiting on his add-on porch when Kendra pulled up in her car. She'd dropped Daisy off at home on her way over and, at the moment, she was glad. There was something about this man that made her feel slightly overprotective, of Madison *and* her dog.

"Hello," she sang out pleasantly, a businesswoman through and through, leaving her purse in the car and unlatching the creaky wooden gate that opened onto the rather hardscrabble front yard. "I hope I haven't kept you waiting."

"Some things," McQuillan drawled, letting his gaze drag over her in a way that was at once leisurely and sleazy, "are worth waiting for."

Kendra felt profoundly uncomfortable and not just

because her last encounter with this man, when he'd warned her about Hutch at the Butter Biscuit Café, still irritated her. Her grandmother's old place was just two doors down, on the other side of the unpaved road, and the old sense of futility and sorrow settled over her as surely as if she'd stepped back in time and turned into her childhood self, abandoned and scared.

"You're planning to move?" she asked sunnily, pretending this was business as usual. McQuillan was, after all, a sheriff's deputy and, even if he *had* stepped over the line with Brylee over at the cowboy bar, there was no reason to paint him as a rapist on the prowl for his next victim.

"I'm not sure yet," the deputy replied, keeping his eyes on her face now, instead of her breasts. "Maybe I'll buy a patch of land and build a house, if I can get the right price for this double-wide."

Kendra approached confidently, with her shoulders back and her spine straight. "I see," she said. "What if it sells right away, though? Where would you live in the interim?"

He favored her with a slow grin that made her skin crawl a little and stepped down off the porch to put out a hand to her. "I haven't thought that far ahead," he admitted, gesturing toward the trailer behind him. "I'm just taking things as they come." He glanced at his watch. "I'm on duty in a few minutes," he went on, handing her a ring with two keys dangling from it. "You go on in and take a look around and, if you wouldn't mind, lock up on your way out. I'll pick up the keys later on and we'll work out the details."

Kendra was used to being alone in houses and apartments with people who made her uneasy—that was part of being in the real estate business—but she was wildly relieved that McQuillan meant to leave her to explore on her own. The idea of being confined in a small space with this man made her more than edgy.

She smiled, though, and nodded. "I'll be back at the office around three-thirty," she said. "You could stop by any time after that."

"Fine," he said, and walked on toward the gate. With a jaunty wave of farewell, he left the yard, crossed the sidewalk and got into his personal vehicle, a small green truck, clearly old but polished to a high shine.

Kendra waited until he'd driven away with a merry toot of his horn, before starting up the porch steps.

The front door stood open, but there was a sliding screen, so she moved that aside to step into a living room exactly like her grandmother's.

Her stomach curled around what was left of her quick lunch, a fruit cup and some yogurt hastily consumed at home while she was getting Daisy settled, and she instructed herself, silently and sternly, to get over it.

She wasn't a little girl anymore and this wasn't her grandmother's mobile home.

Deputy McQuillan's living room was shabby—the carpet, drapes and furniture had all seen better days—but every surface was immaculately clean, like the outside of his truck.

She made a hasty circuit, checking out the kitchenette, the fanatically neat bathroom, the three bedrooms, two of which were desperately small. The master bedroom boasted a water bed with a huge, mirrored headboard, and the coverlet was made of crimson velvet.

Cringing a little, Kendra backed out of that room. It was a silly reaction, she knew, but she had to force herself to walk—not run—through the kitchenette and the living room to the front door.

Outside, she sucked in several deep breaths and resolutely took a tour of the yard. There was a tool shed, a detached garage and a small rose garden encircled by chicken-wire that was painted white. The blossoms inside seemed timid, somehow, like prisoners waiting to be rescued.

Now she was really being silly, she decided.

It was a relief, just the same, to get into her car, shut and lock the doors and drive away.

"I 'POLOGIZED!" MADISON announced when Kendra picked her up at preschool. "Becky and me are friends now! She invited me to sleep over sometime—and she has *horses* at her house—"

Kendra bit back the correction—*Becky and I*—and smiled as she strapped Madison into her car seat. "That's wonderful," she said. "Did you apologize to Miss Abbington, too?"

Madison nodded vigorously, but a frown creased her forehead. "Where's Daisy? You didn't give her back to that lady at the shelter, did you?"

Slightly stunned, Kendra straightened. "Daisy's at home," she said gently. "And of course I didn't give her back, sweetheart. Why would I do that?"

"Sometimes people give kids back," Madison ventured.

Kendra swallowed hard, worked up another smile. Madison had been shunted from one foster home to the next during her short life, so it wasn't difficult to figure out the source of the child's concern, for Daisy *and* for herself.

"You're staying with me," Kendra said carefully, "until you're all grown up and ready to go off to college. And even then, you'll always have a home to come back to, and a mommy, too."

"You won't give me back? Not ever?"

"Not ever," Kendra vowed, fighting tears. "And the same goes for Daisy. We're in this for the long haul, all three of us. We're a family, forever and ever."

"It would still be nice if there was a daddy," Madison mused, though she looked appeased by Kendra's promise never to leave. It was one she'd made a thousand times before, and would probably make a thousand more times in the future.

"I guess," Kendra allowed, getting quickly behind the wheel and starting up the car so they could head for home.

"If I could pick out a daddy, I'd choose Mr. Carmody," Madison went on.

By then, Kendra was beginning to wonder if she was being played, but she didn't hesitate to give her daughter the benefit of a doubt. Carefully, she put the car in gear and drove away from the community center, waving to other mothers and fathers coming to collect their children. "Unfortunately," she explained, "it doesn't work that way."

"How *does* getting a daddy work, then?"

Kendra suppressed a sigh. "It's not like baking cookies, honey," she said. "There's no recipe to follow. No formula."

"Oh," Madison said, and the note of sadness in her voice made Kendra ache.

They drove in silence for a minute or two.

Then Madison spoke up again. "It's not fair," she said.

"What's not fair?" Kendra asked patiently, concentrating on the road ahead.

"That *my* daddy's in heaven instead of right here in Parable with us," Madison replied succinctly. "I want a daddy I can see and talk to."

Kendra didn't trust herself to answer without bursting into tears, so she held her tongue.

CHAPTER FOURTEEN

THAT EVENING, AFTER supper and a story and going-to-sleep prayers—Madison asked God for a daddy and suggested Hutch Carmody as a promising candidate for the job—Kendra sat alone at her kitchen table for a while, a little dazed by all that had been going on lately.

She'd had a heck of a time keeping back the tears while Madison was putting in her request for a father; now, as she sat there with a cup of herbal tea before her, they ran freely.

Daisy, who had been snuggled up at the foot of Madison's new bed only a few minutes before, meandered into the kitchen, came straight over to Kendra's chair and stood on her hind legs to plant her forepaws on Kendra's thigh. Her brown eyes shone with canine sympathy and she made a low, whimpering sound in her throat.

Kendra gave a raw chuckle, sniffled and laid a gentle hand on the dog's golden head. "You're a good dog, Daisy," she said, thick-throated with all the complicated emotions swamping her just then.

Daisy rested her muzzle on Kendra's leg and sighed sweetly.

Kendra continued to stroke the dog, used her free hand to raise her teacup to her mouth.

"I'm so confused," she confided after several sips and swallows.

Daisy sighed again, lowered herself to all fours and looked up at Kendra with those glowing eyes, tail wagging slowly back and forth.

"Listen to me," Kendra muttered, sniffling again. "I'm talking to a dog."

Daisy sat now, watching Kendra alertly, as if waiting for her to go on. *Yes, you're talking to a dog. That's a problem?*

Kendra laughed and brushed away her tears with the backs of her hands. "I'll be *all right,*" she assured the animal quietly. "So please stop worrying about me." Then she got up, took Daisy out into the backyard just once more and returned to the kitchen.

Apparently satisfied that her second-favorite mistress would indeed remain in one piece without her, at least for now, Daisy ambled back to Madison's room, retiring for the night.

Kendra finished her rapidly cooling tea, went into her home office and logged on to the computer. She'd waited this long to see if Brylee had kept her word and had the web picture taken down, but she couldn't wait any longer.

She was too jittery and frazzled to read or take a luxurious bath by candlelight or simply go to bed early, her usual remedies for everything from wrenching trauma to minor frustrations. That was what she did when she *felt* too much—when it all became overwhelming—she read, or bathed, or slept.

While those things were all perfectly okay, in and of themselves, Kendra was beginning to see them as forms of running away now, time-honored methods of avoidance or denial, metaphorical hiding places where she could take shelter from thoughts and emotions that chafed against the bruised and tender parts of who she really and truly was, deep down inside.

She was a woman now, a mother, and while she figured she functioned pretty well in the latter role, the former was beginning to issue some pretty powerful complaints. *That* Kendra was tired of doing everything alone, including sleeping in an otherwise empty bed. *She* wanted a man to hold her when she needed holding, to love her in every way, on every level—emotionally, mentally and, oh, yes, physically.

The problem, she admitted silently, as she clicked her way over to the Down-With-Hutch webpage, was her complete lack of confidence in her own ability to choose the right man.

First, there had been Hutch, not caring enough to fight for her, even after all the dreams and hopes they'd shared, trampling her heart to dust, leaving her self-esteem in shreds. Then along came Jeffrey, the knight in tarnished armor. Had he ever really loved her or had he simply *wanted* her sexually? She'd never thought of herself as anything more than moderately attractive, but she'd had her share of admirers—too many of them shallow and inherently noncommittal.

Sure enough, the picture of her and Hutch in the three-legged race had been taken down, along with the bitchy remark that had accompanied it, but the smear campaign against the errant groom continued, unabated.

That troubled Kendra—made her feel defensive on Hutch's behalf—which was probably just more proof that she was teetering on the edge of the same old dark abyss as before, when he'd essentially handed her over to Jeffrey like a book he'd already read and hadn't found all that interesting in the first place.

She sighed, clicked over to her email.

There were friendly notes from both Tara and Joslyn, along with one from Treat McQuillan. Kendra had, of course, given him the address she used for business, after he'd stopped by the office late that afternoon to pick up his keys. He had seemed pleased about putting his double-wide up for sale and moving on to whatever it was he meant to move on to; they'd come to terms quickly and the contract was signed.

But this was her personal email account—supposedly, only friends knew it.

Hi, Kendra, the deputy had written, as though they were pals from way back. The rodeo is coming up this weekend, as you know, and I was wondering if you'd like to go with me. If you got a sitter, we could have some dinner and stay up late to watch the fireworks. Maybe even make a few of our own.

Instinctively, Kendra lifted her fingertips off the keyboard, as if it had suddenly turned slimy. *Maybe even make a few of our own.*

Was he kidding?

She recalled McQuillan's tirade in the Butter Biscuit Café that morning, when he'd practically ordered her to stay away from Hutch Carmody—as if he had the right to dictate *anything* to her.

And now he had the nerve to suggest *fireworks?* Where did he get off, making a remark like that?

She breathed in, breathed out. Lowered her fingers back to the keyboard, and replied, Thanks for the invitation, but I've already made other plans. Also, I normally try to keep my business and social lives separate. Best, Kendra Shepherd.

The message was short, to the point and only partially true. She *did* have other plans, heaven help her, to go the rodeo, the carnival and the fireworks display with Hutch, bringing Madison along. And socializing was a big part of her business; she did a lot of lunches and dinners, sometimes threw parties for clients, and before Madison entered her life, she'd dated the occasional business contact, too, though only casually.

Seeing Deputy McQuillan on a potentially romantic basis, however, was certainly not in her game plan. She didn't find him attractive, but that was the least of it. She disliked him; it was that simple. He went around with the proverbial chip on his shoulder and the way he'd treated Brylee at the bar that night didn't do him any credit, either.

The male ego being what it was, Kendra fully expected McQuillan to respond to her refusal, however politely it had been offered, by firing her and finding someone else to sell his home for him. There were two or three other real estate brokers in the county, each with a few sales agents on staff, but hers was the only firm in Parable.

A competent businesswoman, through and through, Kendra hated to miss out on a commission, even the relatively modest one she could expect if she found a buyer for the deputy's mobile home, but if things went down that way, so be it. Even at best, real estate was a catch-as-catch-can affair—you showed a lot of houses, the more the better, and if you worked hard and had decent luck, you eventually sold a few.

McQuillan's response popped up in her online mailbox just as she was about to shut down the computer, push back her chair and brew another cup of herbal tea.

You think you're too good for me? was all he'd written, in a line of lowercase letters, oddly spaced and with no punctuation.

A chill slithered down her spine, but anger immediately quelled it. Please see the first email, she responded tersely, and hit Send.

He replied within seconds, but Kendra didn't open the new message. She blocked any further communications from Deputy McQuillan's email address and logged off with an irritated flourish.

Was the man merely obnoxious, she wondered, storming back to the kitchen, or did he present an actual threat of some sort?

She considered calling Boone, not as a citizen of Parable County, but as a friend, but she quickly disregarded the impulse. The sheriff had a wide area to police and, besides, sending rude emails wasn't a crime. If it were, she thought, with a tight little smile, she'd probably be in the slammer herself, with Brylee and her posse for company.

Kendra brewed that second cup of tea she'd promised herself earlier and sat down to drink it, silently reminding herself that she didn't have to make all her life decisions that very night, or the next day, or even next year.

She would stop pushing the river, as the saying went, and just let things unfold at their own pace—even if it killed her.

BOONE AND HUTCH met at the Butter Biscuit Café for breakfast the next morning, both ordering the special, as they did whenever they had a free morning, their joking excuse being that they shouldn't be expected to eat their own cooking day in and day out just because they weren't married.

"Did McQuillan go ahead and file charges against Walker Parrish?" Hutch asked, looking across the table at Boone while they waited for the first round of coffee.

"Hell, yes," Boone said, looking as weary as he sounded. His kids were due to arrive soon, probably on an afternoon bus, and while he seemed anxious to see them, it was obvious that he was already dreading the whole thing, too. "I would have had to arrest Walker, except I called Judge Renson ahead of time and she went ahead and set bail before the fact. Walker paid it, of course, so he didn't wind up in my jail, but he still has to go to court in six weeks or so and answer to an assault charge."

Hutch sighed, swore under his breath. "I've always wondered why Slade didn't fire McQuillan when he was sheriff. Now I'm wondering the same thing about you, old buddy. The man's a hothead—the original loose cannon—not to mention a pain in the ass."

"It's not that simple," Boone answered, "and you damn well know it. We're all civil service, remember, and while my recommendation carries some weight, the powers that be aren't going to let Treat go on the grounds that nobody likes him."

The pancakes arrived, stacks of them, teetering on two plates, and Essie herself did the honors, setting the meals down in front of Hutch and Boone with a deft swoop of each arm.

"On the house," she said, with a sidelong glance at Boone. "Even if you *did* give my favorite niece a speeding ticket last week. Now her insurance premium will go up."

Boone chuckled hoarsely, distractedly. "It's Carmody's turn to pick up the check anyhow," he said, then added, "Tell Laurie to keep her foot out of the carburetor of that little car of hers and *poof,* the problem's solved. No more tickets."

Essie shook her head as though she wouldn't have expected any other reaction from the boneheaded likes of Boone Taylor, and walked away.

"Looking forward to seeing your boys again?" Hutch asked after they'd both drenched their buttery pancakes in thick syrup.

"Of course I am," Boone snapped, downright peckish now. "I just wish I had a better place to put them up, that's all."

"There's no better place than home, Boone, and as far as those little boys are concerned, home is wherever you are."

Boone glowered at him over the towering pancakes. "Excuse me for saying so," he growled, "but you don't know F-all about raising kids, now do you?"

Hutch slanted the side of his fork through the syrupy stack on his plate. "You're already moderating your language," he observed lightly. "That's good. Can't have the munchkins picking up all kinds of dirty words from dear old Dad."

"Shut up," Boone said without much conviction.

Hutch chuckled and took a big bite of his food. While he was still chewing, Slade wandered into the café, taking off his hat as he crossed the threshold.

Hutch waved him over and Slade joined them, drawing back a chair and sinking into it.

"Ever since you stole Opal out from under us," Slade told Hutch, probably only half kidding, "I've been having cold cereal for breakfast."

"What a pity." Hutch grinned with mock sympathy. "Poor you."

"How're Joslyn and the baby doing?" Boone asked between bites.

At the mere mention of his wife and child, a light seemed to go on inside Slade. His eyes twinkled and he grinned. "They're good," he said. Then the grin faded. "I'm a little worried about Shea, though," he added, lowering his voice, since the place was doing a brisk trade, as always.

Essie appeared table-side, wielded the coffeepot she carried and took Slade's order for a pancake special like the ones his friends had.

When she was gone again, bustling off to the kitchen to confer with the fry cook, Boone said, "Shea? She's a good kid—never gets in any trouble as far as I know."

Slade sighed, ran a hand through his dark hair in a gesture of suppressed agitation. "She *is* a good kid," he agreed. "But she's normal, too."

"I don't follow," Boone said, still scarfing up pancakes like there was no tomorrow. To look at him, a person would think he hadn't eaten in a week.

Hutch wondered idly if Shea had gotten herself a boyfriend, thereby rousing her stepfather's famously protective instincts, but it wasn't his business either way, so he didn't ask outright. He just went right on putting away his breakfast and swilling his coffee.

"The Fourth is coming up in a few days," Slade reminded Boone unnecessarily. "You know how it is. During the fireworks, a few kids always climb the water tower to get a better look. Joslyn overheard Shea saying something about it to a friend on her cell phone."

Hutch felt a mild twinge at the mere mention of the water tower, but neither Boone nor Slade would have noticed, being intent on their own concerns, and that was fine with him.

"And you think she's planning to scale the tower with some of her high school pals?" Boone prompted, sounding mildly amused now.

"We've both asked her, Joslyn and I, I mean, and she says she wouldn't do anything that stupid," Slade said. "But—"

"Climbing the water tower is dangerous," Boone agreed, making a gruff attempt at reassurance, "but it isn't illegal, as you know."

"Couldn't you station a deputy out there on Saturday night," Slade pressed, "just to keep an eye on things?"

Boone was clearly regretful as he spread his hands in a gesture meant to convey helplessness. "You ought to know better than anybody, Slade, that I don't have that kind of manpower. And I need the few deputies I have to keep the celebrating down to a dull roar. Folks get all riled up after the rodeo and a few spins on the Tilt-a-Whirl over at the carnival, not to mention the beer and the dancing at the Boot Scoot and then the fireworks to top it all off."

"Damn it, Boone," Slade argued, just as Essie returned to set his plate down in front of him with a thump, "some kid could fall and break their neck. Whatever happened to 'serve and protect'?"

"I can't be everywhere at once," Boone pointed out reasonably. "Neither can my deputies. The best I can promise is that somebody will drive by the water tower once in a while to make sure everything's all right."

Slade seemed to deflate a little. "Then I'll watch the place myself," he said. "During the fireworks, anyhow."

Boone held up his fork, like a teacher about to point to something written on a blackboard. "You're not sheriff anymore," he said. "And you're not a deputy, either. Keep an eye on Shea if you're concerned and leave it to the other parents to do the same for their own kids. That tower is a menace, I grant you, but kids have been climbing it since right after the turn of the last century and nobody's ever actually taken a header off it in all those years, now have they?"

"There's always a first time," Slade grumbled, but he began to eat his pancakes.

Hutch didn't bring up the obvious solution—which was to just pull the water tower down, once and for all, and haul off the debris—because better people than he had lobbied for that for a couple of decades now and gotten nowhere. Besides, he wasn't inclined to remind Slade of that humiliating afternoon when they were kids and he'd gotten stuck up there himself, scared shitless and unable to move until his half brother alternately goaded and cajoled him down.

Now mercifully—at least for Hutch—the conversation took a different turn. Slade asked how long Boone's boys would be staying with him and Boone said only until Sunday night because they were both attending summer school this year.

"Summer school?" Hutch echoed. "Damn, Boone, that's harsh. Summers are for goofing off—for swimming and playing baseball and riding horses until all hours, not beating the books. And, anyway, those kids are what, six and seven years old?"

Boone favored his friend with a reproving glance. "Thank you for your profound wisdom, Professor Carmody," he drawled. "I guess if I wanted to raise a couple of cowboys, that approach would suit me just fine. It just so happens that I don't."

"What's wrong with cowboys?" Slade interjected, being one.

"If you wanted to *raise* Griff and Fletch," Hutch retorted, leaning forward to show Boone he wasn't cowed by his tone *or* his badge, "they'd be living with you, like they should."

Boone flushed from the base of his neck to the underside of his jaw. "Opinions are like assholes," he told Hutch, in a terse undertone. "Everybody has one."

Hutch grinned, picked up his coffee cup and raised it to Boone in a sort of mocking toast. "Good thing you went to college, Boone," he said. "You might not have such a good grasp on human anatomy if you were, say, *just a cowboy.*"

Slade chuckled, but offered no comment. By and large, he wasn't much for chitchat. He'd said his piece, about Shea and the water tower, and now he was probably done talking, for the most part.

Boone huffed out a breath, plainly exasperated. "Tell me this," he demanded in a hoarse whisper. "Why does everybody in this blasted county feel obliged to tell me what's best for *my* kids?"

Slade and Hutch exchanged glances, but it was Essie, back to refill their coffee cups from the carafe in her right hand, who actually answered.

"Maybe," she said crisply, "it's because you can't seem to figure it out on your own, Boone Taylor. Those boys need their daddy."

KENDRA, MADISON AND Daisy passed the fairgrounds on their way to the community center and preschool, and Madison could barely contain her excitement. The carnival was setting up for business; banners flew in the warm breeze and a Ferris wheel towered against the sky. Carousel horses, giraffes, elephants and swans waited to take their places on the merry-go-round, hoisted there by teams of men in work clothes, and cars, trucks and vans were parked, helter-skelter, outside the exhibition hall where vendors and artisans from all over the state were getting ready to display their wares. The Fourth of July weekend was a big money-maker for practically every business in town and it was coming up fast.

"Look, Mommy!" Madison called out as though Kendra could possibly have missed the colorful spectacle taking shape on the fairgrounds. "It's a circus!"

Kendra smiled. "Actually, it's a carnival. And we're going there on Saturday, remember?"

"Couldn't we go *now?* Just to look?"

"No, sweetie," Kendra responded, signaling for a turn onto the street that led to the community center. "It's time for preschool. Besides, the carnival isn't open for business yet."

"When does it open?"

"Not until Friday afternoon," she said. "That's two days from now, so it's three days until Saturday, when we'll go to the rodeo, and then the carnival, and then the fireworks."

"Mr. Carmody is going to ride a bull in the rodeo part," Madison said, mollified enough to move on to the next topic. "We get to watch."

Kendra swallowed. She didn't know which scared her more, the prospect of letting Hutch slip past her inner barriers again—he was bound to score, eventually—or the thought of him riding two thousand pounds of crazy bull, risking life and limb.

And for what? A fancy belt buckle and prize money that probably didn't amount to the cash he routinely carried in his wallet—*if* he won?

He was wild and reckless, a kid in a man's body. Mentally, she added bull-riding to the long list of reasons why Hutch Carmody was her own personal Mr. Wrong.

She made the turn, headed toward the community center.

Glancing into the rearview mirror, she saw Daisy standing with her paws on the back of the seat, gazing out the rear window as the fairgrounds disappeared from view.

"Does Daisy get to go to the rodeo, too?" Madison queried, from her safety seat.

"That wouldn't be a good place for her, sweetheart," Kendra explained. "She could get lost or hurt somehow and, besides, all that noise would probably scare her."

"Won't she be scared if she's all alone at home?" Madison fretted.

"She'll be just fine," Kendra said gently.

They'd reached the community center by then, and a little girl immediately broke away from the crowd of children on the grassy playground, running to greet them.

"That's Becky," Madison said, delighted. "She's my best friend in the whole world!"

Kendra smiled, watching as Becky, a small dynamo with blond pigtails, dashed in their direction. The little girl wore jeans, a ruffled cotton blouse and a pair of neon pink cowgirl boots—possibly the same pair Madison had appropriated—along with a broad grin.

Evidently, all was forgiven.

Madison wriggled out of her car seat and jumped to the ground while Daisy, excited, barked and scrambled around inside the Volvo.

"This is my mommy," Madison told Becky, indicating Kendra, who stood beside the driver's door in her working-mother outfit, a trim beige pantsuit, expensively tailored. "Mommy, this is Becky. She's six already, but she likes me anyway, even though I'm only four."

Becky stopped, looked up into Kendra's face, squinting a little against the bright sunshine and said, "My mom is going to call you on the phone. She says both of you have to get to know each other a little before there can be any sleepovers for Madison and me."

"I'll look forward to hearing from your mom," Kendra said, offering a hand. Privately, she thought Madison was still too young for sleepovers, but she didn't want to cast a pall over the girls' day by saying so now.

The child shook Kendra's hand without hesitation. "Mom says," she went on cheerfully, "that for all you know, we could be a family of ax-murderers."

Kendra chuckled. "I doubt that," she said, though she was a little taken aback by the graphic visual that came to mind. Becky's family must have moved to Parable recently, because she couldn't place them.

Madison waved at Daisy, who had wriggled into the front passenger seat at some point and was pressing her nose against the inside of the windshield, and waited politely while Kendra bent to give her a see-you-later kiss on the forehead.

"Be a good girl," Kendra said.

Madison, young as she was, actually rolled her eyes in what appeared to be comical disdain. "I will," she replied. "Mostly."

"Try to do a little better than 'mostly,' please," Kendra instructed, folding her arms and tilting her head to one side, letting her eyes do the smiling while her mouth pretended sternness.

Madison and Becky clasped hands, giggling, and ran toward the throng of children and playground attendants up ahead.

Kendra watched until they were safely enfolded in the group, then got back into her car, told a fretful Daisy that everything would be all right and drove off.

Deputy McQuillan was waiting on the sidewalk in front of her office, once again in full uniform.

Daisy growled at him, at the same time cowering a little.

"Good morning," Kendra said with a businesslike smile.

McQuillan looked down at the little dog—for the briefest moment Kendra thought he might try to kick Daisy, there was so much distaste in his expression— then turned his attention back to her. "I've decided to get another real estate agent," he announced bluntly. His eyes fairly snapped with suppressed fury.

Kendra shifted her keys from her left hand to her right and unlocked the office door, gently urging Daisy inside. The pup took refuge under the desk Joslyn used when she came in.

"That's certainly your prerogative," Kendra said with cool dignity, setting down her purse and keys. She took their listing agreement from her in-box and handed it across to Deputy McQuillan.

He tore the document into two pieces and threw them at her, before stalking out of the office and slamming the door behind him.

"That certainly went well," Kendra told Daisy ruefully as the dog low-crawled out from under Joslyn's desk, now that the coast was clear.

For the next hour, Kendra busied herself with routine tasks—reading and replying to emails, initiating and returning phone calls, and surfing the web for for-sale-by-owner listings in the surrounding area.

She came up dry that morning, though, and was thinking about locking up the office and playing hooky for the rest of the day when Walker Parrish came in again.

Daisy went right over to him, and he laughed as he bent to ruffle the dog's ears in greeting.

"My friend's decided she'd like to take a firsthand look at your house," Walker told Kendra. Once again she thought how attractive he was, and marveled that he didn't do a thing for her. "Casey's on the road with her band until after the Fourth, but she says she could stop in for a quick look at the place late next week."

"Not Casey Elder?" Kendra asked, surprised to find herself holding her breath for the answer. She'd dealt with a number of celebrities in the course of her job, and she wasn't the type to be starstruck, but Ms. Elder just happened to be one of the biggest names in country music and Kendra was most definitely a fan.

"Well," Walker said sheepishly, "yeah. But I wasn't supposed to mention her name."

Kendra smiled to reassure him. "Your secret is safe with me," she said lightly, "but the minute Ms. Elder sets foot in Parable, everybody is going to know it. She is, after all, a superstar."

Walker chuckled. "She considered wearing a disguise," he admitted.

"A pair of horn-rimmed glasses with a big plastic nose and a mustache attached?" Kendra joked. Then, more seriously, she added, "It must be difficult, being so recognizable."

"Casey copes with her fame pretty well," Walker said, while Daisy sat gazing up at him in her usual adoring way. "And I assured her that while she has a big following around here, nobody's likely to mob her or anything."

That was true enough. People would be curious about her, especially at first, but if Casey Elder decided to become a permanent part of the community, she'd be welcomed with casseroles and supper invitations, like any other newcomer.

"I take it she liked the pictures you took when we went through the house the other day?" Kendra prompted, wondering about the connection between Walker and Casey and immediately deciding it was none of her business. She certainly wasn't about to ask.

"She liked them, all right," Walker answered, looking as though he wanted to say more but wasn't sure he should.

"You told her the asking price?"

"She didn't bat an eye," Walker said with a nod.

He still had that peculiar look on his face.

"Walker," Kendra nudged, "what is it?"

"Casey's from Dallas," he said uneasily. "I'm not sure she understands what it means to live in a small town, even though she writes and sings songs about it all the time."

Kendra folded her arms, tilted her head to one side and waited. What on earth was going on here?

"Casey and I—" Walker began, stopping to clear his throat. "We have a—complicated relationship."

So, Kendra thought, *my hunch was right. They're more than just friends.*

"No need to explain," Kendra said briskly.

Walker looked miserably determined to go on. "We were never married—never even involved, really, but—" He paused, swallowed visibly. "But Casey's kids are both mine."

Kendra barely kept her mouth from dropping open. What he'd said didn't surprise her as much as the fact that he'd said it at all. "I don't—" she began, and then gave up on completing the sentence.

"The thing is, they don't know it yet," Walker went on. "The kids, I mean. Casey and I want to break it to them gently, once they've gotten settled and everything."

"It's a secret, then," Kendra said quietly.

Walker nodded, shoved a hand through his hair, slapped his hat against his thigh once, lightly. "Nobody else knows," he said. "Not even Brylee."

"Then why tell me?"

"I'm not sure," Walker said, looking flustered. It

was odd, seeing him like this, when he was usually so self-possessed.

Kendra made a lip-zipping motion with one hand. "I won't breathe a word," she promised.

Walker's grin was appreciative and she could tell he was relieved. "Thanks," he said. "Casey will be calling you one day soon. To make an appointment to see the house, I mean."

"Great," Kendra said. "I hope she likes it."

"Me, too," Walker said very quietly. Almost, Kendra thought, wistfully.

She shook off the romantic notion. Ever since Hutch had kissed her down by Whisper Creek, she'd been prone to overthink the whole concept of love.

Walker started for the door, and Kendra returned to her chair behind her desk, smiled a goodbye when he looked back at her over one broad shoulder.

"Interesting," she told Daisy, once he'd gone.

Daisy went back under Joslyn's desk and was soon snoring.

Kendra fidgeted. The urge to call Joslyn or Tara or both of them at once to find out if either of them knew anything about Walker and Casey Elder was strong, but she never really considered giving in to it. After all, she'd promised not to tell what she knew, and if there was one thing Kendra Shepherd believed in, it was keeping promises.

CHAPTER FIFTEEN

SATURDAY MORNING ARRIVED right on schedule, although Madison had seemed certain it would somehow be postponed, if not canceled entirely.

The weather was warm and brilliantly sunny, the sky an achy blue that left sweetly tender bruises on Kendra's heart as she stood at the kitchen sink, her arms plunged into hot, soapy water, gazing out the window as she finished washing the breakfast dishes. By her calculations, two bowls, a couple of spoons and the pot she'd cooked the oatmeal in didn't justify running the machine and, besides, she needed to keep her hands busy.

It had been a couple of days since she'd last seen Hutch, but he'd called once, said he'd pick her and Madison up for the rodeo and the other festivities around eleven-thirty, if that was okay with her. He'd sounded almost shy, but that was probably some kind of ruse.

Hutch Carmody didn't have a shy bone in his red-hot cowboy body.

She'd replied in a blasé tone that eleven-thirty would probably be fine and been jittery every waking minute since, much to her private chagrin, wondering if this get-together qualified as an actual *date* or, since Madison was going along, just a friendly outing. Deciding what to wear wasn't a problem: a long-sleeved T-shirt, jeans and sneakers—she didn't own boots—would fill the bill just fine, for both her and Madison. *But what about my hair?* she dithered. What about makeup? She wanted to look her best, of course, but not as though she was hoping she and Hutch could slip away alone at some point and make their way up the mountainside to the magic meadow.

Was she a bad mother for even *thinking* such a thought? Madison had separation issues, though she seemed more secure every day, settling in well at pre-school and in the new house and, anyway, there were only a few people Kendra would feel comfortable leaving her daughter with—Joslyn and Tara, certainly, and of course Opal. But they would all be busy with their own plans, wouldn't they? And, besides, any one of them, if asked to babysit, would instantly guess why Kendra wanted to disappear for a while.

Behind her, Madison and Daisy scuffled on the linoleum floor, Madison laughing with delight, Daisy barking exuberantly, as she always did when they played.

Kendra emptied the sink of water, rinsed her hands under the tap, dried them on her flowered apron, and turned to smile at the pair of them, girl and dog, raising her voice just enough to be heard over all that happiness. "We'd better get going," she said, "if we're going to drive Daisy out to Tara's place and get back in time to meet Mr. Carmody."

Tara had suggested the canine sleepover, reminding Kendra that it would be quieter out there in the country, far from the Fourth of July fireworks, and thus not so frightening for Daisy. Plus, Lucy would be there and the pups could keep each other company. In the morning, Tara could bring Daisy home or Kendra could pick her up on the chicken farm, whichever worked out best.

Madison, fairly bursting with excitement—new boots *and* a day with Hutch Carmody, would wonders never cease?—nodded hard enough to give herself whiplash. She'd been making a ruckus ever since they'd finished breakfast, trying to keep busy until it was time to go.

It was hard to say which event Madison was most excited about: choosing the promised cowgirl boots, watching Hutch ride a bull in the rodeo, going on rides at the carnival, or taking in the fireworks, which weren't even scheduled to begin until ten o'clock, when the sky would finally be dark enough to launch the first sprays of multicolored light against a black velvet background.

This would be a long day for Madison, Kendra thought not for the first time, when they were all in the Volvo, seat belts fastened. She bit her lower lip as she backed the car down the short driveway and eased carefully onto the street. It would be a long day for *her,* too, given that Hutch would be at her side for most of it.

What did they really have to talk about, she and Hutch, once they got past hello? Not the old days, certainly—*how about all that steamy sex we used to have?*—and the present didn't offer a lot of topics, either.

And what if she just kept reliving that sizzling kiss by the creek the whole day and night? She'd be in a perpetual state of arousal, with nothing left of her but smoldering embers by the time it was all over.

"Can we buy Daisy a present at the rodeo?" Madison asked from her safety seat when they were well on their way to Tara's. "And for Leviticus and Lucy, too?"

Kendra knew the little girl was fretting about the

dogs being left alone, thinking they might be lonely or scared, even with each other for company. "I think that's a fine idea," she said, smiling. "Tell you what—while we're looking for those boots of yours, we'll keep an eye out for something they'd like."

Madison cheered at that, and Daisy started barking all over again, sharing in the headiness of the moment.

Tara came out of the main chicken coop when they drove up, wearing work clothes and scattering indignant hens in all directions as she came toward the car.

"You're not going to the rodeo like that, are you?" Madison asked with great concern as soon as they'd come to a stop and Tara had opened the back door of the car to help her out of the seat. "You have chicken poop on your shoes."

Tara laughed and shook her head, but before she could reply, Lucy came bounding down the front steps from the shady porch, barking gleefully. This, of course, got Daisy all worked up again and the canine chorus began.

"I'm not much for rodeos," Tara explained when the din subsided a little and Madison was out of the car seat. "But I'll be in town later for the fireworks." A pause. "Without the poopy shoes, of course."

By then, Daisy and Lucy were playing a merry game of chase, and Madison ran right along with them, transcendence in motion, the sunlight catching in her coppery curls.

Watching, Kendra felt literally swamped with love and gratitude. She was so blessed, she thought. She had everything a woman could want.

Then the memory of Hutch's kiss sneaked up on her,

as it had a way of doing, and heat swept through her in a fiery flood.

Okay, she clarified to herself. She had *almost* everything.

Tara, meanwhile, took in Kendra's French braid, small gold earrings and carefully applied makeup, and looked fondly sly. "Don't *you* look nice today?" she drawled. Then, in a lower voice, though Madison couldn't possibly have heard her over all that racket she and the dogs were making, "Why, if I didn't know better, I'd think you were looking for a little Hutch-action."

"Oh, please," Kendra said, averting her eyes for a moment.

Hutch-action, she thought. *Oh, Lord.*

Tara merely folded her arms and raised her perfect eyebrows. She might have been wearing dirty coveralls and manure-caked shoes, but she still managed to look like the class act she was, right down to the double helix of her DNA.

"Madison will be with us the whole time," Kendra pointed out when her friend didn't say anything more, probably because she didn't have to, having made her point. "What could happen?"

"Nothing," Tara admitted, pleased. "But that doesn't mean all that time together isn't going to crank up the dials. I don't know why you and Hutch don't just—" she leaned in now, and dropped her voice to a whisper "—*do it.* It's going to happen, you know. It's inevitable, fated, meant to be."

"No," Kendra argued too fiercely, "it *isn't* going to happen, because I won't let it!" Deep down, though, she wasn't so sure, because some part of her had been hankering to head for the meadow ever since Hutch had reminded her of the things they'd done there, back in the day. "This is just an outing, nothing more." She counted off the events on her fingers. "Rodeo. Carnival. Fireworks. Over."

"Right," Tara said. She wasn't actually smirking, but she was close to it.

That was when Kendra blurted it out, the thing she hadn't meant to say at all, to anyone. Ever. "What are we going to *talk about* for a whole day?"

Tara's smile turned gentle and she touched Kendra's arm. "You and Hutch don't need a script, honey," she said. "Just let things *happen*. Roll with it, so to speak."

"Easy for you to say," Kendra pointed out. "You'll be here, shoveling chicken poop all day!"

"Some people have all the luck," Tara confirmed wryly as Madison left the dogs and came toward them. Daisy and Lucy were settling down in the shade of a nearby tree for an impromptu nap.

"Let's *go*, Mommy," Madison said eagerly, clasping Kendra's hand. "It's almost time for Mr. Carmody to come and get us, isn't it?"

"We have a little while yet, sweetheart," Kendra assured her child after a glance at her watch.

"Come inside and have some lemonade, then," Tara said. "I just made it fresh this morning, before I went out to do the chores."

Madison looked doubtful. Like most children and all too many grown-ups, she probably thought she could make the minutes pass faster just by force of will, and she was a nervous wreck from the effort.

"I also have cookies," Tara bargained with an understanding smile.

"What kind?" Madison wanted to know.

"Madison." Kendra sighed.

Tara chuckled. "Chocolate chip," she said.

"Just one then," Madison agreed.

"Madison Shepherd," Kendra said. "What do you say when someone very kindly offers you lemonade and cookies?"

"If it's somebody I know, you mean?" Madison asked. "Because I'm not supposed to talk to strangers, am I?"

Kendra suppressed a sigh. "No," she answered patiently. "You most certainly aren't. But Tara isn't a stranger."

Madison beamed, remembering her manners at last, or maybe just willing to use them. "Yes, please," she told Tara triumphantly, like a quiz show contestant coming up with the right answer and thus taking home the prize.

They all went inside, Tara leaving her dirty shoes behind on the step, followed by the sleepy dogs, who both curled up on Lucy's fluffy dog bed in a corner of Tara's kitchen, Daisy's head resting companionably on the scruff of Lucy's neck, both of them awash in the summer sunlight pouring in through a nearby window. They shimmered.

Tara, as charmed by the scene as Kendra was, quietly got out her cell phone and snapped a picture of the pair.

"I'll send you a copy," she said, setting the phone aside.

Kendra nodded, and she and Madison went off to the powder room to wash their hands.

When they got back to the kitchen a couple of minutes later, Tara was pouring lemonade into cut-crystal glasses, and chocolate chip cookies beckoned from an exquisite china plate.

Kendra smiled at the contrast between the old farm-house and Tara's elegant possessions, vestiges of her other life back in New York. Close as they were, Tara had been fairly tight-lipped about her pre-Parable life—she'd admitted to a bitter divorce and a passion to rein-vent herself completely, but that was about all.

Both Joslyn and Kendra figured Tara would open up to them when she was ready and, in the meantime, they were content with things as they were.

Tara, Kendra and Madison chatted amiably while they enjoyed the refreshments, and then it was finally time to go back to town, much to Madison's delight.

The little girl said goodbye to Daisy, who barely opened her eyes in response, and Kendra thanked Tara for everything, offered up a see-you-later.

Madison and Kendra had been home for fifteen min-utes or so when Kendra heard the sound of a vehicle rolling into the driveway.

"He's here!" Madison shouted from the living room. She'd been keeping watch at the window from the mo-ment they got back from Tara's. "And he's in a shiny truck!"

Kendra had never known Hutch to drive anything but one of the battered old pickups used on the ranch—he seemed content to take whichever one wasn't in use at the moment. She, like most people, tended to forget that he had money, and plenty of it, because he lived simply and never flaunted his wealth.

She went out onto the back porch, her heart ham-mering under her sensible shirt, and watched as Hutch climbed out of a red, extended-cab pickup, the rig gleaming in the sunlight.

"New truck?" she asked. Her heartbeat thundered in her ears, but she probably looked calm on the outside.

Or so she hoped.

"I'm taking it for a test drive," Hutch said. His hair was a little too long and slightly tousled, and he wore a black hat, jeans, a colorful shirt and clean but service-able boots. He was, Kendra was reminded, planning to ride in the rodeo later that day. "Like it?"

"It's…nice…" she said, rattled. If she asked him not to enter the bull-riding, would he agree?

She'd never know, because asking was out of the question.

Madison, meanwhile, dashed past Kendra, linger-ing on the porch, and fairly catapulted her small body into Hutch's arms.

He caught her deftly and plunked his hat on her head with a laugh. Her whole face disappeared under the crown. "Hey, short-stuff," he said. "Ready for a big day?"

Madison peeked out from under the hat, transfigured by the sheer magic of Hutch Carmody. "We're buying boots!" she crowed.

Hutch chuckled again, shifting her easily to his left hip. "So I hear," he said. "You look mighty good in that hat, cowgirl. Maybe we ought to get you one of those, too."

Kendra opened her mouth to protest—she worked hard not to spoil Madison, and it wasn't easy because her tendency was to grant every whim—but closed it again in the next instant.

It's no big deal, she told herself.

Hutch's gaze swung back to her then, and he let it roam over her briefly. Appreciation sparked in his eyes.

"Pretty as a mountain meadow," he commented smoothly.

Kendra felt that now-familiar surge of heat go through her. Such an innocent-sounding reference and, at the same time, a bold invitation.

Or was it more of a promise?

"Thanks," she said, hurrying back into the house in an effort to hide her pink face. Once there, she dragged in several deep breaths, struggling to regain her composure, and took her time getting her handbag, making sure all the stove burners were turned off and the doors were locked.

When she came outside again, Hutch had installed Madison and her car seat in the spiffy truck.

With a laugh, Madison plopped his hat back on his head, and it landed askew, pushing down the tops of his ears. He made a goofy face for the child's benefit before straightening it, and Madison found that uproariously funny.

"Ready?" he asked almost gruffly when he turned his attention on Kendra.

It was a loaded question. He was asking about more than the rodeo and the carnival and a fireworks display, and she couldn't pretend not to know it.

She said nothing, because "no" would have been a lie and "yes" would lead to all sorts of problems.

He grinned, reading her well, and held open the passenger door for her. He did give her a brief boost when she stepped up onto the high running board, the way he'd done when they went riding.

She blushed hotly and refused to look at him, staring straight through the windshield when he chuck-led again, shut the truck door and came around to the driver's side.

During the short ride to the fairgrounds, Madison made conversation between the adults unnecessary, if not impossible, chattering away about Ruffles—she couldn't wait to ride again, would they be doing that soon?—and her new boots and whether she should get a pink cowgirl hat or a red one.

The parking lot at the fairgrounds was already burst-ing with rigs of various kinds, but Hutch found a spot for the truck and had Madison out of her safety seat and standing in the gravel before Kendra had alighted and walked around to their side.

Hutch gave her a sidelong look, grinned and set his hat down on her head. "Relax," he said. "You've got a pint-size chaperone here, and that means I'll have to behave myself, now doesn't it?"

The hat smelled pleasantly of Hutch—sun-dried cot-ton, fresh country air and the faintest tinge of new-mown grass—and, for just a moment, Kendra allowed herself to revel in the moment, as happy as Madison had been when she wore Hutch's hat back at the house.

Her hands shook a little as she lifted it off and handed it back, and the question she'd promised her-self she wouldn't ask tumbled out of her mouth with no prompting from her addled brain.

"You're dead-set on this bull-riding thing?"

Hutch regarded her for a long moment, his expres-sion unreadable. "Does it matter?" he asked.

Madison, by that time, had taken his hand and was trying to drag him toward the ticket booth, some fifty yards away.

Kendra sighed. "Yes," she admitted as he took her hand and Madison pulled them across the lot like a little tugboat. "It matters."

"That's interesting," Hutch said. "Why?"

"Why, what?" Kendra was stalling now. She was between a rock and a hard place, and there was no way to extricate herself. If she asked Hutch not to ride, she'd seem controlling, and he'd probably refuse to skip the event just because he was stubborn. If she *didn't* ask, on the other hand, she'd have lost her one chance to make sure he didn't break his damn fool neck in front of her, half the county and, worst of all, Madison.

"Why does it matter?" Hutch pressed quietly.

"I'd hate to see you get hurt, that's all," Kendra said in a light tone that didn't match the urgency she felt. Madison, the human tugboat, was within earshot, after all.

"I'd hate to see that, too," Hutch said, one side of his mouth tilting up in a classic Hutch Carmody grin. "But I don't believe in sitting on the sidelines, Kendra, just to be safe. I *love* the rodeo, especially the bull-riding."

She felt frustrated and something was doing the jitterbug in the pit of her stomach, on icy feet, even though it would be a couple of hours before he actually climbed down off the catwalk and into the chute where an angry bull would be waiting for him.

"You're not scared?" she asked against her will.

They'd reached the winding line in front of the ticket booth by then, and Madison let go of Hutch's hand and fidgeted.

"What if all the boots are gone when we get there?" she fretted.

Hutch touched the top of her head lightly and briefly

and in a very daddylike way. "No worries, short-stuff," he assured the child, though his gaze was still fastened to Kendra's face. "There will be plenty to choose from when our turn comes."

If *she'd* said something like that, Madison probably would have ratcheted up the angst another notch, but the little dickens settled right down after Hutch spoke to her.

Kendra rested her hands on her hips, waited for him to answer her last question.

He grinned. "Walker Parrish has some famously nasty bulls in his string of rodeo stock, and flinging cowboys three ways from Sunday is what those critters do best, so, yeah, I might be a little nervous. I'd be an idiot if I wasn't."

"Then why do it?"

"Because I want to," Hutch said easily, "and because fear isn't a good enough reason to keep to the sidelines when there's living to do."

They'd reached the booth by then, so Kendra didn't reply. She just bit down hard on her lower lip while Hutch extracted his wallet from the hip pocket of his jeans and paid their admission.

Their hands were stamped, so they could come and go throughout the day, and Madison thought that was the coolest thing ever, especially when Hutch told her the mark would show up even in the dark.

Once they were inside the fairgrounds, Hutch crouched in front of Madison, pushed his hat to the back of his head, and looked the little girl straight in the eye. "You stick close to your mama and me, now," he said very seriously. "Will you do that, munchkin?"

Madison nodded solemnly.

Kendra's heart pinched, watching them together. Some things were so beautiful, they hurt.

Hutch straightened, shifted his hat. "Well, then, that's settled," he said. "Let's take a look around."

They headed for the exhibition hall first, where all the vendors had set up booths to market everything from handcrafted silver and turquoise jewelry, always popular with the rodeo set, to custom-made saddles and other tack. There were hats and boots galore, of course, in every conceivable size, style and color.

Madison zeroed in on a pair with a peacock-feather design sewn into the leather and rhinestone accents.

"These are pretty, aren't they?" she said, looking up at Hutch for his opinion.

A little stung that she hadn't been acknowledged, let alone consulted about the boots, Kendra began, "But they're too—"

Hutch silenced her by taking her hand and giving it a light, quick squeeze. "Mighty showy," he agreed thoughtfully, focused on Madison. "But stalls and barn-yards are messy places, and riding horses stirs up a lot of dust. Splashes up some creek water, too."

Madison tilted her head to one side, considering. Kendra might have been invisible, for all the notice the child paid her. Hutch's opinion was apparently all that mattered, at least in this situation.

"Boots aren't supposed to be pretty?" Madison asked, looking mildly disappointed. She was a girly-girl, as well as a sporty type, and she loved tutus, flashy toy jewelry and plastic high heels.

Hutch's grin was like a flash of sunlight on clear water. "Yes," he said. "They can be pretty. But a real cowgirl like you needs to think about how her boots are going to hold up over the long haul."

Madison was clearly puzzled.

"You need boots that will last," Kendra translated, glad to be of some help even if she was on the fringes of the question.

Madison weighed that. "Okay," she finally agreed. "Let's find some that will last *and* look pretty."

"Good plan," Hutch said with another sideways glance at Kendra, fueled by a grin that made her feel as though her clothes had just dissolved. "We'll keep looking until we find just the right pair."

Eventually, they did find the right pair for Madison. They were dark brown and sturdy, with a tiny pink rose stitched into the side of each shaft.

Kendra smiled as she handed her debit card to the merchant and shook her head at the offer of a box. "She'll wear them," she said. "Thanks anyway, though."

Madison, prancing around in the new boots like a little show pony angling for a blue ribbon, had forgotten all about the sneakers she'd been wearing before.

A cowgirl-Cinderella in boots instead of glass slippers, Madison twinkled like a fully lit Christmas tree, showing off for Hutch.

Prince Charming in jeans, Kendra reflected, taking a good long look at Hutch while he was busy raving over Madison's footwear.

Beware, said the voice of Kendra's rocky childhood, and her once broken, barely mended heart. *Danger ahead.*

But there was another voice in her head now, and it repeated something Hutch had said minutes before.

Fear isn't a good enough reason to keep to the side-lines when there's living to do.

Madison brought Kendra back to the here and now by tugging at her hand. "You need boots, too, Mommy," she said earnestly. "So you can go riding with Mr. Car-mody and me."

"True enough," Hutch said with a twinkle. "Boots are a requirement if you're going to travel farther than the creek."

The creek.

The *kiss*.

There she was again, stuck in the same old dilemma. If Madison was set on learning to ride for real—and she obviously wanted that very much—then Kendra, of course, would need to go along, at least until her daughter was older. Which meant she might as well invest in a pair of boots for herself—and it wasn't as if she couldn't afford the purchase. The rub was, doing that meant a lot more than just selecting the right size and style and paying up. It meant she was agreeing to not just one more horseback ride, but very possibly dozens of them.

With Hutch, it seemed, everything had at least two meanings.

It was maddening.

Half an hour later, Kendra was the owner of a pair of well-made and very practical black boots, with no frills whatsoever.

While she and Madison waited in the shade of an awning near the cluster of food concession booths, Hutch took the box out to the truck.

"I wanted to *wear* my boots," Madison said, turn-ing backward on the bench to stick both feet out so she could admire them. "Mr. Carmody says they have to be broken in right."

Mr. Carmody says this. Mr. Carmody says that.

Madison was obviously in love.

"Let me know if they start pinching your toes or rubbing against your heels," said Kendra, ever practical. "New shoes can do that."

Madison turned around, rolled her eyes once, and reached for one of the French fries from the order they were sharing. She swabbed it in catsup and steered it toward her mouth. "Cowgirls don't mind if their toes are pinched," she announced. "They're *tough*."

Kendra laughed, after reminding herself to lighten up a little. This was Madison's first pair of boots and she might remember this day all her life. And Kendra wanted that memory to be a good one.

"Yes," she agreed, "they are. And you are definitely a born cowgirl."

Madison was pleased, and dragged another French fry through the catsup just as Boone approached the table, flanked by two small, dark-haired boys—miniature versions of him.

They wore jeans and striped T-shirts and brand-new sneakers, and they both had freckles and a cowlick above their foreheads. If one of the little guys hadn't been almost a head taller than the other, they could have been mistaken for twins.

Looking at the children, Kendra saw their mother in them, as well as Boone, and a lump rose in her throat. She'd liked Corrie Taylor, and it still seemed impossible that she was gone.

"Well," Kendra said warmly, blinking a sheen of sudden moisture that blurred her vision. "Griffin and

Fletcher. You've grown so much I almost didn't recognize you."

The smaller of the two boys huddled shyly against Boone's side. Like his sons, he was wearing casual clothes; he rarely bothered with a uniform, and today he was probably off duty.

The taller boy put out a manly hand. "I'm Griff," he said. Naturally, he didn't remember her. Most likely she was just another friend of his mom and dad's, faintly familiar but mostly a stranger.

Madison, whose mouth was circled with catsup, regarded the boys with a curious combination of wariness and fascination. To her, they were probably members of an alien species.

Kendra shook the offered hand. "Hi, Griff," she said. "I'm Kendra." She peered around at the other little boy, who was still trying to hide behind Boone's leg. "Hello, there," she added.

"Fletch is sort of shy around the edges," Boone said, sounding pretty shy himself.

"This is my daughter, Madison," Kendra said to all three of them, gesturing.

"I have new boots," Madison said. She got down off the bench, rounded the picnic table, and walked right up to Griff, standing practically toe-to-toe with him. "See?"

Fletch peeked around Boone to take a look. "Girl boots," he scoffed, but there was a certain reluctant interest in his tone.

Boone chuckled and made a ruffling motion atop the boy's head. If the kid's hair hadn't been buzz cut, Boone would have mussed it up. "Of course they're girl boots," he reasoned.

"Because Madison's a *girl,* dumbhead," Griff told his brother.

Boone let out a long sigh. He looked overwhelmed, completely out of his depth, this man who, in the course of his job, feared no one.

Kendra took pity on him. "Join us?" she said, moving over to show that there was plenty of room at the table, with just herself and Madison taking up space. "Hutch took something to the truck, but he'll be back in a couple of minutes."

Boone considered the invitation carefully. "You guys hungry?" he asked.

Both boys nodded quickly.

"What'll it be?" Boone said, indicating the row of concession wagons lined up along the side of the fair-grounds, offering everything from hamburgers and hot dogs to chow mein, Indian fry bread and tacos.

They both wanted hot dogs, as it turned out, and orange soda to drink.

Madison, Kendra noticed, squeezed in beside her and left the bench on the other side of the table to the boys. Like them, she was shy but intrigued.

"Is that your dad?" she asked, nodding toward Boone, who was waiting in a nearby line by then.

"Yeah," Griff said, elbowing Fletch, who sat too close to him for his liking.

Fletch ignored his brother's gesture and shook his head. "No, he isn't," he argued stubbornly. "Uncle Bob is our dad."

Uh-oh, Kendra thought.

And then Hutch was back, all easy charm. He sat down on Kendra's bench, lifted Madison onto his lap, and proceeded to win both boys over in two seconds flat.

By the time Boone returned with lunch for himself
and the kids, Griff and Fletch were grinning at Hutch
and lapping up every word he said.

CHAPTER SIXTEEN

FOR ALL KENDRA'S fears that the day would drag by, the next couple of hours unfolded easily, naturally. She and Hutch and Madison went on most of the rides at the carnival. On the merry-go-round, Hutch made Madison laugh so hard she nearly fell off the pink swan she'd chosen, just by waving his hat around and pretending the blue-and-green tiger he sat upon was sure to buck him off any minute. Kendra, standing protectively beside her daughter while the mechanism turned and the calliope played, watched him, her heart full but on the verge of breaking.

Don't, she wanted to say to him. *Don't make Madison love you. She's lost so much already.*

But it was too late for that, of course. The man had won the child over completely, helping her choose just the right cowgirl hat, and bandannas for the canine contingent. He'd even presented Madison with a giant pink-and-white teddy bear—it had been consigned to the truck for the duration, like Kendra's new boots—having acquired it by getting a perfect score at the target-shooting booth.

Madison hadn't wanted to give up that bear, even long enough to have it safely stowed away until it was time to go home. She'd have preferred to lug the thing around all day, showing it to everyone, recounting the glorious legend of how Hutch had won it for her. He'd been the one who'd finally managed to persuade the little girl to give up the huge toy, however temporarily—Kendra had gotten nowhere with her sensible advice.

She was pleased because *Madison* was pleased, of course, but Rupert, her daughter's beloved purple kangaroo, once her constant companion, formed a lonely figure in her mind's eye. Ever since Daisy had landed in their lives like a space capsule falling out of orbit, Rupert had been forgotten, left behind in Madison's room, albeit in a place of honor. Even though she was having a good time and she knew that Madison's reduced dependence on the tattered stuffed animal was a good sign, Kendra felt a pang when she thought of poor Rupert. She could identify with him.

After the merry-go-round rides—Madison had gone from the swan to an elephant to a giraffe to a regular carousel horse—the appointed hour arrived, and the crowd streamed from the midway into the outdoor arena, where the rodeo was about to start. The bleachers filled quickly, and everybody stood up when the giant flag was raised and last year's Miss Parable County Rodeo sang "The Star-Spangled Banner."

Since the bull-riding would be the final event of the one-day rodeo, Hutch took his place in the bleachers next to Kendra, taking Madison easily onto his lap when they sat down.

A colorful opening ceremony followed the national anthem, and Madison watched, wide-eyed, as pretty local girls rode in formation, each one dressed in a fancy cowgirl outfit and carrying a huge banner. They performed a few expert maneuvers and the loving crowd cheered loudly enough to raise the big sky arching over all their heads by at least an inch.

"I want to do that someday," Madison, having watched every move the girls and their horses made, said with more certainty than a four-year-old should have been capable of mustering up. "Can I do that when I'm bigger, Mommy?"

Kendra smiled, touched her daughter's cheek. For all the disposable wipes Kendra had used on that little face today, it was still smudged with the remains of a cotton candy binge. "Sure you can," she said. "When you're older."

"How *much* older?" Madison pressed.

Hutch chuckled and turned Madison's pink cowgirl hat 360 degrees until it came to rest on the bridge of her nose. "Those girls out there," he told her, "have been riding since they were your size, or even smaller. It takes a lot of practice to handle a horse the way they do, so you'll want to be on Ruffles's back as often as possible."

Kendra gave him a look over Madison's head and a light nudge with her elbow, but he just grinned at her.

The rodeo began and Madison was enthralled with every event that followed—except for the calf-roping. That made her cry, and even Hutch couldn't convince her that calves weren't being hurt or frightened. Calves were routinely roped, thrown down and tied on ranches, he'd explained, so they could be inoculated against diseases and treated for sickness or injury. Privately, though Kendra knew Hutch was right, from an intellectual standpoint anyway, she agreed with Madison; the event wasn't her favorite, and she was glad when it was over.

They watched the sequence of competitions. The

barrel racing—since all the competitors were female—cheered Madison up considerably. She wanted to know if she and Ruffles could start practicing that right away, along with flag carrying.

All too soon, it was time for the bull-riding. Hutch took his leave from them and headed for the area behind the chutes.

Like the other livestock in the rodeo, the bulls were provided by Walker Parrish's outfit, and they looked mythically large to Kendra, milling around in the big pen on the opposite side of the arena.

Her heartbeat quickened a little as she saw Hutch join the other cowboys waiting to risk their fool necks, and her stomach, containing too much carnival food, did a slow, backward roll. Saliva flooded her mouth and she swallowed, willing herself not to throw up right there in the bleachers.

The first cowboy wore a helmet instead of a Western hat, a choice Kendra considered eminently practical, and he was thrown before the sports clock reached the three-second mark.

The second cowboy made it all the way to six seconds before the bull he was riding went into a dizzying spin, tossed the man to the sawdust and very nearly trampled him.

Madison looked on, spellbound, huddled close against Kendra's side. Once or twice, her thumb crept into her mouth—a habit she'd long since left behind as babyish.

Another helmeted rider followed, and lasted just two and a half seconds before his bull sent him flying.

Then it was Hutch's turn.

The whole universe seemed to recede from Kendra

like an outgoing tide. There was only herself, Madison, Hutch and that bull he was already lowering himself onto over there in the chute. He wore his hat, not a helmet, and Kendra saw him laugh as he adjusted it, saw his lips move as he spoke to the gate man.

Then the gate swung open and the bull—the thing was the size of a Volkswagen, Kendra thought anxiously—plunged out into the very center of the arena, putting on a real show.

The announcer said something about Hutch's well-known skills as a bull-rider, but to Kendra the voice seemed to be coming from somewhere far away and through a narrow pipe.

The big red numbers on the arena clock flicked from one to the next.

Hutch remained on the back of that bull through a whole series of violent gyrations, and then, blessedly, the buzzer sounded and one of the pickup men rode up alongside the furious critter. Hutch, triumphant, switched smoothly to the other horse, behind the rider, and got off when they'd put just a few yards of distance between them and the bull.

Eight seconds.

Until today, Kendra had never dreamed how long eight seconds could seem.

The crowd went crazy, clapping and whistling and stomping booted feet on old floorboards in the bleachers, and the announcer prattled happily about how Hutch would be hard to beat.

Madison scrambled onto Kendra's lap. "Is he done now?" she asked, sounding as breathless as Kendra felt.

Kendra hugged her daughter tightly. "Yes," she said. "It's over."

"Good," Madison said. "That boy-cow looks mean."

Kendra chuckled and, to her relief, some of the tension drained away, softening her shoulders and unclenching her stomach. "I think that boy-cow *is* mean," she agreed.

They watched as Hutch climbed deftly over a fence and stood, watching as the next bull and rider came hurtling out of a chute.

For Kendra, the rest of the event passed in a blur of cowboys and bulls and disconnected words booming over the loudspeakers, all of that underpinned by enthusiastic applause. She sat holding Madison a little too tightly, trying not to imagine how Hutch's ride— or that of some other cowboy—*could* have turned out.

The effort was futile, and by the time Hutch and the other winners were announced and the closing ceremony began—the announcer thanked everybody for coming and reminded them to stick around, check out the goods on offer in the exhibition hall, and enjoy the carnival and, later on, the fireworks—Kendra was weak in the knees.

She and Madison met Hutch, as agreed, outside the arena gate.

Seeing him again, up close, all in one piece, Kendra felt a humiliating urge to cry and fling herself into his arms. Fortunately, she didn't give in to that clingy, codependent compulsion.

"Congratulations," she said mildly, stiffening her spine and lifting her chin.

But Madison was much more forthright. She marched over to Hutch, set her little hands on her hips and tipped her head back to look up at him. Her hat tumbled down her back, dangling by the string Kendra meant to snip off with scissors at the first opportunity. "I don't like it when you ride boy-cows," she informed him. "You could get hurt!"

Hutch smiled, crouched down to look into Madison's pleasantly grungy face and gently tugged at one of her curls. "I'm just fine, shortstop," he said quietly. He might have been talking to an adult, from his tone, rather than a child. He spoke firmly to Madison, but addressed her as an equal. "See?"

Madison softened, as he'd intended. "Do you ride boy-cows *a lot?*" she wanted to know.

"No," he replied. "Just once a year when the rodeo rolls around."

Madison mulled that over. Being so young, she probably didn't have any real conception of such an extended length of time. A year, most likely, sounded a lot like forever.

Kendra, on the other hand, knew those twelve months would pass quickly. Would she and Madison be right here when it was rodeo time again, watching this man deliberately take his life in his hands? Or would Hutch have grown tired of them by then, and moved on to some other woman?

She didn't trust herself to say a word in that moment; just stood there, frustrated and scared and wanting Hutch Carmody more than she ever had before.

What was *wrong* with her?

Why couldn't she just stay away from this man, find somebody else—an insurance agent, say, or a school-teacher, or an electrician, if she had to walk on the wild side?

Anybody but a cowboy.

Hutch rose easily from his haunches, bent and hoisted Madison into his arms.

She yawned and rested her head against his shoulder, her pink cowgirl hat bobbing between her shoulder blades.

Kendra slipped the hat off over Madison's head and carried it for her.

"I think a certain little cowgirl could use some peace and quiet," Hutch said, looking at Kendra over Madison's bright tousle of hair. "What if we head out to my place for a while?" Seeing the protest brewing in Kendra's eyes, he immediately added, "Opal's there and the fireworks won't start for hours."

Kendra sighed, then gave in with a nod.

Madison clearly needed a break from all the hubbub and excitement, and so did she.

They left the fairgrounds, Madison asleep on Hutch's shoulder and barely waking up when he unlocked the truck and set her gently in her safety seat.

"Did I miss the fireworks?" the child asked drowsily.

"Nope," Hutch said, buckling her in. "We're going out to the ranch to spend some time with Opal and Ruffles, but we'll be back in plenty of time to watch the sky light up. And look—here's your teddy bear, sitting right here waiting for you."

Madison nodded and smiled and drifted off, her head resting against the bear's plush pink shoulder.

Kendra, evidently relegated to sidekick status and feeling like a third wheel, went around the truck, opened the passenger door and climbed inside quickly. She didn't want to linger, taking the chance that Hutch might goose her in the backside again, the way he had before they left her place.

A wicked little thrill zapped through her at the memory, though.

The drive to the ranch passed in silence, Madison sleeping in back, Kendra at a loss for anything to say, Hutch easy in his skin, as usual, and thinking his own thoughts.

When they pulled in at Whisper Creek, Opal was outside, taking laundry down off the clothesline. Leviticus supervised from beneath a shady tree.

She smiled and waved when she saw them, picked up her laundry basket, and started for the house.

Hutch was carrying Madison, so Kendra took the basket from Opal, after a brief, good-natured tugging match.

"That's one worn-out little child," Opal observed as Madison snoozed on, her small arms wrapped loosely around Hutch's neck. "You were right to bring her away from all that dirt and noise at the rodeo."

"We'll be going back in a few hours," Hutch replied. "She's dead-set on taking in the fireworks."

Opal chuckled warmly at that, and softly. "You put her in there on my bed," she told Hutch, gesturing toward a doorway leading off the kitchen. "That way she'll be able to hear our voices when she wakes up and won't be startled to find herself in a strange place."

Kendra followed Hutch, watched as he laid the child on Opal's quilted bed, tenderly pulled off her new boots and draped a lightweight comforter over her.

There he goes again, acting like a daddy.

Madison stirred and then succumbed to happy exhaustion.

Back in the kitchen, Opal was pouring coffee for Hutch and Kendra, and brewing tea for herself. The counters were lined with a wide assortment of casseroles and home-baked pies.

"Somebody die?" Hutch asked, reaching toward one of the pies. Leviticus stayed close to him, plainly adoring the man.

Opal stopped what she was doing long enough to slap his hand away. "No," she said with a sharpness that was soft at the center, "nobody *died*. We're getting a new pastor—Lloyd's decided to retire, God bless him—and he'll be introduced to the congregation tomorrow morning."

Kendra, who had missed the last couple of Sunday services, felt mildly chagrined that she hadn't known such a change was in the works. She opened her mouth to comment, couldn't think of a single thing to say and closed it again.

"You can have some of that cherry crumble over there," Opal told Hutch, gesturing toward a pan sitting all alone on top of the stove. "I made that especially for you."

"Yes," Hutch said, homing in on the cherry crumble.

Kendra, meanwhile, sat down to sip from the cup of coffee Opal gave her.

"Want some of this?" Hutch asked from across the room, lifting a plate with a double helping of dessert scooped onto it.

"No, thanks," Kendra said with a weary smile. "It looks delicious, but I've had way too much sugar today as it is."

Hutch came to the table, set his plate down and sat. "You keep this up, Opal," he teased, admiring the food, "and I might have to put you on my payroll."

Opal laughed and waved a scoffing hand at him.

"That'll be the day," she said. "Slade Barlow signs my paychecks. I'm only here to keep you from turning into a seedy old coot who hangs flags and blankets up for window curtains and eats every meal out of a tin can."

Hutch laughed at the image and nearly choked on the bite he'd just taken.

Kendra, on edge since the bull-riding competition, relaxed a little and even smiled.

"Anyhow," Opal went on, taking a place at the table to sip her tea, "I'm beginning to think there's hope for you after all, Hutch Carmody." She glanced at Kendra, smiled. "Yes, sir, I do think there's hope."

Kendra, catching the other woman's meaning, squirmed a little. "So," she said with a little too much spirit, "Pastor Lloyd is retiring. Will there be a party in his honor?"

Opal nodded. "Sure," she said. "We're planning it for tomorrow, right after church." An odd, distant expression came into her dark eyes as she pondered, gazing past Kendra's right shoulder and into deep space. "The new fellow," she went on, "is a dead ringer for Morgan Freeman. Went to Harvard. And he's single, too. A widower, like my Willie was."

Hutch chuckled at that, but he was too busy consuming cherry crumble to make any remarks. Evidently, riding bulls took a lot out of a person, producing a desperate need for simple carbohydrates. Subtly, he slipped a bite or two to the dog.

"You've met him?" Kendra asked, mainly to make conversation, though she was a little intrigued by Opal's sudden wistful mood.

Opal shook her head, and the gesture seemed to bring her back from wherever mental territory she'd wandered off to. "I saw his picture, though," she said, and Kendra would have sworn the woman was blushing a little, her mahogany cheeks taking on a rosy glow. "I'm on the pastoral selection committee, you know."

Hutch swallowed, drank some coffee and jammed his fork back into what remained of his cherry crumble. "You hired the man because you think he's good-looking?" he asked in a teasing tone. "Why, Opal, a person would almost get the impression that you're on the lookout for another husband."

She swatted at him, trying hard not to laugh. "You hush," she chortled, obviously embarrassed.

"I'll dance at your wedding," Hutch told her, still grinning.

"You and weddings," she said, and then made a dismissive sound, conveying faux disgust, and rose to leave the table. "There's a combination for you." She paused, sighed, and adjusted the knot at the back of her apron. "I've got a lot of cooking to do," she said, "so I'll thank you to let me get on with it."

Hutch finished the cherry crumble and carried his plate to the sink, where he dutifully rinsed it and set it in the dishwasher, along with the fork.

"I wouldn't mind getting some fresh air," he said.

Again, Kendra felt that strange, surging rush of heat. Her heart struggled up into her throat and pounded there. Was he suggesting…

"It's a beautiful day," Opal said, careful not to look in Kendra's direction. "Why don't you two take a walk or a horseback ride? I'll be glad to look after the Little Miss while you're gone, and Leviticus will be my helper."

Kendra might as well have been back on the Tilt-a-Whirl at the carnival, the way that room seemed to spin and dip around her.

A walk would probably be harmless, but she didn't *dare* go riding with Hutch because she knew where they'd end up.

At the same time, she couldn't bring herself to say no.

To say anything at all.

Hutch looked at her, one eyebrow slightly raised in question.

"Go ahead," Opal told her, blissfully unaware that she, a church-going, Bible-believing woman, was propelling Kendra straight into the dark, raging heart of sin. "Madison will be just fine. Fact is, you'll probably be back before she even wakes up from her nap."

Five minutes later, still dazed, Kendra found herself in the barn, watching as Hutch saddled horses for both of them.

Occasionally, he glanced in her direction, but no words passed between them until he'd saddled both horses and led them out into the afternoon sunshine.

There, Hutch turned to look straight into her eyes. His expression was solemn but not sad, calm but not complacent. He'd been clean-shaven that morning, but now his caramel-colored beard was coming in.

"If you want to stay behind," he told her, "now's the time to say so."

Kendra swallowed hard. Nodded.

Hutch had left his hat in the house for whatever reason, though he was still wearing the same dusty rodeo clothes as before, and he ran a hand through his hair. "You do know where we're headed?" he persisted.

Again, Kendra swallowed and nodded. She walked

over to her horse, the same one she'd ridden that other time, put a foot in the stirrup and almost sprang up into the saddle. She took the reins in hand and waited for Hutch to lead the way.

He sighed, shook his head once and finally flashed a devastating grin at her. "So be it," he said, and they were off.

Kendra followed. It was as though there were two women sharing her body—one sensible and wary, the other reckless and wild.

At the moment, the latter was winning out.

Neither of them spoke as they crossed the range, though Hutch looked back at her once over his right shoulder, before urging his gelding onto the trail that twisted up the mountainside toward the hidden meadow.

Stop, turn around, go back, Sensible Kendra pleaded.

I want this man, countered Reckless Kendra. *I want him and I need him and I don't care if it's wrong.*

There will be consequences, warned her reasonable side.

She knew that was true, but it didn't stop her, didn't even slow her down.

Her mutinous body had taken over, pushing aside her fretful mind with all its dreads and worries.

The meadow was just as she remembered it, shady and secluded and, at the same time, offering a wide view of Parable and the surrounding land.

They dismounted, still without speaking, and Hutch led the horses into a patch of sweetgrass nearby, draping the reins loosely over their necks so they wouldn't trip over them, leaving them to graze.

Kendra, meanwhile, approached the curious pile of stones.

"What's this?" she asked when Hutch appeared beside her, their arms touching.

"A way of getting things out of my system, I guess," he replied.

Kendra frowned, puzzled.

He turned her to face him, resting his hands lightly beneath her elbows. "Those are my regrets," he explained, inclining his head toward the pile of stones. "Every rock represents something I'd like to change but can't. I figured stacking them in a pile was better than carrying their counterparts around in my head."

The statement made an odd kind of sense to Kendra, though at the moment, little else did.

Was she really here, in the secret meadow, alone with Hutch Carmody?

As if in answer, he cupped her chin in his hand, bent his head and kissed her. At first, it was just a light brush of his lips against hers, but then it deepened, grew hot and moist, and Kendra's arms went around his neck, while his tightened around her torso, holding her close.

For Kendra, that kiss was a fiery balm, not just to her body but to her spirit, as well. She returned it fiercely, letting go of everything but the heady sensations Hutch stirred in her, the wild needs, the treacherous joy, the sweet sorrow of knowing that life is short and precious.

"I guess that's a yes," Hutch said with a raspy chuckle when the kiss finally ended.

Kendra laughed, and they kissed again, even more hungrily this time.

They eased downward into the thick carpet of grass

without their mouths parting, did battle with their tongues, pushed and tugged at each other's clothes.

Nearby, the horses grazed peacefully, saddle leather creaking now and then, their bridle fittings jingling as they raised and lowered their heads.

Birds swooped and sang, and tiny creatures scuttled through the grass, and Kendra gave herself up to Hutch, to his hands, his mouth, his husky whispers.

Time slipped away, just as their clothes had. The ground was soft under Kendra's back and their only covering was the sky.

He kissed her until she was so dizzy that the arch of blue over their heads blurred whenever she opened her eyes.

He ran his lips along the side of her neck, across her collarbone, all the while caressing her breasts, one and then the other, with a gentle, calloused hand.

Kendra gasped with pleasure and arched her back, wanting him *now,* not later.

But the excruciatingly delicious foreplay went on—he nibbled at her, everywhere, tongued her nipples until they were pebble-hard, and finally suckled.

It felt so good that she cried out, offering a single, insensible, desperate plea.

Now. Every nerve, every cell in her body seemed to scream the word.

There was, however, no hurrying Hutch Carmody, when it came to lovemaking, anyway—he continued to take his time, stroking her with his hands, exploring every curve and hollow with his lips or the tip of his tongue.

Finally, he came to the core of her femininity, and

touched the soft, moist curls with the heat of his breath, arousing her to an even higher pitch of need.

She begged.

He parted her, took her full into his mouth and sucked.

Glorious heat pounded through her like a drum beat, and her hips rose from the soft ground, seeking, seeking the warmth and wetness of his mouth. She felt his hands, strong, under her buttocks, holding her up so that he could drink from her like some sacred cup.

Passion and pleasure raged inside her, like a lightning storm, clamoring, climbing, driving her ever upward toward...heaven?

She shattered into blazing pieces, splintering across the sky.

Fireworks, she thought, as her body flexed and flexed again, reveling in wave after wave of satisfaction.

When he'd wrung the last throaty cry of release from her, Hutch lowered her gently to the ground. He knelt astraddle of her, breathing hard, and she was aware of him reaching for something nearby, tearing open a packet, putting on a condom.

Without a word, he poised himself to take her, waited the instant it took for her to nod and slide her hands along the muscular length of his back.

He was inside her in a single, powerful stroke, deep inside her, where all her dreams and secrets lived, and the sweet satisfaction she'd felt only moments before turned to fiery need.

She whispered his name, raised herself to him.

Once they'd attained a rhythm, he increased the

pace, then slowed it, now driving into her, now withdrawing almost completely.

His control amazed her, given that she'd lost hers with the first kiss.

Soon, Kendra was flailing in the grasp of an undulating, rippling climax so intense that she thought she might actually die before it ended.

Hutch murmured to her and she saw the muscles tighten along his neck and upper arms as he plunged through the final barrier and let go, giving a low, ragged shout as he spilled himself into her.

Afterward, they lay side by side in the soft grass, still breathing hard, and a soft breeze rippled over them, like a blessing.

The sky and the tree tops, out of focus before, slowly regained their color and shape, but they blurred a little, too, because Kendra's eyes were full of tears she couldn't have explained.

Hutch raised himself on one elbow, looked down at her face, brushed the moisture from one of her cheeks with the side of his thumb. But he didn't ask why she was crying and Kendra was glad, because she couldn't have explained that the things she was feeling were so big, so ferocious and so wonderful that she wasn't sure she could bear them.

He kissed her softly, briefly, this time offering solace, not passion.

They were silent for a long time, recovering, drawing themselves back together like the scattered pieces of a pair of jigsaw puzzles.

Kendra was the first to speak. "You brought a condom," she observed with a little smile.

"Just the one," Hutch replied. "Damn it."

She laughed richly, freely, openly. For the first time in a long while, she felt whole.

Her joy was bittersweet, though, because she knew it couldn't last.

CHAPTER SEVENTEEN

KENDRA'S WELL AND thoroughly loved body thrummed with residual ecstasy as she slowly, carefully put her clothes back on, determined to come away looking as though she'd never taken them off in the first place. Hutch, wearing his jeans again and shrugging into the shirt he'd discarded earlier, grinned at her.

Things like this, she thought, were so much easier for a man.

All men had to do was tuck in their shirt and zip up their jeans and they were good to go, with nobody the wiser. She, on the other hand, probably had grass in her hair, and her French braid was coming undone. And even if she got her clothes and hair right, her eyes surely glowed and her cheeks were flushed, too—both sure signs that she'd just had the best sex of her life.

Fortunately, Madison wouldn't pick up on the signals. But *Opal* might.

Hutch walked over to her, undid the braid completely, and ran splayed fingers through her hair, letting it spill down over her shoulders.

"That's better," he said, quietly grave. "My God, you're beautiful."

Kendra raised her hands, meaning to gather her hair back and replait it, having momentarily forgotten that the rubber band she'd used to secure it was lost somewhere in the grass, but Hutch stilled her, his thumbs moving in small circular caresses against her palms.

"I left the house with a braid," she told him as her normal state of quiet agitation overtook her again, "and I'm going *back* with one."

Hutch chuckled. The way he was touching her made her regret that he'd brought only one condom. With him, once had never been enough; in the old days, they'd often made love for hours at a time, falling asleep in each other's arms and waking up to make love again. And he'd already made her want him again just by touching her and standing so close.

His body was hard and hot and unequivocally male, and she could still feel the weight of it, the power and the thrust, and her own sweet victory found in complete surrender.

"Kendra," he said. His tone was raspy.

"What?" she all but snapped, flustered.

"Your hair looks fine the way it is. In fact, it looks more than fine."

She was looking around for the lost rubber band by then, but in vain. "Opal will guess—"

Hutch rested his hands on either side of her face, so she couldn't turn her head away. "Opal has *already* guessed," he said, amused. "Why do you think she offered to look after Madison so we could leave the house?"

Kendra ached with embarrassment. Of course he was right—Opal was no fool and the ploy had been a pretty obvious one, too—but on the inside, she was still soaring. Besides, for all her jitters, that reckless part of her remained very much in charge. "Awkward," she said, singsong.

Hutch laughed. "What's awkward? Nobody's judging us, Kendra—we're both grown-ups, remember?"

"*One* of us is, anyway," Kendra said, making a rueful face.

He kissed her forehead, then the tip of her nose, before lowering his hands. "Let's go," he said, "before I throw caution to the winds and take you down again, condom or no condom."

"I might have something to say about that, you know," Kendra pointed out, but she couldn't muster up any real annoyance.

"Is that a challenge?" he asked, low and easy. His right index finger traipsed lightly down her cheek, along her neck and once around her breast, in a slow, heated orbit.

Electricity jolted through her, and she jumped back a step, every bit as hot and bothered as she'd been when they first tumbled into the grass. "No," she said quickly. "It *wasn't* a challenge."

He grinned. Then he made a sweeping gesture with one arm toward the placidly waiting horses.

They each mounted up, Kendra moving quickly so he wouldn't "help."

When they got back to the barn, Hutch took care of the horses and sent Kendra inside to see if Madison had awakened from her nap yet.

She hadn't.

Opal remained in the kitchen and a delicious aroma filled the air.

"All three of you need a real supper," the older woman announced firmly. "Not more carnival food." If she'd noticed that Kendra's hair was no longer pulled back in its former tidy braid, she didn't offer a comment or give any indication that she knew anything special had happened while they were out.

Kendra was fiercely grateful for that; she wasn't ready for anyone else to know, not even Joslyn and Tara, and she told them pretty much everything.

She slipped away to the nearest powder room, washed her hands, splashed her face with cool water—her makeup was long gone but the glow made up for it—and inspected her clothes for grass stains in front of a full-length mirror.

When she came out, Madison was in the kitchen, rubbing her eyes sleepily. "Is it tomorrow?" she asked Kendra. "Did I miss the fireworks?"

Kendra swept her up, hugged her, and gave her a smacking kiss on one pudgy cheek. "It's still today," she said. "And we're going back to town for the fireworks after supper."

Madison looked greatly relieved, and wriggled in Kendra's arms, wanting to stand on her own. Even at four, she had a streak of independence running through her as wide as the Big Sky River. "Good," she said looking around the kitchen, nodding a hello at a smiling Opal. "Where's Hutch?"

So it was "Hutch" now, and not "Mr. Carmody."

Kendra wasn't sure how she felt about that—or anything else, really. Her emotions were still in a jumble, impossibly tangled. She knew the regrets would set in eventually—she could feel them circling around her, slowly closing in, like wolves waiting for a campfire to die down to embers—but for now, for tonight, she was going to let things be all right, just the way they were.

"He's in the barn," Kendra answered.

Madison, more and more awake as the moments

passed, tilted her head to one side and studied Kendra quizzically. "What happened to your hair, Mommy?"

Before Kendra could stumble out a reply, Opal came to the rescue. "I could use some help setting the table," she told the little girl, "and I know you're real good at that."

Madison lit up, allowing Opal to take her over to the sink and quickly wash her small hands with a moist paper towel.

Meanwhile, Opal's gaze met Kendra's, full of kind understanding. The woman might as well have said, "Don't worry, everything's going to be all right," her expression conveyed so much tenderness.

Hutch stepped in from outside a moment later, rolled up his shirtsleeves and went through the hand-washing ritual at the kitchen sink. Except for a certain light in his eyes, he looked like innocence personified.

After drying his hands, he took four plates down from the cupboard and set them between the knives, forks and spoons Madison had carefully arranged at each place. He might have been dealing cards, his motions were so deft.

"You ought to come to town with us," he told Opal fifteen minutes later when they were all seated at the table, enjoying her fried chicken, green beans, mashed potatoes and gravy. "Take in the fireworks."

"Thank you very much but no, sir," Opal replied briskly. "I've got a big day tomorrow and I need my beauty sleep."

Kendra sneaked a glance at Hutch and saw that his eyes were twinkling with mischief, as well as recent satisfaction. Still feeling the occasional sweet aftershock herself, Kendra blushed again.

"I knew it," he told Opal. "You've got your cap set for the new preacher."

"I do not," Opal said. "For all I know, he's a rascal. You good-looking types usually are."

He chuckled. "What do we know about this guy?" he asked. "If he comes a-courting, I need to be sure he's on the level."

"Stop it," Opal said, though she was clearly enjoying the exchange. "He's a looker and a widower and he has a divinity degree from one of the best universities in the country, and that's the sum total of my knowledge."

Hutch chewed on that, and a mouthful of chicken, for a few moments, swallowed, and went right on teasing Opal. "A Harvard man," he ruminated. "Makes me wonder why he'd want to live in a place like Parable, Montana. What's this yahoo's name?"

Opal glowered at Hutch, but her eyes were dancing behind the lenses of her old-fashioned glasses. "If you want to know that," she shot back, "just come to church tomorrow and you'll find out."

Hutch huffed out a laugh. "The last time I was there," he said, "all hell broke loose."

"We go to church sometimes," Madison put in, eager to join the banter. "Don't we, Mommy?"

"Yes," Kendra said.

"Are we going tomorrow?" Madison asked. "To see the new preacher from Harvard?"

She smiled. *A little repentance might be in order,* she thought, *for me at least.* "Unless you're too tired," she answered. "It will be very late when the fireworks get over tonight and you might need to sleep in tomorrow morning."

"Can I ride the merry-go-round again?" the child inquired, on to the next thing, like a firefly flitting from bush to branch. "I want to see if the tiger really bucks like a boy-cow."

Hutch grinned, reached out to tousle Madison's hair. "We'll have plenty of time for tiger rides," he told her. "It's still a couple more hours until it gets dark enough out to set off those fireworks."

"I might be awake at *midnight!*" Madison marveled. No doubt there were a few storybook pumpkin-coaches going through her mind, drawn by talking mice. To a small child, Kendra reflected, midnight was a magical hour.

"You might be," Kendra agreed, sure the little girl would be sound asleep on Hutch's shoulder again before the grand finale.

"Wow," Madison breathed. "Midnight is *really late.*"

"Yep," Hutch said affably with only the briefest glance in Kendra's direction, lavishing attention on his dog, instead.

Half an hour later, after Kendra had helped Opal clear the table and set the kitchen to rights—Hutch had taken Madison out to the barn to say hello to Ruffles while the cleanup was going on—the three of them were back in Hutch's truck, headed for town.

There was still plenty of light, though shadows were slowly creeping down the mountainsides to pool in the valley where Parable rested, all lit up in Christmas tree colors for the Fourth.

The man at the entrance gate to the fairgrounds flashed a black light on the backs of their hands, and Madison was thrilled to see the stamp she'd gotten that morning reappear on her skin.

"It's magic," she breathed.

Kendra loved her little girl so much in that moment that she had to restrain herself from grabbing her up and hugging her tight.

They returned to the merry-go-round—like the other rides, it was doing a brisk business because there was still at least an hour to kill before the fireworks began—though Hutch remarked that half the county was probably over at the Boot Scoot Tavern, whooping it up. After waiting in line, Madison rode the tiger, this time with Hutch standing beside her and Kendra taking pictures with her cell phone each time they went by.

It all seemed so normal, though she still had that strange sense of being two people instead of just the usual one. And those two people were definitely at odds with each other.

Are you crazy? one of them demanded from a hiding place somewhere in the back of her brain. *This is the same man who broke your heart. And just a few weeks ago, he abandoned his bride on their wedding day.*

But this second Kendra was having none of it. She wanted to live in the moment, to enjoy the delicious fantasy of being loved and wanted for just a little while longer.

By the time everybody gathered at the edge of the field next to the rodeo grounds to watch the long-awaited fireworks show, Madison could barely keep her eyes open.

She'd had a big day, this very little girl, and despite a nap and a good supper, she was beginning to run down.

Hutch held the child in his arms and they watched as colored light spattered the dark sky, bloomed into a swelling shape of blue or green, red or gold, and gracefully fell away. Even the sparks were beautiful, a rain of shimmering fire.

Kendra realized, with a start, that she was perfectly happy, alternately watching the breathtaking spectacle in the sky and the bright reflections it cast onto the upturned faces of the people around her.

She was, in that instant, so happy that it terrified her.

It was dangerous to open her heart and her mind and her spirit to life, to a certain man, to the singular joys of being a young, healthy woman, with needs to be satisfied. Loving Madison so completely was all the risk she could bear to take—why was she pushing her luck this way? Was she greedy to want more than motherhood, more than her career?

Long before the fireworks ended and the crowds dispersed and she and Hutch and a soundly sleeping Madison were in the truck on the way to her place, Kendra had begun the lonely and singularly painful process of drawing back into herself, like a sea creature retreating into its shell.

Hutch probably sensed the change, but he didn't say anything.

When they got to her house, he lifted Madison from the car seat and carried her into the house. Subdued, Kendra led the way to the little girl's room, where he laid her gently on the bed and stepped back.

He left the room without a word and Kendra found herself listening hard for the sound of the front door opening and then closing behind him as she quickly undressed Madison, put her into a soft cotton nightgown and tucked her in with a kiss.

That night, it was Kendra who prayed.

"Thank You," she whispered.

Hutch was in the kitchen when she got there, leaning idly against one of the counters with his arms folded. He'd brought the big teddy bear inside while she was looking after Madison, and set it, like a jaunty diner, in one of the chairs at the table, a gesture that touched something deep inside Kendra and left a faint bruise in its wake. Her new boots, still in their box, were there, too, filling the room with the clean scent of leather.

"Want to tell me about it?" Hutch asked quietly without preamble.

Kendra wanted to avoid his gaze, but she couldn't seem to pull hers away. "What's to tell?" she asked with a flippancy she didn't really feel. "It's been a long haul and we're both tired, and tomorrow is another day."

"If you think we're going to pretend that nothing happened up there in the meadow this afternoon," he informed her, quietly blunt, "you're dead wrong."

"We got—carried away," Kendra said, trying to smile and failing.

"We made love," Hutch said gravely. "That changes things, Kendra. At least, it does for me."

"You said it yourself," she said, careful to keep her voice down, in case Madison woke up and overheard things she couldn't be expected to understand. "We're grown-ups, not kids. We lost our heads for a little while, but now that's behind us and—"

He crossed the room in two strides, took her gently but inescapably by her upper arms, and pressed her to the wall, held her there with the intoxicatingly hard length of his body. And then he kissed her.

It was the kind of kiss that conquers a woman, lays claim to her, body and soul.

Knowing she ought to break away, Kendra kissed

him back, instead. She couldn't help it, because the old hunger, the one she'd pushed down all this time, was rushing through her again, and it was stronger than ever.

She was blushing when Hutch drew back, released her, stepped away.

Moments later, he was gone, out the door.

She heard his truck start up, drive away.

Kendra crossed the room, turned the lock and sat down in a chair at the kitchen table across from the ludicrously large pink-and-white teddy bear Hutch had won for Madison at the carnival.

It seemed to be watching her and a bit smugly at that.

"Oh, shut up," she told it. Then she sprang out of her chair again, marched into the bathroom and ran herself a hot bath.

There were too many feelings welling up inside her and they were too complicated to sort out. She felt frantic.

Kendra stripped, stepped into the tub, sank into the scented water.

She closed her eyes and instantly she was back in that mountain meadow, lying in the grass, with Hutch Carmody riding her as confidently as he'd ridden the bull at the rodeo and the tiger on the merry-go-round.

Kendra's eyes popped open in alarm, and just like that, she was at home again, in her own bathtub, up to her chin in billowing bubbles.

Realistic Kendra was back on the scene, with a vengeance, while the one that had gotten her into trouble was conspicuously absent. Wasn't *that* a fine how-do-you-do?

She soaked for a while, even tried to read the paperback she'd left within reach on the back of the toilet, but nothing worked.

She was all a-jangle.

Her grandmother's voice echoed in her head.

Now you've done it. You're nothing but a tramp, just like your mother.

Kendra got out of the tub, dried herself with a towel and pulled a nightgown on over her head. She padded into the kitchen, flipped on the light she'd turned off earlier and brewed herself a cup of raspberry tea.

The drink soothed her a little, but total emotional and physical exhaustion were the only reasons she slept at all that night. Her dreams were full of garish carnival rides, scary clowns dressed like cowboys and her grandmother, following her around, shaking a finger at her and repeating the same words over and over again.

You're nothing but a tramp, just like your mother.

The next morning, Kendra woke with a pounding headache and Madison, wearing her boots and her cowgirl hat with her nightie, jumping up and down on the bed beside her.

"Get up, Mommy," she chanted, beaming with fresh energy. "We have to go to church and look at the new preacher!"

Kendra sighed, arranged her pillows and sat up, resting against them.

"Of course we do," she said. "And stop jumping on the bed, please."

She didn't want to look at what the soles of those little boots might have left behind on her formerly pristine white eyelet bedspread.

Madison leaped, agile as a gazelle, to the floor.

Her hat was askew and her eyes were wide beneath the brim.

"Get up!" she pleaded. *"Please,* Mommy!"

Kendra sighed again, tossed back the covers and got up. She padded into the bathroom, opened the door of the medicine cabinet and shook a couple of aspirin into her palm, swallowing them with a gulp of tap water.

Madison prattled nonstop the whole time, reliving the carnival, the rodeo, the purchase of her boots and hat and the bandannas for the dogs, and finally the fireworks.

The aspirin didn't kick in for a full fifteen minutes, during which Kendra listened patiently to her daughter's continuous chatter, nodded at appropriate intervals and chopped fresh strawberries to sprinkle over cold cereal.

"I'll bet Daisy misses us," Madison said, scrambling into her chair at the table and taking her spoon in hand. "Can we go get her right after church? And then can we go back to the ranch so I can ride Ruffles?"

"Whoa," Kendra pleaded, raising both hands, palms out. "Slow down. We'll go to church, stay after for Pastor Lloyd's retirement party, and then drive out to Tara's and pick up Daisy. That's pretty much a day-full, sweetheart."

"But what about Ruffles?" Madison pressed, on the verge of whining but not quite there. "She'll be *lonesome.*"

"She won't be lonesome," Kendra replied patiently, forcing herself to eat a few bites of cereal. If she didn't, her stomach would start growling in church for sure, probably during prayers. "She has all those other horses to keep her company, not to mention Leviticus."

"But I want—"

"Madison," Kendra broke in, kindly but firmly, "we're coming *home* after we pick Daisy up, and that's the end of it."

Madison's lower lip jutted out, but, being a bright child, she didn't push the issue. Kendra didn't believe in spankings, but she wasn't above decreeing a time-out, and Madison hated those, because it meant sitting still and being quiet.

"You're mean," she said under her breath.

"A regular Simon LeGree," Kendra agreed. "Eat your breakfast."

THE REVEREND DOCTOR Walter G. Beaumont *was* a dead-ringer for Morgan Freeman, Kendra discovered when she and Madison were seated side by side in the pews later that morning, right next to Opal. He sat in a chair just behind and to the left of the main pulpit, while Pastor Lloyd delivered his farewell sermon.

It was a good message, though Kendra only heard part of it because her mind kept wandering. She hadn't really expected Hutch to show up, but her feelings about that were mixed. She was disappointed that he wasn't there, as well as relieved.

Pastor Lloyd seemed happy about his retirement, and after the services everybody gathered in the social hall adjoining the church for the party.

There was a lot of food—Opal wasn't the only member of the congregation who'd been cooking up a storm, obviously—and small gifts were presented to the outgoing pastor, who eagerly introduced his replacement and said what an honor it was to have such a learned man in their midst.

Opal barely took her eyes off the Reverend Doctor Beaumont, Kendra noticed with a lot of affection and no little amusement. The man was tall, slender and graceful, beautifully dressed in a dark tailored suit, and his voice was deep and resonant, but not too loud.

He definitely wasn't the hellfire-and-brimstone type, Kendra concluded with relief. She did wonder, though, as Hutch had at supper the night before, what could have attracted this highly educated and obviously sophisticated man to a small, mostly rural community like Parable.

The party was winding down by the time Pastor Lloyd asked Dr. Beaumont to say a few words.

He didn't need a pulpit or a platform; his voice rolled over them like controlled thunder, quiet but forceful, even commanding.

"It's an honor to join this fine community," he said, revealing strikingly white teeth as he smiled, his gaze sweeping, warm, over the assemblage. "I look forward to getting to know all of you, and I look forward to the fishing, too, which I hear is mighty good around these parts."

A twitter of laughter rippled through the friendly crowd. After church, most of the gathering would be heading back to the fairgrounds to shop in the exhibition hall and enjoy some of the carnival rides, but their affection for Pastor Lloyd, and their wish to make the new man feel welcome, kept them there.

Looking around, Kendra felt a rush of affection for these people—*her* people—all of them hardworking, doing their best to lead good and honest lives, glad to live in a place like Parable, where the fishing was good and the Fourth of July was a big, big deal.

This is home, Kendra thought, soothed. *I was right to bring Madison here. No matter what else happens, this is where we belong.*

By then, the children were getting restless—many of them had been to Sunday school and attended the main service afterward, thereby exhausting their limited supply of patience—and the crowd began to thin.

In her turn, Kendra said goodbye to Pastor Lloyd and shook hands with Dr. Beaumont, then rounded up an overexcited Madison and headed for the parking lot.

They drove out to Tara's house, chatted with her for a few minutes, collected Daisy and headed back home.

There, Madison changed out of her Sunday school dress and into shorts, sneakers and a top, and she and Daisy dashed outside to play in the yard. Kendra, still in the simple blue sundress she'd worn to church, kicked off her dressy shoes and went to sit on the porch step, watching them.

She half hoped Hutch would show up, or simply call, and half hoped he wouldn't.

She needed time and space so she could get some perspective, sort through what had happened up on the mountainside the day before. At the same time, she wanted him close again.

The sound of her ringing cell phone interrupted her thoughts; she slipped into the house, retrieved it from the counter where she'd left it before church, and answered, "This is Kendra Shepherd."

"Hello, Kendra Shepherd," said a cheerful female voice that seemed vaguely familiar. "This is Casey Elder. Walker Parrish gave me your number?"

"Yes," Kendra said, surprised to find herself a little

starstruck and right on the verge of gushing. "Hello, Ms. Elder."

"Call me Casey," was the perky response, "and I'll call you Kendra. How's that?"

Kendra smiled. "That's fine," she said, already liking the woman, sight unseen. "Walker tells me you're thinking of moving to Parable."

"That's right," Casey confirmed. She seemed to radiate energy, even over the telephone, which was pretty impressive, since Kendra knew the singer had been on tour with her band and probably performed the day before. "I don't mind telling you, he makes the place sound pretty darn good."

"It's a great town," Kendra said.

"I'd like to come and have a look," Casey replied. "Would Tuesday be all right?"

"Sure," Kendra answered, delighted. They agreed to meet at Kendra's office at ten-thirty Tuesday morning, said their goodbyes and hung up.

She still had the cell phone in her hand when she stepped outside, smiling to find Madison and Daisy both lying side by side in the grass, on their backs. Daisy's four feet were raised, bent at the joints.

"We're remembering the fireworks," Madison explained.

It being early afternoon, the sky was clear and blue and bright with sunlight.

"I see," Kendra said.

"Daisy didn't see them," the little girl clarified, "but I told her all about it."

The phone rang in Kendra's hand just as she took her previous seat on the porch step, and a little trill of excitement went through her.

Let it be Hutch.

Don't *let it be Hutch.*

"Hey," Joslyn said. "It's me."

"Hey," Kendra replied.

"How was the big date?" Joslyn asked.

Kendra bit her lower lip, considering her answer. She wanted to argue that her time with Hutch *hadn't* been a date, but that would be pure denial. After all, she'd wound up making love with the man up there on the side of Big Sky Mountain.

"Fine," she hedged.

Joslyn laughed. "Fine? There's a lot you aren't telling me, I'm guessing."

Kendra sighed, but she was smiling. Even now, hours and hours after the fact, she still felt the lingering effects of several powerful releases. "And I'm not about to tell you, either," she said. "At least, not over the phone."

"Great," Joslyn answered. "Why don't you and Madison come out here for a visit and some supper? Shea and the baby will keep Madison occupied, and you can tell me *everything*."

"I don't think I'm ready for that," Kendra said.

"Something happened," Joslyn insisted gently.

"Yes," Kendra admitted. "And I'm positive I'm going to regret it."

"Don't be so sure," Joslyn counseled. She sounded delighted. "So you'll come for supper?"

"Not tonight," Kendra said. "Madison had a big day yesterday and she needs time to settle down a little."

"I understand," Joslyn replied. "Still up for being Trace's godmother? Slade and I are thinking of scheduling the christening for next Sunday, after church, if the new pastor agrees."

"Of course I'm still up for it," Kendra said. "I'm honored."

"Slade is asking Hutch to be Trace's godfather," Joslyn ventured. She was stepping lightly now, Kendra could tell. "Is that a problem for you?"

"No," was Kendra's reply. "And even if it was, it wouldn't be my call."

"I might come in to the office for a few hours tomorrow," Joslyn went on. "I'd bring Trace along, of course."

"Of course," Kendra agreed.

"You're stonewalling me," Joslyn accused, good-naturedly. "Don't you get it, Kendra? I'm dying for information here!"

Kendra laughed. "Put your curiosity on life support," she said. "Madison is within earshot, and anyway I'm not *about* to fill you in over the phone."

Joslyn gave an exaggerated sigh. "All right, then," she said. "I guess I'll have to wait until tomorrow."

"Guess so," Kendra acknowledged, still smiling. She didn't plan on sharing any of the intimate details, but she was actually eager to discuss what had happened up there in the meadow yesterday, with her best friend anyway. Joslyn was levelheaded, nonjudgmental and totally trustworthy, and talking things over with her sounded like a good idea.

Maybe she, Kendra, could get some perspective on the situation. If indeed it *was* a situation. Men didn't take the same attitude toward sex as women did—there was no implicit commitment.

Still, hadn't Hutch said, just the night before, after that dazzling kiss against her kitchen wall, that making love had changed things?

Time would tell, Kendra thought as she said goodbye to her friend and let the phone rest in her lap while she watched her daughter and Daisy play in shafts of summer sunlight.

CHAPTER EIGHTEEN

GIVE THE WOMAN *some space,* Hutch counseled himself silently that bright Sunday afternoon, as he kept busy grooming horses in the barn, Leviticus close by. He was restless, despite his own advice, wanting to head straight for town, find Kendra and—what?

Talk to her? Make love to her again?

Instinct, as well as knowing Kendra so long and so well, warned that she might run for the hills if he came on too strong, too soon.

No, he'd contain his impatience, go slowly. He'd lost her once, and he didn't want to risk losing her again.

He loved her—that was the only thing he was really sure of.

He was finishing up, wondering what else he could turn his hand to that would use up some more daylight, as well as personal energy, when he heard a rig pull up outside the barn. Leviticus, not much of a watchdog, gave a halfhearted woof.

Probably Opal, back from church, he thought, headed for the doorway. He was grinning a little, remembering how she'd left the house all spiffed-up that morning, flatly denying that she was out to impress the new preacher.

When he stepped out into the sunlight, though, it was Boone he saw, getting out of his squad car. Both boys tumbled out from behind the grate that separated the front seat of the cruiser from the back, grinning a howdy at Hutch.

He chuckled and gave them each a light squeeze to the shoulder—they were dressed up, and it saddened him a little, because these were probably their traveling clothes. Boone had said they'd be leaving today, but Hutch hadn't given the matter much thought until now.

"They want to say goodbye to you before they catch the bus back to Missoula," Boone said, looking as lame as he sounded. He was wan, and he hadn't shaved, and Hutch would have sworn the man was wearing the same set of clothes he'd had on yesterday at the rodeo.

The taller boy, Griff, looked solemn. "We don't want to leave," he said. "But Dad says we have to."

"Uncle *Bob* is our dad," the smaller one, Fletch, insisted staunchly.

Hutch stole a sidelong glance at Boone's face and saw that his friend looked as though he'd just been sucker-punched, square in the gut. He waited for Boone to correct the boy, to claim him, as it were, but he didn't do that.

"Well," Hutch said, holding on to his grin because it was threatening to slip away, "I hope you'll come back for another visit real soon."

Griff's dark brown eyes were bright with angry sorrow as he looked up at Hutch. Something in his expression begged him to step in, change the direction of things, get Boone to see reason, to understand what he was throwing away just because he was scared.

The backs of Hutch's own eyes stung like fire; he hated the helplessness he felt. Bottom line, it was

Boone's call whether the boys stayed or went, and he had no right to interfere—not in front of them, at least.

He'd have *plenty* to say to Boone in private, when he got the chance.

Boone consulted his watch. "We'd better go," he said without looking at his sons. "You don't want to miss the bus."

"Yes, we do," Griff argued. "We want to stay here with you, Dad."

"No, we *don't*," Fletch put in, but his lower lip wobbled and his eyes glistened.

Boone sighed, and his gaze met Hutch's. *Help me out, here, will you?* That was what his expression said, as clearly as if he'd spoken aloud.

"You know what I think," Hutch replied carefully, quietly. "And you can be sure we'll discuss it later."

Fletch wasn't through talking, evidently. He tensed, like he was thinking about kicking Boone square in the shin, looked up at him, squinting against the sun and his whole body trembling, blurted, "You don't want us anyway! You can't wait to get rid of us!"

Boone went pale and, after unclenching the hinges of his jaws, he replied, "We've already had this discussion, Fletcher." He paused, shook his head, tossed a grim, thanks-for-nothing look Hutch's way. "Get in the car, both of you."

After one last imploring look at Hutch, Griff put his hand to his little brother's back and shoved him in the direction of the squad car.

"Damn it, Boone, this is *wrong*," Hutch growled, as soon as the boys were inside the vehicle again, with the doors shut. "Sending those kids away is the same thing as saying straight out that Fletch has it right, you don't want them."

Boone looked at him in stricken silence and for a long time, but in the end, he didn't answer. He just gave a curt nod of farewell, turned his back and walked away.

Hutch watched the retreating squad car until it was clean out of sight.

Then he went inside the house and, with Leviticus close on his heels, wandered uselessly from room to room, too restless to light anywhere and do anything constructive.

When he'd vented some of the steam that had been building up in him since Boone's visit, he took a shower, put on fresh clothes and headed for town in the new truck he'd decided to go ahead and buy.

He still intended to keep his distance from Kendra, much as he wanted to walk right up to her and tell her straight out that he still loved her—had never *stopped* loving her—and meant to marry her if she'd have him.

But he knew all too well what she'd say—that they'd just gotten "carried away," up there on the mountainside. That he was still on the rebound from Brylee and in no position to make any sort of long-term commitment.

He was sure she loved him—her body had told him things she wouldn't or couldn't put into words—but that didn't mean she trusted him. And without trust, without respect, love just wasn't enough, no matter how strong it was.

So he had to wait. Bide his time.

And that was going to be just about the hardest thing he'd ever done.

The carnival was shutting down when he drove by the fairgrounds a few minutes later, the rodeo arena was dark, the vendors outside the exhibition hall loading up what they hadn't sold over the weekend.

It all made him feel lonely, as though a small, special world had opened, just for that brief time, and was now closing again. Shutting him out.

He might have gone to the Boot Scoot for a beer and maybe a game of pool, just to get his mind off things, but it was always closed on Sundays. Even the Butter Biscuit locked up and went dark once the after-church rush was over.

He turned his thoughts to Boone and the sorry situation he'd gotten himself into by letting go of his kids after Corrie died. Hutch started thinking about fear, and what it did to people. What it cost them.

It was a short leap, of course, from his friend's worries about being able to take proper care of a couple of growing boys to the things, he, Hutch, was afraid of. One of them was commitment—he'd be staking his heart on an uncertain outcome if he got married, and if things went sour, he'd lose half his ranch in the divorce settlement. Whisper Creek was *part* of him, and without the whole of it, he'd be crippled on the inside.

The other thing he was afraid of was the water tower.

So he drove there, parked in the tall grass, twilight gathering around him, and looked up. The ladder dangled, rickety as ever, from the side, but something was different, too.

Shea, Slade's teenage stepdaughter, peered down at him, white-faced, from the heights. She appeared to be alone, and a quick glance around confirmed that she *had* undertaken this rite of passage on her own.

"Hi, Hutch," she called down, her voice a little shaky.

"What the hell are you doing up there, Shea?" he snapped, in no mood for small talk.

"I'm—not sure," she replied. "You won't tell Dad and Joslyn, will you?"

"No promises," Hutch said. "Get down here, damn it."

Shea's voice wavered, and even from that distance, with her face a snow-white oval, he could see that she was crying. "I—can't. I tried, but I'm too scared."

Hutch felt the back of his shirt dampen with sweat, and his gut twisted itself into a hard knot. "Come on, Shea," he went on, more gently now. "You got up there in the first place, didn't you? That means you can get down."

"Climbing up wasn't scary," she told him. "Climbing *down* is a whole other matter."

Hutch swore under his breath, moved closer to the ladder. The rungs were old, some of them missing, others hanging by a single rusty nail.

He knew then what he had to do, but that didn't mean he wanted to do it. He kept his gaze fixed straight ahead, because he knew if he looked from side to side, even though he was still standing flat-footed on the ground, he'd feel like he was trying to walk the perimeter of the Tilt-a-Whirl while it was spinning full-throttle.

"Okay," he heard himself say, as if from a distance. Say, the next county. "Hang on. I'll come up there, and we'll climb down together."

"All—all right," Shea agreed.

Terror aside, the approach didn't make a lot of sense to Hutch—Shea probably didn't weigh more than a hundred and ten pounds, while he tipped the scales at an even one-eighty. Expecting that ladder to hold both of them at the same time was anti-logic, pure and simple.

Still, he'd been where Shea was once. He knew she was frozen with fear, knew she needed another human being within touching distance, someone to be with her, talk her down.

Just as Slade Barlow had once done for him.

He closed his eyes for a moment, sucked in a harsh breath and started up that ladder.

He kept his gaze upward, on Shea's face as she leaned out over the edge of the flimsy catwalk, looking down at him. Her eyes were enormous and awash in tears.

"Easy now," he said, addressing himself as much as Shea. "Just take it real easy, sweetheart. You'll be standing on solid ground again in no time."

"You're going to tell my dad," Shea fretted.

The remark lightened the moment, brought on a slight smile that loosened Hutch's tight lips a little. His palms felt slick where he gripped the splintery side rails of that ladder, and his stomach shinnied up into the back of his throat like it meant to fight its way right out of him.

"No, I'm not going to tell your dad," he replied evenly, still climbing. One rung, then another, and for God's sake, don't look down. "*You* are."

"He'll kill me," Shea said.

Better him than a fifty-foot fall from a water tower, Hutch thought, but what he actually said was, "If I were you, I'd worry about that later."

He was almost at the top now, and there was a certain dizzy triumph in that, but he still couldn't bring himself to look anywhere but at Shea, the closest thing he had to a niece.

"Now what?" Shea asked.

A reasonable question, Hutch reflected. "Come on out onto the ladder," he said. "I'm right here with you."

As if he could catch her if she fell.

The things Slade had said to him, way back when he was in Shea's predicament and scared half out of his wits, shouldered their way into his head and tumbled right out over his tongue.

"You can do this," he said quietly. "It's just one step, and then another, and before you know it, we'll both be off this thing."

Shea hesitated, then swung a blue-jeaned leg out over the edge, found a rung with her foot, pushed on it a little to make sure it was sound.

"Easy," Hutch said. "Slow and easy."

Shea was on the ladder, but she clung there for a moment, looking as though she might not move again. "I'm so scared," she whimpered.

"That's okay," Hutch reasoned. "Just take another step. One more, Shea."

He moved down a few rungs to give her room.

One of them split when he stepped on it, and he almost fell, felt slivers digging into the palms of his hands and the undersides of his fingers as he held on, found his footing.

"Don't put your weight on any one rung until you're sure it will hold," he told her calmly, even though he felt like a lone sock tumbling round and round in a clothes dryer. Tentatively, she took another step.

Sweat ran down over Hutch's forehead and stung

like acid in his eyes. "That's it," he said evenly. "You're doing fine."

The descent was a long one—several more rungs broke along the way, under Shea's feet as well as Hutch's—but they finally made it.

Hutch swayed, feeling an uncanny urge to kiss the ground.

Shea threw her arms around him. "What if you hadn't been here?" she whispered.

He hugged her once, then stepped back to look into her tear-stained, bloodless face, taking an avuncular hold on her shoulders. "You'd have made it down on your own eventually," he said, though he wasn't sure that was true. "Are you all right?"

She nodded, hugging herself now, even though the evening was warm. "Thanks," she murmured. "Thanks for showing up when you did, and for helping me."

"Let's get you home," Hutch said. Since he hadn't seen a car around, he knew the girl must have come on foot.

"Dad and Joslyn are over at Grands's house with the baby," she explained. "For Sunday supper."

"We'll head for Callie's, then," Hutch told her.

"Do I still have to tell them what I did?"

"Yep," Hutch answered, opening the passenger door of the truck so she could scramble inside.

"Why?"

"Because you do," Hutch replied when he was behind the wheel with the engine started. "Otherwise, it's a secret and I can't be part of that, Shea. Your dad and I have our differences of opinion now and again, but he *is* my brother, he loves you, and he has a right to know what you're up to." He made a wide turn and they bumped back out onto the dirt road that led to the water tower. "What were you thinking, anyhow, climbing up there?"

It was a rhetorical question, a conversation-starter, really. There *was* no good reason for pulling a stunt like that, but kids did it, year after year, decade after decade, generation after generation.

"I did it because I didn't want to be afraid of it anymore," Shea said.

"I hope that doesn't mean you plan on a repeat performance," Hutch answered, biting back a grin. Damned if the kid didn't have a point—*he* wasn't scared of it anymore, either.

"That," Shea said with a tremulous smile, "would be overkill. Once was enough."

"More than enough," Hutch confirmed.

A few minutes later, they pulled into the parking lot in front of Callie Barlow's Curly Burly Hair Salon. Slade immediately appeared in the doorway of the add-on where Callie lived.

"Tell him," Hutch reiterated as Slade walked toward them, looking puzzled.

Shea sighed dramatically, opened her door and hopped to the ground. Hutch got out, too.

"I climbed the water tower," Shea confessed in a breathless rush, "and then I got scared and I froze and Hutch came up to get me. Am I grounded?"

"You are *so* grounded," Slade told her, cocking a thumb over his shoulder to indicate that she ought to go into the house. All the while, though, Slade was watching Hutch.

When they were alone in that dusty parking lot, Slade nodded to him. "Obliged," he said. He, of all people, knew what climbing that damned ladder had meant for Hutch. He'd have ridden the devil's own bull first, if that would have gotten him out of it.

They shook hands, and Hutch was reminded of the splinters he'd have to remove when he got home.

"See you," he said, turning to get back in the truck.

"Hold on a second," Slade said. "I've got something to ask you."

Hutch turned his head. Waited.

"Joslyn and I—well—we'd like you to be Trace's godfather, if you're willing. The ceremony's next Sunday, after church."

Hutch was moved by the request, but he didn't want it to show. "I'm willing," he said, his voice a little huskier than usual. "But you know how it is with me and churches. Lightning might strike or the roof could fall in."

Slade chuckled. "I'll chance it if you will," he said.

"I'll be there," Hutch told his half brother. "Just let me know what time—and promise me I won't have to rent another tux."

"Just dress the way you normally would," Slade said, his grin lingering. "And Hutch?"

Hutch had the driver's door open and he was already on the running board. "Yeah?"

"Thanks," Slade told him. "For helping Shea out, I mean."

Hutch wasn't wearing a hat, but he tugged at the imaginary brim just the same. "Somebody did the same for me once," he said and got into the truck.

He headed for home, feeling like a different man from the one who'd left it.

By Tuesday morning, Kendra had largely recovered her equilibrium. Discussing the Hutch situation with Joslyn the day before, here at the office, had helped a lot.

Now the storefront space buzzed with anticipatory vibes—even Daisy, who had come to work with Kendra as usual, seemed to sense it.

Sure enough, promptly at ten twenty-five, a powder-blue sports car nosed into a parking space out front and a small woman, wearing jeans, an oversize T-shirt, a baseball cap and sunglasses got out and stood waiting on the sidewalk while Walker parked his truck a few slots over.

Reaching her side, he kissed Casey lightly on the cheek, the way he might have kissed his sister, Brylee, and then held the office door open for her.

Tendrils of Casey's legendary head of red hair were escaping from beneath the cap as she stepped inside, and an impish little smile played on her famous mouth.

She enjoyed being in disguise, that was obvious, so Kendra didn't blurt out the first thought that popped into her head, which was, *I'd have recognized you anywhere.*

Walker, as if guessing Kendra's thoughts, winked at her over the top of Casey's head.

Recalling what he'd told her—that Casey's two children were his, as well—Kendra's curiosity ratcheted up a notch, but of course asking about that was out of the question. Whatever had gone on between Walker and Casey was their own business, not hers.

But she still wondered.

A lot.

She smiled and extended a hand to Casey. "Hello," she said. "I'm Kendra."

"Casey," the other woman replied, shaking Kendra's hand. Her grip was surprisingly strong for such a small person. "Glad to meet you," came out sounding more like, *Gladta meet ya,* since Casey had a Southern accent.

"She thinks she's fooling everybody," Walker told Kendra, grinning. "This is the Casey version of low-key."

Casey removed her sunglasses, revealing her striking green eyes and long lashes, and made a face at Walker. "Let a person have a little fun, why don't you?" she retorted lightly. Then she spotted Daisy and went straight over to her, patting the dog's head and talking to her as she would any friend.

Daisy was instantly besotted with Casey, as she had been when she first met Walker. Kendra took this as a good sign, since she believed dogs and other domesticated animals were excellent judges of character.

"I sure am ready to have a look at that house," Casey announced. "I've been excited ever since Walker sent me the pictures."

"We'll take my car," Kendra said, picking up her keys. She'd vacuumed the interior thoroughly that morning before taking Madison to preschool, and covered the backseat with an old blanket for the trip over, removing it after she'd unloaded the dog, all to prevent messing it up again.

"That's fine," Casey said agreeably, and they all left by the back way, since Kendra's car was parked behind the building, and besides, she wanted to draw as little attention as possible.

Daisy wasn't happy about being left behind and whined pitifully, trying to squeeze through the crack when Kendra went to close the door.

"Oh, let her come along with us," Casey urged.

"She sheds," Kendra said.

"I don't mind," Casey replied.

Kendra nodded and brought Daisy along, already liking Casey Elder for her down-to-earth attitude. She'd fit in well here in Parable—if she decided to stay.

Casey rode in back with Daisy, crammed into the middle because of Madison's car seat, while Walker took the front passenger side. Kendra followed side streets to Rodeo Road, but people peered at them curiously as they passed just the same from yards and sidewalks.

Any stranger would have attracted their attention, but they might well recognize this one—even in disguise, it seemed to Kendra, Casey Elder radiated a sort of down-home confidence that marked her as somebody special.

They reached the mansion without incident and, since the work was done, there were no cleaning or painting crews around.

"Holy *smokes*," Casey said in her trademark drawl, standing at the front gate and looking up. "That is *some* house."

Kendra was already unlocking the front door, Daisy at her side. "You be good," she whispered to the dog.

Inside the massive entryway, Kendra went over the house's best features, but she sensed that Walker and Casey wanted to explore the place on their own, so she left them to it, saying she and Daisy would be on the screened-in porch in back, or in the yard.

Casey smiled and nodded, and then she and Walker set out on their self-guided tour.

Kendra went on through the middle of the sprawling house and out the back door, taking Daisy with her. She let Daisy sniff her way around the yard while she checked the flower beds—the gardeners she'd hired were doing a good job of weeding and watering—and unlocked the door to the guest cottage, so Casey could look it over when she was ready.

She picked a bouquet of zinnias in the garden, planning to put them in the center of her kitchen table over at the rental house later on, and then just stood there, looking around, waiting to feel the sadness of letting go. After all, this had been her dream house once; she'd loved it, lived in it with pride. There were a lot of happy memories, from before and after the break-up with Jeffrey—she'd played here as a child, of course, taken refuge here, and much later, Joslyn had lived in the cottage, when she'd first come back to Parable and found herself falling hard for Slade Barlow—the last man on earth Joss would have chosen. Later still, Kendra had thrown a huge party right there in the backyard, with dancing and caterers and the whole works, to welcome Tara when she'd bought the chicken farm the year before.

No sadness came over her, though.

She knew, standing there with a colorful bouquet of summer flowers in her hands, that Casey would buy this house and make it a home. She would raise her children here.

And that was all well and good.

This house had been Jeffrey's, really—he'd been the one to pay for it, to furnish and maintain it, even after they were divorced. Now it was going to change hands, and the money from the sale would go into a trust fund for Madison, Jeffrey's child, as it should.

Kendra felt a lot of peace in those moments, thinking about all the changes that had taken place in her life since she'd first seen this house, as a lost little girl, hungry to belong somewhere, to be wanted and welcome.

And she *had* been welcome here, with Opal and Joslyn and Joslyn's laughing, generous mother.

But she wasn't that unwanted child anymore. She was a grown woman, whole and strong, with a daughter of her own to love and bring up to the best of her ability. She liked her life, liked who she'd become, knew for sure and at long last that she'd be happy from now on, with or without Hutch Carmody, because she'd *decided* to be.

It was time to leave her fears and doubts behind and go forward, expecting good things to happen, knowing she could cope with the bad ones.

After half an hour or so, Casey and Walker joined her in the yard.

Casey was beaming. "It's perfect," she told Kendra, bending to stroke Daisy's gleaming golden head when the dog approached, wagging her tail. "Where do I sign?"

Kendra glanced at Walker, then looked at Casey again. "Don't you want to think about it for a while?" she asked. As many houses as she'd sold over the course of her career, she'd never had an instant offer like this one.

"Heck, no," Casey replied exuberantly. "It's just what I want. Why wait?"

That was it.

There was no haggling, no having the place inspected, no anything.

Casey signed a contract when they got back to the

office, wrote an enormous deposit check to show good faith and announced that the sooner the deal closed, the better, because she wanted to get her children settled in Parable before school started.

Kendra promised to speed things along in every way she could.

After Walker and Casey were gone, she jumped up and down in the middle of the office and whooped for joy, causing Daisy to slink under a desk and peer out at her with wary eyes.

That made her laugh, and she spoke soothingly to the dog until she came out of her hiding place.

Presently, Kendra gave up on the whole idea of working—there wasn't much to do, anyway—and, after locking Casey's mongo check away in a desk drawer, she summoned Daisy, locked up and returned to her car.

The zinnias she'd picked at the mansion rested on the passenger seat, a damp paper towel wrapped around their stems, reminding Kendra of the fireworks on Saturday night, colorful flowers blooming in the sky and melting away in dancing sparks.

She drove to the Pioneer Cemetery, parked, picked up the zinnias and, leaving Daisy in the car with a window rolled down so she'd have plenty of air, walked along the rows of graves until she came to her grandmother's final resting place.

Eudora Shepherd, the simple stone read, and the dates of her birth and death were inscribed beneath it. No husband was buried nearby, no family members at all.

Her grandmother had been alone in the world, for all intents and purposes.

Kendra crouched and laid the zinnias gently at the base of the dusty headstone.

"You did the best you could," she said very softly, as the breeze played in her hair. "It must have been hard, taking in a child at your age, with money always running short and trouble coming at you from every direction, but you let me stay with you when Mom left, and that was what was important. You fed and clothed me and kept a roof over my head, and I'm grateful for that, Grandma. I'm really, truly grateful."

Kendra stood up straight again, her eyes dry, her heart quiet.

At long last, she'd truly let go, stopped wishing the past could be different. All that really mattered, she realized, was now, what she did, what she thought, what she felt *now*.

She said goodbye to her grandmother, to all the things that had been and shouldn't have, and all the things that should have been, but weren't. She said goodbye to Jeffrey, and goodbye to the reckless boy Hutch had been when she first fell in love with him.

And "hello" to the man he had become.

She was in no rush, though. Things would unfold as they were supposed to, and she was open to that.

HUTCH SADDLED REMINGTON and rode up to the mountainside alone that morning after assigning the ranch crew to various tasks for the day.

He dismounted, left the horse to graze and walked toward the rock pile, pausing briefly in the place where he and Kendra had made love the previous Saturday afternoon.

He smiled. It had been good—their lovemaking—

because it had been right. Not to mention, long over-due, from his viewpoint, anyway.

He went on to the stone monument he'd built in fury, in pain, in frustration, lifted up one of the heavier stones, and set it on the ground.

"It's over, old man," he told his dead father, though only the birds and the breeze and his favorite horse were around to hear. "I'm through hating you for not being who I needed you to be. You were who you were. I don't mind saying, though, that I want to be a differ-ent kind of man. If Kendra agrees, I mean to make her my wife. I'll love her until the day I die, and maybe after that, too, and I'll love that little girl of hers like she's my own."

Hutch began to feel a little foolish then, talking to a dead man, and anyway he'd said what he wanted to say.

One by one, he tossed aside the rocks that made up that pile and finally stood on level ground.

CHAPTER NINETEEN

HUTCH DIDN'T SEE Kendra again until the day of little Trace Carmody Barlow's christening, when he showed up at the church in a pair of slacks, a white shirt and a lightweight sports jacket with a secret tucked into one pocket for later.

Most of the congregation had stayed on after the regular service for the special ceremony, and Hutch was mildly uncomfortable, stealing the occasional anxious glance at the ceiling, willing it to hold.

The new pastor, Dr. Beaumont, opened with a prayer.

Hutch bowed his head, like everybody else, but his eyes were partway open the whole time, drinking in the sight of Kendra standing next to him and wearing a green dress made of some soft fabric that looked supple to the touch.

When the prayer was over, Kendra opened her eyes, caught him looking at her and smiled slightly.

Dr. Beaumont took the baby boy gently from Joslyn's arms, holding him securely and baptizing him with a sprinkle of water, in the name of the Father, and the Son, and the Holy Spirit.

Promises were made all around.

There was another prayer; Slade was holding the infant now, looking as though he might just bust open with love and pride. His resemblance to the old man

was stronger than ever, except, Hutch noticed with a
slight jolt, for the quiet self-assurance in his eyes. That
was the difference—Slade was fine with being Slade,
taking life as it came, but their father had seen it as
a battle instead, something to survive and overcome,
and the effort of doing all that had used up all he had
to give.

The formal part of the christening ended and the
small but enthusiastic crowd was dispersing. Now, there
would be a celebration picnic on the grounds of the Pioneer Cemetery.

Hutch went over there ahead of time and wound up
standing at the foot of his dad's grave.

There was nothing to resolve, really; he'd made
peace with John Carmody, once and for all, by taking
down that monument up at the meadow, rock by rock.

Resentment by resentment, hurt by hurt.

All that was gone now, scattered, just like the stones.

Still, it seemed right to pause and silently pay his
respects, because in spite of it all, he'd loved his father,
known all along on some level that the old man had
given what he had in him to give.

Folks started arriving right away, filling the picnic
tables with food, kids running around, playing, adults
talking and laughing in the shade of the trees.

Out of the corner of his eye, Hutch saw Slade heading in his direction. He'd taken off his suit jacket, Slade
had, and the sleeves of his white shirt were rolled up.

He came to stand beside Hutch.

"You doing all right?" he asked, his voice husky.

"I'm just fine," Hutch answered honestly. "How
about you?"

"Never better," Slade replied. "I've got everything a man could ask for and more."

Hutch looked down at the fancy headstone, bearing their father's name, along with the dates of his birth and death. It was hard to believe that a man's whole life could fit between two sets of words and numbers like that, symbolically or not, but there it was.

John Carmody had been born, lived his life and died.

And behind a single dash, chiseled in stone, was the whole story, much of which they'd never know.

"He should have acknowledged you sooner, Slade," Hutch said without looking at his brother. "Treated you better."

Slade considered that for a few moments. "He gave me life. Maybe that was all he could manage. And he knew Callie would raise me right."

Hutch merely sighed.

Slade rested a hand on his shoulder. "There's a party going on over there under the trees," he reminded Hutch. "How about joining in?"

Hutch lifted his head, grinned when he saw Madison running toward him in a polka-dot dress, her arms open wide.

He scooped her up when she reached him, carried her as he walked alongside Slade. She chattered in his ear the whole way, going on about how she'd missed him and Mommy had, too, and saying she wanted to ride Ruffles again so she'd be ready to carry a flag at the rodeo and compete in the barrel racing when she was bigger.

Kendra, seeing them, broke away from the gathering.

Madison, spotting Shea nearby, squirmed in Hutch's

arms and he set her down. She ran toward the older girl with barely a glance at Kendra, and Shea greeted the little girl with a bright smile and a giggle.

Hutch and Kendra, meanwhile, stood a few feet apart, the grass rippling all around them like a low tide, just looking at each other.

Figuring that he'd put this conversation off long enough already, Hutch cleared his throat and moved in closer, cupping her elbows in his hands. She smelled of lavender soap and sunshine, and her eyes were as clear and green as sea glass.

"I love you, Kendra," he said, on a swell of emotion that made the words come out sounding hoarse. "Maybe it's too soon to say it—hell, maybe it's too *late,* I don't know—but it's true." He reached into his coat pocket, brought out the small velvet box, opened it with a motion of his thumb. His great-grandmother's engagement ring was inside—a simple but elegant concoction of diamonds and rubies. After Joslyn had done a little detective work so it would fit Kendra, he'd had it sized, cleaned and polished at the jeweler's. Now, it caught fire in the sunlight.

Kendra's eyes widened as she looked at the ring, but she didn't say anything right away, and the next few moments were some of the longest of Hutch's life. They'd traveled a rocky road, the two of them, and while he knew she loved him, he wasn't sure she'd be willing to throw in with him for the long haul.

"Are you asking me to marry you?" she finally asked very softly.

Hutch was only vaguely aware of the nearby crowd. For him, time had stopped and Kendra was all there was to the universe.

"Yes," he managed at last. "If you feel the same as I do, that is."

She smiled. "I've loved you since we were kids, Hutch," she told him. "That hasn't changed."

"Then you'll marry me?"

She stepped in close, put her arms around his neck, and looked up into his eyes. "I'll marry you," she agreed quietly. "When we're both ready."

"I'm ready *now*," Hutch told her. God knew *that* was the truth in its entirety.

She laughed. "There are things we have to work out first," she reasoned. "Plans and decisions to make. We have to consider Madison, for a start."

He wanted to adopt Madison, raise her as a Carmody, but this wasn't the place to talk about that. He'd already jumped the gun by declaring himself and shoving a ring at Kendra, in a graveyard of all places, with half the town looking on. This time around, he wasn't going to botch everything, like he had before.

She stepped back and offered him her left hand, and he took the ring out of the box and slid it onto her finger.

He kissed her then, and the town of Parable applauded from the picnic tables under the trees.

One month later...

OPAL DENNISON SAT UP straight in her new favorite pew, one that afforded her the best possible view of the pastor, Dr. Walter Beaumont. She'd taken it over the first time he preached and laid claim to it every Sunday since.

Today, on this bright August afternoon, Hutch Carmody was up front, in exactly the same place he'd stood at his *last* wedding, with Boone beside him as best man, just like before.

The church was packed with guests once again and, since the organ music hadn't started up yet, folks were buzzing with excitement and speculation, most of them wondering, unless Opal missed her guess, if history would repeat itself.

She settled in, Joslyn's baby safe in the infant carrier beside her, since Joslyn and Tara, being bridesmaids, were at the rear of the church, waiting for the ceremony to begin. Slade was back there, too, fixing to give Kendra away, though she was still out of sight, except for a spill of shimmering lace, part of her magnificent dress.

Turning a little, Opal saw Slade's gaze connect with Joslyn's, and it seemed to her that their two souls glowed right through their skin, lighting up their faces and surrounding them with a shared aura.

She smiled to herself, turned her attention back to the groom, waiting up there by the altar with Walter, who looked resplendent in his pastoral robes. Oh, he was a handsome one all right, with his full head of white hair and his dignified manner, but this was Hutch's day, and Kendra's, and Opal meant to focus on them.

Settling in contentedly, Opal exchanged a mental high-five with the Lord. *We do good work, You and me,* she told Him silently. She looked over at the best man, Boone, standing beside Hutch and looking solemn. *Course we've still got* him *to straighten out, don't we, and sweet Tara, too, but we can cross Hutch and Kendra off our list, just like we did Slade and Joslyn. Another mission accomplished.*

Just then Walter caught Opal's eye. A small, mischievous smile tilted his mouth up at one side, and darned if that man didn't *wink* at her, right there in church, with him right up front in full view and holding the Holy Book in his hands.

Or did he?

After a moment, she wasn't sure whether he had or not. Had she imagined it?

The idea warmed her all over just the same, clear to the center of her being, but she didn't wink back, of course.

There was a proper way to go about things, after all, and anyway she was in no big hurry to reel Walter in and marry up with him. She liked him a lot and they'd even gone out fishing together a couple of times and talked and laughed so much they'd scared away all the trout. The Sunday after little Trace Barlow was christened, with Kendra and Hutch standing up as godparents, they'd gone to the Butter Biscuit for brunch together after church, she and Walter, and stayed until Ellie practically kicked them out so she could close the place promptly at two o'clock, as she always did on the Sabbath.

Yes, sir, things were looking real promising on the romance front, not just for Kendra and Hutch, but for her and Walter, too.

All she had to do now was wait and trust and let the Good Lord have His way, since He always knew best.

RAISING HER VEIL, Kendra bent, her eyes brimming with happy tears, and kissed Madison, her flower girl, soundly on the cheek. "Nervous?" she whispered. When the organist struck up the prelude, Madison would be the first member of the wedding party to walk up the aisle.

"No," Madison answered in a stage whisper, looking earnest in her blue silk dress with the ruffled skirt. "I'm getting a *daddy* today!"

The comment carried far enough to raise a gentle twitter of laughter from the pews nearby.

Then the organist sounded the first reverberating note and, on cue, Madison strolled down the aisle, a job she'd practiced tirelessly for several weeks by then, scattering pink and white rose petals as she went.

People crooned and smiled as she passed.

When she reached the front, she went right over to Hutch and tugged at his sleeve with her free hand, holding the now-empty flower basket in the other.

He leaned down and she whispered something in his ear, and he grinned at her and pointed out the place where she was supposed to stand.

The prelude continued, picking up speed, and Tara followed Madison's trail of rose petals, looking fabulous in the soft yellow dress she'd chosen herself. Joslyn, like Madison, wore blue—Kendra hadn't wanted to impose any specific fashion statement on her friends.

Joslyn reached back, gave Kendra's hand a quick squeeze, exchanged glances with Slade and moved gracefully between the two rows of pews, coming to stand next to Tara.

"This is it," Slade whispered to Kendra as she took her arm. "Ready?"

"Ready," she replied, clutching her bouquet of zinnias and daisies and drawing a deep breath.

The wedding march began, but before Slade and

Kendra could take the first step, Hutch left the platform and started toward her.

A hush fell over the guests and the music dropped away, one jumbled note on top of another, into silence.

Kendra held her breath as she watched Hutch approach. He looked impossibly handsome in the tux he'd reluctantly agreed to wear, just for today, and love welled up inside her.

Reaching her, he smiled and offered her his arm.

"I'll take it from here," he told Slade, who grinned and shook his head as he stepped aside.

The congregation let out their collective breath, and the music started again, faltering at first and then filling the little sanctuary to its walls in a joyous flood of sound.

Hutch and Kendra walked arm in arm to the front of the church and stood together before the pastor.

They'd written their own vows, though they hadn't shared them with each other, and Kendra was so overcome with joy and with love for the man standing beside her that she was sure the carefully prepared words had slipped her mind forever. She'd have to wing it, she supposed, but that was all right.

Hutch spoke first, turning to Kendra, taking her hands in his, holding her gaze through the billowing softness of her bridal veil.

"Sometimes," he began, his voice husky but strong, "a man is lucky enough to get a second chance, whether he deserves one or not, and that's what's happened to me. I love you, Kendra. I always have and I always will. I'll be faithful to you and I'll listen to you. I'll protect you and provide for you, and—"

"You'll be my daddy!" Madison piped up, beaming.

That brought on more laughter and a smattering of applause.

Hutch slanted a look at the little girl, grinned and confirmed in a clear voice, "And I'll be your daddy." He paused, asked amicably, "Do you have anything else to say, shortstop, or can we get on with this?"

Madison considered for a moment, finally shook her head, curls flying, and chimed, "No, that's everything!"

The whole congregation chuckled.

Hutch turned back to Kendra and finished his vows.

Kendra swallowed, looking up at his face, loving him with all she had and all she was and would ever be. "I love you, Hutch Carmody," she began, never taking her eyes from his. "I'll be your friend and your partner, as well as your wife, from this day forward, in good times and bad and everything in between. I'll be the best mother I can to Madison and to all the other children I hope we'll have together, and I promise to trust you, always, and to be worthy of your trust in return."

When she'd finished, there was a short silence, during which she and Hutch simply looked at each other, exchanging further vows, silent ones, deeper ones, ones that went far beyond words.

Dr. Beaumont asked them the usual questions then, and they answered with "I do," and slipped wedding bands onto each other's ring fingers.

Finally, in a booming voice of jubilant authority, the minister pronounced them man and wife.

"You may kiss the bride," he added, pretending it was an afterthought, though by then Hutch had already raised Kendra's veil, smoothed it back away from her face and covered her mouth with his own.

The organ soared back to life.

The congregation rose as one, cheering and clapping.

Madison dropped her flower basket, rushed over and wriggled in between Kendra and Hutch, and they each took her by the hand, walking back down the aisle together, a family.

THE RECEPTION, HELD IN the community center, took the better part of forever to go by, as far as Hutch was concerned. There were endless pictures to pose for, hands to shake, a big, fancy cake to cut into. There was food and music and enough presents to fill the back of a semitruck.

Hutch enjoyed the festivities, but he was ready for the honeymoon to start, and he knew Kendra was, too. For various reasons, they'd decided to not have sex again until after the wedding, and they'd stuck to the plan—not an easy matter and now that the finish line was in sight, he wanted to cross it.

They'd be staying on the ranch instead of going on a trip, with Madison spending the first night at the Barlows' place with Opal, who'd just moved back there, and of course, Shea, Madison's own personal teen idol.

The time passed like molasses in January, as the old saying went.

They danced, he and Kendra, and holding her close was sweet torment.

"I can't wait to get you alone, Mrs. Carmody," he whispered in her ear.

"You'll *have* to wait, Mr. Carmody," she teased.

Another hour went by before Kendra agreed to slip away. They said goodbye to Madison, who was on the piano bench beside Shea, learning to play the bass part of "Heart and Soul," and dismissed them with a happy grin and "See you tomorrow!"

The new truck was waiting outside, decorated from front to back with streamers, streaks of shaving cream, and all manner of other stuff, including a big, hand-lettered sign that read Just Married.

He hoisted Kendra into the passenger seat, taking what seemed like an extra five minutes to stuff the skirts of that big dress in behind her. She laughed the whole time.

What a sight they must make, Hutch thought, getting in on the driver's side, him in a tux, and Kendra in all that lace and silk, leaving their wedding in a pickup truck.

Eager as he was to get home to the ranch house and be alone with his bride, to unwrap her from that fancy gown and everything underneath it, he was struck dumb for a long moment, just to look at her.

She was so unbelievably, impossibly beautiful.

And she was his.

Peering out of the billows of white surrounding her, she laughed again, maybe at his expression and maybe for sheer joy.

"I feel like a giant cupcake," she said.

He cocked a grin at her before starting up the truck. "Good enough to eat," he replied, driving away from the church.

When they got home, the house was lit up, even though the afternoon was still bright with sunshine. The night before, he and Slade and Boone had spent hours putting up strings of white Christmas lights, and the whole place twinkled.

Hutch parked the truck near the front gate, got out and came around to lift Kendra off the passenger seat.

He didn't set her down, but looked straight into her eyes and said, "Welcome home, Mrs. Carmody."

Her eyes filled with tears, causing her mascara to run a little. "I love you," she said. "So, so much."

He replied in kind and kissed her to seal the bargain.

Getting the gate open with an armload of woman and wedding dress was tricky, but Hutch managed it, carried Kendra up the walk and the porch steps and over the threshold to boot. Leviticus was right there to greet them, though he soon lost interest and wandered off into some other part of the house.

In the foyer, he set her on her feet, pretending to be winded by the effort of lugging her that far.

She smiled, picked up her voluminous skirts and started up the stairs, looking back at him over one shoulder. She knew where the master bedroom was—he'd shown it to her, along with the rest of that big and formerly empty house—but today was different. Today, and tonight, and every night that followed, they could make use of it.

"Aren't you going to help me out of this dress?" she asked coyly.

"It's the least I can do," Hutch answered, then he bolted up the stairs after her, undoing his tie as he went, shrugging out of his tuxedo jacket and leaving it behind on the rail of the landing.

His cummerbund went next and, by the time he caught up with Kendra inside the bedroom, he was undoing his cuff links.

Kendra, a vision in white, stood looking around, taking in the antique four-poster bed, the old-fashioned

fireplace, the built-in bookshelves, bare at the moment
because Hutch had been sleeping in a room down the
hall since he was younger than Madison was now.

She moved to the mantel, ran her hand along the
face of it, turned to him. "Our room," she said very
softly, almost reverently. "The place where our babies
will be conceived."

Hutch watched her, etching her image into his mind
so he could remember, years and years from now, when
they were an old married couple, how she'd looked at
this moment. "Some of them," he agreed. "I plan on
making love to you in plenty of other places, too."

Kendra came to him, stood on tiptoe, and kissed him
lightly on the mouth. "This will do for a start, though,"
she said with mischief in her eyes. Then she turned,
indicating the long row of tiny buttons on the back of
her dress with a gesture of one hand.

Hutch began the slow, delicious process of unbutton-
ing Kendra's wedding gown. He fumbled a little, now
and then—what was the point of making buttons that
small when a man had big fingers?—but he finally got
the thing open, and she stepped out of it, draped it carefully over the chair in front of the fireplace. It looked
like a fallen cloud, resting there.

"Madison will wear this dress someday," Kendra
said. "And maybe other daughters, too."

The thought warmed Hutch's heart, but it was soon
gone. At the moment, he wasn't thinking long-term, he
was thinking right now.

Even without the gown, Kendra was still wearing a
lot of gear—a big, lacy petticoat-type thing, and a camisole with a bra underneath it. She kicked off her satin
shoes and shed the petticoat, unfastened her stockings

from the sexy garters that held them up, bared her legs and stood there in panties and the camisole, looking like an angel trying to pass as a pinup girl.

For a moment, he couldn't speak.

She walked over to him, unbuttoned his shirt, pulled it out of his pants. "Do I have to do all the undressing around here?" she asked.

He shook his head, pulled her close and kissed her again, deeply this time, thoroughly, holding nothing back. She wrapped her arms around his neck, pressed her warm softness against him and kissed him back.

He groaned, consuming her, unable to get enough.

At some point, they both got naked, though Hutch was too far gone by that point to say when it happened. He lifted Kendra in his arms, carried her to the bed and laid her down.

"No foreplay this time," she whispered, gazing up at him with sultry eyes and a wicked little smile. "I want you inside me, Hutch. It's been too long since we were together—like this—"

"No rush," he ground out. "We've got all the time in the world." He kissed her mouth, her neck, found her nipple and took it into his mouth. "All the time in the world," he repeated, using his tongue.

Fire shot through Kendra as Hutch took his sweet time at her breast, caressing her all the while running a hand over her other breast, down her side, across her belly to the place where her passions lived.

She whimpered, giving herself up to pleasure. There would be no hurrying this husband of hers—he believed in taking her by inches, by *millimeters,* a touch, a kiss, a teasing brush of his fingertips at a time.

Her voice was ragged when she said his name, rose

to a low shout when he put his head between her legs and took her into his mouth.

He suckled until she was near the breaking point and then withdrew to nibble at the insides of her thighs, even the backs of her knees.

Her breath came deep and fast, and she commanded him to *take her,* damn it, but he only took her into his mouth again, and alternately sucked on her and teased her with his tongue.

Kendra's hips began to rise and fall, faster and faster, and she plunged her fingers into Hutch's hair, holding him to her even as she pleaded to be taken.

She was on the verge, whispering, "Don't stop—oh, God, don't stop—" when the eruption finally came. She exploded against an inner sky, like fireworks, and dissolved into flaming sparks that took a long time to fall.

By the time she'd settled back into herself, Hutch was poised above her on the bed, his forearms braced against the mattress on either side of her still-quivering, exquisitely sated body.

He moved inside her, slowly that first time, throwing his head back as he reached her depths.

Instantly, she needed him again and more desperately than before. This time, however, he didn't hold back, but gave her all of himself, one long, hard thrust following another.

Kendra found the ever-rising ecstasy almost more than she could bear. She tossed her head from side to side on the pillow, and their bodies collided, again and again, until they reached the same pinnacle at the same moment. Hutch went still, deep inside her, and she felt the surging warmth of him.

This time, there was no condom.

They'd wasted enough time and both of them wanted a baby.

When it was over, he collapsed beside her, one leg sprawled across her thighs, his breathing ragged.

A long time passed before either of them spoke.

"What is it with you and foreplay?" Kendra asked, her head resting on his shoulder.

He chuckled. "Get used to it," he said, kissing her temple. "Some things shouldn't be hurried, and making love to you is one of them."

She made a slow circle on the taut, washboard flesh of his belly with the fingertips of her right hand. "Really?" she purred. Then she closed her fingers around him, and he groaned, instantly hard again.

"Woman," he gasped, "you are playing with fire."

She worked him harder, faster, but gently, too. "Am I?"

He pulsed against her palm, huge and hot, and gave a raspy moan.

Then, in a heartbeat, he was on top of her.

She looked up into his eyes, batted her lashes, and said, "But what about the foreplay?"

"You win," he rasped, and then he possessed her in one hard, driving thrust.

HOURS LATER, DOWNSTAIRS in the dimly lit kitchen— Hutch wearing jeans and nothing else, Kendra in one of his T-shirts, happier than she'd ever imagined it was possible to be—they nibbled at the lasagna Opal had thoughtfully prepared and left in the refrigerator. Leviticus, recently fed, snoozed nearby on his dog bed.

"I guess this isn't much of a honeymoon," Hutch fretted, sitting across from her, his hair love-rumpled and his golden beard coming in with the twilight. "Maybe we should have gone to Vegas or Hawaii or something."

Kendra grinned at him. "No complaints here, cowboy," she said. "We can take trips later. Right now, we've got a lot of settling in to do."

Hutch looked relieved, and the expression in his eyes made Kendra wonder how she'd ever doubted that they belonged together, for always.

They ate what they could, both of them starved and at the same time too riled up to eat much. They'd showered together and made love under the spray, and while Kendra's body still throbbed with aftershocks from the powerful releases he'd brought her to, she wanted more, and she knew Hutch did, too.

"Think we made a baby today?" he asked.

Kendra moved her shoulders in a little shrug. "All we can do is keep trying," she said.

He laughed, reached out, closed his hand briefly over hers. "I have something for you," he told her, turning serious all of a sudden.

"I hope so," she vamped, making eyes at him.

"Besides that," he said, after a raspy chuckle. He stood up, disappeared into his office off the kitchen and returned with a thick packet in one hand.

Kendra frowned, a little unnerved. They hadn't signed, or even discussed, a prenuptial agreement but now, it seemed, he'd reconsidered the idea. Did he really think she'd demand half of Whisper Creek Ranch if, God forbid, they parted ways before one of them died?

"What's this?" she asked warily.

He smiled, reading her trepidation accurately, the

way he so often did. "It's a deed," he said. "Maggie Landers drew it up."

Kendra's hands trembled as she opened the document, scanned the legalese and made the startling discovery that she was *already* half owner of the ranch. All that was required was a notarized signature.

"I don't understand," she confessed. "This ranch means everything to you—"

"And so do you," Hutch finished huskily when her words fell away. "This ranch is *me,* Kendra—as much a part of me as my arms and legs and my heart. I'd do just about anything to keep it. But if you divorced me tomorrow, well, so be it, you'd still be half owner of Whisper Creek."

Kendra was overcome, touched to the tenderest part of her soul. Hutch wasn't just giving her his love, but his complete trust. He was staking everything he held dear on their marriage, their commitment to each other and to a lifetime as man and wife.

She held the document to her heart for a moment, not because of what it offered but because of what it *meant,* and then she set it down on the table between them.

"I'm going back upstairs, now," she announced. "Coming?"

Hutch laughed and scooted back his chair to rise. "Definitely," he said.

* * * * *

BAD NEWS COWBOY

Maisey Yates

CHAPTER ONE

KATE GARRETT HAD never much belonged to anyone. And that was how she liked it.

She didn't have the time or desire to deal with anyone telling her what to do or how to act or how to sit. If she wanted to ride across the field like a bat out of hell and let her hair tangle in the wind, gathering snarls and bugs and Lord knew what else, she'd do that.

It was the perk of independence. Compensation from life since it hadn't seen fit to give her a mother who was around to tuck her in at night. The consolation prize that came for living with a father whose every word was scented with whiskey, who moved around her as if she existed in a different space. As if she wasn't even there.

But who needed warm milk and itchy tights and whatever the hell else came with being hovered over for your entire childhood? She'd rather have freedom and the pounding of a horse's hooves on arena dirt.

Or on the soft soil of the Garrett family ranch, which was what she had today. Which meant it was a damn good day. She had to be at the Farm and Garden for work in a couple of hours, so she would have to cut the ride shorter than she'd like. But any ride was better than none, even if she'd rather keep going until her face was chapped from the wind and her lungs burned.

The sun was getting high in the sky and she knew

it was time to haul ass back. She grimaced and slowed her horse, Roo, turning sharply, as she would if they were going around a barrel, before picking up the pace again on the way out of the loop and galloping back in the direction she'd come.

Wind whipped strands of dark hair into her eyes and she cursed her decision to leave it loose. So maybe nobody yelled at her for letting her hair get tangled, but in the end she had to comb it out and that was always a pain.

She would braid it before work. Because when she'd gotten her horse ready to be put away, she wasn't going to have time to get herself looking pretty. Not that she needed to be particularly pretty to man the counter at the Farm and Garden.

She would settle for not looking homeless.

She slowed Roo as they approached the horse barn, and she dismounted, breathing hard, the early-morning air like a shot of ice to her lungs on every indrawn breath. She led the horse inside and removed her bridle, then slipped on a halter and looped the lead over a hook. She didn't even bother with tying a quick-release knot on Roo when they were at home. She knelt down and loosened the girth on the saddle before taking it off completely, along with the bright blue blanket underneath. In spite of the chilly air that marked the shift from summer to fall, Roo had worked up a sweat during the ride.

She pulled the towel off a nearby rack and wiped Roo down, making sure she was dry and that the saddle marks were removed. Then she took her bright yellow pick out of the bucket and ran her hand down Roo's leg, squeezing gently until the horse lifted her foot. She picked out any rocks and mud that had collected during the ride, humming softly as she did. She repeated that step on the other three legs and was nearly finished when she heard footsteps on the ground behind her, followed by her oldest brother's voice.

"You're up early, Katie."

"I wanted to get a ride in before I headed to work. And if you call me Katie one more time, I'm going to stick this pick in your eye."

Connor only smiled at her threat, crossing his arms over his broad chest, his wedding band catching her attention. In the seven months since he and Liss had gotten married, it had stayed shiny. It was some kind of metal designed to break if it got caught on anything, since ranch work was dangerous for men wearing jewelry.

She liked the reminder, though. The reminder that he was happy again. Connor had spent way too much time buried in the depths of his grief, and Liss had finally been able to lift him out of it.

As an added bonus, Liss had allowed Kate to wear jeans and boots to the wedding. Which was more than her future sister-in-law, Sadie, was letting her get away with for her and Eli's upcoming mammoth nuptials.

"Sorry, Kate," Connor said, his smile getting wider.

"You're cheerful this morning," she observed, finishing with Roo's last hoof before straightening.

"I'm pretty much cheerful all the time these days."

"I've noticed. Which is more than I can say for your wife."

"Her ankles are swollen. It's all my fault," he said, but he didn't look at all abashed. In fact, he looked rather proud. Love did weird things to people. It was kind of strange being surrounded by it like she was now.

Watching both of her older brothers fall fast and hard.

And she was just alone. But then, she was kind of used to that. And she liked it. She wasn't beholden to anyone. It was secure. It was familiar.

Anyway, it made for a lot of free time available to ride her horse.

"Yeah, she makes a good case for staying far away from marriage and pregnancy—" Kate tucked a strand of hair behind her ear "—what with all the complaining."

"Suits me just fine if you stay away from it for now," Connor said. "Nobody's good enough for you anyway."

"I don't know about that. But I haven't met anyone with the balls to keep up." That wasn't strictly true. It was more true to say she hadn't done any serious looking.

Really?

She gritted her teeth and ignored that thought.

"That doesn't surprise me. What time do you get off?" he asked.

"Pretty early."

"Are you coming out for poker?"

She was usually invited to the family game these days, after years of them behaving as though her presence stifled conversation. No matter whether she was three, thirteen or newly twenty-three, Eli and Connor looked at her like she was a child. Of course, Sadie and Liss weren't much better.

And Jack was pretty much the worst.

She ignored the slight twist in her stomach when she thought of her brothers' friend.

"Isn't it my night to bring dinner?" she asked.

He leaned against the barn wall. "That's one reason I was making sure you're coming. If not, I was going to have to cook something."

"By which you mean opening a frozen pizza box?"

"Yes. Because that is the extent of my skills and if I ask Liss to cook anything right now, I'm going to end up with a ladle shoved up where the sun don't shine."

Kate winced. "Well, out of concern for your…that, I promise to bring dinner."

He pushed away from the wall. "Excellent. See you tonight."

She hesitated before asking the next question. But she did need to know. "How many of us will there be?"

Connor screwed up his face, clearly doing mental math. "Six counting you."

So that meant everyone was coming. Which wasn't all that remarkable. It was more common than not. Considering that, her stomach should not have felt the way it did when she took an extra-sharp barrel turn while riding Roo.

"I might bring fish and chips from The Crab Shanty."

"You don't have to do that. It's expensive. And greasy." He paused for a moment. "You realize that expensive was the negative and greasy was the positive."

She waved a hand. "I'm sick of pizza. I'll spend my money however I damn well please. Anyway, I still have some cash from my last win." The purse for the last amateur barrel racing event she'd won hadn't been very big, but it had been enough to continue giving her the luxury of working part-time at the Farm and Garden while she kept honing her skills.

It was too expensive to jump into the professional circuit without the ability to back it up.

"Fine. Spend your money on seafood. In which case, I'll take the lobster, thanks."

"Liss isn't the only one who might stuff things in places, Connor. I'd watch it."

He reached out and mussed her hair, like she was a damn toddler. Or a puppy.

"Watch it, asshole," she grumbled.

"Sorry, did I break one of the eggs in that bird's nest of yours?"

She scowled. "I hope your wife punches you in the face."

"That isn't a far-fetched hope."

"Excellent," she said, knowing she sounded bloodthirsty. She felt a little bloodthirsty.

"I hope you don't plan on treating your customers the same way you treat me."

"No, I perk up for actual people."

"I don't really care how evil your mood is if you bring food. And money to lose."

"Shut it, Garrett. You know you aren't going to get any of my money."

Connor's smile turned rueful. "No. Because Jack is going to end up with everyone's money."

The outright mention of Jack's name made her skin feel prickly. "Well, that's true," she said. "I don't know why you invite him."

Connor looked mystified. "I don't think anyone does. He just shows up."

"Ha. Ha." Kate scuffed her boot through the dirt, leaving a line behind.

"I have to get a move on," he said. "These cows won't castrate themselves."

"Damn lazy beasts. Also—" Kate held her hands up and wiggled her fingers "—no thumbs."

"Right. It's thankless work. It's also the only magic trick I know."

She narrowed her eyes. "Magic trick?"

"I'm off to go change bulls into steers. With the help of my lovely assistant, Eli."

She snorted. "Yeah, well, enjoy that. I'm going to give thanks that I'm not on ranch duty today."

"See you tonight." And with that, he turned and walked out the alley doors.

Kate grabbed her brush out of the bucket, then tossed the pick back in. She straightened and ran the bristles quickly over Roo's hair before taking the end of the lead rope and guiding her into her stall.

She unhooked the rope and patted Roo on the nose before scratching the white star on her forehead. "See you later," she said, unable to resist dropping a kiss on the horse's nose.

A day that started with a ride and ended with a poker game surrounded by her family could only be a good day.

And the presence of Jack Monaghan didn't matter at all.

IT WAS A strange thing knowing that whenever a random expense came up, he had the means to handle it. After spending most of his childhood in poverty, Jack Monaghan was still getting used to having money. Not

just in his pocket but in his bank account. In stocks and
bonds. He even had a savings account and some set
aside for retirement.

If someone looked at his finances, they might think
he was responsible. Stable. Because on paper, he looked
good. A person might be tempted to draw the conclusion that Jack was a steady, staid family man.

Yeah, that motherfucker would be wrong.

But Jack didn't care either way. Because today his
tractor was broken, and he was headed over to the Farm
and Garden to get a replacement part and he didn't have
to beg anyone for a loan.

He killed the engine on his F-150 and got out of the
truck, walked to the front door of the store and pushed
it open. The little bell that was strung overhead sig-
naled his arrival and a dark head popped up from behind the counter.

"Hey there, Katie," he said making his way across
the store.

The youngest Garrett narrowed her brown eyes, her
glare as penetrating as a rifle bullet. "What are you
doing here, Monaghan?"

"I'm a paying customer, twerp."

"Did you just call me a twerp? Because I have the
right to refuse service to anyone." She flipped her braid
over her shoulder, her expression remaining fierce.

"Yeah, that would go over real well with your boss.
Especially since I'm here to drop decent money on a
freaking carburetor."

"We're probably gonna have to order it. You could
always go to Tolowa and pick it up at one of the bigger stores."

"I'd rather get it here. Keep my business in Copper Ridge."

The corner of her lips turned up in a bad approximation of a smile. "That's appreciated."

"It's okay, Katie. I know you don't appreciate much about me."

"If you called me something other than Katie, I might."

"I just called you twerp and you didn't seem to appreciate that, either."

"Maybe if you pulled your head out of your ass and realized I was a grown-up and not a child, we wouldn't have so many problems." She crossed her arms beneath her breasts—which he knew she had; he wasn't blind —and cocked her hip to the side.

"We don't have problems. You have problems. *I* am fine." He pulled a piece of paper out of his pocket that had all of the relevant make and model information for his tractor. "Well, except for a carburetor problem." He handed her the paper and she took it from him, studying the information before scrunching her nose and turning to the antiquated computer on the counter.

The monitor was practically the size of a hay bale, big and square, off-white. Like something they had used back in the junior high school computer lab.

"Doesn't that thing drive you crazy?" he asked, indicating the machine.

Kate frowned, entering numbers in slowly before turning to look at him. "Why would it drive me crazy?"

"Because it's so outdated I'm surprised you can't hear gears turning inside when you give it a command."

"It works fine."

"Isn't it slow?"

She blinked. "Compared to what?"

"Do you have a computer?"

"Why would I need a computer?"

He looked at the completely earnest and completely confused expression of the younger sister of his two best friends in the world. Kate was pretty enough even if she didn't choose to make the most of her assets, not a bit of makeup to enhance her features, her hair rarely in any configuration other than a single braid down her back. Invariably, she wore slightly baggy T-shirts or flannel button-up tops tucked into either a pair of Wrangler or Carhartt jeans.

Kate dressed for functionality, not decoration.

He had no issue with that. Kate was… Well, as women went, she was more functional than decorative, so it fit.

"I think most people would say they couldn't survive without one," he said.

"Well—" Kate flashed him a smile "—look at me. Surviving and shit."

"Good job." He tapped the counter. "Now let's see if you can order me a carburetor as handily as you can survive."

"Watch it, Monaghan," she said, still typing numbers into the computer. "I am bringing dinner tonight, and I don't have to bring any for you."

"Oh, do we have the option of excluding people from dinner now? I'll remember that when my turn comes around."

Lately, Kate was usually prickly as a porcupine when he was around. He was never sure why. But then, he seemed incapable of leaving her be. He wasn't sure why that was, either. She brought out the devil in him.

Of course, the devil in him seemed to live real close to the surface.

It hadn't always been like this. Sure, they'd always hassled each other. But beneath that, he'd known where he stood. Somewhere in the vicinity of her brothers. Both of them had had some pretty shitty home situations. His mother stressed, angry and resentful of his presence. While Kate's mother had been gone, her father a slobbering drunk.

Eli and Connor had done their best to take care of her, but when they'd needed help? He'd been all in. Making her smile had been his goal. Because she'd been so short on reasons to smile.

An only child, he'd had no one around to take care of him. To cheer him up when he'd been smarting from a slap across the face delivered by his mom. He'd had the Garretts. And he'd soon realized that the void he'd felt from having no one to take care of him could be filled by offering Kate what he'd so desperately wished for when he'd been young.

Somewhere along the way they'd lost some of that. Something to do with her not being a kid anymore, he supposed.

The bell above the door rang again and Alison Davis walked in, carrying a white pastry box with a stack of brochures on top. "Good morning, Kate." She offered Jack a cautious smile, tucking her red hair behind her ear and looking down at the ground. "Good morning."

"Hi, Alison," he said, softening his tone a bit.

Though she'd left her abusive husband a year and a half ago, Alison still seemed skittish as a newborn colt. Maybe that was just him, too.

"What brings you by?" Kate asked.

Alison appeared to regroup in time to focus on Kate. "I wanted to bring you a pie. And also to ask if it would be all right if I put a couple of advertisements for the bakery here in the store. I have two new employees, both women who just left men who were...well, like my ex. I'm happy to have them working for me, but now I need more business to match the expense. One of them hasn't had a job in fifteen years and no one else would hire her." Alison let out a long breath. "It's hard to start a new life."

"I'm sure," Kate said. "Yeah, I'll take a whole stack of those ads. I don't think Travers will have a problem with it. But if he does, I'll tell him he's being stupid. And then he'll probably change his mind because he's pretty cool."

"I don't want to get you in trouble," Alison said.

Kate snorted and planted her hands on her hips. "Nobody gets me in trouble unless I agree to be in trouble."

"I appreciate it." She set the bakery box on the counter and took the brochures off the top of them. Then she lifted the lid, revealing the most perfect meringue he'd ever seen in his life. "Lemon meringue," she said. "I hope you like that."

"I do." Kate took the pie and moved it behind the counter. "I gladly accept. I promise to refer customers to you, too. If anyone comes in with a pie craving I can send them right down the street."

"I appreciate it. Really I appreciate what everyone has done. I thought when I quit the diner, Rona would be mad at me. But instead she decided to order all of her pies from me now that I'm not making them there."

"That's great!" Kate smiled.

Yes, she seemed perfectly capable of being nice to other people. So it was him.

"I have a few other businesses to go to. And I don't want to distract you from your work."

"Great—just leave the brochures here on the counter."

"Thanks, Kate." She offered a shy wave, then turned and left the store.

Jack watched her go, then turned his attention back to Kate. "That was nice of you."

"I am nice," she said.

"To some people."

She scrunched up her face. "Some people deserve it."

"Oh, go on, Katie. You like me."

Kate looked at the computer screen, a slash of pink spreading over her cheeks. "I like my brothers, too, but that doesn't mean I don't want to punch them in the face half the time."

She was blushing. Honest-to-God blushing. But he didn't have a clue as to why.

"That embarrassing to have to admit that I'm not the worst person in the world?"

"What do you mean?" she asked, looking back at him, her dark eyes glittering.

"You're blushing, Garrett."

She pressed her palm to her cheek before lowering it quickly. "I am not. What the hell would I have to blush about around you?" She turned her focus back to the computer screen, her expression dark now.

"You wouldn't be the first girl I made blush."

"Gross."

"Are you bringing that pie tonight?" He thought it

was probably best to change the subject, because something about it was making him edgy, too.

"I don't know. I might hide it back in my house and keep it all for myself."

"You can't eat a whole pie."

"I can absolutely eat a whole pie. And will."

"Better idea. Only you and me know about the pie. Save it, and I'll come back to your place with you."

Kate blinked rapidly. "No."

"What?"

"I don't think it's a good idea for you to come to my house. I mean, I think we need to share it."

He wasn't sure why it was so difficult to find a topic that didn't make her mad or...weird. Jack never had problems talking to women. Women liked him. He liked women. The exception seemed to be Kate. And seeing as he'd known her the better part of her life, he couldn't fathom why. Usually, their banter was pretty good-natured. Lately, he wasn't sure that was the case.

"Your total is one ninety. That includes shipping," she said, the change in topic abrupt.

"Great. When do you expect it to be here?"

"Should only take two days."

"Even better." He reached into his back pocket, took out his wallet and handed Kate his debit card. "I might actually swing by the bakery and pick up another pie on my way home."

"Yeah, I wish there was more I could do to help. For now, all I can think of is increasing my pie consumption. Which I'm not opposed to. But there has to be more that can be done."

Ideas started turning over in Jack's head. His brain was never still. Not unless he was on the back of a bull intent on shaking him loose. Or riding his horse so hard and fast all he could hear was the pounding of hooves on the ground. In those moments he had what he imagined was tranquility. Outside that, it never happened.

"If I think of anything, I'll let you know," he said. He was already determined that he would think of something.

The printer whirred, spitting out a receipt that Kate tore off and handed to him. "You're all set. Someone will give you a call when it's in."

"Great." And then, for no other reason than that he was curious whether or not he could make her cheeks pink again, he tipped his hat, nodded his head and treated her to his patented Monaghan smile. "See you later, Katie."

He didn't get a blush. He didn't even get a return smile. Instead he got a very emphatic middle finger.

Jack laughed and walked out of the store.

CHAPTER TWO

"I COME BEARING FISH! And chips. Well, French fries. But you knew that." Kate pushed her way through the front door of Connor's house holding two large white takeout containers. One held the fried fish fillets, and the other the fried potatoes.

"I'm starving." Kate rounded the corner and saw her sister-in-law, Liss, standing in the center of the dining area with her hand on her rounded stomach.

"You're eating for two," Kate said. "Or so I've heard."

Liss screwed up her face. "That would make sense. If I knew I was gestating a ravenous wolverine rather than a human child."

Kate laughed and walked over to the table and set the cartons down. The only other thing on the scarred wooden surface was the big green Oregon Ducks ice bucket her brother put his beer in. Well, beer and soda now, since Liss was pregnant and Connor barely drank anymore.

"Although, if it isn't a wolverine, it just means that I lack restraint." Liss groaned. "I can't pass Rona's without going in for a milkshake. And I can't pass The Grind without getting an onion cheese bagel. I'm a cliché without the pickles."

Connor leaned in and kissed his wife on the cheek.

"You're having a baby. You can be a cliché if you damn well please."

Kate's heart squeezed tight as she watched the exchange between Connor and Liss. Connor's first wife, Jessie, had been an influential figure in Kate's life. The two had gotten married when Kate was only nine, and seeing as she didn't have a mother, Jessie was as close as she'd gotten to a female influence.

Jessie's loss had been devastating for everyone. Though she knew it had been the worst for Connor. Considering that, him falling for and marrying Liss was only good in Kate's eyes. And Liss had always been a fixture around their house, seeing as she'd been best friends with Connor since they were in high school.

Having her as a sister was a bonus that Kate quite enjoyed.

"Ugh. Can I be a cliché eating French fries?" she asked, sitting down at the table and digging a Coke out of the ice bucket.

"I'll get you a plate." Connor turned and walked back into the kitchen just as they heard a pounding on the door.

"Who even knocks?" Liss mused.

She had a point. Jack, Eli and Sadie never knocked. "I'll go see." Kate walked back out to the entryway and jerked the front door open, freezing when she saw Jack standing there holding a stack of four pastry boxes. Her heart did that weird thing it did sometimes when she was caught off guard by Jack. That thing where it dramatically threw itself at her breastbone and knocked against it with the force of a punch. "Were you kicking the door?"

"I couldn't open it. Not without setting all of these down."

Kate looked up, studying his expression. He was so very tall. And he always made her feel...little. Sure, Connor and Eli were tall, too, but they didn't fill up space the way Jack did. He was in every corner of every room he inhabited. From the spicy aftershave he wore to his laugh, low and rough like thunder, rumbling beneath every conversation.

Kate stepped to the side and held the door. "What do you have?"

"Pies. From Alison's."

"Four pies?"

He sighed heavily and walked past her into the dining room. She shut the door and followed after him. "Yes." He placed the boxes on the table next to the fish and chips. "Four pies."

Liss's eyes widened. "What kind?"

"I'm not sure. I just bought pies."

There was something about all of this that made her feel weird. A little bit weak, a little bit shaky. He'd done this for Alison, which was...touching. Definitely touching. And nice. Beyond nice of him. And a little bit curious. Because he was Jack, and he had a tendency to be kind of a self-centered asshole. So when he did things for other people, it was notable.

And strange.

And it made her throat a little bit dry. And her face a little bit hot.

"Is that going to be your solution for her?" Kate asked. "Going on a four-pie-a-day diet?"

"Obviously not," he said, sitting down at the table and snagging a beer out of the bucket.

"What solution are we talking about?" Liss asked, crunching on a French fry.

Connor returned then, setting a plate in front of Liss before setting places in front of the rest of the chairs, then taking his seat next to his wife. "Hey, Jack," he said.

"Hey," Jack replied, putting a handful of French fries on his plate.

"I brought fish," Kate said. "It's healthy. And you people are eating French fries."

"Don't worry, Kate," Jack said. "We'll get around to eating your healthy battered fried fish in a minute."

"Solution?" Liss prompted, her eyebrow arched.

"Alison stopped by the Farm and Garden today," Kate said. "She had brochures for her bakery. And she mentioned that she's hired on a couple of other women who just got out of circumstances similar to hers. But of course, it's a new business, and she has a lot more overhead now since she's renting out store space. Anyway, Jack and I were talking earlier about how we wish there was more we could do."

"So Jack was also at the Farm and Garden?" Connor asked.

"I had to order a carburetor." He ran a large hand over his jaw. His very square jaw. And she heard it. The brush of his palm over his dark five o'clock shadow. She swore she could feel the friction, deep and low in her stomach. And it wrapped itself around the general feeling of edginess firing through her veins.

For some reason the line of conversation was irritating to Kate. Possibly because it was preventing her from figuring out just what Jack's motives were where

Alison was concerned. And even more irritating was the fact that she cared at all.

For some reason a lot of little details about Jack's life sometimes ended up getting magnified in her mind. And she overthought them. She more than overthought them; she turned them over to death. She couldn't much explain it. Any more than she could make it stop.

"So you obviously stopped by the bakery and bought pies," Kate said, trying to speed things along.

"Obviously," Jack said, sweeping his hand in a broad gesture, indicating the still-stacked boxes of pie.

"It was nice of you." She was pushing now.

"I don't know that I'd go that far," he said, shrugging his shoulder before pushing his fingers back through his dark hair. "But you know I was raised by a single mom who couldn't get a lick of help out of her deadbeat ex. Stuff like this… I don't like hearing about men mistreating the people they're supposed to care for. It sticks with me."

Kate felt as though a valve had been released in her chest and some of the pressure eased. "Oh. Yeah. That makes sense, I guess."

Jack arched a black brow, his blue eyes glittering. "I know you don't think I make sense very often, Katie. But there's usually a method to my madness."

"Don't call her that," Connor said. "She hates that."

"Thank you, Connor," Kate said, feeling exasperated now. "But I'm perfectly capable of fighting my own battles. Especially against Monaghan. He's not the most formidable opponent."

"I'm wounded, Katie."

He'd said it again. That nickname that nobody else but Connor ever called her. But when Connor said it, it rubbed the wrong way, made her feel as if he was talking down to her. Like he was still thinking of her as a kid.

When Jack said it, her skin felt as though it had been brushed with velvet, leaving a trail of goose bumps behind. It made her feel warm, made it hard to breathe. So basically the same as being rubbed the wrong way. Pretty much.

Either way, she didn't like it.

"You're a slow learner, Monaghan."

He chuckled and leaned back in his chair, crossing his forearms over his broad chest. "There are quite a few women who would beg to differ."

Her cheeks caught fire. "Shut. Up. You are so gross," she said, picking up her plate with shaking fingers and serving herself a heaping portion of fish. No fries. Ungrateful bastards not eating her fish.

She heard the door open again, and then Eli's and Sadie's voices. Now the gang was all here. And she could focus on playing cards, which was really what she wanted.

Sadie led the charge into the dining room, holding her now-traditional orange-and-black candy bowl in front of her, a wide grin on her face. Eli was a step behind her looking slightly abashed. Probably because his fiancée was breaking sacred football laws by bringing the colors of an opposing team onto hallowed ground.

But she did so every week. And every week, Connor made a show of not eating the candy in the bowl. Eli didn't eat it either but didn't make a big deal out of it. While Jack ate half of it without giving a crap what anyone thought. Which summed them all up, really.

Kate always ate the candy, too. If only because she didn't see the point in politicizing sugar.

"Fish and chips!" Sadie exclaimed. "That makes a nice change from pizza. And pie!"

"The feast is indeed bountiful tonight," Liss said, eyeing the pie. "We have Kate to thank for that."

"Excuse me," Jack said. "I brought the pie. I will have you all know that Katie has a lemon meringue pie hidden back in her cabin. And she did not bring it to share with you."

Kate lifted her hand to smack Jack on the shoulder, and he caught her wrist. Her heart hit the back of her breastbone so hard she was afraid it might have exploded on contact. His hand was so big his fingers wrapped all the way around her arm, holding her tight, a rash of heat breaking out from that point of contact outward.

Her eyes clashed with his, and the sharp remark she'd been about to spit out evaporated on her lips.

She tugged her wrist out of his hold, fighting the urge to rub away the impression of his touch with her other hand. "I didn't bring it because I don't want to share my pie with you," she said, looking at Jack.

"Selfish pie hoarder," he said, grinning at her in that easy manner of his.

And her annoyance tripled. Because him grabbing her wrist was a whole event for her body. And he was completely unaffected. That touch had been like grabbing ahold of an electric fence. On her end. Obviously, it hadn't been the same for him.

Why would it be? It shouldn't be that way for you. Yeah, no shit.

"I am not." And she cursed her hot cheeks and her lack of snappy remark.

"I might have to side with Jack on this one," Liss said, her tone apologetic. "Or maybe I'm just on the side of pie."

"Traitor," Kate mumbled.

"Though, on the subject of pies," Jack said, turning his focus to Sadie, "we were trying to figure out if there was something that could be done to help bolster Alison's business."

"Hmm." Sadie piled food on her plate and sat down, Eli taking a seat beside her. "I'll have to scheme on that for a while."

"You have to watch her. She's a champion schemer," Eli said.

"The championest." Sadie smiled broadly.

"Scheme away," Jack said.

"You don't have to tell her to scheme," Eli said. "She can't stop scheming. This is how I ended up with an annual Fourth of July barbecue on my property."

"I'm delightful." Sadie nodded, the expression on her face comically serious.

"She is," Eli agreed.

"Are we going to play cards?" Kate asked.

"So impatient to lose all of your money," Jack said.

This was a little more normal. A more typical level of Jack harassing her.

"To me," Sadie said, her grin turning feral. Sadie, it turned out, was a very good poker player for all her wide-blue-eyed protestations to the contrary when she first joined their weekly games.

Kate opted to stay silent, continuing on that way while the cards were dealt. And she was dealt a very good hand. She bit the inside of her cheek to keep her expression steady. Sadie was cocky. Jack was cockier. And she was going to take their money.

By the end of the night Kate had earned several profane nicknames and the contents of everyone's wallets. She leaned back in her chair, pulling the coins toward her. "Listen to that. I'm going back home, dumping all this on the floor and swimming in it like Scrooge McDuck."

"No diving in headfirst. That's a sure way to spinal trauma. It isn't that deep of a pool," Connor said.

"Deeper than what you have. I have all your monies." She added a fake cackle for a little bit of dramatics.

"Then I will keep all the pie," Liss said.

"That's my pie," Jack said.

"You have to stay in fighting form, Monaghan. Your bar hookups won't be so easy if you lose your six-pack," Liss said cheerfully.

"I do enough work on the ranch every day to live on pies and still keep my six-pack, thank you very much."

"You aren't getting any younger," Sadie said.

The conversation was going into uncomfortable territory as far as Kate was concerned. Really, on all fronts it was getting to an awkward place. Jack and sex. Jack's abs. Yikes.

"I would return volley," Jack said, "but I'm too much of a gentleman to comment on a lady's age."

"Gentleman, huh?" Eli asked. "Of all the things you've been accused of being, I doubt that's one of them."

Jack squinted and held up his hand, pretending to count on his fingers. "Yeah, no. There have been a lot of things, but not that one."

"Anyway," she said, unable to help herself, "you comment on my age all the time."

"I said I never commented on a lady's age, Katie."

She snorted. "I am a lady, asswipe."

"I don't know how I missed it," he said, leaning back in his chair, his grin turning wicked.

For some reason that comment was the last straw. "Okay, hate to cut this short, but I have an early morning tomorrow." That was not strictly true. It was an optional early morning since she intended to get up and spend some time with Roo. "And I will be stopping by The Grind to buy a very expensive coffee with the money I won from you."

Jack stood, putting his hands behind his head and stretching. "I'll walk you out. I have an early morning, too, so I better get going."

Dammit. He didn't seem to understand that she was beating a hasty retreat in part to get away from him. Because the Weird Jack Stuff was a little more elevated today than normal. It had something to do with overexposure to him. She needed to go home, be by herself, scrub him off her skin in a hot shower so she could hit the reset button on her interactions with him.

She felt as if she had to do that more often lately than she had ever had to do in the past.

The thing was, she liked Jack. In that way you could like a guy who was basically an extra obnoxious older brother who didn't share genetic material with you. She liked it when he came to poker night. She liked it when he came into the store. But at the end of it she was always left feeling…agitated.

And it had created this very strange cycle. Hoping

she would see Jack, seeing Jack, being pissed that she had seen Jack. And on and on it went.

"Bye," she said.

She picked up her newly filled change bag and started to edge out of the room. She heard heavy footsteps behind her, and without looking she knew it was Jack. Well, she knew it was Jack partly because he had said he would walk her out.

And partly because the hair on the back of her neck was standing on end. That was another weird Jack thing.

She opened the front door and shut it behind her, not waiting for Jack. Which was petty and weird. She heard the door open behind her and shut again.

"Did I do something?"

She turned around, trying to erase the scowl from her face. Trying to think of one thing he had actually done that was out of line, or out of the ordinary, at least. "No," she said, begrudgingly.

"Then why are you acting like I dipped your pigtails in ink?" he asked, taking the stairs two at a time, making uncomfortable eye contact with her in the low evening light.

She looked down. "I'm not."

"I seem to piss you off all the time lately," he said, closing the distance between them while her throat closed itself up tight.

"You don't. It's just...teasing stuff. Don't worry about it."

Jack kept looking at her, pausing for a moment. She felt awkward standing there but also unable to break away. "Okay. Hey, I was thinking..."

"Uh-oh. That never ends well," she said, trying to force a smile.

"What does that mean?"

"I've heard the stories Connor and Eli tell. Any time you think of something, it ends in…well, sometimes broken bones."

"Sure," he said, chuckling and leaning against the side of his truck. "But not this time. Well, maybe this time since it centers around the rodeo."

"You don't ride anymore," she said, feeling stupid for pointing out something he already knew.

"Well, I might. I was sort of thinking of working with the association to add an extra day onto the rodeo when they pass through. A charity day. Half-price tickets. Maybe some amateur events. And all the proceeds going to…well, to a fund for women who are starting over. A certain amount should go to Alison's bakery. She's helping people get jobs. Get hope. I wish there had been something like that for us when I was a kid."

Kate didn't know anything about Jack's dad. As long as she'd known him, he hadn't had one. And he never talked about it.

But she got the sense that whatever the situation, it hadn't been a happy one.

And now mixed in with all the annoyance and her desire to avoid him was a strange tightening in her chest.

"Life can be a bitch," she said, hating the strident tone that laced its way through her voice.

"I've never much liked that characterization. In my estimation life is a lot more like a pissed-off bull. You hang on as long as you can, even though the ride is uncomfortable. No matter how bad it is on, you sure as hell don't want to get bucked off."

"Yeah, that sounds about like you."

"Profound?"

"Like a guy who's been kicked in the head a few times."

"Fair enough. Anyway, what do you think about the charity?"

Warmth bloomed in her stomach. "Honestly? I think it's a great idea." She couldn't even give him a hard time about this, because it was just so damn nice. "We only have a couple of months until the rodeo, though. Do you think we can pull it off?"

"We?"

Her stomach twisted uncomfortably. "Well, yeah. I think it's a good idea. And I would like to contribute in any way I can. Even if it just means helping the pros tack up or something."

"When are you going to turn pro, Katie?"

She gritted her teeth, and it had nothing to do with his unwanted nickname for her. "When I'm ready. I'm not going to waste a whole bunch of money traveling all over the country, entering all kinds of events and paying for association cards when I don't have a hope in hell of winning."

"Who says you don't have a hope in hell of winning?" he asked, frowning. "I've seen you ride. You're good."

The compliment flowed through her like cool water on parched earth. She cleared her throat, not sure where to look or what to say. "Roo is young. She has another year or so before she's mature. I probably do, too."

He reached out and wrapped his hand around her braid, tugging gently. "You're closer than you think."

Something about his look, about that touch that should have irritated her if it did anything, sent her stomach tumbling down to her toes.

Then he turned away from her and walked around to the other side of his pickup truck, opened the driver-side door, got inside and slammed it shut. He started the truck engine and she felt icy spots on her face. She released her breath in a rush, a wave of dizziness washing over her.

You'd have thought she'd been staring down a predator and not one of her family's oldest and dearest friends.

Freaking Jack and all the weirdness that followed him around like a thunderclap.

She walked over to her pickup and climbed in, then started the engine and threw it into Reverse without bothering to buckle. She was just driving down the narrow dirt road that led from Connor's house to her little cabin.

The road narrowed as the trees thickened, pine branches whipping against the doors to her old truck as she approached her house. She'd moved into the cabin on her eighteenth birthday, gaining a little bit of distance and independence from her brothers without being too far away. Of course, it wasn't as if she'd really done much with the independence.

She worked, played cards with her brothers and rode horses. That was about the extent of her life. But it filled her life, every little corner of it. And she wasn't unhappy with that.

She walked up the front steps, threw open the front door that she never bothered to lock and stepped inside. She flipped on the light switch, bathing the small space in a yellow glow.

The kitchen and living room were one, a little wood-stove built into a brick wall responsible for all the heat-ing in the entire house. The kitchen was small with wood planks for walls that she'd painted white when she'd moved in. A distressed counter-height table divided the little seating area from where she prepared food, and served as both infrequently used dining table and kitchen island.

She had one bathroom and one bedroom. The house was small, but it fit her life just fine. In fact, she was happy with a small house because it reminded her to get outside, where things were endless and vast, rather than spend too much time hiding away from the world.

Kate would always rather be out in it.

She kicked her boots off and swept them to the side, letting out a sigh as she dropped her big leather shoulder bag onto the floor. The little lace curtains—curtains that predated Kate's tenure in the house—were shut tight, so she tugged her top up over her head and stripped off the rest of her clothes as she made her way to the shower.

She turned the handles and braced herself for the long wait for hot water. Everything, including the hot-water heater, in her little house was old-fashioned. Sort of like her, she supposed.

She snorted into the empty room, the sound echoing in the small space. Jack certainly thought she was old-fashioned. All that hyperconcern over her not owning a computer.

Steam started to rise up and fill the air and she stepped beneath the hot spray, her thoughts lingering on her interaction with Jack at the Farm and Garden. And how obnoxious he was. And how his lips curved up into that wicked smile when he teased her, blue eyes glittering with all the smart-ass things he'd left unsaid.

She picked up the bar of Ivory soap from the little

ledge of the tub and twirled it in her palms as she held it beneath the water, working up a lather. She took a breath, trying to ease some of the tension that was rioting through her.

She turned, pressing the soap against her chest, sliding it over her collarbone.

Yeah, Jack was a pain.

Still, she was picturing that look he got on his face. Just before he said something mouthy. She slid the bar of soap over her breasts just as she remembered her thwarted retaliation for his teasing tonight. The way his fingers had wrapped around her wrist, his hold firm…

She gasped and released her hold on the bar of soap. It hit the floor and slid down between her feet, stopping against the wall.

She growled and bent down, picking it back up, ignoring the pounding of her heart and the shaking in her fingers.

The shower was supposed to wash Jack off her skin. He was not supposed to follow her in.

Another jolt zipped through her at the thought because right along with it came the image of Jack and his overbearing presence sharing this small space with her. Bare skin, wet skin…hands on skin.

She turned and rinsed the soap off her chest, then shut the water off, stepped out and scrubbed her skin dry with her towel, much more ferociously than was warranted.

She needed to sleep. Obviously, she was delirious.

If she didn't know better, she would think she was a breath away from having a fantasy about Jack freaking Monaghan.

"Ha!" she all but shouted. "Ha ha ha." She wrapped

her towel around her body and walked to her room before dropping it and digging through her dresser for
her pajamas.

She found a pair of sensible white cotton underwear
and her flannel pajama pants that had cowboy hats, las-
sos and running horses printed onto the fabric.

There could be no sexual fantasies when one had on
cotton panties and flannel pants.

With pony pajamas came clarity.

She pulled a loose-fitting blue T-shirt over her head
and flopped down onto her bed. Her twin bed. That
would fit only one person.

She was sexual fantasy–proof. Also sex-proof, if the
entire long history of her life was anything to go by.

"Bah." She rolled over onto her stomach and buried
her face in her pillow. She had arena dirt, pounding
hooves, the salty coastal wind in her face, mixed with
pine and earth. A scent unique to Copper Ridge and as
much a part of her as the blood in her veins.

She had ambitions. Even if she was a bit cautious
in them.

She didn't need men.

Most of all, she didn't need Jack Monaghan.

CHAPTER THREE

JACK ROLLED INTO the Garrett ranch just after nine. He'd finished seeing to his horses earlier and was ready to ambush Kate with coffee and a plan. It was her day off, and he knew she wasn't still in bed lying low while the sun rose high. It wasn't her way. Which meant he would have to track her down on the vast property.

But that was fine with him. He didn't have much else happening today.

His equine operation had gotten to the point that it was running so smoothly he often felt as if he didn't have enough to do. He had people who worked on the ranch seeing to all of the horses' needs and a housekeeper who took care of all of his needs. He was forging great connections in competitive worlds. Both the Western riding community and dressage. And he was very close to signing a lucrative deal to breed one of his stallions to a champion hunter jumper, Jazzy Lady.

Now that all that was falling into place and he wasn't traveling with the rodeo, he was left with a lot of free time.

His mother had said idle hands were the devil's workshop, usually before she booted his ass outside so he'd stay out of her hair. But then, he'd never had much use for worrying about things like that. In part because he never worried all that much about the devil. He'd gone to church once when he was a boy with a friend from his first-grade class. The pastor had said something about Joshua the son of Nun. And after the service the boy who had been his friend when they'd walked into the building had decided Jack the son of Nun was a fitting nickname for him since he didn't have a daddy.

Jack had punched that little son of a bitch in the face and had never darkened the doors of any holy institution from there on after. He hadn't stayed friends with the kid, either. In fact, the only people he had stayed friends with were the Garretts and Liss. He'd raised too much hell over the years to keep many other connections.

Hell, he'd taken to it as if it was his job. And when he'd transitioned from causing trouble in town to bull riding, it had just been a more legitimate method.

And another way for him to try to get his old man to take some notice. To make his mother look at him for more than thirty seconds.

It hadn't worked. His success hadn't changed that, either.

But he had Eli and Connor.

Together they'd knit a strange and dysfunctional group that continued on to this day. He liked to think they were all a little more functional now. Well, the rest of them more than him, he supposed.

Though he had some stability now with his ranch. He might not be married and procreating like his friends, but he wasn't a total lost cause.

And he knew that in and of itself was a big surprise to most people in Copper Ridge. Oh, sure, they were all polite enough, but he knew for a fact no one wanted him dating their daughter or their sister.

Though now they were happy to have him spending money at their establishments.

He killed his truck's engine and got out, grabbing hold of the big metal thermos he always carried with him during the workday and two tin mugs.

This was a peacemaking mission, which meant he had come prepared. He shoved his truck keys into his jeans pocket and crossed the gravel lot, heading toward the newly built barn, Connor's pride and joy, with the exception of his wife and unborn child.

Just then Connor walked out of the alley doors and Jack called out to get his attention. "Morning," he said.

"You brought me coffee," Connor said, flashing him the kind of smile that up until a few months ago had been absent from his friend's face.

"Sorry. You're out of luck. The coffee isn't for you."

"I'm hurt," Connor said, putting his hand on his chest. "You're bringing coffee to another man, Monaghan?"

"Nope. It's for Katie."

Connor's brows shot up. "Uh-oh. What did you do?"

"Nothing. But I do need to convince her to help me out planning this charity rodeo day. I can use some contacts with the pro association. I've been in touch with a few people since I stopped competing. But she's in a better position with the locals."

"You could probably seduce help out of Lydia. Or just ask."

Jack thought of the pretty dark-haired president of the chamber of commerce. Yeah, Lydia would be into it, no seduction required. The charity event, not sleeping with him. He let his brain linger on that thought for a moment, if only because it had been a while since he'd seduced anyone or been seduced in return.

"Sure," he responded.

"You don't sound enthused."

"I'm not *un*enthused."

"Yes, you are."

Jack shrugged. "Not interested, I guess."

"Are you sick? Because she's female, so she's your type."

Jack couldn't argue with that. "I don't need to seduce her into helping. It's a good idea. You make it sound like women only want to listen to me because of my body," he said, arching a brow. "I'm more than just a pretty face."

"I want to say something right now...but I have a feeling I could dig myself into a hole I'll never get out of."

"You probably shouldn't say it," Jack said. "However, if you were thinking that I'm also a very sexy ass, you would be correct."

"You better wash your mouth out with soap before you bring that coffee to Kate. Or she'll probably end up throwing it in your face."

"She's not my biggest fan."

Connor offered him a skeptical smile. "Actually, I think she's a pretty big fan of yours." Jack puzzled over the words for a second before Connor continued. "You're like another brother to her. Which is why she gives you hell."

Jack let out a hard breath. "Lucky me. Do you have any idea where the little she-demon is?"

"She took Roo out for a ride. But she should be back in soon."

"Which way does she normally go?"

"She rides out through the main pasture toward the

base of Copper," Connor said, talking about the mountain that the town was named after. "And she comes back around behind the horse barn."

"Thanks. I'll head that way."

Jack turned away from his friend and started walking down a dirt path that would lead him toward the horse barn and hopefully bring him into line with Kate.

The cloud cover hadn't burned off yet, gray mist hanging low over the pine trees, pressing the sky down to the earth. The air was damp, thick with salt from the sea, and he had a feeling it would rain later. Or if they were lucky, the moisture would burn away, leaving clear blue skies.

But he doubted it.

He cut through a little thicket of pines and came out the other side on another little road. This was the one that led all the way back to Kate's cabin, but if he crossed that and cut through a little field, he would make it to the barn in half the time. So he did, wet grass whipping against his jeans, dewdrops bleeding through the thick denim.

He could only say thanks for good boots that would at least keep his feet dry.

He hopped the wire fence that partitioned the next section of the property off from the one he'd just left and stood there in the knee-high weeds, staring off into the distance. Then he saw her, riding through the flat expanse of field, strands of dark hair flying from beneath her hat, her arms working in rhythm with the horse's stride. As she drew closer, he could see the wide smile on her face. It was the kind of smile he rarely saw from her. The smile of a woman purely in her element. A woman at home on the back of the horse.

He felt the corners of his own mouth lift in response, because that kind of joy was infectious.

He stood and watched her as she drew closer, hoofbeats growing louder as she did.

He could pinpoint the exact moment she saw him, because she straightened, pulling back on Roo's reins and slowing her gait. He started to walk toward her, and she dismounted, her smile faded now.

"I have coffee, so you can stop frowning at me," he said, holding up the thermos and the mugs.

She squinted, her expression filled with suspicion. "Why do you have coffee?"

"Because I want to talk to you about something. And I figured it was best to try and bait you."

Kate screwed up her face, wrinkling her nose and squinting her eyes. "I am not a badger. You can't bait me."

"Sure I can, Katie. I bet I tempt you something awful," he said, holding out the thermos and unscrewing the lid.

Kate rolled her eyes. "Tempt me to plant a boot up your ass."

He left one mug dangling from his finger and straightened the other, then poured a measure of coffee into it. "Be nice to me or I won't give you what you want."

He watched as the faint rose color bled into her cheeks, lit on fire by the first golden rays of the sun breaking through the cloud cover, adding a soft glow to her face. "You seem to be forgetting who you're talking to, Monaghan," she said, her voice gaining strength as the sentence picked up momentum. "Boot. Ass."

"You do need your coffee. You're cranky." He held

out the mug and she took it, wrapping her fingers around it like claws.

"I *wasn't*."

"Well, stop. I want to talk to you about the rodeo."

She took a sip of the strong black coffee and didn't even grimace. But then, she would have trained herself to never make a face. She drank her coffee and her whiskey straight up and never complained about the burn. Kate never seemed to show weakness, never appeared to have any vulnerability at all.

In that moment he wondered what it might be like if she did. If she softened, even a little bit.

Dark brown eyes met his, a core of steel running straight on through, down deep inside of her. Yeah, there would be no softening from Kate Garrett. "Then talk," she said before taking another sip.

"Who do you think you can get to volunteer to ride when there's no score or purse at stake? I mean, we can keep score, but it won't count toward anything. Just winning the event."

"I'm not sure as far as the pros go. We'll probably have to reach out to the association. But I know some people who can do that. You being one of them, I assume."

One thing about the rodeo he'd liked. He'd come in with no established baggage. Nobody cared that he didn't have a dad, that he'd grown up poor. His luck with buckle bunnies and his propensity to fight in bars had also added to his popularity.

But the circuit wasn't real life. It was like living in a fraternity. Too much booze, too much sex—it was all good there. It just wasn't real life.

Of course, real life was often hard and less fun.

"Yeah, I've got a lot of buddies from back in those days."

"You make it sound like it was a million years ago."

Only five, but it felt like longer sometimes. "It doesn't just have to be all pros," he continued, pitching an idea at her he'd had the other day. "We can do amateurs against professionals. That would make for a fun event."

"Well, you know I would do it. And a few others might. I bet Sierra West would."

At the mention of Sierra's name Jack's stomach went tight. Her involvement in this could be a slight complication.

He gritted his teeth. No, there was no reason to consider the Wests a complication. Sure, he shared genetic material with them, but the only people who knew that were his mother, the man who had fathered him and Jack himself. As far as he knew, the legitimate West children knew nothing about it, and Kate certainly didn't.

If he were a sentimental man, he might have been tempted to think of Sierra as a sister. But he couldn't afford sentimentality. And anyway, he'd accepted quite a bit of money to pretend he had no clue who his father was. And so he was honor bound to that. Well, not exactly honor bound. Bought and paid for, more like.

"Great. Sure."

"If you don't want my suggestions, don't ask for my help," she said, her tone cutting.

"I *want* your suggestions," he bit out.

"You sound like you want my suggestions like you want a root canal."

If he was this transparent at a mention of Sierra's

name, then dealing with her while coordinating the rodeo events would be somewhere way beyond awkward. Which meant he had to get it together.

"Sorry, honey," he said, not quite sure why the endearment slipped out. Because he was trying to soften his words maybe? "I do want your suggestions. That's why I came to you for help."

She chewed her bottom lip. "You really do want my help?"

"Yes."

"Why? I mean, there are a lot of people you could get to help you. People who aren't kids."

"I don't think you're a kid."

He could remember her being a kid, all round-faced enthusiasm, shining dark eyes, freckles sprinkled over the button nose. Usually, she'd had dirt on her. Yeah, he could remember that clearly. But that image had very little to do with the woman who stood before him. Her cheeks had hollowed, highlighting the strong bone structure in her face. Her nose was finer, though still sprinkled with freckles. Her dark eyes still shone bright, but there was a stubbornness that ran deep, a hardness there developed from years of loss and pain.

She cleared her throat. "That's news to me."

"Consider yourself informed."

"Now that we've established we're on equal footing—"

"I didn't say we were on equal footing. I said I didn't think you were a kid."

"What is that supposed to mean?"

"I've been pro, honey badger," he said, combining her earlier assertion that she was not a badger with his accidental endearment. "I know the ins and outs of these events. My contacts are a little bit out of date, which is where you come in, but the rodeo is still my turf."

"Bull riders. The ego on y'all is astronomical."

"That's because we ride *bulls*. Those are some big-ass scary animals. A guy has to think he's ten feet tall and bulletproof to do something that stupid."

"It's true. You are kind of stupid." A smile spread over her face. Sometimes, it turned out, Kate did smile at him. But usually only after she was done insulting him.

"I'm wounded."

"Don't waste your time being wounded. First, we're going to have to find out if the Logan County Fairgrounds are available for the date we would need it. Probably the day before the actual rodeo starts or the day after."

"You know who to call for that?"

"Yeah, but I might want to go through Lydia."

"Good call," he said. "See? This is why I asked for your help."

"Because I'm a genius."

"Sure." He shrugged. "About a couple things."

"Aren't you going to have any coffee?" Kate asked, something searching in her brown gaze now. He had no clue what the hell she was looking for, but even so, he was almost certain she wouldn't find it.

"I have to run," he said. He didn't have to run. He didn't have anywhere to be. Except for some reason he felt averse to prolonging this moment here in the field with her. "When is the next local meeting?"

"Tomorrow night. You should come."

He'd stopped going to the amateur association meetings in Copper Ridge years ago. He'd turned pro when he was twenty, using the money that the man who was, according to genetics, his father had given him to keep his mouth shut about his existence.

Sometimes it felt like his attempt at being seen when he'd been paid to disappear. A way to demand attention without breaking that damned agreement. Other times it had all felt like an attempt to bleed that unwanted blood right out of his veins, let it soak into the arena dirt until the Wests weren't a part of him anymore. But that feeling had faded as he turned that initial bit of money into yet more money through event wins and investments and sponsorship deals.

Though at thirty-three, he felt too damn old to get trampled on a regular basis. He'd felt too old five years ago when he'd quit. Not just too old for the getting-trampled part but the hard living that went with it. He knew there were plenty of guys still out there riding, but he didn't need to and he felt lucky to have escaped with as little damage as he had.

"Sure, I'll be there. I'll do the hard sell and see if anyone else has more ideas."

"Do you want to ride together?"

He nodded slowly. "Yeah, let's do that. Do you want to drive?"

"I think your truck is a little bit cushier than mine, but I appreciate the offer."

"Okay, then, I'll pick you up… When?"

"Seven."

He gripped the brim of his hat with his thumb and forefinger and tipped it slightly. "Okay, then, see you at seven."

SHE HEARD A car engine and raced to the window, her heart pushing against the base of her throat. But she didn't see anything. No truck. No Jack.

"Oh my gosh, calm down, me."

It was probably just one of the ranch hands headed out to the barn, or maybe Eli getting home from work. There were three whole minutes before Jack was supposed to show up, after all. And she was being ridiculous about it. Completely overcome by the sense of hyperawareness that often assaulted her when dealing with Jack-related things. And she would picture him pulling up, and her stomach would turn over sharply, her breath catching, and there was nothing she could do to stop it. The response was completely involuntary, and it was so strong it made her legs shake.

Anyone would think she was waiting for a date.

She gritted her teeth and closed her eyes tight just as she heard another engine sound. Her eyes popped back open and she brushed the curtains aside again just in time to see Jack's truck rumbling up the drive.

She put her hand on her stomach. "Stop it," she scolded herself. It did nothing.

She grabbed a jacket and her bag and jerked open the front door, then walked out onto the front porch as she slung both over her shoulder. She wasn't going to sit in her living room and wait for him to come to the door. She was not going to encourage her weird bodily reactions.

She scampered to the truck and flung open the passenger-side door, then braced her foot on the metal running board before climbing into the cab. She slammed the door shut and buckled. "Let's go."

"In a hurry, Katie?"

"I would like to be on time," she said, battling against her urge to bristle.

She didn't want to bristle. She wanted to be sleek. She wanted to have no reaction to him whatsoever. None at all.

"Is it still at the Grange Hall?"

"Yes, it is. And I hope you ate, because they still serve store-bought sugar cookies and watered-down punch."

"Ah yes, the official small-town meeting food."

"I don't mind the cookies. I don't even really mind the punch. I just don't know why people think they go good together."

He put the truck in Reverse, then turned around and drove back down the narrow driveway that fed into the wider main driveway that eventually curved onto the highway.

"It's one of the great mysteries of our time," Jack said. "Personally, I think overearnest meetings like this should come with whiskey."

"I would have no problem with that. But somehow I don't think the budget allows for alcohol."

"Well, that's an oversight. What has to be cut to make room in the budget for alcohol?"

"There really isn't much to cut. We kind of pay for our own stuff. In addition to paying dues to be a part of Oregon's Amateur Riders Association. But you know, support system. Training. And we do get to use the arenas of the fairgrounds a couple times a month at no extra charge."

"I guess next time I'll bring my own whiskey," he said.

"There won't really be a next time, though, will there?"

"I suppose that all depends on whether or not I'm creating a monster with this."

"You feel pretty passionately about it, don't you?" She so rarely asked him sincere questions that he seemed stumped by this one. Well, she was, too. She had no idea what she was doing. Why she wanted to know more. Why she wanted to dig deeper.

"I do," he said finally. "It feels like half the time the odds are stacked pretty high against women."

"Seeing as it was my mom that screwed everything up, I can't say that's been my experience," Kate said.

He huffed out a laugh. "I suppose in your life it was different. Not just because of your mom, but because Connor and Eli would kill anyone who hurt you. You're surrounded by people who love and protect you. There are a lot of people who aren't. A lot of kids, a lot of women. They're either abandoned and left to their own devices, or worse, they're actively hurt by the people who are supposed to love them."

Kate immediately felt stupid for her earlier comment. "Did your dad... Did he hurt your mom?"

"No. Thank God all he did was leave. But even that didn't make it easy. It just... This kind of stuff gets me. I don't want a wife. I don't want kids. Because I know myself. It doesn't make any sense to me, these men who have kids just to leave them. Who get married just to mistreat the women they made vows to. At least I know my limitations."

"You wouldn't hurt anyone, Jack." Kate's voice was small when she spoke the words.

"Not with my fist." He tightened his grip on his steering wheel.

She studied his profile, the strength in his hands,

the muscles in his forearms. He was tan from hours working out in the sun, strong from all the lifting and riding he did.

And regardless of how he treated her sometimes, regardless of the fact that he had been around since she was a little girl, he was most definitely not her brother.

She swallowed hard, her throat suddenly dry. "I'm sure that you… I mean…if you wanted to…"

"I don't. So it isn't an issue."

His response, so hard and sharp, definitive, made her feel stupid. Young.

He took a hard right just before Old Town, moving farther away from the ocean and into the less quaint part of Copper Ridge. The Grange was a tiny little building nestled between a modern grocery store and the edge of a residential neighborhood. It looked as if it was built out of Lincoln Logs, and Kate imagined it was supposed to be quaint, when really, years of repainting and foul weather had left it looking worse for wear.

An American flag and an Oregon flag flew high in the parking lot, which was already filled with pickup trucks. There was no place for Jack to park, so he pulled up to the curb, put the truck in Park and shut it off.

"Maybe we should have warned them?" she asked.

"With what? You can't email them—you don't have a computer."

She snorted. "I could have called."

"You don't have a cell phone."

"I have a landline."

"You could send smoke signals."

"Jack," she said, exasperated, opening the passenger door and sliding out, not waiting for him. She went ahead and walked into the building, greeting everyone who was in attendance, already seated in a semicircle in the back room.

The front room had permanent seating and a stage for community theater. But they met in the back in a sterile environment that had a little kitchenette with bright orange countertops, a white linoleum floor and fluorescent lighting.

Long folding tables were set out with the promised punch and cookies. They looked mostly untouched.

The lonely punch and cookies weren't all that surprising. They were more of a formality. An offering of refreshment because if there was going to be a gathering, refreshments had to be on offer. The laws of small-town etiquette.

There were only two vacant chairs, and it so happened that they were right next to each other, so any hopes she'd had of getting some distance from Jack were thwarted.

Her friend Sierra waved, but there were, of course, no open seats next to her. Sierra somehow managed to exude both femininity and strength. Kate had no fucking idea how you were supposed to exude femininity. Yet Sierra managed. Her blond curls were always perfectly set; her brightly colored eye shadow made her blue eyes glow. She was the classic sequined rodeo queen. Kate couldn't even fathom trying to wear a sequin. It would just feel like trying too hard.

She wasn't the type to ride with turquoise and rhinestone.

But sometimes Sierra made her wish that she was.

Eileen, the president of the group, was reading minutes, so Kate took her seat as quietly as possible. She kept her eyes fixed on Eileen and jumped when Jack took a seat next to her. Did he have to be so…warm? Yes, he was warm. Uncommonly warm. She could feel it even with a healthy bit of air between them. And it was distracting. And disturbing.

She looked down at her hands, which were folded in her lap. But then she saw Jack's denim-clad thighs in her peripheral vision and became completely distracted by that. They looked hard. And if they were like the rest of him, they were probably uncommonly hot. Temperature-wise. Just temperature.

She forced herself to glance away.

When Eileen got to the part where everyone brought up relevant business, Kate didn't speak up, because she didn't want to speak first. And also, the dry throat.

When it finally seemed that topics had been exhausted, from a need for new barrels for the arena they trained in at the fairgrounds to shared transportation to amateur events on the West Coast later in the year, Kate opened her mouth to speak. But Jack beat her to it.

"Hi," he said, clearing his throat. "If you don't know me, I'm Jack Monaghan. I used to ride pro in the circuit, though I haven't for a few years. But I wanted to come today to talk to you about the possibility of doing a charity day at the upcoming rodeo here in Logan County."

Eileen brightened visibly. "What sort of thing did you have in mind?"

"Well, Kate and I have been talking, and she was the one who told me I should come tonight." He gestured toward her and she lifted her hand, twitching her fingers in an approximation of a wave. "We were thinking that it would be a chance for this group here to take part in some events. And I could get in touch with some of the riders I know coming through with the pro association. See if maybe they wouldn't mind participating, either. You could all compete against each other. And we would work with the chamber of commerce both here and in some of the other towns to get food donated, as well. I have plans for the proceeds to go to a couple of the battered-women's shelters and to help a local business that's been trying to get disadvantaged women back on their feet after they leave abusive situations."

"Well, provided we can secure the space, I think that sounds like an excellent idea," Eileen said. "Can I get an informal count of who would be interested in participating?"

Nearly every hand in the circle went up, and Kate's heartbeat increased, satisfaction roaring through her.

"That's a good start," Eileen continued. "We'll just want to see which day the fairgrounds might be able to accommodate us. I'm willing to do that."

"That would be great," Kate said.

She was more than happy to let Eileen use her connections with the board at the county expo.

"Kate and I will work on the roster and the schedule of events." Jack was speaking again, and volunteering her for things, things that they would work on together. She wasn't sure how she felt about that. "So you can get in touch with either of us if you want to participate, and we'll get you added to the list. If you don't want to compete, we could still use the help. We'll need a lot of volunteers to try and keep costs down. Because if it gets too expensive, we won't have anything to donate."

After that, much-less-organized conversation broke out in the room, a buzz of excitement surrounding them.

"Okay, I think that concludes official business for the evening," Eileen said above the din.

Kate stood, and Sierra rushed across the circle and to her side. The other woman spared a glance at Jack, a half smile curving her lips upward, a blush spreading over her pale cheeks. She was doing it again. *Exuding.* Sierra West was beautiful—there was no denying it. She was even beautiful when she blushed, rather than awkward and blotchy. Kate had a feeling that *she* was just awkward and blotchy.

"This is such a great idea," Sierra said. She reached out and put delicate fingers on Jack's shoulder, and everything in Kate curled into a tight hissing ball. She did *not* like that.

"I can't take much credit," Jack said. Except he really should have been taking all the credit.

"I'd love to participate in a barrel racing event," Sierra went on.

Jack cleared his throat and took a step away from their little huddle. "Well, just give Kate a call about it and she'll add your name."

"And anything else I can do to help…"

"We've got it," Jack said.

Sierra looked confused at Jack's short reply, as though no man had ever turned down the opportunity to spend extra time with her. "Okay. I will…call Kate, then."

Jack nodded, his jaw tense. And Kate was perversely satisfied by the fact that Jack didn't seem at all enticed by Sierra's clear interest.

On the heels of her satisfaction came annoyance at said satisfaction. Jack could do what he wanted with whoever he wanted.

Though Sierra was one of her few female friends and

she had to admit it would be weird if the other woman was sleeping with someone Kate was so close to.

Jack. Sleeping with Sierra.

Immediately, she pictured a messy bed and a tangle of limbs. Jack's big hands running down a bare back. Long hair spread out over a white pillowcase. Only, for some reason, the woman in her vision wasn't a blonde with a riot of luxurious curls. Instead she had straight dark hair...

Kate bit down on the inside of her cheek. "Yes," Kate managed to force out, "call me."

"Hey, some of us are headed to Ace's," Sierra said. "You want to come?"

"I came with Jack..."

"That's fine," Jack said, cutting her off. "She can go. We'll both go."

"Great." Sierra smiled brightly. "See you there."

Kate rounded on Jack, the tension from earlier taking that easy turn into irritation. "Did you just give me permission to go somewhere?"

"I'm your ride."

"Yes. My ride. Not my dad."

He chuckled. "Oh, honey, I don't think for one second that I'm your dad."

"Stop calling me that," she said, ignoring the rash of heat that had broken out on her skin when he'd spoken the endearment.

It made her angry because she was not his honey. Not now, not ever. She clenched her teeth and her fists, turned, and walked out of the room, headed out into the warm evening air.

"I can't call you honey, I can't call you Katie. I can't win," he said, his voice coming from behind her.

She turned around to face him. "You could call me Kate. That's my name. That's what everyone calls me."

"Connor calls you Katie."

A strange sort of desperation clawed at her chest. "Connor is my brother. If you haven't noticed, you aren't. Now let's go to Ace's."

CHAPTER FOUR

JACK WAS FEELING pretty irritated with life by the time he and Kate walked into Ace's. He was pretty sure his half sister had attempted to make a pass at him, and Kate was acting like he'd put bugs in her boots.

He also couldn't drink, because he was driving.

Irritated didn't begin to cover it.

He was getting pretty sick and tired of Kate's prickly attitude and now he'd gotten himself embroiled in a whole thing with a woman who was the human equivalent of a cactus.

He really needed the drink that he couldn't have.

Though maybe if Kate had one, she would calm the hell down.

"Can I buy you a drink?" he asked.

"A Coke," she said.

"You want rum in that?"

"No."

"Why not?"

"Because making an ass out of myself in front of a roomful of people is not on today's to-do list. I'm a lightweight."

He laughed. "Okay, I'm a little bit surprised that you would admit that."

"Why?"

"You're the kind of girl who always has to show the

boys up. I would think you'd want to try to drink us under the table."

She arched her brow. "I'm way tinier than you. I'm not drinking you under any table."

"All right, one Coke for you."

He turned and headed toward the bar, and to his surprise, she followed him rather than going over to the table where her friends were already seated. "Why are you buying me a drink?"

"I was hoping to trick you into getting drunk so you wouldn't be so uptight," he said, because he always said what was on his mind where Kate was concerned. Neither of them practiced tact in the other's presence.

She sputtered. "I'm not uptight."

"You're something."

Kate's lip curled upward. "Now I don't really want you to buy me a drink. I don't like your motives."

"I'm not going to sneakily give you a rum and Coke. I'm ordering you a soda."

"But it was not born out of generosity."

"Will you please stop making it impossible for me to do something nice for you."

"But you aren't doing something nice for me," she insisted. "You were trying to…calm me. With booze."

He turned, and Kate took a step back, pressing herself against the bar. He leaned forward, gripping the bar with both hands, trapping her between his arms. "Yes, Katie, honey, I was."

Her dark eyes widened, her mouth dropping open. Color rose in her cheeks, her chest pitching sharply as she drew in a quick deep breath.

He looked at Kate quite a lot. He saw her almost

every day. But he'd never really studied her. He didn't know why in hell he was doing it now.

There wasn't a trace of makeup on her face, her dark lashes long and thick but straight rather than curled upward to enhance her eyes. There was no blush added to her cheeks, no color added to her lips. It exemplified Kate. What you saw was what you got. Inside and out.

And for some reason the tension that had been gathering in his chest spread outward, spread around them, and he could feel a strange crackling between them. He wasn't sure what it was. But one thing he was sure of. He'd made a mistake somewhere between calling her "honey" the first time, days ago, and the moment he'd pressed her up against the bar.

Everything he knew about her had twisted. The way Kate made him feel had shifted into something else, something new.

If it had been any other woman at any other moment, he might've called it attraction.

But this was Kate. So that was impossible.

And then the sort of dewy softness in her eyes changed, a kind of fierce determination taking over. She took a step away from the bar, a step closer to him, and reached up, gripping his chin with her thumb and forefinger, tugging hard, bringing his face nearer to hers. "Look, Jack," she spat, hardening every syllable, "I think you need to back off."

Her skin was soft against his, her hand cool. Her hold was firm, uncompromising, like Kate herself.

Unlucky for her, he didn't compromise, either.

He leaned in, closing some of the distance between them. Her lips parted, and for just one moment he saw Kate Garrett soften. But it was only a moment. Then the steel was back, harder than ever. He waited for her to back down, waited for her to step away and hiss at him.

But she didn't. She simply stood there, holding him fast, her breasts rising and falling with each indrawn breath.

The noise faded into the background, and the people around them turned into a blur as his focus sharpened on Kate. The only thought he had in his head was that this was without a doubt the strangest moment of his entire life.

They were playing chicken—he knew her well enough to realize that. She was challenging him, and she thought he would back down.

That was fine. It was almost normal. It was the undercurrent beneath the challenge, the one making his heart beat faster, making his stomach feel tight, that was giving him issues.

She leaned in slightly and without even thinking, he took a step back, breaking her hold on his chin. Breaking whatever the hell thread had wound its way around them.

"I'm going to get you that soda," he said, knowing his tone sounded way harsher than he intended. "Go hang out with your friends. I'll meet you over there."

He expected her to argue, but she didn't. She just nodded and moved around him cautiously, her dark eyes glued to his for a moment before she averted them and made her way to her group.

He let out a breath he hadn't realized he'd been holding.

Well, that was fucking weird.

"Monaghan," Ace said, sidling over to his end of the bar. "Can I get you something?"

"Two Cokes," Jack said, resting his forearms on the bar.

Ace laughed and pushed his flannel shirtsleeves up. "Sure. You want me to start a tab for that?"

"I'll pay now," Jack growled.

Ace grabbed two glasses and filled them with the nozzle beneath the bartop. "So... Kate Garrett?"

"What about her?" Jack asked, feeling irreversibly irritated by the other man now. Because he could feel himself being led somewhere, and he didn't like it.

"You and her are..."

"What? No. Fuck no."

"It looked like something to me. So I wondered."

"It was nothing," Jack said, ignoring the rush of heat in his blood that made him wonder if it was more than nothing. "Just messing with her."

"That's what I'm saying," Ace said, smiling broadly. "Anyway...why not?"

Anger surged through Jack's veins. "For one because I like my balls where they're at. And if I ever touched Katie, Connor and Eli would remove them. And then Liss would sew them onto the top of a winter hat as a festive decoration. Additionally? She's a kid."

"She's not a kid," Ace said, his eyes fixed across the room. "And I'm not the only one who realizes that."

Jack turned and looked and saw Kate nearly backed up against the wall by some asshole cowboy who had his hat tipped back and his jeans so tight his thighs were probably screaming for mercy. He was leaning in, holding her hostage.

Because he was an asshole. And never mind that Jack'd had her cornered only a few minutes ago. It was totally different. No matter what Ace thought, he wasn't trying to get into her pants.

But that guy was.

"Excuse me," Jack said, grabbing the sodas and moving away from the bar.

He stalked across the room, his eyes on Kate and the cowboy. And then he stopped, the two frosty glasses sweaty in his hands. He had no clue what the hell he was doing. About to bust in on Kate flirting with some guy... Chad something, if Jack remembered right. Your standard frat bro with spurs.

Not the kind of guy he would recommend she talk to. But she could if she wanted to, and he had no say in it.

She was right. He wasn't her older brother.

A fact he was very aware of right then.

So instead he paused at an empty table for two and set the drinks down, flicking an occasional glance over to Kate. But he didn't sit. Not until he got a read on the situation.

She looked over the guy's shoulder and locked eyes with him, just for a moment, and then her expression turned defiant. She flipped her hair over her shoulder, batting her eyelashes in a near-cartoonish manner.

Then she arched her back, thrusting her breasts outward, and Jack about choked on his Coke. She was... Well, she was being pretty obvious but Jack wasn't sure she knew what the hell game she was playing.

She isn't a kid.

No, she wasn't, but she flirted like a fifteen-year-old who'd only ever seen it done in bad teen movies. Why hadn't anyone ever...talked to her about this shit?

She was over there throwing herself to the wolves. She was playing the game, and she had no idea what the prize was.

He thought back to his rodeo days. To the way he

and the other guys had been with women. Love 'em and leave 'em…fast. But those women had known just what they were asking for and Kate so clearly didn't.

Watching her with this guy, who couldn't touch the skill the guys on the circuit had, Jack had a sudden vision of her surrounded by the type of guy he knew waited for her in the pros…

Yeah, lamb to the slaughter was what came to mind.

She was just so damned naive.

She tilted her head to the side, putting her hand on the guy's shoulder, laughing loudly enough for him to hear her.

Then the cowboy leaned in and said something, and Kate's face flushed scarlet, her posture going rigid against the wall. She was saying something back and then the guy leaned in closer.

Jack took a couple of steps closer to the couple—so he could tell Kate her ice was going to melt and make her Coke taste like sadness, not for any other reason—and it put him in earshot of the conversation.

"If you want to get out of here," Chad was saying, "we can get in my truck and I'll take you for a real ride. Especially if you're into giving a little head."

And in a flash Jack saw Kate walking out of the bar. Getting into that truck. Undoing that asshole's belt and lowering her head to…

"Okay. Enough." Jack took two long strides forward, his blood pounding hot and hard. It was time to intervene.

KATE FELT A SHIFT in the air, and it was welcome. Her conversation with Chad had started out well enough, and she could tell it had annoyed Jack. Which was sort of the idea after the shit he had pulled earlier.

Buying her alcohol to make her sweet, pressing her up against the bar, looking at her like she was a fucking sunrise or something. Setting off a burst of heat low in her stomach that made it impossible to pretend anymore that she didn't know what was happening.

Attraction. That was why his presence made her feel itchy. Made her feel restless and hot, like a spark ready to ignite.

It was the worst. It was literally the worst. Worse than knocking over a barrel at a key moment, worse than a fresh cow patty between your toes and even worse than trying to eat a salad without ranch dressing.

Worst. Worst. Worst.

And so she had decided to try to parlay that attraction into an interaction with Chad. Because if she was that hard up for a little male attention, Chad was certainly a better bet. Also, the idea of being into Chad didn't fill her with terror and a whole lot of "dear God no."

But that was before he leaned in and told her just what he'd like to go in the back parking lot and do with her.

And she had no idea if she was supposed to want to, if she was supposed to be flattered, or if she was supposed to punch him in the face. She was just too shocked to process it. Fascinated, really. That somehow a little conversation and back arching had turned into…that.

But she didn't have any time to process it, because a deep voice broke the interaction between her and Chad and broke into her muddled thoughts. "Is there a problem here?"

It was Jack. And she wondered then if him moving closer was the shift she had felt. Disturbing. On so many levels.

"I don't think there's a problem here," Chad said, tugging his hat down, when only a few minutes earlier he had pushed it back. "Kate?"

"No," Kate said, "no problem." She was feeling completely at sea and in over her head, but she wouldn't admit that, not to Jack. She would fight her own damn battle. If she was even going to fight it. Maybe she would go in the back parking lot with Chad and undo his belt in his truck as he had suggested.

The thought did not fill her with arousal. In fact, it kind of made her feel sick. So she supposed she wouldn't be doing that. But Jack didn't have to know that.

"You look uncomfortable, Kate, and from where I was sitting, it looked like this bonehead was blocking your exit."

Chad turned to face Jack, pushing his hat back again. That was one annoying nervous habit. "How is it your business, Monaghan?"

Jack chuckled and crossed his arms over his broad chest, the muscles in his forearms shifting, and in spite of herself, Kate felt her heart rate pick up a little bit.

"It's my business because anyone who's bothering Kate has to deal with me."

"Oh, really?" Kate all but exploded. "Anyone bothering me has to deal with *me*, Monaghan. End of discussion." And now she was just pissed. She turned her focus back to Chad. "And you. I wouldn't go out back with you and do…that…even if you bought me a whole dinner at The Crab Shanty."

"Oh, come on, Kate. You are obviously asking for it,"

Chad said, his tone dripping with disdain now. "Shoving your tits in my face like that."

And suddenly, Chad was being pulled backward, then spun around and slammed up against the wall. Jack was gripping the collar of his shirt, his forearm pressed hard against the other man's collarbone. "If you're in the mood to get your jaw broken tonight, then keep talking," Jack said, his voice a growl. "Otherwise I'd walk away."

A hush had fallen over the bar, all eyes turned to Jack and Chad.

And on her, too. She had lost control of the situation, and she didn't like it at all.

"Jack, don't," Kate said.

"Are you actually defending this dickhead?" Jack was incredulous.

"No. But I don't need your help to say no. Let go."

Jack released his hold slowly, but there was still murder glittering in his blue eyes. "Whatever you want, Katie."

And then Chad lunged at Jack. It was a mistake. Before Kate could shout a warning, Jack was in motion. His fist connected with Chad's jaw, the sound rising over the lap steel that was filtering into the room from the jukebox.

"What'd I tell you, asshole?" Jack looked down at Chad, his expression thunderous. "I would've let you off because she asked. But since you made it about you and me... Hopefully, you don't have to get that wired shut. Drinking out of a straw for six weeks would really suck."

Jack stepped over Chad's crumpled form and walked out of the bar. Kate looked around the room. The only

446   BAD NEWS COWBOY

people who were still watching were members of the rodeo club. Everyone else had gone back to their darts and their drinks. A punch-up in Ace's wasn't the rarest of events. But seeing as Jack had just punched out one of their own, the club was still interested.

"Well, he was being an ass," Kate said, turning and following the same path Jack had just taken out of the bar.

It was downright chilly out now, the fog rolling in off the ocean leaving a cool dampness in the air. She could hear the waves crashing not too far away but couldn't see them because of the clouds.

The moon was a white blur of light mostly swallowed up by the thick gray mist. She could see only the faint outline of Jack, walking to his truck, thanks to the security light at the far end of the parking lot.

"Are you just gonna leave me here?" she shouted, breaking into a jog and going after him.

"I figured you could get a ride," he ground out.

"I did not need you to come over there and intervene." She stopped in front of him, and he turned around to face her.

She could only just make out the strong lines of his face, could barely see the way his brows were locked together, his expression still enraged. "It looked like you did. Don't be such a stubborn child all the time. If Connor or Eli had been here, they would've done the same thing."

"You aren't Connor and Eli," she bit out.

"No," he said. "But I'm something. And I'm not going to apologize for being mad about a guy talking to you that way."

"Maybe I wanted him to talk to me that way." She hadn't.

"Then raise your standards."

"As high as yours?" she asked.

"At least I know what I'm doing. You're like a…lamb being led to the slaughter."

She laughed, an outright guffaw, in spite of the fact that she found very little about this funny. She was attracted to Jack, she had just caused a major scene in Ace's, and now this. "Does anything about me look adorable and woolly? I didn't think so. I'm like a…a bobcat. I'm not a lamb."

"I thought you were a badger."

"That is beside the point. Maybe I'm a badger-cat. Anyway, the point is I don't need you to take care of me."

"Maybe not. But I'm not going to stand there while he says things like that to you."

"Why not? Why do you care?"

Her words hung in the silence, resting on the mist. And she wished they would just go away, because they felt exposing. And he was looking at her, making her heart beat faster, making her stomach seize up. Now that she knew, it didn't seem so irritating. It seemed like something else entirely.

Her shower the other day, the way her skin had felt so sensitive, the way Jack had flashed through her mind, rose up to the top of her thoughts. She nearly choked on her embarrassment then and there.

But she didn't say anything. She didn't back down.

"Because I could tell he was asking for things you weren't ready for," he said, his voice muted now.

"You don't know what I'm ready for." She forced the words out, her throat scratchy and dry.

He took a deep breath, lifting his head, his expression concealed by shadow. "I guess not. But I'm going to go ahead and assume based on knowing you and the way you were flirting that you don't have a whole lot of experience."

Heat flooded her face. "I don't really want to talk about this with you."

"Why not? As we have established," he said, his voice lowering slightly, "I am not your brother."

A shiver ran down her spine and settled in her stomach, leaving it feeling jittery and uncomfortable. "Right. That's been well established."

He looked pained. "I mean, look, you could maybe... talk to Sadie about this? Or Liss?"

"I'm not looking for advice," she said. "Anyway, Liss feels like crap, Sadie's busy, and they would both rat me out to my brothers, who would... It doesn't bear thinking about."

"Right."

"And I'm good at flirting, Jack."

"You're not."

"Yes, I am. I could have closed the deal with him. All I had to do was shove my boobs in his face and he was good to go. It's not like it's hard. I mean, I didn't really expect for him to say...all that. But it's not like I repelled him."

"That's not how you flirt. That is how you get...not a date. You get something else. And really, what you did had less to do with it than...just the guy you were talking to. You have to understand some guys are just after one thing. You have no idea what you're doing."

The air felt thick between them, and she couldn't blame it on the fog. It was just like earlier, when he dropped her at the bar. When she reached out and grabbed his chin, his stubble rough beneath her skin, so undeniably masculine, so undeniably *something* she'd never felt before.

Damn him, he was right about her experience. Or lack of it.

She'd never even been kissed. Which put Chad's offer firmly in the no column. But…what would it be like to kiss Jack? To feel his lips, warm and firm, and that stubble, all rough and…

"Maybe I'm the one who's wrong," he said. "Did you want to leave with him?"

Jack's question pulled her out of her fantasy. And she was relieved. "No." She was certain about that.

"So obviously, shoving your… Doing the… That isn't what you want to be doing."

Jack tongue-tied was almost funny enough to make the conversation less horrifying. Almost. "And you're an expert?"

"More than you. Look, what is it you want? The way you were acting is definitely going to work for one thing. But if your end goal is a date, you might want to approach it in another way."

"If I want a date?" she asked, blinking slowly, not exactly sure how they wound up in this conversation.

"Yes, a date. And not like…an invitation to go down on a guy in his truck."

Her face burned. "It's not my fault he said that stuff."

"I know," he said. "I'm not blaming you. But you know…if you set a trap for a horny dillweed, that's all you'll catch. And there's a lot of those in the circuit. If you intend to go pro, you're going to be exposed to a lot of it."

She let out an incredulous sound. "Are you…are you actually offering to help me hook up?"

"No. I'm not offering to help with that. But obviously, you could use a little bit of help figuring out how to deal with this kind of thing. Teaching you how to use…different bait."

"Instead of horny-dillweed bait?"

"Yes," he said. "I can help you."

"I'm twenty-three," she said.

"I know. And you're fast and strong and smart. You're the best damn barrel racer around, whatever you think about yourself. You're ready to go pro and take the circuit by storm. You're a hard worker and a good sister."

"So what exactly are you…offering?"

"If you're going to flirt, you should flirt with me."

CHAPTER FIVE

JACK WASN'T QUITE SURE what devil was possessing him at the moment. The same devil that had possessed him when he crossed the room and intervened in Kate's interaction with Chad. Something hot and reckless, which he was used to but not in connection with his best friends' little sister.

You're just looking out for her.

True. It might not be God's work, but it was Eli and Connor's work. He was helping.

Leading her not into temptation, and away from idiots who only wanted to get into her pants.

"Chad didn't hit you, did he, Jack?" Kate asked, her tone suddenly filled with concern.

"No. Why?"

"Because you're talking like someone who has a hcad injury."

"Lesson one," he said, his tone firm. "Don't insult the guy you want to hook up with."

Kate took a step back, her expression hidden from him by the dim evening light. "I don't want to hook up with you."

"Obviously." He felt like a moron for phrasing it that way. Things had gotten weird in the past hour and this wasn't helping. "I didn't mean that. I only meant that I can teach you how to talk to men."

"I was raised by men," Kate said, holding her hands wide. "I know how to talk to men. I know about horses, sports and even some of the finer points of tractor mechanics. I even like to compare scars."

Jack's throat clamped down hard on itself at the image of Kate shuffling clothing around to show off the various scars she no doubt had on her body.

Want to compare scars, baby?

Yeah, that might actually work as a pickup line. The other stuff, not so much.

"You know how to talk like a man, Kate. That's different than knowing how to talk to men. And it's also different than talking to them the same way you would your brothers but adding the…back arching you were doing."

"How?" she asked, sounding totally mystified.

"It just is. I mean, I don't talk to women the way I talk to Connor and Eli."

"You pretty much talk to me the way you talk to Connor and Eli. Except condescending."

Jack let out a heavy sigh. "Get in the truck."

"See? You're all ordery."

"Kate," he said, through clenched teeth, "get in the truck."

This time something in his tone spurred her to obey and she got in the passenger side of his black F-150. He breathed into his nose and then let a slow breath out through his mouth. He was insane.

He shook his head as he got into the truck, slammed the door behind him and started the engine before Kate could say anything.

He put the vehicle in Reverse and drove out of the

parking lot, gripping the steering wheel tight, tension creeping up his shoulders.

"So," Kate said. He had known his reprieve wouldn't last. "What exactly would this flirting boot camp entail?"

Okay, so she hadn't forgotten. Which meant he was committed. No turning back now. Anyway, there was no reason not to go through with it. Kate was just Kate. End of story. "I figure since we're working together on the rodeo, we might as well work on this, too."

"Why?"

The question of the year. "I don't want to babysit you the whole time we're organizing this. And when you go pro, Kate Garrett, there are going to be cowboys all over you."

"And what? You think I'm so stupid I'm gonna get tricked into bed? Like I don't know my own mind? Or are you trying to help me get some?"

The tension crept higher, climbing up into his neck. "That isn't what I said."

With any luck, him taking control of the situation would keep her from getting taken advantage of. Not that it would be wrong for Kate to get laid.

Even thinking about it threw up a big fat stop sign in his brain, warning his thoughts not to go any further.

Okay, so it wasn't as if he expected she never would. Or even that she hadn't. Because, as she had pointed out a few times, she was twenty-three. And you didn't exactly have to be smooth to get a guy into bed.

But she deserved better than an ass clown like Chad.

"Okay, what you do with my teaching is up to you," he said. "But forewarned is forearmed. If you want to get better at talking to guys, I'll help you. And what

will help mc is if I know that you'll be more prepared
to deal with jerks should any approach you. And that
you understand you don't have to do anything with them
just because they asked."

"Good grief, Jack. I know that," she muttered.

"Just don't ever sell yourself short."

"Why not? Men do it all the time. I don't understand
what all this protecting me from shallow creeps who
are only after one thing is about. You *are* that creep.
I mean, obviously, with other women, not with me."

He nearly choked on his tongue. "That's different."

"How is it different?"

There was no way for him to say how it was different
without sounding like a total jackass. So he kept quiet.

But Kate wasn't content with that. Of course she
wasn't. "Come on, Jack. I'm waiting for an explanation."

He let out an exasperated breath. "It's just that there
are different kinds of women. There are the kind that
you marry. And there are the kind that you…"

A hard crack of laughter filled the cab of the truck.
"Are you kidding me? Are you trying to tell me that you
marry good girls and sleep with bad girls? And that if
I keep pushing my breasts out, the boys will think I'm
a bad girl and corrupt me?"

"It's not good and bad." He had no clue how to dig
his way out of this. Sure, it sounded wrong when he
said it like that. Maybe it was even bad to think it. But
the bottom line was there were women who were fair
game in his mind, and then there was Kate. And she
was an entirely different category.

"All right, then. What kind of girl am I?"

Jack tightened his hold on the steering wheel. "The
type that could get taken advantage of by assholes."

"You think I'm stupid?"

"That isn't what I said. Stupid and inexperienced are two different things."

"You think I'm wholesome."

Yes. It suited him just fine to think that Kate Garrett was as wholesome as whole grains. "Comparatively."

"Compared to what? The women you sleep with?"

Heat lashed Jack's face. "You're determined to take this the wrong way."

"Enlighten me. What is the right way to take this? You're sitting here telling me there's a certain type of woman it's acceptable to mess around with and a kind that isn't acceptable to mess around with, and you're putting me in the category that isn't allowed to mess around."

"It's not just women," he said.

"Okay, then. What kind of guy are you, Jack Monaghan? Are you the kind of guy a girl marries? Or are you the kind we're supposed to want to bang?"

Hearing the provocative words on Kate's lips made his stomach wrench up tight. "Kate…"

"Go on. Tell me. It's hardly fair, since you have such a comprehensive assessment of me. I deserve one of you. So tell me, Jack," she said as he turned the truck into the narrow drive that would take them to the Garrett ranch and on to Kate's house, "are you the sort of guy that a girl should dream of getting in a tux? Or are you the kind of guy that a girl should think about getting naked with?"

He slammed on the brakes, without thinking, without meaning to. But he could not drive while she talked like that. "Dammit, Katie."

"For such an experienced man, you're acting very prudish."

"You want to know what kind of guy I am, Kate?" He shouldn't challenge her, and he knew it, but he couldn't help it. Because she was pushing. And when Kate pushed, he had to push back. Now and always. "Let me lay it out for you. I'm not the guy you marry. I'm the guy you stay up all night with. I'm the guy who doesn't call the next day. I'm the guy your mama would've warned you about if she had stayed around."

The last words barely made it out of his mouth before Kate grabbed ahold of his shirt and tugged him toward her. "Now you're being a jerk on purpose," she said, dark eyes glittering in the dim light, clashing fiercely with his.

"You wanted to know what kind of guy I was. I think that should answer your question." He felt like a tool. He'd lost sight of what the end goal was in this weird game they were playing. All he knew was that she was pushing, and he was pushing back. All he knew was that his blood was burning, and his heart was pounding faster than it should have been.

"You did. You're an ass. Question answered."

She raised her hand as if she was going to hit him, and he caught her wrist, holding her steady, their eyes still locked. She was breathing faster than he was, and suddenly, the anger riding over the heat burning in his blood fizzled out. The heat remained, his heart still thundering hard, steady. And he was still holding on to Kate's wrist.

The feeling that had surrounded them back at the bar had returned. Deeper. Stronger. And there was no pretending he didn't know what it was. He could feel her pulse fluttering beneath his thumb, faster and faster the longer he held her.

Fuck.

He released his hold on her and put both his hands back on the steering wheel. "I am. I'm an ass. I'm sorry. I'm sorry I said that."

"Why did you?" she asked, her voice small now.

"I don't know," he said, lying through his teeth with the truck still idling in the middle of the driveway.

"It was offensive. Not just what you said about my mother."

"I know. I didn't start out meaning to be offensive. Saying it out loud, I realize it's stupid. But definitely in my mind I think of the kind of women that I would pick up in a bar and the kind I wouldn't. Or more specifically, the kind who wouldn't go with me. Of course, saying it out loud forces you to listen to how stupid it is."

"It is stupid."

"I know."

"So," she said, folding her hands in her lap now like a good student. "You're going to teach me to flirt."

He didn't want to. He didn't want her flirting with the guys who were part of her group. He didn't want her flirting with the cowboys who would come in with the rodeo.

And considering what had just happened a few seconds ago, that meant it was exactly what he *needed* to help her learn to do.

As long as he focused on protecting her, as long as he focused on the right angle, the weirdness between them would evaporate. It had to. It was an aberration, something he would have liked to blame on alcohol. But he couldn't, since all he'd had was a Coke.

He could blame it on the full moon or on the way she had grabbed his chin. All things that had passed and would pass.

And since they were going to be working on the rodeo together, he really needed to get a grip.

"Yes. That's exactly what I'm going to do." He eased his foot slowly off the brake, and the truck started rolling forward.

"But chastely."

"I will give you certain tools. What you do with them is up to you. And does not need to be shared. And none of this should be shared with Connor or Eli."

Ultimately, he had Kate's best interest at heart, he really did. But since he wasn't related to her, he was being slightly more realistic than they would be. They would probably lock her in her room and not care about the fact that she was twenty-three.

"Okay. It will be our secret."

He turned his truck onto the little road that led to her cabin. And he tried not to dwell on the way the word *secret* sounded on her lips. Illicit and a little bit naughty. Nothing he and Kate talked about should sound naughty or illicit.

He swallowed hard. "Yeah."

He breathed a prayer of thanks when he rolled up to Kate's house. He needed to get home and get his head on straight. Tonight felt like some kind of weird detour out of his normal life. Suddenly, he'd become aware of some different things about Kate. Some things that he would rather have never been aware of.

And with that had come a thick, heavy tension that just wouldn't clear up.

A new day would fix that. The sun rising over the

mountains, bathing everything in golden light, chasing away the shadows that rested on Kate's face now. The shadows that accentuated her high cheekbones and the fullness of her lips. The darkness that blanketed the whole situation and made it seem fuzzy. Made her seem not quite like Kate. Made him feel not quite like a man who had known her since she was a whiny two-year-old.

He put the truck in Park but left the engine running. "Good night, Kate," he said, opting to use the name she preferred. All things considered, it seemed safer.

"Do you want to come in?"

His pulse sped up. "Why would I want to do that?"

"For some tea? For a flirting lesson?"

"Let's hold off on that," he said, his throat constricting. Right now he needed to get away from her.

"Okay. Thank you for coming tonight." She took a deep breath. "And thank you for punching Chad in the face. He's a doofus."

Jack laughed. And for a moment things felt as though they might be back to normal. The kind of normal they had before the past year or two, when everything he'd said and done had been wrong in Kate's eyes. "He really is. I hate that guy."

"I guarantee that he now hates you," Kate said, opening the passenger-side door and sliding out of the truck. "See you later?"

"You know you will. Probably a whole lot sooner then you'd like."

She didn't say anything to that. She simply smiled and slammed the door. He watched her walk all the way into the house. Because he had to make sure she was safe, after all. Not for any other reason.

Once she was inside, he put the truck in Reverse and

backed out of the driveway. The air quality in the vehicle had changed since Kate had left. He could breathe easier.

He wasn't going to overthink it. It would be a non-issue by tomorrow.

The sun would rise, he would be able to put Kate back in the proper place in his mind, and life would go on as it always had.

PERFECT. JUST PERFECT. Now that she'd made the critical mistake of admitting it to herself, it was as if a veil had been torn from her eyes and she could no longer feign ignorance of any kind. She was attracted to Jack.

Heart-pounding, bone-tingling, heavy-breathing, thinking-about-him-in-the-shower kind of attraction. How she'd spent so long pretending it was anything else was a mystery.

Self-preservation. That was clearly the answer. That and deep denial that ran all the way to her bones. Because nothing was ever going to happen with Jack. Never, ever, ever.

On a personal level, she liked Jack okay except when he was being a pain in the ass. Which was always. So often she liked him only minimally.

Apparently, though, liking him or not had nothing to do with sex feelings.

She let out a heavy sigh and dropped her bag on the floor. She had sex feelings for Jack. And it was undeniable. When she imagined getting in Chad's truck and doing all that dirty stuff to him, it made her feel vaguely unsettled and more than a little disgusted.

She allowed herself, just for a moment, to imagine she was back in the truck with Jack, the light low, his blue eyes fixed on her. And she imagined him putting his hand on her cheek. His fingers would be rough, calloused from all the hard work that he did. No matter how much Jack tried to pretend he didn't take things seriously, she knew it wasn't the truth. He was a hard worker, and everything he had was a result of that hard work.

She was sure his touch, his skin, would reflect that. Then she imagined him leaning in, those eyes that were usually all filled with mischief turning serious as his focus narrowed onto her face.

And then she imagined him whispering all those filthy things to her. Except he didn't say the words quite the way Chad had. Not in her fantasy. Of course, what he did say was all very vague and murky because Kate wasn't exactly up on dirty talk.

But she knew Jack would be way smoother than Chad. His voice would go all deep, the way that it did when he talked about something serious, which was so rare it was like finding gold. And it would get a little bit rough, the way it did when he called her Katie.

When she thought of touching Jack, of taking her clothes off for Jack, she didn't feel disgusted. She felt shaky and afraid, and given that this was only a fantasy, she could only imagine how terrified she would be if she found herself in this moment in reality. But she didn't want to run away. She wanted to lean in.

Shit, shit, shit. Undeniable sex feelings.

She turned to her couch, bracing her knees against the arm and falling forward over the side. Then she buried her face in one of the throw pillows and let out a long, drawn-out moan. What the hell was she supposed to do with this? Attraction to Jack, of all people.

It was the worst thing ever.

In his eyes she was nothing more than a kid. A kid he had to protect from herself. As though her flirting was tantamount to running with scissors. And he was going to teach her how to do it right. Just more reinforcement of the fact that he did not see her as an adult woman. And even if he did, there was no point in going there. He was the baddest bet around and everyone knew it.

He was an unapologetic manwhore who did whatever he wanted with whoever he wanted and never, ever made a commitment.

She tried not to find that assessment of him exciting. She should have found it disgusting. She should have found *him* disgusting. But she didn't. She couldn't. She never had.

From the time she was a little girl, running wild through the fields until she couldn't breathe, until the wind tangled her hair into knots, Jack Monaghan had amassed a whole mountain's worth of admiration in her soul. When the world had been bleak, he'd made her smile. Simple as that.

She wasn't a child now. She was a twenty-three-year-old virgin who had never even been kissed, who still ran like lightning through the grass and let her hair get tangled into a mess. And no matter how hard she tried to fight it, he still held his claim on that turf in her soul. The way Jack walked around doing what he wanted was more than a little appealing to someone who felt sheltered beyond reason.

Plus, the man was so hot it was entirely possible that women's clothes incinerated on contact. And if that happened, what was a guy to do but say yes?

She clicked her teeth together, annoyance at her own

self coursing through her veins. She was making excuses for him. And for her.

So, two things she knew. She wanted him. And she shouldn't.

The rest she would have to figure out later.

CHAPTER SIX

THE ONLY PROBLEM with the weekday at the Farm and Garden was that it provided far too much time for thinking. Kate didn't want to think. Not right now. At the moment her thoughts were lecherous and traitorous and she didn't really want to deal with either thing.

But there had been very few customers today and she'd spent the past forty-five minutes dragging a giant hose around and watering the plants in the back. Which meant thinking.

About last night. About her misguided flirting attempt with Chad. About what a jerk he'd been. About the way Jack had looked when he'd strode up looking like an outlaw ready to start a gunfight. And then he'd punched Chad. She had no idea how something like that could be...sexy. Yes, it had been sexy.

Oh yeah, there was also the fact that she was acknowledging that Jack was sexy now.

Thankfully, there were still no customers or they would all have been looking at her blushing right now.

Then there was the flirting thing. He had offered to teach her how to flirt. With other men.

She'd spent the entire night in her bed tossing and turning, trying to figure out what to do with that offer. It was a weird, patronizing offer. One she would normally have been tempted to tell him to shove up his ass.

But given her recent revelation, she was looking at it a little bit differently.

She was attracted to Jack. He had punched a guy for her, and it had been sexy. He wanted to teach her to flirt.

Doing the Jack math on that equation was leading her to some interesting places.

If he was giving flirting lessons, they would potentially find themselves in some interesting situations.

Situations that might give her an opportunity to try to seduce him.

She dropped the hose into the planter that was right in front of her, covering her face with both her hands. *Seducing* Jack. She'd never even thought of seducing a man before. Much less this man. The idea filled her with a strange kind of tingly horror and an excitement that mixed together so well she couldn't sort out which one was which.

She supposed at this point it was all the same, really. The fear of the unknown, the fear of a missed opportunity.

But one had far fewer consequences, that was for sure. Because Jack was a person she had to deal with on a fairly regular basis. Of course, the problem with living in a small town was that any guy she chose to get involved with would be someone she had to deal with on a regular basis.

She was not in the market for relationship. She wanted to go pro with her barrel racing and that would mean traveling all over the place, which would not leave any time for a guy. Which, provided things wouldn't get all weird after, actually made Jack the best bet of all. Because he wouldn't want anything more, and neither did she. Because she knew him, knew he wasn't, like, a secret ax murderer or anything. And because she trusted him.

That all had to count for something.

She pointed the hose at a little azalea that was placed in a pot on the ground. She was so focused on that, and on her seduction thoughts, that she didn't realize she had company until said company spoke.

"If you keep making that face, it will get stuck that way."

She jumped and splashed water on her hands with the hose, looking up to see Jack standing there grinning at her. "You scared the piss out of me!"

He made a face. "So that's not all just from the hose?"

She looked down and saw she'd misdirected the stream and that the water was puddling at her feet. She scowled and directed it at the plants again. Her face was hot, embarrassment over her choice of words lashing her. Which was stupid, because she shouldn't be embarrassed to say the normal things she always said in front of Jack. Seduction plans or no.

"What are you doing here?"

"You have two strikes against you already, Katie bear," he said, dodging the question.

"How did I get strikes? I'm not playing baseball. I'm watering azaleas."

"In the flirting game, little missy."

She decided to ignore the fact that he'd called her *little missy*. "Is it three strikes in flirting, too?"

"No idea."

"You're supposed to be the expert."

A slow grin spread over his face, the expression positively wicked. "I don't know, because I've never struck out before." She felt the heat in her face intensify, spread over her cheeks. "I made you blush. So I'm doing something right."

"You're not supposed to be practicing on me. I'm supposed to be practicing on you," she said, irritated that she was so transparent.

"You might want to turn your hose off."

She scowled and turned around, twisting the faucet handle then discarding the hose. "There. Off."

"Lesson one—don't look at the object of your affection like you want to stretch his scrotum out and wrap it around his neck."

"But what if that's what I want to do?" she asked, keeping her face purposefully blank.

"I didn't realize you were kinky," he said, arching a brow.

She bit the inside of her cheek to keep from reacting. "There's a lot you don't know about me, Jack."

"Oh, really?"

"Yeah, really. I'm a complex woman and shit."

"Of course you are." His blue eyes glittered with humor, and anger twisted her stomach. He still wasn't taking her seriously. Still looking at her as if she was a little girl playing dress-up.

She'd never played dress-up in her damn life. Her mother had left when she was a baby, taking every frill, every pair of high heels, every string of pearls with her. And Kate had seen two things in her household. She had seen her father sit on the couch and waste away, and she had seen Eli and Connor get out every day and bust their butts to make a better life for her, for themselves.

So she'd worked. From the moment she'd been able to. And none of it had been a game.

If Jack thought this would be any different, then he hadn't been paying attention.

"Somehow I don't think you believe me," she said, keeping her eyes locked with his.

"Sure I do." He reached toward her, and her heart stuttered. Then he grabbed ahold of the end of her braid and tugged lightly, in that patronizing, brotherly way that he did.

And that was the end of her rope.

Kate was the kind of girl who rode harder and faster whenever there was a challenge placed in front of her. And this was no different.

So she tilted her head to the side, following the direction he was tugging her braid. And then she reached toward him, but since there was no braid to grab, she reached around behind his neck, sifting her fingers through his hair, ignoring the way a whole shower of sparks skittered from her fingertips to her palm, down to her wrist.

She made a fist, pulling gently on his dark hair. Then something different flared in his eyes. A heat that matched the one burning inside her stomach. The heat she had just identified last night.

Holy crap.

She took in a shaking breath, her heart pounding so loudly she was certain he could hear it.

She leaned in, running her tongue along the edge of her suddenly dry lips as she did. Jack's posture went straight, his body shifting backward slightly, betraying the fact that she had now succeeded in making him uncomfortable.

The realization sent a surge of power through her, one that helped take the edge off the shaking in her knees. She moved her mouth close to his ear, the motion bringing her body in close to his, her breasts brushing against his chest, her pulse an echo like hoofbeats on the dirt.

She took a breath and was momentarily stunned by Jack. By his scent, clean and spicy, soap and skin. Being surrounded, enveloped, by his heat. By him.

A jolt of nerves shook her, and she felt tempted to bolt. And that temptation spurred her on. Because she didn't run.

"If you were telling me a lie," she said, lowering her voice to a whisper, "if you really think you know everything there is to know about me, I hope you consider yourself enlightened now." She moved away from him, her cheek brushing against his, his stubble rasping against her sensitive skin.

The sensation sent a shock of pleasure straight down to her core. She looked up, her eyes clashing with his. They were close enough that if she leaned in just a fraction of an inch, the tips of their noses would touch. And from there, it would be only a breath between their lips.

Jack lifted his hand again, taking ahold of the end of her braid and wrapping his fist around it. But rather than giving it the gentle tug she had become accustomed to, he simply held her.

Kate's heart thudded dully, her mouth so dry she felt as though she'd sucked on a piece of cotton. Everything in her was on hold, wondering what he would do next. Would he release his hold on her? Or would he pull harder on her braid, closing the distance between them?

Oh Lord, she could barely breathe.

Then he winked, releasing his grip on her and straightening, as though all of that tension between them had been imaginary. As though he hadn't felt it at all. "Good job," he said, his tone light, dismissive. "You might be a better student than I thought you would be."

She cleared her throat and flipped her braid over her shoulder so he couldn't grab it again. "Maybe I'm not the hopeless little innocent you think I am, Jack. Maybe—" she made direct eye contact with him, doing her best to look unflappable while she was internally quite flappy indeed "—there are a whole lot of things you don't know about me." Then she looked down, very purposefully, to the bulge just below his belt that she usually worked very hard to avoid looking at and back up, meeting his eyes again. Her heart was pounding so hard now she felt dizzy.

But she was going to win this weird game of one-upmanship they found themselves in, because she would be damned if she walked away with him still seeing her as a kid. With him making her feel like a kid.

"Maybe not." His voice was rough now, sort of like she'd fantasized it might be when she'd imagined him propositioning her.

She opened her mouth to say something else, something sassy and sensual and undoubtedly perfect. Undoubtedly perfect before she was interrupted and unable to say it.

"Hi, Kate. Hello, Jack."

Kate turned and saw her sister-in-law, Liss, standing there, her head tilted to the side, arms crossed over her rounded belly.

"Liss," Jack said, nodding his head. "I have to run. See both of you later."

He beat a hasty retreat, leaving her standing there alone with Liss.

"I thought I'd stop by and see if you had time for lunch. I'm in town grocery shopping and things. Generally killing time."

Kate cleared her throat, feeling unaccountably guilty and as if she'd been caught with her hand in the cookie jar. Her hand had been nowhere near Jack's cookie jar. She had no cookies. So that was ridiculous. Still, her face was all hot. "Sorry, I can't take a break yet. No one's here to relieve me for another hour."

Liss wrinkled her nose. "Okay. I'd love to wait for you, but I can't. I need fried fish with more malt vinegar than one person should reasonably consume. And I need it now."

"Yeah, go eat. I'm fine."

Liss did not leave. Instead she stood there, rocking back on her heels, bunching her lips up and pulling them to the side before taking a deep breath. "Kate, I love Jack like a brother. You know that."

Deeply uncomfortable anticipation gathered at the base of Kate's skull and crawled upward, making her scalp prickle. "Yes. I know that."

"He's bad news, Kate. I mean, as far as women are concerned. Nobody's going to reform him. Not even you."

Kate inhaled, preparing to say something. To protest. But instead she ended up choking. She covered her mouth, trying to minimize the coughing fit that followed. When she straightened, tears were running down her cheeks and her throat felt raw. Liss had made no move to help her; rather, she was just standing there looking at her. "Why exactly did you think I needed that warning?" she asked, her voice sounding thin and reedy now, certainly not convincing.

"I see the way you look at him."

"Can you look at someone a certain way? I just thought I was looking at him like I look at any normal human." Lies.

"If you don't need the warning, feel free to ignore me. But if there's any chance you might need it, take it."

Kate was just completely done being treated like everyone's little sister. "Thank you," she said, her voice tight. "I will keep that in mind just in case. Though I'm not sure if you noticed, but I'm not sixteen anymore. Or twelve."

Liss was not cowed. "I did notice. And I bet I'm not the only one. Which is what concerns me. Older, more experienced women than you have suffered a bad case of the Jacks."

"I've known him my entire life. I think it's safe to say I'm immune." Lies. Lies. Lies.

"Forget I said anything. Unless you need to remember that I said this," Liss said, looking extremely skeptical.

"Okay. Should I ever feel like I'm in danger from Jack, I will remember this."

"Great." Liss continued gazing at her for longer than was strictly necessary. "Okay. I'm going to go eat."

"Great. Enjoy your vinegar."

"I will. In fact, I have to go quickly so that I don't die."

"Don't die. Feed my little niece or nephew."

Liss smiled, the weirdness from a moment ago dissipating. "Oh, I definitely will. No worries about the baby skipping meals. Or even going a couple of hours without. See you later, Kate."

And Liss left, leaving Kate there alone to examine both what had just happened between Jack and herself and Liss's observations.

She didn't really care what Liss thought about Jack and whether or not he was good or bad news. Because that had nothing to do with how she felt about Jack. She was attracted to him. She didn't want forever and ever and a picket fence with him.

Still, she was a little bit unnerved that Liss seemed to read her so well. It made her wonder if Connor and Eli could read her just as plainly.

She immediately dismissed that. Unless it was printed on the back of a cereal box, neither of her brothers were going to read too deeply into anything.

Anyway, there was nothing deep to read.

It was just a case of a little harmless desire. And if given the chance, she imagined she could burn it out nicely.

A slow smile crossed her lips. Yes, that was what she wanted.

And with her decision made, Kate went happily back to work.

JACK DID HIS absolute damnedest not to reflect on anything that had passed between Kate and himself in the past twenty-four hours. Because he was sitting in his living room with her two older brothers, his very best friends, men who were like brothers to him. Men who would snap him in half like a matchstick if they had any idea of the thoughts that had run through his mind earlier this morning.

No matter how fleeting said thoughts were.

They had been brief, but they had been way, way outside the boundaries of Safe Kate Thoughts.

For a moment there, when she'd curled her fingers through his hair, those serious dark eyes on his... Yeah, for a moment there he'd thought about cupping the back of her head and closing the distance between them...

And he was going to stop thinking now.

He heard a sudden and violent outburst of profanity and realized he'd missed something on the game.

"Pass interference my ass!" Connor shouted.

"Must be nice to have the refs in your pocket," Eli grumbled, leaning back on the couch.

"Yeah," Jack said, only pretending to have any clue what was happening.

Connor snorted. "I just got a profane text from Liss."

"Is she watching the game in between female bonding moments?" Eli asked.

"You don't think Sadie is watching the game?" Connor asked.

"She pays just enough attention to football to irritate all of us. Though I imagine that if Kate is around, she and Liss will have banded together to commandeer the remote."

"Had we opted to watch the game as a group, I imagine she would have showed up wearing orange and black and rooting for the Beavers. Even though they aren't playing."

"You chose a real winner there, Eli," Jack said, happy to be on any topic other than the one his brain seemed intent on focusing on.

"Our love transcends football," Eli said, lifting a bottle of beer to his lips.

"And my love for Liss doesn't have to," Connor said.

"And I'm single, assholes," Jack added, grinning broadly.

"I don't envy you," Eli said.

"Because you've forgotten."

"Forgotten celibacy? Feeling lonely, depressed." Connor shook his head. "No, I have not forgotten that."

"Some of us are not celibate," Jack said. Though, come to think of it, it had been a lot longer than usual since he'd picked someone up.

Which could explain some of the weirdness between him and Kate.

And now he was back to Kate.

"So you and Kate are working on a charity thing?" Eli asked.

A sharp sensation twinged in his chest. It was almost as though Eli could read his mind. Which was a dangerous thing right now. "Yeah. Has she mentioned much about it?"

"No, not really. I was curious."

"Well, it isn't just me and Kate," he said, feeling unaccountably guilty. "We've got the whole amateur association involved. And I'm working toward reconnecting with some contacts in the pro association to get them to help, as well. So it's a whole group effort."

"To help Alison?" Connor asked.

His question had a tone to it. A suspicious tone. "Yes. Her and other women in her situation. I'm impressed with what she's doing, improving not only her situation but the situations of others." Which didn't sound defensive at all. Not that he had any reason to feel defensive about Alison. It was the entire situation.

"Is there something going on with her?" This question came from Eli. "You and her, I mean."

Jack was almost grateful they were so far offtrack. "No. I'm sure she's lovely but hooking up with vulnerable women is not exactly my thing." Which was a nice reminder. "They want what I'm not going to give."

"You seem to be giving things," Eli said.

Well, this was the story of his life. He couldn't possibly be doing something nice just to do something nice. He must have ulterior motives. Probably extremely dishonorable ones.

"Because I'm a nice person, jackass."

Eli held his hands up, palms out. "Of course you are."

"I do selfless things."

"Uh-huh," Connor said.

"I have." Maybe not very many.

"Fine. I believe you," Eli said.

Jack snorted and stood up, making his way into the kitchen to grab another beer. Of course, he couldn't be too mad, since Connor and Eli were his oldest friends and they had a lot more context for his behavior than most people did. Still, the citizens of Copper Ridge tended to sell him short. And yeah, some of that he'd earned. But not all of it.

He liked to make people laugh; he liked to provide a good time. He liked to have a good time. And somehow people tended to mistake that to mean he didn't take anything seriously. As though his ranch ran on charm rather than labor. As though he had lucked into his position on the circuit.

Maybe if he did a good job organizing this charity thing, the town would have to realize that he had the ability to see something through. To do something right, to do something noble, even.

Yeah, *noble* wasn't a word typically used to describe him.

Maybe, though…maybe he could get noticed for doing something good. Maybe he could change some things.

Everyone liked him well enough, but no one took him all that seriously. He wondered if that would change if the townspeople had any idea that he carried the same genes as the venerable West family.

No doubt it would, since the oldest of the West children had a fairly large scandal in his past, and yet the town never seemed to talk much about it. As though the influence of Nathan West was mixed into the mist, settling over everything. All-seeing, all-knowing.

But he had no claim to that name; he'd sold it when he was eighteen years old. A little bit of hush money to get his life going, to permanently separate himself from a man who had never given a damn about them anyway. It had seemed like a no-brainer at the time.

Now sometimes he felt a bit as if he'd sold himself. Pretty damn cheap, too.

And the Wests were part of the town—the mortar in half the brick buildings on Main Street. Jack felt somewhat obligated to slide under the radar. Oh, sure, he'd been a pro bull rider; he was a ladies' man; he lived in the same town he was born in. The people paid him no mind, because they thought he was harmless. Thought he was laid-back. Thought he was haphazard, that he came by his successes accidentally.

They underestimated him, and he allowed it.

And he was pretty tired of it.

He jerked open the fridge and pulled out another bottle of beer before slamming the door shut again. Yeah, he was pretty damn tired of it. So he was going to put an end to it.

This charity rodeo was going to be a success. One of the biggest things Copper Ridge had ever been a part of. Maybe it would even be something that caught on. Something that was annual, at least here, if not in other counties.

It would be work. Hard work. And people would have to acknowledge that.

Hell, that was the entire point of his horse breeding operation. No one knew it. No one but him. But he was amassing a reputation for having some of the finer stock around, and he was most definitely gunning for Nathan West. To overthrow him. To diminish the man's empire.

To meet the man at the top of his own game and beat him at it.

Maybe it was petty. To want something just so he could prove to the man who would never lower himself to call himself Jack's father that he wasn't just a little bastard brat who could be swept under the rug. That if he was given money, he wouldn't just go drink himself into a stupor with it because he was poor and unworthy and didn't know what to do with cash. Oh no, he was making himself legitimate competition.

And the old man had provided the seed money that allowed Jack to do it.

It was poetic justice, albeit private poetic justice, that he had been enjoying greatly for the past couple of years.

This would be just a slightly more public showing. The middle finger to his dad, a bid for legitimacy. A way to flaunt himself without violating their agreement. His dad's dirty secret shining in the light, and even if no one else knew it, the old man would.

Yeah, he was all in. No question.

He turned and walked back into the living room, offering Eli and Connor a smile they didn't see, since they were glued to the game.

"Since I've been a pretty awesome friend to you lousy pieces of flotsam and jetsam for the past twenty-some-odd years, I was thinking you could help out with the charity."

"How?" Connor asked. "I feel invested in helping, if for no other reason than Eli and I saw the way that husband of Alison's treated her."

"Time donation, monetary donation, spreading the word. Whatever you feel like you can give."

"You've got it," Eli said.

"It will be good for your reputation anyway, Sheriff," Jack said.

"Well, now you're acting like I need to have ulterior motives to contribute to charity."

"I'm just adding incentive."

"Your pretty face is enough incentive, Jack. It always is," Connor said.

"I'm flattered, Connor but you're a married man, and I'm not a homewrecker."

"That's too bad. Liss is pretty open-minded."

"If I took you up on what you're pretending to offer, you would scamper into the wilderness and never return," Jack said drily.

"Damn straight."

"And I'd run in the opposite direction," Jack added.

"Okay, that call was balls. There is no way this game isn't fixed," Eli groaned.

And after that, they didn't talk about charity, and Jack didn't think much about it. He didn't think about Kate, either. Well, not much.

Sure, there had been some tension between them recently. But ultimately, she would always be the little mud-stained girl he'd helped distract while Connor and Eli had dealt with their drunken mess of a father.

It had given him a place to be, something to focus on besides his unhappy home.

The simple fact was the Garretts were more than friends to him. They were family. Connor and Eli were his brothers, a dream an only child like himself had never imagined could be realized.

Then he'd grown up and found out he had siblings. Half siblings, but other people who shared his DNA. At that point he had another realization about just how little blood mattered.

Colton West was his brother by blood, but he doubted the man would ever cross the street to shake his hand. He doubted the other man had any idea.

Connor and Eli had always been there for him. And they always would be.

Nothing on earth was worth compromising that over. Nothing.

THE LIST OF PARTICIPANTS for each event had grown. And thanks to Jack's hard work it included several people from the pro circuit. Kate felt downright intimidated, she couldn't lie. She was signed up to compete against some of the best barrel racers around, and even though it was just a charity competition, she felt as if it would be some kind of moment of truth.

About her skills. About whether or not she had an excuse to hold back from turning pro. About a whole lot of things.

She looked down and kicked a stone, watched it skim across the top of the fine gray dust in the driveway. She'd come out to get a ride in before the meeting tonight. Before Jack was due to pick her up and take her over to the Grange again. But she sort of felt numb, sluggish, frozen. Not in the best space to do a run around the barrel she had set up in the arena.

But she supposed she had to. She kicked another stone.

She hadn't seen Jack since that day at the Farm and Garden. They had only shared one phone call, where he had rattled off a list of names that had made her stomach heave with anxiety. All the while, her heart had been pounding faster because of the deep timbre of his voice. She didn't need professional psychiatric help at all.

She let out an exasperated breath and shoved her hands in her jacket pockets as the wind whipped across her path. She upped her pace as she headed toward the barn.

Her fingers were still numb as she tacked Roo up. She pulled the girth tight and checked everything over once. Then she leaned in and kissed Roo right over the star on her forehead. She inhaled her horsey scent, shavings and the sweet smell of the hay. It was like slipping into a hot bath, a moment of instant relaxation.

"Okay," she said. "We can do this."

She led Roo outside before mounting and taking it slow over to the arena. Roo was a soft touch, and it took only a little gentle encouragement to urge her horse to speed up. Then she let out a breath and spurred Roo to go even faster, leaning into her horse's gait, making the turn around the first barrel easily.

She wondered what her time was. She should have grabbed the stopwatch that was hanging on the fence. She leaned back slightly and Roo sensed the change, shaking her head and knocking against the second barrel as they went around.

"Shit." She looked over her shoulder and watched it topple. So that was it. That was her run.

She slowed considerably when she approached the third barrel, then made an easy loop around it before stopping Roo inside the arena. She cursed again, the foul word echoing in the covered space.

She lowered her head, buried her face in her hands and just sat there. Feeling pissed. Feeling miserable.

"It was a pretty crappy run."

She raised her head and looked up, saw Jack standing against the fence, his boot propped up on the bottom rung, forearms rested on the top.

"What are you doing here, Monaghan?"

"I decided to come a little early and see Eli and Connor. Neither of whom are here."

"So you decided to come over and poke me with a stick?"

He lifted his hands and spread them wide. "No stick."

"Verbal sticks, asshat."

"Sure. I have verbal sticks. Why the hell did you suck so bad?"

"What does that mean? Why did I suck so bad? I didn't suck on purpose."

"No, you didn't. But you can do better. So the question is, why did this run suck so bad?"

"I don't think there's an answer to that question," she said, sitting up straighter on the back of her horse and crossing her arms.

"There is always an answer to that question. And if you want to be a lazy-ass rider, then the answer to the question is that your animal acted up. But if you want to get better, then the answer is that you did something stupid. Always put the control with yourself. Then it's your fault when you lose, but then it's up to you to win."

"Are you going to have me wash your truck now? Wax on, wax off."

"I kind of am your Mr. Miyagi at the moment. Your flirting guru. I might as well teach you how to win rodeo events, too."

"No one asked."

"But I am the only one of the two of us who has competed on a professional level. And if it is something that you really want, maybe you should accept my help instead of being stubborn."

"I'm not being stubborn."

"Babycakes, you eat stubborn-Os for breakfast." He wandered over to the open arena gate and grabbed hold of the stopwatch that was looped over the top rung of the fence. Even while he was here witnessing her failure, annoying her, she couldn't ignore how damn sexy he was. The way his jeans clung to his muscular thighs.

Did women look at thighs? Was that even a thing? Or was it just a bad case of the Jacks?

"I'll reset your barrels." He walked into the arena and made sure everything was lined up, lifted the one she had knocked down. Then he walked back to the fence. "Reset yourself, Katie."

She flipped him the bird while obeying his command. She had some pride, after all.

Then she shut him out. Shut out his voice, shut out his presence and focused. The horse started to move, and she knew that Jack would have started the time at that moment. The start was a little bit slow, and she faltered going around the first barrel. Then she shook her head, spurring Roo on harder into the second. That went better. But she knew she wasn't at top time. Not even her own top time. She was too in her head, and there was nothing she could do about it right now. Not with Jack here. Not with that whole list of professionals she was going to be competing against in front of people.

Not when she was going to be faced with the undeniable proof of whether or not she had the ability to compete professionally and win. And down went the third barrel.

Kate growled, bringing Roo to a halt. She slid off the back of the horse, walked over to the barrel and reset it herself. "I'm gonna call it good now," she shouted.

"Do it again."

"No. I've done it twice—that's enough."

"Your horse can handle more than that. You know that."

"I'm done, Jack," she said, feeling a whole lot angrier than the situation warranted. But she didn't care. Because all of this felt like a little bit too much. Because she wanted Jack, and yesterday, just when she thought he might want her too, he had walked away. He had walked away and acted as though it didn't matter.

And now he was here again, getting in her face, treating her like a kid. He was the worst. He was worse than the run she had just done.

"Do you want things to go well when you compete next month?"

"No," she said, her tone dripping with disdain. "I want to fail miserably in front of a thousand people."

"With those skills, you will." There was an intensity to him that was unusual. And it matched her own.

This was weird. All of this was weird. Sure, she and Jack sniped at each other, but this wasn't normal.

None of this was normal, and she had no freaking clue what to do about it.

She turned away from him and started fiddling with the barrel position again.

"You going again?" he asked.

"Nope," she said. "I already told you that."

"Stop being a baby."

She snorted. "Kiss. My. Ass."

"I don't think I'll kiss it, actually." She didn't see his next action coming. Literally, because she was turned away from him. The sharp crack on her backside with his open palm didn't hurt, but it sure as hell shocked her. "Now, get that pretty ass back on the horse and do it again."

Shock, anger and undeniable lust twisted together in her stomach, forging a reckless heat that fueled her next set of actions.

He had too much control. She let him set the terms in the Farm and Garden, let him mess with her, let him ramp up her attraction and walk away. He thought he was the teacher, in everything, in all things, because he thought she was a kid, easily dealt with. Wasn't that what all of this was? Just him dealing with an obnoxious kid. Teach her how to flirt, keep her out of trouble. No way. No more.

He had too damn much control, and he was too confident in it. She was going to take it. Now.

She reached out, grabbed ahold of the collar of his shirt and pulled him forward, catching him just enough by surprise that she managed to knock him off balance and close the distance between them as she stretched up on her toes to press a kiss to his lips.

She realized her mistake a split second too late.

She'd seen it as a moment to seize power, but what she hadn't realized was that all semblance of control would flee her body like rats off a sinking ship the moment his mouth made contact with hers.

There was no calculation, not now. There was no next move that she could think of. There were no thoughts at all.

There was only this. There was only Jack. The heat of his body, the sensation of his lips pressed against hers. The fact that this was her first kiss was somehow not at all as important as the fact that she was kissing Jack.

And he wasn't pushing her away.

He didn't move for a moment, simply standing there and receiving what she gave him. But in a flash, that changed.

He wrapped one arm around her waist, holding her hard against him, crushing her breasts to the muscular wall of his chest. So tightly she could feel his heart raging.

Somewhere in her completely lust-addled mind, she was able to process the fact that he was affected by this, too.

She angled her head, trying to deepen the kiss, wanting more, *needing* more. Just as she did, she found herself being propelled backward, released.

Jack turned away from her and walked about four paces before whirling around again.

She felt cold. Shaky. She had kissed Jack. *Actually* kissed him. And for about two glorious seconds he had kissed her back.

And then he had…shoved her.

"Don't do that again," he said, his tone hard.

"If you're going to slap my ass, I expect a kiss on the lips first," she said, not quite sure how she was managing to keep her tone steady.

Her insides certainly weren't steady. They were rocked, completely turned on end. But at least her voice was solid.

"Don't…do that again," was his only response.

"Why not? I thought you were going to teach me how to flirt. Doesn't that fall under the header?"

"That falls under the header of playing with fire, little girl."

Her heart thundered faster, her lips impossibly dry. "Maybe I want to."

"Spoken by a girl who's never been burned," he said, taking another step backward.

"Spoken like a man who's afraid I might be kerosene to his lit match." Apparently, being stubborn and unwilling to back down handily took the place of having experience and confidence.

Good to know.

"We're not going to do this."

"Why?" she asked, not quite as pleased with the tone

of her voice this time. She sounded needy. And she hated that.

Her mother had walked out when she was two; her father was a drunk. She'd never had the chance to be needy. Frankly, she didn't like the way it looked on her. She was making a mental note to avoid it in the future.

"You know why."

Because he thought of her as a kid? Because he wasn't attracted to her? Because Connor and Eli would kill him and bury his body in a far-flung field? She didn't know *why*, because there were too many whys. But she wasn't going to go on. She wasn't going to do the needy thing. She was not going to beg.

She had her pride. Sure, she'd never been kissed before today, but she had never really wanted to be kissed by any of the guys she had known. She would go find someone else before she would make a fool of herself in front of Jack Monaghan.

Though it was hard not to beg when her lips still burned from the touch of his. When her body ached in places she hadn't given all that much thought to before.

Yeah, that made it a lot harder.

"Get on your horse. And do the run again," he said, his blue eyes level with hers.

"Still?"

"Are you a quitter?"

"Fuck you."

"Shout that at me all you want when you're doing the run again. Go."

She walked back over to Roo and got on. They walked back to the starting point. Then she looked at Jack, who was standing there holding the stopwatch. She took a breath and started. And her mind was blank.

Blank of anything but what had just happened. Blank of anything but the heat and fire burning in her blood from the anger, from her arousal. That moment when her lips had touched his. When he had pushed her away.

She rounded the first barrel and it seemed slow, easy, in comparison to the confusion that was pouring through her. They straightened up and she went to the second, slowing down the moment in her mind so that she could capture the memory of his lips on hers. It had only been a second. A fraction of one, even. But it had felt so important. So altering.

Before she knew it, she was rounding the third barrel, the impression of the heat and firmness of his mouth still on hers as she let out a breath and finished the run.

It was fast. It was clean.

It was good.

She looked up, saw the stopwatch hanging on the fence where it had been before Jack had come.

And Jack was gone.

CHAPTER SEVEN

KATE SHOWED UP to the meeting late and pissed. All things considered, Jack didn't really give a fuck about her mental state.

The little wench had kissed him.

Sure, he'd been baiting her to do something. He couldn't deny that. But never, not once, had he imagined she would do that.

Somehow, in the moment, slapping her on the rear had made sense.

He'd shown up at the ranch, and neither Eli nor Connor had been there. Then he'd run across Kate. Riding her horse around the barrels, so obviously holding back it had made him angry for some reason.

Probably for the same reason her putting off turning pro made him angry.

She was selling herself short. Holding herself back. Making herself so much smaller than she should.

He hated that. It was something his mother had done, always. Accepting defeat. Receding into it. A woman who hadn't been wanted by her rich lover, so she'd refused to take anything from him. Refused to fight. Curled so deep into herself she couldn't even love her son, because she couldn't see her value or his.

He didn't want to see Kate doing it, too.

But then she compounded her sins by being...not

the Kate he was used to. When she'd done her second run, he'd been far too aware of how her body moved with the horse's. And it had been far too easy to imagine her riding astride him as he gripped her hips, as she followed his rhythm.

Something in his brain was short-circuiting. And that had been confirmed when she'd started running her mouth, and in his mind it had seemed a perfectly acceptable solution to give her a smack on the ass. Nothing more than a sports pat, something to prove he was in complete control of himself. That she was one of the guys, or just a little sister to him, or something.

It had backfired in a very spectacular way.

Not only because the contact had felt decidedly unbrotherly on his end but because then she had turned around and kissed him.

And it had damn near knocked him on his ass.

More accurately, it had damn near taken them both to the ground, where he would have taken things a lot further than a simple kiss.

He tried to think back to a few weeks ago. When Kate had simply been Kate, the younger sister of his two best friends in the entire world. A woman he'd known for so many years he didn't spare her a second glance when she walked in the room. There had been no need to look at her. He had her memorized already.

No makeup. Long dark hair either hanging down her back or tied back into a braid. And her body... He'd never even bothered to look. Not in a serious way.

He wanted to go back to that time. Sadly, he couldn't. Which meant when Kate stormed into the Grange Hall looking furious, he did look at her.

At the flush of rose in her cheeks that betrayed just

how mad she was, at the dangerous glitter in her dark eyes. The way her hair was disheveled, probably from the ride earlier, but it made him think of the kiss. The possibility that it had been messed up by him.

The kiss had been too brief for that. He hadn't had the chance to sift his fingers through her hair. Hadn't had a chance to do anything much other than brush his lips briefly against hers. Because he had come back to his senses and fast.

He shouldn't be regretting that.

He gritted his teeth and tried to focus on what Eileen was saying about the progress sheet made for their rodeo day. Kate, meanwhile, had taken a seat opposite him in the circle, making such a show of not looking at him that it made her anger all the more apparent.

Okay, so leaving her during her ride and then not taking her to the meeting as they'd agreed had probably been a jerk move. But he didn't really appreciate the kiss, so as far as he was concerned, they were even.

Except for the part where Kate Garrett had made his dick hard and nothing would be right in his life or his head ever again.

So yeah, there was that.

Eileen called on him to speak and he rattled off the list of riders he'd gotten to agree to be a part of the competition.

With the venue confirmed, enough riders on board and enough livestock owners willing to have their bulls and broncs involved in the extra day, everything was ready to move forward.

And he could barely pay attention, because the kiss, the kiss that never should have happened, was still burning his lips.

Shit, he was the one acting like a virgin, not Kate.

The word sent a shock of heat through his body. A virgin.

The odds that Kate was a virgin? Very high. Very, very high and he shouldn't care or ponder that. He shouldn't think of Kate and sex or Kate and no sex at all.

Except he had thought *Kate* and *sex* a lot in the space of the past few minutes, and dammit, he needed a distraction. He needed to chop wood. No, that wasn't good enough. He should go pull a tree down with his bare hands. Anything to expel the extra testosterone currently roaring through his body.

He could sleep with someone else, he supposed. Kate wasn't an option and the best way to deal with being horny was to get some. A simple problem with a simple solution.

He raised his eyes and scanned the room, purposefully avoiding looking anywhere near Sierra or Kate. There were some hot cowgirls in the building. Chicks in rhinestone jeans and pink hats with tight tops and big breasts. Girls who would stay long enough to complete the ride, so to speak, and then get on their way. No hang-ups, no nothing. Just his type.

Except looking at them right now was just like looking at a sunset. Real nice, real pretty, but he didn't want to fuck it.

Not that he wanted to do that with Kate. There was a lot of mileage between a kiss in an arena and full-on... bedroom events.

But the fact that it was on his mind was a bad sign.

By the time the meeting adjourned, Jack wasn't in the mood to stick around and socialize, even if he should. Especially with the pretty cowgirls.

He didn't feel like it.

He stood and made his way out, looking at Kate one last time. Kate, who was still very definitely ignoring him.

Fine. He walked out the door, and thankfully, no one stopped him. Probably because he looked about as happy as a guy chewing glass.

He crossed the street to where he'd parked his truck. The days were getting shorter, dusk already lowering itself down to the tops of the mountains and blanketing the town in deep blue. There was something peaceful about it like this. The familiar shrouded in darkness. He'd traveled all over the country during his stint in the rodeo, but he'd never found another place he felt as if he could call home.

On the road he'd found what he did or didn't do meant nothing. Because no one who mattered was there to see it.

Copper Ridge, for all the history, good, bad and ugly, was his home. No doubt about it.

Eli was here. Connor was here.

And the Wests are here. And you're still wishing he'd see you.

No. Hell no. The old man could rot, for all he cared. He wanted to be a thorn in his side, sure as hell, but he didn't want attention. Didn't need admiration.

"All right, asshole."

Jack turned and saw Kate storming across the street, her hands clenched into fists at her sides. She painted a sharply contrasting picture to some of the other women in the group. No sequins, no pink.

Oh yeah, and she was looking at him like she wanted

to kill him with her bare hands and feed his body to the seagulls.

"What do you want, Kate?"

"Why did you stand me up?" she demanded.

"Why did you kiss me?"

"Because you're sexy and I wanted to. Now, why the hell did you stand me up?" she asked again, her voice cracking. "I waited for you."

"I wasn't in the space to deal with you. And you think I'm sexy?"

"No, dumbass. I think you're a fucking troll—that's why I kissed you." She was mad. And not the normal Kate mad. Not the kind where she wanted to slap his arm and call him a name and call it done. He'd never seen her this mad.

"We can't," he said, because it was the only thing he could think to say.

"You can't say you're going to take me somewhere and then not show up."

"That has nothing to do with the kiss."

"So you didn't leave me stranded because I kissed you?"

It was exactly why he hadn't brought her with him to the meeting. "I didn't strand you," he said. "You have a truck."

"I have waited on too many damn curbs for a man who was at home drunk off his ass to spend ten seconds waiting for you," she said, her voice breaking now.

Kate wasn't just mad. Kate was hurt. And he would have fed his own body to the seagulls about now if he wasn't so attached to it.

"Kate... I didn't... Look, I just thought it was best if we had some distance. I sure as hell don't know what's

been…" He trailed off because he couldn't find a way
to finish the sentence that didn't force him to confess
more than he wanted to.

He looked through the hazy light and saw that her
eyes were glittering, filling with tears. The mighty Kate
Garrett, whose face he hadn't seen streaked with tears
since she was nine years old, sitting on the step outside
her house while her dad raged and threw things inside,
was about to cry.

Because of him.

She was right. He was an asshole.

He wanted to tug her into his arms and give her a
hug. But hugs, touching of any kind, had turned an unexpected direction. Like a mean bull on a bad day. And
there was no way he could reach out to her now.

"Katie," he said, his voice rough even to his own
ears, "please don't cry."

"I'm not crying," she said, but the catch in her voice
told another story.

"Damn it all to hell." He took a step forward and
wrapped his arms around her shoulders, tugging her in
close. "I'm sorry. I didn't mean to hurt your feelings. I
thought we could use some…distance."

She looked up at him and the vulnerability in her
eyes caught him off guard, punched him in the gut.
"You want distance? From me?"

There was no good way to answer that. "I don't…
want…" He released his hold on her and took a step
back. "Things are weird right now. You get that, right?"

"You never want distance from me. We're around
each other all the time."

"Yeah. And up until today we'd never kissed. So
things change."

"It was only a little kiss," she said, sucking her bottom lip between her teeth and chewing it.

"Big enough," he said, his gut burning as the memory flashed through his mind again.

"That you need distance from me."

"Kate…"

"You're supposed to be teaching me to flirt."

"You took it too far."

"Why?"

"For God's sake, Kate, drop it," he ground out, turning toward his truck and starting to open the driver's-side door.

"Is it because you didn't like it?"

He whirled around. "It's because given a few more minutes or a few less thoughts, I would have had you down on the ground and out of your clothes, badgercat, so unless that's the sort of thing you want to mess around with, I'd suggest giving me the distance I ask for."

Kate's eyes widened, her lips dropping into a rounded O shape. "You liked it, then?"

"This isn't going to end anywhere good." He didn't know if he meant the conversation or what was happening between them. It could be either. Or both.

People were filing out of the Grange Hall now and looking in their direction.

"Can we get inside your truck?" Kate asked, her voice small.

"For a minute." Only because he still felt like such an ass for making her tear up.

She rounded to the passenger side and got in and Jack paused outside the truck, taking in a deep breath of non-Kate-filled air before opening the door and climbing in.

"Okay," he said, slamming the door. "What else do we need to talk about?"

"You said you would give me flirting lessons…"

"And I already told you why that's over."

"And you said you'd coach me with my riding."

He rested his elbow against the place where the window met the doorframe. "You don't need coaching. You need to stop holding yourself back. Get out of your head and just ride. There. I'm all done."

"And I don't want distance."

He let out a long, slow breath, then turned to face her. Speaking of distance, there was less of it between them now than he would have liked. But then, at the moment, a whole arena wasn't distance enough. Hell, a whole small town didn't seem to be enough.

She didn't have tears in her eyes, not anymore. Instead she had that look. That fierce, determined look she got when she was ready to dig her heels in and fight. He'd seen that look many times over the years and he knew her well enough to know there would be no placating her. There would be no gentle words to get her to back down.

When Kate had an idea in her head, she went with it, and he would be a damn fool to do anything but meet it head-on.

"All right, then. You don't want distance. What do you want?" he asked.

"I want… I want more of what happened today."

Shit. "What? You want…you want me to lay you down on the bench seat and screw you senseless, is that what you want? You want me to treat you like you're just any old buckle bunny and not Eli and Connor's sister?"

She wasn't looking at him now. She was looking

past him. It was dark in the truck, so it was difficult to tell, but he was pretty sure she was blushing a very deep shade of red. "You're getting ahead of me," she mumbled. "I was thinking maybe we could kiss a couple more times."

Shame lashed him like a whip. He was being a serious dick because he had no clue what to do with everything rolling around inside of him. And pushing her away by shocking her, dealing with his rage at himself by speaking the fantasies he was actually having into reality, as if they were so ridiculous they were only worth mocking, not doing, was the only strategy he had at the moment.

"It's not a good idea," he said.

He looked out the window and noticed that most of the cars were gone, everyone who had been at the meeting dispersed, headed over to Ace's, he imagined.

It was just the two of them now.

And there was no damned distance.

"You were a bull rider for like five years. And at no point in time is it ever a good idea to get onto the back of an angry bull. But you did it a lot. Being smart isn't really a requirement for you."

He wanted to tell her he didn't see her that way, to say it wouldn't work, because she was more kid sister to him than she was a woman.

And a few weeks ago, it would have been true.

But tonight it was a lie.

"I would rather take my chances with a bull than with your brothers."

"Is that the only reason you don't want to…kiss me again, because of Eli and Connor and the likelihood that they would kill you dead?"

He paused, knowing he had no good way to answer this. Sensing he'd started on a bad road long enough ago that there was no turning back now. "It factors in."

"What other factors are there?"

"Dammit, Katie. I do not want to have this conversation with you."

"We don't have to talk. We can kiss."

He clenched his teeth together, so tight he was afraid he might break them. "Do you know why I wanted to teach you to flirt?"

He was going to try a different tactic.

"Because you need a hobby?"

"Because I wanted to protect you. I don't want you getting screwed over by some asshole. Connor and Eli are great. They're my best friends. But I bet they didn't talk to you very much about...dating and things."

"You're acting like I'm sixteen." Kate's frustration was obvious. But too damn bad. He was frustrated, too. And it was her fault.

"No, I'm not. I'm acting like you're someone with a hell of a lot less experience than I have. I'm not wrong, am I, Katie?"

There was a slight pause, and he heard her shift next to him. He resisted the urge to look. "Since I have not slept with half the eligible population of Copper Ridge, I think it's safe to say I have less experience than you," she said, her tone honed to a razor's edge.

"I'm not going to apologize for my actions. Not to you."

"I didn't ask you to."

"You don't have to be young to be naive. My mother was twenty-five when she had me. She wasn't young. She wasn't stupid. She was blinded by her feelings for a jackass who didn't use a condom. And who sure as hell had no plans of sticking around and helping her raise me. So forgive me if I don't trust my species around you."

"You don't need to trust your species around me. You just need to trust my aim with a .30-06." He didn't say anything, and she continued staring at him. "That means I can take care of myself."

"I don't want you to get hurt."

"Ever?"

His stomach tightened uncomfortably. "Yeah. Ever. Why would I want you to get hurt?"

"Getting hurt is a part of life. I've been hurt plenty." He looked at her then. Because he couldn't stop himself. "I don't really think some guy seeing me naked and never calling is going to hurt me more than my mom abandoning me when I was two. Or my dad dying after spending most of my life as a worthless drunk. Or losing my sister-in-law, who was pretty much the only woman I had around. Yeah, I guarantee you sex will hurt less than that." She blinked rapidly, looking straight ahead. "There are some things I'm inexperienced with, Jack. That's true enough. But I have more experience with all kinds of other shit than any one person should have. And I'm still standing. I'm not all that breakable. So you can stop with the gallant crap. I didn't ask for it. I don't need it."

"So instead you want me to do my damnedest to hurt you?" he asked, his voice rough. "I don't want to add to that."

His head was pounding, the pressure building behind his eyeballs. And his cock was still hard. He was pretty sure it had been since their lips had made contact in the arena. He had just more or less successfully ignored it during the hours since. He was less successfully ignoring it right now. Because the cab of his truck smelled like the no-nonsense soap Kate washed her skin with. It also smelled like hay and grass and sunshine. Stuff Kate had tracked in.

Hell, it *was* Kate.

She was the earth with everything unnecessary stripped away. Leaving behind a kind of beauty a man couldn't make with his hands. As wholesome as a damned apple pie. And for some reason that wholesomeness had worked its way beneath his skin until it had settled in his gut, growing into a dark and twisted need. A need he would have to try to choke out.

He nearly snorted at that. That was potentially a bad way to phrase that. Even internally.

"How could you hurt me?" she asked. She was innocent. So damn innocent.

He could think of a hundred ways. Ways that would be fun for a while but could very well destroy them both in the end. So he didn't say anything.

"I'm serious," she continued. "I know you. I know exactly what I would be getting myself into."

"If you're propositioning me, Kate Garrett, you had better be sure you know what you want," he said, his patience snapping.

She didn't hesitate. "Kiss me."

That need, the one that was all knotted up inside him, started to bloom like a poisoned flower. Spreading desire through his veins like a sickness. When he had no hope in hell of fighting. Not now. Not anymore. And even though he knew it would lead them straight to hell, he let it grab hold of him.

He reached across the distance, pressed his hand against her back and drew her forward, his lips crashing down on hers with a desperation that would have shocked him if he hadn't been beyond that.

She gasped, the little intake of breath giving him the perfect opportunity to do what he'd held himself back from when she'd grabbed him in the arena. He slid his tongue against hers, the illicit friction sending a shiver of pleasure running down his spine, then settling lower, making his cock hard. Heavy.

He was very aware that these were Kate Garrett's lips beneath his. Because that scent that had been teasing him from the moment they had gotten into the truck wasn't just surrounding him now. It was in him. He inhaled deeply, trying to recapture his earlier thoughts. That she was somehow simple, wholesome.

But that connection was gone now. Her scent was now linked, inextricably, to her kiss.

And her kiss was nothing like apple pie.

She still smelled like grass and sunshine, but now he could only think of pressing her down into the grass, exposing her skin to the golden rays of the sun while he kissed every last inch of her.

His head was still screaming at him that this was wrong. But his heart was raging, and his body was on fire. And so his brain was outvoted. Two against one, poor bastard.

Kate. It's Kate.

The mantra his mind was pounding through him like a drum didn't do anything to satisfy the hunger that was roaring through him like a hungry animal. The only thing for that was to get more of what he craved. And right now that was Kate.

He lifted his other hand, cupped the back of her head and held her hard against him, deepening the kiss. She whimpered, arching against him, closing some of the distance between them. Then she rested her hand on his thigh, and heat exploded in his gut.

Too much. Too fast.

He couldn't force himself to care about that, either.

Kate had asked for a kiss, and his instincts were racing five steps ahead. To what it would feel like to strip her top off. To what her breasts would look like without the boxy shirt she favored concealing her curves.

She wore the most unflattering clothes. And right now he appreciated it. It left a whole lot to his imagination. He couldn't guess what he might find when he unwrapped the beautiful present that was Kate Garrett.

Would she have a long slender torso that gently curved into hips? Or did she have a more dramatic contour to her waist?

And her breasts... It was impossible to tell just how large they were. Whether they would be tight and perky or whether they would dip softly, perfect for him to cup in his hand.

He wanted to know. He needed to know. And at the same time he wanted to draw out the torture. To leave the questions unanswered for as long as he possibly could so he could revel in the pain, in the deep, intense longing that had sunk its teeth into his throat.

A raw sound escaped Kate's lips, vibrated through her entire body and through his own.

She was wearing denim, dammit. And a big-ass belt with one of those big-ass buckles. It would have been so much easier if she were wearing a skirt, something he could shove up her hips quickly while he pushed her panties to the side.

But she didn't have on a skirt. Because the woman had never worn a skirt in her life.

And he well knew it because he had known her for most of it.

Kate. It's Kate.

Holy shit.

He wrenched his mouth away from hers, his chest heaving, breathing a serious challenge. He straightened, facing forward, his hands on the steering wheel. "Get in your truck."

"Jack…"

"Go get in your truck. Please." He didn't mean the last part to sound quite so much like begging.

"Or what?" Her question was muted.

She was baiting him. And he was tempted to take that bait. To try and shock her. To say something to her he had no right to say to a woman he should think of as a sister. But he didn't take it.

"There is no or, Katie. Get in your truck and go home."

He expected her to argue. She didn't. He listened to the sound of the truck door open, and he didn't watch as she got out.

"We're going to have that distance we talked about earlier," he said, his voice rough. "No more flirting lessons. No more rodeo instruction." He raised his head and looked at her, only for a second. "No more kissing."

Her expression was defiant, flat. Her eyes were glittering again and he knew that she was going to go home and cry. And it would be his fault.

He couldn't stop her. So he looked away from her instead.

She didn't say anything. And he didn't look at her again.

Didn't even look when she slammed the door.

He waited a few minutes, then looked at her truck, watched as the headlights came on, as the engine started and as she drove away. He looked at the truck. He wouldn't allow himself to look at her. But he assumed that as long as the truck was making it away from the Grange safely, so was its driver.

Now all he had to do was put distance between himself and a woman he saw every day. Without rousing the suspicions of her brothers. Who he also saw every day.

He would have to relearn to look at her and not wonder about what she looked like naked. He would have to look at her and forget that he had ever wanted to know about the mysteries of the curve in her waist.

Easy. It would be easy.

He started his truck and let the rumble of the engine drown out everything else. But it didn't quite manage to drown out the voice in his head that was telling him it wouldn't be easy at all.

CHAPTER EIGHT

ONLY FORTY-EIGHT HOURS ago Kate would have said nothing could've possibly made her dread the bridesmaid dress fitting for Sadie's wedding more than she already was. But she had officially found a way to make herself dread it even more.

A dress fitting with only a crappy night's sleep and a few hours between making out with Jack and getting rejected by Jack made the situation seem even worse.

She still couldn't quite believe she'd kissed him twice. That she had gone from kissing virgin to fully initiated since just yesterday. And that it had been him. Jack.

Her face burned and she leaned forward in the driver's seat of her truck, pressing her forehead against the steering wheel. She'd been sitting out in the parking lot of the bridal store for the past ten minutes, avoiding going inside.

Because she was afraid that last night's transgressions would be written across her face in red ink. And if not quite literally, the permanent blush she'd acquired would do so metaphorically.

Sadly, she couldn't avoid facing Liss and Sadie forever. She allowed herself a fantasy where she managed to dodge both of them, and wearing a dress.

Alas, it was only a fantasy.

Still, if recent events with Jack were any indicator, sometimes fantasies came true.

Or at least half-true.

She thought of the way his big hands had moved over her back, the way he'd cupped her head. The way his tongue had felt against hers.

She shivered, restlessness growing between her thighs.

Who knew that having a man's tongue in her mouth could be so damned erotic? It wasn't as if she didn't know she wanted sex. She'd been very aware of men as a species for a while. Quite a while. And had taken great pleasure in tormenting Eli and Connor with her awareness simply because…well, she was their sister and tormenting them was what she did right along with breathing.

But her fantasies on the subject had been hazy, confined mainly to enjoyment derived from looking at men, rather than deep imaginings of what it would be like to be kissed by them. To be touched by them.

And all of that was changing because of Jack Monaghan.

The thought was becoming less and less disturbing. Because kissing him felt so good.

It wasn't like she wanted a relationship with him. She wasn't sure she wanted a serious relationship with anyone, ever. Her parents' marriage hadn't exactly been something to aspire to. Then there was the heartbreak Connor had experienced with his first marriage.

And sure, everything was going great for him now. And Eli was in love, blah blah blah. But they were also in their thirties. She had a long time until she was in her thirties. She didn't know the ins and outs of the love lives of her brothers, and she frankly didn't want to. But she doubted that either of them, Eli especially, had been monks before falling in love.

Frankly, she felt as though she had to have some sex before she ever worried about marriage. And sex with Jack... If he was half as good in bed as he was just kissing in the cab of his truck, it would be electrifying. Altering. Potentially ruining her for other men.

No. She wouldn't let it.

Of course, it was kind of a moot point since he had rejected her. And what was she supposed to do? Beg?

Just get on her knees in front of him, eye level with his...belt buckle. And then she would put her hands on said belt buckle, pull the thick leather of the belt through the loops, undo the fly and button on his jeans...

Holy sock monkeys, she was having a full-on sexual fantasy in the parking lot of the bridal store. And she still had to go face Sadie and Liss.

She pulled her keys out of the ignition and slowly opened the driver's-side door, pressing her foot down slowly onto the blacktop, listening to stray gravel grind against the hard surface. She was in no hurry. Officially in no hurry.

She looked at the store, at the three large windows in front, each with two glittering dresses on mannequins displayed proudly in it. And the building was purple.

The whole thing was Kate repellent.

She'd never seen the point in this kind of thing.

The cowgirls she raced against always complained about rhinestones falling off their jackets and hats. Kate, for her part, didn't have rhinestones on her jacket or hat and therefore never had to worry about them falling off. Really, her take on life seemed a whole lot more practical to her.

But she was a twenty-three-year-old virgin. And she doubted Sierra or the other girls had that same issue.

Maybe men were like magpies and their dicks were attracted to shiny things?

She kept pondering that as she walked through the door and into a ruffle-and-rhinestone wonderland.

Sadie and Liss were standing at the front counter, and both smiled broadly when she entered. For some strange reason Kate had the feeling of walking into a lion's den with two hungry predators staring at her. Only instead of the background being littered with bones, it was littered with silver racks full of gaudy, shimmering dresses. It was not, in her mind, a less grisly prospect than seeing the picked-clean carcasses of previous victims.

Bones or gowns, it spelled doom for her either way.

The pristine dresses were packed in tightly, covered in plastic. Probably to catch falling rhinestones. Maybe her fellow cowgirls should consider wrapping their hats in plastic.

She had a feeling that idea wouldn't go over well.

"There you are," Sadie said, reaching out and grabbing hold of Kate's arm, drawing her in close. As though Sadie knew that Kate was a flight risk. She was not wrong. "Lisa May already pulled a few dresses in your size. They're waiting in the fitting room. Along with my wedding gown. Because I'm going to put it on and you're going to stand next to me. To assess visual compatibility."

"She's gone full Sadie," Liss said, somewhat apologetically. But Kate noticed that Liss was not prying

Kate's arm out of Sadie's grasp. No, Liss was interested only in saving herself.

"This is a huge wedding. And since we had to put off fitting and style selection till the last minute because of—" Sadie waved her free hand in front of Liss's baby bump "—that, now we have to get cracking."

They'd already known special order would be futile, since there was no way to know just how Liss would expand. They'd also decided that matching dresses wouldn't work, because the same style wouldn't be flattering on Kate's slender frame and Liss's ever-rounding one.

And by *they'd decided*, Kate meant that Sadie had decided.

Sadie pulled Kate along to the back of the store with her. There was a row of dressing rooms, each separated from the public by a purple curtain.

Three were open, one with a wedding dress hanging inside and two with an array of dresses in various shades of fall colors.

Eli and Sadie were having a barn-set harvest-themed wedding, which meant absolutely nothing to Kate. Apparently, it meant burnt orange to Sadie.

"Okay, they've been organized by the order you're supposed to try them on in, because some of them pair with each other more nicely than others," Sadie said, releasing her hold on Kate in order to make broad hand gestures. "Of course, there will be some leeway for mixing and matching. I want you both to feel comfortable in the dress."

"You want me to feel comfortable in a dress?" Kate asked. "Because that isn't going to happen. I say just pick what you like. I'm not going to *like* anything."

"Kate," Sadie said, "I love you. But you're going to have to try to love the dress and make me feel good about it, or I will kill you."

Kate made a mental note to lie about whichever one Sadie looked the most enthused about. As long as it didn't have ruffles.

"I'll try. Because I don't want to be dead," she said, stepping into the dressing room and unhooking the curtain from the pullback before tugging it closed.

She started to undress, her mind blessedly blank until Liss's voice penetrated through the connecting wall of the dressing room. "So how are all the charity plans coming along? Do you all have the venue confirmed?"

Kate pushed her jeans down her hips and turned to face the dresses. "Yes. All that's taken care of."

She picked up the first dress, one with fluttery orange ruffles all down the skirt. She ran her fingertips over the fabric, watching as it caught the lights above. It was shiny.

She pulled the zipper down and lowered the dress to the floor, holding it gingerly by the straps as she stepped into it.

"Has Jack been helpful?"

Being forced to think of Jack while tugging the slippery, soft fabric of the dress up over her mostly bare body made her skin feel hypersensitized. "Yes. He's been very…helpful." Oh yes, Jack had been *very* helpful in a few *very* specific ways. Such as turning her on to a point that was nearly painful.

She felt as though her voice was thick with that unspoken comment.

"Not driving you crazy?" This question came from Sadie.

"Or bothering you?" This one from Liss, and it was spoken a little bit more sharply than necessary, in Kate's opinion.

"Why is my interaction with Jack suddenly so interesting?" She reached behind her back and pulled the zipper up, then stepped out of the dressing room and into the main area of the store. She caught her reflection in the wall of mirrors across from her and stopped, blinking rapidly.

She couldn't remember the last time she'd worn a dress. If she ever had. She'd worn jeans and boots to homecoming. She hadn't gone to prom.

She hadn't had a date for either.

"Kate, that looks beautiful," Sadie said, her face getting all soft.

Kate turned her focus to Sadie. And it was Kate's turn to stare. Sadie was beautiful. Her blond hair tumbled past her bare shoulders, light makeup on her face. Simple. And the wedding dress she had chosen had that same light, simple beauty that her future sister-in-law possessed in spades. A layer of lace sat over a heavier silk layer, which conformed to her curves, while the lace flowed out gently, delicate and sheer, catching the sunlight that was streaming through the window. There were a few scattered beads sewn in, just enough to add a little shimmer. It reminded Kate of webs, heavy with dew in the early morning, strung between wildflowers in the fields on the ranch, catching the light just so and making the ordinary into something that was worth stopping and staring at.

"Oh, Sadie," Kate said, her heart feeling too big for

her chest. She was having what might have been the first girly moment of her life. She was about to cry. Over a dress.

But it wasn't that simple. It was more than that. It was everything it represented. "Eli is going to... I don't even know."

Kate looked over at Liss, who was wearing a short cream-colored dress with orange flowers in a style that flowed over her rounded stomach. And she was crying. There was no *almost* about it. "Damn pregnancy hormones," she sniffled.

For some reason Liss's comment twisted the moment. And Kate looked between the woman her brother was about to marry and the woman her other brother *had* married, was having a child with. She was acutely aware of how much things had changed. How much they were changing still.

She'd clung to the ranch, to Eli and Connor, to the safety of sameness for a long time. Because in her life change had rarely been good. So she had held on tightly to the only things that were good. Family. Stability.

Which, more than money, might be the real reason she hadn't gone pro a couple years ago.

She'd been afraid to do any leaving. And now she was afraid of being left behind.

She thought that if she stayed rooted to the spot resolutely enough, she could keep things stable. Keep the world from turning itself over again, leaving everything scattered and out of order. Leaving her to try and rebuild yet again with reduced materials.

But it hadn't worked. Things were changing again. They were just doing it around her, leaving her feeling unsure of her place. Unsure if she even had one.

These thoughts, these concerns, felt treacherous in a way. Because she loved Sadie; she loved Liss. She wanted Connor and Eli to be happy.

But it didn't make all of this any less unknown or scary.

Didn't make her feel any more certain about her place in all of it.

It left her feeling desperate to race forward and try to get ahead of it all. To make a change, to make a move, that would help her feel like she was keeping up.

"Do you hate your dress that much?"

Kate snapped out of her internal crisis long enough to realize that Sadie was talking to her. "I don't hate it."

"You look upset," Sadie said.

"I'm just… I'm really happy for you. I'm happy for you and Eli. And you and Connor," she said, turning to Liss. "I'm emotional about it." The flat tone of her voice undermined the statement.

Sadie laughed and reached out and patted Kate's cheek. "I guess this is the Kate Garrett version of emotion?"

Kate cleared her throat. "Yeah, sort of unrefined. Like the woman herself."

"*Refined* just means that all the dangerous, interesting bits have been sifted out. Never refine, Kate. It would be disappointing," Sadie said, her blue eyes suddenly serious.

Kate felt doubly bad about her moment of fear over Sadie's upcoming marriage to Eli. Because Sadie was wonderful in every way. Sadie had a way of making Kate see things differently.

Also, Sadie had taught her how to bake quiche.

An invaluable skill if there ever was one.

This wasn't the kind of change she needed to be afraid of. But understanding that didn't make her feel less stagnant. Still didn't make her feel any less of a desire to move.

Maybe that was why this change was so scary. It made her feel so conscious of how far behind she was.

Of the fact that while she stayed in her comfortable little place, the people around her would move forward, with or without her.

"Okay, next dress," Sadie said, all of her authority firmly back in place. "I don't think these are the ones."

Kate was relieved. Because *ruffles*.

She turned and walked back into the dressing room, trying to shake the heaviness of the moment off her chest. She was just trying on dresses. She needed to get a grip.

The next dress had no straps at all. It was a deep cranberry color, the neckline shaped a bit like a heart. She shrugged off what she was wearing and started getting into the new one.

"What the hell bra are you supposed to wear with this?" she called out.

"Not one," Sadie shouted back.

"That's not going to work," Kate said.

For some reason she could only think about how she would feel wearing this in front of Jack. She would feel naked with just the dress on and nothing underneath it but a pair of panties.

"Just put it on."

Kate unhooked her bra and threw it on the floor, obeying Sadie's command. She held the dress over her breasts and reached behind herself, struggling with the zipper while fighting to keep the fabric in place. Finally, she gave up and turned it sideways, then zipped it up and twisted it so it faced the front.

There was no mirror in the dressing room, so she had no idea how it looked. She gritted her teeth and swept the curtain aside, walking out into the main area. Liss and Sadie assessed her, far too closely for her liking.

"You have to adjust your girls, Kate," Sadie said.

"Excuse me, what?" Kate asked.

"Hoist your boobs up," Liss supplied helpfully.

Kate could see in the mirror that her face now matched the dress. "Why would I do that?"

"So that the dress fits properly," Sadie said, her tone even. "And so men can ogle your cleavage."

Kate nearly choked. "And I want that?"

"Kate Garrett," Sadie scolded, "this is not the time for you to go acting maidenly and modest. We have checked out construction-worker ass together."

"That's different than trying to get them to check *me* out."

Sadie waved a hand. "It is not."

"I'm not sure Eli would appreciate you giving me such advice."

"He isn't here. And I don't ask him permission for everything. I don't ask him *permission* for *anything*. And I certainly hope you don't."

"Of course I don't." But she worried an awful lot about his approval.

"Okay," Liss said, "lean forward."

"Like this?" Kate bent slightly at the waist.

"Yes. You reach down into the top of your dress and pull your boob up and push it in toward the center of the neckline."

"Are you serious?"

"Yes, I am serious. This is a valuable life skill. Now do it."

Kate turned away from Sadie and Liss and reached down beneath the fabric of her dress, following Liss's instructions.

"Okay, do your other boob."

Kate cringed but did as she was told. "Done."

"Now straighten up and admire your work."

Kate did, then turned to face the mirror. She watched her eyes widen, watched her mouth drop open in shock, because she scarcely recognized the woman she was looking at.

First of all, she was a woman and not a girl.

Kate knew she was a woman, but there were a whole lot of days when she didn't exactly feel like one. There was no denying it now.

The color was rich and brought out a lick of brandy color in her brown eyes, reflecting a similar shade in her hair. The dress left her shoulders bare and exposed a healthy amount of pale, slender leg that she had never before given a whole lot of thought to. But the bit that really shocked her was her cleavage. And the fact that she had achieved it. Now that she had done as Sadie and Liss had told her, the dress no longer sat over her curves. The dress was now shaping itself to her body, the dark berry color shocking against the pale white of her breasts, which looked rounder and fuller than she had ever imagined they could.

There was nothing ambiguous about this. It screamed out to anyone who saw that she was a woman. A woman who wanted to be looked at. A woman who was worthy of being looked at.

A woman Jack would have to look at.

Her breath caught.

"That's the one," Sadie murmured.

"Oh yeah," Liss agreed.

"You can wear cowgirl boots with it," Sadie said. "They would look cute."

"Uh-huh." But Kate wasn't really listening anymore, because her mind was stuck on what Jack's face might look like when he saw her in this dress. On what he would think of her. On how he would react.

On whether or not he would be able to tell her no again.

She needed to change. And this was a change. But it wasn't enough.

She was ready to do something, something crazy, something reckless.

She was tired of sitting still. She was tired of being where she was.

She wanted Jack. And she was going to have him. The Kate standing in front of her right now could have him.

"Yes," she said, finding her voice again. "This is definitely the one."

CHAPTER NINE

JACK MONAGHAN'S DAY had been terrible from moment one. It started when he opened his eyes. He didn't feel rested, and he was hard. That wasn't unusual, not at all. Just your standard-issue morning erection easily solved in a routine morning shower.

But this was no generic morning erection. At almost the exact moment he became aware of it, the events from the night before flashed back through his mind. Kate. Her mouth, her lips, her tongue. Her hands. Her body.

And no matter how hard he tried, he couldn't banish those images from his mind. And he could not make his erection a generic one. He grabbed ahold of himself in the shower with the mind to get some relief. But then Kate joined him.

He couldn't even picture her naked. Because he still had no idea what her body looked like.

And what kind of idiocy was that? Fantasizing about a woman when he didn't even have a handle on what her figure would be like. Literally or metaphorically.

Kate was slim and strong, capable. She had a bit of light muscle tone in her arms from all of the hard work she did. A stubborn set to her jaw, brown eyes that were shot through with golden flame, and hair that hung lank and straight no matter how much humidity blanketed the air.

Oh yeah, and she was the virginal younger sister of his two best friends, and she kissed like a wicked little goddess.

There were a lot of things he didn't know, but apparently, he knew enough to fantasize.

To imagine what it would be like if it wasn't his hand wrapped around his cock but hers.

Yeah, he'd given up at that point. He'd gotten out of the shower, unsatisfied and in a foul temper. He'd gone on about his ranch chores in the same manner. Hard and pissed off about it.

He'd figured if he couldn't work his sexual frustration out in the preferred method, he would do it with actual physical labor. Too bad it hadn't worked.

It was a gray day, the air cool and wet. Even so, by the time he headed back from the barn to his house, sweat was rolling down his chest and back.

He let out a long sigh when his boot hit the bottom step that led up to the deck. For some reason as he walked up the heavy wooden steps, he remembered the feel of the hollow metal steps that had led to the front door of the single-wide trailer he'd grown up in on the outskirts of Copper Ridge.

He paused when he reached the top, moving his fingertips over the railing. It was hard to believe how far he'd come. From the place he'd been too ashamed to invite his friends to, to a custom-built home on a successful ranch.

He took a lot of things for granted. That he could talk his way out of trouble. That he could get laid if he wanted to. He didn't take this for granted. Never. Not one day of his life.

The front door of the house opened and his house-keeper, Nancy, stepped out, practically wringing her hands. "There's someone here to see you, Jack."

Jack frowned. "Inside?"

She nodded. "I told him you were busy, but he said he would wait."

Nancy was friendly, and the presence of a visitor wouldn't normally have her acting nervous. That was enough to make Jack's stomach tense. He wasn't sure why. Unless he was about to get served or something, but he couldn't think of a reason.

There were no outstanding debts or bills to be paid, not anymore. So it wasn't that, either. Though a holdover from a childhood spent in poverty was a lingering anxiety about bills and bill collectors that was hard to shake.

His mail sometimes made him nervous. Because a stack of envelopes had never meant anything good when he was a kid. It had meant stress. It had meant his mother closing the bedroom door and crying. She didn't think he knew, but he did.

For some reason this moment reminded him a lot of that.

"Did you get his name?" Jack said, striding across the deck and following Nancy into the house.

If Nancy answered, Jack didn't hear, because the moment he saw the tall lean figure of a man in a white Stetson, facing away from him, Jack knew exactly who it was.

"What the hell do you want?" He had never spoken to this man in his life. Had never seen him any closer than across a crowded bar or the street. But he knew who he was. And he knew he didn't like him.

The stranger turned and Jack felt a strange release of tension in his muscles. It was both a relief and an utter horror that the man in front of him was just an aging gray-haired human with lines around his eyes and mouth, rather than the imposing monster his mind often chose to play stand-in.

A relief because who wanted to face a monster? And a horror because it meant dealing with the fact that a very average man held so much control over what Jack did and why.

"I came to talk to you."

Jack looked around the room and noticed Nancy had made herself scarce. "Well, you don't want to engage in father-son bonding. I know that much. Because I took a fuck-ton of money from you to keep quiet about our relationship. Such as it is."

"You got that damn straight. I'm not here to talk to you about that. We're never going to talk about that."

The moment felt surreal. Jack was, for the first time in thirty-three years, face-to-face with his father. There had been no warning and no fanfare. Just the specter that hovered over Jack's every action and decision made manifest in his living room.

"Then what are you here to talk about?"

"I came to talk to you about a horse."

The hair on the back of Jack's neck prickled. "None of mine are for sale."

"I don't want your horses. I just wanted to tell you in person that Damion Matthews isn't choosing your stallion to sire Jazzy Lady's foal."

"What the hell are you talking about?"

"I know the two of you had been in talks. Just about
to sign an agreement."

"Yes," Jack bit out.

"Then you punched his son in the face, and he's not
real happy with you. I'd rather not take a win just because your low-class bastard genes took over your better instincts in a bar fight, but make no mistake, I *will*
take it."

Fire burned through Jack's blood. "I'm only a bastard
because you don't know how to keep it in your pants."

"You're a bastard because you were born one. That
kind of blood outs itself eventually. Genetics are important. You don't breed a Thoroughbred to an over-
used plow horse. The same is true for people. You're
the end result of that."

Jack had a sudden flash of what would happen if he
lost his temper. If he hauled off and punched Nathan
West in his smug face. He would probably get arrested.
Probably by Eli. And whatever reputation he wanted to
cultivate would be completely destroyed.

Yeah, none of that made him feel less inclined to
do it.

But his feet stayed rooted to the spot, and his hands
stay down at his sides, clenched into fists.

"I didn't think we were going to talk about me," Jack
said, a hint of the violence pounding through his body
evident in his tone.

"Don't think I don't know what you're doing, boy.
I'm well aware. You starting this ranch, stepping on
my turf. There was a day when there would've been
no question as to which breeder people would come to,
and now there is. But it won't last. It can't last. You're
not wired to be better than you are."

"I would punch that jackass one hundred times even if I knew I would lose the deal. And I'm happy not to work with him. Because I have ethics. We both know you don't."

"According to your reputation, you and I have some similar ethics. You are my son, after all. But your mother's half is the one that will hold you back. Don't forget. You're out of your league. You're only here because of me, because of the money I gave you. If you had one bit of shame, you would have taken the money and got out of town. But you don't have any. So you stayed here and set up a ranch designed to compete with me. A ranch I bought for you."

Rage flared up in Jack's stomach, molten heat that spread through him, testing his control. "I entered rodeo events with your money. I made smart investments with your money. At this point, it's difficult to tell what you paid for and what I paid for."

"Don't pretend you earned it. Without me you would be nothing."

"Without you deciding you wanted to ensure that no other living soul ever found out that I was your son? That's more accurate. Don't act like you did me a favor."

"Oh, I won't. I'll go back to not thinking of you at all soon enough. This little venture of yours is doomed to fail."

"Are you going to sabotage it for me?"

He laughed, walking past Jack, bumping into him on purpose with his shoulder. "I believe you'll do that for yourself, son. You already have."

"Get out of my house. Don't come back here."

"Which part did you buy with my money?" his father asked, deep blue eyes making contact with his own.

They were Jack's eyes. Staring back at him without even a glimmer of warmth.

His mother's eyes were a light grayish blue, different from his own. This was where the color had come from.

The realization made him feel unclean somehow.

"I think I used part of your money to dig out the septic. You're welcome to come back and stand in that, if you have half a mind. Otherwise, keep off."

"You do remind me of your mother." And Jack knew he wasn't being complimented.

"And you remind me of a piece of shit I stepped in once."

The old man shook his head, chuckled and walked out the door.

It wasn't until the front door slammed shut that Jack realized he was shaking. Shaking with the effort of preventing himself from punching his father in the face. Shaking because for the first time he had been within punching distance of the old man.

Shaking with pure disgust, directed at himself, because in spite of the fact that his dad was nothing more than a prick with money, a part of him had hoped he'd been here to tell him he hadn't ignored him after all.

But no. Instead he'd been here to remind him of something Jack had been doing his best to forget. That he was a bastard. A bastard who would never earn this town's approval. Who would never permanently rise above the circumstances of his birth.

"Bullshit," he said, into the emptiness of his living room.

His custom-built living room, which was part of his near-million-dollar home on a massive parcel of land. Because he had transcended his birth.

That kind of blood outs itself eventually.

Yeah, like when you grabbed hold of your best friends' little sister and kissed her the way you kissed a woman you intended to take to bed.

Oh yeah, that was bleeding every bit of bad out for all to see. Staining his hands. Hands that had been all over Katie. No doubt he'd gotten it on her, too.

He was ready to put a fist through the wall of his custom home.

The phone in his pocket vibrated and he reached his hand inside and pulled it out, opting to deal with that rather than punching a hole in his house.

It was Kate. He took a deep breath and answered the call. "I thought I told you I needed distance."

"I'm distant."

"You're on my phone."

"It's not like I'm physically pressed against your ear, Monaghan. I'm at home."

"Calling me is not distance."

"What happened to you? You sit on your spurs?"

"I got a visit from my dad," he said, his voice hard. He had not intended to tell her that. He hadn't intended to tell anyone that. Because he could never tell anyone that Nathan West was his father. So what was the point in bringing it up at all? There was no point. There was no point to any of this. To wanting his approval, to believing anything that he said. And yet he couldn't erase the words the old man had spoken into the room.

Bastard. Bad blood. Bastard. Bad blood.

"I'm coming over," she said, no hesitation at all.

"That would be doing a pretty piss-poor job of distance."

"You shouldn't be alone."

"It's a great time to be alone with a bottle of alcohol."

"Connor and Eli would be lousy at helping you deal with this."

"I don't need help dealing with anything."

"Clearly not. You sound extremely well adjusted at the moment."

"I don't need to talk right now," he said, his bad blood boiling over now. That was what was driving him. No question. "I could use your mouth for one thing right about now, and it isn't talking."

He hated himself more than ever. For proving his father's point, for believing him. But he didn't know what else to do. Didn't know how else to be.

And hell, his dad was right. He was doing a good job building his business, and he'd punched that asshole Chad in the face and lost himself a lot of money. He couldn't even blame it on the fact that he'd simply forgotten the connection between Chad and his father. Even if he had remembered that Chad was Damion Matthews's son, he would have punched the ever-loving hell out of him because of the way he'd talked about Kate.

Because that was who he was.

The silence on the other end of the phone spoke volumes about the fact that he'd finally gone over the line. Good. Maybe she would stop messing with him now. Maybe she would understand just who it was she was dealing with.

As long as she'd been a little sister to him, she'd been safe. But she was determined to play with fire, and he needed her to understand the fire burned.

"I'm coming over, Jack," she said finally, her tone even.

"I'm telling you right now, Katie," he said, his voice

rough as he searched for just the right words to make sure she would stay away, "if you come over tonight, you're not leaving my house a virgin."

Silence settled heavy between them, no sound but her breathing coming over the other end of the phone. And then the line went dead.

He'd finally done it. He'd succeeded in scaring her away. Well, it was about damn time.

He looked up and saw Nancy standing in the doorway, looking pale.

"You have a comment?" he asked.

Now he was being an ass to Nancy. Fantastic.

She shook her head slowly. "No. Your dinner will be out of the oven in half an hour. I'm going home."

"Whatever you heard…none of it's repeatable."

"I figured as much. I'm sort of insulted you felt you had to tell me that."

"I have some trust issues," he said, his tone hard.

Nancy arched her brows and took her purse off the hook by the door. "I can see why." Then she paused for a moment, her hand on the doorknob. "Don't do anything stupid."

"Like drink myself under the table?"

"As long as you do that at home, it's probably your safest bet. Get drunk, pass out, don't do anything you'll regret."

And with that, Nancy left, taking her judgment with her.

He imagined she had heard him talking to Kate, and while she wouldn't know who it was, it didn't really matter, seeing as everything he'd said was offensive no matter the context.

Fortunately, he wouldn't be given the chance to do

anything he regretted, because Kate had hung up on him. Because Kate clearly wasn't coming to comfort him, since he'd likely succeeded in putting her off him for life.

It was for the best. Definitely for the best.

He went into the kitchen and opened up the oven door. There were enchiladas. That wasn't terrible. It was the one part of his day that wasn't terrible.

He put his hands flat on the kitchen counter and lowered his head, replaying the conversation he'd just had with Kate.

He had no right to talk to her that way. But he had even less of a right to touch her, and with him in the state he was in, if she came over now, begging for him to kiss her...

Yeah, it was better to warn her off.

Because that's how low you are. You would screw Kate if she asked for a kiss because you can't control your damned dick.

Yeah, that was where his dad had things wrong. It wasn't his mother's genes he worried about. It was the West genes. The ones that made you walk around like you were an invincible, bulletproof paragon capable of doing whatever the hell you wanted without having to pay for the consequences.

He raised his head when he heard a sharp pounding on the front door. He wondered if Nancy had forgotten something.

"Come in," he called.

He heard footsteps on the hardwood floor, and they stopped right around the kitchen doorway. "I don't... I don't have sexy underwear or anything."

"Oh, fuck."

Kate was standing there looking like she was out of breath. The color high in her cheeks, and her braid in disarray, stray tendrils escaping, hanging loose around her face. She was wearing a T-shirt that was shaped like a rectangle, not doing anything to accentuate her figure, and a pair of jeans that had most certainly seen better days.

And she was the most terrifying, unwelcome, enticing sight he could have imagined.

"I got here as quickly as I could," she said, her dark eyes trained on him.

"You weren't supposed to come." It was all he could think to say. Well, he could swear again. But other than that, he had nothing else to say.

"I was never very good at doing what I was supposed to."

"Katie." He just said her name, because he was out of words. His mind wasn't forming sentences anymore; he was just feeling. Angry, desperate, turned on beyond what he felt capable of handling.

She took a step into the kitchen, a step toward him. "I have to keep telling you not to call me that."

"Yeah, well, I'm a bastard. In every sense of the word."

"You can be. But you aren't always."

He blinked hard, trying to superimpose the image of Kate as a girl over the image of the woman walking toward him. It seemed like not that long ago that when he thought of her, he still thought of that skinny long-limbed girl with freckles and scrapes on her elbows. But not now.

And as hard as he tried, he couldn't recapture that vision now.

The past wasn't in the room with them, and he wished like hell it was.

Her dark eyes met his, concern evident in the crease between her brows. She reached out, pressed her hand on his face, her smooth skin scraping across the stubble on his jaw. "Are you okay?"

For just a moment he thought of the past. Thought of driving up to the front of the Garretts' house, seeing Kate sitting on the porch, a blank look on her face.

Kate rarely cried. She was too tough for that. Too tough for her own good.

Eli and Connor had been nowhere to be seen and he'd heard a crash coming from inside the house that told him they were probably dealing with one of their father's drunken benders.

So he'd sat down beside her, put his hand on her shoulder. "Are you okay?"

And now she was asking him.

It made his chest feel tight, made it hard for him to breathe.

"I've never met him before." Just like the admission he'd made on the phone, this one just spilled out.

"Why today?"

He forced out a laugh. "It wasn't for a reunion."

"Tell me."

"I can't."

She put her other hand on his face, holding him steady, her eyes never leaving his. "He's an asshole." Her voice was fierce, shaking.

"I didn't even tell you anything about him."

"I don't need to know anything about him. If he knew where you were and he never met you until today, then he's useless. The worst piece of garbage in the world. Almost as bad as a mom who walks away from her two-year-old daughter and her two boys. She knew where we were and she never came back. It was her address for sixteen freaking years. She knew how to get back to it. She just never did. She's bad. Not us. He's bad. Not you."

"Do you believe that?" About himself, about herself.

"Sometimes," she said, the shaking in her voice becoming even more pronounced. "And sometimes I'm sure it was my fault even though I can't remember her face. I'm sure I must've done something."

"He never even met me. I guess he just knew that I wasn't worth it," Jack said.

"You are, though, you know."

He reached up and grabbed her wrist, tugging her hand down from his face to his chest. "Do you think so, Katie?" His heart was raging, the promise he'd issued to her over the phone looming large over them.

"Yes."

"You don't even like me. Everything I do makes you mad."

"I do like you. Maybe that's why everything you do makes me mad."

He knew exactly what she meant. Because the more he started to like her, the more tense he felt. His body's attempt at convincing itself he didn't want to be anywhere near her, when in fact he wanted to be as close to her as humanly possible.

For what purpose? To have those questions about her body answered?

It didn't get much more selfish than that.

But maybe that's just who you are.

Yeah, selfish was the only thing it could be. Because

he couldn't give her anything else. The realization of how wrong it was to touch Kate made him feel slightly sick about his entire adult sex life. Because if it felt wrong to use Kate for sex, with nothing else on offer, it had been quite possibly wrong to use other women that way, too. Though they had most definitely been into it.

Still, he had made his excuses based on a sorting system in his brain that said some women were okay to have a good time with, while women like her were off-limits. He'd never thought it explicitly, not until that conversation with Kate about flirting. But once he outlined it then, he'd realized what a dick he was. And this was all underscoring it.

But no matter which way he twisted the reasoning, there was no justification for following through with the attraction that had popped up between Kate and him.

None at all.

But still, he had his hand wrapped around her wrist. Still, he was holding her palm to his chest.

"I never told you I was a virgin," she said, her voice thin, almost a whisper.

"But you are."

She looked down, swallowing hard. His heart rate increased as he waited for her to respond. That was one of those things that shouldn't matter, either. Even if she had slept with someone before, she was still off-limits to him.

But if she hadn't…

It would make their encounter more significant. Hell, he remembered his first time and there had been a lot of times after. Still remembered the woman. Two years older than him, more experienced. It had been fast and disappointing. For her. He had enjoyed the hell out of it.

But he had learned quickly that if he didn't figure out what he was doing, women wouldn't come after him for a repeat performance. So he'd gotten good. And he'd gotten good fast.

But in a long line of sexual experiences that had been hotter, better, that first one still stood out.

Being that first one for Kate would mean something. And he wasn't good with meaningful sex. Meaningless was the name of his game.

"Yes," she said. "I am."

He swore, but he didn't move away, keeping his hold on her. "Why do you want this?"

"Because I know you. I trust you. I know you'll make it good." Her words were a balm he didn't deserve on his scarred, mangled-up soul. No one trusted him. Kate seemed to trust him. "But you have to want it, too. I don't want my first time to happen because I talked you into it."

"You don't need to talk me into it," he said, his voice almost unrecognizable to his own ears. "I've spent the past week trying to talk myself out of it. Because I can't offer you anything. Nothing more than sex." He raised his hand, traced the outline of her upper lip with the edge of his thumb. "Make no mistake, badger-cat, it'll be good sex. I'll go slow. Taste every inch of you, not just because it'll make you mindless, not just because it will make you beg, but because I want to. Because I crave you. It will be more than good—it will be amazing. But it will still stop at sex. Nothing else."

"A good first time isn't nothing." Her cheeks were bright red, her words a thready whisper.

More evidence that he should back off now. She was too sweet. Too innocent.

"It's less than you deserve."

"What did you want from your first time?"

"To get off. Simple as that."

She closed her eyes, the blush remaining on her cheeks, a smile curving her lips. "I want that. I really want that." Her lashes fluttered, her lids opening again. "I realized today that I've been standing still for a long time. Everyone is moving forward and I'm just the same. I'm tired of being the same."

"This will change things," he said.

"I know. I want things to change. More than that, I want you."

He looked into her eyes, let his gaze drop to those soft, sweet lips. Kate Garrett contained the promise of hell wrapped up in a pretty little bit of heaven.

It would feel so good, but once it was all over, there would be nothing but regret and purgatory to deal with.

He knew it. It was wrong. It was bad. It was a betrayal of the two men who had stuck by him all of his life.

He'd protected Kate from some of the pain that came from living with a drunk. Had done his damnedest to make her laugh at impossible situations. Had punched Chad for daring to overstep with her.

He'd locked the door on so many of life's evils, shielded her from them. Only to discover he'd locked her in with an even bigger threat. Himself.

He was the fox in the henhouse. But even knowing that didn't stop him from wanting to eat her.

"Kiss me, Katie."

CHAPTER TEN

THE ROUGH COMMAND on Jack's lips was enough to send Kate over the edge then and there. She was trembling. Had been ever since she'd hung up on him during their phone call earlier.

She'd been certain of two things during that call. He needed her, and he was trying to push her away. She'd decided she wasn't going to let him get away with that.

Someone had to be there for him. She wasn't going to leave him to go through this alone, not when he'd been there for her countless times over the years.

Anyway, his "threat" just wasn't all that scary.

He'd promised her that she wouldn't leave his house a virgin. And she was very much hoping he followed through with that promise.

But she wouldn't worry about that just yet. For now, she would just follow that deep, throaty command, enjoy the way it made her feel. Enjoy the way he said her name.

Katie.

That lush sensation of having velvet rubbed across her skin. The one she had resisted for so long because it had frightened her. Because it had confused her.

She wasn't confused now.

Though she was a little scared. The virginal nerves were to be expected, probably. She had never actually talked to anybody about virginity loss before. Because she'd had a tough time bonding with girls when she was in high school. And by the time she was out of high school, it was weird that she hadn't lost it—at least, she assumed. So she didn't really want to ask anyone anything, because that would mean admitting her status.

She liked her friends well enough, but she didn't really trust them with information like that. The commonality between herself and her friends was horses, not boys.

But her nerves were going to have to take a backseat, because Jack wanted her to kiss him. So she was going to.

She trailed her fingertips along the edge of his jaw, relishing the feel of his stubble beneath her fingertips. It was such a masculine thing.

She was used to men. She'd grown up in a house full of them. She was used to whiskers, used to heavy exposure to the top half of men's bodies as her brothers traipsed through the house in towels or just sweatpants. Accustomed to the way they talked, the way they swore, the way they kept house—or, in Connor's case, didn't.

But this was different. Different from all those easy, domestic male things she had been exposed to all of her life. Different from watching shirtless men sweat and build decks and barns, which she'd spent a fair amount of her time enjoying.

That kind of distant observation left her a degree removed. Allowed her to feel a little bit of excitement while holding herself back. Without ever risking anything.

Sort of like barrel racing on the amateur circuit when she could probably go pro.

She shook off that thought. She didn't need to have any serious non-Jack thoughts right now. And so she let her world shrink down, reduced to nothing more than the feel of his whiskers beneath her hand. Nothing more than the beat of her heart and the echoing beat at the apex of her thighs.

Her heart beat out a rusty, unfamiliar rhythm against her breastbone, one hand still rested on his chest, held there by his iron grip.

She leaned forward, hoping he couldn't tell that she was shaking. She slid her thumb along the outline of his lower lip, mimicking what he'd done to her earlier. A short, deep sound rumbled in his throat and she took it as confirmation she'd done something right.

"You're sure taking a long time to kiss me," he said.

"I'm thinking."

"Second thoughts?"

"No. Just thinking about how sexy you are," she said, deciding she wasn't going to turn into a shrinking violet just because the prospect of getting naked with him loomed. He was still Jack. And she'd never been very good at watching what she said around Jack. "I've never seen a naked man before."

A gust of air escaped his lips. "Dammit, Katie."

"I'm looking forward to it," she said.

"What if you don't like it?" he asked, leaning forward slightly, his breath fanning across her cheek.

"I'd say the odds are pretty low. I mean, I like the way you look with clothes on. But I really like your skin. Your throat."

"My throat?"

She swallowed hard, ignoring the little rash of embarrassment that broke out across her skin. "Yes. It's hot. Your Adam's apple. Because it's very much a man thing."

"That's the strangest compliment I've ever gotten."

"Well, I'm not finished yet."

He chuckled, but it wasn't an easy sound. "Sorry, I didn't mean to interrupt you."

"Your forearms."

"Those are good, too?" he asked, a smile curving his wicked mouth.

"Really good," she said, her throat dry now. "Your muscles, the dark hair. Your wrists. Your hands."

He moved in just a little closer, his lips so close now all she would have to do was tip her chin up just slightly and she would close the distance between their mouths. "What about my hands?"

"They look strong. And when I imagine having them on me...all over me..."

"What do you imagine me doing to you with my hands, Katie?" he asked, his voice almost a whisper now.

"Touching me."

He made a sound that was somewhere between a groan and a growl, one that resonated deep inside her. "Not good enough. Tell me more. Tell me what you want."

"T-touching my breasts." She closed her eyes to try and get the rest of the words out without melting into a puddle of embarrassment. "Sliding down my back, holding on to my hips."

"What about touching you between your thighs, baby?" he asked, his voice so rough now it was like a stranger's.

She opened her eyes and they clashed with his intense blue gaze. "Yes. I want that."

"Good. Now, are you going to stop talking and kiss me?"

She figured that was a rhetorical question. So her answer was to press her mouth against his. There was no anger between them this time, no challenge, no dare. But it didn't defuse the heat, the passion that burned between them.

His lips were hot and firm, commanding. He directed the kiss with unerring skill, delving deep, sweeping his tongue across hers, the slick friction sending a sweet honeyed sensation down through her veins, all the way down, leaving her wet with wanting him.

He released his hold on her wrist, wrapping his arms around her and tugging her body tightly against his. He was all strength and warmth, comforting and terrifying at the same time. She could feel his arousal hardening against her stomach.

Jack Monaghan was hard. For her.

She couldn't help but smile at that. And then a little giggle bubbled up in her throat and managed to escape.

Jack broke the kiss, his mouth still hovering near hers. "Something funny, badger-cat?"

"No," she said, unable to suppress the smile.

"Good." Then he leaned forward and bit her bottom lip before kissing her again, harder than before.

The sharp pain from the bite shocked her, especially followed closely by the deep, unending pleasure that came from his wicked, skillful tongue. And then she couldn't remember if the bite had hurt at all or if it had just felt good. It all felt good. Jack felt good.

He moved his hands down her back, just as she'd told

him she wanted him to. All the way down to her hips, holding her steady, held tight against his body, against his hardened erection.

This time she was the one who pulled back. She studied his face and was struck by how familiar and different he was all at the same time. This was Jack. Her Jack. The one who would always try to make her smile even while the world felt as if it was crumbling around her. The one who always gave her a hard time and tugged her braid and called her Katie.

He was that, but it was like she'd always been looking at him through a fog and suddenly it had lifted, revealing details, facets of him she'd never been able to see before. She'd caught glimpses of them, little moments of intensity, a look, a smile, but this was different. More. Like looking full on into the sun.

And she didn't want to look away.

"What?"

"Just looking at you," she said.

"And?"

"You're the most handsome man I've ever seen," she said, immediately feeling out of her league as the strange old-fashioned compliment hung in the air between them.

Something sharp and hot passed through his eyes. "Is that so?"

"Yes."

He moved his hand to her shoulder, then down the length of her arm, and curled his fingers around her wrist and drew it close to his mouth, pressing his lips firmly against her palm, his eyes never leaving hers. "You're beautiful, Kate Garrett."

She shifted, leaning in and kissing him again. Because she was afraid that if she didn't, she was going to cry. And she'd already cried in front of him one too many times. Crying was stupid. It was passive. It didn't accomplish anything.

It most especially wouldn't accomplish her number one goal of the night, which was to get in bed with Jack.

The thought sent a shock wave down through her body. It was really happening. She was going to bed with Jack. Which was also a terribly old-fashioned way of thinking about things. But her thoughts had suddenly gone a little bit coy now that actual sex was imminent.

"I'm going to pick you up now," he said, his lips moving against hers as he spoke.

"What?" But even as she asked the question, she found herself being swept up off the ground, cradled close to his chest.

"We're going upstairs."

She looped her arms around his neck and held on while he carried her from the kitchen, through the living area and up the wooden stairs that led to the second floor of his home. She'd never been upstairs at Jack's house. There were only bedrooms up there. And she'd never been in his bedroom.

She shivered.

Jack paused midstride. "You okay?"

"Yes," she said, her teeth chattering.

"I'm only going to ask you this once. From this point forward I'm going to assume this is what you want. That even if you're nervous, you want this. You tell me right now if you aren't completely certain."

She didn't hesitate. "I'm certain."

"You are certain about what?" he asked, his voice uncompromising.

"I want to make love." She could have bitten off her tongue. Why couldn't she have said something dirty like *screw*? Or at least straightforward like *have sex*? Why was she suddenly shy?

"You understand what this is, don't you? Nothing outside the space, outside the house, outside tonight, changes."

Her heart twisted. "I understand."

He nodded once, then continued on his journey up the stairs, down the hall. His bedroom door was partly cracked and he shoved it open the rest of the way with his knee, then kicked it closed behind him.

It was a big bedroom, with wood floors and a braided rug in the center. Beyond that was a large bed with a rustic wood headboard and footboard and a quilt spread over the mattress.

If there were more details to take in, she didn't grasp them. She was focused simply on the way Jack was holding her, on the purpose with which he was walking through the room, toward that bed.

He set her down on the edge of it and took a step back, looking at her.

Then he gripped the hem of his T-shirt and tugged it up over his head, exposing his body.

Her mouth went completely dry, her heart thundering so hard she was afraid it would sprout hooves and gallop straight through her chest.

She'd seen Jack without a shirt before, but she'd always done her best not to look. Always done her best not to feed the wicked little monster that lived inside of her, harboring a Jack obsession she'd always tried to pretend wasn't there.

So now she indulged herself. Taking in every detail, every inch of exposed skin. More than that, she let herself feel. Let the full impact of him hit her square in the chest and spread out, all the way to her toes, and hitting some very interesting places in between.

His chest was broad and muscular, tapering down to a narrow waist with well-defined abs. He had just the right amount of dark hair on his chest, thinning out as it spread downward, then becoming more pronounced again in a line that disappeared beneath the waistband of his pants. A line she most definitely wanted to follow.

Happy trails to her indeed.

He took a step closer to her, and her eyes were drawn lower, to the front of his jeans and the aggressive bulge that was now at eye level. The fantasy she'd had earlier today in the truck outside the bridal store flashed through her mind.

She reached out, grabbing hold of his belt buckle, but he took firm hold of her and lowered her hands. "No. Not that. Not yet."

"Why not?" she asked.

"Because we're not starting with something that's about me."

She cleared her throat, feeling nervous, embarrassed. She'd been confident a moment ago, but maybe that wasn't something a woman was supposed to want. "I… I mean… I want…"

"Me, too. But I don't think I can handle it right now."

"We're going to have to stop talking in euphemism, because I'm kind of worried we are talking about the same things, and I'm worried that I don't understand you," she said, the words flowing out in a nervous rush.

He laughed, his chest pitching, his abs rippling with the motion. It wasn't an easy laugh; it was forced, strange. "I don't want you to suck me off right now, because I'll come in about ten seconds. Was that straightforward enough for you?"

Her face felt like it was on fire. "Yes."

"Were we talking about the same thing?" She nodded, swallowing hard. "Good. I'm glad you want to."

She felt relieved by that statement. Relieved that it was okay for her to want to taste him. Relieved that they were tracking.

He looked at her for a moment, then moved forward, putting his knee down on the mattress right next to her thigh. Then he leaned in, kissing her, propelling them both backward so they were lying on the mattress. He was holding himself up, palms flat on either side of her shoulders, his body not making any contact with hers.

She arched upward, desperate for something, desperate for more.

"Be patient," he said, angling his head to kiss her neck.

Desire ignited in her, a spark meeting a pool of gasoline. And it was just a kiss on her neck. But it was unexpected, and it was new. And it was so much more powerful than she'd imagined simple contact could be.

His lips embarked on a journey down to her collarbone, half his kiss landing on her T-shirt and the other on her bare skin. He raised his hand, curled his fingers around the fabric and pulled it down low, making a V that peaked between her breasts.

He looked up at her, hungry blue eyes meeting hers, and a sharp stab of anticipation hit her low and deep.

He kissed her then, on the curve of her breast, and she let her head fall back, let her eyes close again.

Abruptly, he abandoned her, straightening up, sitting on his knees. She looked at him on the bed, so close to her, and she knew she was staring with an expression of dumbfounded wonder on her face, but she couldn't bother to care.

Yes, she had seen plenty of shirtless men, but not like this. She'd never realized before that there were different kinds of nakedness. There was the kind where men stripped their shirts off while they were working, wiping sweat from their skin before going about their business. The kind you saw at the beach, when shirts off was the casual dress code for every male in the vicinity.

And then there was this. An intimate, raw kind of nakedness. Where the knowledge that they would touch each other, taste each other, all over their bare skin hung between them.

A kind that promised more secrets would be revealed, along with more skin. A kind that made her whole body feel electrified.

His eyes were unreadable, watchful. As though he was assessing her, deciding what to do next. She wished he would hurry and make up his mind, because she was afraid she would burn up and incinerate into a little pile of Kate-shaped ashes before he did.

His next move was fast, fluid. Suddenly he was over her again, taking hold of the bottom of her T-shirt and wrenching it over her head. He looked at her, his gaze dark, intent on her. He swore, harsh, hard.

She watched his face as the intensity in his eyes sharpened, as his lips parted slightly, his jaw slackening. He looked like... He looked an awful lot like she imagined she had only a few moments ago when she'd been examining his body.

"Why are you looking at me like that?"

He dipped his head, kissing her neck. "Because you're so damn sexy I can hardly stand it."

"But you've seen a lot of naked women." She didn't feel jealous about it. She was about to benefit from the fact that he'd seen and touched a lot of naked women, so she was hardly going to be shrewish about it now.

"But I've never seen you." His words moved over her like warm oil, soothing and arousing all at once. "And believe me, I've put quite a lot of thought into this over the past few days."

"You have?"

A wicked smile curved his lips and he reached down, unfastening the button on her jeans, the sound stark and loud in the bedroom. "Hell yeah."

She didn't really know what to say to that. So she didn't say anything. Instead she relished the slow torture of him lowering the zipper on her pants, tugging them down her legs and throwing them down onto the floor.

She wasn't wearing anything now but her underwhelming white seamless bra and matching cotton panties. There was nothing exceptional about the cut of said panties. They provided full coverage, both in the front and the back, and while she was somewhat grateful for that considering there were some scary things involved in being naked in front of someone for the first time, she was also aware that men didn't exactly get hot and bothered over demure underwear that covered more than your average bikini.

But judging by the blue flame burning in Jack's eyes, he wasn't really bothered by the style of her underwear.

"Told you I didn't have any sexy underwear," she said, her tone apologetic.

"But you've got a hell of a sexy body," he said, resting his hand on her rib cage, then slowly letting his fingertips drift down her torso, tracing the line of her slight curves down to her hips, down to those nondescript panties. "I've been torturing myself wondering about your shape. Wondering what your breasts look like. Damn, baby, you hide yourself well."

She sucked in a sharp breath. "Nothing special."

"I'm going to be the judge of that. And one thing I need you to be really sure of is that I'm not comparing you to anyone else. I can't even remember anyone else right now."

His words quieted some of her nerves, identifying the source in a way she hadn't been able to and cutting them off at the root. There was no room for doubt. Not when the way he looked at her proved the truth of every word he'd just spoken.

He pressed his forefinger to where bra cup met skin and traced a slow line upward until he reached the strap. He curved his finger around the fabric, drawing it down her shoulder. Then he repeated the motion on the other side.

He looked at her, lowered his head, his tongue following the path his finger had just taken. Instinctively, she reached for him, threading her fingers through his hair, holding him tightly to her as he teased her with his mouth.

He reached behind her, unhooking her bra and sending it the way of her jeans and T-shirt.

Raising his head, he looked at her, a ragged breath shaking his frame. "Katie," he said, his tone reverent as he lifted his hand to cup her breast, slowly sliding his thumb over her nipple.

Pleasure so sharp it cut like a knife sliced down through her. She wanted to close her eyes, to block out some of the sensory input battering like a ship against the rocks, but she was desperate to watch his face. Desperate to hold on to every moment.

Because this was her moving forward. Running forward full tilt.

And she didn't want to let one moment blur, let one escape without turning it over, fully experiencing it.

"Beautiful." He cupped her with his other hand, teasing both tightened buds with slow precision. Then he bent, drawing her deeply into his mouth, pulling a harsh, hoarse cry from somewhere deep inside her.

She worked her hips in time with the expert rhythm of his tongue, trying to ease the cavernous ache that was building, building, building between her legs.

He shifted his denim-clad thigh and she rocked against him, a white-metal burn scorching through her, internal muscles tightening.

She reached out toward his belt buckle again, and this time he didn't stop her. This time he let her get it undone, let it hang loose while she went after the button on his jeans.

But from her position it was awkward, and after watching her struggle for a few moments, he relieved her of her burden. He stood and shucked his jeans, keeping his eyes trained on her as he straightened and pushed his underwear down along with them.

She was in entirely new territory now. She'd never before seen a naked, aroused man.

But she had been right in her theory. Jack had nothing to worry about, because she liked it. She liked it a hell of a lot.

Although along with the liking came the return of her nerves. Because big. He was very big. Not that she had any basis of comparison, but at the moment she felt she didn't need one.

He leaned forward, grabbing hold of her hips and dragging her down toward the edge of the bed, then hooked his fingers into the waistband of her panties, tearing them from her body.

"I'm all out of patience." He adjusted her position, drawing her even nearer to the edge of the mattress, then lowered himself to his knees, turned his head and pressed a kiss to the inside of her thigh.

Her stomach tightened, every muscle in her body tensing as she waited for him to make his next move. He cupped the most feminine part of her with his large, warm hand, parting her slick flesh, his breath fanning over sensitive skin as he moved closer.

She curled her fingers around the quilt, bracing herself. But her feeble attempt at preparing had been for naught. Because there was no preparing for the extreme altering sensation of Jack's tongue over the part of her that had been screaming for his touch.

He tasted her, slow and deep, thorough. It was so strange and alien, something she had never even fantasized about and yet something he had known she had wanted. In spite of the fact she hadn't known she'd wanted it.

He continued to lavish attention on her with his tongue as he shifted his position slightly, his finger teasing the entrance to her body. She swore and arched her hips, pressing herself more firmly against him, demanding more.

He pushed his finger deep inside of her, testing her, working it in and out of her slowly, the sensation new, joining a whole host of other new sensations that she hadn't even begun to grow accustomed to before he added another.

A second finger joined the first, slowly stretching her, uncomfortable where the first had been easy. But she realized what he was doing. What he was getting her ready for. And she was thankful, yet again, for his experience.

Slowly, the discomfort faded and pleasure built inside of her. He increased the pressure of his tongue over that sensitive bundle of nerves and pushed her over the edge with effortless precision, her muscles tightening around his fingers as wave after wave of sensation pounded over her.

He withdrew from her, stood and walked over to the nightstand. He opened the top drawer and pulled out a strip of condoms. He tore one packet off the rest, then made quick work of getting the protection on.

She was fascinated watching him, his strong, masculine hand rolling the latex over his thick erection. It was strange, incongruous and perfect seeing Jack in this context. She couldn't look away.

"Scoot up," he said, his voice strained.

She complied, her legs feeling a lot like wilted asparagus stems as she tried to will her trembling, useless muscles into doing her bidding.

She lay back, her head rested on the pillow, her thighs parted slightly. She forgot to be embarrassed about the fact that she was naked in front of him. Really, how could she be embarrassed about anything now that he had put his mouth there. Now that he had tasted her in the most intimate way possible.

Well, she supposed she *could* be. But it would be a little silly.

She still hadn't touched him in the way she wanted to. Still, she hadn't put her mouth on him. She wanted to slow things down, ask for more. Because she was afraid this was all he would give her. And it wasn't enough. Not nearly enough.

But before she could say anything, his body was covering hers, and he was kissing her deep, a reminder of her own pleasure flavoring his lips and tongue.

He flexed his hips, the head of his arousal testing her, teasing her. The hollow ache was back, a new orgasm building inside of her already. Impossible, she would have said. But Jack seemed fully capable of accomplishing the impossible where her body was concerned.

Abruptly, he ended the kiss, lowered his head, buried it in the curve of her neck as he moved, wrapping one hand around both of her wrists and pushing them up over her head while he thrust deep inside of her.

She couldn't hold back the sharp, shocked sound that was forced from her in time with that deep thrust. She'd heard years of horse riding made this kind of thing easier, but if this was easier, she was going to thank God for her horse habit every day for the next five years.

Because easier or not, it still hurt like hell.

She screwed her eyes shut tight and waited. She couldn't hear anything but his ragged breathing in her ear and her thundering heartbeat echoing in her head.

Slowly, she became less aware of the pain between her legs, more aware of the viselike grip he had on her wrists, the pain there slowly intensifying as the pain at the place they were joined lessened. As though it was simply draining from one part of her body to another.

She opened her eyes and met his fierce gaze. She nodded slowly, answering the unspoken question she saw there.

It was all he needed. He withdrew slightly, then thrust back home. She gasped, but this time not because of pain. He went slowly at first, allowing her to get used to the sensation of being filled by him. Until she went way past being used to it and crossed over into needing it, craving it.

She arched toward him, resenting the fact that he was holding her hands captive, but he didn't respond to the clear physical request that he release his hold. Instead he bent his head to her breast, tracing the outline of her nipple with his tongue before scraping it lightly with his teeth.

Jack was in her. Deep inside her. And it wasn't just pleasure overtaking her but the unending sense of being part of another person. Of him being part of her.

Not just anyone. Jack.

Always Jack.

She'd had no idea. She'd really had no idea.

He kept full and total control of the movements, keeping her pinned, trapped by his strong hold and the weight of his body. It was maddening, drawing out the building pleasure to almost unbearable intensity. With his other hand he traced the outline of her lips, her jaw, sliding his hand down, curving it around her throat, the subtle show of his strength and power sending another electric surge of pleasure through her.

Then he moved on to her breasts, her waist, her hip,

where he gripped her tight, pulling her hard against him in time with his thrusts. He was going to kill her. He was honest-to-God going to kill her with a promise of release not delivered, keep her poised on the edge forever.

She wiggled, managing to break free of his hold. She cupped his face, pulling his head down to hers, kissing him deep before moving her hands down to his muscular shoulders, over his back, down to his ass. She hadn't gotten a good look at it, not yet. Later. She would look later. For now, she would just feel and enjoy.

Something about her exploration tipped him over the edge, and she could feel the moment his tenuous control snapped. His movements were no longer measured, his thrusts no longer even. It became wild and desperate, the ride of a cowboy hanging on for dear life.

She moved in time with him, pushing them both closer to the brink. He pressed his forehead against hers, a long, low growl rumbling through his body, the clear sign of his desperation ramping up hers.

If there had ever been any doubt that he wanted this, if there had ever been any fear that he was only doing this to keep her out of trouble, because he felt sorry for her, that growl effectively frightened it off into the very far distance. It was raw; it was real. And it was all for her.

Then he froze above her. She could feel him pulsing deep inside of her. And it was as if the heavens had broken open inside of her, pouring forth torrential downpours of pleasure. She had a thunderstorm raging beneath her skin. Heavy and electric, loud. Roaring through her with the force of a tornado. Powerful, devastating and no less destructive.

All she could do was cling to him. All they could do was cling to each other until it passed. All she could do was hope they both survived the aftermath.

JACK WAS PRETTY SURE he was dying. At the very least, he had set a foot on the road that would lead to death the moment he had touched Kate. Because if Connor and Eli ever found out, they would kill him. Spectacularly. Slowly.

A damn harsh truth to have to consider with the flavor of Kate still on his tongue. But it was a factor in this whole thing.

"Just a second," he said, pushing up from the bed, trying to ignore the chill on his skin caused by separating from her beautiful body.

His questions had been answered. Her breasts were just the right size to fit in his palm, her nipples a pale pink. Perky. That was his official description. Her waist ran more straight up and down than hourglass, her skin paler, softer than he had imagined it would be. Her hips were perfect. Perfect for holding on to while he slid into her hot, tight body.

He was getting hard again. He was such a bastard.

He turned away from her, walking into the bathroom that was connected to his bedroom. He discarded the condom and caught sight of his reflection in the mirror. Yeah, he was still himself. And he'd just taken a good long look at Kate, so he was certain she was still herself.

And he had just taken her virginity. He felt a little bit sick.

He walked back out into the bedroom, and Kate was still lying there at the center of the bed, completely naked. She sat up when he returned, dark hair sliding over her shoulders, only part of it remaining in a now nearly wrecked braid. She looked up at him, questions in her dark eyes. Questions he knew damn well he didn't have answers to.

Because he didn't know much of anything right now. He really knew only one thing for certain. He was one hell of a son of a bitch. She was so young. An entire decade younger than he was. So much more in terms of experience.

"Well," he started.

At the same time she said, "So…"

He stopped talking and decided to wait for her. Because hell if he knew what to say.

"Should I go?" she asked.

She looked so vulnerable. So young.

"Don't go," he said. But he knew even as he said the words that he couldn't allow himself to touch her again. Shame was crawling over his skin like ants, unfamiliar and unpleasant.

Bad blood. Dirty.

Oh yeah, he'd more than proven that.

He bent down and retrieved his T-shirt from the floor and tossed it over to Kate. "Why don't you put this on?"

She obeyed, even though she looked confused while complying. Though the sight of his white T-shirt settled over her bare curves didn't do much to quiet the arousal that was roaring through his veins like a beast. He could see the outline of her nipples through the thin fabric. And now he knew what they looked like. Now he knew what she looked like all over. And he would never be able to forget.

He wasn't about to compound his sins by sending her out into the cold or by touching her again. Those two things were kind of at odds, since he had proven he did a lousy job of keeping his hands off Kate when she was anywhere near him.

"I have some things to do. Before I come to bed."

Her eyes got larger. "Oh." She scrambled to the edge of the bed, swung her legs over the side of the mattress and stood. "I thought we might…talk, maybe?"

His chest got tighter, breathing almost impossible now. "Later," he said. He had no intention of talking to her later. He had every intention of avoiding his bedroom until she was asleep.

She frowned. "If you have something to say, you should just say it."

"Sometimes, Katie, things need to be left unsaid."

She looked hurt. Confused. Shit, he was a bastard. "We never leave things unsaid."

"Yeah, well, until tonight we never had sex before, either."

"I would have thought we would talk more now that we've seen each other naked."

He tried to force the corners of his mouth to lift into a smile. He imagined it was closer to a grimace. "That's not how it works."

One side of her mouth pulled sideways, straight across. He imagined that was her attempt at a smile. Then she lifted her shoulder, as if shrugging off his words of more experienced wisdom. She reached up, sliding her hand around to the back of his head while she stretched up on tiptoe and kissed him.

And he was weak. Just a man. So he let her. More than let her—he wrapped his arm around her waist, held her to him for a moment, relishing the feel, the softness of her breasts pressed against his chest.

"I'll be here," she said, getting back into bed, slipping beneath the covers.

And he would be anywhere but there, because his resistance was low. "Get some sleep."

He walked out of the bedroom and down the hall, down the stairs. He didn't have anything to do. It was almost 10:00 p.m. and all he wanted to do was climb into bed with the soft, beautiful woman upstairs.

But the soft, beautiful woman upstairs was someone he never should have touched in the first place.

Dammit. Why had his conscience shown up now? He'd been more than willing to let it all burn earlier. It should have arrived before he'd taken Kate to bed or not at all.

Unfortunately, his ability to justify had run out.

Mainly, it was because of the way she'd looked when he'd come out of the bathroom. That gut punch of reality that had hit him square and hard.

No matter what she said, he was going to hurt her. He probably already had, probably would even leaving it at this once. But continuing on wouldn't make it any better.

He'd made it his mission to protect Kate from some of the uglier things in life when she had been younger and surrounded by ugly things. Surrounded by empty booze bottles, the smell of alcohol and her father's disconnected, slurring speech.

He'd been there when her father had died. And had comforted her when Connor's first wife, Jessie, had been killed. And after all that, knowing everything she'd been through, knowing how battered her heart was, he'd done this. But he was going to fix it.

He was going to protect her, as he always had.

He'd let himself lose sight of that, mired in his own shit. But he wouldn't forget again.

CHAPTER ELEVEN

IT WAS POKER NIGHT. Somehow Kate had forgotten last night when she'd decided it would be a good idea to go to Jack's to comfort him and see if he would make good on that dirty promise he'd issued over the phone. Somehow she'd forgotten that he and her entire family would be getting together to play cards only twenty-four hours later.

She'd been dreading it for most of the day. At least, once she'd stopped turning over and over the events of the night before. And once she'd stopped dealing with the very real desire to curl up into a ball and lick her wounds. Wounds left behind by what had followed the most incredible sex anyone had ever had.

Not that she knew about all the sex that had been had, but there was no way in hell it could top what had happened between Jack and her.

The sex had been perfect. It had been the unspoken weirdness that had occurred after. In many ways, she wished he had freaked out. Wished he had yelled and said he was never touching her again. Wished he had thrown things and shouted and said it was a terrible idea and they should never touch each other again. But he hadn't. He had left, saying nothing. Promising he would be back. He hadn't come back. She had lain in bed awake for hours after he had gone downstairs, waiting for him. She hadn't been able to move. Glued to the mattress as though he'd stuck her there. She didn't wait. Never. Not for anything.

But last night she had.

Had lain there with her eyes open, gritty, until the sky outside had started to lighten. Finally, she had drifted off, only to wake up two hours later. The bed was still empty of anyone but her, cold except for where she was nestled beneath the quilt.

When she had finally gotten up, she had dressed. Except she had kept his T-shirt on in protest of his abandonment. And then she had gone downstairs looking for him, but he hadn't been there.

She'd thought about calling him. Thought about looking around the property.

Then she'd realized that this was probably what he did with every woman he slept with. And they probably all felt needy and desperate after, searching high and low to see if they could find him, to see if they could talk him into touching them one more time.

She had a case of the Jacks. She'd promised herself she wouldn't get those.

She had promised she would be cool and sophisticated. Because she didn't want a relationship anyway, so there was no reason to let him hurt her feelings. Though she did want more of what they'd done. There was so much left for her to experience. And right now she couldn't fathom being with anyone else. Not when he was still her primary obsession.

It wasn't just that, though. He'd hurt her feelings. She didn't want him to have that kind of power, but he did.

Still, she was balanced. So she had spent only half the day fetal over all of that. She'd spent the rest of it panicking about the poker game. About whether or not he would be there. If he was there, it would be incredibly awkward. If he wasn't there…

Knowing he was avoiding the house because of her would hurt. Seeing him for the first time since they had been naked together, with Connor, Eli, Sadie and Liss looking on, would be terrible.

Of course, she could always skip the game. But it would be suspicious because she never had other plans. Which was why she was tromping over to Connor's house, her hands stuffed in her pockets, her boots crunching on the gravel.

Jack's F-150 wasn't in the driveway. Her heart slammed against her breastbone, then slid all the way down into her stomach. She gritted her teeth and stomped up the stairs, the noise created by her feet hitting the solid wood doing a little bit to satisfy the irritation that was rioting through her.

She opened the door to her brother's house without knocking and shut it firmly behind her. Not even the smell of pizza in the air offered her any comfort.

She walked into the dining area and saw that everything was all set and ready to go, the green-and-yellow Oregon Ducks bucket sitting in the center of the table filled with beer and soda. She was not messing around with soda tonight. "Beer," she said.

"Did you get kicked by Roo?" Eli asked.

"No," she said, sitting down at the table and scowling at her older brother. "Why?"

"Because that was a strange little one-word greeting. I thought maybe you were having trouble stringing thoughts and sentences together."

"Just had a bad day," she said without thinking. She

shouldn't have said anything, because now they would ask for an explanation. Well, Connor and Eli probably wouldn't. But Sadie and Liss...

"Oh," Sadie said, the sympathetic sound grating across Kate's nerves, "what happened?"

"Work stuff," Kate lied. Because it had been her day off. But sometimes her schedule got shuffled around, so it was feasible that they might not realize.

"Drama with a flat of pansies?" Connor asked, his mouth curving upward into a crooked smile.

Kate nodded, her expression mock serious. "Yes, pansies are the most dramatic of all flowers."

"Azaleas are the most apologetic," Sadie said, laughing at her own joke. A wide grin spread over Eli's face, too. Kate remembered the apology azalea that Sadie had purchased from her more than a year ago in an effort to engender some of Eli's goodwill.

Obviously, it had worked. Or if not the azalea, maybe something else.

Maybe she should buy Jack an azalea.

"What about petunias?" Liss asked. "What are their dominant emotional characteristics?"

"I hear petunias are the hardened criminals of the plant world," Eli said.

"I'm sure you would know," Sadie said, kissing Eli on the cheek.

Kate heard the sound of the front door opening and her heart scampered up to her throat, resting there, fluttering madly like a nervous animal. Because there was only one person it could be. Only one person who would show up on poker night and not knock.

She looked down at the center of the table, determined not to watch the doorway.

Her pulse was pounding in her ears, and if there was conversation going on around her, she couldn't distinguish it from the roar of blood that had taken over all the space in her head.

She heard shoes on the hard floor and knew that she couldn't keep not looking, because not looking would eventually appear a lot more suspicious than looking. She lifted her head slowly, trying to prepare herself to face Jack for the first time.

Preparation had been futile.

It was Jack, Jack, whom she had known for almost her entire life. He was familiar, from his dark hair, nearly black, to his blue eyes, always glittering with humor. Broad shoulders, muscular frame. The very same Jack she had always known. But more. So much more.

There was an intimacy to having been with someone that she'd never realized existed. The source of the special looks that passed between her brothers and their respective lovers.

Like different kinds of nakedness, this was another new discovery. She had known Jack before, but now she *knew* Jack. Had learned things about him she could never unlearn. Knew what his skin tasted like, felt like, looked like all over.

Knew how he shook when she traced her tongue along the line of his jaw. Knew how his whole body shuddered as he found his release. Had heard that feral growl as he thrust deep inside of her.

She hadn't just been skin to skin with him; he had been inside of her, as close as two people could possibly be.

Wow, so much for trying to act casual about all of this. She was not feeling casual.

And now she had passed from normal looking at Jack in greeting to staring.

But…she realized that Jack was staring, too. He was frozen in the doorway, his lips parted slightly, his eyes trained on her.

"Hi," she said, knowing she sounded subdued. But she felt subdued, so all things considered, it was fair enough.

"Hi, Katie," he said.

She didn't correct him.

He walked into the dining area and sat down in the only available chair, which was—thank God—between Eli and Liss and not next to her.

"So are you all ready to lose your money?" he asked.

There, that was slightly normal. She was struggling with normal. She was struggling with anything beyond guppy dry-drowning on land.

"I don't know," Eli said. "I'm feeling lucky tonight. I'm getting married in two weeks to the most beautiful woman in the world. Frankly, I'm untouchable."

"Your wallet is very touchable. And I'll prove it," Jack retorted.

"I think you're all forgetting that last time I cleaned up," Kate said.

Jack turned his electric-blue gaze to her. "I suppose you did."

"No suppose about it. If we had kept going, you would have left wearing a barrel, because I would've stolen the pants right off you."

She regretted her words, but not until it was too late to do anything about it. Not until she had spoken them, not until they were hanging awkwardly in the air like dazed fruit bats.

"I bet you would have, Katie bear," he said, his jaw tensing.

The group seemed oblivious to the tension between them. Which was insane, as far as Kate was concerned, because it felt so thick, so real. A physical presence in the room rather than a simple feeling. She felt as if the tension was sitting there drinking a beer, holding a sign that said They Totally Had Sex Last Night.

"Deal. Somebody deal," she said, hoping that no one took note of the edge of desperation in her tone.

"Kate's in a hurry to lose," Connor said, grabbing the deck and setting them up for a little bit of five-card draw.

"More like your face is in a hurry to lose," she said. Admittedly, it was not her finest comeback. But she was not on top of her game. Since most of her brainpower was devoted to not looking at Jack to see if he was looking at her.

"His face lost at birth," Eli said.

"Nice." Liss smiled with approval.

"Can you believe that? My own wife." Connor shook his head, but he didn't look irritated in the least. Instead he just looked pleased to be able to say the word *wife*.

"Wives are the worst," Sadie said. "I can't wait until I'm one."

"Soon." Eli looked at Sadie and smiled. That secret smile that Kate suddenly understood. They looked as though they had secrets because they did. Because there was a wealth of knowledge they each held about the other that no one else would ever have.

And she'd gone and given herself all that knowledge

about Jack. She hadn't realized. Hadn't realized how much it would change. It was as if she'd spent her entire life thinking that *Old Yeller* had ended before the final chapter and had been suddenly introduced to the actual ending years later.

Because then a heartwarming story about a boy and his dog became something else entirely. All of the previous story was there, but that last bit changed everything. Changed all of what it was.

That was what sex with Jack had done.

He wasn't a hideous dead-dog book. In fairness, the sex they'd had was hardly a tragic final chapter. It was just…different. He was different.

Everything that came before this new chapter had taken on an extra facet. Given her new understanding. It was so much more than she'd expected. So much more than she'd wanted.

Unsurprisingly, she lost miserably. Her poker face was off because she was putting all her energy toward applying it to keeping Jack feelings off her face.

Jack didn't win any rounds, either. It was Eli, in keeping with his bold prediction, who won the night.

"You suck, Eli," Liss said, eyeballing her diminished pile of change. "Stealing money from a pregnant lady."

"Unless pregnancy hormones interfered with your bluffing abilities, I don't see what it has to do with anything," Eli responded.

"If you make her mad, it's on you," Connor said.

The banter continued for a few more moments, but Kate and Jack sat it out. She stole a glance across the table at him, the first time all night that she'd chanced anything more than looking in his direction but looking through him.

The corner of his mouth lifted slightly, and she felt the impact of that small gesture down deep. She couldn't think of anything to say, couldn't think of anything to do, so she just stared at him.

Thankfully, no one else noticed. She took a sharp breath, noticed his eyes lowering to look at her breasts. She felt a flush creep up her neck and over her face.

It reminded her of the expression on his face last night. Reminded her of that sharp need in his eyes as he'd thrust inside of her.

She felt like she'd stuck her head in a barrel of bees.

"You look tired, Kate." This comment came from Connor. "Were you out late last night?"

"What? No."

"I saw you pull out around eight. You got back after I was in bed."

Horrified heat punctuated by pinpricks of ice flooded her face. "I just… I mean, it wasn't late to me. I guess to an old guy like you, maybe ten or eleven or whatever is kind of late."

"An old guy," Connor said drily. "Do you hear that?" He addressed the group. "We are old."

"Maybe you all are," Sadie said, "but I'm not."

"Where were you?" And the interrogation started with Eli.

"Am I supposed to give you an accounting of my whereabouts now?" She knew that she was sounding guilty now, which was stupid. She should have just played it off. The defensiveness was making it worse. But she hadn't been able to hold it back. Because she wasn't good with subterfuge. She had never engaged in it.

If only she had realized that being a straight arrow

for so many years would come back to bite her in the butt one day. She might have worked harder at cultivating a little rebellion earlier.

"I just went over to Ace's for a drink." She couldn't look at him, because she was lying, and she was a terrible liar. She'd been told by more than one customer at the Farm and Garden that she had an honest face. Honest faces tended to do strange things when dishonest words were being spoken.

Sadie and Liss exchanged glances, and Kate knew that more questions were imminent. "I met *girl*friends," she said, heading them off at the pass. "Sierra West and some of the other women who barrel race." Neither of them would probably ever talk to Sierra about it. Her alibi was most likely never going to get checked.

"Hope you had fun," Sadie said.

Kate had a feeling Sadie didn't believe her. Which hurt her feelings, really. Silly, since she was lying. But she wasn't exactly rational at the moment.

"I did. But now that you mention it, I am tired. I think I'll head to bed. I have to be at work early." She stood, the chair sliding inelegantly behind her, causing her to stumble. "See? Tired."

She waved halfheartedly and walked out of the dining room. Once she put some distance between herself and the dining room, her breath left her body in a gust, and she realized she had been taking in only shallow bits of air and releasing it very slowly ever since Jack had walked into the room.

She heard another chair scrape against the floor, and instinctively, she knew it was Jack's. She wanted it to be Jack. She wanted to talk to him. She also wanted to avoid him.

Her feelings made exactly zero sense at the moment.

She couldn't hear what he was saying, but she could feel the rumble of his deep voice, feel it moving through her, making her all soft again. Wet again.

The man was made entirely of wicked magic.

She heard his heavy footsteps and froze, waiting for him. Of course she was waiting for him. She was predictable. She would love to walk out and scurry back to her house as quickly as possible. But she wouldn't. Because no matter how upset she was for the way things had gone earlier, she wanted to be near him again. She wanted to hear what he had to say.

Anyway, she saw him all the time. They had to work it out. She couldn't avoid him forever, so she might as well not ever start.

He appeared in the doorway of the dining room, and their eyes clashed. She nodded once and turned, heading out the front door and into the chilly, wet night air. There was a breeze blowing in off the sea, the sharp, briny smell mixing with the smell of earth and pine.

Kate folded her arms, shivering but not from the cold.

A moment later Jack appeared on the porch, casting a quick glance back at the house before walking toward her.

"Did you drive?" he asked.

"No."

"I'll walk you back."

"You sure I won't try to jump you again?" she asked, knowing that she sounded pissy and not really caring.

"As long as you aren't worried about me jumping you," he said, his tone dry.

"*Worried* isn't the word I would use."

"Come on, let's walk and talk." He took two strides, evening his position with hers. Then they both started back down the road that led to her cabin.

She shoved her hands in her pockets, keeping a healthy distance between them. Jack seemed content to do the same.

"So—" she kicked a pinecone that was in the middle of the driveway and sent it flying "—why did you leave me in bed alone, asshole?"

"Because I'm an asshole," he said, surprising her with the frank admission.

"Okay, that's honest, but it doesn't really help me."

"Because I didn't want to be tempted to do that again."

"Why? Just…once? How is that even…reasonable?" She snorted out a breath. "Wait, never mind. You probably have sex with a random woman one time with great frequency."

"I can't dispute that," he said, his tone somewhat rueful.

"I know you can't. Your reputation is pretty well established. And I know it, Jack, I do. It isn't like I want anything serious. I just thought maybe more than one time."

"Sure. I mean, it would be great. I can't deny that. There's no sense in denying it. What we have… It was explosive. I'm not going to pretend differently. I had to leave because if I had stayed, I would have pinned you down to the bed and had you again. There is no question. I had to leave because my good intentions are about as easy to strip off as that T-shirt of mine you were wearing last night."

"I stole that T-shirt," she said, her voice raspy then because his words had affected her so deeply.

"You can keep it."

"If you want me, why won't you let yourself have me? I mean, you aren't exactly known for your restraint."

"Because you are Connor and Eli's younger sister. Because they are two of the most important people in my life and if they found out that I... I kind of joked about them killing me, but I actually think they might."

"They wouldn't kill you."

"Maybe not. What little respect of theirs I have, I would lose. I would lose their friendship."

She knew he was right. No matter how angry it made her, no matter how unfair it seemed that his actions, her actions, be dictated by the potential reaction of her brothers, she couldn't pretend that there would be no reaction. Couldn't pretend that it wouldn't upset their lives. She never talked about sex with Connor and Eli, but she had a feeling her brothers would take a dim view on whomever she decided to sleep with. If they found that Jack was having sex with her just for the sake of sex...

Yeah, that would go down about as easy as swallowing a hedgehog.

But it didn't erase her longing for him. Just because she understood, didn't mean she was opposed to changing his mind.

She opened her mouth to say something. Something like "They don't have to know." Or "We can keep it a secret." But she realized she was verging on begging. She was inexperienced, sure, but even she knew that wasn't ideal.

They walked on in relative silence, the only sound

their feet crunching on the rocks and pinecones as they made their way down the dark tree-lined road that led to her little cabin.

Too soon they rounded the slight curve and her little outdoor light came into view, shining a welcome, representing tonight's finish line. The end of this new development in her relationship with Jack.

An end she wasn't ready for.

She half expected him to turn and leave then, but he kept going with her until they reached the steps.

"Really quick," she said, sensing he was about to leave, not ready for him to go, "I just wanted to tell you that it was good. And I'm glad you were my first." She bit the inside of her cheek, battling stupid, unwanted tears that were starting to fight for escape. "It was good."

It wasn't exactly the eloquent speech she had felt building in her chest. Not exactly the sophisticated and magnificent parting words she might have hoped for. But they were true. And she needed him to know.

I've wanted you forever.

She left that part unspoken, because it was too revealing. Not just for him but for her. She didn't want to say the words out loud, because she didn't want to ignore all of them or what else they might mean.

He nodded slowly. "It was."

She took a timid step toward him, half expecting him to move away, but he didn't. He stood rooted to the spot, watching her. The glare from the porch light cast deep shadows on his beautiful face. Highlighted the sharp cheekbones, the straight line of his nose, the squareness in his jaw. The perfect curve to his lips.

And now she knew for sure why his lips had always been so fascinating. Knew why staring at them for too long had always made her stomach feel fluttery and tight.

Because her body had been reading the promises there, and now that she'd seen them fulfilled, she felt it all even more vividly.

Just one more time. One more kiss.

She put her hand on his face, stretching up on her toes, pausing just for a second before she leaned in. He raised his hand and curved it over hers, holding her to him, looking intently at her in the dim light. It was all the consent she needed. She angled her head, kissing him deep, and he returned it.

It occurred to her then that she'd never kissed Jack goodbye before. And that that was what she was doing now. She screwed her eyes shut tight, softening her lips, opening for him, submitting to the sensual assault that originated where their mouths met and carried through her entire body.

She was going to have to try to unlearn all the things she knew, going to have to try to forget the new chapter she'd read. This was goodbye to Jack as she had come to know him.

There would be no secret looks for them to exchange, no little touches that served as brief and electric reminders of what they shared behind closed doors.

There would be none of that. Because it was over. Because this was it.

Too soon the kiss ended. When they parted, they were both breathing hard.

She curled her hands into fists, digging her short fingernails into her palms, biting the inside of her cheek to keep herself from asking him if he wanted to come in.

He had already given his answer, he had given his reason, and it wasn't wrong. She'd told him he wouldn't hurt her. Told him she knew what to expect. So now, even though it hurt, even though she had expected more, she had to pretend none of it was happening.

"Good night," he said, his voice low, rough. "See you tomorrow, Kate."

Don't call me that.

Those words were on the tip of her tongue. In that moment she hated the sound of her preferred name on his lips. Because it wasn't what he called her. It wasn't teasing. It wasn't designed to get a rise out of her. He was treating her the way everyone else treated her.

And he used to treat her like she was special. She realized that now, an epiphany that had come at the very worst time.

"Good night," she said, turning away from him and walking up the stairs to her front door, ignoring the gnawing feeling of incompletion that grew with each bit of distance she put between them.

CHAPTER TWELVE

IT WAS A CLEAR, crisp afternoon and Kate hoped that was a good omen for tomorrow. Because tomorrow was Eli and Sadie's wedding and she wanted very much for it to be perfect for them. Eli deserved perfect.

He had given up so much to ensure that she didn't feel the neglect of her father, who'd wandered around the house like a drunken ghost who couldn't interact in the mortal realm.

Connor had spent his days working on the ranch, keeping it running, keeping them fed, making sure they had a roof over their heads. Eli had done everything he could to keep the house clean, to keep her taken care of. He had brushed her hair, braided it, picked her clothes out for her. He had ridden his bike with her on the back in a special seat down to a day care every morning so that he could be sure she was being taken care of while he continued going to school.

He had done everything in his power to make sure the residents of Copper Ridge thought their household was running as normally as a home could after the woman of the house had up and left her family.

Eli had made their house a sanctuary even while a good portion of the storm raged inside the walls.

In many ways, Connor and Eli had been her parents. She'd been raised by two teenage boys, and she couldn't begin to thank them enough if she started now and kept going for the rest of her life.

"It's sunny," Liss said, a smile on her face as she looked out the kitchen window of the Catalog House, one of the oldest structures on the property, ordered by her great-great-grandpa from the Sears catalog. Eli and Sadie would be spending the night separately, with all of the girls bunking in Sadie's B and B.

"Yes, but the weather here is a fickle mistress," Sadie said. "So hopefully, the fog won't roll in before tomorrow."

"I guarantee you it will roll in at least three times before tomorrow," Kate said. "We just have to hope it rolls back out again at the right time."

"True enough," Sadie responded.

"But the sun will shine on you," Kate said, with a certainty she felt all the way down to her toes. Because God, the universe, whatever, owed her brother a sunny wedding day.

"I will take your certainty as prophecy." Sadie patted Kate on the cheek.

"I don't really mind a little bit of cold," Liss said, her hand on her stomach. "It does not take much to make me sweat. I would rather not sweat all over my bridesmaid dress."

"You can sweat on your bridesmaid dress. I don't mind," Sadie said.

"Alternately, you can reschedule your wedding for after I give birth."

"Nope. I have roughly three hundred dinners—fifty salmon, two hundred and fifty filet mignons—scheduled to be brought tomorrow to feed very hungry people. There is no rescheduling this wedding. Oh, and I love Eli and cannot spend one more minute without being joined in the bonds of holy matrimony."

"You've been abstaining for your wedding night, haven't you?" Liss asked.

"Yes. Yes, we have. There will be no rescheduling," Sadie said.

Kate blinked, trying not to think about any of this information too deeply. Liss, on the other hand, seemed highly amused. "Why are you doing that? It was his idea, wasn't it?"

"He thinks it's romantic and traditional. I told him not exactly since we have been sleeping together since before we were actually in a relationship. He did not take my point."

"This is hilarious," Liss said, her smile wide.

"Don't be smug," Sadie said, eyeballing Liss. "It isn't like you can get up to anything at the moment."

Liss's smile turned naughty. "That isn't true. We're very creative."

Kate was suddenly applying all of this personally rather than feeling indignant or disgusted, as she normally would have. Because this wasn't forcing her to think of her brothers as sexual beings; it was forcing her to think of herself as one. Of what long periods of abstinence would mean for her now that she knew just how good it could be. And a long period of abstinence was most definitely what she had stretching in front of her.

Also, there was the small matter of her wondering what all being "creative" might entail.

She imagined that Jack could be very creative.

"I think Kate is getting ready to stuff her socks in our mouths," Sadie said.

Kate felt her ears get hot, because that had not been

what she was thinking at all. "Yeah. I don't need to hear any of the sordid details about your personal lives. I like you, no offense, but you know."

"Sure," Liss said.

"It's time to head out for the wedding rehearsal anyway," Sadie said. "Okay—" she took a deep breath "—this is going to be fine, and I'm not going to trip on my way down the aisle."

Kate had never seen Sadie trip. "You aren't really known for your clumsiness," Kate pointed out.

"But if I was ever going to contract a case of the clumsies, it would very likely be on my way down the aisle."

"Probably," Kate said. "But if you fell, Eli would just come and help you up. That's what he does."

Sadie's blue eyes misted over and she grabbed hold of Kate, pulling her into a tight hug. "You're right. You're so very right." She released her quickly and slid her forefinger beneath her lashes, wiping the moisture away. "Okay, let's do this."

ELI, CONNOR AND JACK were standing around in the field, having just set up six rows of chairs in front of an arbor that was heavily laden with flowers.

"You ready?" Connor asked, the question directed at Eli.

"It doesn't seem like a strong enough word." Eli's voice rang with certainty. For a moment Jack envied that certainty. Eli knew who he was; the community knew who he was; he knew what he wanted. Jack didn't know shit.

Holly, the wedding coordinator, walked up the aisle, a clipboard in her hand. "The ladies are ready. We have the music cued up. Connor and Jack, I need you. Eli, you're going to go wait over by the sound booth. Tomorrow you will have the pastor with you." She looked at them expectantly. "Okay, move."

Connor and Jack exchanged a look and followed Holly back down the aisle and around behind the barn. Sadie was there, her blond hair piled high in an exaggerated bun, a bouquet made of wrapping paper and ribbons in her hand, Liss by her side.

But it was Kate who made him feel as if he'd been hit in the chest with a ton of bricks. He had pretty successfully avoided her for the past couple of weeks. Bachelor-party stuff had taken the place of the poker game, and he'd made vague noises about work commitments when he would normally have come by the ranch to visit or help with an extra project.

He had been avoiding things because of her. Because no matter what he had said about their need to be finished with the kissing, and the sex, and the completely inappropriate attraction, his body wasn't on the same page. His body saw her and growled, starving for her in spite of the fact that she was wearing another of her ill-fitting T-shirts and shapeless jeans.

"Okay," Holly said, interrupting his thoughts, "I will be back here during the ceremony to cue you when it's time to go. The music will start—" and just then the music did start "—and then we'll give it a few seconds. Eli will walk out with the pastor. Liss, you and Connor walk out together, followed by Jack and Kate. Then Sadie."

The music changed and she pointed at Connor, who took Liss by the arm and began to walk back with her down the aisle. Kate looked at Jack, catching his eyes. He tried to smile as he extended his arm to her.

"Okay, badass badger-cat," he said, trying to sound brotherly, "no chewing on the ankles of the guests on your way down the aisle."

She squinted one eye, the left side of her mouth pulling down. "What?"

"You have to be a lady. This is a wedding." Somewhere in the murky depths of his brain, he thought maybe this would be the key to getting things back on track. If he treated her like he had before he'd started noticing her breasts and things, before he had kissed her, they would revert back to the way they'd been.

So he would just ignore the feeling of being scorched currently assaulting his forearm where she had her hand placed on him and move forward.

She didn't get a chance to respond to his comment, because a few seconds later they got their cue, and they were making their way toward the arbor. He could feel her tense up. He leaned in and whispered in her ear. "Easy there, Katie." Because that was what he would have done before. So that was what he was going to do now.

It didn't work. She only grew more rigid with each step.

They parted at the head of the aisle, Kate going to the left, while he went to the right. He looked across the way and saw that she was glaring at him, her dark eyes blazing with anger. He gritted his teeth and turned his focus to the aisle again, to Sadie, who was practically skipping toward them.

Holly was hot on her heels. "Okay, then Sadie says her piece when prompted by the pastor—" Jack noticed that Eli looked slightly confused by this but said nothing "—and comes up to join Eli. Vows, kiss, the song will start, you will be presented to the guests. Then we walk out. Reverse order, Eli and Sadie first." She made a sweeping gesture indicating they should walk back now. They complied. "Jack and Kate."

Jack shot Kate a look and they both started walking, meeting in the middle, where he took hold of her arm again. The contact sent a shot of sexual hunger down to his cock that rivaled some of the better blow jobs he'd had.

Which got him looking at her mouth and wondering what it would be like to have it on him. She had a pretty mouth. He had never put much thought into it before.

He was now.

Get a grip, idiot.

He needed a distraction. Possibly to meet another woman. A woman at the wedding tomorrow. A little bit of casual sex to burn the feel of Kate from his skin.

He ignored the violent twisting in his stomach, the instinctive and emphatic *no* that screamed through his body. This was, in his estimation, a lot like getting bitten by a snake. You had to inject yourself with more venom to fix what was wrong. Which meant having more sex. With someone else.

That had made more sense before he had actually thought it through with actual words.

Still, it was the only solution he had.

That and to treat Kate like he really wanted to want to treat her. Which was the golden rule or some shit, he was pretty sure.

Soon they reached the other side of the barn, and she

released her hold on him a little bit too quickly. "Afraid you're going to get cooties?" he asked.

The glare she shot his way could be described only as evil. "I'd say I probably already have them," she said, her tone deadpan but dangerous.

Eli and Sadie seemed oblivious to the exchange. They were too busy talking to each other in hushed tones and gazing deeply into each other's eyes.

It was on the tip of his tongue to say something about how she couldn't have caught anything from him, seeing as he'd used a condom. But that would have been crossing the line. Even if her older brother hadn't been standing right behind him, it would have been over the line.

Screwing her in the first place was over the line.

Yeah, no argument. Which was why he was fixing this.

Or at least, was trying to fix it.

Judging by the stormy look on Kate's face, he was failing.

Connor and Liss joined them in the back of the barn then, and Holly clapped her hands, her red curls bouncing. "Okay. That went great. So now all you have to do is the exact same thing tomorrow, but also you'll be married at the end of it."

"So are we done?" Kate asked.

"Yes," Holly said. "Really looking forward to this wedding. It's going to be beautiful."

"I just need to go back to the house and get some clothes," Kate said, directing her comment at Liss and Sadie. "I'll be by the B and B later."

She turned and walked away from the group. He knew he was risking looking suspicious, but he felt like he needed to go after her. Because they needed to get something settled between them tomorrow before the wedding.

"I just need to go ask her something about the rodeo thing," he said, realizing when he spoke the words that the excuse seemed more suspicious than a simple *I'll be right back* ever would have. But it was too late now.

He broke into a partial jog, headed after Kate. "Katie," he said.

She stopped, her shoulders straight, her back stiff. "What?" She started walking again, not turning around to face him.

"Hey." He reached out and tugged lightly on her braid. "Are we okay?"

She whipped around, her expression angry. "Don't do that. And you know what? Just...do what you did that night after the game. Call me Kate. Don't call me Katie."

"I don't want things to be different. I would hate to think that what happened messed things up permanently. Avoiding you like I have been doesn't work."

"If you don't want to...be more than friends, or whatever we are, that's fine. That's fine." She reiterated the last bit. "But things won't be the same as they were before. It's impossible." She turned and started walking away again.

"That's bullshit."

"This whole thing is bullshit," she said, spreading her hands, still not stopping, still not looking at him.

He reached out and grabbed her arm, forcing her to stop. But she refused to look at him. "I don't want things to be different," he said, his voice rough, his hand burning from the intensity of touching her. Mocking everything he was saying.

"They are. Honestly, Jack, I thought I was the stupid virgin." She pulled out of his hold and this time he didn't go after her.

If he hadn't already known it, this proved it. He was the King Midas of fuckups. Everything he touched turned to shit.

This was why he liked it easy. This was why he liked things surface. Charm could fix everything when no one was overly invested. A smile, a joke, a round of beer… It solved whatever problem he had.

But he couldn't fix this thing with Kate no matter how hard he tried. Feelings. Too many of them.

Guys like him had to stick with simple for this very reason.

Bad blood.

Yeah. But if no one saw you bleed, they never knew.

Too bad Kate Garrett had seen him bleed. Too bad he'd bled all over her.

Yeah. Too damn bad.

It made him wonder if the charity event would prove anything at all. Or if it was just another thing he was destined to destroy.

THE DRESS DIDN'T seem as special as it had when she bought it for the purpose of seducing Jack. Now it just seemed pointless. She'd seduced Jack already. In a T-shirt, jeans and cotton undies. And it was over without him ever having seen this.

She looked at herself in the mirror. Her hair was down and straight, since as far as she knew, curling was not in the listed skills on her hair's résumé. Liss had promised she would weave some flowers into it so that it matched hers. And while that was going on, Sadie was going to do her makeup.

Kate had never worn makeup before. She wasn't sure how she felt about it.

Well, she might have been excited about it if she'd had a seduction to look forward to. As it was, she had an awkward postseduction walk down the aisle to look forward to. Which was not the same thing.

She didn't have time to worry about Jack. Didn't have time to allow herself to be derailed. Once the wedding was over, she was going to redouble her focus on the barrel racing. Getting ready for the event at the charity day. Getting ready to kick some serious butt.

Her stomach tightened with anxiety when she thought of that. If she really did this, if she really did well, it was just one more change. One more step forward. She was starting to realize how difficult that was for her. How much it scared her.

But even though it sucks, you survived Jack.

Yes, she had. Maybe that was it. She needed to look at it as a step forward where her foot had landed in a cow pie, and she had slipped and fallen on her ass. But it was still a step forward. Still a change. And now she'd been with a man. One of life's great mysteries was now known to her.

Progress. Progress towing a boatload of awkwardness and hurt feelings, but progress nonetheless.

Liss walked into the light, airy bedroom Kate was currently standing in. "You look beautiful, Kate." Her tone was a little bit too kind.

"Thank you?"

"Was that a question?"

"The tone of your voice is strange."

Liss lifted her hand, showing a little bunch of baby's breath with little dried roses mixed in. "Not intentionally. I'm just here to fix your hair. Sit on the bed."

Kate obeyed, and Liss started fiddling with her hairstyle immediately.

"So," Liss started. And here it was. Kate had instinctively known something was coming. "Are you okay?"

"Why?"

"You're acting weird. And so is Jack. And I am not stupid."

Kate's throat tightened and her stomach along with it. "It's fine," she said, knowing she was completely unconvincing.

"If he did anything to you, I will kill him. Cheerfully." She sounded cheerful but lethal.

For some reason that made Kate mad. Which was strange, because she was mad at Jack. Or more accurately, she was hurt because of him. But she didn't like the implication that what had passed between them was him "doing something to her." She had wanted it. She had asked for it. He hadn't done anything she hadn't wanted except stop. And she couldn't imagine why Liss, who had known Jack almost as long as Kate had known him, would act like he was someone or something Kate needed to be protected from.

"You know, Jack is a good guy," Kate said, her tone defensive. "He would never do anything to hurt me. He would never do anything to hurt anyone."

"But that's the thing about Jack," Liss said, her tone more firm. "He doesn't mean a lot of things. He can be… He's very charming, but he can be selfish."

Kate thought about the evening she'd spent in Jack's

bed. Selfish was the last thing she would call him. Even now, even while she was upset with him, she couldn't say that anything he'd done was selfish. In fact, he was thinking of Connor and Eli and their relationship. Was considering her feelings, even if it was in a way she didn't want them considered.

"Jack isn't selfish," she said. She knew she sounded upset, and she didn't really care. She was comfortable being mad at Jack. She was not comfortable listening to Liss talk about him this way. "Who do you suppose helped take care of me when my dad was miserably drunk and Connor and Eli had their hands full? Jack did. And he's helping with this charity thing, and he's offered to help coach me on my riding so I can win this event. Because it's important to me, and he cares about that. And yeah, he pisses me off. Because he can be obnoxious. But he's a good man. You're supposed to be his friend. I wouldn't think you'd have a hard time seeing that."

Liss continued calmly weaving flowers to Kate's hair. "I am his friend, Kate. Which means I have a realistic viewpoint on his shortcomings. It's difficult to have a realistic viewpoint when you have feelings that go somewhere beyond friendship."

"And if I did, maybe it would be a problem," Kate said, her teeth clenched.

"There are easier men to set your sights on. Jack likes a good time, but he won't stay around for a long time."

"Easier men? Is that the goal? Because if so, I don't think you ever would've married my brother."

Connor had been the grumpiest, most closed-down man in town until Liss had managed to get him to fall in love with her and, along with that, drag him up out of his grief.

"I'm not telling you what to do. Or what not to do. I'm just telling you I've observed that there is something different between you and Jack. And if you need to talk to me, you can."

She swallowed hard. "Don't say anything to Connor?"

"I don't keep secrets from my husband. But right now I don't know any secrets," she said, her tone full of meaning.

"There aren't any to tell," Kate lied.

"Okay. If you say so. Anyway, your hair is done. Sadie will be up in a second. She's just getting the finishing touches done on her makeup. Then she'll do your face before she gets into her dress."

Kate nodded mutely. Liss turned to go. "Wait," Kate said. "Thank you for looking out for me. I've lost every woman who has ever come into my life. But now I have you. And Sadie is here to stay… I'm glad you're my sister, Liss. And I appreciate you offering advice."

"Anytime," she said, smiling slightly before leaving the room.

A few moments later Sadie came in, a bag of makeup in her hand. "Ready?"

Kate took a look at her reflection, which was still barefaced. Her hair was partially pulled back, some of the strands twisted around blossoms. There was something satisfying about how different she looked. As if her outside finally matched her insides. Ever since that night in Jack's bed, something had felt off.

Now at least she looked a little bit more like a woman. Sure, she'd always been a woman—the loss of her virginity didn't change that. But Jack had made her aware of just how much of a woman she was.

"Yes," Kate said. "I'm ready."

JACK HADN'T WORN a suit since Connor's first wedding. His wedding to Liss had been casual, jeans and button-up shirts, no ties, down by the swimming hole they'd frequented as kids. The casual dress had been due in large part to the cold weather of the winter wedding, but it had also been a reminder of their past. Of the good things in the past, while they walked into the future.

Eli and Sadie's wedding, on the other hand, was not casual at all. Sure, it was all wrapped up in the rustic flavor of the Garrett ranch, but everything was elegant and styled, down to the most minute detail. Much like the bride. Sadie had that way about her. That effortless, free-spirit vibe. But beneath all of that she was much more thoughtful, much more purposeful.

All in all, someone he was glad to see marrying his best friend. Even if he did have to wear a suit.

The wedding was due to start soon, the seats placed out in the field filling up with guests.

He'd been assisting in the seating arrangements, but soon it would be time for him to take his position behind the barn with Sadie, Liss, Connor and Kate.

Kate, who he was no closer to fixing things with.

So much for his attempt at bringing things back to normal. He'd spent a good portion of last night pissed at himself about that and mad that he couldn't even get drunk, because he couldn't afford a hangover on the day of his friend's wedding. He scanned the crowd, spotting a host of familiar faces.

Instinctively, he homed in on the single, attractive

female faces. Lydia was here, Holly the wedding coordinator and Alison. Alison was still a no-go, as far as he was concerned. But Lydia and Holly didn't have any relationship baggage that he knew of. Neither of them had a reputation, but that didn't mean they were opposed to a good time. It just meant they were discreet.

And that was fine with him. He wasn't looking to flaunt, wasn't looking to hurt Kate in any way.

It was just his snakebite theory. Kate Garrett made him feel snakebit. He needed antivenom.

Still, neither of those possibilities created even a kick of excitement in his gut. Which was dumb. Lydia was beautiful. Dark hair, dark eyes, petite, feminine frame. Holly was tall, willowy and pale with curly red hair and freckles across her nose. They represented some fine variety. Either one of them should do something for him. But no. Nothing.

His gut clenched tight, his whole body freezing, when an unexpected set of guests walked in. Nathan West, his beautiful wife, Cynthia, and three of the adult West children. Sierra, Madison and Gage. Colton, predictably, wasn't anywhere to be seen. But he very rarely was.

Of course the Wests would be here. All of them. Eli was a prominent figure in the community, and so were they. They had deep pockets and donated large sums to the sheriff's department. So obviously, they would be here for the wedding of the sheriff. For some reason Jack simply hadn't been prepared.

He started walking toward them, his stomach churning, anger firing through him. Nathan caught his eye, a warning look in the icy depths of his own, and Jack stopped. What the hell was he doing? He was going to make a scene at his best friend's wedding? For what purpose? There was none.

Jack stopped, but Nathan kept walking. He didn't look away from Jack, his eyes fixed on his.

"Mr. Monaghan," Nathan said, extending his hand, a smile on his face.

Jack felt sick. But he wasn't about to be outdone. He took his father's offered hand and returned volley with a smile of his own. A smile that was far too similar to the older man's for his taste. "Mr. West."

"I had to come shake the hand of my most worthy competition. Enjoy the wedding. Tell the bride and groom congratulations on my behalf."

Jack squeezed West's hand. "Absolutely." He released his hold, continuing away from the seating area and toward the back of the barn, rage now a living thing inside of him.

Nathan West got to walk around without ever having his reputation questioned, while Jack had to work his ass off to get any respect. There was something wrong with that.

There was also something deeply wrong with the fact that Jack had now made eye contact with his father twice. And there was no satisfaction in it.

Attention. Acknowledgment. It was a cold and bitter thing.

Big surprise—life wasn't fair. He'd known that from moment one. He just wished he didn't have to be reminded so damn frequently.

And then he felt a little bit like a prick for complaining, because at least he'd gotten a payout to keep his identity a secret. A lot of bastards just had to deal with the stigma and never got the reward.

It was all the child support his mother had never accepted. And then some. She had been furious when she found out he'd taken the money. When she found out he'd lowered himself, his pride, to that level. She'd sworn she'd never speak to him again. And she hadn't.

He still couldn't regret it. His mother'd had the power to give them something else and hadn't. Realizing that, he'd been angry, too.

They were both still angry.

Though now some of his anger was at himself.

He'd sold himself, but he hadn't sold himself on the cheap.

The first thing he saw when he rounded to the back of the barn was Sadie. Jack had never harbored any fantasies about getting married, but he could well imagine that any man who had would immediately want to snatch her up and carry her to the nearest church. She looked perfect, like an angel, like everything Eli deserved.

Then he turned and saw Kate. After that there was just nothing else.

She was wearing a dress the color of cranberries, little flowers in her dark hair, which hung loose around her shoulders. She so rarely left her hair down. Even the night they'd been together, it had been back in a braid. And he wanted desperately to sift his fingers through it, to feel the softness, the weight of it, to spread it out over his pillow.

Her eyes were highlighted with gold makeup, picking up all the subtle color she had naturally and making it even brighter. And her lips…painted the same color as the dress. He'd become increasingly aware of those lips in recent weeks and seeing them highlighted like this was torture.

They were vivid in his mind's eye now, softening for a kiss, parting so that they could wrap around his hardening—

He wasn't sure he would survive this wedding.

Sadie let out a long, slow breath. "Okay. Nothing to be nervous about," she said.

"Nothing at all," Connor said, putting his hand on her shoulder. "Welcome to the family, Sadie Miller. I had to call you that since you're going to be a Garrett in a few minutes."

She smiled. "Oh, come on. I've been one. This just makes it official."

"True," Connor responded.

The music changed, and the sounds of the crowd noise dissipated as everyone took their seats.

Silence fell between the five of them, too. Waiting.

Instinctively, he went to stand next to Kate, seeing as it was his position for the wedding. Also, his body wanted to be close to hers. Simple as that.

She looked up at him, her expression shaded by her lashes, which looked longer, thicker and darker than usual. She didn't say anything, and neither did he.

Holly cued Liss and Connor. Connor took hold of his wife's arm, his smile broad, and the two of them began their journey to the aisle.

He extended his arm to Kate, who slowly accepted it, her eyes never leaving his. Because he couldn't resist, he leaned in slowly, his lips next to her ear. "You look beautiful."

She shivered. "Thank you," she said softly.

Holly pointed at them and mouthed the silent "go"

and then he started to lead Kate around the barn. They walked through the field and to the aisle, now flanked with full chairs. He refused to look at any of the guests. He wasn't taking a chance on making eye contact with West. Not now.

Instead he kept his focus on walking that straight line up to the arbor. And then narrowed his focus still. To the feel of Kate by his side. Her fingertips digging into his forearm as she held on to him. Her shoulder brushing against him with each step.

He stole a glance at her out of the corner of his eye. Red lips. Her beautiful red lips.

In that moment, he let them become his whole world.

Because the real world wasn't something he needed to deal with just now.

They reached the head of the aisle, and he reluctantly released his hold on her, going to stand beside Connor.

The music changed and so did the atmosphere out there in the field. It was as if suddenly everyone in attendance had taken an indrawn breath at once. As if they were all holding it. Waiting.

And then Sadie appeared, backlit by the sun, making it look as if she had a halo around her face. She was most definitely glowing. Jack glanced at Eli, and he was pretty sure he was glowing, too. Without the benefit of the sun. It was just Sadie.

Sadie stopped at the head of the aisle and Pastor Dave, a man Jack knew only by reputation rather than by any time spent in church, smiled at her.

"Traditionally, this would be the moment when the bride is given away. But Sadie has something she would like to say instead," the pastor said.

Sadie smiled, her focus on Eli, as though he were the

only person there. "I left here when I was seventeen. And I spent most of those years after that alone. Wandering around, never settling. Not belonging to anyone. Then I came back here. And I found you. Right where I left you. Now I give myself away. To you, Eli Garrett. Because I trust very much that you will honor my gift. Now and forever."

Eli broke away from his position and went down to stand with Sadie, taking her hand and leaning in to kiss her. "I give myself to you, too," he said.

For some reason the declaration made Jack search for Kate. It must have had the same effect on her, because when he looked in her direction, their eyes locked. Heat streaked through him as the words echoed inside of him.

I give myself to you.

A trade. A choice.

"Wonderful," Pastor Dave said. "Now let's begin."

THE CEREMONY WAS OVER and Eli and Sadie were officially Mr. and Mrs. Garrett. Kate was seated at the bridal party table, picking at a piece of cake, watching them dance beneath the hanging lanterns in the barn.

She felt Jack's presence before she saw him. "What do you want, Monaghan? Come to harass me more like yesterday?"

She still felt jittery and unsettled from his compliment earlier.

You look beautiful.

He'd said the same to her when she was in a T-shirt and jeans. He was probably just being nice. And it shouldn't have mattered. But it did.

"Why aren't you eating your cake?"

"Because. It's a carrot cake. Which is a horribly

named food. Maybe, *maybe*, you could call it a muffin. And then I wouldn't find it so offensive. But it isn't cake. It certainly isn't wedding cake. Sadie has good taste most of the time, but I question this."

"That was probably Eli's decision. You might not know this but we used to go to Rona's for his birthday. Back when we were thirteen, fourteen and maybe a little older. No one at home made a cake. She used to give him a piece of carrot cake on his birthday."

Kate's heart twisted, her breath stalling out. "Really?" She looked back down at the previously offensive cake. "He always made my birthday cake."

"I remember. They were ugly-ass cakes. He used a mix so they tasted okay but he couldn't frost worth a damn."

"He always made sure I didn't go without. Him and Connor." She cleared her throat. "And you."

"Well—" he sat down in the empty chair next to her and she squished her legs together, making herself smaller, in an effort not to touch him "—it's nice to know I wasn't always a source of bad feelings for you."

"You aren't a source of bad feelings. Don't be dramatic. Again, you're the one that's kind of acting like a virgin," she said, careful not to look at him as she spoke the offending words.

"I don't want you to be upset."

"Sorry, not sorry. I have the right to be upset. I thought… First of all, I thought there would be a little more to it than that. Second of all, whatever I said about how I would react isn't really valid. I didn't know. I had never done that before. My inexperience absolves me."

"It does not," he said.

"It sure as hell does. No jury in the world would side with you on this. You're the town stallion."

"Everyone has had a ride, ha ha ha."

"So you've heard that one before?"

"It's just maybe not as clever as you think." He leaned in and her breath caught. "And anyway, it isn't true."

"It isn't?" she asked, her tone a tiny bit too hopeful for her taste.

"Yeah, come on. That's ambitious, even for me. There are quite a few women I haven't slept with in Copper Ridge. Though you have to take into account the fact that I spent a lot of years traveling on the circuit."

"Right," she said.

"Jealous, Katie?" And if she wasn't mistaken, his tone sounded a bit hopeful, too.

"Why should I be jealous? I had you, didn't I?"

"Once."

She looked down, taking a deep, furious breath. "That was your decision, not mine. I wanted more."

"What do you think I can give you? It's an important question, and I need to know the answer."

She stared down more determinedly at her cake, catching sight of his thigh in her peripheral vision. He was wearing a suit, which wasn't normally her thing, but he made it look sexy. And now, with the ceremony hours behind them, he had ditched his tie, the top two buttons on the white shirt undone, his jacket discarded, his sleeves rolled up to his elbows. He looked disheveled and dashing, and there was no point pretending she thought otherwise.

But there was a point in doing her best not to look at him so that he couldn't tell she felt that way.

"I'm tired of being afraid," she whispered, surprised

at the words that tumbled out of her mouth. But as soon as she said them, she knew they were true.

"What are you afraid of?"

"Change. It's why... It's why I haven't gone pro. Because if I do, I'm going to have to leave. Because if I do, I'm going to put distance between myself and Connor and Eli and the ranch. Everything that matters to me. I've lost enough. I want to keep it all close. I like things to stay the same. So... I work at the Farm and Garden and live on the same property I was born on, and I had never even gone on a date. Never kissed anyone. Because doing different things and being different is so scary. But with you...it wasn't scary, Jack. Because it's you. It couldn't have been anyone but you."

She chose that moment to look at him and the expression in his eyes made her heart flutter around her chest like a terrified bird. Lust, need, naked, raw and completely undisguised, burned from those familiar blue eyes. Rendering a man she knew as well as her own flesh and blood a total stranger yet again.

She knew without a doubt there were more chapters of Jack to read. And she wanted to read them. To devour them.

The craving for that knowledge was so strong she ached with it.

"It has to be me?"

She nodded slowly. "Yes."

CHAPTER THIRTEEN

KATE'S WORDS WERE BALM for a wound he hadn't known he had. Or maybe he'd known he had a wound, but he'd just imagined it was a different one. But he'd been searching for something—approval, accolades, from the town, from his father—for as long as he could remember.

Had been seeking out just one person who might realize he was more than easy smiles, pure dumb luck and shallow affairs.

Right now he saw it in Kate's eyes. That simple gift he'd spent so many years chasing. With wild behavior. Bull riding. Ranching.

She *knew* him. She understood him. More than that, she needed something from him and believed that he had the ability to give it.

And he wanted her, dammit. Wanted those perfect red lips on his mouth, on his neck and everywhere else.

"It's already weird," he said slowly.

"What is?" She blinked rapidly.

"You and me. We did it once, and not doing it again didn't make it normal again. Like you said, it can't be normal. It changed."

"Jack. Please, please don't tease me."

"I'm not."

Her face turned pink and she directed her gaze down

to the uneaten cake on her plate. "And I don't want you to sleep with me again because you feel sorry for me. Or because you're trying to fix something you already broke."

The simple fact was he had come to the wedding with the aim to fix something broken. He'd thought he would pick up another woman, that he would have some easy, fun sex that would have no emotional implications. Sex that wouldn't be hard and wouldn't threaten the most important relationships in his life.

But it wouldn't work. He'd ignored the most essential part of the antivenom principle. It had to come from the same sort of snake.

That meant either he had to keep sleeping with Kate until he was cured of his desire for Kate, or he had taken the metaphor too far. But he was going with option one since it meant he got to sleep with her again.

Yeah, he would have loved to believe he was being altruistic. That he was simply trying to restore order, that he was trying to give her what she wanted. The simple fact was it was just a side effect, albeit a pleasant one. He wanted her. Beginning and end of it. And somehow over the course of the wedding, over the course of the day, he'd begun to lose sight of the other things.

The fact that she was Connor and Eli's sister. The fact that she was ten years younger. The fact that he was a lot more experienced and should know better than to fool around with her.

All those things were somewhere way off in the distance now. And Kate was so close he could smell the clean, simple scent of her soap, of her skin.

"I don't feel sorry for you. And I'm not trying to fix the damn thing." His voice sounded like gravel, his words strained, but there was nothing he could do about it. He was beyond control. Beyond himself. "I want you." He lowered his voice, conscious of the fact that they were still in a room full of people, though most everyone was out on the dance floor, music playing heavily over top of their conversation. "I can't tell you how it changed. When exactly it began. I *realized* it changed that day you kissed me. But it was different long before that." He looked around to make sure they hadn't caught anyone's attention. They hadn't. "It would only be physical. I don't have anything more for you than that."

"Good thing. I don't have anything more for you or anyone beyond that. I told you, I'm tired of being afraid. I'm making changes. I'm going to go pro, and that means I'm going to be traveling, pursuing my dream. I'm not going to be hanging around here mooning over a boyfriend." She cleared her throat and raised her eyes to meet his. "Or a lover."

Hearing the word *lover* on Kate Garrett's painted lips was one of the most erotic experiences of his life, and he couldn't possibly begin to break down why.

"Sounds like we're on the same page, then."

"I'm going to go for a walk," she said slowly. "Down to the old barn."

Heat pricked the back of his neck, and guilt pricked his conscience. He knew exactly which barn she was talking about. Mainly because he had taken a woman there nearly a year ago with the express intent of getting it on with her during Eli's election party. He had been thwarted since he'd encountered Connor and Liss making out, before anyone had known they were more than friends.

That memory should have been enough to get him to tell her no. Should have been enough to highlight the differences between them.

At least, it would have been if he were a decent human being. He wasn't.

"And I'm going to get a phone call a couple minutes after you leave. And I'm going to have to go check something back at the ranch." He chose his words carefully, and Kate clearly understood.

"Okay." She stood, taking the napkin that was in her lap and setting it on the table, her eyes never leaving his. "See you later."

He watched as she slipped through the crowd, kept an eye on any and every hint of crimson he could catch through the thick knot of people. This part, the waiting, would be torture.

So he wasn't going to wait. No one was paying attention to them anyway. Eli was dancing with Sadie. Connor and Liss were across the room, Liss's feet propped in Connor's lap while he rubbed her ankles.

He opted to go out a different door, following a different path from the one Kate had just taken. He cut across the driveway that led back to the Catalog House to a different road that went back to the old barn.

Kate deserved better than a quick, rough screw in a barn during her brother's wedding. But then, she deserved better than him. So he supposed it was all in keeping with the theme.

He broke into a jog, not caring anymore that he wasn't acting casual, fully committed now to his need. How different this was from the last time he had come out here with a woman. That had been...normal. He had wanted the person he'd been with, but not like this. He hadn't felt desperate, hadn't felt desire and guilt claw-ing at his insides in equal measure, each one agitat-ing the other, making it fight harder for pride of place.

He hadn't been shaking with need, ready to tear his clothes off during the walk over so that things would go faster once he was inside.

No, this wasn't like that last time at all. It was un-like anything.

He pushed open the barn door and saw Kate crouched down in the corner by a lantern, turning the switch, the artificial flame lighting up.

"Well, that's handy."

Kate straightened and turned to face him. "I thought so."

"Come here."

Crimson lips turned upward. A small, wicked smile. Just for him. "If I don't?"

"Then I'm going to have to go get you."

Her eyes sparked with humor and a streak of defi-ance so uniquely Kate it hit him in the gut like a sucker punch. And the realization, the reminder, that this was Kate only made him want her more.

Amazing to see another facet of a woman he'd known for so long. To know for sure and certain beneath her makeup was the person he'd always known. Who could keep up with the boys, who was full of strength and sass. But that she was also this woman. This siren who was seducing him with such little effort.

With no resistance on his part.

"Why don't you come get me, then?"

He began to walk toward her, slowly undoing the buttons on his shirt, her lips going slack, her eyes wid-ening slowly. Watching Kate watch him was an im-

mensely gratifying experience. One he never could have
predicted. When it came to sex, he considered himself
jaded. But he'd never been with a virgin before. Much
less a woman who had never kissed anyone else. The
novelty of being her first, her only, was more intoxicat-
ing than he could've imagined.

The way she looked at him, awe mixed with admiration, was like a shot of Jack Daniel's that went straight
to his head. He shrugged his shirt off and let it fall to
the floor before putting his hands on his belt. She licked
her lips and he felt the impact resonate in his groin.

"That lipstick should be illegal."

She blinked, her expression one of genuine surprise.
That was another thing about Kate. She possessed no
guile. None of this was an act, a show or a game. She
was experiencing it for the first time, sharing it with
him, making him feel as if it was a first all over again
for him, too. "Why?"

He reached out and slid his thumb along the line of
those lips. "Because it makes me want to do damned
dirty things to you. Do you know what I've been thinking about ever since I saw you this afternoon?"

"No," she said, taking a step backward, her voice
a whisper.

"Of course you don't." Because she was innocent.
And he was a bastard. By the end of tonight, she would
know. And the next time he, or another man, told her
her lipstick was giving him dirty ideas, she would know
exactly what it meant. That made him feel guilty. It
made him feel angry, because he was thinking about
her with another man. And she would be with another
man someday.

But right now she was his.

"When I came around the back of the barn and saw you," he continued, "my heart about exploded. All I could think about was you kissing me. Leaving your lipstick behind on my skin. I'd already been thinking impure things about your pretty mouth. But that lipstick made it that much worse. Made me want to see your lips on my cock."

Her face turned the same shade of scarlet as her mouth from her perfect, beautiful cleavage up to her hairline. He'd gone too far, and he knew it. But he felt compelled to push. Maybe because he thought if he did, she would back out. Except when he really thought about it, that made no sense. Kate Garrett had never backed out of anything. And presenting a challenge would only make her push back harder.

Maybe that was the real reason he was doing it.

"If you want it, come over here and get it. It seems like I kiss you an awful lot, Monaghan. A girl doesn't like to feel like she's the one doing all the chasing."

"She says with her two weeks of experience."

She tilted her head, a familiar stubborn set to her jaw. "I know what I like. I know what I want."

He felt his lips curve upward into a smile as he continued to slowly work his belt, tug it through the loops on his dress pants before undoing the ridiculous hooks that held them closed, drawing the zipper down and pushing them onto the barn floor, kicking off shoes and socks along with them. They would be dirty. Very obviously so. But he didn't care.

He pressed his hand over his hard, heavy erection. "You want this?"

"Yes." There was no hesitation, none at all.

"Good." He quickened his pace, closing the distance

between them and wrapping his arm around her waist, cupping her chin with his thumb and forefinger, looking deep into her dark eyes, searching for any sign of fear, of potential regret. There was none of that. There was nothing but need, a desire that burned as bright as his own.

It didn't surprise him. In some ways Kate's insides matched his own. Wild, fierce.

A bit too bold. A bit too reckless.

Just one of the many reasons that the moment attraction had begun to spark between them, there was only one place it could end. Neither of them knew how to back down. He should have seen that from the beginning. Should have seen that this was the only place it would ever end.

"If I had known a dress would make a man look at me like this, I would've started wearing them a long time ago," she said.

"When was the last time you wore a dress besides today?"

"Never. At least, not that I can remember. They've always seemed pretty useless to me."

Arousal burst through him like an electric jolt. "They have their uses. They have their conveniences."

"Is that so?"

"Let me show you." He bent his head and kissed her neck, embraced the roar of satisfaction that rocked him as she shivered beneath his lips.

"I didn't expect that."

"This will be the only time I surprise you tonight." He kissed a line along her jaw to her chin and from there to her lips. He thought his heart was going to burst, thought he might come on the spot, just from the taste of her, from the feel of her slick tongue sliding against his own.

He could feel her perfect little breasts pressed up against his chest. He was going to taste her again. And suddenly, he couldn't wait. He broke their kiss, lowering his head and tracing the deep V of her cleavage with the tip of his tongue. She'd worked some kind of voodoo magic with this dress, and he wasn't complaining at all.

A rough, hoarse cry escaped Kate's lips and satisfaction rolled over him in a wave.

"Do you know what I like about dresses?" he asked, his voice almost unrecognizable to his own ears. It was broken, rough. Not the voice of a man who was used to casual hookups, not the voice of a man who treated sex like something easy and fun. It was the voice of a man who was desperate, close to shattering.

"They let your man parts breathe?" Kate asked, each word punctuated by a heavy breath.

He let out a laugh. "Try again." He moved his hand down between her thighs, reaching beneath the soft, flowing skirt, tracing the edge of her panties where they met her inner thigh, slowly, teasing them both.

"Oh. Oh!" She gasped sharply as he delved deeper, encountering sweet, slick wetness that let him know just how much she wanted him.

"Easy access," he said, pushing deeper, sliding a finger into her tight passage.

She raised her hands and gripped his shoulders, clinging to him tightly, her fingernails digging into his skin. "Yes, Katie." She clung harder, pain burning through him at the point where she held him. "Leave a mark, baby."

He brushed his thumb over her clit and she leaned

forward, pressing her lips to his collarbone before parting them and biting down. The intensity of the sensation sent a white-hot flame burning a trail from his shoulder down to his dick. He'd never been into this kind of thing before, but for some reason, with Kate, everything felt good. More was only better.

"You're so wet for me, Katie," he said, pushing a second finger deep inside of her. "I love that you want me so much."

"I do. Only you." Her words were broken, a sweet sob that soothed wounds deep inside of him.

"I'm the only one that's ever touched you like this," he said, not a question, because he knew. Still, she answered with a nod, her bottom lip clenched tight between her teeth. "The only one who's kissed you. The only one who's been inside of you."

"Yes," she said, breathless.

"You have no idea how fucking hot that is. And it shouldn't be. I should be disgusted with myself for taking advantage of you. But I'm not. Because that first kiss was mine. This is mine," he said, pushing his fingers deeper, sliding his thumb in a circle over her clit.

"I'm glad it was you," she panted.

He withdrew from her body, slid to his knees, shoved her dress up over her hips and wrenched her panties down her thighs. "Spread your legs for me," he said. She complied without argument. "You're much nicer to me when you're naked."

"Well, you're nicer to me when I'm naked, too," she said.

He chuckled, leaning in, inhaling her sweet, musky feminine scent. "Very true. So beautiful." He took a long leisurely taste of her, enjoying everything. Her flavor, the way her body shuddered beneath him, her fingernails going back to his shoulders, digging into his skin.

He tasted her as deeply as he could, relishing the evidence of her arousal, taking each and every cry of pleasure on her lips as his due. His reward. He continued on until she froze, until he felt her climax wash over her, sending his own arousal up another notch until he was so hard it hurt.

He stayed down there on his knees, one hand cupping her ass. "What do you think about dresses now?"

"They are a lot more practical than I imagined," she said, her voice thin, breathy.

Never in all his life had he thought he would say things like this to Kate Garrett. Never once had he imagined he would hear her familiar voice sounding out her climax, hear her speak to him in the aftermath of her pleasure.

He'd never imagined it, but now he wondered how he'd ever lived without it.

"Stand up," she said, her voice stronger now.

"You think you're giving orders now?"

"Stand up. And show me your—" she swallowed "—cock."

He wasn't about to say no to an order like that. He rose to his feet, carefully removed his underwear and kicked them to the side. They would be full of hay and dirt just like his pants and he honestly didn't care.

"It's my turn," she said, her eyes locked with his.

She reached out, wrapping her hand around his dick. His breath hissed through his teeth, fire lashing over him, so hot, so destructive he was sure it would consume him.

"I didn't get to touch you last time. Not like this." She squeezed him, her expression full of wonder. Wonder he sure as hell didn't deserve. But wonder he was most definitely going to take. "You're so hard. Big."

That kind of thing shouldn't turn him on. But it did. Normally, that was just a line. Thrown out to boost a guy's ego. But Kate meant it. That did things to him, touched things that went a whole lot deeper than ego.

She lowered herself slowly down in front of him and he had the suspicion that somewhere along the way, between when he had stood up and she had begun to kneel down, they had traded experience. Because he was the one shaking now; he was the one left in wonder of what might happen next.

Then right in front of him, his darkest, dirtiest fantasy, the one he had indulged in at his best friend's wedding, began to play out in front of him. He raised his hand, cupped her face, slid his fingers back through her hair. He didn't want to guide her actions, didn't want to direct her. Kate was the fantasy. It wasn't about a woman going down on him and giving him pleasure. That was generic. Nice under some circumstances, certainly, but generic. He wanted to know how Kate would do it.

She parted her lips slowly, then flicked out the tip of her tongue and tasted him. Instinctively, he tightened his fist in her hair, pulling up as she went down. She looked up at him, a smile curving her lips. And he knew right then and there he would never be able to pull on Kate Garrett's hair in that playful way he'd done for years without remembering this moment.

It didn't seem fair that a few stolen moments could obliterate years' worth of history, but he had a feeling it could. Could and had. Or maybe *obliterate* was the wrong word. Maybe it was more like mixing two handfuls of sand. One that represented their past and one for this.

Put them both together in a jar, and you would never be able to separate the two again. They would be mixed forever.

Though right at this moment, with Kate's tongue sliding over his length, he couldn't imagine why he would want to. He closed his eyes, trying to shut out everything but the way she felt. His knees nearly buckled when she opened her mouth and took him in as deep as she could. It wasn't all that deep, her movements hesitant. He could tell this was her first time doing this.

Why did that make it hotter? Why the hell did that make it sexier than anything else he'd ever experienced?

It was Kate. And she was doing it all for him. Well, for her, too.

And that was the answer to his question.

She reached up, taking hold of the base of his shaft, squeezing him tight while she kept working her own strange kind of magic with her lips and tongue.

His thigh muscles were shaking, the joints in his knees turned to liquid. He was having trouble standing. Having trouble hanging on to his control.

He opened his eyes and looked down, his eyes meeting Kate's. It was as if all the air had been pulled from his body, and along with it every bit of restraint.

"Stop," he rasped, the word weak and ragged.

She moved away from him, the color high in her cheeks, her expression full of confusion.

"I have you again," he said. "We're not finishing like this."

614 BAD NEWS COWBOY

"Do you have a...condom?"

Shame lashed him with the force of a whip. Because he did and he was far too aware of why.

"Yes."

Thankfully, she didn't question it. He abandoned her for a moment, going after his pants, his wallet and the condom he'd placed inside just this morning.

He looked back at the barn door, which he had closed behind them, a bit of unease gripping his throat. Guilt. *Because you should feel guilty, you prick.*

He did feel guilty. About a few things. But not guilty enough to stop.

He strode back across the empty space to Kate. He grabbed hold of her waist and propelled them both deeper into the back of the barn, beneath the hayloft, behind the ladder. "Give us a little warning in case we get interrupted," he said, then kissed her deeply.

Her eyes widened. "We won't, will we?"

"We don't have to do this."

She grabbed hold of his shoulders and tucked him toward her, moving them both backward until she was up against the barn wall. "Yes. Yes, we do."

She kissed him again and he just let himself get lost in it.

He tore the condom open without breaking the kiss and used one hand to roll it over his cock before shifting their positions. He put one hand on her side, pulling her leg up over his hip, opening her to him, while he held tightly to her with the other arm, bracing her against him, trying to shield her from the rough wood as best he could while he pushed in deep.

White spots exploded behind his eyelids, pleasure so acute it was almost pain as her tight, wet heat surrounded him. His mind was blank. Of any previous experience, any other women, anything else but what it was like to be inside her.

He forced himself to open his eyes, to meet her gaze, to watch her face so that he could be certain he was doing it right. He had no other way of knowing. He was lost at sea right now, any and all skill he might have claimed to possess completely forgotten in the moment.

He flexed his hips and coaxed a small sound of pleasure from her. He repeated the motion, his movements growing more frantic with each and every thrust. He did his best to keep his focus on her, on her responses, on her pleasure. Because if he didn't, if he let go, he was going to lose it before she did.

He couldn't remember the last time he'd done that. But experience didn't matter. Whoever had come before didn't matter. They weren't Kate. This was Kate.

So he had to hold on. Had to hold on until she let go.

He moved one hand to her breast, sliding his thumb over her nipple as he bent his head to kiss her neck. Both actions made her moan with pleasure, sending a kick of satisfied desire through him. "Is that good, Kate?"

He felt her nod, her hold on him tightening as he moved deeper, harder inside of her, pinching her nipple lightly between his thumb and forefinger as he did. "Good?" he asked again.

Again, he got a silent nod.

"Say it. Tell me it's good," he said, repeating the action.

"Yes. Yes, it's good." The words sounded torn from her.

And before he could stop them, stereotypical, asinine words he'd never uttered in his life spilled out of his mouth. "Say my name when you tell me it's good," he said, an edge of desperation there that he couldn't fathom.

And she complied without hesitation. "Jack. It's good, Jack."

He lost it then, pressing her firmly against the barn wall, any rhythm, any finesse to his movements, gone completely. "Kate," he ground out, "come for me."

He was begging now, because he didn't have it in him to hold back. Not anymore.

And with her name on his lips, she gave it all up to her release, her internal muscles tightening around his cock. His mind went blank, his world reduced to the slick hot feel of her, the sensation of her pleasure around him. Her soft skin beneath his fingertips, her breath in his ear. If there was anything else in the entire world, he didn't know about it, and he didn't care about it.

His climax seized him like a wild animal, tearing at him, threatening to consume him. And he let it.

CHAPTER FOURTEEN

As THE FOG of pleasure receded, Kate couldn't help but wonder if she would be wearing the evidence of this encounter on her skin for the next few months. It had all been fine and dandy during the main event, but now she was afraid she had splinters the size of tenpenny nails driven deep into her back. And she was feeling it.

Of course, she supposed that could be a metaphor for every sexual encounter she'd had with Jack.

It seemed like a good idea at the time...

She winced as she pushed away from the wall, watching Jack dress slowly, the contraception discarded somewhat haphazardly in a little hole he'd made in the dirt floor. She felt as if she'd been scrubbed down with poison oak, the burning and itching on her skin getting worse with each passing moment. And along with that was a growing sense of dread. Because she knew that any moment now Jack was going to turn to her and tell her what a giant mistake they had made.

Though that was probably a bit confrontational for him. Maybe he would just take off again. Flee into the night and leave her naked in the barn by herself.

He pulled his shirt over his head and straightened, looking at her and frowning.

Here it came...

"Why are you looking at me like you want to stab me clean through with a pitchfork?" he asked.

"I'm not," she sniffed, turning to the side to see if she could find her panties, doing her best to right her dress.

"Holy shit," he said.

"What?"

"Your back."

She reached around and touched her shoulder blade, wincing when she came into contact with a splinter. "Yeah."

"You should have said something."

She let out an exasperated breath. No real surprise—he was trying to tell her what to do. "I was too focused on getting what I wanted. I wasn't really bothered by it."

"But you are now."

"If you try and use this as a teachable moment regarding the heat of the moment and certain consequences, I'm going to knee you in the balls."

His dark brows shot upward. "I need those. If you want to keep enjoying what we just did."

"What do you mean, keep enjoying?"

"We tried ignoring it. We tried going back to normal. It didn't work. From where I'm standing, that wasn't enough to take care of it."

She squinted. "By *take care of it* you mean…"

"It wasn't enough."

Her throat ached. "You really want me, Jack? I mean, you *want* me?"

He let out a long, slow breath. "Do you have to ask? After all of that, you have to ask? I can't control myself around you."

"What changed?"

He just stared at her like he'd been hit in the back of the head with a two-by-four. "I think you did."

The words made her stomach flip, a strange, uncomfortable tightening working its way from there up her throat. "I haven't changed." It was a reflexive response, a funny one considering this had been about moving forward. About making sure she wasn't left behind. Really, it was about changing. But she'd been thinking more of changing her position in life, not herself.

"It's not a bad thing."

"I think maybe you changed. Because it used to be that I looked at you and saw a guy who was basically another brother. Who was great and funny and made me mad and made me laugh. But then…then my skin started feeling too tight when you were around. And you made my scalp prickle and my heart beat too fast."

"You have a crush on me," he said, his lips curving into a wicked smile.

"I don't… That's not… You make it sound juvenile."

"You were mean to me because you liked me. That's juvenile."

She shoved his shoulder. "Making fun of me for it isn't any better."

"I never said I wasn't juvenile. Completely childish. Like I said, I'm not the one who changed."

"How did I change?"

He looked down at her cleavage pointedly. "Well, other than the obvious."

She put her hand over her uncharacteristically exposed bosom. "Yes. Besides that. You aren't that simple. You can have whatever boobs you want—you don't need mine. Particularly since mine are aggressively average."

"I'm going to have to stop you so that I can correct you. There is nothing average about your rack."

"It's not that big."

"Quality, honey. Not quantity."

Humor tugged at the corners of her mouth. "You are naughty."

"And you like it."

"I do. And it surprises me a little."

"It surprises you, Kate Garrett? I've seen you leer at passing men with all the subtlety of a construction worker."

"Looking and touching are two very different things," she said.

What struck her most about this exchange between Jack and herself was that it was easy. Easier than quite a few of the interactions they'd had since attraction had combusted between them. At least, it was easy now that she didn't feel so much like he was trying to protect her without actually listening to her.

"They definitely are," he said, looking his fill.

"Okay, calm down."

"You know what else changed?"

She blinked. "No. You have to tell me."

"You have been Connor and Eli's younger sister since the moment I met you."

She snorted. "Of course I have been."

"No. That's not what I meant. That's the number one thing you've been to me. They cared about you, so I cared about you. Because they are like family to me. And because of that, so were you. But I don't know... Every year, you seem to become more you to me. Not Connor and Eli's sister. Kate. And what I want, and what we do, doesn't have anything to do with them."

"You don't care what they think?"

"I wouldn't go that far. But I'm not going to make decisions based on that. I know that if they found out, there would be hell to pay, and that's one bill collector I'd like to dodge for as long as possible. And seeing as this isn't ever going to turn into anything beyond the physical, I don't see why they have to know."

"No. I wouldn't tell them no matter who it was. I'm not looking for marriage or even a long-term relationship. My brothers don't need to know about my sex life. Also, I don't want you to die."

"Yeah, they would kill me." His eyes held a glimmer of humor.

"So we should keep doing this."

"Until we don't want to."

"Simple," she said.

It was difficult to fight the feeling of smugness that built up inside of her. She was a late bloomer, there was no disputing that, but here she was handling a physical-only relationship like a pro.

"We can keep working on the charity event. I can help you with your riding. And when we feel like it, we can take some very rewarding breaks."

"I like the sound of that."

"Right now we better go back."

She cleared her throat, nodding. There really was no excuse for missing more of her brother's wedding reception. But she didn't really want to go back to reality. Didn't want to stand in a crowd of people and pretend that things were as they'd always been with Jack and herself. Not when things had changed on such a deep level.

She wanted to go into the woods alone, spend some

time in the quiet turning over her newest treasure, studying it, holding it close to her chest.

Too bad that wasn't an option.

She started to walk toward the door and Jack swore harshly. "Your back."

She added a matching swear word to his. "What are we going to do about that? I must look like I got into a fight with a porcupine."

"Yes. If that porcupine was a barn wall you got banged against. It looks like exactly what it is."

"Okay. We walk back. I'm going to hang around outside the edges of the reception. You give me your jacket. You left it back at the reception, right?"

"Yes."

"Okay. I'll pretend to be cold. You pretend to be a gentleman."

Jack laughed, smiling, his whole face lighting up. And Kate's heart lit up right along with it. "I'll try."

JACK SLIPPED HIS JACKET from the back of the chair sitting at the table that was designated for the bridal party and walked back out of the new barn to where Kate was standing on the outskirts of the celebration. "Here you go, badger-cat. So you don't get chilly."

She began to reach for the jacket but he stepped to the side, sliding the sleeve over her arm, drawing it around behind her and doing the same on the other side. "So." She gave him a sweet, shy look that burned straight down to his gut. Now that the guilt had been washed away by that last encounter, it was just lust. Simple, not pure at all. "You're just going to call me badger-cat now because I'm not on your ass about calling me Katie?"

"I miss being yelled at," he said.

"I can yell at you."

He looked over his shoulder and saw that no one was nearby. He leaned in, his lips touching her ear. "I could make you scream again."

Kate looked at him, a self-satisfied smile on her lips. It made him feel warm all over. "Probably not tonight."

"I could."

"It wasn't doubt about your ability. It's just… It's Eli's wedding. And I need to stay. And you need to never have your truck parked out in front of my place overnight. And I won't be able to leave inconspicuously."

"Why don't you come to my place after work tomorrow. Hitch up your trailer and bring Roo. You can do a run on some barrels there. We'll do a little planning for the charity day. And I'm sure we'll find some free time in there." He listened to himself constructing a careful alibi for the express purpose of getting her naked again and keeping it secret. And he felt more than a little bit like a dick. But he wanted it. She wanted it. So he wasn't going to waste too much time worrying about it.

"Sounds good."

"We'd better get back," he said, stepping away from her, putting a careful distance between them.

She nodded and started to walk ahead of him, the sleeves on his coat hanging down to the tips of her fingers, the bottom hitting just above the hem of her dress. His gaze was linked to her, almost as if it was chained there. And the sight of her, petite but strong, covered by something of his, tightened that chain around his throat until he could barely breathe.

They walked back into the barn, the heated barn, which made it a little silly for Kate to be wearing the jacket, but it was a whole lot less silly than her displaying her war wounds to the roomful of people. He felt bad about that. Bad but also perversely satisfied that he'd marked her somehow.

Because dammit, she'd done something to him.

Sex for him was easy. A quick road to satisfaction. And it had never much mattered to him who it was with. He liked his partners, but he didn't need them. He needed Kate. Had woken up every night since she'd kissed him aching, with a hard-on that wouldn't quit. And fantasies that would only take the shape of her.

He would have been pissed about it if it didn't feel so good. He had no clue how the hell this woman had taken on this new form. To slip beneath his bedcovers, to slip beneath his skin.

It was the slow shift. Because he'd never put distance between himself and Kate, had never believed he might need to. So he'd had no defenses in place when she moved in for that kiss.

When she'd been all covered up in dirt and clothes and a scowl, she'd been Connor and Eli's little sister. But now that she'd smiled at him, kissed him, stripped for him, he'd seen the whole woman. And then it hadn't mattered anymore. Who she was related to, what they might think. She mattered. On her own. She was every inch herself. All strength, dreams and meanness when she got poked too many times. In bed she was fire. Unschooled, uncontained.

Now in his mind she stood alone, not attached to anyone else. She wasn't just a woman; she was a whole storm. Too much to be simply someone's sister.

It was a damn shame that he couldn't reach out and uncover all that again. That he had to stand here and pretend she was just Eli and Connor's sister when the secret was out and he knew different.

Kate stepped deeper into the barn, getting caught up in a group that contained some of the people from the amateur association. He held back, in part because he wanted to be near Sierra West like he wanted a screwdriver to the scrotum, and in part because he didn't want to stand near Kate and pretend.

Not right now.

Not while it was all still raw. Not while his blood was still hot and he could still feel her on his skin.

"Now it's just you." Jack jumped and turned as Connor clapped a hand on his shoulder. "Well, and Kate."

Discomfort wound its way through him. "Uh... what?"

"You're still single. You're the last holdout. Kate isn't really a holdout yet. She's just a kid."

Jack bristled. "She's not really a kid."

"She damn well is. And that's good, as far as I'm concerned. Better to be young when you're young and... whatever."

"Are you drunk?" Besides the occasional beer, Connor had given up drinking a little over a year ago.

"No. Just thinking. I want you to find someone."

Jack nearly choked. "Uh. Thanks. I'm fine. Without."

"You think you are, but come on, all the whoring around has to get old."

A sweet, illicit memory of recent "whoring" flashed through his mind. Made instantly ten times more awkward by the fact that he was standing in front of his partner's brother. "No. It really doesn't. I know that was never what you were into. I respect that. But... I don't want marriage and babies and domesticity. It's not me."

"Yeah." Connor's gaze drifted off and Jack followed his friend's line of sight. To Kate.

"She was cold," Jack said, knowing he sounded defensive. But she was standing there in a jacket, and he was without one, so he felt as though he had to throw in an explanation.

"You've always helped take care of her," Connor said. "I appreciate that. I was always busy on the ranch, and Eli had to pick up all the house and Kate slack. Sometimes I think I should have done more."

"Oh, hell, Connor. When? You were a kid and you were running a ranching operation while your dad soaked his liver in booze." Jack looked away from Kate and back to his friend.

"Still. I worry about her. A hell of a lot more than I worry about you."

"She's tough," Jack said, his throat getting tight, his heart suddenly too large for his chest.

"She is. But she reminds me of a spooked horse. They're scary. Tough. Could mess you the hell up. But they're afraid. Afraid to let you touch them."

"Because not every horse needs to be broken," he said, feeling as if the analogy, which was bad to start with, had broken down completely.

"She's pretty amazing when she's wild."

Another image. Kate with her head thrown back while he thrust deep inside her tight little body...

"She sure is," Jack said, knowing that if he hadn't been hell bound before, he was now.

"But I don't want her to be alone. I don't want to think we messed up so bad she couldn't...have this," he said, indicating the decorations, the event around them.

"Maybe she doesn't need this. Maybe she just needs barrels and some dirt. That's happiness, too."

Connor let out a long sigh. "I suppose. I think sometimes you see her a little bit more clearly than any of us. You were always able to cheer her up when she was a kid."

Jack waited for the guilt, but he didn't feel any. Yeah. His conscience was seared like flesh stuck in a fire. To the point where he didn't feel a damned thing.

Hell. He was going to hell.

"But you gave her stability," Jack said, making a belated and weak attempt at atonement. "And she should believe in love and commitment, because you and Eli gave her that. You gave it all up for her. I just came by and made jokes when shit was tough. There's a difference. You both stayed. And you're still here. If she doesn't end up with anyone, it'll be because she chose it, not because you did anything wrong."

As far as inspiring speeches went, it wasn't bad. It also wasn't his to make. Because he had a feeling if things went south with Kate at any point after this, it would be his fault. That if she didn't end up with a guy, it would be his fault.

Ten-gallon ego you got there, Monaghan.

Yeah. But it was because she'd been a virgin. Because he was the first. If he fucked up, then he would pave a bad road for the bastard who came after him.

A small evil part of him was satisfied by that thought. He wanted things to be hard for the bastard who came after him. He wanted to kill the bastard who came after him and he didn't care whether that was fair or whether or not it made sense.

If he didn't want forever, he couldn't fault everyone who would come once they were over.

But he did.

Because her kisses were for him. Her body was for him.

If she could get a look at his thoughts right now, she would tie him to the train tracks, but he didn't care.

Connor was looking at him funny. "Why are you single?"

"What the hell, man?"

"I mean, that was a good speech. If I was half that good at making speeches, Liss would want me dead a lot less often."

"I'm single because I'm good in small doses. Like I just said. I'm not the guy who stays." He let out a long breath and his gaze drifted over to where Eli and Sadie were just leaving the dance floor. "Speaking of, I think the couple is about to leave."

"Well, then, let's go send them off."

CHAPTER FIFTEEN

KATE DIDN'T WASTE any time getting Roo into the trailer after work. She'd hooked it up to the truck before leaving, and now she was ready to spend the afternoon with Jack.

Practicing her barrel racing, specifically. And also planning the charity event.

Okay, and the sex.

She had spent only a little bit of extra time laboring over her underwear selection. Black. Black cotton was the sexiest she had. She needed to remedy that. Practical underwear took on a whole new meaning when their primary objective wasn't simply not riding up your ass crack. Seduction added a new dimension to panty requirements.

And since seduction panties looked as if they would do just that, she was thinking she'd need seduction panties and everyday panties.

Being a woman was exhausting. She bet Jack was just going to stick with the one kind of underwear.

Her internal muscles clenched unexpectedly as she thought of just how he filled out said underwear.

She blinked and revved the engine on the truck, pulling forward to the long driveway. Her old truck bounced and groaned over the potholes until she turned out onto the two-lane highway. It still groaned as it rolled over the asphalt, but it bounced less.

Sex was a whole thing, she was discovering. She hadn't given it a whole lot of thought before she'd had it, and now she seemed to ponder it a lot. Along with underwear.

She'd known sex would change things between herself and Jack—she wasn't an idiot, even if she was innocent—but she hadn't realized sex would change so much of what she thought about.

That it would change the context of simple things like underwear.

She turned left off the highway and onto Jack's property. A wooden frame arched up over the road, an iron sign hanging down that read Monaghan Ranch.

Every time she came here, she was in awe all over again. About what he'd accomplished with his life. About how far he'd come.

So far from his days in a single-wide buried in the brush by the sea. She'd been to his house only once, and she'd waited in the car on Eli's orders.

She'd been little, but she remembered. She'd rolled down the windows and taken a good look at the little yellow mobile. Stained by salt, moss climbing the side, a product of the eternal dampness.

The smell of cigarettes had soaked through the walls, pushing on to the driveway, combatting the brine-and-seaweed scent that lay heavy in the air.

Bleak, washed out, so unlike the young man she knew. It had made her wonder where Jack got all his humor. Because he certainly hadn't collected it on the dirty, bramble-covered beach near his house.

This ranch, the place he had built for himself, was

much more in keeping with who he was. A little bit over the top, a little bit showy, but functional, and pure country. She drove past the house, headed toward the arena. Jack was already there, facing away from her, his arms spread wide, hands rested on the top rail of the fence. She took a moment to admire that broad chest, narrow waist and very, very fine ass.

An ass she had touched.

She couldn't hold back the smug smile that pulled at the edges of her mouth.

She put the truck in Park, killed the engine and took the keys out of the ignition, hesitating for a second before opening the door and climbing out. "Hey," she said, walking over to where he stood.

He turned, a blue flame flickering in his eyes for a moment. "Hey."

For a moment she wasn't sure what to do. Her instinct was to launch herself at him and kiss him, but she wasn't sure if that would be okay. She wasn't really sure what the protocol was for a temporary sexual arrangement with your brothers' best friend. And then she figured she didn't really care. Because this was only temporary. And anyway, she and Jack had already waded through a whole swamp of awkward. If emphatic greetings weren't acceptable they would talk about it. And it couldn't possibly be more of a minefield than previous discussions.

She picked up her pace and closed the distance between them, wrapping her arms around his neck and stretching up on her tiptoes, kissing him as deep and long as she wanted. Jack put his hands on her hips and held her steady while she explored his mouth. The slow glide of his tongue against hers, the warm firmness of his lips.

She slipped her hand from around his neck, sliding her fingertips across his jaw, his stubble rough beneath her fingertips.

She pulled away, rubbing her nose against his, following some instinct she hadn't known she'd possessed. "You remind me of a sexy outlaw," she said, then kissed him quickly again.

He arched a dark brow. "An outlaw?"

That question knocked a bit of the shine off that perfect moment of clarity and confidence she'd just experienced. For a while she had been convinced that there was nothing she could do wrong. Now she was questioning that. She was a novice, after all. A novice who still possessed nothing more than cotton panties of the most demure variety.

"Yeah," she said, her tone less certain now. "Because... kind of...dark and dangerous. And..."

He cupped the back of her head and pulled her in for a hard kiss. "Dangerous?"

"Stop making me feel silly."

"You shouldn't feel silly. I like hearing what you think about me. It's a lot better than having you snipe at me."

She pulled away from him, snorting. "I do not snipe."

That earned her a smack on the butt. She yelped and rubbed the spot he'd just made contact with. It didn't hurt. If anything, she liked it. "You snipe."

"If I do, you deserve it."

"Honestly, I like talking to you rather than just circling you. I feel like that's what we've been doing for a while."

Kate took hold of her own hand and started picking at the dirt beneath her thumbnail. "Maybe. But it was pretty off-putting to realize I wanted to kiss you more than I wanted to punch you."

"Out of curiosity, when did you realize that?"

She dug deeper beneath her nail, putting most of her focus and energy onto that task. "I don't know if I fully realized it until after."

"After we kissed?"

"After we had sex." She cleared her throat. "Before that, I was still on the fence about whether or not kissing would be more satisfying than punching."

A strange smile turned up the corners of his mouth. "But sex officially tipped you over."

She dug harder at her thumbnail, then realized she was standing there picking dirt out from under her nails in front of her lover. Reflexively, she grimaced and put her hands down at her sides. Her lover. Jack was her lover. Having a lover was weird enough; having it be Jack was weirder still. Or maybe not. She couldn't actually imagine assigning that label to anyone else.

"Well, you presented a convincing argument."

"Did I?"

"Yeah. Your um…body made a very convincing argument."

"Stands to reason. My dick did very well on the debate team in high school."

"Debate? I would have thought that PE was more your dick's forte."

"Possibly. Though my member is very convincing. Even without words."

This was weird, talking about more intimate things in a tone they would have used prior to actually having experienced anything intimate together. A strange mixture of old and new.

"Well, as difficult as it is to believe, Monaghan, I did not come here to discuss your penis, or the virtues thereof. I came here to ride."

"That begs the question if we're still on the subject of my manhood, or you actually brought a horse in the trailer."

"I brought a horse. And if you don't behave yourself when I'm done riding Roo, I might not *ride* you."

"I don't believe that, baby."

Kate's heart fluttered and she rolled her eyes, mainly at herself, but she was content to let Jack believe that the expression was directed at him.

"Your ego is stunning."

"It is, isn't it? I'm glad you notice, because I just got it resized."

"Did you?"

"Yes, it's gone up about three sizes ever since Ms. Kate Garrett decided it was better to kiss me than punch me."

How did he do that? It was a stupid thing to say. Arrogant and obnoxious. And yet somehow it made her feel all warm inside.

"Well, Kate Garrett giveth, and Kate Garrett taketh away. I'm expecting you to coach me through a few runs on the course first. Otherwise, I will have to leave you with nothing but a shrunken ego."

"Shrinkage is never good. Get your pony out, and let's do this."

She shot him a deadly look before turning, heading back toward the trailer and opening it up. She readied Roo and led her out, the horse's hooves clopping on the ramp that went down to the gravel, where the sound changed to a muted crunch. Kate brought her to the arena and looped the lead rope over the fence before opening up the side of the trailer and setting out to get her tack ready.

"Roo is not a pony, just so you know."

"Thoroughbred. I know. I was being an ass."

"You *should* know, Mr. Rodeo. I'm counting on the fact that you have actual expertise to help me through all of this."

"I do, I promise you. Not just from the rodeo." He hesitated and she looked at him. He reached back and rubbed his hand over the back of his neck. "You know, the breeding operation is going really well."

She was tempted to say something in the same smart-ass vein as he just had. To banter back. But somehow she sensed it wasn't the time. He was looking for something.

Approval. Her approval.

Which was strange, because she had never thought of Jack as needing approval from anyone, least of all her. And yet it was there in his voice. She couldn't deny it. And she wouldn't deny him.

She offered him a smile, continuing her work on Roo. "This whole place is amazing." She turned her focus back to Roo's tack. "And I've never liked all this talk about luck where you're concerned. I've never seen anyone work as hard as you and change their position in life so drastically."

He shrugged, a halfhearted laugh on his lips. "I only moved about five miles down the road. Not sure that counts as changing position."

"You did," she said, thinking about that washed-out trailer again.

"I think you're the only one who sees it that way."

"Well, everyone else is an idiot. I'm pretty confident in that assessment."

"One of the many things I like about you."

Kate tightened the girth on Roo's saddle and straightened. "Okay, I'm riding right now. So I guess you just stand there and yell at me if I do a bad job?"

"Yeah, I can handle that."

Kate mounted Roo and rode her over to the open gate, staring down the course with determination. She remembered the last ride. The one that Jack had walked away from. The one she'd never seen the time for, because her timekeeper had taken off after the angry kiss.

She had been thinking of *him* during that ride. Not about success, not about failure, but about Jack.

Of course, thinking about Jack was as natural as breathing.

She took a deep breath, made her mind a blank space until she saw nothing but the barrels in front of her.

And then she went.

Her movements blended with Roo's body, adjusting to the rhythm. It felt easy to slide into it, to follow the leads of Roo's movements. And she felt that in turn Roo followed hers.

Kind of like kissing. She hadn't known what she was doing, but paying attention to the subtle way Jack moved his lips, flicked his tongue, had made following along intuitive.

This was similar in a way. Required an awareness of her whole body so that she could sense subtle shifts and respond with perfect control.

Memory blended with the present, memory of what it had been like to be pressed up against Jack only a few moments ago, her muscles languid as she let arousal roll over her. Every touch, every taste, every shift of his hands working together.

And before she knew it, she had rounded the last barrel. Nothing was knocked over, and nothing felt slow.

"Holy shit!" She didn't bother to hold back the exclamation. "It was good."

"Yeah, it was," Jack said, smiling. He was holding a stopwatch that he hadn't shown her before, and he looked at the time. "Damn good, Katie."

"One more?"

He nodded. "Do one more, and then we'll get on with this charity stuff."

And get on with the rest of their afternoon together.

He left the rest of it unspoken, but she heard it all the same.

The second run was as successful as the first, and Kate was on a high by the time they sat down in Jack's living room with the details of the charity rodeo day spread out in front of them.

Kate picked up one of the spreadsheets, reading the extensive list of business names. "I can't believe you got all these vendors confirmed."

Jack leaned back on the couch, his hands behind his head, displaying his extremely tantalizing biceps, thanks to his very tight black T-shirt. Another thing about sex. It made her think of words like *tantalizing*. Usually words like that were reserved only for pie.

"Lydia had a hand in it—I can't take all the credit. Plus, Eileen has been on top of things. And Ace is overly generous. When Ace gets involved with something, the other business owners tend to follow. Plus, the guy is always willing to donate beer, and that is about the most valuable thing I can think of."

They were both sitting on the couch, with about a foot of space between them, trying to keep focus on the task at hand. Kate wanted to close the space and press her body against his. Just so she could touch him. Though like the "kiss or not to kiss?" dilemma from earlier, that wasn't strictly sex, either.

The spreadsheets for the charity event were working so well she was considering suggesting making a spreadsheet of the particulars of their arrangement. An arrangement was all it was, really. It wasn't a relationship, that much was certain.

Which meant she was going to go ahead and speak the words that were rolling around in her head, making her tongue restless. Because before they'd started doing *stuff* together, she would have spoken them.

She looked up at him. "If you didn't minimize your contributions to everything, maybe people wouldn't think all of your achievements were dumb luck." As soon as she spoke the words, she realized how accurately they described Jack.

He was quick to extol the virtues of Connor and Eli, to remind her of everything they had done for her, and yet he never brought up all the ways he'd been there. In fact, when she tried, he often changed the subject.

And now he wouldn't even accept a compliment for the event that he had inspired.

He shrugged, leaning forward, the casual gesture exposed for the lie it was by the tension in his jaw. "I'm being honest. I'm not the kind of guy who has to trumpet his own achievements. I know a lot of people assume I am, but I'm not."

It hit her then what a funny mix of things Jack was. He had an easy kind of cockiness, and only moments ago she had accused him of having a massive ego. But when it came to important things, he was quick to shift the credit.

In contrast, he never shifted blame.

He was quick to call himself a bastard or a jackass or any other derogatory name, all while laughing it off. She wasn't quite sure why.

"Jack, it's more than that," she said, her tone grave.

He raised his brows. "Listen to you, missy. Pulling rank now like you gained a decade on me instead of being one down. Why? Just because we've…"

"Shut up," she said. "I'm serious. If you're going to be an ass just because I stepped into some thorny business, then shut the hell up right now. I'm not in the mood to listen and separate out what you said just because I scared you and decide what should offend me."

"Scared?" he asked, his tone incredulous.

"Yes. Scared. You know how I know it's scared?" She didn't wait for him to answer. "Every time I took a shot at you, it was because I was scared. Of what you made me want. Of what you made me feel. I was so scared I shoved it down deep enough that I couldn't recognize what it was. So scared I never let myself think the word *want*. But it didn't change the fact that I felt it. And you know what? It's better this way. Brought up to the top and dealt with. Naked and…and…and raw and real. It's better than pretending it isn't there."

He was silent for a moment. Then he leaned back, his gaze assessing. Dark. "But in your scenario you got sex instead of sexual frustration. What will I get?"

She gnawed on the inside of her lip. "Release? From…issues?"

He snorted and shook his head. "Right. Because you're so into talking about your feelings?"

She frowned. "What do I need to talk about my feelings for? I'm fine."

"So am I," he said.

She rolled her eyes. "We just had a discussion about the not fine."

"You had a discussion. You drew conclusions. All on your own. I think it's bullshit."

She stared him down, that familiar feeling of uncontrollable determination gripping her, anchoring itself deep in her gut. When she had that feeling, backing down wasn't an option. Ever. Sometimes it got her in trouble.

It had earned her a scar on her shoulder blade when John Norton had dared her to walk the top of a fence like a tightrope back in second grade. And right now who knew what it would get her. But in the moment the consequences never mattered. Only the win.

"Jack…"

He looked back down at the papers in front of him, pen in hand, discussion clearly closed.

Her anger reached its peak, and there was no one left to help Jack Monaghan now except for God. And she doubted Jack would ever even ask *him* for help.

Jack would never ask. And he was apparently done listening.

Fuck. That.

She gripped the hem of her T-shirt and stripped it up over her head, that bullheaded determination steering the ship now. And now that it was, there would be hell to pay.

It just remained to be seen whether hell would bill Jack or her.

She reached back and unhooked her bra, then let it fall to the floor with a soft thump. That garnered Jack's focus.

His blue eyes connected with hers, then lowered, heat flaring bright and hot in their depths. For a moment she lost the thread of her intentions completely. She could only stand there and bask in her newfound power.

She'd always been strong. Hell, she'd been able to beat up every boy in her class before they started growing body hair. She was tough, and no one had ever questioned that. She hadn't, either.

But this power? This was new. This was different.

Her body had the power to turn some kind of tide inside the infamous Jack Monaghan. To take him from anger, to take him from purposefully ignoring her to looking at her with the kind of keen focus she'd never seen him train on anything.

She'd known there was power in strength. In a closed fist and a quick tongue. In the ability to ride faster than the boys, fix the fence with better skill. But she hadn't realized how much power there was in her body. In its softness, its innate being. No walls up, no clothes on. No front of bravado or show of toughness.

She'd already realized that she'd discovered a hidden layer of Jack, a deeper level of who he was. In this moment she realized she'd found the same in herself.

She took a step toward him and pressed her knee down beside his thigh on the couch before following suit with the other, sitting on his lap, facing him. "Is that paper still more interesting than what I have to say?"

His eyes flickered downward. "No. But now you

have the issue of what you have to say not being quite as interesting as how you look."

Completely against her will, a smile tugged at the corners of her lips. "I've heard women complain about that, but I don't think I've ever had that problem. It's certainly an interesting one."

"I'm being offensive. At least have the decency to get mad at me." He reached up and cupped one of her breasts as he spoke, teasing her nipple with his thumb.

"Can't," she said, her voice thin now, breathless. "It's impossible to be mad at you when you do that."

"That's interesting," he said, flashing a wicked smile at her. "Makes a man want to try."

He wrapped his arm around her, planting his palm between her shoulder blades, holding her steady as he let his other hand drift down to her stomach, all the way down to the waistband of her jeans.

"Somehow I don't think you're trying to make me mad."

"No. But I might be trying to change the subject." He flicked the button on her jeans open and drew the zipper down slowly.

"And I might allow it. For now." She had achieved one portion of the victory she'd been aiming for. She hadn't allowed him to push her away. So she would stick a little flag in that and claim it as a triumph for Kate Garrett.

It was either that or she was weak.

She didn't really care which it was at the moment.

He slipped his hand down between the fabric and her skin, his fingertips teasing the edge of her underwear. His expression changed, the mischief, the wickedness gone, replaced by that intense focus he'd treated her to earlier. As all-consuming as the things he made her feel were, as intense and wonderful as it was when he dipped his fingers beneath the fabric of her panties, gliding through her slick folds. Watching the intensity on his face as he set about the task was almost more compelling. Almost.

His touch set her on fire, created a deep, restless ache, the impression of a spark that was about to burst into flame.

She touched his stomach, hot and unbelievably hard, pushing the hem of his shirt up before pulling it resolutely over his head. It forced his hands away from her body, but it was a small price to pay to earn the pleasure of seeing him.

Of giving herself another chance to look at him and really feel what it did to her. Rather than trying to push it down, rather than getting angry, rather than acting disgusted. She had spent so long pretending because she hadn't been able to deal with what it meant. That gnawing, beastly ache in her stomach that seemed to appear whenever Jack was around. It grew more intense when he lifted something heavy or stripped down to nothing more than his jeans.

She remembered, vividly, when he'd done that during the rebuilding of Connor's barn. The show she'd put on about being irritated that he was showing off.

No wonder Liss had figured it out. With hindsight, with less innocence, Kate could see her own excuses for the paper-thin constructs they were.

"You've gone very still," Jack said. "Either there's a rabid wolverine behind my head about to attack, or you're thinking."

"Wolverine. Stay perfectly still if you value all of

your body parts." He went still beneath her hands, his muscles tensing. She leaned in, kissing his neck, angling her head and biting his ear.

"I'd say I have to worry more about the badger-cat than the wolverine," he said, his voice rough.

"It's true. I am fearsome." She pressed her mouth to his, then nipped his lower lip.

She reached between them, making quick work of his belt, opening his jeans, then pulling his underwear down to reveal the package beneath. He shifted, raising his hips and reaching behind him, digging in his back pocket until he produced his wallet. "Very important," he said as he opened it and fished out a condom.

"Very."

He took care of the necessities, his jeans only partway down his hips still since she hadn't ceded her position on his lap. "Katie. I'm desperate." He sounded it. And she would have been lying if she said she didn't like that.

She stood, getting rid of the rest of her clothes before moving back to him, over him. She waited for nerves, for uncertainty. She'd never done this before, and it was putting a lot of the control into her hands when their other two times Jack had firmly led the way. But her nerves didn't show. The confidence she had found in a fleeting moment during their kiss outside, and more permanently when he'd demonstrated just how much she affected him, held fast.

She put her hands on his shoulders and rose up on her knees, adjusting her position carefully, reaching down and taking hold of his thick arousal and guiding it slowly inside of her body as she lowered herself onto him. He wrapped one arm around her waist, anchoring her, and reached up, gripping her chin between his thumb and forefinger, tilting her face down, forcing her to meet his eyes.

Jack was big on eye contact, and that was another thing that sent a wave of satisfaction through her. He wasn't tuning her out, concentrating only on the physical feeling. He was forging a connection between them. Far from denying that she was the woman he was with, the way he looked at her, with such focus, proved that he was embracing this. That he wanted her, not just the way sex made him feel.

She moved above him, trying to recall the way he did things when he set the pace. The speed and pressure at which he seemed to lose control. She rocked forward and he released his hold on her chin, moving his hands to grip her hips, holding her steady without taking the control.

"Is that okay?" she asked, breathless, barely able to force the words out.

He didn't say anything. His only response was to kiss her, deep and savage, none of his skill or carefully learned moves on display. But it was okay. She liked it. Jack was all around her, in her. And she was more than happy to be consumed, by him, by this. By the firm grip of his hands on her hips, his lips, his teeth, his tongue. And those blue eyes that looked into hers, unflinching, uncompromising.

Emotion expanded in her chest, blending with the pleasure unfurling in her stomach, both of them bleeding out and meeting the other, mixing together until they were one and the same. It was so all-consuming, so very much, that she could barely breathe.

And all the feelings down deep beneath that layer

she had uncovered today rushed up inside her. It was too much, too much for a woman who had only just discovered that all of this existed within her. And now she was being pelted with it, like raindrops, hard and sharp, threatening to break through her skin in the downpour.

And the only thing keeping her from succumbing, from being completely destroyed, was those blue eyes. Familiar where everything else was so foreign.

"Jack." She hadn't meant to say his name out loud, but she was beyond thought, beyond control.

His grip tightened as he began to meet her thrust for thrust. And then she lost the thread of who was in control and who wasn't. It was equal, a joint pursuit. Him following her, her following him, each of them recognizing what the other needed, what the other wanted.

His movements became erratic, rough, pulling her body down on his as he thrust up to meet her. He moved one hand from her hip and placed it on her cheek, drawing her down nearer to him and kissing her throat, his teeth scraping over her delicate skin. She tightened her hold on his shoulders, bracing herself as he flexed his hips one last time, pushing her from the outskirts of the storm into the center of the tornado.

It roared over her, in her, through her, but Jack held her steady. Even while his own release shook his frame, he held her.

When it was over, she raised her head, half expecting to look around the room and find furniture upended, papers scattered everywhere. But everything was the same. Even the spreadsheets they'd been looking at before were in their place, completely undisturbed by what had just passed between them. It didn't seem possible. The disconnect between what had happened inside of her and the state of the room was too sharp for her to process.

He patted her thigh and somehow she recognized it as a signal he needed her to move. She complied. He disappeared from the living room and returned a few moments later with his jeans done back up and the protection taken care of. She hadn't bothered to get dressed again. Instead she took the blanket that was draped over the back of the couch and pulled it over her body.

He returned to the couch, sitting next to her, his denim-clad thigh pressed against her blanket-covered knee. She wanted to say something, to use words to connect them now that their bodies were separated. She poked at the woven elk on the blanket, considering, flashing back to the conversation they'd been having right before they'd stopped talking altogether.

"I don't remember our mother at all." The words slipped out before she'd fully committed to speaking them. Jack had that effect on her. Always had. "Sometimes I think maybe that's a good thing. How can you miss something you don't even remember?" She swallowed hard, her throat getting tight. She resented the emotion that was creeping over her. It was messing with all of the good things Jack had just made her feel. And she didn't like feeling anything on the subject at all. "But…at least if I had a memory, it would be clear. The pain, I mean. Instead it's just this weird ugly black hole that opens up inside of me sometimes. At the strangest moments. Not on Mother's Day or anything like that. Just sometimes when I see a woman taking care of a child. I remember one time I saw a little girl pestering her mother in the store, and the woman looked so tired. And she was frustrated, it was obvious. Obvious that parenting wasn't easy or fun all the time. But she was there, Jack. She stayed. And I... I just stood there staring. Wondering why my mom couldn't stay for me. I don't have an image of her in my mind, nothing specific to even be angry at. But sometimes I am." She cleared her throat. "I don't even feel like I have the right to be. Eli and Connor gave up everything to take care of me. They are the ones that should be angry. I didn't lack for much, because of the way they handled things. Why should I feel sad at all?"

She searched his face, because part of her really wanted an answer to that question.

Jack was staring straight ahead, his jaw clenched tight, his gaze distant. "The way I figure, if people have a right to leave, if they have the right to never show up at all, we have the right to be as angry as we want to be. Appreciating what Connor and Eli did for you doesn't mean you can't be hurt by why they had to do it."

"Are you angry?" she asked, the question almost a whisper.

"All the time."

She studied his profile. Strong, visually perfect. Straight nose, square jaw, dark brows and a fringe of lash that somehow never, ever made him look feminine. He appeared to have it all together. He seemed happy, carefree. Her brothers had often commented that Jack never had to try, that good things fell in his lap, that luck followed him around like a slobbering puppy.

But he was angry. And in that moment she saw it. In the hard lines of his face, the tension in his muscles. *All the time.*

He was angry all the time.

"You don't show it," she said, her words strangled.

"You don't show yours, either."

"I don't feel like I deserve it." She sucked her lower lip between her teeth. "How would it make Eli and Connor feel if they knew…?"

"Screw them, Kate." He turned to her, his eyes blazing. "This isn't about them. Your feelings aren't about them."

"But they—"

"Right. They're wonderful. And they love you and they cared for you, but shit, that doesn't mean that everything was fine. It doesn't mean that being raised by your teenage brothers was as good as two functional parents would have been. Of course you're angry. Of course you are."

He spoke with such strength, such conviction, and she knew that beneath those words, that vein of anger running through them, was rage for himself.

She had a feeling she would have to show hers first. That he needed permission to let his out. Well, hell, so did she. So maybe they could give that to each other.

"I am angry," she ground out, "because…because my mom left and what the hell was I supposed to do when I needed a bra? Or…or pads or tampons or whatever? Ask my brother's wife. Ask a school nurse." She should have been embarrassed, but she was too upset to feel embarrassed. She had never talked to anyone about this before, had barely let herself feel it. "I sure as hell wasn't going to talk to my drunk dad. Sometimes Eli and Connor would need him to pick me up from something. And he would…get drunk and forget. I remember being in junior high and sitting there waiting. Teachers just look at you all sad and kids wonder who gets forgotten. What must be wrong with you."

"He was a drunk, Katie. That's why he forgot."

Her throat became impossibly tight, an ache spreading down from her chin to her chest, blooming outward. "I don't think he really forgot."

"Of course he did."

She shook her head. "No. I think he hated me. I think he was punishing me." She felt as though she'd just ripped back the skin on her chest and exposed a dark, ugly secret that lurked beneath. Exposed all her blood and organs and a darkness she'd never wanted anyone else to see.

"Why would you think that?" Jack asked. And she was glad he hadn't tried to tell her she was wrong.

"I reminded him of her. Not because I looked like her, but because I was... I was the reason she left. I was an accident. The kid they weren't supposed to have. The one that tipped it over into being unmanageable. The one that made her leave." Her voice broke and she forgot to be horrified by the show of emotion. "I'm the one who made her leave."

Jack leaned in, folding her up into his strong arms, holding her against his bare chest. "You didn't make her leave. Best argument she could make in her defense is that her demons chased her away. Though in my experience, demons like you where you're at. The better to torment you. She walked with her own two feet, and nobody made her. Certainly not a two-year-old girl who deserved her mother. There was nothing for you to earn, Kate. That's the kind of thing we're supposed to be given from the moment we come into the world. The love of our parents. I've earned a lot of bad things in life based on my own actions. But I didn't earn my father's abandonment. Not right at first."

"Are you talking about when you met him? A few weeks ago."

She hadn't asked him about that. Not since that night. Because he hadn't brought it up, and she wanted to respect his silence. But they had gone somewhere past careful respect in the past few minutes. She was open; she was exposed. And she craved something similar from him. So that she didn't feel like she was alone, sitting here on his couch with her heart out in the open.

"I didn't know my father. I still don't. But I've known who he was since I was eighteen."

"You…you have? Do Connor and Eli know that? Does anyone know that?"

"No. Because I found out who my father was the day his attorney offered me a payoff to never tell anyone. They thought I knew. I didn't. But I took the money. And I signed their nondisclosure or whatever the hell it was. I paid to make myself disappear. I sold myself." She wished that she could see his face, but he was still holding her close. She wondered if the look in his eyes matched the bleak tone in his voice. "It wasn't luck that made me rich. It was my father."

CHAPTER SIXTEEN

JACK DIDN'T KNOW why he was sitting here opening a vein and bleeding all over Kate. Maybe because she had gone first. Because he wanted her to know she wasn't alone. Because for the first time he didn't feel alone.

A strange shift had happened in his life, and he could hardly figure out how or why. Eli and Connor had been his best friends for as long as he could remember having friends. And he'd never even been tempted to talk to them about this. In turn, they'd never spoken about the way they felt. With their mom leaving, their dad a drunk, their entire life focused on the responsibility of caring for Kate and the ranch. Of course they hadn't. They were men and men didn't talk about their feelings.

And he'd never had a long-term relationship with a woman. Never been in a situation where he wanted to talk to women about anything but which position they liked best.

Kate was different. She was different from those women, and she was different from a friend.

She was Kate. That was the beginning and end of it.

"Your dad gave you money in exchange for you... keeping yourself a secret?" Kate's tone was incredulous, and he couldn't blame her.

"Yes. And I took it. It was all the child support money my mother had refused all of our lives. And then some. I was so angry, Kate. So angry when I found out, because we had lived in that trailer that was falling down around us for all of my life. Because she wouldn't take his money. Because she had too much pride. She was disappointed to discover that I didn't suffer from the same problem."

"Is that why she...?"

"Why we don't speak? Why she moved into a different trailer about fifty miles away? Yeah, I think so." He laughed, leaning his head back, tightening his hold on Kate, suddenly very aware of the warmth of her body pressed against his. "I traded a lot of things for that money. My relationship with her. My fantasy of ever having a relationship with my old man. My fantasy that he was somehow decent, just unable to be with us for some reason. My self-respect. It's tough to feel proud about that kind of decision. So I felt like I better make damn sure I used that money well."

"That's why you ended up in the rodeo."

"Something I never would have been able to afford to get into otherwise. Without it, I don't know. I would probably be working at the gas station store or working as a hired hand for Eli and Connor. Sometimes I think that might've been better. There's a lot of honor in something like that. Working for every bit of what you have instead of getting ahead of the game by taking a handout."

"That isn't what you did. What your father had was yours."

He shrugged. "Is it? I mean, I get that legally he owed us a certain amount. I get that morally you could make the argument that what a parent has also belongs to their children. But I'm not sure that in reality it made his money mine."

"You were eighteen. Of course you took it. And you should have. Look what you got because of it!" She waved her hand around, indicating the large living room around them. The high ceilings with natural log beams running across them, the expansive windows that provided a view of the mountains, of the spread that Jack owned. His land. "You can't regret it. You achieved your goal. You made what you needed to."

"It doesn't always feel like it. I mean, I have all of this, and I'm happy to have it. I love my house. I'm proud of it. I'm not going to pretend that I'm somehow above the money, not when it's created the kind of life I always wanted. But I do wonder what would've happened if I had just told him to go screw himself. I think that's what my ranch is, honestly."

He was treading a dangerous line, one that risked violating legal papers he'd signed. He wasn't sure he cared. He prized this moment over any of that. This moment of honesty like he'd never had before.

"I'm still listening," Kate said, her way of asking for more.

"Nathan West is my father." He knew he didn't have to impress upon her how important it was she kept it a secret. Knew he didn't have to demand her silence, because she would give it. He believed that down to the core of his being.

She said nothing. She simply went perfectly still in his arms. He listened to the silence for a while. To the sound of her breathing, the tick of the clock that he never looked at on his wall. That the interior designer had insisted go there because that was the kind of thing that went in houses like this. He'd had to hire someone to put furniture, and the blanket Kate was currently wrapped in, in his house. Because he'd lived in a glorified cracker box and he hadn't known where to begin in terms of filling a house this size with things. In part because there were things for houses he hadn't even realized existed.

"Sierra flirts with you," Kate said, breaking the silence. "That is seriously messed up."

He laughed—he couldn't help it. Of all the things he'd expected her to say, that wasn't it.

"Oh my gosh," she continued, "what if you didn't know? This is a really small town. Sierra likes you. She would… If you didn't know…"

"Stop. Stop right there. You're turning this into an after-school special."

"I'm just saying."

"I'm sure he never thought it would be an issue. Seeing as I'm sure he never thought one of his daughters would ever want to slum it with me."

"How can he think that when he wanted your mother? And I don't mean that your mother is slumming it. I just mean that it's awfully hypocritical."

"Yeah, well. He's a hypocrite. A very comfortable hypocrite, by all appearances."

"You have brothers and sisters," she said, her tone muted.

He nodded slowly. "I traded them for this place, too."

"Well, I suppose, especially when you're eighteen, money means a whole lot more than half siblings who might be as terrible as your dad."

"That's about the size of it."

"What happens if you tell?"

"I have to give the money back."

"Can you?"

He stared straight ahead at a knot on the wooden wall. "Yes. I can. But I've been so focused on building a competing empire and messing with them I haven't really wanted to yet."

"You got his attention."

"I guess I did. I think maybe I even scare him." He swallowed. "It's less satisfying than I imagined it would be."

"Why?"

He laughed. "Good question. Maybe because it means my dad is a dick. And there's no alternate scenario, no outcome other than that. It just is what it is. And now I can't pretend different."

"If it helps, my dad is dead. And I lost the chance to yell at him."

"What's that supposed to help?"

She snuggled deeper against him. "I don't know. Misery loves company?"

"You're pretty good company."

"Good miserable company." She yawned and he wished that she could stay the night. He never wished women would stay the night. They never did. But he wanted her to. Because she was different. So he wanted to keep feeling different.

He took hold of a lock of hair, tugging it gently. "You're a pretty fantastic little misery, it has to be said."

She reached up and covered his hand with hers, slowly locking their fingers together before lowering them so their clasped hands rested on his knee. He wasn't one to sit still. He worked, and when he was with a woman, they went about their business, and then she left. Jack was only still when he was sleeping.

Except now. And he found he didn't want to do anything but sit here. It was the most productive bout of stillness he'd ever been a part of. Whether because of the words that had just been spoken or because of the calmness that came from sitting next to her, he didn't know. But it felt more substantial than a whole day of hard work.

"I suppose you should go," he said after the minutes had turned the hand on his largely ignored clock halfway around.

"Probably." She angled her head and he responded to the invitation, bending down and kissing her. They didn't have time for the kiss to be anything else, and there was something deeply sensual and desperate that he couldn't quantify in that. Kissing for the sake of kissing had gone extinct in his life once he'd lost his virginity. He was starting to think that had been some shortsighted stupidity on his part.

He let himself get lost in the softness of Kate's lips, the slow slide of her tongue, the little sighs that rested on the back of her indrawn breaths.

"I have to go. We're all having dinner tonight."

"I was invited, actually," he said, feeling a kick of guilt that he hadn't mentioned it before.

She looked at him, her expression hopeful. She wanted him around. It shocked him how much that assurance meant to him. "Are you going to come?"

"I don't have to. If it's weird."

"It's weird. But I would rather see you again than avoid the awkwardness."

"I think that's the best compliment I've ever gotten."

"Good." She kissed him again, then stood, holding the blanket around her body. "You better come." She started to collect her clothes and he grabbed hold of the edge of the blanket, tugging hard until he seized possession of it. She squeaked, holding her clothes to her chest as she scurried across the room toward the bathroom.

A smile tugged at the corners of his mouth. He wasn't quite sure how Kate managed to take him from one of the hardest subjects he'd ever talked about to smiling in the space of a few minutes. His smile broadened. Because he would see her again tonight, and that was about the best thing he could think of.

CHAPTER SEVENTEEN

IT WAS A fine day for a rodeo. She could only hope tomorrow was, too. The weeks had passed quickly, much more so than Kate had anticipated. The leaves had changed, dramatic red, orange and gold replacing the vibrant green. Though the mountains remained that particular shade of pine that earned the name *evergreen* with ease.

The day was crisp and clear, and vendors were setting up around the outside of the expo's indoor arena without fear of rain.

As she walked down to the gates where the competitors would assemble, her stomach flipped. A twitching feeling in her stomach like a horde of spiders skittering around overtook her for a second. She had to stop, pressing her palm flat against her midsection. She took a breath, in slow, out slow.

A few of them had volunteered to spend the night at the fairgrounds over the next four days, keeping an eye on the booths. Kate was one of the volunteers, and she had brought a small tent to put up near her horse trailer and the stall Roo would be in.

Tomorrow. Tomorrow was the competition. And even though it didn't count toward overall scores or earnings of any kind, it felt like a big deal to her. She was competing against Jessica Schulz, Sierra West, Maggie

Markham and basically anyone else who was considered a contender in barrel racing, professional or otherwise.

But as she stood there, nerves immobilizing her, she realized that she wasn't afraid to win anymore. She had been. She'd been afraid that wanting this was somehow disloyal, that wanting to leave was wrong. She'd been afraid to go off and create a life apart from Connor and Eli because they had invested so much of their lives in her.

But they were happy now. They had Sadie and Liss.

And Jack... Well, Jack had told her it was okay to be angry. She had been turning that over ever since. Thinking about all the implications. About the fact that maybe, just maybe, her life, her emotions were separate from theirs.

Such a small sentence, and yet it had echoed through her like a pebble tossed into a canyon.

"There you are. Sierra told me you were around." She turned around and saw Jack walking toward her. In a tight black T-shirt, a cowboy hat and jeans, the man was lethal.

A part of her had imagined that after such frequent exposure, particularly to his naked body, he would have less impact upon sight. That part of her had been very, very wrong. The T-shirt enhanced his muscles, reminded her of how strong he was, how it felt to be held in his arms. The jeans, hugging very relevant parts of him, reminded her of secrets about him that she knew intimately. His hat and the dark stubble on his jaw added to the outlaw fantasy. That was just for fun.

"Yes, I am standing here and processing nervous excitement."

"Oh yeah?" He rubbed his hand along his chin, the

sound of his whiskers scraping against his skin reso-
nating inside of her. "What are you nervous about?"

"I've never competed in a venue quite this spectacular. This is reserved for the pros."

"Reserved for you."

"Not quite."

"After this. You're going to turn pro after this."

She lifted her shoulder. "Maybe."

"If it's money, Katie, let me help." His blue gaze was
so earnest she couldn't be offended by the offer. Especially since she knew he would make it whether they
were sleeping together or not. Because Jack took care
of her. He always had.

Whatever his track record with past relationships,
Jack Monaghan had been faithful to her for about
twenty years.

"I have the money."

"Then we won't argue about it. I did find something
out you might be happy to hear."

She hopped in place, stirring up some of the fine
gray dust that surrounded the gravel on the ground.
"Tell me."

"Today's event is sold out to capacity. With the rental
fee waived for the day, that means we've raised well
above what we projected we might. Enough to make a
sizable donation to local battered women's shelters and
Alison's bakery, specifically to establish a training program for work experience."

Kate close the distance between Jack and herself and
wrapped her arms around him, pressing her body close
to his. He hesitated for a moment, then pressed his hand
to her lower back, squeezing her gently. She was tempted

to kiss him, but she knew that with so many people hanging around, it was a chance she couldn't take.

The realization made her chest ache, which was strange, because keeping it a secret hadn't felt like a problem before. She'd been fine with the fact that it was just between them. Perfectly happy to keep it a secret because it was never going to progress beyond where it was now.

So why did it feel as though it already had? Something had changed. Something in her, something in him. She didn't know what it meant. She didn't want to.

She pulled away from him. "I volunteered to spend the night tonight. Here, I mean. We won't have much time to be together this weekend."

They were still stealing moments in the afternoon when they could. Once, she had left much earlier than necessary for work and ambushed him on his way out the door to do chores. But in the interest of maintaining secrecy, neither of them had thought it would be a great idea to park at each other's places overnight. Sure, they could have circumvented that, but a lot of cloak-and-dagger would've had to be involved. And that was a lot of work to go to simply to spend the night together, when that was obviously taking a step deeper into the relationship than either of them were supposed to want.

"That's handy, because I volunteered to spend the night, too. But I didn't bring a tent," he said, his blue eyes intense.

"Well, if somebody asks where your tent is pitched, what are you going to tell them?"

"That when you're around, my tent is pitched in my pants?"

She snorted out a laugh, reluctantly amused. "Except no, you can't say that ever."

"Right. Because romantic declarations are off the table."

"That was not a romantic declaration."

"It's the best I've got."

She shoved him, a thrill rushing through her because she got to touch him again. He caught hold of her wrists, holding her steady. Another moment that was reminiscent of things they'd shared prior to their relationship becoming more. But now the playfulness was wired with electricity. She liked it.

Though on the heels of the electric shock came the concern that this would always be there. That going back to normal was the real fantasy.

She pushed that thought away, because she didn't have time to deal with it right now.

"In all seriousness, if anyone asks, I'll say I'm sleeping in my truck. But what I would like to do is sleep with you. Really."

"It's a tent."

"Then you will have to be quiet."

"Okay, Monaghan, but that means you're going to have to lower your game."

"On second thought, if anyone asks, in the morning we'll just say it was coyotes."

She narrowed her eyes. "I do not sound like a coyote."

"No. You sound like a badger-cat. But in fairness, most people won't be familiar with the call of the badger-cat." He reached toward her and pulled on her braid, the gesture entirely welcome now rather than irritating. She wondered if it had never really been irritating. "Don't be nervous. You're going to be amazing."

"Thank you."

"Just 'thank you'? Not 'thank you, asshole'? Or 'thanks, I couldn't have done it' without me?"

"No. Just thank you." She looked down below his belt buckle pointedly. "Now, are you just going to stand there pitching a tent, or are you going to help me with mine?"

"OKAY, I HAVE made the rounds. Thanks to no help from you," Kate said, climbing inside the tent and zipping it up tight before kneeling down next to where Jack was reclining.

"I'm being discreet."

"Oh, is that what you call it?" She pushed at his shoulder. "You sort of planned this thing. You might want to make a show of helping out."

He grinned at her, and her heart turned over. "I'm letting others have the glory now. And I'm protecting your reputation, Ms. Garrett. You should be thankful."

"I can protect my own reputation, thank you."

He frowned slightly. "All right, then, maybe I'm protecting me. Because people would want to run me out of town on a rail. Whatever the hell that means. Probably with pitchforks and torches."

She adjusted her position, lying down, resting her head on her hands. "You think so?" Of course, thinking of how Liss had reacted when she had imagined there was something going on between her and Jack, she had a feeling he was closer to the truth than either of them would have liked to believe.

"I have a certain reputation. And it's not unearned. I

won't pretend that I was chaste before we got together."
The way he said that, *got together*, made her stomach
turn over. "I've fooled around with a lot of women.
And people know that. Like I told you before, there
are some things that happened to me that aren't earned.
But I went out of my way to raise hell and now that I
would rather be known for something other than that,
the town hasn't exactly changed their perception of me
on a dime. Can't say that I blame them."

"Maybe not. But if I don't hold your past against you,
I wouldn't think it was anyone else's business."

He reached out and wrapped his arms around her,
pulling her up against his body. "One of the many things
I like about you. You see through my bullshit. No one
else does. No one else even tries."

"I've always seen through your bullshit." She smiled
and leaned in, kissing him.

They just looked at each other for a moment, and
then the light in his eyes changed, sharpened. "Are you
feeling brave?" he asked, his voice wicked.

"Is that a trick question, Monaghan? I always feel
brave." Such a lie, because her insides were quaking.
Had been for some time now. But in spite of her fear,
she wouldn't back down. She never did. Whether that
was a handicap or an asset, she wasn't certain.

"Brave enough to let me have you out here? All those
people who know us are just a canvas wall away. Seems
a little bit naughty."

His words sent a shiver through her body. She was a
lot of things. But naughty had never been one of them.

"I'm not...opposed to naughty."

"Good. I like that. But you're gonna have to try not to
scream my name when you come." His blue eyes were

electric, intense. "You're going to have to be very quiet. Do you think you can do that?"

She should have been appalled by his ego. Instead his words were pure heat, setting fire to her blood, making her insides melt like honey.

"You might have to give me something to bite on to," she said, not certain where the words came from. She was a different person when she was with Jack. Or maybe she was the same person. But she'd changed. Had found whole new parts of herself, things that she wanted that she'd never known before, things she could say, things she could do that she had never imagined she could.

She'd grown up without much female influence in her life. No one much to talk to about love and sex and flirting. She'd just imagined she wouldn't be much good at it.

The fact was, she was damn good at it. And she was extremely pleased with herself.

"I can give you something to bite," he said, a feral light in his blue eyes. "If you behave. Or don't." He assessed her slowly, sending a shiver through her. "This tent is a pretty cramped space. You're going to have to get naked for me. I can't wrestle around with your clothes without making a scene."

She snorted. "You've got to get naked for me. Tit for tat and all that shit."

"I love it when you talk dirty." Without hesitation, he stripped his T-shirt up over his head and set to work on his belt buckle.

Never one to be left behind, Kate undressed as quickly as possible, freezing when she looked up and saw Jack. Naked and so hot she was surprised he wasn't burning a hole through the tent wall. She still marveled at the sight of Jack's body, every damn time, but it was amazing how that awe combined with comfort. There was a familiarity to those acres of bare skin, the satisfaction of secrets known. Only to her, only to him.

She wasn't embarrassed to show him her body. She knew that he liked it. From every angle, no matter what. He had never given her a moment to be insecure about the fact that she wasn't soft or particularly chesty, because he was so quick to speak his appreciation. He had never once made her feel like he was comparing her to other women. Had never made her feel like she should compare *herself* to other women.

And even if she'd had men in her past to compare him to, she knew there would be no comparison. Not really.

"Damn," he said, the reverence in his tone reinforcing the confidence planted there and grown by him. "I have woven whole fantasies around what your body might look like, and I'm honored and a little bit surprised every time I get to see it. Every time I realize that you've let me know it so well."

Her face heated. "Same goes."

"You feeling adventurous?"

She frowned. "Depends on what you mean by *adventurous*. I'm not exactly in the mood to go climb a mountain. I'd rather fuck."

He laughed. "Well, that is what I had in mind. Not the mountain climbing. I just thought you might want to try something we hadn't."

Her scalp prickled. "Well, that depends, too."

He leaned in, his voice low, husky. "Trust me, Katie."

"I do." She realized how very true that was the moment the words left her lips. Jack had never given her a reason to doubt his word. He was reliable, dependable, another person in her life who had stayed.

If the town of Copper Ridge couldn't see that, if Nathan West couldn't see what a wonderful man his son was, then they were blind-ass idiots.

"Not sure I deserve your trust," he said, "but I'll take it. Which maybe says some bad things about me."

"You're only bad in a fun way."

"We'll see if you still think that in a few minutes. Get on your hands and knees. Show me your pretty ass."

Those words, those surprising, dirty words, sent an arrow of heat straight through her midsection that hit its target, fear rippling through the tailwind. But still, she didn't hesitate, stopping now never occurring to her.

She liked Jack like this, all rough and commanding, because she knew he got that way when she pushed him to the limit, pushed him straight to the edge of his control. She'd learned that she was never more in power than when Jack was making demands, and she knew that she could push that power, push his control, further by obeying him.

Strange, maybe. But she was discovering that the politics of sex were different from anything else.

She held her breath, waiting for his next move. A firm, warm hand slid across her backside, the friction over her skin hot, perfect. He moved his hand lower, teasing the entrance to her body with strong, blunt fingertips before pushing his finger deep inside of her.

She'd been with Jack countless times over the past weeks, and she'd started to think they'd done all there was. This was different. She couldn't see him, couldn't guess what might be coming next.

She heard him tearing a condom packet, knew that now he was rolling it over his thick length. She knew this routine well, knew just how long it took to go from grabbing the pack to protected to inside of her.

She held her breath and she waited, but he didn't do anything yet. He simply waited, one hand firm on her hip, the other moving between her legs, drawing the moisture from inside her body and sliding it over her clit.

That was one of the new sexy words in her vocabulary, added thanks to Jack and his very dirty mouth.

"You're ready for me, Katie," he said, his voice rough. "So wet. So hot."

"Yes," she whispered, "I'm ready."

He replaced his fingers with his cock, pushing inside slowly. This new angle of penetration was a revelation. She felt fuller, and he went deeper. And she saw stars. But she couldn't see his eyes. This was a departure from the way they typically made love, his gaze trained on hers as he thrust hard and deep.

She couldn't see him now; she could only feel him. The intense fullness of him being inside of her, the strength in his hold, the sound of his breath. There was familiarity in his rhythm, because she knew exactly the way that Jack moved to bring them both to orgasm.

This position should have felt more distant, but it didn't. If anything, it felt more intense, more intimate somehow, because it was up to her to know him by touch, by sound, rather than by sight. She did. She knew his body; she knew his strength. It was Jack. Only Jack.

It could only ever be Jack.

He shifted, bringing his hand forward to tease her

clit, intense, deep need riding through her as he did, bringing her closer and closer to climax.

Her arms were shaking from the exertion of holding herself up, because while she had strength from lifting bales of hay, demanding her muscles work properly while being subjected to this assault of pleasure was a bit much.

Unable to hold herself up any longer, she relaxed, lowering her upper body down to the sleeping bag, while Jack thrust hard into her from behind.

She pressed her face into the pillow and let it capture all of the sound she couldn't control as Jack propelled them both over the edge. Release roared through her, stars bursting behind her eyelids. Little pops of white light that burned bright before fading, leaving behind impressions of flashbulbs and fireflies.

His fingers dug deep into her hips and he froze behind her. Made a low, harsh sound, no concession being given to the fact that they were not in a soundproof environment.

Maybe, just maybe, the people around them wouldn't guess what that sound was. But she knew. She knew it intimately.

Jack. It's Jack.

He withdrew from her body, releasing his hold on her for a moment before tugging her up against him, his chest pressed against her back, his breathing hard and uneven. He held her like that until they had both settled a bit, the aftereffects of their climaxes fading slowly. Their muscles relaxing, sleep edging closer. It was an amazing thing to be so in tune with another person. To reach the heights at almost the same time and to come down together.

"Just a sec, baby."

Jack moved away from her, rustling around in his things for a moment before coming back to her. "I came prepared for contraceptive disposal," he whispered, his voice husky.

"You make it sound so classy," she whispered.

"You know me better than that." He kissed the back of her neck and pulled her more tightly against him, nestling her bottom up against him.

"Hell, Jack, you know *me* better than that."

He traced his fingertip down her arm. "Yes, I do."

"I'm glad that you don't have to leave."

"I'm glad I don't have to leave."

This felt right. Staying together, holding each other after they'd made love. Rather than both of them getting dressed hurriedly and her scurrying home. She had told herself that this would be awkward. But spending the night was unnecessary, because she hadn't known what to do with the steadily growing feeling that separating from him afterward was wrong. That growing sense of wrongness was... Well, it was *scary*. Because it proved what she wanted to deny. That whatever was happening between herself and Jack wasn't stagnant. It was growing; it was changing; it was moving forward.

Which was balls, because the sex was supposed to be a vehicle to help her move forward. They weren't suddenly supposed to be moving forward together.

She shivered and he moved his hand down to her stomach, so warm and perfect, strong. Firm. And she figured she would just let this moment be. It was hard to worry about the future when the present felt so nice.

She had been short on luxury in her life. She was a hard worker, and to the same degree she tended to ig-

nore sore muscles and fatigue, she ignored all too often
the velvet feel of grass under her feet and the perfect
warmth of the sun on her skin. She didn't get caught
up in the details.

But she was letting herself get caught up in this. In
the luxury of being held against Jack. The strength in
his arms, the warmth in his body, the sound of his heart
beating steadily behind her. That was better than grass
between her toes any day.

And it was a better way to earn sore muscles than
doing ranch work.

She rested her hand over Jack's and forgot to worry
about what any of this meant. For a while she was just
going to let herself have the luxury.

CHAPTER EIGHTEEN

JACK HAD WOKEN UP early the next morning, before anyone else, because it had been important that he get dressed and get his ass out of Kate's tent before anyone saw. Fortunately, he'd managed. He was starting to think she didn't much mind anybody finding out about them, but that wasn't the way to go about it. And there would be an order to things.

Which was a shame, because he really liked his balls where they were, and he wasn't entirely certain that Connor and Eli would let him keep them when the truth came out. But it would have to. The only other option would be ending things, and soon, because sneaking around wasn't doing it for him anymore. And he wasn't doing that. Ending it. No way in hell.

He hadn't wanted to get up. He'd wanted to lie there with her forever. Still. Calm. Tranquil.

The first time in his life he'd ever found peace in stillness. A revelation.

It was tempting to think, as he often did, that the feeling was an illusion of darkness. That with the sunrise, things would change. But the sun hadn't changed a damn thing. It'd just shone a light on them. Made it that much clearer.

He had something with her...something he'd never

had with anyone else. Something he'd never even imagined he wanted.

How had he ever thought she would leave things inside him the same as they'd always been? Kate Garrett was a gale-force wind, and he'd believed he could tangle with her and come out unchanged.

That was some kind of dumb arrogance.

He took a deep breath, trying to dispel the weight that was settling on his chest, and looked around. People were already filing into the fairgrounds, the first event starting soon. Thankfully for both his nerves and Kate, barrel racing was event number one. He had told her not to get worried and not to be nervous, but he couldn't follow his own advice. He wanted her to win. He wanted her to see what he saw. That she was good enough. More than good enough, she was brilliant.

She had the potential to be whatever she wanted. And sure, the idea of her going on the road with the rodeo was kind of a tough one. It would mean being separated. But that was just one more reason they needed to go ahead and figure out how they were going to navigate this relationship.

He felt like he'd been sucker punched. Relationship. Well, that was what it was. He had never before made a habit of spending the night with a woman. Had never spent multiple nights with the same woman. Maybe a few here and there, but not more than a month. He had never wanted to. But he wanted to hold Kate forever, and he supposed that meant it was a relationship.

He took a sip of his coffee and sighed as the hot, strong liquid slid down his throat. It was a fairly clear day for autumn but the air was still cool. A nice day for the events since neither horse nor rider would get as sweaty as usual.

Kate had already gone off to get ready and to get Roo warmed up, and he was trying to be inconspicuous and not hover over her. Since he had a feeling if he got anywhere near her, no one would confuse his attachment to her. He was most definitely more lover than older brother, and that much would be clear if anyone so much as saw him look at her.

He was loitering back by where the riders would come in, rather than going to the stands, because he figured however this shook out, Kate would need a big hug afterward. And he would be the one to give it to her.

His pocket buzzed and he reached into it, pulling out his phone. It was Eli. "Hello?"

"Are you at the fairgrounds?"

"Of course I am. Just ready to watch her ride." He didn't bother to specify who. And he realized that it was awfully familiar of him, but then, they were awfully familiar. Right now he couldn't bother with trying to act like it was different.

"Are you in the stands?"

"Nope. Hanging out by where they come in."

"Are you going to come and sit down?"

He cleared his throat, turning in the direction of the stalls. And he saw Kate walking toward the arena. She was wearing a pair of tight black jeans and a button-up shirt, also black, with little silver stars up by the collar. She had on her black cowgirl hat with the silver buckle on the band, her long dark hair in its usual braid.

Some of the other women had their hair loose, in bountiful curls, bright pink lipstick, turquoise and gold.

But Kate was the one who stood out to him. Kate shone the brightest. Because she was Kate. It was that simple.

"No," he said, his chest tight. "I'm going to stand back here. Just in case. I mean, I've been coaching her and stuff." It was a lame finish, he knew.

"Okay," Eli said, no concern in his tone at all. Which made him feel like kind of an ass. Because no matter how obvious he felt the relationship change with Kate was, Eli clearly suspected nothing. Because, of course, as far as Eli was concerned, there was just no chance of Jack ever touching Kate. Because she was too young, because she was Connor and Eli's sister.

But those things were so small to him now. Minimal parts of the complex beauty that made up Kate Garrett. And he couldn't bring himself to care.

"Talk to you after." He hung up, walking toward the temporary fences, keeping his distance. He didn't want to distract her. But then he noticed she was looking around, searching. Probably for Connor and Eli, Liss and Sadie. Her family. Probably not for him. But just in case, he took a few long strides down toward where she was, keeping himself across the arena from her. She turned and saw him. And the smile that lit up her face felt like the best, most undeserved gift he could've ever received.

He smiled back, gratified by the blush that colored her cheeks.

Then she turned her focus back to the task at hand. She wasn't searching anymore. Which meant she had been looking for him. That did something to him. Made it almost impossible to breathe.

The first rider went, then the next. But he didn't pay attention. His eyes were locked on Kate, who was staring straight ahead at the arena. When she was next up, she mounted Roo and took her position in the chute.

The ride ended to thunderous applause, and Kate was motionless, waiting for her gate to open. He let his eyes flutter closed just for a moment, and for the first time in his memory, he uttered a prayer.

He took a breath, and the gate opened. And Kate flew.

Her braid bounced against her back, dirt flying up behind the horse's hooves. She went around the first barrel clean, picking up the momentum she had lost on the turn and burning flawlessly into the next. When she finished, he cheered the loudest.

The next three riders went. Then it was all reset for the second round. More waiting.

Her turn came around again too fast and not fast enough. She turned back and looked at him, the first time she had looked at him since before her run. He wished that he could touch her. Tug her braid. Give her a kiss. Judging by the flush of color in her cheeks, she understood what he wanted.

"Go, badger-cat," he whispered.

She nodded once, then turned her attention back to her ride, taking her position in the chute. For a moment everything inside of him went still. His heart, his breath. All of it frozen.

This was it. There were good times on the board, and she would have to do better this time than last time to pull ahead.

Her gate opened and she was quick off the mark. He didn't watch the timer on the board; he watched her, willing her to go fast, to go clean. And she did.

When she finished, her time had blown away everyone that had gone before her. And he knew without a doubt no one would ever catch her.

Because no one could catch Kate Garrett. Not in the arena, not in life. She was too far out ahead of the crowd. And for some reason she saw something in him. That strong-willed, determined woman who had survived and thrived even with the abandonment by her parents, both physically and emotionally. Who had lost more than any one person should, who'd had burdens placed on her slim shoulders that men twice her size could never have carried.

She saw good in him.

If the whole town never saw it, if his father never saw it, he didn't give a damn. Somehow, over the course of the past month and a half, he'd lost that drive to prove himself by organizing this charity. Had started caring about only one person seeing him at all. Because it didn't matter. It didn't matter what anyone thought. Not when Kate saw who he was.

She came around to the back of the arena just as the next rider was breaking out of the gate. And he didn't care if people saw, didn't care what they thought. He jogged toward her, slowing as he approached her horse.

He reached up, and she looked down at him, arching a brow.

"Come here," he said, no room for argument in his tone.

She began to dismount and he caught her, holding on to her waist and lifting her down to the ground. She smiled, a small one that curved the edges of her lips up just so. He wanted to kiss them. Right at the curve, then again at the lush center.

Too bad he couldn't. Not here. Not now. But he didn't want to release her, either. Not yet.

"Kate! That was amazing."

He stepped away from Kate slowly, not responding to the jump and wiggle on her end. He turned and saw Connor, with Eli, Liss and Sadie trailing behind, a broad grin on his face. Again, the intense trust his friends had for him was evident in the way neither brother raised a brow over his physical contact with Kate.

"It isn't over yet," she said, scuffing her boot through the dust, her eyes fixed on the trail she left behind.

"No one is going to beat you," Connor said.

She lifted her shoulder. "Sure. Probably not. But you paid for your tickets. You should probably watch the end of the event."

Eli grinned broadly. "Who cares about all that. We were here to see you."

"You guys suck. You're going to make me cry," Kate said.

"I didn't think you had tear ducts," Connor said.

"Turns out I do. Please don't make me use them."

"I'll do it for you," Liss said, "since I'm an emotional mess."

"I'm not even pregnant," Sadie said, "and I might."

"I haven't won yet."

"Just one more ride. She didn't even have a better score than you in the first round." It was Jack who pointed this out.

"Stop with your logic," she said, waving a hand. "I'm not going to watch. I'm going to go put Roo away. You come get me if I win."

"You should go after her," Eli said, when Kate was out of earshot.

"Me?" Jack asked.

"Yeah, you were her coach. Go say something encouraging. We'll keep watch."

He'd wanted to go after Kate; he just hadn't figured he would do it in front of her family. But he would now. "Text us as soon as the results are in," he said. Strange how easy *us* had come out of his mouth. Or not strange at all considering the things he'd been turning over lately.

"I'll text you," Liss said. "That brick Kate calls a phone probably can't get text reliably."

Jack nodded and turned away, headed toward the stalls. He went ahead and walked behind Kate, enjoying the view. She paused midstride and turned to look over her shoulder, one brow arched. He was caught.

"What are you doing?" she asked.

He jogged up to her. "They sent me after you to act coach-like."

"They wouldn't have done that if they had any idea."

"Oh, sure as hell not."

"Thank you for coming," she said.

He wasn't sure if she meant now or to the whole event. "Of course." That answer worked either way. "You're going pro now, Kate Garrett."

"We don't know if I won."

"You don't need to win. That was a winning ride, whether it wins this particular time or not. You're going to do this."

She laughed nervously, brushing a strand of hair out of her face. "You want to get rid of me that badly?"

"I don't want to get rid of you at all. I want you with me, in my bed, every night. You have to understand that my telling you that you need to do this is just because I believe in you that much."

She looked up, startled. "Why?"

"A man has to believe in something. I'm going to go ahead and believe in you."

"You sure that's smart?" she asked, a forced laugh laced through her words.

"I'm known for my luck, not my smarts."

"But it's there all the same."

He smiled. "Then how dare you question me?"

"Sorry, Monaghan. It will never happen again. I promise to preserve your ego at all costs."

It occurred to him just then that it wasn't his ego he cared about. "I want to take you on a date."

Her blue eyes widened, and she blinked rapidly. "You...what?"

"You. Me. A restaurant, a walk along the harbor. A date."

"In public?"

"In public. Out of bed. With clothes on."

"That...doesn't sound like as much fun as the way we normally do it."

A strange sharp sensation lanced his chest. "Maybe not. But it is what normal people do."

She looked over his shoulder, likely squinting to see her family in the distance. "But they'll find out."

"I know. I'm starting to think they should."

"But this..."

"Can't be anything if we don't move forward."

Kate hesitated, moving her hand over Roo's neck. "I thought... I thought we said..."

"We did. But things change. Dinner. Tomorrow night. We'll have it in Old Town."

She thrust her chin into the air, wrinkling her nose. "And what will I be wearing, Mr. Monaghan?"

"Provocative. We're going to have to deal with that later."

Her cheeks turned pink. "Well, you're being all demanding."

"And you like it. Wear whatever you like, but I'm picking you up at six."

The phone buzzed in his pocket and he took it out. There was a text with one word: yes!!!

He couldn't hold back the smile. The flood of pure joy that burst in his chest like a firework and crackled outward.

"You won, Katie," he said.

She looked at him, shocked. "I did?"

Just then Eli and Sadie appeared, out of breath. "Connor stayed back with Liss. They're on their way. She can only waddle," Sadie said. "You won! Kate, you're amazing!"

"I... It was because of Jack." Her brown eyes met his and he felt everything in him tighten. "I couldn't have done it without him."

Liss and Connor found them, and immediately their excitement took over the conversation. He looked past everyone, at Kate, and mouthed, "Six."

She looked at him, her face serious, and nodded slowly.

It wasn't emphatic, but he would take it.

CHAPTER NINETEEN

IN KATE'S OPINION, she was just acting stupid. She had seen Jack a million times, at restaurants, at her brothers' houses, at the rodeo only last night. He had seen her dressed in her Sunday worst for when she worked at the Farm and Garden and he'd seen her in her rodeo clothes. He'd seen her naked, for goodness' sake. There were no surprises left.

So there was no reason on earth to start getting worked up now over what she might wear to go out to dinner with him. It wasn't as if she owned a dress, other than the bridesmaid dress, or makeup. It wasn't as if she was going to do anything with her hair but put it back in a braid.

She looked at her reflection in the mirror, at her heavy straight hair, hanging free. Okay, maybe she would leave it down. Just for something slightly different. She was regretting the fact that she hadn't made it over to the mall in Tolowa to pick up some underwear. Maybe she would have gotten a pair of jeans she hadn't bought folded on a shelf at a sporting goods store. Probably not, though.

She sighed heavily. It was what it was. Jack would be by to get her in fifteen minutes, so she supposed she needed to make a decision.

She thought back to that night he'd stood her up before the meeting at the Grange. She knew without a doubt he wouldn't stand her up tonight—that wasn't why she was reflecting on that night. She was just reflecting on her nerves. On that feeling of excitement, as if he was coming to get her for a date. And now he really was. Strange how a couple months changed things.

She decided on a pair of black jeans and a white button-up top that had a faint floral pattern etched in tan all over it, along with some fancy pearl buttons. It was more of a competition outfit, but nowhere near as flashy as what a lot of her contemporaries considered a competition outfit. Really, she was probably still underdressed for a date.

A date. They really were going on a date. He didn't mind if people found out about them.

The strangest sensation gripped her, one of fear, exhilaration. Like riding her horse full speed through a fog bank. No clue what was ahead. Unable to slow down. She had no idea what was on the other side of tonight, what it would mean for each and every one of her relationships. For her future.

Then there was the small matter of making the decision to compete professionally next year. And that would change things, too.

Suddenly, she wanted to strip all her clothes off and scamper back to her room, crawl under her covers and hide her face. Will herself back in time to the simple ranch girl she had been before she'd tasted Jack Monaghan's lips. It was all his damn fault. He was the one who had changed things. Who had reached inside of her and rearranged all of the familiar scenery into something she couldn't sort through.

Damn Jack Monaghan.

Damn him to... Well, not to hell. But maybe to a city. That was close enough.

She didn't strip her clothes off. And she didn't hide. Instead she took one last look at herself in the mirror, at her dark hair tumbled down loose, at the way her outfit hugged her curves, showing off a bit of her figure in a way that was honestly not that unpleasant.

She took a deep breath. She was a lot of things. She was tough, and lately, she was even naughty. She was also brave. Which meant she was going on this date. Her nerves didn't get to tell her what to do.

KATE WAS TWITCHY and borderline sullen the entire ride from the ranch down into Old Town, and her twitching only increased when she saw the restaurant they would be dining in.

"Beaches?" she asked, wrinkling her nose at the white facade of the historic building. It was right on the harbor, overlooking the bay on one side and the ocean on the other. It was one of the nicer places Old Town Copper Ridge had to offer. Unassuming for all its fanciness, bleached and weathered from the salt water and wind, but it was the freshest seafood around and they made their own beer batter for the fish and chips, which in Jack's mind meant it was a damn respectable date restaurant. At least, if one was going out with Kate Garrett. He wasn't all that experienced in terms of going out on dates. Generally, he met women at Ace's or at one of the bars in a surrounding town. He met them out; he didn't take them out. There was a difference.

Which only underscored the difference with Kate. And why he had to do this. She was different in every way, so he was damned if he was going to treat her like some dirty little secret. Like it was just another physical affair.

Like his father had treated his mother.

She wasn't a dirty secret. She was the most beautiful secret a man could ever have, and he was too damned proud to hide it anymore.

"Yeah. First of all... I don't want to keep this a secret."

Kate shifted, tucking her hair behind her ear. "Right."

"But this isn't the way I want Connor and Eli to find out, either. So I figured we would go somewhere off the beaten path. Then we can talk about what to do from here but I thought we should...test the waters first."

She cleared her throat. "Right. Because you want to tell them."

"I don't want to keep sneaking around, Kate."

She nodded mutely. "Still. Beaches is fancy."

"I'm a classy bastard. If you hadn't noticed." Likely, she hadn't. Because, really, he wasn't. But he was trying to do right by her. Trying to prove to her that he was sincere. That he could do this. Screw the town. Screw his dad.

All that mattered was Kate.

"Well, obviously. I just figured we'd go to The Crab Shanty and sit on the dock and I would pretend to pinch you with a dismembered crab claw."

He had to smile, because that did sound like her. "It's not too late for that. Sounds fun."

She hesitated, the war in her eyes so very transparent. She wanted this, but for some reason she was nervous about accepting it.

"No," she said slowly, "you planned this. So we need to do it."

"But I did it for you. So if this isn't something you want, you need to let me know."

"No, we'll do the unsophisticated crab thing when I take you out," she said, her tone firm. "But I'm very messy."

"I'll lick the butter off your fingers."

"Ew."

"You like me," he said, unable to suppress the smile that was tugging at his lips.

She shrugged. "You're okay," she said, swinging her head in the motion that normally sent her braid slapping against her back. But she'd left her hair down, and instead it rippled, a shimmering wave that he itched to touch. It was a tease. Because usually, Kate's hair was only down like this when they were in bed. "I'm hungry," she said, arching her brow and walking toward the restaurant.

He caught up to her, grabbed hold of her hand and placed his fingers through hers. "We'll get you food."

She froze, her expression nervous. "Pretty bold," she said, but she didn't let go of his hand.

"Yeah, well, I am."

They walked toward the restaurant and he paused at the door, pulling it open for her, releasing his hold on her hand and waiting for her to go inside first.

"Fancy."

"Kate, stop looking at me like I'm going to bite you on the neck and suck your blood."

She winced. "Okay," she said, walking past him and into the restaurant.

The hostess wasn't anyone he recognized, someone young, probably someone from the high school. Which was good. Since Kate was twitchy as a bull facing the prospect of becoming a steer.

The young woman led them to a table that was right up against the windows, providing a view of the rolling waves. There was, in fact, a candle in the middle of the table. It was romantic. He and Kate Garrett were engaging in romance, which individually would've been strange enough but with the two of them combined would be a damned spectacle if anyone in the restaurant recognized them.

"Are you getting a hamburger or fish and chips, Katie?" he asked, skimming his menu quickly, finding he didn't actually care what he got.

She raised her brows. "Maybe I want the tuna tartare, asshole. You don't know."

"Do you?"

"No. Fish and chips. And a beer."

"Me, too. What beer?"

"A Caldera."

"Sounds good."

The conversation was a little bit inane, but he couldn't think of anything better to talk about. If he did, he might start speaking in poetic verse about the way the candlelight flickered across her hair, the way it highlighted the hollows of her cheeks, making her look like a classic painting.

He had a feeling she would excuse herself and run off to the bathroom if he did something like that.

He didn't know what the hell was wrong with him. He was almost sick over her. Sick over Kate Garrett. Ten years younger, practically a virgin. And he was losing his shit for her.

After their waitress, also blessedly a stranger, came

and took their order, they made small talk about how well the rodeo had gone, Kate being careful not to compliment him too profusely, likely so that he didn't have to shift credit. Since she had already identified that he did that. She saw him so clearly. Much more so than anyone else. Much more so than he did.

He said something funny—he didn't even really pay attention to what—and Kate laughed, putting her head down, her hair sliding over her shoulder, full lips curving into the most beautiful smile he'd ever seen. She was out of his reach. Being the man he'd always been wouldn't be enough with her. He would have to change. He would have to want more. He would have to be more.

It hit him then just why he wasn't comfortable accepting accolades. Why, no matter what he said about wanting to improve his reputation, he never really took steps to do it. When he got positive attention, he was quick to shift the focus. Because striving for more was hard. It demanded all the time. Living down to a bad reputation was a lot easier than living up to a great one.

He'd watched Eli live beyond reproach from adolescence. He knew how hard it was. Knew what it cost. He'd never had that kind of confidence in himself. But then, he'd never really had incentive. Kate was that incentive.

He was going to be good enough for her, because he had to be. Because she deserved the best, and even if he could never be the best, he would be everything he could.

Because his other revelation in that moment was that he simply couldn't live without her. And he wouldn't. He wanted more than to just take this public; he wanted to take it legal. Permanent. He wanted her forever.

He loved her. He motherfucking *loved* her.

Their food appeared a moment later, and Kate grabbed the bottle of Portland ketchup from the center of the table and popped the lid off, then smacked the bottom with gusto, trying to get some on her fries.

She looked up, her expression sheepish, her hand poised presmack. "Sorry. Fanciness isn't my strong suit."

"You have to get your ketchup somehow."

She set the bottle down and placed a knife inside the narrow neck, drawing out as much as she could. And even completing this silly, clumsy task, she was the most captivating creature he'd ever seen.

Yeah, it was love. What else could it be? Love, he was pretty sure, was watching someone smack a ketchup bottle while wanting to drag them into the bathroom and have them against a wall.

Well, it was more than that. But that was part of it.

She dipped her fry in her hard-won ketchup, crunching loudly.

"I need to tell you something."

She paused midcrunch, her eyes widening. "What?" she asked around a mouthful of potato.

"Something I should have realized sooner."

"If you brought me here to tell me things are done..."

"Why would I do that? Why the hell would I do that?" He was defensive now, and he knew it. Because she was supposed to know him better than that.

"I knew this felt like a bad idea."

"Is that right, Katie?" he asked, anger firing through his veins. "Then you don't actually know anything. I brought you here because I'm tired of sneaking around. Because I'm tired of hiding the fact that we are together.

I don't care what anybody thinks about it. No, I don't deserve you. Everyone here knows that. But I have you, and I'm so damn proud of that fact. And I'm going to do everything I can to be a man who's worthy of you."

She was still holding her French fry up by her mouth, her lips parted slightly. "What exactly are you saying?"

She didn't look happy. She didn't look hopeful. She looked… She looked scared, and when a man was making confessions, shaking down to his core, that wasn't what he wanted to see.

But it was too late to turn back now. The burning that had been growing, spreading in his chest for a while now, had taken hold completely, and there would be no stopping it until he said this, until he admitted it.

"I'm trying to say that I love you." He waited for a smile. For something that looked even a little bit like happiness. But Kate just sat there, her eyes glittering, darting back and forth as if she was looking for an exit. Looking anywhere but at him. But he'd never been accused of being a fast learner. So he kept talking. "I love you, Kate. I want more. I want everything."

Kate braced her hands on the edge of the table, like a passenger grabbing hold of the dash when she saw an accident coming that she couldn't do anything to stop. "Jack… You can't… That's not what this is." She looked wild, panicked. Like he'd told her he was dying of a terrible disease, not like he'd confessed to having feelings for her. "You said. You told me this would be sex only. Only sex."

"Yes. I said that. And in the beginning, I meant it. I've never had anything more with anyone else. It changed. I changed. That's what it is now." He took a deep breath and looked at her, at the woman he'd known for so many years. The woman who had been part of his life for so long he couldn't imagine living without her. The woman who had recently become his entire world. Whether her hair was braided or free, her lips naked or painted red, she made his heart beat. "I love everything about you, Katie. Probably always have. You see me. You're the only one who sees me."

She blinked hard, her brows locked together. "But that doesn't mean…that doesn't mean that I love you. That doesn't mean that I can love you. Or that I want… Jack, I'm going to go professional next year. I'm going to travel all around the country."

"Yes. I know. And I'll… I'll go to some of it. I'll travel with you sometimes. Or I'll just stay here and wait for you if that's what you want."

"You… You told me… You were the one who said this was only physical. You were the one who was worried about me getting hurt. You can't just change the rules," she said, her eyes glittering, her voice fierce.

And it hit him then what an arrogant asshole he was. Because in his momentary revelation he hadn't imagined she might tell him no. He'd been so focused on his own journey, on his revelations about himself, that he hadn't stopped to think she might not be on the same page. That she might not love him.

Looking at her now, at the anger, at the terror in her eyes, he knew he had miscalculated, and badly.

She was rejecting him. She was honest-to-God rejecting him. He'd never been rejected by a woman in his life.

Because you never asked for more.

And now that you have…

He gritted his teeth against the searing pain, the burning anguish in his chest.

"I have to go." She stood up, pushing her food back to the center of the table and turning away from him, then walking quickly out of the restaurant.

He would have bled less if she'd shot him. As it was, he was just sitting there feeling like he'd sustained a mortal wound with nothing to staunch the flow.

He reached for his wallet and dropped sixty dollars on the table, knowing he was overpaying and not caring. He stood and followed the path Kate had just forged with all of her righteous indignation, well aware that everyone in the restaurant was looking at him. Well aware that everyone had just seen him get rejected by a woman he didn't deserve.

If there were people in there who knew them, and there very likely were, they had just seen Jack get put in his place. They had just seen his unworthiness confirmed on a grand stage.

He walked outside, his breath visible in the cold air. People were dining out on the front deck, outdoor heaters lit, the warmth warping the air around them. And Kate was standing there, wringing her hands and looking both ways. Probably pissed because she'd just realized she'd stormed out on her ride.

"Kate," he called down to her. He realized that he'd captured the attention of the outdoor diners, but he didn't care. "Come back. Let's talk." He started down the steps toward the street and she turned partly away from him. As if she didn't want people to know he was talking to her.

And it hit him then. She wasn't the dirty secret. She never had been.

It was him.

Of course it was. He was no good. The town bike, bike that everyone had ridden once. The bastard son of no one.

She was Kate Garrett, sister to Connor and Eli Garrett, the best men in town. She deserved better and everyone knew it. Apparently, so did she.

He took a deep breath, the salt air burning his lungs, his heart pounding heavily in his head, and asked himself how the hell he'd gotten here. Breaking into pieces over a woman he would have called a girl only a few months earlier.

She had been honest when she'd said she didn't want more and when he'd decided he'd believed he was being honest. But he was a liar. Apparently.

He just stood there, his hands clenched at his sides. He was holding back a flood of heartbreak and poetry, and neither were anything he had experience with. And behind the poetry were small mean things that he wanted to say to hurt her, to get a reaction out of her. To make her understand what he was feeling.

All of it was better left unsaid. He might not have any experience with this kind of thing, but he knew enough to know that.

Too bad he was past the point of giving a damn. There was no point in pride, no point in preserving any damn thing when his heart was already broken. She was ashamed? She wanted it to be a secret?

Too bad. He didn't.

Because he was proud of her. Proud of what he felt. He didn't deserve her shame. He deserved for her to at least listen to him. To say it to his face if she didn't want him.

His father had sent a damned legal team and payment to get him out of his life. He needed at least a conversation from Kate.

"Fuck it." He strode toward her, and she turned away, starting to walk in the other direction. "Kate! Wait. Listen to me."

"No."

"You don't have to commit to anything. Not right now, but we need to talk. You are not running from me."

He closed the distance between them and she looked up at the audience they'd gained. "I'm not having this fight with you in front of half the town."

He looked up at the diners. "That's not even close to half the town. And you're trying your best to not have this fight with me at all, and I'm not going to have it."

"I didn't ask your permission to not have it. I'm not having it." She turned away from him again and he caught her arm.

"You're gonna run away with your tail between your legs like a scared little animal?"

She whirled around, jerked her arm from his hold and planted her hands on his chest, shoving him back. "I am not afraid."

"Could've fooled me. You look like you're running scared."

She took another step toward him and he wrapped his arm around her waist and pulled her up against his body. "Don't," she said, her tone warning.

But he had never been very good at taking warnings.

He dipped his head and kissed her.

It wasn't a kiss to try and seduce her around to his way of thinking. It wasn't even a show for the crowd. He just wanted her to taste his anger. So that she could feel the desperation he did. So she could feel how wrong it was for them to be anything but together.

She didn't push against him. Instead she kissed him back, giving him a taste of her own rage.

Fine. He would take that. It was better than her walking away. Better than her refusing to fight. He would rather fight. Would rather go down in a blaze of bloody glory than offer her his heart and watch her walk away in a huff as though they'd done nothing more than disagree about politics.

He would drag it all out right here so everyone would know it had existed. That it had been real. She wanted it to be a secret? She wanted it to stay hidden? Too damn bad.

It was too big for him to hide, too big for him to walk away from unchanged. And he was tired of being invisible. He would be damned if she tried to make him invisible to her, too.

All those stunts he'd pulled, all the things he'd done to get his father's attention… They were a boy's rebellion. A boy's bid for what he'd been denied.

This…this was a man's desperation. From deep within his soul.

He wanted her to cry for them, for this. Because he would cry. He wanted her to break, because he was shattering inside like glass.

If she was going to walk away, he wasn't going to make it easy.

She was holding tight to him now, clinging to his shirt, but in spite of that, he found himself being propelled backward.

"What the fuck, Monaghan?"

Jack found himself off balance and staring at the

hulking silhouette of his best friend Connor, standing there backlit by the streetlight, his hands clenched into fists. Jack was having a hard time figuring out what the hell Connor was doing in town, and in the middle of that confusion was the instinctive fear he felt for his safety.

Even with the darkness keeping his expression vague, Jack knew that Connor had murder on his mind.

Jack was having trouble making his mouth work. So it wasn't a huge surprise when the words that came out of his mouth were both asinine and self-destructive. "It's exactly what it looks like."

That had been a mistake, and he knew it. When it came to physical strength, if it were Eli, Jack was pretty sure he would have a fighting chance. They were about the same height, with lean muscle. Connor, on the other hand, was roughly the size of a rodeo bull and, much like a rodeo bull, had no qualms about stepping on your head.

"Connor," Kate said, "just… Don't…"

"Stay out of this," Connor said, his voice hard.

"No. I will not stay out of it. I'm in it. What are you doing here?" Kate asked.

"I was out having dinner with my wife and I got a text from our friend Jeanette saying you two were out here making asses of yourselves on Main Street. That's what I'm doing here. I don't know what I expected but that," Connor said, pointing to Jack, "that was not it."

"Connor," Jack started, but his words were cut short when Connor's fist connected with his face. Jack went down, the sharp, hard crack of the sidewalk on his knee enough to offset the throbbing in his head.

"Connor?" Another voice was added to the chorus calling out Connor's name. Liss had just appeared behind Connor, holding on to the edges of her coat, the yellow streetlights igniting her hair like a red flame.

"He was kissing her," he said, pointing down at Jack. Then he turned his focus back to Jack. "I saw you two yelling at each other. Heard you yell at her. And I saw you grab her and make her kiss you."

Yeah, as things went, that was probably the worst way ever for Connor to discover his relationship with Kate wasn't entirely platonic. The yelling. The kiss, which could be viewed as somewhat of a rough kiss.

"I care about her," Jack said. "And you know me. Think about those things right now."

"You care about her?" Connor asked, his tone incredulous. "Like you care about all the women you pick up at bars and fuck?"

"Don't," Jack growled. "Don't say that shit when you don't know what you're talking about."

"You," Connor said, rounding on Kate now. "How could you be that stupid? You know him. You know what a damned ass he is. Tell me you're not sleeping with him."

Kate had her arms wrapped around her midsection, as if she was trying desperately to fold into herself and disappear. "Connor... I..."

"Shit," Connor bit out. Then he turned his focus back to Jack. "Give me one good reason not to kill you here and now."

"Two. There are witnesses and your brother is the sheriff. I'd hate for Eli to have to arrest you." It was a bad time to make a joke. Though it wasn't entirely a joke. He half believed Connor would kill him where he stood if he didn't give him a good reason not to.

"I swear to God, Monaghan..."

"I love her," Jack said. His pride was dead and buried anyway. Might as well make it roll over in its grave. He directed his gaze to Kate. "I do. I love you. I'm proud to love you. I want more. I want more than just sneaking around. I don't care if he knows it. I don't care if they know it," he said, gesturing up to the people who were now avidly watching the scene unfold. "Maybe I'm not good enough for you. No, hell, I know I'm not. But I thought you at least knew me well enough... I thought you trusted me. You know my past—everyone here does. I thought you knew I was more than that."

Kate was shivering now, her eyes resolutely dry, her teeth chattering. "I do know you. That's the problem."

The last bit of hope he carried died a slow, howling death inside of him, begging for mercy as Kate's words pushed it to a place beyond healing.

Connor was just standing there looking grim. Liss was a few paces back, her skin waxen. And Kate was in the center, determination in her face even while she shook so hard he thought she might rattle apart.

All of them standing away from him.

A clear line.

He stood alone. As always. He'd been a fool to think it could ever be different.

"Perfect." He turned away from them, the feeling of isolation growing inside of him. Pain bleeding outward, pain no one else saw or cared about.

Because they saw only what they wanted to when they looked at him. Maybe in the end, they were right. Could everyone be wrong about him? It didn't make much sense.

Maybe, all this time, he'd been the one who was wrong.

He'd been such an idiot. He had imagined that if he tried, he could be good enough for Kate. But he should've known. Bad blood. He would never be good enough for her; he would never be right for her. Even the people who were supposed to love him most felt that way.

He'd told Kate that he was wrong for her. But somewhere along the line he had stopped believing it. But she still did.

Damn himself for being so convincing.

KATE WATCHED AS JACK walked back to his truck, started it up and drove away. Then she turned and looked at her brother and at Liss, who were both staring at her awaiting an explanation she wasn't sure she could give. She wasn't giving any sort of explanation right now, because her throat was too tight, and her head was throbbing.

He loved her. Jack loved her. He had said the words and everything had frozen inside of her.

And now everyone around her seemed frozen, too. She couldn't face it.

"I need a ride home," she said, the words sounding far away and fuzzy. Not just like someone else was saying them—but like someone in another time and space was saying them.

Liss moved to her, wrapping her arm firmly around Kate's waist. "Of course."

Kate didn't want to be touched. She felt so damn fragile. As if a touch might break her. But she also wasn't about to push her pregnant sister-in-law away from her.

They walked down the street, Liss holding her tight, holding her together, Kate imagined now, since she felt as if her body was made entirely of cracks and splintering glass. Connor was behind them, acting like a shield against everyone rubbernecking to get a look at the situation.

Liss opened the door to Connor's truck and stood waiting for her to climb in.

"I... Can you sit in the middle?" Kate asked.

Kate needed an easy escape. She didn't know if she would survive the ride home. She needed to let part of the splintered bits of herself break open entirely. To let some of this pressure escape so it didn't dissolve her entirely.

"Sure." Liss climbed in ahead of her, surprisingly agile given her advanced stage of pregnancy.

For the first time ever in her whole life, Kate really wondered what it would be like to have a baby. A whole new wave of longing broke over her. Dreams, desires she'd never once let herself have, clawing up from deep inside her, threatening to overtake her.

Her stomach cramped and she got in quickly, slamming the truck door behind her just as Connor got in and closed the driver's side.

She wasn't going to think about shit like having babies. She'd never thought about it before.

She thought of Jack. Jack's hands on her skin. Jack looking at her, his blue eyes so deep and earnest.

I love you.

That meant...that meant this stuff. Getting married. Having babies.

The pang hit harder, echoing through her, a metallic taste lingering on her tongue.

No. She couldn't do that. He would depend on her then. A child would be depending on her...

Shit. No. Shit. No.

That mantra echoed in her head the entire ride back to the ranch, Connor and Liss, blissfully, letting silence fill the cab of the truck, letting it surround her like a fuzzy blanket, cushioning her from reality.

From the pain of the moment.

They pulled into the driveway and Kate felt her body start to tense. They would want to talk tonight. And she would have to explain.

And she couldn't explain. Not without the dam bursting and her becoming a whole flood that washed away everything she knew. Everything she was.

They pulled up in front of the main house. Of course Connor wasn't taking her home. Of course he was bringing her here. And Liss would make cocoa and they would want to talk and she couldn't. She couldn't.

She felt for the handle and flung the passenger door wide, undid her buckle and stumbled out of the truck.

She had told him she wasn't running. But she was. And she was going to do it again. She turned away from Connor and Liss and she ran. Not toward her house, toward the barn. If there was any clarity to be had, she would find it there.

There was no sound around her, only the desperate gasp for breath and the sound of her feet on the ground. She closed everything out and listened closely to that rhythm, counting footsteps, counting breaths. That at least did something to stem the pain.

She wrenched open the side door of the barn and walked inside, waiting for the immediate peace and calm that always came when she breathed that air in deep.

Instead it broke loose that frozen block that had

lodged itself in her heart. All the cracks that had formed on the drive over breaking apart, bit by bit. And once that happened, the sob that had been building in her chest all this time released.

Tears flooded down her cheeks and she didn't make any move to stop them. She walked over to Roo's stall and pushed the door open. Stepping inside, she put her hand on her horse's rump, sliding her fingertips along up to her neck before wrapping her arms around the animal and burying her face against her. And then she cried like she didn't remember crying in her whole life. Not when her dad died, not when Jessie died.

She had cried—of course she had. She had grieved. Because she had lost. But something in her, a wall of some kind that she'd built up strong around herself, had held the flow in check.

That wall was gone now. And she was certain it had something to do with Jack. Stupid Jack. Stupid Jack who probably had Connor's knuckle prints in his cheek. She should have felt bad about that. Later she would feel bad about that. But right now she was glad that someone who was stronger than she was had knocked him flat. She wanted him to hurt the way she did, to feel afraid, to feel as if the rules had been changed.

Because she was small and petty. And she wasn't brave.

She had spent so long pretending to be brave. Convincing herself she was brave. Because she ran into everything with guns blazing. Because she didn't cry— she gritted her teeth and got to work. But the truth was, she did that only because she was afraid of all the other emotions she might accidentally feel. Bravery wasn't just being tough. And she was only just now realizing that fact.

Fine, then. She was a coward.

But things were changing too fast. She had changed; what she wanted had changed. And she was afraid she would keep on changing until she got to a place where she didn't recognize herself anymore.

This is what happened to Mom.

Fear gripped her throat and shook her hard, a sob racking her shoulders.

"Kate?"

The sound of her brother's voice penetrated her weeping.

She looked up, dragging her arm over her cheeks, wiping the tears away. "Shouldn't you be out rallying the townsfolk with pitchforks and torches?"

"Did you want me to? Because I would happily go torch Monaghan's ass. He would deserve it."

She sniffed loudly. "Why are you so convinced of that? You haven't even asked me what my part in all this was."

"He deserves it, because you're my sister. And you're upset. There's only one side for me to take."

"You probably shouldn't hate him."

"I don't know. I was sort of thinking I should call up Eli and make sure he hates him, too."

She shuddered, another sob working its way through her. "Don't."

"I do have to tell him. Otherwise the gossip chain is going to wrap itself around him when he goes to get that foofy coffee of his tomorrow morning before his shift. I imagine you would rather have me controlling the conversation instead of some old busybody."

"I guess we did make gossip. But it was his fault."

"Then I'll ready the pitchforks," Connor said, his tone casual.

She wiped at a tear that was running down her cheek. "No, you dumb asshole. I meant the spectacle was his fault. Because he wouldn't just…"

"Kate Garrett, this is the first time I've seen you cry outside a funeral since you were a little girl with two skinned knees, two scraped elbows and a split lip from a very ill-advised stunt you pulled climbing around in the hayloft. Which in my mind means Jack Monaghan might need killing. But I would rather know for sure before I go risking jail time over the demise of my oldest friend."

She paused for a moment. "Well, on the one hand, if you did kill him, Eli might help you cover it up."

"Kate. He said… He said that he loved you. The only thing I have ever heard Jack say he loved is a hamburger and a piece of pie. He doesn't do things like that. He doesn't get attached to people. Well, people other than me and Eli. He doesn't get attached to women."

Another tear trailed down her cheek. "I know."

"Maybe tell me what's been going on with few enough details that I don't end up emotionally scarred."

She blinked rapidly, trying to stem the flow of moisture that was running endlessly from her eyes. "We've been…together. You know. Together."

"Yes. I know exactly what you mean. Picnics in the field with a good foot of space between your bodies. The begrudging allowance of hand-holding after several dates. That is what you mean."

"Well…"

"No. For the purposes of this conversation. That is what you mean. Continue."

A reluctant laugh pushed through her tears. "Right. Picnics. And it was supposed to just be picnics. That's what he said. That's what I wanted. It's what I agreed to. But then…then tonight happened. He told me that he loved me. And I just…" Tears and misery struggled to the forefront again, choking off her words. "I can't. Connor, I can't. How can I? With everything… With Mom…"

Suddenly, she found herself being tugged away from her horse and pulled into Connor's embrace. "Whatever Mom's issues were, they were hers. Only hers. You're not why she left, Kate. I'm sure there were a million reasons, but you weren't one of them. You weren't the reason she left. But you are damn sure the reason we stayed. You were our glue, Katie. You're the reason Eli and I didn't just give up and go off and do Lord knows what while everything here fell apart. We didn't stay for Dad. It was all for you. So don't for one moment think that you somehow can't have love."

She took a shuddering breath. "At the risk of sounding a little bit egotistical, I actually do know that, Connor." She took a deep, shuddering breath. "You and Eli did such a good job of letting me know that you never resented me. And letting me know just how special I was. All of the baggage and crap that I have because of Mom and Dad… That's all on them. And it's so much smaller than it probably should be. Because of you."

"So what's the matter, then, Katie? If you don't love him, you don't love him. And that's fine. But you're in here crying like someone reached in and pulled your heart out. You look like someone who just lost love. I'm the last person on earth to push anyone toward Jack. I know him well enough to know what he's done, and that when it comes to love he's unproven. But I don't want to see you like this." He released his hold on her. "Do you love him?"

"It isn't that simple."

"Bullshit it's not. It's completely that simple."

"No, it's not. I'm not afraid of not being lovable. You've proved to me that I am. Eli has proved it. I'm afraid of… I'm afraid of me. I've changed so much just in the past couple of months. I tried so hard not to. For a long time. But then I saw myself being left behind. You're married. You're having a baby. Eli is married. I was still just me. I got afraid. And I thought maybe I needed to do something. So I started aiming harder for the rodeo stuff. And…and then there was Jack. I know you worried about being Dad. That's not what I worry about. I worry that I'm Mom. So I spent a hell of a long time just working hard, trying to be everything good that you and Eli were. And then I allowed just a little bit of change, and everything feels outside my control. Where will it end? I'm afraid of what I'll change into. I'm afraid that someday I'll be the one who walks out the door. On my husband. On my kids. Dad always… I swore when Dad looked at me, he was seeing her. I'm better off just doing the rodeo thing. I'm better off if nobody needs me."

"Katie," he said, his voice rough. "I love you. That's a load of shit. You have to get out of your own way."

"Easy for you—"

"Think real hard before you finish that sentence," Connor said, his voice hard. "I know all about life kicking you in the balls. I know better than most. I would venture to say I know better than you. I also know that there's a point where you can't blame other people or even fate for the crap in your life. If you hold on to her too long, it's all you get." He sighed heavily. "I almost lost Liss. And it wouldn't have been anyone's fault but mine."

"But what if I—?"

"Who controls your life, Kate? Sure, none of us chose the parents we had. I didn't choose to lose Jessie. But you? You control you. If you don't want to leave, don't leave. If you want to be faithful to your husband, be faithful to your husband. If you want to have children, and you want to be a good mother, choose to do that. Don't you let people who abandoned us determine how happy you'll be. Don't you let them stop you from having love. And don't you ever let fear decide what you'll become." He grabbed hold of her arms and looked her in the eye. "I don't care what you do. If you ride on the circuit and only come home off-season. If you marry that asshole Jack and have ten babies. As long as it makes you happy. Be happy."

She swallowed, her throat so dry it felt as if she'd swallowed a handful of dust. "I'm scared." It was a hard thing to admit, a hard thing to say. She'd lived so long thinking she was brave.

"That's okay. Me, too. I'm about to be a father. I don't know how to do that. But it isn't the fear that's the problem. It's what you do with it. It's whether or not you let it win." He patted her shoulder and looked at her hard.

"Connor," she said.

"Yes?"

"You do know how to do that. How to be a father.

Listen to all the things I just told you. About how I never felt unloved. You're going to be great."

The corner of his mouth lifted. "Thanks. I needed to hear that. But if I'm going to listen to you, you need to listen to me. You aren't anyone but you, Kate. Remember that."

She nodded slowly and watched him walk out of the barn.

She didn't feel relieved at all. In fact, she was starting to feel angry. He wasn't listening to her excuses. They were good excuses. They would keep her safe. They would keep her from getting hurt.

Like you aren't already hurt? You're in here crying like an orphaned calf.

Yes. She was. But pretending to be tough, shutting out every emotion, every deep desire, meant that she couldn't get her heart broken. If she didn't pay attention to her heart, what would she care if it was, anyway?

But she did care. Right now she did, because she felt like she was dying. Maybe it was just too late for all this self-protection. Maybe this was as bad as it got.

This misery of her own making was possibly the most painful thing she'd ever experienced.

Did she love him? She was afraid to answer that question. Connor was right—she could control herself. She could control what she did. And for the majority of her life that had meant protecting herself. As life had raged on around her without asking what it should or shouldn't do, as people had been torn from her life in various different ways, she had built up walls around herself, stronger, higher. Had honed herself down to the basics. Tough. Hardworking. Loyal. Those things were simple; those things were sure.

But the rodeo had been the start of it. The start of wanting more. And once she had opened up that desire inside of herself, more had followed.

But no matter how well she protected herself, no matter how tightly she controlled her desires, she couldn't control life. She wouldn't be able to build a wall around Jack that contained them both, that kept them safe from everything.

It was easier to forget him. To curl up into a ball and find the bricks that had been destroyed by the shattering weeks with him and start to rebuild.

She had been blindsided by life too many times. Had felt like nothing more than a helpless little girl who was at the mercy of stronger forces. She had found ways to shield herself from that, and she had been stupid to forget them.

She could control herself. So she would.

CHAPTER TWENTY

THE WEST RANCH was one flipping fancy place. From the gated entry to the sprawling Spanish-style mansion and the top-notch boarding and riding facilities.

For one moment, one brief moment, Jack allowed himself to imagine what it might have been like to grow up here. To spend his days wandering across the manicured lawns before meandering idly down one of the paths that led to the stables.

But it was a very brief moment.

He hadn't grown up here. He'd grown up in a dirty, moldy trailer that had made his skin break out into a rash. Because even his mother had felt as though she had to pay homage to the mighty Wests by not even asking for the child support she was due. Well, he was done.

He was done being anyone's dirty secret. And if that meant becoming the dirty laundry spread out all over the yard, so be it. But he wasn't hiding. Not for anyone.

He made his way up the manicured walk and rapped the brass knocker against the door. Apparently, the place was too damned fancy for something as practical as a doorbell. And God forbid any of the invited guests tax their knuckles requesting entry.

He waited. And he realized that he had no guarantee of who might be behind the door when someone answered. If someone answered. It could be Sierra. Could be the older West daughter, Madison. Or one of the sons. The other sons. The ones who weren't him.

It could also be Nathan West's wife.

And he could be standing on the doorstep holding the final nail in the coffin of their marriage. It was hard to say.

Even if you are, it isn't because of anything you did. It's because she's married to a bastard.

A bastard who produced more bastards.

He heard footsteps on the other side of the door and his muscles tensed. Momentarily, nerves took over, and they were almost strong enough to blot out the pain that had been radiating around his heart since the moment Kate had rejected him. Almost.

The door opened. It was Madison, one of the Wests he'd had very little contact with. She was younger than he was by quite a bit, older than Kate or Sierra. She always looked like she was irritated to be wherever she was, her expression tight and restless. As though she was in far too much of a hurry to deal with whatever was in front of her.

She was looking at him like that right now.

"Is your father home?" he asked, just barely restraining himself from asking if *their* father was home.

She blinked slowly. Even her blink was bored of him. "He is. May I tell him who's here to—?"

The door opened wider behind Madison to reveal Nathan West. "Whatever you want to discuss, Mr. Monaghan, we can do so outside privately."

"Fine with me," Jack said, taking a step away from the threshold.

Nathan moved past his daughter, closed the door and

led them a few paces away from the house. "Am I going to have to call the police on you?"

"I doubt it. You should know that the sheriff is one of my best friends. So." At least, the sheriff had been one of his best friends. As it stood, Eli might arrest him cheerfully.

"What is it you want? We have an agreement."

"That's actually what I'm here about. I'm here to release myself from that agreement." He reached into his pocket and pulled out an envelope. "There's cash in here. You can count it. It's the exact amount you gave me. It's my hush money. And I'm paying it back because I'm not going to be quiet anymore. And now you can't make me." But it was different now. This was about freedom. He wouldn't be making more bids for attention, wouldn't ever care if Nathan West looked his way again.

Nathan's eyes blazed. "You can't do this. You're just going to walk around ruining my reputation? Ruining my family?"

"This may come as a shock to you but I have no desire to ruin you—" as he spoke the words, he realized they were true "—but I'm not going to pretend. I'm not going to hide. And I'm not going to owe you a debt. Now, I know I needed your money to get the start I got. Because frankly, growing up like I did, with nothing, it would have made getting to my position a whole lot harder, if not impossible. But I'll take the loan as my due, since you were able to dodge child support for the first eighteen years of my life. I'll consider it payment for keeping the secret all that time, for allowing you to stay married to a woman who probably has no idea what a jackass you are. For letting you keep your family intact while your kids grew up. You know, the kids you acknowledge. And now I owe you nothing. That's the most important thing I can think of."

"Did you expect I would respect you for this? Because I don't," Nathan said, sticking the envelope in his pocket. "I don't think much of anything about you."

Jack waited for pain, for a sense of rejection. There was none of it. Nathan was just a man. An old man. And he might have been responsible for some of Jack's genetic material, but not for anything else. And now there was no debt between them. Whatever Jack wanted to do about their relationship, if he wanted to do anything at all, he wasn't bound by any sort of agreement.

"Did you expect me to cry when you said that, Dad?" Jack asked drily. "Because I promise you I won't. I'm going to go home, to my nice house. I'm going to figure out a way to win the woman I love, and when I do, I will treat her like a queen. I will stay faithful to her all my life. That's a lesson you taught me, whether you meant to or not. Because I've seen the other side of it. I will never be you. And I am glad of that. I know you think I should be proud that you're my dad, that you should be ashamed I'm your son. But nothing could be further from the truth. I may go on hiding the fact we're related because I'm ashamed of you."

Jack turned away from the old man, not waiting for a response. And with every step he took, he felt as if he was shedding years of weight from his shoulders. And as he reached his truck, he felt as though a tether snapped between himself and his father. Whatever he owed him was settled. It was done.

And now he was going to make good on the promise he had just made to his father.

He was going to win Kate's heart. And when he did, he was going to do everything in his power to keep it.

THE WAITING ROOM at the birthing center was filling up with friends. Where the Garretts were short on family, they didn't lack for support.

Kate was sitting next to Eli and Sadie, her fingertips biting into the pink patterned fabric that covered the arms of the waiting room chairs. She had underestimated just how terrifying Liss giving birth would be. Everyone around her seemed calm, firmly accepting that this was the normal order of things. That women had babies, and everything was fine. But Kate was terrified.

Because life wasn't always fine. And she knew it.

She couldn't fix it. She couldn't control it. Here in the waiting room, she was just a little girl, sitting on the step at the school, waiting for a father who would never show. At the mercy of the wind or life or whatever it was that saw fit to play so dangerously with her.

She hated this. She hated everything about it. Why was life so fucking scary?

It was so much easier when you didn't have all these people to love, all these opportunities to bleed.

Jack was just one more. And she just couldn't. She couldn't.

"Are you okay?" Eli asked, his tones hushed.

"Fine," she lied.

"Connor told me a little bit about what happened with Jack," Eli said, his voice measured.

She was almost relieved that he was asking about Jack instead of dredging up the deep brokenness that was in her. The screaming, knowing little fear beast that exposed her for the coward she was.

"He told you?"

"Yes. I had to talk him out of killing Monaghan, so you should be grateful he came to speak to me." Eli paused for a moment. "Unless you want him dead."

"I don't want him dead," she said, her heart fluttering. "I don't even like to joke about that. We are kind of a lightning rod for crap, if you hadn't noticed." The entire situation had set her on edge.

"Of course we're not going to kill him," Eli said. "But I do have questions."

Sadie's head appeared around her husband's shoulder as she leaned in, her expression keen.

"Obviously, Sadie has questions," Kate said, her voice monotone.

"About a thousand," Sadie said.

"There isn't anything to say. It happened. It's not happening now."

"But how did it happen? Why did it happen? How long did it happen?" This was from Sadie, and Eli just sat there looking visibly uncomfortable.

"I don't think Eli wants the same level of detail you do," Kate said.

"That is a fact." This came from Eli.

"What happened?" Sadie asked, deciding to be more selective in her questioning, clearly.

"Things. Stuff and things," Kate said. "I'm over it," she lied.

Just then the thing she was most definitely not over walked into the waiting area, a fluorescent green visitor tag on his shirt.

Eli simply stared at him, not offering a greeting.

Sadie looked from him to Kate, then did a noncommittal half wave.

Then Eli stood. "What are you doing here?"

"I was looking for everyone. Stopped by the Farm and Garden to see if Kate was there and was told you were all here. So now I'm here, too."

"Nobody called you," Eli said.

Guilt twisted Kate's internal organs. Because if not for her, him and all of the fallout, there would have been no question about him coming today. He had been friends with Connor and Liss for years, so of course he would have been here for this. She had ruined it. They had ruined it.

"I'm well aware nobody called me, Eli. But I'm here all the same. Because I'm not about to let something that happened between myself and your sister, who is an adult, by the way, keep me from supporting Connor through this. Liss is a friend, too. Why would I miss this? Just because you're pissed right now? Anyway, I'm pretty sure I would be mad in your situation, too, but I'm not sure you have the right to be. Kate makes her own decisions. She always has. There is no pushing her when she doesn't want to be pushed—you know that. I've recently had a reminder of that. She does what she wants. She knows her own mind. I didn't talk her into anything."

Kate could barely tear her eyes off the ground to look at him, but even though it was hard, she did. "You should also know that Kate doesn't like being discussed like she's not here."

"I didn't figure you were speaking to me," he said.

"Well, I didn't figure you were speaking to me."

"I went looking for you, didn't I?"

"Not sure why you would."

"The little matter of being in love with you."

Eli straightened a little bit at that. "What?"

"So you didn't hear about that part," Jack said.

"No," Eli responded.

"It doesn't matter. That shouldn't matter. And let's not discuss this now," Kate said. "Better yet, let's not discuss this ever. Jack and I have said everything that needs to be said to each other, and the rest isn't your business."

She wrapped her arms around herself, holding herself tight. Protecting herself. She would be tough.

But you aren't being brave.

Yeah, well, screw bravery. She didn't want to be brave.

She wanted to be safe.

Of course, Liss was in there giving birth, and Connor was in there trying to cope with that. The people around her seemed to refuse to climb into her little bubble and insulate themselves. And what could she do about that?

Then there was Jack, who was trying to tear it all open, expose her to the elements.

In this moment, she hated them all.

"I'll just go sit over there." Jack turned away and went to a row of chairs that was unoccupied, then sat there resolutely, his arms crossed over his chest.

Her heart felt as though it was cracking open all over again. How did other people not see the faithfulness of Jack Monaghan? He was here. Even when he wasn't wanted. Here because it was right. That was how deeply he cared, how true his loyalty ran.

How could anyone think he was fickle? How could

anyone think he was nothing more than bad blood? Even Liss had doubted him, and he was still here for her.

She would have been proud of him if she wasn't so irritated with the bastard.

Minutes stretched into hours. Kate got up from where she was sitting and walked down the hall toward the water and ice machine that was there for their use.

She heard heavy footsteps behind her and she didn't have to turn to figure out whose they were.

"What?"

"I want to talk to you," Jack said.

"Not now," she said.

"Fine. After."

"Assuming everything is okay."

"Of course everything is okay." In spite of herself, she looked at him. "Everything is going to be fine."

He could see straight through her; more to the point, she let him. She showed him her fear. She didn't know what it was about him that compelled her to do it.

"You don't know that," she choked.

"I guess I don't," he responded. "I guess we can never really know for sure. But without hope, what do you have, Katie?"

"Protection? Protection from disappointment."

"Do you really think expecting bad things to happen makes bad things hurt less?"

She shook her head slowly. "I don't know. But all we can do is survive the best we can, right?"

He looked at her for a long moment, his blue eyes assessing. "I would have agreed with you not too long ago. But now I think maybe we should try for better than surviving. I think maybe we should try living."

Living. It was an entirely different image than survival. Survival conjured up a picture of her huddled in a cave, knees drawn up to her chest, arms wrapped around herself while the storm raged outside.

Living made her think more of dancing in the rain, daring the lightning to strike.

She wasn't sure she could do that. The cave wasn't all that appealing, but it was safe.

"I can't talk about this right now." She turned away from the machine and headed back to her seat, only realizing once she was in view of Sadie and Eli again that she had forgotten to get the water she had gone to fetch in the first place. Great.

Just then the door to the delivery room cracked open, and the nurse came out. "She's here. Healthy. A beautiful baby girl."

All of the breath in her lungs escaped on a rush, her ears buzzing. "Everything is okay?" she asked, unable to disguise the fear in her voice.

"Everything is okay."

The nurse disappeared for a moment, then reappeared. "Kate? Your brother wants you to come in and see the baby."

Kate stood, her legs wobbly. "He wants *me* to come in?"

The nurse nodded. "We'll start with you."

Kate walked forward, and any pretense of being fine and together was out the window. They walked into the room, the sounds of bustling and a baby crying hitting her hard. The nurse swept the curtain aside. Liss was lying in the bed, her feet still up in stirrups. Kate chose to look away from that. It wasn't hard anyway.

Because Connor was standing there, big and strong and as infallible as he'd always been in her mind, with the smallest baby she'd ever seen nestled in the crook of his arm and a tear on his cheek.

He looked up from the baby, only for a moment, meeting her eyes. "She's just perfect, Katie. Isn't she?"

Kate felt like she'd been punched in the chest. "Yes."

"A girl," he said, smiling now. "My daughter. Ruby. I have a daughter."

She looked at the baby, at Connor, at his wife. At a whole second chance playing out right in front of her that would never have happened if Connor had chosen to simply survive.

Something felt as though it was swelling inside her. Growing too large for her to breathe around. She couldn't breathe.

"I'm so happy for you," she said, her voice barely a whisper. "I'll let... I'll let Eli and Sadie come in now."

She turned and walked out of the room, and then she walked out of the waiting room, out of the hospital. She got in her truck, and by the time she started the engine, tears were streaming down her face, matching the rain that was starting to fall from the sky.

WHEN KATE GOT back to the ranch, she parked her truck in front of the barn, killed the engine and got out, her boot pressing down deep into the muddy ground.

The rain was falling hard and fast now, and a smart person would take shelter. That was how you survived, after all. She should go back to her house and light a fire in the woodstove, put on her sweats and hunker down. That was surviving.

She was tired of surviving.

She was tired of being stripped down to the essentials. She kicked her boots off, and the mud was slick between her toes, the gravel that was mixed in painful as it dug into her tender skin. But she could feel it.

She moved toward the stretch of green field in front of her. She walked through a gap in the fence, the mud deeper now, velvety blades of grass creating a barrier between her and the squishy ground. She just stood there for a while and looked up at the sky, letting the rain roll down her face, mixing with the tears she was certain were falling now.

Standing here, stretched out like this, facing the broad expanse of sky, she could feel the stiffness inside of her, the strain from having been curled up, stagnant for so long. She was never one to sit still physically, perhaps in part because it gave too much voice to the internal.

So she stood still now, and she let herself feel. The cold, the rain, the grass, the mud. And her heart. Beating steadily, painfully.

Beating for Jack.

Emotion rose up inside of her, grew, expanded. Love. She loved him.

And it was worth every risk, every possible outcome. Because she would so much rather stand out in the storm than keep hiding.

She thought of Jack's face, of the pain in his blue eyes when she had rejected him. She had hurt him. She had been so focused on her own fear, on her own trauma, that she hadn't paused to consider what he had risked. She hadn't thought of his pain, because she hadn't imagined she could possibly hurt him.

She had. She had made him feel as if she thought he was a secret, as if she was ashamed of him.

Protecting herself had hurt the man she loved most.

And if she had needed any other bit of confirmation that she had to change, that was it.

She heard the slam of a car door and turned to see Jack standing by his truck. The sound of the rain must have obscured the sound of the motor.

She stood there frozen as the rain washed down her cheeks, watching as he approached. He was wearing his hat, that hat that never failed to make her heart squeeze tight, the tight black T-shirt that outlined his perfect body and the jeans that knew him almost as intimately as she did. It was like watching her soul walk toward her. And the closer he got, the more complete she felt, the more right everything felt.

"Did you follow me, Monaghan?" she shouted over the rain.

"Yes, I did. I wanted to make sure you were okay." He moved through the same gap in the fence that she had and stopped when he was about a foot in front of her. "And I wanted to make sure you didn't weasel out of our talk."

"Nothing quite that calculated. I just needed… I just needed some time."

He swallowed, his Adam's apple bobbing up and down. "And have you had it?"

"Yes," she said. "You were right. I was being scared. I've spent my whole life being scared."

"You, Kate Garrett? Scared?"

"Yes. Me. My mom left when I was two. My dad died when I was in high school. My sister-in-law… Life has always been kind of a scary, unpredictable thing for me. But the one thing I could do was make myself tough. Make it so I didn't feel it quite so deep. I told myself I was fine because I had Connor and Eli to take care of me. Because I had you. Except then things changed between us. It wasn't just you taking care of me, making me smile. You broke me open and made me feel. That was scarier than anything. Scarier than going pro, scarier than facing down an angry mama bear. Scary. I told myself I was upset because of the changes. Because I might turn into something I didn't want to be. But the simple truth was, I was just afraid to feel. When you feel, when you want, loss can hurt you. Not just hurt, devastate. It changes things inside you that you can never put back. It's a terrifying thing to sign on for, Jack."

He cleared his throat. "I can't even pretend to know loss the same way you do, Kate. I know in some ways I have more experience, but in other ways I feel like you've lived more life than I have. And not life I envy."

"Connor tried to talk to me, but I wasn't ready. Then today... I saw him with Liss. Their baby. Jack, he has all of that because he refused to give in to fear. He has life—he made life. I want that. More. Everything."

"Everything?" He took a step toward her, gripped her chin with his thumb and forefinger. "Really, everything?" His expression was fierce, his voice hoarse. "Does that mean you love me, badger-cat?"

She didn't even bother to hold back the tears that welled up in her eyes. "Yes, Monaghan. I do. I love you. I did even when I said I didn't. I didn't mean to lie, but I was too afraid to even think it."

His blue eyes, normally so wicked, glittered with moisture, too. "Well, I'm glad to hear that. Damn glad."

She expelled a breath on a broken sob. "I have so many sorries to say to you. For hurting you. For making you think I was ashamed, rather than admitting that

I was just a coward. Jack, I don't deserve your forgiveness. I don't deserve for you to love me."

He leaned down, kissing her lips lightly. "That's where you're wrong. You deserve for me to love you always. No matter what. Kate, don't you understand that you are the reason I'm not ashamed of myself anymore? I spent a lot of years sabotaging myself. Telling myself I wanted approval while going out of my way to make sure I didn't get it. Because I was ashamed of what I had done. Ashamed of who I was. Wanting recognition I couldn't have, because I'd signed that away. But I'm free of that now. You saw me more clearly than I ever saw myself, and it took that for me to finally change." He swallowed hard. "I gave the money back to Nathan West. And I don't know if I'll ever tell anyone that he's my father. But I could. I'm not hiding anymore. Not where I come from, not who I am. That's all you, baby."

"I guess we both helped each other."

"I hear that's what love is for. To make you better. To make the person you love better."

"I believe it."

"I still want you to do the rodeo. Because you want to."

She smiled up at him.

"Really?"

The rain slowed, the clouds parting slightly, pale yellow light breaking through.

"Yes. And I will support you however you want me to. By going with you. By staying away… Bribing judges. Holding a bake sale."

She laughed. "You would do all that for me?"

"Happily." He tightened his hold on her and bent down, sweeping his other arm behind her knees and lifting her up, cradling her against his chest. "Do you know why?"

"Because I let you do me in a barn?"

"That doesn't hurt. But that's not why."

"Because I am a badass badger-cat and you fear me?"

He laughed and kissed her nose. "No. Because you're mine. And I love you. Which means nothing on earth will ever separate us. Even distance. I'm in this. For real. Forever."

Kate put her hand on his cheek, angling her head up so that she could kiss him. "Same goes, Jack Monaghan. Same goes."

"Well, I am awfully glad to hear that."

Kate Garrett had never much belonged to anyone. And that was the way she had liked it. But as Jack carried her through the field, down the driveway and back to her house, she couldn't help but think that belonging to someone, having someone belong to you, was a whole lot better than being alone.

And when he laid her down on the bed, the bed that she'd thought was big enough for only one, and pulled her into his arms, she knew for a fact that spending the rest of her life living with him would be a much better adventure than simply surviving on her own.

EPILOGUE

IT HAD TAKEN a little bit longer than usual to get the game started. But Ruby Kate Garrett ran the show these days, even though she was only two months old. Named for her hair and for her fearless aunt, she had taken over the Garrett ranch with ease.

She was the cutest thing any of them had ever seen. Also, a grumpy little pink cuss. In that way, she took after her father. Though Connor didn't seem to mind putting up with his daughter's crankiness. Far from it—it was the happiest Jack had ever seen his friend.

Right now she was asleep in the crook of Connor's arm, while he balanced both her and his poker hand, which Jack had caught glimpses of. Enough to know that Connor was definitely not the one who was going to win tonight.

Not that Jack cared either way. As far as he was concerned, he had a winning hand no matter the cards that were dealt to him.

He had Kate. He didn't need much more than that.

"So how are the new digs, Katie?" Connor asked.

"Jack has a housekeeper," Kate said, putting her hand on his thigh beneath the table. He fought the wicked impulse that told him to move it up a little bit higher. "It's pretty awesome."

"That's the only reason she moved in with me. She sleeps in the guest room," Jack lied cheerfully.

"I don't mind that," Eli said, grinning.

The moment Jack and Kate had told her family that they were in love, the issues they'd all had with the two of them as a couple had vanished.

"You act like such a prude," Sadie said, digging her elbow into Eli's side. "Sheriff in the streets, freak in the sheets."

"I like that," Liss said. "I would come up with one for Connor but he's pretty much only one way."

"I'm genuine," Connor said. "And honest."

"And less grumpy than you used to be," Liss said. "Which I appreciate. And I assume everyone else does, too."

They all raised their various beverages in salute.

"Nice. Thank you," Connor said, touching the edge of a little pink blanket around his daughter's sleeping form.

It was an amazing thing, this new normal they were creating. With couples and a baby and love. And for the first time in a lot of years, Jack truly felt like part of a family. Oh, sure, the Garretts had always made him feel like one of their own. But with any luck, soon he actually would be.

They played a few more rounds until the new parents started getting droopy from lack of sleep. Then they divvied up the food, Kate snagging all of the dessert, and headed out. It was a strange and wonderful thing to be leaving together. Going back to the same house.

A house that was a home now, because she was in it.

It was dark outside, the air holding a sharp chill that

stabbed deep into his lungs like an ice pick. Or maybe that was just nerves.

Once they were on the bottom porch step, Jack pulled Kate up against him. She clutched the boxes of pie closer to her chest. "Don't make me drop this. It's a s'mores pie. I don't know if you understand how much that means to me."

"Of course I do. I would never do anything to compromise your pie."

"Sure." She wiggled her hip against his. "Is that a rock in your pocket or are you just happy to see me? Fun fact, I totally didn't get what that meant until after you and I... Well, you get the idea."

"That's adorable. And while I am always happy to see you, I actually do have something in my pocket. Incidentally, as with the other option, it is also for you."

She blinked, her eyes wide. "What is it?"

"It might be a ring box," he said, his throat getting tight.

"Oh, really?"

"I know you're not big into sparkly things, but I thought you might like this one a little bit. To wear while you compete this summer."

"Jack Monaghan, I have never worn a piece of jewelry in my life." She stretched up on her tiptoes and kissed him. "But I know for a fact that I'll wear this one for the rest of it."

* * * * *

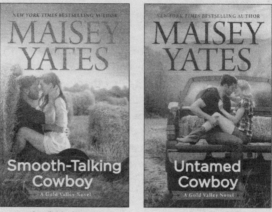